LURCHING TOWARD YONDER

Renardo Barden

Anhinga Press

DEDICATION

To three indispensable witnesses:

for Rohana, finally,

and in memory of
my son Michael
and
an irreplaceable friend Harris Nolan

'46 Mercury

"Take a pencil and map out your Magic Circle fun right now.
You've got the car, and if you're missing out on this kind of driving,
you aren't enjoying half of what your car offers you."
Published by Ethyl Corporation, New York,
to help you get more enjoyment out of your car.
Look, *May 12, 1959*

One hot summer afternoon when I was five, my dad returned from a New Mexico fishing trip with a snapping turtle locked in the trunk of his plum-colored '46 Mercury.

Junior Wong and I spread the word that when they finished their beers, my dad and his fishing buddy, Pep, would come out in the backyard, topple the big oil drum containing the "dinosaur ancestor," and chop its head off. After being diced into little green cubes, the turtle would be tossed in the pressure cooker for soup. Being a big boy, I would have to at least taste it.

Pep Mangus explained that we had to watch from on high because if the turtle saw us on the ground, it would charge and chomp our toes, or maybe even pinch our little peters off. Junior, who was eight, scrabbled up beside me on the ash pit at the alley end of my backyard. Safely out of reach, he helped three of his younger brothers up for a view of the action.

Moments later, my dad emerged from the house with a newly honed hatchet in one hand and a quart of beer in the other. Mangus followed him, setting his own bottle down beside my dad's in the dirt. He looked at my dad and said, "You ready, Bert?"

For an answer, my dad spit on the blade of his hatchet and toppled the barrel. The turtle—way bigger than a hubcap— charged Mangus, but then wheeled quickly and darted at my dad's leg. My dad made a kind of hopscotch step, swinging the hatchet. He missed once, then twice; then he cleaved the turtle's neck. The shell walked backwards up the sidewalk, leaving its head to hop up and down in the dust. I imagined the head was either looking for its shell or furiously hoping to luck into my dad's ankle. To avoid those bounding jaws, my dad skittered this way and that. Mangus lowered a big black boot on the turtle's shell and kept it there until the flippers ceased to row uselessly in the dirt. The bullet-shaped

1

head slowed, twitched a few times, and, like a toy winding down, became very still. When a trickle of dark blood drooled from the hollow neck sagging out of the shell, my sister Leslie—old and tall enough to watch from the far side of the fence—squealed with delighted disgust.

My dad wiped the hatchet blade with a rag and lit a cigarette. Mangus slugged from his beer bottle, put it down, then swooped, hugged the turtle's body to his chest and carried it inside. Junior and I jumped down in a hurry and ran toward my dad. When he refused our request to examine the turtle's head—tendered in the name of science—the two of us sighed and walked together down the alley to talk about dinosaurs and cars.

My dad drove a big Mercury with lots of dents. Junior's dad drove a green Willys. When Junior grew up he was going to be a chemist and drive an Oldsmobile Rocket with Hydra-Matic Drive. I was going to become a paleontologist and haul fossils in my own Studebaker Commander or Hudson Hornet.

At the dinner table that night my dad insisted the turtle had died as soon as its head was hacked off, but I took this as another of his attempts to put a stop to my questions. My dad was not a liar, but he would say anything to avoid explanations. In particular, my inquiries about the workings of cars made him slap himself in the forehead and claim not to know—even when he clearly did. When I pressed him for more information, he sweated profusely and said in a voice filled with impatience and pain, "What!?" When he yelled like that, it wasn't a question but rather a warning not to talk anymore. Sometimes my mom explained things, but only when she had the time, and only if she thought I was old enough to understand.

Junior was my best source and when he wasn't around to answer my questions, I explored our alley or city block, thought about what I knew was true, what might be true, and what I could ask him about later. When he was available, I plied him with questions and listened avidly to his explanations.

The day after I tasted turtle soup, Junior and I sat under the shade of a maple tree with our bare feet sticking out where the sun could shine on them. The neighborhood smelled of bacon grease, dandelion killer, burned rubber, cottonwood trees, gasoline, and strange flowers.

"My dad said the turtle died as soon as its head came off. But the turtle kept moving for a long time and I say it died later."

"Your dad is right, Tim." Junior explained. "The turtle had death throes."

"It didn't throw anything."

2

"Death throes are like what your baby brother does when your dad's not home and your mom yells at him to go inside. He gets down on the ground, kicks, waves his arms, and makes all kinds of noises."

"Temper tantrums?"

"Yeah, death throes are like temper tantrums."

"Okay, I get it. Animals who don't want to die throw themselves around because they're mad they gotta die."

"Yeah. But never mind that for now. Get your rake and shovel. We have to go back to our fossil dig."

Our fossil dig was the vacant lot at the end of the block. It was baked hard by sun and thick with weeds, a neighborhood jungle and junkyard with many hiding places. When digging proved arduous I proposed that we get some dynamite and blow holes where we thought the fossils were. Junior didn't think this was a good idea because, he explained, in digging for dinosaurs you had to be careful not to blow up their bones. We sat down together on the little dry mound beside our ditch. "We have to get used to hard work and travel," Junior said.

"Why?"

"I've made an important discovery. Do you still want to be a famous paleontologist?"

"Yes," I said, "I think so."

For reasons I didn't understand very well, Junior's oldest brother had forbidden him to teach me Chinese. Seeing how disappointed I was, Junior agreed to teach me biology, botany, chemistry, geology, physics, geology, or paleontology. He explained that paleontology was about dinosaurs that lived in Colorado when it was still a swamp. Paleontology involved learning about the Triassic, Jurassic, and Cretaceous Periods, digging with my toy shovel, being prepared to wash petrified bones, and then nail and glue them into skeletons for museums. The hardest part of paleontology was learning to pronounce *Tyrannosaurus rex*, *Allosaurus*, *Triceratops*, *Stegosaurus* and *Diplodocus*. Helping me with all those syllables, Junior pointed at the letters in a dinosaur book, and I began to read. Once I started reading, I couldn't stop. I hid my mom's magazines under my pillow and carried them into the bathroom late at night. Junior read his oldest brother's college textbooks in much the same way. I wanted to be a Chinese-speaking paleontologist. Having learned to read by listening to Junior and looking at letters in a book, I was sure I'd learn Chinese by listening alone, eavesdropping on the Wong family.

"Okay," Junior continued, "I've figured out how we can both become famous scientists."

"How?"

"What's the fastest car in the world?"

I didn't hesitate. "A Hudson Hornet."

"And cars are getting faster and faster all the time, correct?"

"Yes."

"Okay, well, this is the part that's going to be hard to understand. I've been reading my brother's physics and astronomy books and doing some independent research." Looking at me, he wrinkled his nose. "According to a property hidden in curves of time and space and discovered by a man named Albert Einstein, if cars keep getting faster, we can soup up a Hudson Hornet, maybe put some wings on it, find an empty road down a long hill, get it going as fast as we can, and drive it off a high cliff. When we're in the middle of the air, we'll have to crash through this sound barrier, which has already been done by jet planes by the way. Once we get past it, if we can keep going faster and faster, we'll be able to approach the speed of light and steer carefully and meet the world back where it was a long time ago. Then where do you think we can get to?"

"China?"

"No, we don't have to get going faster than light to go to China. What prehistoric age would you like to go to?"

"The Cretaceous Period. To see the tyrannosaurs!"

"So, about 125,000,000 years ago?"

"Yes."

"It's theoretically possible for us to do that."

"It is?"

"Yes. All the old ideas about time have been shot to holy hell, as your dad might say."

"Wow."

"The question is, do you have the scientific vision to believe this?"

"I don't know."

"That's okay. You've just started to read. You remember that the snapping turtle is a close ancestor to many prehistoric forms of life, right?"

I nodded.

"Okay, well, think about this. If your dad, who has an old Mercury, can drive slowly to New Mexico, drinking beer all the way, and then come home with a dinosaur ancestor, isn't it possible that sometime in the future, with bravery, scientific vision, and a souped-up Hudson, we could drive the speed of light to the Cretaceous Period?"

"Maybe," I hedged.

Much as I wanted to see live dinosaurs, I wasn't sure I wanted to risk getting burned up by light, crash a car, and then have to deal with carnivores bigger than a house. What I was sure about was wanting to grow older, drive a car through China, and meet Chinese people, especially old women like Junior's Grandma Wong. I didn't want to meet the Red Chinese, though. Just the ones whose skin colors matched Junior's.

Junior scratched his head with the handle of my little shovel. "We both have a lot more to learn before we can undertake such an expedition, of course."

Maybe Junior was right and one day we would climb out of a fast car and wander prehistoric jungles where pterodactyls hatched eggs big as Nash Ambassadors. But I hoped we could start by going a little slower and driving to China first.

Junior looked at me. "Hey, your dad's calling you."

I picked up my rake and shovel and ran home. When my dad called, I had learned to come in a hurry, even if it was only to go for what he called "a little ride."

When my mom worked late, my dad often paid off the babysitter, then hurried my sister and me into his Mercury. I didn't mind the little ride. What I hated was the big wait after the little ride was over. Typically, my dad refused to answer any questions about where we were going. He parked on a street with nothing of interest to see and, before getting out, always said the same thing in the same unassailable tone of voice.

"I'll be back in a minute."

My dad's impatience with my questions, his swats and rages out of all proportion to my offenses, were bad enough. But, as far as I was concerned, the worst thing about my dad was that he often left me and my sister in the car while he drank in beer joints.

Waiting for him to return, Leslie and I argued about how long he'd be gone. We bickered about how mad he'd be and what he'd do if we told him how long he'd been gone; we disputed the color of her blouse, disagreed about whether or not Superman could lift the entire planet, or whether or not dinosaurs could eat a grown man in one gulp. What mattered most was that we took fixed, contrary views and insisted on them until my dad finally returned and told us to shut up. Sometimes he was gone so long we ran out of things to argue about. When that happened, Leslie would clamp her hands over her ears while I did or said everything I could think of to make her speak or laugh.

Often it was just my dad and me. In my dad's absence, I scooted behind the steering wheel and made up songs about driving Ford Mainlines and Nash Ramblers through the far countries of the world.

There were times when he was gone so long I worried he'd decided not to return because I asked too many questions and spilled too many things. Once, after hearing a car backfire, I cried, certain that he'd been shot by someone in the beer joint. It was bad to think about such a thing, and as my sister Leslie said, it was a big sin to hope it would happen.

I couldn't please him or quit trying to please him. Tying my shoes was something I was slow to master, even though I wished he would stop stooping over and dripping sweat on me and calling me "a goddamned idiot." The sandals and cowboy boots I favored required no laces, so I considered that learning to tie shoes was a waste of time. I was more in earnest about cars than in learning to tie little bow knots, because I was sure that once I'd learned enough about cars, Junior and I could drive the All Can Highway into "the frozen wastes" I'd been reading about. Furry parkas and fur-lined boots would be necessary on such a journey. I hoped we'd make our drive without the transmission troubles experienced by the men depicted on highway billboards and in magazines. Of course, before we could launch our expedition, we would have to learn what transmissions were and how to fix them. Also, I'd have to know how to keep brakes from bleeding and learn why men like my dad enjoyed making them bleed in the first place.

Meantime, I would continue living in what my parents, Bert and Jean Barlow, described as a "mixed neighborhood." I'd go on waiting for my dad outside beer joints, arguing with my sister Leslie, and putting up with my baby brother Mike. Luckily, I'd have friendship and some answers. The other half of the duplex where we lived was filled with Wongs: Junior and Grandma, eleven Wongs in all. My not-so-secret plan was to finagle an invitation into the Wongs' house. Junior understood this, yet he couldn't invite me in without permission. And I couldn't ask Grandma Wong myself without knowing Chinese.

One day my mom said the Wong boys were quarantined with a contagious disease called ringworm. True, their hair had fallen out and they wore little caps, but they didn't act sick, and anyway, I regarded a funny hat as an acceptable price to be paid—like eating fish—for the privilege of associating with the Chinese. The caps didn't slow the Wong boys down or diminish their interest in the bowls of odd food they carried out to the front porch to eat with polished sticks, so I didn't understand why the doctor had said they couldn't be outside.

My dad said you got ringworm from being dirty, though I viewed his saying so with suspicion. He knew how to weld, how to drive safely with a cigarette in one hand and an elbow draped out an open car window, how to belch loudly—how to yell, tie his shoes, and blow marvelous smoke rings at the dinner table. But his answers were always too short and incomplete, and he would almost never answer two questions in a row. When I asked him why the Chinese were dirtier than other people, and how the Wongs got so dirty, he glowered at me and sent me out to play.

I had pored over all my mother's magazines searching for articles about ringworm, and read a lot of not-so-interesting stuff, and was very happy when Junior finally knocked on my door again. We towed a battered red wagon up the alley to rummage through trash in search of whatever might prove useful for our scientific experiments.

Halfway down the alley, Junior held a sticky half bottle of cough syrup up to examine its redness in the sunlight and said it was worth keeping as a possible antidote.

Instead of asking him about antidotes, I said, "My dad claims you get ringworm from being too dirty. He said the Chinese are a dirty people. Are you clean now?"

"Your dad's not very scientific. We're always clean. But you know what?"

"What?"

"Even if the Chinese were dirtier than other people, it would be all right because we invented the soap white people love so much. Plus, we invented compasses, arithmetic, firecrackers, wheels, pinwheels, and magic. Most of the best things in the world."

"What did white people invent?"

"Fords and communism and ideas about people who aren't white."

"I asked my dad how much money it would cost to go to China."

"What did he say?"

"He said, 'Jesus H. Christ.' Then he hit himself in the forehead with his hand."

"Your dad cusses a lot."

"Yeah."

Junior put the cough syrup bottle in a corner of the wagon. "We couldn't go to China anyway. Not for a while."

"Because of the communist rabble?"

"You're reading about communists now?"

"I read some stories in my mom's magazines. The Commies have to live behind an iron curtain."

"It's not really iron, and there isn't any actual curtain. You know what a metaphor is yet?"

"Yeah."

"What?"

7

"A kind of hardwood that only grows in the tropics?"

"Oh boy. We got to get you straightened around. A metaphor is just a bunch of words that secretly mean something else."

"Like Chinese?"

Junior towed the wagon to the next trash barrel. After peering inside he climbed up on the wagon, bent over and fished out an empty box of birthday candles. "A metaphor is like this. You've read about the Communist Party. If you didn't know about metaphors you might think it was a bunch of Communists blowing out birthday candles. But it's not. Just the same as when they say the Red Chinese. There's no Chinese people who are red. There isn't anybody who's red. Not even Indians."

"How do you find out about this stuff?"

"The best way is through reading and writing and traveling. One of my brother's books said that the secrets to a good life are communication and transportation. In other words, talking and going places." Momentarily, Junior examined a length of narrow pipe.

"What good is that pipe?"

"Well, if we can manage to sterilize it, we can turn it into a blowgun and kill things if we need to."

I was distracted by an empty tomato can. "If you smashed this can flat and put another can beside it and then another, and you did it a thousand times, would it be a mile?"

"A thousand times?" Junior looked at me, smiled, and shook his head. "You have to learn your numbers better so you can start on measurements. Remember, the seven is an upside down and backwards L and the two is a mirror image of an S. Why do you want to know about a thousand cans?"

"I read about an All Can Highway and wondered how they made the cans stay put and how many cans it would take to make a road all the way to the frozen north."

"It's Al-Can. Al is short for Alaska, and Can is short for Canada."

I nodded my head. "Oh, I get it! Like a metaphor!"

"Yeah, that's right. The Al-Can Highway runs from Canada into Alaska where they have big bears and seals and stuff. Hey, do you think you can sneak in your house and steal some stick matches?"

"I don't know."

"Well, let's go see if you can. With these clothes pins and rubber bands, I'll show you how to make a match gun."

The next afternoon, while my dad was in a beer joint, I made up a song about metaphors and decided that when I got home I would apply some of my mother's bleach to the brown leaves falling in our front yard. After turning the leaves into paper, I would write a book about dinosaurs. Then I fell to considering problems posed by car speed.

Recently, I'd realized for the first time that my dad didn't control the car's speed by how fast he moved his hands on the steering wheel. I had been considering the possibility that car speed had to do with the *placement* of the hands on the steering wheel—or maybe with how hard the steering wheel got squeezed. If car speed was a matter of hand placement, where did my dad move his hands to slow down—to the right or left? Did one hand draped over the steering wheel make the car back up? How did a steering wheel recognize a hand or wrist? Was a *Brontosaurus* footprint bigger than a truck tire? Why did God let all the dinosaurs die in the tar pits instead of just killing a few of them? And assuming extinct meant dead for good and becoming petrified bones in tar pits, how could Junior and I hope to survive crashing through a sound barrier? How could we travel through light and then emerge elsewhere, alive among amazing prehistoric creatures? How would all the skin and blood and teeth get back on the dinosaur bones before we got there?

Stumped, I considered Junior's theory that the secret of life had to do with talking and moving. Because I liked to talk, read, and listen, I was convinced I'd be good at the first part. The second part, moving—big people called it transportation—was scarier. It was one thing to grow up to become someone who could trick and persuade people to let you do what you wanted, and another to learn to control powerful machinery so it would take you where you wanted to go.

From watching my dad, I knew that transportation meant learning to drive and fix cars. It also meant cutting your knuckles on dirty car engines, drinking alcohol, smoking cigarettes, and doing other things that hurt the throat and hands. The more I thought about it, the more it seemed to me that transportation was probably more important than talking, if only because people like my dad did all right, even when they yelled to keep from having to talk or listen. Plus, there were other people who rarely spoke, like Junior's dad. Yet, from what I could tell, nobody was exempt from having to travel and obey the real bosses of the world, the bosses my dad called management cocksuckers, say, or the teachers of Junior Wong. Even Grandma Wong needed transportation. Each week she took the bus downtown and returned home toting strange little sacks filled with smelly items my mom called whatnots. Whatnots were small objects my mom didn't want to talk to me about.

Communication allowed you to understand things. But transportation provided you a chance to look more closely at whatever you didn't understand. With transportation, you could get to a doctor when you needed a transfusion, or find a banana split. Transportation could provide a feeling of exhilaration, like taking your feet off a trike's pedals when you were going about twenty miles an hour. But, from sitting in my dad's old Mercury, I knew transportation also led to fear and boredom, to beer joints, places so smoky and stale they made you gag. Neighborhood bars were old destinations. New destinations meant new problems. For one thing, until you realized you had already arrived at a new destination, you never knew quite how far it was to where you wanted to go; you never knew what might happen before you got there. Then, after arriving, you didn't know how long you'd have for things to get right. Sometimes instead of getting right, they got very wrong.

Though Junior and his brothers and sisters spoke perfect English, the Wong kids always talked Chinese to one another. I listened to them through the walls. Chinese was a beautiful, singing language. It could be chanted and howled but, apparently, never shouted in anger. When a Wong sliced open a hand with a knife or carried a dead pigeon into the house, everybody in the family chanted about it in the same long slow tones they used to celebrate family birthdays. No Wong ever shouted and hit the wall with a fist, or threw a beer glass across the room, or called anybody a goddamned idiot. Junior said this was because the Chinese were an ancient and noble people and, to avoid hurting the feelings of loved ones and strangers, they had deliberately left bad words out of their language. When I explained this to my dad at the dinner table, he slapped himself on top of the head, groaned and said, "Oh, bullshit!"

In my house only my dad could say bad words or call people goddamned idiots and make them shut up or cry. In the Wong house, two people imposed silence, without shouting or cussing: Mr. Wong and Grandma Wong. When Grandma Wong talked, I liked to press my head to the wall, close my eyes, and picture a huge magical duck quacking from the farthest shore of the world. When she fell silent, no small Wong voices wailed or piped up for a long time. One day, I hoped to ring the Wong doorbell and ask Grandma Wong, in Chinese, if I could come inside. Once she heard me speak Chinese, I was sure she would smile with happy surprise, unhook the screen door, and let me in for a long look around.

On cold mornings in our house I squatted beside the hot-air register until the heat from the basement furnace turned my hands pink and burned my tailbone. I listened for the sound of a Wong laughing or crying or shouting in anger. Junior said they never cried or shouted in anger and that they sometimes laughed at us because we shouted and cried so often. My mom said it was rude of them to laugh at us and that Junior was lying because it was human nature to be upset sometimes. I was determined to find out who was right. More than that, of course, I hoped to solve the mysteries of Chinese. One morning when my mom asked me if I wanted more cereal I said, "Yow bang yow" and thought it sounded pretty good. But when I tried it out on Junior he was not impressed.

In warm weather I liked to stand near the Wongs' open front door and take in the sour and bitter smells that came from inside. Once, when Junior's younger brother Marshall was trying to keep me from getting a good look at a bowl of food he'd carried out to the front porch, he dropped his bowl and started to cry. Junior's explanation to Grandma Wong that I was naturally curious rather than mean or rude didn't make any difference. My hope to be invited into the Wong house seemed more and more remote.

The Wongs kept a big, rust-colored Chow dog named Low Foo Doy, which, Junior said, was Chinese for lion. For the most part, Low lived on a pile of rags on the screened-in Wong back porch. But Low could leave the porch for the backyard whenever he wanted to by poking his head and shoulders through a small door made just for him. My mom told everyone in the neighborhood that Low had bitten the mailman and the iceman. I heard a lot of racket one afternoon, carried an empty wastebasket into the yard, and watched Low bite the man sent over to read the Wong's electric meter. Grandma Wong came running out and hit both the man and dog with the handle of her dust mop. She flailed at the man because she didn't like people who didn't speak Chinese. She whacked the dog for not having bitten the man from the electric company right away, for not having bitten him harder when he finally did bite him, and for being underfoot when she was trying to plant herself better to whack the man harder.

My mom said the electric company might sue Grandma Wong. When I asked Junior about this, he said because we were children, we weren't allowed to know much about money and should mind our own beeswax and concentrate on our studies. When I complained I didn't have any beeswax or very many studies, Junior went inside and brought out a book called *Bodies in Motion*. That day I discovered the accelerator pedal and discarded my hand-placement theory.

One day my friends Lee and Jimmy proposed that the three of us climb the fence from their yard, race across the Wong yard, and clamber into my yard before Low could catch and bite us. My mom was always worried that Low might get loose and bite me, but I had studied his expression through the screen door and was not afraid. I liked the idea of testing my own instinct against my mom's fears, but more than that, I hoped to come to Grandma Wong's attention in some dramatic way. If I couldn't go inside the house, I wanted to experience the full focus of her authority, feel whatever it was that made Junior, Victor, and Marshall Wong hang their heads whenever she spoke.

I took my turn scaling the fence, dashing across the Wongs' yard, and dropping to safety. But however hard I ran, however much my hilarity made me stagger, Low showed no interest. Nor did Grandma Wong come howling demonically from the back porch to scold or hit me across the back with a stick.

One of the things I liked most about my mom's magazines was looking at the black and white photographs of car wrecks and thinking up punishments for the drunken drivers who made them happen. These "roadside tragedies" were caused by many of the hard, sharp things attached to cars.

I learned about these hard, sharp things in a small way when I tripped on a corner of the warped linoleum on the back porch and fell on the trunk lid my dad had removed from his Mercury. In falling, I raked my forearm across the license plate still attached to the trunk. While blood soaked through the sleeve of my favorite cowboy shirt, my dad drove me to the doctor, yelling at me most of the way to stop howling. Junior had already told me about transfusions, but I didn't know how much a quart was, how long it took to bleed one, or how many quarts were in my body. As it happened, I didn't need a transfusion. The doctor sewed up my arm like a coat sleeve and sent me home to wait for my arm to grow a long white line called a scar.

That night I dreamed about traveling to China with Junior. We were given the choice of riding with my dad in his Mercury or traveling by ourselves in a mechanical dragon designed by the Ford Motor Car Company. My dad was going to China to teach the Chinese how to cuss and prevent ringworm. If we went with my dad, we'd be able to see landscapes and oceans through the car windows. We also knew, though, that we'd have to ride in silence because he didn't like kids talking while he drove. For that reason, and because we didn't know how many beer joints my dad would want to stop in along the way, we decided to travel in the dragon. We navigated the flying dragon by turning an internal crank as fast as we could. When our progress was rapid, we were cheered by passengers riding in a glassy bubble we towed behind us, but whenever the dragon slowed, the riders threatened to throw us overboard.

When the crank came off in our hands, someone shouted down that without brakes, there could be no stopping in China, or anywhere else. Eventually, we were issued an ultimatum. Unless we designed perfect brakes by the time the dragon passed over Japan, we would be killed with an internal combustion engine. I woke up sweaty, whimpering, and worried. I'd planned to travel far and wide and fast, but I had never thought enough about the problems associated with stopping until then.

"Think of brakes," Junior explained the next day, "as little greasy hands that come down out of a car's fenders to grab the tires and keep them from spinning." Again, Junior brought out a book. When I still didn't understand, he promised to work up another scientific experiment. Before we got to it, though, my dad picked me up from nursery school in a rented truck and sent me inside a big, strange house far from the Wongs to sit on a box with a coloring book and some broken crayons. I cried, not so much from grief but from the discovery that nothing about you mattered very much to other people until you owned and controlled your own transportation and destinations. Where I wanted to be for a long time was almost anywhere but our "new" house. More than any place, I wanted to be back in what my mom called the dangerous mixed neighborhood. I wanted to sit on the front steps with Junior naming every year of every car that rolled down the street.

Tulips and roses grew in front of the freshly painted porches on which wooden swings creaked in the wind. There was no street life beyond the fertilizing, watering, and cutting of lawns. When I roamed the alleys, I saw a lot of unfriendly washed kids playing on swing sets behind newly painted gates. There were no musical parades on dirty streets. No interesting trash littered the alleys. Everyone had refrigerators, so there were no icemen staggering up the alley with gleaming blocks of ice in rusty tongs. People went to the neighborhood supermarket, so no battered trucks loaded with watermelons inched down streets; no Chinese or Mexicans or black men stood awkwardly among mounds of melons, singing out the names of various fruits and vegetables over and over again. There were no stray dogs, or good, rich smells, no loud noises, and from what I could see no prospects of murders or dirt clod fights with neighborhood kids. The boys all wore crew cuts and stared and didn't speak. Their sisters favored braids and fresh dresses and looked carefully before crossing streets without much traffic. My mom was happy about how safe the new neighborhood was, but I thought it was as boring as waiting in the car for my dad to come out of a beer joint.

One morning, while thinking about brakes, I lobbed a broken mop handle through the spokes of a little neighbor girl's tricycle as she pedaled furiously down the sidewalk. The spokes bit down on the stick and whirled it up against the trike's front fork with a clunk, and the girl went over the handlebars. The trike flipped and bounced sideways in the grass. The rider landed on her hands and knees on the sidewalk and started crying. More to minimize certain punishment than to comfort her, I helped her up, dusted her knees, and petted her white blond hair. To my surprise, she didn't connect her fall with the thrown stick. When her mother came scampering down the street, I leaned the mop handle against the far side of a tree trunk and resumed my honeyed ministrations. The woman was beautiful, smelled like a garden, and told me what a wonderful little boy I was. Swept away by the fragrance and the unforced gratitude of both girl and mother, my conscience never had a chance.

That night, I thought about how the girl might have been hurt, about how it was wrong to pretend I'd had nothing to do with her fall, and about justice, punishment, and Grandma Wong. I'd seen my dad blow up and make everybody cry. I'd heard Grandma Wong induce sincere reform with two or three words. It seemed to me she could make wrong things right just by singing a single dry musical note and curling a wrinkled index finger. I wondered what Grandma Wong would have done if I had been her grandson and she had seen me throw the stick or learned of my deception. Would she have scolded and shamed me, beat me on the shoulders like she did the meter man? Would God punish me? Could I punish myself before God got a full report? What would be the right punishment, neither too much nor too little? How did justice differ from punishment and mercy?

Sometimes, when I forgot my table manners and scraped my teeth with my fork, my dad used the flat blade of his butter knife like a drumstick on the top of my head. About as often, he swatted me on the butt with an open hand for going outside without shoes or socks. Sometimes he hit me when he was mad. At other times, he stepped away and punched a door or threw a dinner plate. Occasionally, he just grunted and made threatening, bearlike motions. Even if he could recognize justice, I didn't think he'd ever be able to control his anger enough to administer it. Nor would he ever take the trouble to describe what it might be. My mom often kept him from finding out about and punishing my accidents or rebellions, but her gift was for mercy, not justice.

My dad compulsively watched over me, hurrying me, preventing and obstructing me, and standing over me to make sure I did what I was told in just the way and at just the rate expected. Because his scrutiny always led to a shout and often to a swat, I decided early on that supervision itself was a form of punishment. Wherever my dad couldn't see me became the place I most wanted to be. Remaining there as long as possible became a deep pleasure. It was also clear to me that if my dad ever learned of what happened with the broomstick, he'd manage not only to punish me, but to rob me of a growing sense that my life would eventually become something I could learn to hide or steer away from him. Throwing the broomstick was the first thing I ever did I felt certain he would never find out about. It was as if I'd stolen an apple he didn't know existed and chewed to sweetest fructose all evidence of the theft. Before I fell asleep that night I decided that secrecy was something I was going to have to live with. I might have to undergo some punishment from God for hurting the little girl, but I would never confess to the girl or her mother or anyone what I'd done, lest the shame take away my first experience of whole-hearted human praise. Sin and secrecy self-tangled themselves in my mind. A secret was a private wealth only you knew you had.

Later that summer my grandpa, Lester Barlow, provided me with my first significant transportation: an old, red twenty-four inch bike. He held my thin shoulder as I wobbled and gathered momentum, hurrying alongside as I cranked precariously down the sidewalk. Then, just at the moment I thought it might prove possible to stay upright on two tires, he pushed hard between my shoulder blades, uttered a few winded words of encouragement, and drifted back behind me as I wobbled up the block. The white picket fence in front of the little girl's house shimmered and quivered in the afternoon sun. My bike's front wheel banged into the fence and I went down in the grass. Smarting from the pain in my knee and foot, I got up, examined the bike, and sneaked a look at the big picture window. To my disappointment, the little girl and her mother were not looking out.

  That afternoon I crashed into the fence so often that even my normally patient grandpa succumbed to frustration. Somehow, my response to this was to bash into the fence at an even higher rate of speed and fall that much harder on the lawn. Still, however much I hurt, and however slowly I got back on my feet, no sweet face appeared at the window or emerged from the house to pity or comfort me. Just before dinner, I twisted and went over the handlebars, cutting my right eyebrow on a fence picket. My dad was out of town and my mom was busy doing laundry. After the application of Mercurochrome and a Band-Aid, dinner was a mess of leftover spaghetti eaten slowly, while Lester mawkishly rambled about the wonders of self-confidence and the importance of positive thinking.

Because of a broken stretch of sidewalk and a one-way street on the other side of the block, pedaling in any other direction was out of the question. But in any case, Lester's view of manliness allowed for no detours or whimpers of reluctance. You rode directly at your fears, you took your lumps, established competence, gracefully accepted compliments, and hid your pleasure behind modest little thank-yous; this was how good boys became worthy men. I remember the old man holding his long, weathered arm out and saying that the road to growing up began beyond the banged- up white fence. He urged me to see the fence not as a barrier but as a challenge. "Positive thinking can soften the hard objects of the world," Lester said. I didn't understand this. But by then, I had become aware that as long as I could keep from falling so hard that I cried, crashing into the fence was harder on the bike and wood than it was on me. By late the next morning several pickets were chipped and a few of the wooden fence posts were cracked. A bike pedal was torn, the handlebars were slightly bent, the front fender was dented, and the seat was scuffed and abraded. Even the bike's thick red patina was streaked with chalky white paint. Heartened by a sense of my potential for delivering as well as receiving injurious force, I pumped past the fence all the way to the end of the block. There, not quite prepared for the adventure of turning a corner, I dropped in a heap and managed to keep clear of the falling bike. Soon, with a little stomp on the elevated pedal, I learned to launch myself and glide past the fence. By late afternoon, I was negotiating turns and marveling that the bike would stay upright on its two narrow tires. With my grandpa standing next to me, I was looking down the next block as far as I could, wondering how far I could ride without stopping.

That evening, while my grandpa was listening to Mozart, I asked my mom why my grandpa was so nice and my dad was so mean. She stopped what she was doing and said that Lester had probably once been as impatient with my dad as my dad was with me. After that, I made a point of watching the two men and concluded there was something to this. Somehow, whatever I did and didn't do, whatever I was told and whatever I wasn't, caused my grandpa and dad to bicker, yell, and pout.

I had already ruined my relationship with my dad by spilling things, complaining about waiting in the car, crying too often about things that "didn't really hurt," and taking so long to learn to tie my shoes. I quietly took my grandpa's part. The older man rewarded my loyalty with shiny coins, ice cream, and a smothering kind of love that inevitably tailed off into reminiscence and lecture. Sometimes, I wanted to get away from him, too.

Frustrated by my clumsiness, my dad often called me "a goddamned Chinaman." Since I considered that Junior and Grandma Wong had lives and interests so compelling that they never got angry or cried, and since Junior had convinced me the Chinese had invented everything of any importance, I didn't mind being thought of as a "Chinaman." The "goddamned" part I didn't like. From the neighborhood branch library, I checked out a book about Marco Polo and concluded that I was more a Marco Polo-in-waiting than a "goddamned Chinaman." The China in my mind was a country where it was okay to be slow, dreamy, and fascinated. It was a place where people always kept their voices melodic and free from anger and resentment, a realm where everything smelled bitter or fried or hot. There, instead of getting whacked for something before you realized what it was you'd done, you could walk around and eat with sticks, or use either hand. And you could even suck on your fingers when you were finished.

Perhaps, as Junior insisted, the ancient past flourished beyond a sound barrier and a field of light. But I wasn't quite ready for crashing barriers and speeds of light. What I was able to accept was the fact that my dad, in his slow, smoky '46 Mercury, had captured a living prehistoric creature on a New Mexico fishing trip. What Junior didn't seem to fully realize was that a good part of the past seemed to live on just over the horizon. To reach it, it didn't seem necessary to get a Hudson Hornet going faster than the light accelerating out of a light bulb. You just had to have transportation and the freedom to explore, beginning, I hoped, with a bike deliberately pedaled beyond parental boundaries.

One summer morning I sat across the table from my grandpa, sharing the newspaper. He stirred his instant coffee and read the front pages while I spooned the last milk from my cornflakes and pored over the comic strips. When he muttered that the world was a jungle, I hoped he was right. The world he saw as a giant, godless dirtball, a violent garden filled with evil Germans, teenagers, and other unpleasant surprises, I considered a verdant park of endless diversity; the best part of my life would begin once I had the run of such a place. I had my new bike, permission to ride in the street, and an invisible fence, boundaries set by my mom that I couldn't wait to ride beyond. While my grandpa exclaimed over the horrors on the front page, I savored Vincent Hamlin's Alley Oop, the hairy caveman who rode in high style, going through the past and future, wisely avoiding the present, on his pet dinosaur, Dinny.

My best friend Donnie Kelly had his own bike, understood the life of Oop, and lived a five-minute ride away. Donnie was freckled-faced, and near-sighted, his shirts constantly working free of the trousers into which, under the stern eyes of the St. Francis de Sales grade school nuns, they were tucked again and again. What he lacked in athletic ability, he made up for in ardor, pacing back and forth, scolding and praising, hurrying the endless schoolyard football games toward conclusions they never reached. His bloodied elbows were skinned and scabbed and skinned again. Shirts torn and spotted with food or blood, he hectored the half-hearted for messing up or wasting time and would fight anybody over any matter of honor whatever. Since he was in a hurry to get back to the game, he never pressed a fight once he'd gained an advantage. Nor did he cry when he was whipped as he was now and then, or when, in a scramble for the miniature airborne football, he belly-flopped or tumbled in the paved yard. As often as not in getting to his feet, he solicited help in finding his errant specs. And when they were broken, he stuffed their three or four pieces in his shirt pocket and returned fierce and half-blind to the game. When his glasses were on his face, they were greasy with fingerprints and partially reassembled with rubber bands or transparent tape. Even newly repaired, his glasses had a way of sliding down his dripping nose, which he wiped with big, shoulder-driven motions of his sleeved forearm—snot or blood—white shirt or plaid. Better a soiled shirt, Donnie would mutter, than a smudged face.

We went to the movies to celebrate Donnie's eighth birthday. While we ate bags of popcorn, his mother, Miriam, and her priestly brothers-in-law made funeral arrangements for Donnie's father, Ralph.

Ralph had been driving home from a department store in the family's Plymouth Cambridge. The car blew a tire, jumped the curb and hit a street lamp. The car lacked seat belts and the heavy steering wheel did its worst. Ralph died of internal injuries in an hour.

To me, the drama of Ralph's funeral was more diverting adventure than tragic event. In my presence at least, Ralph's death never seemed to interest Donnie much, except to get him more attention than he wanted from his priestly uncles, each of whom was now more sure than ever that Donnie ought to "be given every chance to develop a vocation" and become a priest. As Donnie's friend and fellow altar boy, I, too, squirmed before these strange men who talked so mysteriously of Christ and souls and states of grace.

For Donnie and me states of grace were motions of our own devising—running, riding a bike, and free falling. We spent after-school hours "bailing out," by which we meant scaling garage roofs, goading each other to jump, spreading our arms, stepping forward, and shocking our kneecaps and hips with the delicious violence of gravity.

When the streets were iced-over, we sneaked out of the house in our good, leather-soled Mass and Communion shoes and loitered at strategic corners. Waiting beside stop signs, we ducked down, grabbed rear bumpers, and often managed to ski two or three blocks on our slick leather soles. Occasionally, we hit dry patches of pavement and tumbled like shirts in a dryer.

When the streets were no longer slippery, we took up positions between houses and threw snowballs in long, high arcs at passing cars. Running between houses, flinging open gates, dashing through fenced yards, we hid from angry drivers wherever we could—even in doghouses. After a time, we grew older and bolder and disdained hiding. The chief pleasure became staying just out of reach and listening to the names we were being called.

Once, an undetected cop caught us and drove us to Donnie's house. Though Donnie got a licking when his mother came home from work, the next day we just switched neighborhoods and started all over again.

Occasionally, cab drivers and truckers took exception to our snowballs. Cab drivers shoved their cabs in reverse and backed them up at outrageous speeds. Or they skidded down alleys, crept up side streets, and found an unexpected approach, appearing again just when we thought we were safe. Truck drivers enjoyed explaining how they might slap us silly and drive off and never be caught or prosecuted. While I found this persuasive and feigned a show of contrition, Donnie proved harder to intimidate. Though he got slapped a time or two, he once got us out of a jam by telling a trucker with a missing front tooth that he had memorized the truck's license plate, then proved it with a recitation.

The cars I'd admired on billboards, in magazines, or from the safety of my front porch insinuated themselves more deeply into my life. Unable to drive, I relished interacting with and tormenting those who could.

Increasingly, my allowance and snow-shoveling money went for model car kits, plastic husks of '57 Impalas and '32 Roadsters, assembled from plastic branches laden with tiny, scrimshawed axles, carburetors, valve covers, and steering wheels. In my haste to enjoy the completed model, I skimmed the written instructions and, departing from the assembly sequences, ended up with models that lacked seats, fan blades, floor mats. Small parts were broken or glued on wrong, or fouled with black, gummy tumors of noxious rubber cement. Decals, which were easily torn and difficult to manipulate with smudged fingers, proved particularly vexing. Called to dinner, I left the caps off the tiny bottles of bright lacquer or put paint-loaded brushes down to dry on the tabletop. The final product usually had bubbled or gritty paint and was marred with black brush bristles.

My grandpa disapproved of the decals and iconography, though he made a point of appreciating my completed models. The manufacturers, the old man claimed, had dedicated themselves to the task of teaching growing boys important lessons about patience, preparedness, and following instructions. To me, this sounded disappointingly like classroom talk and I began keeping my models in places where Lester wouldn't notice or critique them.

Donnie's models were even messier than mine. One snowy afternoon, we held a Demolition Derby in Donnie's basement, dashing our models forcefully into one another until they began breaking up into pieces. Donnie's grandma came down to check on us and became very upset. She told me to go home, and when Donnie resented her proprietary attitude, she let him have it. Neither models nor cars were toys, she said, and she was in no mind to be bullied out of her indignation by boys hell-bent on destruction so soon after the tragic death in the family. Sullen, Donnie gave me all that was left of his model cars. Shard by shard, I gathered up the fragments and carried them home in a grocery bag, determined to re-glue and repaint each one, imagining myself with a fleet of creatively reconstructed models beautified in ways never seen before.

At three o'clock one morning when I'd been given permission to spend the night at his house, Donnie and I tiptoed through the Kellys' dark kitchen, eased the door open, and stepped out onto the wet lawn. Our bikes leaned against an elm tree. We walked our bikes to the backyard gate, which squeaked as we guided them through. When the house remained dark after we took three or four breaths, we mounted our bikes and pedaled up the alley, drawing a manic energy from the cool night air and a city so quiet we could hear the hum of street lamps. On a downhill stretch of Logan Street, I let go of the handlebars, folded my hands behind my head, and leaned back on the seat of the bike, whereupon I saw a glowing white orb move low and rapidly across the sky.

"Donnie," I shouted, grabbing my handlebars again, "what the hell is that?"

The giant, luminous balloon shape accelerated and moved out of sight behind an apartment house. Donnie glided up to join me. "Wow! A UFO!"

Reappearing, traveling parallel with nearby Cherry Creek, the light dipped soundlessly, seeming to hide itself behind a blue spruce tree. Hoping not to lose sight of our UFO, we pumped furiously for the end of the block and a better view of sky. Once clear of the obstructive houses and trees, we stopped pedaling and dismounted, awestruck, watching. Oncoming headlights distracted us. A red-and-white Ford Galaxie passed, stopped quickly, and zoomed back toward us in reverse.

"Shit!" I said. "It's my dad!"

The light skated north and seemed to dissolve. Donnie wheeled round, stood upright on the pedals, and cranked as hard as he could for home, riding the wrong direction down a one-way street. I started to do likewise, but my dad cut me off. He jumped out, leaving the car door open and the interior light on. From the grotesque angles of his graying hair, I knew that for some reason he'd been roused from sleep.

"What the hell do you think you're doing, getting me out of bed in the middle of the night?" His breath was sweet from port wine.

"Dad, a UFO! We just saw a UFO! It just now disappeared behind that row of trees!" He swung at me, but I ducked and the open palm of his hand glanced off the top of my head.

"Goddamned sneak! I'll give you a UFO," he said. "Liar."

"Dad, I swear we just saw a UFO!"

He cuffed me again.

More scared than hurt, I dismounted and placed the bike frame like a fence between us. "I'll never do it again," I promised. He got the handlebars and ripped them away, flinging the bike down in the street. A porch light came on and the headlights from another car came toward us.

"Donnie's grandma heard you sneaking out. She called after you, but you didn't turn back." He kicked the bike toward the car and gestured toward the trunk. "Get that thing in there before I take it down and throw it in the goddamned creek!"

I knew it was the wrong thing to say, but blurted it out again. "Dad, we saw . . ."

He moved on me again and stopped himself. "No more shit about UFOs. Unless you want to become one yourself!"

I stowed the bike and opened the back door, but he would have none of that. He wanted me in the front seat, in harm's way, physically accessible to any other necessary outburst, visible and squirming. The big Ford jumped and squealed. He had remembered to bring his bottle. He uncapped it, sipped, and cradled it between his two thighs. His belt was unlooped and he hadn't bothered to zip his slacks or fully button his sports shirt. He took corners too quickly, all the while proposing exaggerated punishments and voicing whatever vague threats occurred to him.

My mom was in the kitchen, wearing her robe, sipping from a cup of tea and nibbling a slice of toast. She'd already poured my dad a mug of beer and she chided me, knowing she was expected to, understanding that if she sounded angry and disappointed enough, she might make things a little easier on me. I said nothing about the UFO, pinned the whole scheme on Donnie, true but treasonous, behaved with acceptable remorse, and did my best to look exhausted.

My dad was on his third beer by the time I was allowed to retreat to my room. I got a penlight from a drawer, found a pencil stub, and wrote down a description of what I'd seen, noting that, while extraterrestrial beings contemplated the physical geography of North America for good or evil purposes, my dad was sitting in his favorite chair downing beers and listening to *Tosca* on the stereo. I added that what my dad was fond of calling the "real world" demanded too much compliance, obedience, and drudgery. Worse, it excluded whatever adults were too busy to notice.

'58 Ford Station Wagon

"If there are two children in your family, one of them,
statistically speaking, will be killed or injured in a traffic accident."
Attributed to Dr. Amos E. Newhart,
The Institute of Public Safety at Pennsylvania State University,
from, "Your Car and You," by Siler Freeman
Look, *May 12, 1959*

There were three worktables in my grandpa's basement on which he handcrafted fishing rods for family members and special friends. His hunting arsenal, which he kept in a cabinet nearby, consisted of a .22 semiautomatic, a double-barreled .20 gauge shotgun, and a bolt-action 30-06.

I had a part to play in his dream of bagging an elk in the high Rockies. At seventy, his vision might be deteriorating, he admitted, but his hands remained steady and his heart strong. Together we would bring down the mighty Wapiti. The old man's fantasy, too often introduced at family dinners, worried his wife Nina, irritated my dad, and often strained my adolescent capacity to deal with simultaneous surges of pride and embarrassment.

Evenings in Lester's basement workshop, I memorized NRA safety rules and cleaned and polished the guns. While I cleaned them and oiled their dark stocks, he produced battered photo albums bulging with fading snapshots of his life in Chicago, where he'd lived and worked until his retirement, and the North Woods, where he'd spent several years as a younger man in a logging camp. Among my favorites was a photograph of a young Lester holding the flute he'd once played in camp orchestras. It had been taken, he said, shortly after a brawl in which he'd fought alongside Jack Dempsey, the legendary heavyweight-boxing champion of the 1920s.

Engaged for a lumber camp smoker, "the Manassa Mauler" happened to be backstage when Lester and a group of musicians were mobbed by logging camp drunks unresponsive to the classical music being played for their refinement. When the melee was over, the champ praised Lester's right cross. Recalling the story, the old man studied the thin white hairs on the back of his sturdy fist and nodded to himself.

There was another picture of Lester with his flute, but he couldn't encounter it without muttering about the "son of a bitch of a German" who had accused him of overblowing the instrument and fired him from the Chicago Symphony Orchestra.

Most of the photographs documented game and fish. Very visible were bewildering numbers of men with forgotten names, bad teeth, straw hats, old cars, shabby suits and ties, and heavy-duty camping gear. Better illuminated and more prominently displayed were the fish. Smaller fish were dangled on stringers. "Lunkers," mostly muskie and pike, were draped over tree branches. Dead game was embraced by squatting hunters. Deer and black bear were held in wrestler's headlocks, sad faces directed into the camera lens. It seemed both marvelous and unfair that my grandpa had landed so many big fish from the once-bountiful waters of Wisconsin and Michigan, when my own biggest fish had been a fifteen-inch rainbow trout. But it saddened me that my grandpa believed the best part of his life was visible in a few dozen cracked and yellowing photographs of dead animals and forgotten men.

One night he flipped to an image of himself smoking a cigarette and holding up an empty pint bottle. Embarrassed, he clucked his tongue and claimed, once again disdaining to provide details, that drink and cigarettes had ruined his life. Although curious about his real or imaginary debaucheries, I knew better than to press him; he was already inclined to twist autobiographical anecdotes into object lessons. He was too fond of lectures about the evils of smoking cigarettes, which I was already sneaking, and drink, which I hoped to try at an early opportunity.

When we came on a photograph of a big-hipped woman whose long hair seemed precariously contained in a grotesque bonnet, he told me it was his sister Lottie, with whom he hadn't spoken in almost forty-five years. Since her likeness invariably produced a glistening behind his bifocals and a head-shaking silence, I wondered why he didn't take the picture out of the album and, if not throw it away, or at least put it in an envelope where he could find it only when he wanted to savor his regrets. I never suggested this, of course, and just sat tapping my foot while he muttered his hopes that I would never know the manifold disappointments and betrayals he'd experienced in his life. In my mind I was already planning my liberation from my dad as something permanent and irrevocable, but I didn't think there was going to be any disappointment or betrayal connected to that. Still, it scared me to think that someone else in my family might engender so many unacknowledged tears and so much bitter head shaking. Eventually, my mom told me that Lester and Lottie's falling out dated from her failure to attend Lester and Nina's wedding.

Sometimes, particularly after an argument with my dad, Lester's photographs elicited mutterings about a curse on the Barlow men. When pressed to elaborate, he invariably began with a rambling account of his own grandfather, a man said to have been denied a veteran's pension because he remained the town bully, though one of his hands had been shot off in a Civil War battle. For Lester, further evidence consisted of the Germanic origins of the family name. Except for Beethoven, Mozart, and half a dozen composers, Lester held a generational dislike of Germans, whose gifts, he said, were limited to music, machinery, obedience, and murder. Whenever he heard Lester bad-mouth Germans, my dad never failed to point out that Lester also held against all Germans the arrogance of a certain conductor who had fired him fifty years ago from the Chicago Symphony.

Lester's dismissal from the Chicago Symphony Orchestra had figured prominently in the life of his son, so when we were alone, whenever the subject of the firing came up and Lester tried to talk about the German character, I tried to steer the conversation toward the enigma of my dad, Bert, who, judging from the scarcity of photos of him, seemed to have been an almost minor character in his father's life.

Most of what I knew of my dad I culled from brief interviews with my grandpa or from eavesdropping at the boozy dinners my dad occasionally hosted for fellow book salesmen. Lester had gone to White Sox games while Bert stayed home to practice his oboe. Lester went fishing while Bert stayed home to play scales. Whatever might damage the nimble fingers or affect the boy's ability to work the keys of his oboe was forbidden. To hear Lester tell it, Bert had enjoyed the life of a privileged prince and ultimately won a full four-year musical scholarship to Carlton College in Northfield, Minnesota. It was there, Lester lamented, that things began to go wrong.

Once enrolled, freshman Bert Barlow threw himself at a junior named Catherine Patterson. When she found his lack of a suitable religious background and his proposed musical career unacceptable, he vowed to convert to Roman Catholicism and give up the oboe — even renounce his budding love of the forbidden jazz. Married students on scholarships were unwelcome at Carlton in those days, so Bert left school, got hitched, and then divorced in a little over a year. By then, he had hocked his oboe for gas money to the West Coast and, far away from Lester, took welding work in Bay Area shipyards.

By the time I'd come to resent my dad's impatience with and all-consuming anger at the most trifling of ordinary frustrations, Lester, my grandmother Nina, and my mother were all attributing Bert's worst behavior to his abandonment of music. The outlines of the Bert Barlow myth seemed to be Lester's creation. But my mom, with her predilection for Methodist fatalism and penchant for the Shakespearean, filled it out and added a literary twist. I say Methodist fatalism because my mother seemed to derive consolation from the belief that somewhere in the great American unknown was a practicing Catholic harridan named Catherine who, in some convoluted way, was responsible for damaging the lives of the Barlow children. She encouraged this fatalism in us and we grew up convinced that if Bert had chosen music instead of Catherine our lives might have been better. Since nothing could be done about the past, my mom encouraged us to make the best of an intractable situation.

My grandma's hunting lunches consisted of smoked-sausage sandwiches, apples, milk, and shortbread cookies. Thus provisioned, my grandpa and I regularly drove off to roam the fallow fields on the high plains east of Denver in search of suitable small game.

One cloudy afternoon, Lester parked his black-and-white '58 Ford station wagon under a big cottonwood tree and knocked on the back door of a farmhouse. A handsome, middle-aged man with clear gray eyes and faded freckles studied us carefully before introducing himself as Ted Seecrist. After a few minutes of embarrassing small talk, my grandpa got us permission to hunt jackrabbits on Seecrist's land.

Once cured of buck fever, the tendency to open fire instantly on anything that moved, I became a good shot with the semiautomatic .22. Since I didn't much care to watch the jackrabbits die, I usually gave them a long running start in the hope they'd be done thrashing by the time I tracked them down. Since my mom and grandma refused to dress or cook our game, we left the carcasses in the fields. This was not a wasteful or a horrible thing to do, Lester explained. As hunters, we were bold benefactors in leaving fresh rabbit to injured hawks, lame coyotes, and sick badgers.

Whenever my grandpa lingered in Ted's basement to talk about ammunition loads, impact statistics, and feet-per-second, I tramped the fields, imagining myself a cold-blooded bounty hunter, a wounded Wild West sheriff who looked enough like Elvis to be surrounded by delirious girls. Rabbits were remorseless bushwhackers, guilty of horrible predations committed at private girls' schools where the students all resembled Diane Watson. I wielded the .22 from the hip like a television cowboy, coughing and spitting like a world-weary Doc Holliday, as the rabbits died.

Down in the hollow I smoked cigarettes that I'd pilfered from my dad's shirt pocket earlier in the morning. I lit one, coughed, and thought about Diane Watson's sea-green eyes, her dramatic eyebrows, and the dainty bra that rode upon her developing breasts. At a teen club dance held in the school gym decorated to look like a jungle, I had put my right hand on her hip and marveled how the hand had worked itself up the small of her back as our bodies moved together. My foot glanced off one of hers and she laughed softly, without blame. Drinking in the fragrance of the spicy perfume at her throat, I had prayed for Johnny Mathis to sing forever. About then the gym lights went up and Sister Margaret yanked the needle from the record with a squawk and began extemporizing about occasions of sin. When the sermon was over, one of Sister Margaret's darlings appeared at the turntable and called out for everybody to form a circle and "Do the Hokey Pokey."

Loitering in a hollow not far from Seecrist's house, I puffed and struggled to reduce to a bare minimum what I wanted Diane to know: that I would never think of her tits in the way I sometimes thought about the amazing fleshy globules I sneaked looks at in drugstore magazines. More than that, I wanted her to know I was searching for an opportunity to demonstrate my unique capacity for suffering and self-sacrifice when it came to any and all matters touching on her honor or safety. There was a dress the color of a robin's egg she wore sometimes. In my fantasies she was wearing such a dress, kneeling at my bedside, weeping copiously over bloodstained sheets on which I lay wounded after having successfully defended her life from evil-minded Protestants. Sister Margaret would be there, too, fingering her rosary at a suitable distance, shaken to her soul, and amazed by the depth of the love she perceived between two of her geography students.

Due back at the house for lunch, I stuffed a stick of gum in my mouth, and ran for Seecrist's house. While we ate soup, baked potatoes, and Mrs. Seecrist's special deviled eggs, Ted talked about the coyote footprints he'd discovered last week near his chicken coop. He proposed that we pile into his old Ford pickup and drive down to the dry creek bed where the varmints lived, where I might even earn a little bounty money with the .22. I rode in the back of the truck cradling the .22, wondering how I might explain killing rabbits and coyotes to Diane Watson.

Ted and my grandpa spent much of the afternoon adjusting the telescopic sight, blasting targets they painted on trees with my grandpa's 30-06, while I roamed freely in search of coyote tracks, and well downwind of the men, smoking the last of the Camels I'd pilfered from my dad.

On the rough ride back to the house, a big jackrabbit got up in front of the truck and dashed up a long slope. Ted leaned out the window and said, "Hold your fire, Timmy. Let's see what the old man can do with the heavy gun."

Lester opened the passenger door, rested the rifle stock in the open window, and held it to his cheek. At the top of the hill the rabbit stopped and turned back. It seemed to fly straight up in the air as the rifle blast echoed in the fields. Three hundred yards away, we found the bloody rag of fur and bone.

Years spent throwing snowballs at cars had convinced me there wasn't a bigger pleasure than gloating after an exciting escape. All the rabbits I'd shot had been on the run, dying in the numb ferocity of terror. If my grandpa had allowed himself more pleasure in the accuracy of his shot, I might have gone on hunting rabbits. As it was, I stood up on the windy hill, thinking about how cruel it would be to die after thinking you were safe.

My grandpa gave me my first driving lesson when I was fourteen. After an hour or two on Seecrist's rutted farm roads, he urged me out onto one of the slightly busier section roads. Later, when we started for home, he insisted that I continue to drive down Highway 40 toward Denver. We'd gone only a few miles when a highway patrolman pulled me over, issued Lester a ticket, and then escorted us to the house of a nearby justice of the peace. After the old man paid up, we stopped for pie and milk at a truck stop and he swore me to secrecy.

The next week I came home from school and saw my dad at the kitchen table, drinking beer from a chipped root beer mug. My grandma sat nearby, sipping port from a shot glass. Lester was pensively stirring the remains of a cold cup of instant coffee. I knew I was in trouble, tried to think what I had done, and drew a blank.

My dad looked at his watch. "Did you have to stay after school?"

"No."

"What took you so long to get home?"

I shrugged and rolled my eyes.

"Now Bert," my grandma Nina said. "He's a sweet boy. He has to have a little time with his friends." Her silver hair was neatly pinned to the top of her head. She was a strange, highly-strung nervous woman, a font of pity for all living things. I didn't understand how she had stayed married for almost fifty years to my grandpa or how my dad could have such a mother.

"Hi Gramma," I said, kissing her doting cheek.

"His friends!" Bert snorted, "Dollops of goddamned smelly grease on their hair combed into duck's asses, pants worn down round the knees."

"You should count yourself lucky to have such a son, Bert," she said. "He's sweet and he's smart."

My dad belched and lit a cigarette. "We'll take up the subject of his intelligence and school grades some other time."

I relaxed. Once again, too much was to be made of too little. Once again, my grandma would protect me.

Lester cleared his throat. "Your grandma discovered the canceled check I wrote to the justice of the peace," he said. "I was tempted to tell her a fib, just so she'd worry a little less, but then I remembered some of the things I'd been saying to you about the importance of the truth."

"You're not really in trouble, Timmy," Nina explained.

Lester clucked his tongue. "Anyway, since I still have the floor and might not get it again for a while, there is something more your grandpa wants to tell you. Your grandpa has tried hard to teach you the value of respect for others, and I hope that no matter how big and strong you get, and no matter how your dad acts or what he says in the future, you should never call him a goddamned idiot."

"Dad," Bert said, drumming his fingertips on the table, "I didn't call you a goddamned idiot."

"Yes you did."

"I said around your own grandsons you ought to show a little more respect for the law."

"Well, I don't criticize the drinking or driving habits of parents in front of their children, but you may not be the best person in the world to preach respect for the law."

Bert did not rise to the bait. "And I told you not to ACT like a goddamned idiot."

Lester wiped his lips. "Well, let's spare your mother and son the sorry spectacle of a father and son who have always failed to understand each other, shall we?"

"Dad, let's spare ourselves the goddamned handkerchiefs, shitcan the melodrama, tell him what we agreed to tell him, and get him downstairs on his homework." Bert swigged from his beer. "No more driving lessons, Buddy Boy. Not from your grandpa, not from anybody. You'll wait and get your learner's permit when you're sixteen, along with everybody else."

Though still a ways from being qualified for a learner's permit, the thought of it made me smile. My dad didn't want me smiling just then. He poured more beer, and looked at me sharply. "Provided you get those grades back up where they belong and come up with your own goddamned car insurance money."

"Bert," Nina said. "I wish you'd watch your language."

"Your grandpa appreciates you, Son," Lester said. "And there will come a day when your dad does, too." The old man smiled at me. "Bert's dad may be a goddamned idiot, but for a forty-dollar fine, he's bought himself a little peace of mind. Now at least your grandma and dad will know that if an old man has a heart attack next season in the high mountains hunting the mighty Wapiti, or on the way home from the sporting goods store, he's got a wonderful grandson who, legally or not, knows the rudiments of driving a car and can get the old idiot to a hospital emergency room."

One afternoon a few weeks later, Lester walked into the neighborhood drugstore and caught me reading a copy of *Hot Rod* Magazine. He didn't say anything, but the next Saturday on the way to Seecrist's, he turned off the highway and into a wrecking yard just outside the dusty farm town of Bennett. There, after obtaining permission, he escorted me to the yard, where we inspected a torn and dented Dodge Meadowbrook recently totaled in a head-on collision with another car. Reading the newspaper clipping that just happened to be folded up in Lester's pocket, I learned that seven people had died in the wreck, four of them children.

Under the broken window glass scattered like gravel inside, I noticed a Donald Duck comic book and a blood stained full bottle of orange soda, the only unbroken glass in the crumpled mass of steel and upholstery. Knowing that in the eyes of adults I always seemed to notice the wrong things, absorb the wrong lessons and draw peculiar conclusions, I said nothing about the bottle and listened solemnly to a lecture about the dangers of speeding. I nodded mutely and looked away, not wanting my grandpa to read my mind and discover how curious I was to know if Chevies were really faster than Fords.

I never drank orange soda after that.

Pennants, colored papers, tapes and washable sprays described a dubious but gleaming inventory at Happy Hanks Used Cars. An old Hudson with a fur-covered steering wheel was a cream puff; an Olds '88 with half-moon hubcaps was hot as fire; a Jeep minus a left front fender was a Troutmobile. A pink Studebaker Champion was a cherry jubilee; a Dodge Coronet was fit for a king, and an inky blue Kaiser with a missing headlight and cracked windshield was rock solid, as evidenced by five cartwheeling exclamation marks. Unfortunately, all the cars were kept locked and Hank's salesmen patrolled the lot. My buddies and I were told to beat it several times.

Irv Blocker, who owned a lot nearby, didn't go in for plastic flags or plentiful dollar signs with exclamation marks. He bought his cars at auctions and conducted most of his business from a house trailer or on a lot under three or four stringers of streaked light bulbs. The salesmen, more at liberty to haunt neighborhood coffee shops and beer joints, left his cars unlocked and made no attempt to police the lot.

Best of all, keys were often left in car ignitions, enabling me and a friend or two to start engines and even sit a while and listen to Top 40 Radio. We understood, as the occasional salesman reminded us, that radio and cigarette lighter use ran car batteries down, but saw ourselves as future customers. We got our hands on hot rod magazines and thumbed through them while sitting in Blocker's beaters, dreaming of shiny carburetors protruding through holes specially cut in car hoods. We smoked our pilfered Winstons and talked of shackling, chopping, and other ill-understood modifications, anything that might make us feel cool and garner the attention of older girls.

My friends were interested in what these cars could be and didn't know what to make of my fascination with them as hideouts and refuges and cultural artifacts. I often sat in them by myself, breathing in the wonder of their musty, smoky smells, studying stains and cracks, discolored slipcovers, ashtrays half-filled with lipstick-stained butts, fascinated by what they were already and what they had been. Under seats and in glove compartments there were strange discoveries, Matchbook covers from Florida nightclubs, scrawled addresses, candy wrappers, washers, bolts, screws, unpaid electricity bills, wrapped cigars, beer openers, nails, golf tees, Kleenex, sanitary napkins, packets of sugar, emery boards, lipsticks, and envelopes. Chipped, pitted, cracked, nicked, broken, rusted, and altered, if not museum worthy, to me they were cocoons from which flight had been taken. Their very existence on Irv's lot was consoling and redemptive; they were promises of days to come.

One afternoon, I was sitting in an old Mercury Marquis, listening to Fats Domino on the radio and puffing on a cigarette when the back door opened and a man sat down behind me.

"Put the damned cigarette out, Kid. Nobody likes to buy a smoky car."

"Oh. Sorry."

"Everybody's sorry." It was Irv Blocker. "Sometimes that's good enough, and sometimes not."

I was scared. "I mean . . . ."

"What DO you mean, Slim?"

"I'm saving my money."

"Good for you."

"You know, I'm going to be buying . . ."

"Yeah, well before that, you're gonna be cleaning."

"Huh?"

"You're gonna be doing some window-washing for me, Kid. Either you and me are going to talk to the cops and your folks, or you're going to be rubbing some cigarette smoke off the insides of these windows. You little bastards have been hanging around here way too much. I can see you, you know, when I'm on the phone."

"Okay," I said, "that's fine. I'll do some cleaning."

"And not just this one, either. You and your pals been doing some big time smoking in all my cars."

"Okay." I didn't like the confined quarters of the car and opened the car door.

"Sit back down a second, Kid." Blocker said. "I ain't going to hurt you." He lit a cigarette of his own.

I swallowed a sarcastic remark about how nice it was that his own cigarettes didn't seem to contaminate his merchandise or smudge the windows and then turned sideways, dangling my feet out the open driver's door. Blocker had a weathered face, gray eyes, heavy, black-framed glasses. I didn't know what to make of him. There were faded yellow sweat stains under the arms of his shirt. A wide tie with green and white diagonal stripes had slipped toward one side of his shirt collar. Pens bloomed from a discolored plastic envelope in his shirt pocket. His mouth was a salvage yard of crooked teeth. "What's your name, Kid?"

"Tim Barlow."

"Well, I'll be damned."

"Pardon?"

'Pardon' was appropriate for nuns and priests, but Irv seemed to disapprove of the expression and wrinkled his nose. "What I said was I'll be damned."

"Oh."

"You know why I said that, Tim?"

"No."

"Because your dad bought me a couple of beers last night over at Cliff's Bar and Grill and told me what a good lot boy you'd make. This could be fate, right here."

"My dad?"

"In fact, I told him to send you over here Monday after school to fill out an application." Irv chuckled. "I told him I wanted a kid to wash and polish and clean up cars, shovel snow, and keep the neighborhood delinquents from sitting around in my cars wearing their batteries down and getting them all smoked up with cigarettes. And here you are, already several hours in debt to me."

A couple of weeks before, my dad had caught me with a burning cigarette and hit me in the head with his fist, knocking me down. He threw me a snow shovel he'd bought years ago and sent me out to hustle walk-shoveling jobs. More recently he'd gotten me a job pushing the wheelchair of a neighborhood quadriplegic newspaper seller, and when that hadn't worked out, made me get a paper route. I didn't make any money delivering papers, so I began exaggerating the amount of time it took me to make my monthly collections from subscribers and let my school grades lapse, knowing my mom would insist that I give up the route. Though my dad didn't know it, often, when I pretended to be out collecting on my route, I was sitting around in Irv's cars dreaming of being far away, smoking, loitering, and now apparently blowing a job opportunity. I was going to be in big trouble when my dad heard about this.

"Well, I ain't paying you nothing for your first couple of hours this afternoon."

I opened my eyes. "Okay." Had I heard an implication in Irv's statement? I risked a shrug and a small smile.

"There's some chamois, rags, and a bucket over in that trailer. I've got a couple of phone calls to make. After a bit, I'm going to come out and sniff this car. If it still smells like smokes and old piss—well hell, let's look on the sunny side. Make this car garden-fresh in half an hour, then go tell your buddies to keep the hell off the lot and we'll take it from there. Maybe you've got a job."

"These windows will shine like diamonds."

"Yeah, they better. And keep them rolled down if you're smoking cigarettes in 'em."

"Okay."

"But then you'll have to check the lot before you leave work. I find any snow melting in these cars because you forgot to roll up the windows when you took off, you'll go back to your paper route."

From the way I nodded, he must have known I had something else to say. He winked at me. "You're going to have to work extra hard to keep me from telling your pop you're smoking cigarettes. You know that, don't you?"

"Yeah," I sighed.

Blocker shook his head. "Hell's sake, Kid. Take a joke! I won't tell your dad."

For two hours after school each afternoon, I washed, polished, dusted, and wiped. In bad weather, I swept snow from hoods and bumpers and scraped ice from windshields. Blocker was big on spotless dashboards and dashboard gauges, so as long as I kept moving I had license to sit unsupervised in the plush front seats of big Chryslers, filling their roomy ashtrays, listening to radios, when they worked, and dreaming of girls, real and imaginary.

There were dark times, too, moments when I realized that following my older sister's advice, cutting the belt loops off my pants and coating my hair with floral wax, then shaping it into a ducktail, would only get me so far. My sister knew nothing about what it took to be a man on south Lincoln Street, and I knew only a little more. As nearly as I could understand, you had to pretend to be, perfect your performance of being, a man before people would start to take you for a man. And you had to be taken for a man before you could begin to understand what all the fuss was about. Like a cereal box trinket, manhood couldn't possibly arrive unless you filled out the form, sent in your quarter, and waited with appropriate impatience. Meantime, I was an impostor, lost in a shuffle of masks, scrutinized by older friends more natural, or at least more adroit, at their own performance of manliness.

With tedious, chummy exhortations to be brave and self-effacing, my grandpa touted "fair and square" values as sweet, musty, and intolerably dated as the Tom Swift novels the old man pressed on me. Lester clucked his tongue at anything I did that reminded him of my dad, whose personal failings could be lamented with a few mutterings, if not actually discussed in my presence.

For his part, my dad styled himself the beleaguered pragmatist, a man beset with intolerably petty problems entirely caused by "all the goddamned idiots" who surrounded and delayed him at home, in check-out lines, at traffic lights, and on the job. My dad did what he could to prepare me for manhood by attempting to eradicate in me traces of what he saw as his own father's useless, hardheaded idealism and my mom's bookish dreaminess. My dad saw himself as the appointed spokesman for "the real world," a nose-to-the-grindstone sort of place that, from what I could tell, demanded first the renunciation and then the obliteration of all that was slow, stubborn, independent, or inward.

I was on my own, overwhelmed by how much energy I expended to keep the traces of boyish fraudulence off my pouty face. My cheeks were acquiring a coating of soft white hair when what was called for was wiry whiskers. Pimples appeared overnight, invariably on the end of my nose. My arms were shaped like Popeye's, before spinach, and, though less visible except in gym, my legs were too long and gangly and deformed by knees the size of coconuts. My chest was a shapeless pod, and between my legs was this little, hairless bobbin. And these were just my physical deficiencies.

Most of my friends knew more about cars and life than I did and were at some pains to point out to me how my loyalties and attitudes were dead wrong. What did I stand for? Jesus, Mary, and Joseph, the Dodgers, the Democratic Party, and the Ford Motor Car Company?

My friends held, most convincingly, that Fords sucked and that a loyalty to Ford was probably less a sign of ignorance than a symptom of some pathetic congenital malaise. That Fords were the only thing I knew my dad and grandpa to agree on made it that much harder to switch to Chevy. Any mention of my dad and grandpa's loyalties to Ford, though, was out of the question, suggesting as it did deficiencies in manliness and discernment. After shaking his head in disgust at my dad's relatively new Mercury Monterey, Mick Langford, one of the toughest older guys in the neighborhood who outweighed me thirty pounds, suggested that some polluting strain of impotence and womanliness seemed to run through my family's bloodline. Chevies were outperforming Fords everywhere, Langford sneered, adding that he had no doubt that my own first ought to be a Nash Rambler.

Loyalty to the hapless Dodgers was part of the same inadequacy. Why couldn't I admit that the Dodgers were basically a bunch of hitless base-stealers who couldn't manage to play .500 ball without Koufax and Drysdale, and that in the weaker league?

And as Terry LaConner said right outside the church, "The Virgin Mary? Get off it!" I wasn't about to allow myself to speculate about whether she had or hadn't been a virgin, but as I brooded in one of Stocker's battered Caddies, it hadn't done my immortal Catholic soul any good to have stood and listened and laughed when his greaser buddy started making all those jokes about Joseph's hard-ons.

Manhood involved learning to recognize and accept the truth, advancing deft combinations of action and claim, truth and bluff. Manhood required convincing public performances, and these things could be worked on and maybe almost perfected, but what else was involved? How to tell the swagger from the walk, the tools and pilfered war trophies from glory on the battlefield? In the neighborhood where I lived a real man could keep a car running, manage an acetylene torch, clean a septic tank, operate a backhoe, add a spare bedroom, or build a boat from blueprints published in craft magazines. A real man might never get rich, but as long as he could keep his Chevy running, he could remain independent enough that he wouldn't "haffta take shitoffa nobody." A contemptuous independence defended with fists and expletives was as close to happiness as any man was allowed to hanker after. Apart from cars and big metal things that produced smoke, heat, strong smells, and perhaps the risk of death or serious injury, a real man was not allowed to be interested in very much at all. Motors with eight big cylinders and loud, smelly, pneumatic thingamajigs were not so much toys that gave pleasure as objects of necessary veneration and torment. An interest in cars, like an interest in women, was something sustained with the help of glossy magazines. Cars and women had a lot more in common than position on magazine stands. The more of a real man you were, the more conversant you were with their similarities. You fiddled with both of them while wearing a crooked sneer of contempt. You showed them off to your buddies, got mad at them when they wouldn't do what you wanted, and never ever said anything nice about them in front of your friends. When somebody said something good about either your car or your chick, you hoped to be standing outdoors where you could stuff your hands in your pockets, spit on the sidewalk, and act like nothing at all had been said. As a man, you had to make yourself impervious to accusations of boyhood. The best way to do that was with a toolbox. I'd been around enough older guys by now to know that nobody ever attacked a man's self-esteem when he was rebuilding a carburetor or gapping spark plugs. What's more, I had noticed I could talk all I wanted to about being a man around some younger guy whose ass I could kick if I had to, but on the streets of the real world, which was related to, yet decidedly and confusingly different from my dad's "real world," you could not risk a full-out assertion of manhood until after you'd "popped" your first cherry and completed your first head gasket or valve job. Apparently, valve jobs and fucking were alike, too. You had to do both of them regularly or you began to lose power. The world was ruled by crabby, alcohol-reeking grease monkeys who disdained foreign cars and six-cylinder engines out of the same bottomless reservoir of contempt. How could I approach these gods whose limp dicks were probably bigger than torque wrenches and try to learn about gasket sealers and gapping spark plugs? How could the scared face in the Studebaker's rear view mirror, the impostor cursed with the little hairless Ping Pong balls in the crotch of pants which wouldn't stay up on his nonexistent hips, how could I manage to slip through the gates of the real world into real manhood? How long would I be able to go on straining and faking that I had already arrived?

Dynaflush

"Deep down inside the Dynaflow unit itself, a series of
little propeller-like blades bite into the swirling oil
when you open up the throttle, just like a modern
airplane's propellers bite into air."
*Advertisement, **Life**, January 4, 1955*

The cold war intensified. The space race became a national obsession. Artists and scientists were visiting the White House, and with an enthusiasm that surprised me, my dad gave up selling welding supplies and used cars in favor of encyclopedias. While he was putting a lot of mileage on successions of bigger and newer cars and telling the working people of western Colorado about the importance of alphabetically organized knowledge, I was settling into a newer, bigger house in a better neighborhood. I grew four inches in one summer, put on weight, started caddying at a nearby country club, made new friends, and emerged, more or less intact, from the first phase of my glandular entropy with a driver's license.

By then, some of my friends had driver's licenses and cars. In warm, dry weather, supplied with chrome polish, wax, and window cleaner, these lucky few cruised Washington Park, selecting shady spots where they could rub, and be seen to rub until it gleamed, each steely automotive surface. With car doors slung open and radios blaring Martha and the Vandellas or Jan and Dean, some of them even went so far as to get down on their haunches and scrub their white sidewall tires with foaming toothbrushes.

Automotive styles differed from neighborhood to neighborhood, but it was universally agreed that you had to drive not just a car, but some kind of emphatic statement, even if you were going to run stock. Whatever was or wasn't under the hood, and however sluggish the car might be, it was important to get it tricked out to look loved, fast, and abused. Even a "wreck" should be done up to look capable of breaking the sound barrier, in style. We're talking sound and fury. If you had a crappy car you could do small things to at least make it louder.

I had the fever and considered myself fairly glib when it came to the lingo. But the actual workings of cars were mysterious to me. With mechanical aptitude, older brothers, or friends, not to mention money, suitable tools and shop equipment, you could "drop" in a 327-cubic-inch Chevy engine and modify your gear ratios, whatever they were. Even without the ideal engine, unnecessary louvers could be cut in the hood over the motor. Shackles and huge clamps installed to compress suspension systems imparted a desirable low-slung, supersonic fighter plane look. With access to welding equipment and heavy clamps, you could chop and lower the roof, reduce your windshield to approximately the size of a ventilation window at the top of an outhouse. Grills could be reshaped into shark's teeth and gaping cobra-like mouths could be poked through the hood, sucking cool air down into what might or might not be a fiery power plant within, threatening to bite or strike the world.

Other things could be done, even without money or aptitude. Some neighborhoods were big on gem-studded mud flaps, fender skirts, and hubcaps known as Checkerboard Fiestas. Car paint, as in bright and thick, could be embellished with spidery pinstripes or flames, the hotter-colored the better. And special shiny mufflers, which some held were illegal, made even smoky rattletraps sound like dragsters or Indy 500 cars. Somehow, if you were going on to college, it was permissible to forgo the glossy paint job. For a more *waspy* college-bound look, you could get by with primer; flat gray, the color of cigarette ash, was the preferred hue. In such cases, you avoided the mud flaps and garish extras, favoring the minimalist hubcaps known as moons, half moons, and dulled half moons.

You could mount fist-sized pot metal skulls to gearshift levers, or clamp clear, plastic red or green-tinted knobs to steering wheels, enabling you to turn a corner with one hand. For the truly expressive, there were steering wheels made from specially welded chain links. Rear view mirrors could be lined with white or pink synthetic furs, and mirrors, sun visors, or broken radio knobs could be dandled with rabbits' feet or beer can openers known as "church keys." Catholic scapulars, for protection, or dangling dice or baby shoes were other viable options. There were plastic shrunken heads with tufts of wiry black hair, statuettes of the Virgin Mary or St. Christopher, on whose shoulders the Christ child rode piggyback, or sulky figures of an adult Christ. And for the defiantly irreligious, there were decals of monkey-tailed Satans, pouncing tigers, fire-spitting dragons, or glossy panthers with red-stained maws. To customize or decorate, of course, meant either owning your own car or having a pliable mother.

Those of us with neither, lacked not only transportation, but the means to be taken seriously. At a party, Mark Whiting, a football jock with a midnight-blue '58 Chevy Impala, referred to me and my friend Harley Rosenszweig as "bus boys." When Harley insisted that we hadn't taken the bus or mooched a ride, but that we had arrived in his mom's two-tone blue '57 Buick, Whiting called us "mama's boys." Because he was big and surrounded by football cronies, we made the best of things. At least, being a "mama's boy," driving your mom's car was half a step up from being a "bus boy," taking the bus.

Like an apparition from an old Flash Gordon comic strip, Harley's mom's Buick was chock-a-block with chrome and pot metal, finished off with shiny portholes inset decoratively and uselessly in its front quarter panels. One of the heaviest cars ever built, it wheezed, floated, and bobbed, expending huge efforts and copious gas in going nowhere. On each front fender it sported chromed badges, reading "Dynaflow," but Harley called it "Dynaflush." We both hoped to avoid being seen in it by certain girls, but for a while, at least, it was all the transportation we had. And even when it was no longer all we had, it remained our car of choice for Sunday afternoon outings to Rocky Mountain Raceways, a drag strip near Castle Rock, about thirty miles south of Denver.

Admission to the drags was on a per-person basis, and since Dyna's trunk could accommodate two or even three limber bodies, my friends and I climbed into its trunk just outside the grounds, having already spent our admission on six-packs of 3.2 beer. Colorado was one of several states where 18-year-olds could legally drink beer containing up to 3.2 percent alcohol. The Colorado-based Adolph Coors Company, and several other breweries, serviced this booming market by producing thinned-out beers for apprentice drinkers. Getting drunk on three-two was easy, though something of a workout for the bladder. Even so, sixteen-year-olds with nerve and heavy beards like Harley's could often buy the harder stuff. In fact, Harley liked to claim he sometimes needed the harder stuff to deal with the derision he experienced being seen behind the wheel of Dyna.

Over time, Harley acquired the wit to seek to make a virtue of the Buick's distended bloat, or at least the spunk to try. Plenty of people drove cool cars, he taught himself to say, but there was a decided shortage of guys willing to drive a car so completely given over to useless chromed bloat and swank. To accentuate its chrome and doodads, he occasionally washed and polished and bleached the Buick's little white sidewall tires. At my urging, he read Cyrano and taught himself to orchestrate choruses of laughter, even occasionally going so far as to vocalize the impotent whoosh of the Buick's giant engine. Sometimes he invited hecklers to go for a ride, during which they could watch the all-too-visible fall of the gas gauge needle as the Buick wheezed nowhere in particular. Under pressure, he readily agreed that while, yes, they who drove Chevies, Plymouths, and Pontiacs would no doubt beat Dyna in any kind of race, perhaps without even bothering to shift into third or fourth gear, he would bear the humiliation knowing that in a world where football was a national passion, brute heft and weight counted for a great deal, so much so he'd gladly weigh in against them in a Demolition Derby. On such occasions he'd swat Dyna's massive front fender and refer to it as "the Tank."

Although there were always parties and rumors of parties to crash, gas money to get to them could be hard to come by. Partly for that reason, the neighborhood McDonald's, with its recently expanded parking lot, served as town square and high-school potlatch. There, when inspiration was scarce and finances low, friends and rivals and those unable to borrow gas money could slump against fenders, flip straws loaded with milkshake at one another, lick salt grit from the bottoms of french fry sacks, and critique the clothes and cars of all comers.

One hot summer night, Harley and I sat on Dyna's hood, sucking rum-spiked Cokes through straws and hoping for action.

Sylvia Casey, driving her mother's Jeep, pulled into the empty space next to Dyna. The Jeep glistened with newly applied polish and its engine gurgled and hissed with impressive power. At our urging, Sylvia popped the hood and showed us the souped-up 327-cubic-inch Chevy V-8 engine recently installed by her mother's boyfriend. Two chromed carburetors gleamed from the scrubbed block.

I had been appearing in high-school plays and competing in school-sponsored speech meets whenever it would get me out of school. And I knew Sylvia from three or four speech meet performances she'd given on behalf of the rival high school she and Harley attended.

She was gamine, pretty, and high-strung. Outspoken and contentious, she was quick to deflate pretensions and not easily daunted or cowed into playing the sex object. For her refusal to remain on the periphery of conversations, her willingness to flip guys off, punch them in the arm, or challenge them to repeat to her face any lewd remarks aimed her direction, Harley and I accorded her honorary "guy" status. No fashionably teased hair or pencil-darkened eyes for Sylvia. She wore a pageboy and held that most girls were dreadfully boring, especially those she openly accused of trying to call attention to their tits. Sylvia believed that after her face, her best feature was her butt. One of the things that

Harley and I liked best about her was that after a couple of beers, she could be coaxed into shaking her ass competitively at more socially accepted stuck-up girls with "fatter butts and better boobs."

After having openly admired her mother's Jeep, Harley poured rum in Sylvia's Coke and, with drunken irony, solicited her opinion of Dyna. She shrugged. "Everybody knows it's a poor person's Caddy. Tell your parents I hope they make better money next year, so they can buy the car they really want. By the way, word is that the reason Susie Baumholtz wouldn't go out with you is because she didn't want to be seen in it."

Harley looked to me for understanding and said, "She's a social-climbing bitch. The only reason I even asked her out was as a favor to my mom. I happened to have some free tickets to a concert. No big deal."

Observing other people wandering over and warming to the subject at hand, Sylvia said, "I'm surprised she wouldn't go with you. Those big wide seats in that ugly Buick would certainly support her fat ass."

Harley laughed. "Why won't you go out with me?"

"Well, two no's don't make an absolutely never. But, since you ask, let me offer you some pointers. Don't ever call me up the night before again. Ask me to go somewhere I might actually like to go, and afterwards don't expect to take me out in the middle of nowhere to cop a feel." She looked at Dyna and raised her eyebrows. "And now that I think of it, you'd have to buy the gas so I could drive my car. I wouldn't want to be seen tooling around in that thing."

Stung, Harley raised an eyebrow. "Mama's Jeep."

"Well, mama's Buick to you, too," she laughed. "I mean, I hope it's still your mama's car. I'd hate to think that you drove that pimpmobile by choice."

Harley struggled for a response. "I'd expected you to look a little deeper than that."

"I did look deeper," Sylvia said. "And I saw that it could double as an army tank."

Harley smiled and weaved slightly. "A pimpmobile and a tank. Yes, I agree on both counts. In fact, Buick built tanks for the war. However, Dynaflush is also a spaceship and a royal coach, providing my every comfort."

"Oh, right!"

"What's more, owing to my greater driving skills, I can go in Dynaflush wherever you can go in the Jeep, more reliably, probably faster, certainly in much more comfort."

"Oh, give me a break, Rosenszweig."

Harley was not finished. Splashing more rum in her cup, he said, "Plus, wherever you go you have to ride on those uncomfortable benches. Me, I'll be sitting on Dyna's plush couch, cruising along in cushy style in H.M.S."

"H.M.S.?"

"Harley's Mom's Shitmobile."

Sylvia joined the general laughter. Encouraged, Harley lit a cigarette and inhaled deeply. "Dyna has power windows and an ashtray the size of a serving bowl. Speed is important, of course, but driving skills, automated swank and shiny chrome still count for something in this world."

"Just not with Baumholtz," Sylvia laughed and winked at me. "Harley, the only thing you *would* do in Dyna that I *wouldn't* do in my Jeep is give that bitch a ride around the block. The only thing you *could* do in that that I *couldn't* do in mine is maybe collapse a driveway."

Harley smiled. "Perhaps you'd like to put up a little money on that."

"Aha! The male competitive juices are pumping now. What do you have in mind?"

"Say a little all-out test of roadworthiness and driving skill?"

"Such as?"

"Well, let's do a two-part contest. A race followed by a test of driving skills on a stretch of rough road."

The audience groaned and Sylvia laughed. "You've got to be joking."

"I'm not talking about a race from a standstill," Harley explained. "That would be absurd. We'll pull up alongside each other at twenty-five miles an hour and race to the Celebrity Bowling Alley five blocks from here."

"And the second part?"

"Well, there's a little road that parallels Cherry Creek under Colorado Boulevard. It goes down under the bridge beside the water and comes out on the other side of Colorado."

"What, that thing with all those rocks and big chunks of concrete? Gimme a break. I mean, I could probably make it, but you certainly couldn't. That behemoth's got all of six inches clearance."

Harley was beaming. "But with superior driving skills much can be done."

"Fine," Sylvia said. "Just give me a week to raise some money, so I can make your humiliation profitable."

"No way," Harley said. "I'd never see you again."

She shrugged. "All I've got is three bucks."

Harley looked at me and shrugged. "As it happens, that's about all we can raise, too."

"Tim," Sylvia suggested, "talk some sense to your drunken friend."

A glance at Harley made it clear to me that an expression of my loyalty had become essential. "You've got a Jeep with a hot engine," I said. "But that doesn't mean you know how to drive it."

"Okay," Sylvia said, "then go down with him in a blaze of glorious humiliation."

Contest conditions were negotiated and refined while two dozen bystanders hooted and clapped and predicted disaster for Harley, the hero whose willingness to risk his mother's car would keep the evening from being a perfect disaster for as many as thirty people.

There were no busy intersecting streets along that stretch of Colorado Boulevard, so the Buick and Jeep could pull alongside one another at twenty-five miles an hour in front of the McDonald's, then race to the edge of the main driveway of the nearby bowling alley. When Sylvia expressed alarm about the length of the proposed course, Harley pointed out that even after passing the finish line, there would be three blocks to slow down before the next traffic light. When there was nothing more to be said, Sylvia climbed in her Jeep and Harley and I got in the Buick.

Harley and Sylvia got their respective racers nose-to-nose at about thirty. Then, at a signal given by a kid with a flashlight, Harley straightened his leg and arched his back to apply maximum pressure on the accelerator. Dyna wheezed while the Jeep thundered and jumped in front. Predictably, Harley was counting on his opponent's failure to appreciate how soon the Jeep would hit sixty and how long it would be necessary for Sylvia to go on increasing her speed to preserve the lead and win the race.

Dyna continued to lose ground until an unwitting driver in a red Oldsmobile signaled and drifted obliviously into Sylvia's lane. She had a brief window to an empty third lane, but her brake lights flashed when she hesitated, then flashed again as she doubted and double-checked her margin of safety. Harley's lane stayed clear and Dyna gained ground. As Sylvia jerked into the empty lane, she over steered and touched the brakes again to correct her course. Dyna groaned past the Jeep and won by four or five feet.

Pale and angry, Sylvia appeared in the bowling alley parking lot to demand a rematch. But Harley, knowing all witnesses would take his part, if only because they wanted to watch him try to drive the Buick under the bridge, couldn't stop shaking his head and grinning. Sylvia glared at us all, then without a word, hopped back in the Jeep and started for Cherry Creek.

The road descended steeply under the bridge, entered the shallow creek water, and emerged again seventy-five yards away on the other side of the busy street. It wasn't the road remnant's steepness or muddiness that was discouraging, but the rocks and chunks of cement, the jagged bits of tire-ripping teeth-like shapes visible above the water's surface. From one end to the other, what looked to have once been an old fire road of some sort was choked with broken concrete pylons and the sharp, boulder-sized chunks, the washed-out remains of an earlier bridge.

"Settle for a draw, Harley," I advised him. "Even if you could maneuver around all those shards, you'd still get blowouts in all your tires. It's completely impassable."

"Yeah, I know," Harley said. "But, the thing is, she agreed to go first. She won't make it so we'll win by default—just by having won the race down Colorado."

I looked at him and shook my head. "You know what I think?"

"What's that?"

"I think that you're hoping she gets stuck and asks for your help. I think that you imagine succeeding in the Jeep where she failed. You want a chance to drive that Jeep. That's what I think."

Harley sighed. "You know me too well."

By detouring and splashing through the fouled, shallow waters, Sylvia somehow managed to avoid the worst of the sharp rocks. Confronted at the other side by her flushed, triumphant face, Harley had too much at stake and convinced himself that he, too, could maneuver Dyna through the obstacle course.

"I saw the route," Harley assured me. "There are three major rocks to avoid. My only concern about this whole thing is whether or not we can get up the traction on the far side of the bridge to drive up the incline in all that mud."

I stuffed my hands in the front pockets of my pants. "You want me to ride with you?"

"Yeah."

I didn't want to earn a night's ridicule, though I guessed I would if I had to. "I mean, don't you think you'd have a better chance without my added weight?"

"Nah, come on. I need you as a coach, somebody to help me look around when things get hairy down there."

With the crowd gathered round, we shared the last of the cheap rum, saluted Sylvia, piled into Dyna, and started down.

46

Once he'd bypassed the initial chunks of broken cement and pavement, Harley turned the wheel and goosed Dyna into what he assumed was ankle-deep water. It proved to be deeper. Attempting to back out, he scraped Dyna's rear bumper on a sharp rock and stalled. Thinking he was about to concede, I smiled and shrugged and looked out the window at the shallow water we'd have to wade through. But Harley shot me a quick reckless look, restarted the engine, put Dyna in low, and stomped on the gas. Over the whooshing motor and the sloshing water, I heard hoots and jeers. Expelling white clouds of defiance, the Buick gained the top of a protruding concrete fang and lost traction. Back tires skating starboard, she dropped with a mighty two-ton clank on a submerged rock. Harley goosed her again and rocked her into reverse. This time, the front wheels drifted apart and settled slowly into a muddy pit where the engine gurgled and died. Harley shrugged, lit a Pall Mall, and got out laughing and telling onlookers that with a length of chain and the help of the Jeep, Dyna would be back up on the pavement again in no time.

Not one of the grinning spectators admitted to having a chain or rope. Gloating and insisting she was already in violation of her curfew, Sylvia reminded us that we had almost killed her minutes ago. She muttered something in my direction, started the Jeep and roared off down Colorado Boulevard. There was no way Harley and I could budge the monster Buick. None of the assembled onlookers could be persuaded to help us.

"I ain't about to ruin my pants and catch my death of disease in that shitty ol' water," said one boy in a baseball cap sitting on the hood of a Dodge smeared with primer paint.

"Just leave it down there where it can't be seen from the streets," suggested his buddy. "You'd be doing your bit to beautify America."

We were soon left alone with the beginnings of hangovers. Pooling our resources, we calculated we had enough for coffee at a nearby coffee shop, a package of gum to mask the smell of the rum we'd been drinking, a tip for the waitress, and hopefully, change for the necessary but dreaded phone call.

Harley's mom Ethel said there was "no way in hell" she would give me a ride home. Worse, nothing Harley could say to her was going to prevent her from phoning my dad, blaming me for the whole debacle, and telling him to keep me away because she didn't want Harley hanging around with gentiles.

After a long walk home, I learned from my mom that my dad had already absorbed most of the details of our adventure in a heated telephone shouting match with Ethel. Having slammed the phone down, my dad had gone out for a beer, my mom said, leaving word with her that I was grounded for two weeks and forbidden to see Harley ever again. I was surprised my mom was taking my dad's part in this. The next day my brother Mike told me that my mother had chided him for calling Ethel "a goddamn kike," a reprisal, or so he told my mom, for Ethel's calling him a "fucking goy."

'55 Ford Fairlane

"Hey, Mom, is this Fairlane a sporty car to drive?"
"Hey, Mom, is it really a family-size car?"
"Hey, Mom, did it really cost as little as Dad says?"
"Yes, and don't stick your heads out the window."
*Advertisement, **Look**, November 5, 1963*

One Saturday afternoon a few weeks later, I stood at the front window watching for the arrival of a '59 Chevy with dual clutches and brakes. My driving instructor, Harry, coughed gobs of phlegm into a filthy handkerchief and erupted in profanity whenever my touch with the clutch failed me, or whenever I turned a corner or pulled away from the curb without employing arm signals. I didn't enjoy being called a cocksucker, especially by a wrinkled old lizard in a Mickey Mouse shirt, but I consoled myself with the knowledge that Harry and his unfiltered Chesterfield cigarettes would soon pass from my life forever. And once Harry was out of the picture, I would enjoy reduced car insurance premiums and, whenever I could wheedle it, access to my mom's recently acquired red-and-white '55 Ford Fairlane.

I was disappointed that it was a six cylinder, but as soon as my dad brought it home, I began secretly developing plans to modify its appearance. The first time I drove it on my own, I went around the block, got out, and popped the standard hubcaps and put them in the trunk, hoping my mom wouldn't notice their absence. She noticed, of course. And when I told her where the hubcaps were, she sent me outside to pop the hubcaps back on, then followed me outside and stood over my shoulder while I did, letting me know there was no way she was going to let me install a tachometer on her steering column, lower the car's front end, or even hang a pair of felt-covered dice from the rearview mirror. Resigned to her conservatism, I made the best of things by stowing a large screwdriver under the front seat. Before every date or important outing, I drove the Fairlane around the block, popped the hubcaps, and then reinstalled them again before parking in front of our house.

Three weeks after getting my driver's license, I was down in my basement bedroom. My dad shouted for me to come to the phone and talk to somebody named Casey about a possible summer job. I didn't know anybody named Casey, but I picked up the phone anyway.

"Tim?"

"Yeah?"

"This is Harley."

"Hi."

"Your dad's not on the other extension, is he?"

"No. I'm fine, Casey, how are you?'

"Listen, I can't talk long. You still looking for a summer job?"

"Uh, yes, I'm interested." I looked at my dad and spoke more loudly. "I wondered if that job might come through when I applied for it, of course. What kind of job is it, exactly?"

"Kumpf Motors, this Lincoln-Mercury dealership downtown. Shagging cars. They just fired a guy. If you get over there early tomorrow morning and ask for Hal, he just might hire you."

"All right," I said. "I'll definitely be there, Casey. Thanks for calling"

"The thing is," Harley added, "don't tell them you know me. I got the job through a relative, you know. Word could get back that I'm hanging out with you again."

"I got you, Casey," I said. "See you tomorrow morning."

Hal, the service manager, expressed distaste for my studiously disheveled clothes and my long, unkempt hair, but told me he'd give me a chance to drive the company pickup truck, picking up and delivering car parts, if I'd be willing to "do something about my hair." The idea that I could be paid driving a pickup truck around town without a lot of supervision was magic. I went around the corner and paid for a trim.

My job was to drive an old battered pickup all over the city, shuttling Lincoln and Mercury parts to garages and dealerships. Hal was given to watching his wristwatch and badgering me to hurry. I didn't like hurrying through the parts department, but I was happy to oblige once I was behind the wheel of the dealership pickup, racing through intersections as though every yellow traffic lights was an invitation to accelerate.

After about a week, having come to a rare complete stop at a stop sign a few blocks away from the dealership, I was rear-ended by someone who hadn't been looking. Although the accident was clearly not my fault, I lost the parts delivery job owing, Hal explained, to a company policy of dismissing immediately any parts driver involved in an accident.

Just as I was about to slink home to brood about the unfairness of life, the head mechanic manager waved me over and offered me a job as a shag boy, working alongside Harley. I couldn't understand why, after being fired from the parts department, I would be hired to drive customers' cars to and from nearby storage lots and mechanics' stalls, but

I was glad to start right away, and gladder still to be able to eat lunch every day with Harley.

Gone now was the need to locate obscure addresses, check part numbers, and lug heavy greasy parts down long hallways. There were no more scoldings for dripping battery acid on new showroom carpets, no more wrestling clanking tailpipes through narrow doorways. Shagging cars meant hustling to one or another of five or six nearby company lots, climbing into big Lincolns and Mercurys, slamming their doors, twisting their keys, and burning rubber all the way to crowded mechanic stalls in the service garage.

By the middle of my second week, I was already holding my own against Harley in an ongoing competition to see who could elicit the longest squeals from the tires of the most expensive cars while managing to avoid stationary objects, mechanics, salesmen, and secretaries. Thankfully, I supposed, car owners were confined to the soundproofed showroom and denied access to the garage where their cars were subjected to varieties of gleeful, heavy-footed resentment. Mechanics were paid by the job and didn't like standing around. They scowled and complained whenever it took too long for us to bring them their next job. I soon found that if I made a big Lincoln's tires whistle and trill all the way into a stall, slammed on the brakes, and threw it into park so hard the car rocked back and forth, that the waiting mechanics smiled appreciatively and even offered words of encouragement.

One afternoon I was summoned to get a Lincoln Mark IV out of a stall and replace it with a red Mercury Marquis. The replacement maneuver was complicated by the fact that several other mechanics and a couple of cars were obstructing my most direct route. Since the waiting mechanic was a personal favorite, I took an indirect, high-risk route, which called for backing down two different lanes in the garage, then honking and proceeding backwards and blind across an alley. I was making headway, filling the garage with a squealing melody of Goodyear urgency, when a big Lincoln Continental bashed me coming out of nowhere. Headlight glass, signal lights, and bumper parts went tinkling and clanking across the concrete floor of the garage. Harley got out of the car shaking his head, accepting his share of the blame, and smothering a grin.

Fired and issued our paychecks early, we drove his mom's repaired Buick to Cherry Creek Dam to enjoy the last of a summer afternoon.

Over illegal beers, I mused that having driven recklessly to deliver car parts, I had been rear-ended while sitting at a stop sign. Then having been fired for being the victim of an accident involving a worn-out pickup truck, I was hired to drive luxury cars by another department. Having hurried and driven recklessly as I had been encouraged to do, I'd been involved in an accident and fired. On reflection there seemed two ways of thinking about this: that the real world was paradoxical and horribly unjust, or that the world of cars was subject to laws which varied somewhat from the real world principles that operated elsewhere.

Harley agreed with this. But he also pointed out that since school was about ready to start up again, there was probably no need to confess to our families that we'd been fired.

School started up and Harley and I continued to hang out. We didn't confide our drag-racing ambitions to many, but we did begin making plans to drive both his mom's Buick and my mom's Ford up to the starting line at Castle Rock Raceway and show what, with the help of moms' cars, we and those cars could do.

After consulting with experts, we learned that owing to its engine size, year, and weight, the Buick would be assigned to the L class. We quickly realized the Buick's sluggish acceleration would be regarded as a joke. It would suffer successions of humiliating and laugh-inducing defeats while providing race fans with moments of high hilarity. In contrast, we were convinced that once we removed some of the Fairlane's excess weight, and its air cleaner, I would tear up the N class in my mom's Ford. Knowing she'd be horrified at the prospect of her car in a drag race, we decided what she didn't know wouldn't hurt her.

With visions of trophies in my head, I practiced power shifting, racing the engine, and popping the clutch, while Harley monitored the howl of the Fairlane's motor and held a cheap stopwatch next to the odometer in order to time the Ford in the quarter-mile. As the engine went from a roar to a scream, I rammed it into second, held the gas pedal down, then ripped it into third just before, I imagined, the frantic pistons were about to launch themselves like greasy rockets through the wall of the engine and the little pinkish car hood.

With its flathead six, in first and second gears, the little Fairlane couldn't do much more than howl in automotive pain as it fell back behind the cars we began to challenge on the street. We always had good excuses for losing these street drags and consoled ourselves by speculating about our competition, and the four-barreled carbs and racing cams we supposed were under the hoods of our victorious opponents. Harley knew more about these things than I did, but not much more. As we drove the streets in search of new opposition, we talked of installing hotter plugs, of tune-ups, and a heavy-duty clutch. We grinned and agreed that with my timing and power shifting down pat, the time for us to finally blow our competition off the line at Castle Rock had nearly come.

One summer night just after the Fairlane had been tuned-up by my mother's favorite garage of the month, we piled in and headed to a "kegger" in Boulder. Keggers were frat parties where University of Colorado students paid two-dollar admission fees to stand in line and drink warm, foamy 3.2 beer from ten and twenty gallon rented kegs. As fund-raisers, the University of Colorado fraternities preferred "keggers" to car washes. Not only did they produce more revenue for less labor; they were a lot more fun. Under-aged high-school juniors and seniors also took an interest in these events. As long as cops weren't working the door, no frat brat we came across ever asked paying guests to prove they were of age.

In the knowledge that we'd be spending energy and needing self-confidence later in the evening when we tried to talk with "older chicks," Harley removed the hinges from his dad's liquor cabinet and we downed three screwdrivers each before we headed out. At a station not far from his house, I filled the Fairlane's gas tank and checked the oil.

On the Boulder Turnpike out of Denver, we rolled down the windows to enjoy the balmy spring night air. We had a good idea about how long it would take the Ford to cover a quarter of a mile from a standstill. What we didn't know was the Fairlane's top end. With traffic scarce and the dark road empty before us, it seemed a perfect night to find out. I leaned back and floored it. The long, slightly downhill grade leveled out about the time we hit eighty. Harley slipped immediately into the role of a tense captain in a World War II submarine movie.

"Eighty-five and rising," Harley said. "Ninety and holding steady."

The car was light on the road and the little engine wailed with pain.

"Ninety-five!"

Harley was very excited because Fred Davis, who knew more about cars than either of us, insisted the Fairlane would never get over ninety and certainly would never approach a hundred. Suddenly, skimming the Boulder Turnpike, we both laughed, knowing the little car had more to give. I gritted my teeth, marveling how, at higher speeds, the Ford was harder to steer and much more inclined to take to the air.

Then, Wham! The little Fairlane roared forward in total darkness. A bump at high speed and the hood had come flying up and over the windshield, totally blocking all view of the road.

"Take your foot off the gas!" Harley shouted.

I backed off, but I was blind and we were going so fast that I was scared to hit the brakes too hard. The Ford rocketed toward Boulder.

"Slow down! Don't slam on the brakes!"

I didn't know if I was saying these things or if Harley was.

"Slow down! Slow down! Take it easy!" Even as he screamed directions, he stuck his head out the window. "A little farther right! No, not so far. Back left! Easy! A tiny bit right! There. Easy, easy, easy."

The Fairlane rolled to a stop and we got out on the edge of the road. In the cool night air by the road shoulder we realized that after checking the oil, I had forgotten to close the hood tightly. Now it was bent and wrapped around the windshield, held only by a metal hinge, partly torn through. We worked it like a loose tooth, secured it in the trunk, and drove back to Denver to develop a plausible story for my parents. By the time we got to the consolations of Harley's dad's liquor cabinet, however, it seemed clear to both of us that only a tamed-down version of the truth would be believed.

The next morning, I told my mom about forgetting to close the hood but halved the speed at which we'd been traveling. She bought the story, but when my dad came home he tugged the hood out of the trunk to conduct his own investigation.

"Forty-five miles an hour my achin' ass! Forty-five miles an hour wouldn't reshape that thing into a goddamned potato chip." He swiped at me, but I wasn't there anymore. Luckily, my mom had appeared on the scene. "The insurance deductible is coming out of his savings account. And he isn't leaving the house for a month!"

By the time I was granted limited car privileges again, the drag-racing season was over. When Kennedy was shot that November, my interest in drag racing also became a casualty.

I was sneaking a cigarette behind the gym when JFK was killed. And sitting in front of the television watching hair grow from the shins protruding from my shrunken pajamas when Ruby shot Oswald. After that, it seemed clear to me that priests were full of it, that God was nothing but a fanciful shiver in the fearful hearts of men, and that I owed it to the world to begin carrying such messages to the human race, beginning, I supposed, with my cohorts at South High.

Mister Strassman wore a crew cut and long sideburns, and masochistically enjoyed preparing his history students for the blood sacrifices sometimes demanded by democracy. He hopped from Lincoln to Kennedy, jumped to Korea where his oldest brother had served, and then on to Vietnam, where his favorite cousin had flown helicopters. I suggested that he might be right about the importance of defending

54

democracy, and that if so, on the basis of some reading I'd been doing lately, perhaps it would be best to call the troops home from Asia and send them to Mississippi and Alabama where Negroes were being beaten, bombed, and tortured for attempting to register to vote.

The 60s were starting a little late, but they were coming hard and fast.

The next week my friend Ray was sent home from school to shave. Two days later, he returned to school with a thicker beard and a letter from an attorney friend of his mom's. After a couple of days it quietly leaked out that senior boys would enjoy somewhat more relaxed dress codes and were to be allowed to wear neatly trimmed beards. To celebrate, Ray's mom, Shawna, gave him an eighteenth birthday bash. Not only did she rent a motel room for the occasion, she showed up to chaperone the party. A station wagon full of booze was off-loaded into the room, and about three dozen of us started going at those bottles pretty hard.

Trouble started when Johnny, a kid who lived directly across the street from me, drank gulps from a pint of Jim Beam, vomited all over himself, and took to bellowing like a dying bull. While steady and responsible Ray drove home in search of clean clothes for Johnny, I teamed up with a couple of other guys to hold Johnny fully dressed under a cold shower until he agreed to stop with the caterwauling

Damp and fatigued, I rejoined my date, Lisa, just as somebody flung open the door of the room and announced the arrival of the cops. Towing Lisa into the bathroom, I opened the window and pushed out the screen. With a line of clamoring refugees forming behind me, I helped Lisa through the window and scrambled down to join her in the alley.

Seeing a darkened house protected by a high wooden fence, I urged Lisa through the gate and into a back yard, then coaxed her to join me in a bush bordering the fence.

She whimpered briefly when a squad car cruised the alley with a weaving spotlight, but when we went undetected, she began to relax a little. I tiptoed to the gate, opened it a crack, and looked back toward the motel. Cones of headlights quivered through the heat generated by idling cop car engines. Radios sputtered and squawked. Cops came and went, speaking to one another in businesslike tones. There were other voices, too, familiar but hard to make out, sad and dismayed, some clearly frightened. In the harsh light, I glimpsed Ray's checked sports coat, then saw the red of his mother's dress. There were four police cars in the parking lot and several more, apparently, in front of the motel where I couldn't see them. One by one, the cars drove off and, after a time, a normal hum settled over the motel again.

Thirty minutes later Lisa and I were parked and sitting awkwardly in front of her house. I wished that I'd parked farther down the block and away from the brilliance of her porch light. I was stirred toward the conclusion that for better or worse, the life I'd always known was ending now. If possible, I wanted to communicate something of that sense to Lisa.

She shifted in her seat, putting more distance between us, and leaned against the passenger door. To my dismay I realized that she was more troubled by the stain on her skirt, acquired when she was climbing out the window, than she was by the arrests of our friends. And there was, I realized, another source of irritation. She was due home at twelve-thirty, and it was only ten after eleven. "Some night," she said.

I smiled ruefully. "I hope your life won't be dramatically changed by it." I lit a cigarette. "I know the lives of some others won't ever be the same."

She frowned at me and wrinkled her nose. "That sounds so ominous. You're so melodramatic. What are you going to do?"

"I don't know. I'm already on probation at school for smoking in the bathroom and ditching class, so I'll probably be expelled for attending the party."

"They won't expel you," Lisa argued. "You can say you left once you found out there was booze there. We can say we were at McDonald's hanging out." She sighed. "Even my mother will confirm that you brought me home at eleven."

I had the sense we were being observed by her mother through a crack in Lisa's front room curtains. "I have too many enemies," I said, "and I know the way the cops work. 'Tell us who else was involved or we'll make things a lot worse.' On top of that, I left my poetry book there, in plain sight."

"You didn't have any book."

"Ray borrowed it last week. He put it on the table by the lamp and reminded me not to forget it. It has my name in it."

"Ray won't rat on you."

"No," I agreed. "But somebody else will, I'm sure of that." I aimed a smoke ring at the windshield and regretted it immediately. Lisa frowned, disapprovingly. The smoke ring came apart forcefully against the glass. "I think I'll head out to California, get a job selling surfboards somewhere, go to night school." The prospect scared the hell out of me but I said it because it seemed like a plan that might somehow impress her. Once uttered aloud, it began to look like a great idea.

Nonplussed, Lisa took a tissue from her purse and used it to work the stained skirt.

I felt bad and wanted her to break the silence. When the stain proved resistant she looked over at me and said, "What are you thinking?"

"I think we are in rat's alley where the dead men lost their bones.'"

She shook her head. "What's that supposed to mean?"

"I don't know, exactly," I admitted. "It makes me think of high school. It's a quote from a poem in my book left in the motel room. *Collected T.S. Eliot.*"

"You know, Tim, I think you just want the worst to happen. You're bored and you just want an excuse to do something different." Lisa looked very mature.

"Maybe so."

She moved closer, not a lot closer, but a little. "The first time we went out, I thought, you know the guy's a little strange, but he has interesting ideas. The second time we went out, I thought that maybe we could have some fun together. I mean, I don't want to give you the wrong idea, but I'm not as chicken as a lot of girls are. Not when I like a guy." She looked at me and shook her head. "I like you, Tim, or at least I did like you. But now, I'm getting the idea that I'm too mature for you."

Quickly, she kissed her fingertips, and touched them to my cheek. "Call me if you stay," she said, "but don't call me to say you're gone." She opened the car door and ran for the porch. It seemed like a scene from a movie I'd seen before. When she turned back, I saw that over and above everything else, some half-promised radiance was being removed from my life forever. Having gained the porch, she wheeled and ran half way back. She cupped her hands to her mouth and hollered. "And don't write me from California if you leave."

According to carefully laid plans developed the week before, I was to spend that night at Stephen Cragmont's house, a friend who lived two blocks away. Since Stephen's parents routinely went to bed at eleven, trusted him utterly, and never stayed up later, the invitation came with the opportunity to stay out as late as we wanted. Lisa had told me that Cragmont had been right behind us when the cops showed but had run off with his date in the other direction. From Lisa's house I drove to Cragmont's and sat out front in the car, smoking and experimenting with stories that might enable me to emerge relatively unscathed from the busted party. After a few minutes, Stephen pulled in behind me. He parked and let himself into the Ford.

After making good his own escape, he and his date had driven past the front of the motel and seen two paddy wagons. Among those being boarded he named kids I knew would be only too glad to describe me as one of the organizers of the event.

While I'd been waiting for him in front of his house, Stephen had been parked under a willow tree, several houses down the street from mine. Almost immediately, a carload of revelers, other escapees, pulled up out front to drop off the still drunken Johnny Wagner. Stephen had ducked down and watched the proceedings over the top of the dashboard.

Johnny, whose house was directly across the street from mine, got out bellowing, challenging every real man in the neighborhood to come out for a fight. Among those invited had been me, Stephen said. I was a loudmouth communist, a pacifist, and for my offense of having held him under a cold shower, he was going to kick my ass, he shouted. While those who had driven him home tried to hush him, Johnny crowed that after he was finished with me he was going to take on my dad, not only for his crimes against me, but for his crimes against the human spirit in general.

Stephen solemnly reported that my dad stepped out of the house and onto the front porch clad only in his undershorts, toting his ubiquitous quart of beer. Stephen surmised that my dad was preparing to light into Johnny, and maybe would have, but for the fact that Johnny's widowed mother, Daisy, dashed out of her house in a muumuu, charged her son, and dumped a pail of ice water over his head.

Drenched for the second time that night, Johnny shouted that he was drunk, that wherever I was, I was drunk and a communist atheist to boot, but that even Commies had a constitutional right to get drunk, and that there was going to be hell to pay when Johnny Wagner felt better, because he was going to set the world to rights by beating up everybody in the neighborhood. After absorbing a pair of none-too-motherly cuffs to the head, Johnny allowed himself to be dragged into the house, bellowing all the while that he had a certain affection for communists and atheists and was thinking of becoming one himself, and would certainly do so if his mom didn't let go of the ear she pulled him by. Stephen said my dad lit a cigarette and stood alone a long time on the front porch before my mom finally came out and coaxed him into the house.

I considered that this was very bad news indeed and was pretty sure my dad would wait up all night for me to come in. Stephen and I agreed that some of those who'd been arrested would almost certainly give our names to the police, meaning, I felt sure, certain expulsion from school. We agreed that even as we talked Bert was probably sitting in his chair with another quart of beer waiting to attack me on sight. My guess was that if he got himself mad enough he would turn after a time from me and go dashing across the street to turn on Johnny, who was fatherless. I found myself exaggerating my dad's lack of self control and told Stephen there was a good chance that if my dad's rage lasted long enough, he'd jump into his big Chrysler, drive it right up on Cragmont's front lawn, barge into the house, and give Stephen's reflective, sorrowful-faced dad a lesson in how to discipline a drunken liar of a son. This prospect seemed to scare the hell out of Cragmont, so we drove a few blocks from his house and I introduced my plan.

The best, if not the only, solution to our predicament was to run away. We would drain our savings accounts, pool our limited funds, and go to California, home of the Beach Boys, there to start at the bottom of the ladder of success by becoming surfer-bum dishwashers. Eventually, of course, we would take the high school equivalency test, enroll in college, and achieve fortune and fame, the hard way. Being, of course, true middle-class white boys of the sixties, we knew college was the admission price, and California both the circus and the promised land of no constraints whatever. No doubt, once we established ourselves as competent surfers, neither of us having never more than waded in the Pacific, we would open a series of surfboard shops up and down the coast, buy ourselves convertibles, and gradually reestablish family ties. As our aging parents regretted their old fashioned ways, we might even drive east for a visit.

When we compared savings account balances, it was clear Stephen had about three times more money than I did and that, even so, we would have to scrimp and save for a time. We agreed to share our resources fifty-fifty and formed a tight partnership. There was nothing for it now, we agreed, but to part company for an hour or so, go home alone, and pack our bags. We hoped to be on a train for California before the police put out one of those all-points bulletins on us.

Sneaking alone into the house at four in the morning without waking my parents proved easy enough. But once down in my basement bedroom, waves of memories and associations made me dizzy and scared. My bedroom had been the one place in all the world where I felt free to dream, to recite Samuel Beckett and Eugene O'Neill in front of a mirror, to stand over my record player chanting sneering ecstatic duets with Bob Dylan.

Besides, lately, I'd been having trouble blaming all my misery on my parents. Recently they had begun to lose something of their former power to either influence or oppress, and seemed increasingly more like the hapless, weak-willed appointed representatives of some far more odious authority. I saw a sadness and weariness to my dad's anger and tried to shake it off. My fear of my dad was real enough, but by now I was using it as an excuse, dreading more than actually fearing it. While my dad might well have gone out in the street and slugged Johnny, or tried to, Johnny, who was taller than my dad, might well have hit him back. My dad might take a swing at me before my mom managed to calm him down, but any such attack was likely to be short-lived, and I figured if I could succeed in making him feel guilty for overreacting afterwards, I might even manage to reduce my own punishment for participating in the party. There even followed an awareness that, however secretly, my dad would probably grudgingly admire me for managing to get away when so many others got caught. In my room, my reasons for running away from home began to crumble away. Lisa's words about my boredom still resonated, though, and it seemed up to me to show her I wasn't just a wild kid full of empty talk.

Tossing shirts, socks, and sweaters in a suitcase, I thought about my thirteen-year-old brother Mike, snoring and grinding his teeth in an adjacent bedroom. I wondered what my eight-year-old brother Jeff would think on learning his oldest brother had left home for parts unknown in the middle of the night. They who had seemed such pests a few hours earlier, now impressed me as a pair of innocents whose only real shortcoming was that they had yet to grasp the depths of evil and hypocrisy in the world. I decided I would come back and rescue them, probably sometime after college.

I took a last long look at my lamps, the whale vertebra my grandpa had given me for a paperweight, my desk, and my unmade bed. I considered the photographs tacked to the wall, my books, magazines, bike, and baseball mitt. Then, rather than risk the squeaky back steps, I climbed up on a chair and let myself out the basement window, closing it gently behind me as I squatted outside on the frozen grass. It was a cold, dark morning to leave home.

At Union Station we learned that while we'd been hiding out in a downtown coffee shop waiting for the banks to open so that we could drain our accounts, we'd missed the morning trains to California. We sat down on a wooden bench and began arguing about the advisability of waiting around till that evening for the next train west. When a beat cop showed signs of taking an interest in us, we ducked into the men's bathroom and agreed to catch the next train out of town and worry about getting to California later. Twenty minutes later, a train went creeping along the South Platte River. Safely aboard it, we argued about whether Kansas City was in Kansas or Missouri.

After an expensive dinner in the dining car, we counted our money and warned each other how soon we'd have to find jobs and a cheap room. Depressed by the prospect of dishwashing jobs in Kansas City, we adjourned to the smoking car to steel ourselves for an arduous future dominated by night school and greasy dishwashing machines.

In the smoking car, two big-boned boys about our age left off discussing game strategy with their cigar-gnawing basketball coach. Farmers and old men in suspenders stopped talking all at once. I lit a cigarette and tried to look relaxed and self-assured. Seeming to anticipate that everyone in the car would soon want a clear view of the newcomers in their ski sweaters and penny loafers, the farm boys repositioned themselves and turned back toward us, shifting from one foot to the other and blinking at us with the bovine acceptance of grazing domestic animals.

Stephen fetched a magazine from a back pocket and rifled it loudly. I smiled to myself, amused by Stephen's way of reminding fellow travelers it was impolite to stare. I composed my own face into an expression of weary insouciance intended to convey my indifference to conversations with any past or present 4-H member. I considered my knuckles and puffed, rehearsing my story, just in case.

If pressed I would say we were two brothers en route to Kansas City to visit an aunt and uncle. Calculating that every city had streets named after American presidents, if needed, I planned to say they lived on Lincoln Street and then become as taciturn as the two gum-chewing basketball players staring at me.

A farmer sitting directly across from me scored his corncob pipe with a pocketknife and wiped gobs of black tar on a red handkerchief. A thinner man sat next to him, tapping his foot, perhaps in time to the tune he'd left off whistling when Stephen and I entered the car.

The man folded his knife and dropped it in a breast pocket of his overalls. "Yep," he said, apropos of nothing but seeming to address his companion and the basketball players, "I reckon the world can be an unfriendly sort of place."

Train wheels chattered. The smoking car rocked from side to side. Stephen's magazine pages rattled furiously.

The foot-tapper looked from me to Stephen to the more polite basketball players. He squeezed a knee, regulating his foot, then commenced rolling a cigarette. "Didju boys ever run off from home?"

Stephen froze, though the question had been put to the basketball players. The gangly boys chortled. It wasn't altogether clear whether they were amused by Stephen or by the thought of premature independence. The taller athlete decided it was up to him to answer. He corrected his slouch and said, "No, sir. We wunt have no reason."

"Well, I did, wunst," the foot-tapper said, lighting his handmade smoke. "But I soon learned my old dad knew what he was talking about when he said there ain't but few places in this world where a fellah can go and not be in somebody's way. I reckon that's what a home is. The sad thing is, fer some less fortunates, probably pert near all a home is." The man looked over at me, so I blew a smoke ring, aiming, without seeming to, right at the wart on his nose.

The speaker paused, perhaps to admire my skill, smiled, tapped his foot three or four times, blew smoke out his nose, and turned back toward the basketball players. They squirmed and said nothing.

The man with the pipe thumbed tobacco into its bowl. "I was under the impression, Fred, that you were about to tell us about the time you run off from home."

"Wasn't much, really. Got in a little scrape with the minister's boy after church one Sunday, and I just knew that strap would be waitin' for me when I got home. Well, a town boy I knew, name of Jimmy Peters, his dad practiced a little dentistry on the side. Jimmy and his family had moved over to Hutchinson the year before. And shucks, I figured Hutchinson for the edge of the world, so I took off and went over there."

The basketball players chortled. The man with the corncob tightened the pipe stem with a big, weathered hand. "How did things go for you over in Hutchinson?"

Fred used an index finger to blot a tobacco flake from his front tooth. "How do you think?" He smiled at the memory. "What I never will forget, though, was what happened after dinner that first night. It seems Mrs. Peters had made but one apple pie earlier that day, and since neighbors had dropped by unexpectedly, warn't but one tiny slice left for each of us. Ol' Doc, as even Mrs. Peters called him…course, I don't think he was really a doctor, just another farmer who could lie and tell ya it wouldn't hurt much and then pull yer tooth. Well, Doc had been out in the fields all day and was lookin' kinda weary, but spirited. And seein' how fast my own slice of pie disappeared, he wouldn't hear but what I was going to have his rightful sliver as well. And I remember he and

Mrs. Peters, and maybe even Jimmy, got into a little discussion about it. But Doc tells Mrs. Peters, 'Now, Enid, be still. This young fellah needs that little pie to fortify his strength and courage because tomorrow morning he's got to begin to come to terms with one of the harder truths of this world.' Ol' Mrs. Peters tried to soften what she sensed was coming by asking him how it was he had come to know so much about the harder truths of the world when he didn't know a book jacket from a pig's toe. But Doc just eased that sliver of pie over to me and said, 'Eat it up, son, and enjoy it, because tonight you're our welcome guest. But when you wake up tomorrow it will be as our hand, and things'll get a little easier for my boy Seth. Maybe you haven't never seen the kindness of yer own dad, though I allow that you probably have. But my guess is workin' out there with me in the next little while you'll come to see that it isn't that a dumb farmer wouldn't like to be kind to his own hand, but that when he has to choose who to spare and who to send on to school, he can't send the hand off for school and work his own son.'"

Fred chortled at the memory. "I guess I musta gone a little stiff in my chair about then, because Mrs. Peters told me not to mind the Doc's rudeness and that he meant well even if he did have a sorta morbid way of saying things. But Doc just waved her off again and pointed to that little wedge of pie and said that there was another reason why it was fitting that I eat it, if not tonight then come morning."

Stephen's neck was going red from concentrating on a photo caption in his magazine.

The man with the pipe rubbed the bridge of his nose with his pipe stem. "Well come on now, Fred. What exactly was Doc's other reason for saying you should eat the pie?"

"Doc said that as he had come to understand things from reading the Bible and a newspaper now and then. God had created a world that was not particularly well disposed to runaways, colored folk, or strangers. And he said there was even some reason to think God regretted having made things so hard for such folk. So, according to the Doc, God built a little consolation back into the order of things. Way he did it was to arrange things so that respectable strangers got the good and sweet and the bonus part of life toward the beginning of their misadventures. In that way, the Almighty, in his everlasting goodness and mercy, gave them a few good memories that would make the hard and bitter part of their lives that was yet to come a little easier for 'em to bear."

Stephen slapped his magazine shut, jumped from his seat, and headed for the door. Not wanting to seem to have been affected by a story I was pretending not to hear. I yawned and lit another cigarette.

63

The man with the pipe puffed and moistened his lips. "So how'd things turn out?"

"Well, I will say a couple of things about how they turned out, thanks for asking. First thing is, when I woke up the next morning, the sun was well up in the sky and the house was empty as Monday church. Nobody around. Not even Mrs. Peters. Beside my bed somebody had left a Bible with all them little ribbons tucked in at the story of the Prodigal Son. I read that, listening to the hum of that empty house, knowing they was all out in the fields at work, and felt pretty low. Well, sir, when I finally walked out to the kitchen that table was clean as a whistle but for that sliver of pie. Except for a fork and saucer, that kitchen was like a modern magazine photograph it was so clean."

"And?"

Fred seemed to welcome the chance to express a little irritation. "What do you mean, 'And?' I ate that pie up, washed that fork and saucer, wrote a thank-you note on the napkin, and slipped off home for the strapping I had coming."

The smoking car was quiet. I tried to look bored. The storyteller was sitting back now, confident that I couldn't quit the car without at least a glance at him. I tried to sneak a quick look, but got caught. Fred's eyes were waiting, glittery, but far less ignorant and malicious than I expected. Fred started to laugh. "Last strapping I ever got in my life." I turned away, but my guess was he probably saw the smile forming on my face.

Stephen was back in his seat sleeping, or feigning sleep, as the train slowed into yet another rural station. Outside, tiny snowflakes fell through the pink light of early evening. A dozen passengers, preparing to board, wrestled with suitcases and packages. With a sharp twinge it occurred to me that since my own savings account had been smaller than Stephen's, I was virtually broke and about to become Stephen's guest as well as his traveling companion. I opened a book of short stories and tried to read. Not only were we traveling away from the Golden State, we were heading into frigid weather with clothes more suited to fantasies of beach life than the realities of a Midwestern winter.

It was dark and bitterly cold the night we got to Kansas City. Glassy hard crystals of snow covered the sidewalks. The city smelled of stockyard excrement and model airplane glue. We still didn't know if we were in Kansas or Missouri, had no sense of direction nor any idea where we might find a cheap room. Suitcases in hand, we walked the frigid downtown streets, hoping to stumble on a cheap hotel, trying to keep the bitter wind out of our faces.

A police car appeared out of nowhere. The driver honked, rolled down the window, and beckoned us into the back seat. My heart raced with the fear that Stephen would climb in and blurt out our entire story. I stepped in front of him so that I could get in first.

"Evening, Officer," I rubbed my hands together and blew on my cold fingers, composing and deleting a number of distracting comments I was tempted to offer on the subject of the weather.

The cop looked at me with a decided suspicion. "You boys got some identification?"

"Sure do," I said, reaching for my wallet, and elbowing Stephen out of his trance. "Kind of hard to find the bus stops in this city, isn't it?"

"It's always a little hard to find your way around when you don't know where you're going," the cop offered, using a small flashlight to scrutinize my driver's license.

I took a quick breath and hoped that I wasn't coming across like a scared runaway trying to improvise a consistently believable story. There was no turning back now.

"The guy we talked to a few minutes ago said to walk three blocks, turn right, and look for some hotel near a car dealership. But we never came to any car dealership. And we never found the inexpensive hotel he was talking about either."

The cop seemed particularly absorbed with Stephen's identification. Had we been reported missing? Was the cop about to learn over the radio about a couple of Colorado runaways wanted for under-aged drinking?

"Denver, Colorado," the cop said to himself, as if he'd heard of the place once a long time ago.

"Denver," I said, trying to keep my anxiety in check, jumping at the chance for distracting banter. "The Mile High City!"

Stephen elbowed me and stared morbidly at the big shotgun mounted to the car's dashboard. What did Stephen want me to do or say? Was he seriously worried that we'd be shot for sounding like members of a junior chamber of commerce?

Finally the cop spoke. "Pretty cold and late on a school night for a couple of boys from Denver, Colorado, to be out wandering the streets of a strange city, isn't it?"

As long as he didn't reach for the radio, I planned to agree with everything he said. "We were just talking about that. How hard it was to find our way around here, how we should have made a better plan. Is there any chance you could, uh, give us a ride to that hotel, that one by the car lot? You know which one I'm talking about? It's supposed to be inexpensive. I forget the name of it."

"Suppose you take a minute and tell me what it is you're doing here first?"

"Well," I began, "we came to town a couple of days early for an important speech meet," I gulped. "The Greater Midwestern High School Forensics Championships."

Stephen kicked me sharply in the shin.

The cop turned around in his seat. "The which?"

The kick was painful, but I was scared and fought off the temptation to return it. "Forensics is a kind of old fashioned word for debating. It starts Thursday, the championship does, and runs all weekend practically." I tried to voice a certain disappointment. "You haven't seen anything in the papers about it? We heard it was going to be in all the papers."

The cop shook his head, but seemed to appreciate the explanation of the word "forensic."

I tried to sound as bland and friendly as the basketball players on the train. "Problem is," I explained, "we decided to come earlier than everybody else, to visit Stephen's Uncle Mitch. Then we missed the earlier train out of Denver and got here so late at night that we didn't want to call and get him, Uncle Mitch, out of bed and everything. We decided the best thing for us to do tonight would be to find a hotel and call them in the morning."

The cop turned half around. "You a debater, too?"

When Stephen hesitated, I dug his ribs with my elbow.

Stephen laughed anxiously at his own hesitation, grateful, perhaps to have been spared a kick. "Yes, I am. Not as good as he is, though."

"Well," the cop said finally, handing back our licenses, "you're not about to find buses around here this time of night. I don't know their room rates, but the Dodge City Motel's about half a mile from here. I can swing you by there, but if they're full up or too expensive, you'll have to call a cab."

Our enthusiasm at escaping the cop and the cold night was cut short by the cost of the room and the knowledge that come morning we'd be back on the frigid streets of Kansas City clad only in sweaters and jackets.

Stephen sat on the motel room bed he had claimed for himself and lit a cigarette. "We got to get out of here," he said.

"We just got here," I said.

"It's ugly, cold, and smells like hell. Besides," he added, "that cop wrote our names down."

"So what? I'm sure he's written a lot of names down this week."

"Don't you get it? Before and after cops go on duty, they spend time down at the police station going over paperwork. There are all these lists of wanted people and stolen cars and crap. That cop's going to come on our names, remember driving us over here, and then the heat will be on."

"You think the cop will pay that much attention? I mean, he's got plenty of other stuff to do."

"Well, you made yourself memorable with all that forensics debating society shit. You got a lot of guts, Barlow. But you have to learn not to call so much attention to yourself or we're going to find ourselves in a bad way. Come morning, I say we head south, out of the bad weather, get to some place warm."

"Well, I won't argue too hard with you on that."

"While you were taking your shower I looked at a map in the phone book. We can't afford to turn back west for California. Little Rock, Arkansas, is a big city south of here."

"We're almost broke. I thought you said as soon as we got here we'd have to look for the cheapest dump in town and get jobs all on the same day."

"It's not quite that bad. Yet. Besides, it's probably cheaper to go to Little Rock than buy winter coats and stay here where it smells like cow shit all the time. And I'd like to see some palm trees, wouldn't you?"

"Little Rock isn't exactly the Bahamas you know."

"You ever been there?"

"No."

"Well," Stephen said, snuffing out his cigarette, "maybe you should practice saying less until you know more."

"Okay, fine," I said. "I'll go to Little Rock if you promise that after we get our first dishwashing checks and there are no palm trees, you'll pay me five dollars."

"Dishwashing. That the best we can do, you think?"

"Dishwashing will be a good thing for a while. Dishwashers eat free, you know. If we work different shifts we can sneak each other food. In no time, we'll save up to buy us an old Chevy and head for California."

"A Dodge," Stephen said. "Dodges are hot. Better still, if we can find one, we should buy an old wood-paneled station wagon. Woodies are the cars to have in California. If we could pick one up here, we could get in good with the surf bunnies out there. If we can't find a Woody, definitely a Dodge with a big V-8. Thing is, if we had a Woody, we could start buying and selling surfboards right out of our car once we get to California."

Unable to sleep soundly that night in the overheated motel room, we conked out late morning early afternoon on the southbound bus, and roused ourselves in the late afternoon when the all-but-empty bus pulled into a sorry-looking gravel driveway. A sign in the window of a stained shack boasted of homemade pie.

Inside, a jowly man at a corner table warred with a squadron of flies, determined to enjoy his plate of meatloaf and gravy. He waved at and cussed the insects and then, to our ill-concealed amusement, searched out gravy on his cheek with a long, brown tongue. Between dripping gobs of meat and swipes at the buzzing swarm, he glared at us and muttered. I unfolded a map of the Midwest I'd bought earlier that morning and speculated on our whereabouts.

A middle-aged waitress in a hairnet waddled over with two grease-streaked glasses of water. She stood over us, scowling silently. We stared expectantly at her until she stomped her foot. "Wail, you gonna move the GOTamned map or you want yer water all over it?" The man drooling over his meatloaf looked over and guffawed.

I hurriedly refolded the map and stuffed it in my pocket. The water glasses were slammed in front of us like pistol shots. Amazed at the rudeness of the woman, we put in for coffee and pie.

"Jesus," Stephen whispered when she walked off toward the coffee urn, "I don't know. Did you see those fingernails with all the dirt under them? Maybe we should forget about the pie. Either that, or ask her to let us get it ourselves."

Using bread as a fly swatter, the man with the platter of meatloaf waved one of two slices then loaded the other one with gobs of lumpy gravy. Snapping at the fly on the hand that fed him, he groaned with an animal pleasure as the bread and gravy hit home.

The waitress delivered our pie with a look calculated to let us know she didn't favor strangers who were openly amused by the eating habits of her regular customers. But I'd made up my mind that if I was old enough to live on my own, I was old enough to handle a crabby fat lady in a lopsided hairnet.

"What town is this?" I asked.

"Whaat?"

I was not going to back down. I was going to speak slowly and enunciate, isolate each word; tongue, lips, glottis, all doing the work speech and drama teachers had urged on them. "What town is this?"

"Tau- au-n?" The word acquired three syllables.

"Tau-au-n," I agreed, not exactly mocking her, but not exactly not, either.

She snorted like a bull and tugged her hairnet down until it covered part of her forehead. In exasperation, she turned halfway back to the man with the meatloaf. "Saw the beat of this ever?"

Meatloaf Man now waved at the flies with a coffee spoon while jabbing at rubbery green beans with a fork he held in a fist. Between moans, slurps, and angry waves of the spoon, he managed a reply. "Neber in mah life."

Stephen shook his head as a way of urging me to give up on talking to the waitress. I wouldn't consider it. "What town is this?"

She wheeled, waddled toward the counter, and didn't stop until she reached a stack of water glasses. Our eyes met again in a mirror. "Vaeyduh."

Immensely pleased with myself, I unfolded the map and studied it again. After a few moments, I scooted my chair back, cleared my throat, and raised my voice. "I didn't quite make out what you said. Is this Nevada, Missouri?"

Meatloaf Man left off his slopping and emitted a little contemptuous howl. The waitress jumped as if she'd been prodded with a fork. She hurried out from around the counter and started toward us. After three or four steps, she changed her mind, put her hands on her hips and wagged her elbows like inadequate wings. Folds of skin on her neck quivered as she spoke. She looked like an enraged old turkey hen. "I tail you wat and tail you good! We don't go sashaying' out thur to that desurt in all that sin and watchamacallit an tail them how to pernounce the name o thur stay-ate. And we'll be blamed if we'll sit here and let um tell us how to pernounce the name of our tau-au-n. Nehvaeduh!" She swallowed hard and put her hands on her hips to spell it out. "Aen. Aaee. Veee. Aaee. Deee. Aaee. NEH-VAED-UH!"

Writhing with humiliation, Stephen headed for the bathroom. Staring at me, Meatloaf Man allowed the flies an unmolested moment with his dinner. Unable to close his mouth for laughing, he lifted another slice of white bread to his lips to keep the gray meat from falling back on to his plate.

Returning, Stephen reached for the check. "Let's pay up and get out of here." When I didn't rise immediately, he tossed exact change on the table and started for the bus.

"I'll leave the tip," I said.

"Leave that ol' biddy a tip? You must be crazy."

69

Slurping the last of my coffee, I steeled myself and walked for the cash register. The woman swiped at a toaster with a dirty rag. Looking up she shook her head and clacked several sugar dispensers together. Straightening her hair net, she waddled slowly over to where I stood, put her folded hands momentarily atop the cash register, and took a deep breath. I had composed a smart remark and held it like a rattlesnake under my tongue. Meatloaf Man dropped his fork on his empty plate.

At last the woman spoke. "Pahz-on me."

"Beg your pardon?"

"Pahz-on me," she said. "Reckon I was a little pert in the face of yer ignorance. Coffee and yer dussert's on me."

I coughed and swallowed my remarks about the latex piecrust being on a par with the service. My mouth dropped open. "Why, thank-you!"

"Gwon and get out of here now."

I started for the door, then remembering the tip, started toward the table.

"Forget the tip and jest be on your way," she said.

I shrugged and went for the door.

"An when you get back they-uh," she hollered, "tail 'em all how to pernounce the name of our tau-au-n!"

Back aboard the bus, I tried to cheer Stephen by proposing makes and models for the kind of car we might eventually buy and drive to California, reminding him, for starters, that Ray had told us that most of the girls in LA carried rubbers in their purses. We could pay cash for an old Chevy, I proposed, and on our way west avoid drive-ins and diners buzzing with flies. If we kept our wits about us, we might even sneak a quick visit to Denver on our way to California. Stephen muttered darkly that things might not go as well in Little Rock as we hoped, then wadded his jacket up against the window, secured it in place with his head, and fell asleep.

Surprised to feel so homesick, I kept watch for signs of milder weather. Unpainted houses with boarded-up windows marked the outskirts of each town. Yards were overgrown with weeds and bushes. Trash barrels and bits of machinery propped up weathered and broken fences. Tire swings hung from old trees over patches of bare dirt. Partly dismantled cars rusted in driveways. Dogs, lean and mangy, trotted into wide streets to bark listlessly at the passing bus. Toward the center of these towns, the houses were trimmed in brilliant green. Little lawn statues of "darkies" held lanterns out toward the street. Wagon wheels and weather vanes and television antennas; everything had an out-of-date feel, tidy, bored, and mail-ordered. Old and waiting to be torn down or carted off. It was a relief to reach the outskirts each time again on the way south. The broken gates, the chickens loose in the yard, the dogs pissing on rusting refrigerators all suggested that for people living on the edge of things, there was more to life than just planning and tidying up. There was making messes. And then the highway wound up into the mountains again, into a thick gray consciousness of hardwood forest, axon and dendrite, naked of foliage, bereft of synapse. The trees themselves seemed a Druidical petrification, a bio-alchemical remnant of a long-gone state of mind.

Little Rock! I remembered magazine photographs of leather-faced white men flinging rocks at gaunt, threadbare Negroes who hoped to be admitted to all-white schools. Stone-faced national guardsmen standing in front of ugly white girls snarling under their braces or blowing bubbles with their gum, while giving the frightened Negro children the finger. "Coloreds," they called them. "Negras."

Over breakfast in the Little Rock bus station the next morning, I called Stephen's attention to two drinking fountains, pointing out that the "colored-only" fountain was rust-stained and ancient, while the other one was newly polished and offered refrigerated water. Irritated, Stephen urged me to remember we were strangers, objects of curiosity, and that we could easily be overheard. In a more subdued tone of voice, I countered that Thoreau and others had insisted that bad laws ought not to be obeyed. Hailing as we did from the north, I speculated, we could probably just feign ignorance and do our bit for Negro rights by drinking from colored-only drinking fountains. Stephen put his coffee down and wiped his mouth with a napkin. "You can do whatever you want," he said. "But if you're going to do something like that, give me warning so I can leave first and don't have to stick around to watch you get your ass kicked."

Just then two men sitting a few feet away at the counter pushed away their empty plates, dismounted from their stools, and approached our table. The heavier man grinned at us, displaying a mouthful of yellow and brown tooth stumps before pushing his thinner friend ahead of him to do the talking. Stephen concentrated fiercely on his eggs and hash browns. The spokesman adjusted his overalls straps and offered us a flinch he clearly intended as a bow.

"Is you boys from England or someurs?"

While I scanned the men's faces in search of hostile intentions, Stephen looked like he was about to make a pro segregation speech

"In fact, yes," I said. I spoke with a stiff formality, biting the ends off syllables, attempting an English accent. To improve my inflections, I pictured David Niven and used the fingertips on both hands to smooth the lapels of an imaginary dinner jacket. "On the way to your St. Louis, actually."

Stephen rubbed his forehead and glared at me. His ears were turning red.

The men grinned and nudged one another.

"What city do you boys hail from over there?"

I stiffened, wondering if it was possible they had been to England. I raised my eyebrows until I felt my forehead wrinkle. "Little city, actually. Name of Manchester. Don't spose we've ever heard of it, have we, chaps?"

"No, neither of us ever hab," The smaller man admitted, pointing at the fat man. "Ol' Robbie, though, when we wuz sitting over at the counter says, 'Look at them boys's hair. Way they combs it looks like they could be in one of them English rock-and-roll groups.' We figured you boys wouldn't mind a little expression of polite curiosity."

Stephen kicked my shin under the table. From novels and movies I'd gathered that the better classes of Englishmen amped up a blustery haughtiness to discourage overtures from the less fortunate. I fancied myself with my hair slicked back, a long cigarette holder in my fingers. I conjured Basil Rathbone's Sherlock Holmes, sat stiffly and smiled condescendingly at my flummoxed Dr. Watson. "Well, Robert, I daresay you're an observant chap. And characteristically frontiersman-like, no two ways about it. Alas, I regret to report we haven't yet formed a rock band, nor managed yet to meet the bloody Beatles." I looked at Robbie's more intelligent friend. "Damned lot of people in England, you might say."

Stephen attended to his fork as if he intended to bite the tines off. I now turned a cool smile on our visitors, hoping to convey that I realized that they, good men of Arkansas, were a couple of quite jolly American blokes whose bloody curiosity had momentarily gotten the better of manners their parents and teachers ought to have more persuasively urged on them.

The men squirmed, turned, and uncertain whether or not to offer their hands, made little bows to Stephen. Stephen nodded, smiled without speaking, and looked at his platter of dubious food.

Robbie pulled his friend's forearm. "Nahs meetin' you fellas. Hope yew enjoy yer stay in the Yewnited States."

I smiled and hoisted a stained Melmac coffee cup. "Cheers," I said.

That night the sore throat Stephen complained of turned into a fever. Shortly after breakfast, he paid two nights on the slummy motel room we'd rented, and I spent the next day walking the Little Rock streets, smoking cigarettes and trying to screw up the courage to apply for dishwashing jobs at the few restaurants I discovered. By the time I came back to the room, jobless, I was running a fever of my own.

On the third morning, I came out of the bathroom thinking I hadn't been so sick since grade school. Stephen was sitting on the edge of his bed, smoking. "Being sick wasn't so bad," he announced. "You know why?"

I groaned and climbed under my damp bed sheets.

"Because," Stephen said, "I felt too shitty to be homesick. Today I feel good enough to feel homesick again. I'm going home. You want to go back with me?"

"No," I lied. I felt scared and sicker than ever.

"I'm going to buy a bus ticket to Denver. I'll figure out how much money I need to eat on and then loan you all I can spare—maybe enough to last another week if you can find a cheaper place than this one. You can pay me back, wire me the money, when you get a job. Or even after you get to California."

I felt abandoned and betrayed. At the same time, I appreciated Stephen's generosity.

Stephen finished dressing, looked at me, and shook his head. "You want me to buy you a ticket, too?"

"No," I insisted. "Just turn out the light when you leave."

I got up and took more aspirin and tried to recall the exact state of mind that prompted us to run away in the first place. Out of foolish pride and an adolescent fear, I walked away from a life that now, maybe a week later, seemed very nearly ideal. In exchange for a little obedience and a show of politeness, I enjoyed all the good things I could think of: girlfriends, dates, a part-time job, spending money, the use of my mom's Ford, roles in high school plays, friends who tried to understand me, beer, books, my own room, Friday and Saturday nights, warm weather, and summer vacations.

The aspirin was working its magic and I was sitting in the room's only chair when Stephen returned. "When does the bus leave?" I asked. I was chagrined that I said "the" bus rather than "your" bus, as if anyone, anyone, anyone at all, could be aboard it.

If Stephen felt guilty about abandoning me, he was determined not to show it. Unwilling to plead or coax, he had settled on a strategy of encouragement. "Why don't you change your mind?

"I've got my pride," I said.

He considered my statement. "Yes, I guess you'll always have that. I mean it'll come back in a week or so, right?"

I didn't really approve of his words, but his tone seemed just right. "Well, I don't really want to go back."

"You're smart," Stephen said. "You should go to college and do something with your life besides criticize the world, offend stupid people and tell tall tales."

"Why don't you wait a couple of days?" I suggested. "Maybe I'll go, too. At least let's wait till we've tried to find jobs. You look good. And mature. I bet you could find a job today."

He shook his head. "We can't afford to wait for a paycheck. If we paid a couple of more night's rent here we wouldn't have enough money to eat during the ride back. We'll just have to ride home sick. We'll have to eat cheap, too. No more expensive chocolate shakes."

The thought of Stephen denying himself his favorite comfort food made me laugh and cough at the same time.

"Coffee and burgers," Stephen said. "And smokes. That's all we'll be able to afford until we get to Denver." He coughed and lit a cigarette.

I lit one of my own. Then, sullenly and slowly at first, I began to pack.

The westbound bus howled over potholed roads. Garrulous servicemen in the back slumped all night in illuminated funnels of blue cigarette smoke, handing perfect strangers snapshots of girlfriends and waking me up again and again with endless talk of loved ones, commanding officers, buddies. I was a feverish ache in a fog of aspirin. Every bump was a punch, every stop a bone-chilling shiver, every human voice a deliberate affront. Cold, I sat on my hands and napped until my hands tingled and burned.

In what seemed a dream but wasn't, an old woman spread a tattered blue blanket over me and moved off. A warmth filled my chest. A few minutes later, the bus slowed and stopped in some podunk town and I looked out and I saw the blanket-donating woman lower herself into nowhere, south Kansas. The sky was the color of ink. According to an illuminated green clock in a window, it was just after four-thirty. The bus driver descended and dragged a heavy red suitcase from the bowels of the bus, used his knee to nudge it toward her, then ran back up to his seat. I shook my head to clear it of sleep, put a hand to the window and held it there, hoping the woman would look up to see my expression of gratitude. I turned my reading light on so I might be seen to thank her for the blanket. Squinting, she stopped and grabbed the suitcase with both hands. She stood a moment, exhaling big puffs of white, rocking and testing the reliability of her sausage legs and thick ankles. Then she staggered down a street bordered by dark houses.

When I woke up, the blanket was soaked with sweat. I lit a cigarette and tried to talk to Stephen, who was sitting across the aisle from me. He responded sullenly that he was glad to be going home, determined to apply himself in school, appreciate his family, and make the most of his opportunities in life. He was humiliated, tormented by guilt, and he wrestled with regrets I couldn't share. I regretted mostly the circumstances that had brought about my return. I was sincere about persuading my parents I would settle down, though without being altogether sure I could or really wanted to. I'd tell my friends about my adventures and win some deeper admiration from them; my parents would accept me back, but not welcome me as Stephen's would; it was something that could be known but couldn't be said. Not to him.

The closer the bus came to home, the clearer it became to me that something that could not be breached now divided us. Having been gone eight-and-a-half days, we got off the bus in downtown Denver and boarded a local bus home, staring out the window at the familiar but now transformed streets. We parted without speaking. I raised my arm to wave goodbye and found it much heavier than expected. Stephen nodded grimly and looked down the street toward his house.

In the glow of the porch light, my house looked smaller and cozier than I remembered. I tiptoed up the cement porch steps and peered into the dining room through a gap in the front room drapes. A brilliant white light fell on a supper of turkey and roast potatoes. Four Barlows sat, restless and distracted over the meal. My dad and mom looked older, my two younger brothers, Mike and Jeff, more impish and silly than ever. Everything looked scaled-down, hollowed-out, makeshift; a parody that could not be called what it was. When my dad finished racing through pre-meal grace and reached for the gravy boat, I took a big breath shook the stiffness out of my shoulders, and put a thumb to the doorbell.

My mom's face showed an irritated curiosity as she approached the door. Close enough to reach for the knob, she recognized me through the small glass window and shook her head with the understated happiness I expected her to show. And even as she started saying, "Well, well, well," for the benefit of the people at the table, I knew she was already thinking of ways to smooth things over with my dad.

Mike and Jeff looked at me with expectant grins, but they knew better than to speak or attempt to break the tension. At dramatic moments, the first word belonged to our dad. Fór my part, I knew the worst was over when, rather than flying into an immediate rage, he contented himself with a single, mildly contemptuous grunt.

My mom brought me a plate of food while my brothers gulped milk and stared at me expectantly. No family meal prepared by my mom could be eaten until my dad had critiqued it for temperature and salinity and found it tepid, burned, undercooked and otherwise unworthy. My dad let it be known that once again his wife and oldest son were to blame for allowing the cold night air to get to his meal before he could enjoy it. Between grumbles and complaints about the food and occasional raised eyebrows when I mentioned Arkansas, he forked boiled carrots into his mouth and chewed them as if they were leather. Once she deemed it safe, my mom set the tone for my homecoming. She said she was glad I was home. Now if only I would buckle down at school things were sure to get better for all of us.

Johnny Wagner's drunken shouting in the street was never mentioned. Neither was the party.

I went to bed that night disappointed that no one in my family seemed interested in where I'd been or what I'd seen, and felt lonely in my room in a way I never had before.

A month or so after coming back from Arkansas, it occurred to me that the guys with hot cars never drove them very far and often left them at home while they struggled to raise money for new parts and bragged or whined about how much they spent on upkeep. Money spent making your car look cool, I told Harley, was money you didn't have for gas and oil or a six-pack of beer. Unless your parents had the money and inclination to indulge you, a cool car meant lots of hanging out, lots of looking for admiration instead of driving to admirable places. I told him that what I wanted now, now that I had seen a little of the real world that these dolts were oblivious to, was basically any old reliable car plus plenty of gas money so that once I got out of school I could drive to a place where people weren't afraid to say what was on their minds, and truth and self-expression counted for something. Such a place didn't really exist, Harley said, taking what I thought was too much pleasure from saying so. I was happy to differ. Out there somewhere, I insisted, were most definitely wonders and places where cool cars and the admiration of idiots standing around hawking goobers in a parking lot were less important than ideas and adventures. Somewhere far away from high schools and McDonald's a few whole-hearted people would be glad to meet me. I was sure of that.

The '60 Triumph TR-3

"Believe me, I had not now the power to resist the soft
pleasure he now caused me to taste by the sweet to-and-fro
friction of his voluptuous engine, that terrible machine
which had so furiously agitated me with pain."
The Lustful Turk, by Emily Barlow

Rick Kissler didn't agree with all my ideas, but he willingly challenged or disputed them. His hair was red and curly and his tiny blue eyes glinted when he was excited. To prevent his glasses, worn from early childhood, from slipping down the long, thin arch of his nose, he'd formed the habit of holding his head tilted back, and looking at the world from the bottom half of his glasses.

Instead of an American car "loaded with horsepower and chrome junk," Rick aspired to a car that would handle the curves on Berthoud and Loveland Passes. With that in mind he bought a 1959 green Triumph TR-3. Not being a jock, and determined not to look "too Jewish," Rick confessed that he considered the Triumph an investment in his own sexual initiation. He had a sister who took him to foreign films and he admitted that the Triumph's purchase had been inspired by Marcello Mastroianni's sexual successes in Federico Fellini's movie *La Dolce Vita*. He insisted however that his desire to get laid differed from Mastroianni's, but also from the "put-a-bag-over-her-head" randiness of most the other guys we knew. Early on, Rick spoke of "hoping to understand chicks." To me, this was a kind of dislocating and exotic idea. It had, till then, never occurred to me that there was anything special to understand about the girls slowly but vividly drifting into my life.

Rick's dad, a well-known internist, had provided him with a box of rubbers and quietly sympathized with his son's philosophical restlessness. Safely out of earshot of Rick's mother, the good doctor encouraged his son's agnosticism and turned a mild if not protective eye on the beer-fueled, all night rec room parties that turned into talks about the meaning of existence.

Rick's mother Grace didn't seem to approve of very much about him. Rick said that she felt that only her son's acceptance at a "good" college would stabilize her social standing. Her academic demands on Rick seemed to differ from week to week. One week, she enforced a brittle behaviorism, in which skiing and other blandishments were to be earned with improved grades. The next week, science gave way to tears. Cool logic collapsed into bitching or hysterical tantrums.

Shortly after Rick and I made plans for a weekend's skiing in Winter Park, his mother fined him for unacceptable school grades, deflating his wallet. Just when it looked like we'd have to cancel the trip, he phoned a lodge manager and arranged for us to "ski bum." In exchange for a few hours of hard work, we'd be provided a place to sleep, free meals, and tow tickets.

Fortified by an early dinner, we were handed brushes, soap, sponges, mops, overalls, a six-pack of Coors, and marched to a meat locker in the cellar of the Winter Park Ski Lodge.   After venturing into a malodorous steel room the size of a garage, we opened our first beers. Little flecks of rancid meat and fat were spoiling on the warm walls and floor and a thick, suety wax adhered to every surface. We started by using trowels on the floor. Even then, though, the floor remained slippery. We mopped the floor three times just so we could start on the ceilings and walls. When we'd done the floor nine times, the manager agreed the locker was clean enough and escorted us to a nearby pair of picnic tables, stored in the basement for the winter, on which we could bed down for the night. Once we'd been provided with keys to our basement bedroom so we could let ourselves back in if everyone was in bed, we carried Rick's prized Martin guitar out into the winter night, and still warm from mopping and scrubbing, piled into his Triumph for a night on the town.

The highway high in the Rockies cut a narrow gorge through ten-foot walls of snow. The TR-3's plastic windows were cracked and its heater was inadequate despite our warm clothes. After a ten-minute drive, we reached a small town buried in snow and glowing with an odd, reddish light.

From a recently plowed parking lot we heard the bawling of a country and western jukebox. Our steps in the frozen packed snow squeaked as we walked toward a brightly lit bar constructed of peeled and varnished logs. The puffs of our exhalations were blue and the night acquired an aroma of heavy wood smoke. We kicked our toes against the stairs to clean them of snow and pushed inside toward the heat of a stone fireplace. Rick's hard-shell guitar case earned us a drunken cheer. It was Betty the barmaid's birthday and now there would be not only a lively rendering of "Happy Birthday," but live music. Heavy on the Peter Paul and Mary and Kingston Trio repertoire that we were learning to scorn.

Rick rubbed warmth into the neck of his guitar, while Betty carried us our first free pitcher of beer. Rick strummed and fingerpicked his way through "dumb" songs he refused to sing at high school hootenannies. To earn my own drinks, I sang along with him, muttering tunelessly when I forgot the lyrics, and, between mugs of beer and vodka gimlets bought for us by a man in a straw hat, hollering out remembered choruses.

Sometime after midnight, a pair of highway department workers fetched an old push broom from a closet and Betty the barmaid pulled me off my stool to do the limbo. I was winning the contest, bending backward and scooting under the stick, when I learned that copious amounts of beer punctuated by sweet mixed drinks were incompatible with rigorous physical activity.

I did not remember mounting stairs to get into the bar hours ago, so was surprised to discover them as I launched myself through the front door gut sick, then crashed, barfing and retching, into a the frigid mercy of a snow bank. After a few moments, I found an area uncontaminated by my vomit and put my head back in the snow to watch the stars in the black sky whirl.

The next thing I knew, I was back in the Triumph imploring Rick to turn the heater up. I remember being glad when the car finally stopped moving, thinking that maybe with a few minutes' rest, I'd be able to stagger to the ski lodge basement and scramble up on our picnic table bed, where, if I couldn't sleep, I could at least die the death I craved in the warmth of a sleeping bag.

Rick kept bothering me.

"Barlow."

"What?"

"We've got to get out of here."

"Lemme rest."

"Barlow, we've got to get out of here."

"You go on in. I'll come in a couple of minutes."

"We're stuck in a snow bank."

"Lemme rest."

"Barlow. Wake up. We've got to get out of here."

"Go away."

"We could freeze to death."

Just then, the prospect of freezing to death didn't seem that bad, as long as I didn't have to open my eyes again. I planned to continue to say anything that came to mind in order to keep Rick talking and postpone, perhaps forever, having to open my eyes or move ever again.

"What happened?"

"We skidded and crashed into a snow bank."

"Too bad."

"Barlow, we've got to get out of here."

"You walk on up. I'll be along in a few minutes."

"We're still ten miles from the lodge."

"Don't worry about it."

"Barlow, it's 2:30 in the morning and 20 below zero. If I fall asleep we'll both freeze to death."

"I appreciate your keeping me advised of the climate conditions."

Rick got out of the Triumph, slamming the door so hard it terrified me into a moment's consciousness. Angry and feeling guilty, I opened the small passenger door and fell out into the snow. Headlights brilliant against the snow bank, Rick started digging doggie style in an effort to free the car's front end from the frozen wall. I scrambled to help, but fell back down again, coughing and retching, unable to stop my empty stomach from turning itself inside out.

After a time, bright lights shone on us and I became aware that a group of people were using a chain to tow the Triumph backwards and onto the pavement again.

Later, as Rick helped me climb on my table bed, I told him I was looking forward to the death I was sure would soon occur.

"You know why?" I asked Rick.

Though I could hear his irritation and knew he wasn't much interested, I decided to tell him anyway.

"Because when I'm dead, I won't have to smell myself."

Less than a month before high school graduation, I heard a door open and woke up from a nap in an old hotel room in Glenwood Springs, and stared, not at my roommate Bruce Parnell, but at Sylvia Casey, the Jeep brat herself. She wore a white blouse and her face was flushed. There was something vulnerable and defiant in the way she stood in the hallway, hands stuffed in the back pockets of her sand-colored Levi's.

"Well hello, you jerk."

Groggy from the heat of the afternoon and at a loss to compose a suitable rejoinder, I stepped back and rubbed my eyes. "Nice greeting, Sylvia."

"I know you're still pissed about the night that I left you and Harley in Cherry Creek. However, I'll remind you that I tried to offer you a lift when you were stranded. You brushed me off. It was a matter of loyalty, I guess, for you to stay with Harley. No way was I taking that asshole home after he'd insulted me and nearly gotten me killed."

"Excuse me for not following this conversation very well, Sylvia. I've been taking a nap. How did you know I was here?"

"I saw you check in. I got your room number from your roommate Bruce when I saw him a few minutes ago."

"I didn't know you knew him."

"I don't. I saw the two of you enter the hotel together."

"You've been drinking?"

"What the fuck do you care?"

"Well, it's afternoon, but I really don't. Still, you look a little upset."

"Well, I am little fucking upset, thank you very much. For some reason that I can't remember now, I'd been looking forward to seeing you at this speech meet, which was why I knew when your school bus was scheduled to arrive and why I was hanging out in the lobby when you walked past me as if you never fucking saw me before in your life. And, in fact, right now, it bugs me that you're trying not to look at me as if I'm humiliating myself."

"Oh, for god's sake." I stepped to one side and made a theatrical gesture. "Come on in and sit down, Sylvia."

"Thank you."

"You're welcome." She stepped inside, but not before sticking her head back out to see if she was being observed. "But don't bother closing the door. I'm not staying."

"Okay, fine."

"Well, don't look so hurt. I mean, all I need right now is for your school chaperone or friends to come barging in and jump to the usual lewd conclusions."

I rubbed my forehead with both hands and sat on the edge of my bed. "First of all, Sylvia, although it pissed me off a little at the time, I don't hate you for leaving Harley and me in the lurch when we got stuck in Cherry Creek. I don't know what's been happening in your life, but my own has been going by pretty hard and fast. That whole episode was light years ago. If I passed you in the hotel lobby a little while ago without speaking, it is because I didn't see you and you convinced yourself that you were in some obvious position to be seen. Now that I do see you and I'm a little more awake, I'm glad to see you."

"You didn't pretend not to know me because of a bunch of nasty things you've heard about me?"

"The fact is, I haven't heard anything about you, nasty or otherwise, for a long time. Other than being drunk in the middle of the afternoon, how are you?"

"Fucking terrible."

"What's the matter?"

"You know, I hate it when you talk to me in this tired, world-weary tone of voice. I mean, you'd think, that with all your acting talent, you could see that I'm upset and at least try to make me feel better by at least acting glad to see me."

I walked across the room for my cigarettes and an ashtray. "It's a big world, Sylvia. There's no shortage of phonies and hypocrites, but I'm beginning to think there may be a few people out there who aren't always playing games and actually respect honesty. In fact, I'd tended to think of you as one of those people."

"I'm sorry to be such a bitch," she apologized. "And thank you for the compliment. I guess I was hoping we could skip the crap about the weather and families and talk a little bit."

"Sure."

"Can I sit nearer on his bed? Your roommate's? You think that would be all right?"

"I'm sure it would be fine."

"I mean, I can go away if you need to go back to sleep or shower or something. Maybe we could meet later. If you want."

"You're really acting weird, Sylvia."

"Could we not talk about me for a while? Would that be okay?"

"Yeah," I sighed. "What do you want to talk about?"

She dropped to a precarious position on the edge of Bruce's bed. "Well, let's see." She inhaled sharply, as if she was about to dive off the high board at a public swimming pool. "Congratulations," she said, steadying herself on the bed with both hands, "How about your recent successes in the oral interpretation of *lisherature*."

I laughed. "Shank you very much."

"No, I mean it, even if I didn't quite say it right. When I saw you playing Mercutio in the city drama festival, it was like I understood every word Shakespeare wrote. You must have spent weeks on that Queen Mad speech alone."

"Mab," I corrected her. "In shape no bigger than an agate stone on the forefinger of an alderman."

"Mab, Mab, Mab," she laughed. "You were better than anybody, including the hot shots that got all the awards." She got up from the bed, steadied herself, and wandered over to a mirror to fuss with what might have been her recently brushed brown hair. "I guess you know that your buddy Bruce is known all over the city. I read in the newspaper that he started playing Mozart on the piano at three years old and just got a full four year scholarship to Princeton."

84

"He's smart. But he tends to think of himself as peculiar and beleaguered rather than special. We scoff at some of the same things. "

"You're weird. On the one hand you hang out with guys like Harley, run off to Arkansas, and on the other you read strange books, recite Shakespeare, and show up at speech meets on the other side of the state. Anyway, how is everybody else?"

"Everybody else?

"All your friends who don't go for the theater and books. Harley, and that dumb broad with the big tits." She turned and looked at me with an expression I found impossible to decipher. "Tell me how everybody you know is, and then tell me all about you."

"Well, Harley's got a job at a driving range, shagging golf balls."

She laughed. "And, I heard, practically going steady with Susie Baumholtz"

"Jealous?"

"Him? Her? Get serious. Now your friend with the big jugs, that's another question. With your grasp of Shakespeare I wouldn't expect you to be so hung up on tits. You know my dad is big on Eugene O'Neill. He acted in a couple of his plays in college."

Embarrassed, I fumbled for a cigarette and said nothing.

"Is she putting out for you?"

"Boy, you're really something, aren't you?"

Sylvia laughed and rolled her eyes. "You're so predictable. I thought you were going to say that I have a lot of nerve."

"You do, don't you?"

"You won't answer my question?"

"Why should I?"

"Because I'm curious."

"So what?"

She shrugged and sighed. "What pisses me off is, I bet that whether she is or isn't, you've told all your buddies she is. Isn't that the way it's done when you're a guy, Tim? Under pressure, you say you screwed her even if you haven't. Build your manliness on the ruins of girls' reputations."

I dragged on my cigarette and let myself flop backward on my own bed. I blew an angry stream of smoke at the ceiling. "Not everybody does it like that, Sylvia."

"Mr. Honorable, is it? Johnny Trueheart? Okay, but let me ask you this. If she was putting out for you and I asked you as a friend, as somebody who wouldn't get mad at you whatever you said, would you tell me the truth?"

"I dunno. Probably not."

"Okay, fine. See, what I want you to notice, Tim, is that if I ask an honest question and somebody gives me an honest answer, I don't get upset and act all high and mighty, even if the answer upsets me. She's hurt you, I can tell."

"Get serious. When I came back from Arkansas, which I don't know how you found out about, I called Lisa twice before she deigned to talk to me. She told me that her mother and friends agreed I was immature and asked me not to call anymore for a couple of years."

"I'm sorry you've been hurt."

"I wasn't hurt! I don't always have very reliable judgment, that's all. More than hurt, I was surprised and educated; she turned out to be somebody who craved the admiration of people who didn't interest me."

Sylvia offered me a wicked smile. "Then it won't bother you particularly to know that I saw her making out with some guy at the drive-in. It was Sid, I think, the captain of your wrestling team."

"Big deal!"

"You don't have to be that way with me."

"What do you mean?"

She smiled. "I mean hostile, on guard, afraid I will tell someone you have feelings. I'm not a member of your little gang of puffed up theater hypocrites. If you show me just a little honesty you'll get the same thing back from me. Go ahead and ask me a few questions you think I won't appreciate." She let her hands fall in her lap. "Madame Sylvia reveals all."

"Okay, let's start with these. What are you doing in Glenwood? Did you come to compete in the speech meet? What are you going to perform? Why are drunk in the middle of the day? Why are you so interested in Lisa? And why are you going on about your reputation? Did somebody ruin yours, Sylvia?"

She clapped her hands, very softly. "See? I knew you'd insist on my telling you what you really want to know. I like analyzing what people say and the way they say it in search of what they really mean. By that last question, I think you mean, am I a virgin or did somebody already screw me and talk it up. I also like answering questions in my own sweet time. It's a part of what this school shrink calls my 'maladaptive neurotic patterns.' Anyway, I'm here with the Lincoln High drama and speech class because I've been scheduled to give a speech about the future of our relations with Cuba tomorrow at 1:15. I'm drunk because I've been drinking while everybody else is rehearsing. And finally, yes and no and maybe. If I'd had a reputation to ruin it would be ruined, but since I

86

haven't had a reputation for some time, it's only more deeply besmirched. For your information, I'm not interested in Lisa. Only in getting you to admit you've been hurt so that you might become a little easier to talk to. It's all over your face, the hurt, that's all. Do you want to ride back to Denver with me on Sunday afternoon, once the speech meet is over?"

"You *drove* over here?"

"I couldn't stand the thought of riding the bus with all those idiots, singing stupid songs, looking at me like they know all my secrets." She turned to reconsider her reflection in the mirror again. "Anyway, if I don't decide to drive back tonight, I'd be happy to drive you home after the awards have been given out."

"Having come all the way over here, why would you go home tonight?"

"Because I'm drunk and may get drunker, and because talking to you I've already decided I'm not going to compete tomorrow, no matter what."

I shrugged.

"Just don't try to talk me into relenting. My mind is made up. I'm not saying why and I'm not doing it."

"Okay, your mind is made up. You're not telling me why and I'm not raising the issue again."

"Thank you. I came over here thinking that if you weren't an absolute jerk to me I'd take you out to dinner. But not around here. I'm not talking about a date or anything," she added. "I just want to make up for having ditched you that night."

I looked at her. There was something I was trying to understand.

"Maybe some other time. Oh, come off it," I said. "Don't act all hurt."

"I'm sorry. For some reason, it just never occurred to me until now that you probably have a date anyway."

"I don't have a date," I said. "Do you know of some place close by?"

She brightened. "It doesn't matter where we go. I've got the Jeep."

"Yeah, but you're too drunk to drive it."

"Well, you can drive it then."

I shrugged as if to suggest I wouldn't mind doing her such a big favor in exchange for her buying me a dinner. "Okay."

"But no hot rodding. My clutch is slipping."

Never having driven a car with such a big engine before, I thrilled at the responsiveness of the 327-cubic-inch Chevy that her mother's boyfriend had installed in the Jeep. In order to keep driving I found fault with every restaurant we passed. For a time, Sylvia pushed her head back against her seat and closed her eyes. The sun was setting over Utah and I was wondering how close to California we could get if she were to fall deeply asleep and I was to go on driving until we ran out of gas. Finally, Sylvia placed a hand on my shoulder. "Where are you going?"

"I don't know exactly," I admitted. "It's a beautiful evening for a drive, though. "

"You didn't like the look of any of those places we passed in town?"

"Not really, did you?"

"A couple of them looked fine to me."

"You're really lucky to have this car, you know that?"

Sylvia was crying.

"What's the matter?"

"You're just trying to sober me up! You've got all the windows rolled down and you want to drive a long way out of town so nobody from the speech meet will see us together."

"No, that's bullshit. I don't care if you're drunk. And I am not embarrassed to be seen with you. I just like driving your Jeep and rolled the windows down so I could smoke. "

She studied me. "Well, smoke your fool head off then. In fact, give me one so I can smoke, too, Then, if you don't mind, I'd like you to roll the windows up and turn around and go back to that place with the carving of a mountain lion on skis out front."

I shrugged and turned back. The roadside river was a mercury color, reddish at the banks, taking on the color of the cliffs where it had rained hard earlier in the day. The evening sun made the highway look molten. I wanted to drive and didn't feel like talking, but Sylvia was crying, so I tried to make my face look tender and turbulent, like James Dean. Putting one hand on her neck seemed safe enough. "What's the matter, Syl?"

"Nothing," she said, dabbing her eyes with a tissue. "I'm so damned ugly when I cry, that's all."

"They say everybody looks their best when they're smiling, but you're not ugly, Sylvia. Not even when you cry."

"Thank you. I guess I'm just plain is all."

"Don't say that. The truth is, you're very pretty. You must believe that, at least sometimes."

"A month ago everything seemed different. But never mind that. I feel better, even if you're lying and stretching the truth."

I found a parking spot near the skiing mountain lion. At the table, we didn't say much for a while, until the waitress brought our order and Sylvia laughed at me.

"What's so funny?"

"You scraping off the mayo. You could have asked them to leave the mayo off, you know."

"I always forget."

"You don't like onion, either?"

"Nah."

"I do, but I'm sure my breath is already bad enough," she said removing her own slice.

I wondered if the white slab of onion on the edge of her plate suggested that she hoped I might kiss her later, a prospect that was beginning to appeal to me. Her greenish eyes were wide open and her chin turned to a particular angle. It seemed frighteningly possible that we were going to talk to each other in a way neither of us had ever talked to anyone else before. Ketchup leaked from the corner of my mouth.

"I'm not laughing about that," Sylvia said, handing me a napkin. "Not exactly."

I dabbed at my mouth, swallowed, and couldn't keep from smiling. "Why are you laughing, then?" I hadn't realized how much fun it could be to flirt.

"Do you know what I have out in the Jeep?"

"No."

"I have most of a quart of hot buttered rum and nine cans of beer."

"3.2?"

"Six percent."

"Is it cold?"

"Probably not very. But the rum's in a thermos and should still be nice and hot. We can share it later— but only if you'll agree to answer a few questions."

"Go ahead. Ask questions now," I said.

"Well, I'll start with an easy question and save the harder ones for later. Why do you eat your french fries with a fork?"

"I dunno. I don't like getting ketchup all over my fingers."

"Is that the best you can do?"

"What do you mean?"

"I mean, I think you eat your french fries with a fork because, at least partly because, you don't want to be just some french-fry-inhaling, 3.2 beer guzzling teenager. You like Shakespeare and books. You're tired of not being grown up already."

"Does that make me a phony?"

"It makes you maybe a little dishonest. Maybe that's normal. I don't know how grown up you are."

I fumbled for a response, but she had already pushed her chair back and started toward the front of the restaurant. Two older men at a nearby table watched her butt, disturbing my proprietary pleasure. I turned my attention to the last dreary gray clumps of lettuce on my plate. When Sylvia returned, she smelled of spice and flowers. I pretended not to notice the lipstick that she'd applied and brushed breadcrumbs from my side of the table onto the floor.

"I drove a road out of the canyon and found this totally neat place earlier this afternoon," she said. "It's light for another hour. There's stones in a circle and firewood. We could make a fire and drink rum and beer over there."

I liked the idea very much but felt reluctant to show it. Instead, I nodded and chewed my celery to threads.

"Unless you have to get back to rehearse your performance or something."

Remembering I'd agreed to do just that, I squirmed. "No, not at all," I said. "I've got my reading down pat. In fact, a couple of beers would go down real well."

She took the road out of the canyon and climbed a series of loops through stands of lodgepole pine and Engelmann spruce trees. After a few minutes, the road went muddy and deteriorated into a pair of stony ruts. We got out and stumbled together past a tumbled-down abandoned cabin and through a stand of aspen. The daylight was fading fast.

While I gathered fistfuls of pine needles and poured them over wads of dinner napkins we'd harvested from the restaurant, Sylvia stepped into the shadows under a stand of trees and emerged with a small log. From down on my haunches by the growing fire I sipped a beer and watched the firelight flicker on her face and throat. She sat on the log and laughed. "There's room for two on this log," she said.

I got up and swaggered her direction, but I felt shy and managed to move only a few feet and stare glumly into the fire. Something I wasn't sure that I was all that up for seemed expected of me. The fire popped and sparked. "Good beer," I said. "Still pretty cold." It took me a while to summon the nerve to look at her

"I feel bad that you want to keep so far away from me," she said. "I took a mint already."

I shrugged. "There's a broken branch sticking up right next to you. That's all."

She scooted down along the log and made room for me. I poured beer onto my fingers and wiped two streaks of soot from her face. For a long time we sat silently, listening to the hissing campfire. Filling my lungs with the cool night air, I said, "Go ahead and talk to me. Unburden yourself."

"I'm just hoping, you know, that some day some ugly chubby bald guy with glasses will come along. He could even have a big wart on his nose. Just so he doesn't try to impress anybody. Some guy who will talk to me and answer a question or two without lying. Somebody who won't fuck my half-sister the first time I turn my back on him."

I was shocked. "Fuck your half-sister?"

"Babs," she said, bitterly. "Why? Do you want to fuck her, too?"

"I don't know what you're talking about, Sylvia. I've seen her, what, twice, always flirting with some ass." There was agony on her face and I was irritated that sex and suffering seemed somehow existentially connected. I had read a little D.H. Lawrence. He seemed turgid and quaint.

"I'm sorry."

"I never know quite what you're going to say or how you're going to respond to something I say. Having a conversation with you is like, I don't know, approaching a horse with a reputation for bucking. A growling dog."

"It's not quite that bad, is it?" She took a nugget of spearmint gum from her mouth and tossed it in the fire. "I guess I admire you a little and I'm trying to understand what's going on with everybody else. Sometimes I say exaggerated and outrageous things just to catch of glimpse of how somebody really is. It's a neurotic device, I'm told. I think of it as a defense against liars and hypocrites."

"You want another beer?"

"Yes," she said, "and one of your cigarettes."

I watched her smoke, amateurishly, paying too much attention to the way she handled the cigarette. I saw she was in life over her head, a little like me. I moved a little closer. She used a finger to draw a circle around a stain on my pants. "I can't make up my mind," she sighed.

The fire sizzled and snapped.

"About what?"

"Well, I need somebody to talk to, but I want you to think well of me. I'm also worried, though, that if I don't hurry up you'll go back to your room and forget about me. We'll graduate, you won't call, the summer will go by, we won't see each other again, and then we'll disappear without really knowing each other."

"I'm not going to college, but I will call you on the phone. We can do a few things this summer, before I leave town."

"I'm not trying to elicit promises. I swear. Tell me something. Have you ever thought of suicide?"

"As a little kid, I guess."

"As a kid? God how horrible! Why did you think of killing yourself as a kid?"

"I don't know. Curiosity maybe. I don't remember thinking of myself as being unhappy, though I guess I was. I still have the curiosity about what might yet be, but the fear's too strong now. Besides, it seems like in most cases suicide might be a mistake made by people who worry too much about what other people think about them. After I came back from Arkansas, I started worrying a whole lot less about other people's opinions and things have been quite a bit easier since I did. This summer I'm getting a job and my own car and going where the people don't know my name. There's a folk song with that phrase. When I first heard that lyric I felt, I don't know how to describe it, terrific, understood, challenged. Something like that. You know, ever since I saw you this afternoon I knew something bad happened to you."

She was crying again. The firelight reddened her hair. I put an arm around her shoulder and towed her toward me. She buried her face in my neck. Her tears were cool on my throat. I had to move my shins away from the heat of the fire. When I shifted, she jumped up and flung two medium-sized logs into the fire, setting off an explosion in red and gold. A huge cloud of sparks ascended toward the stars. The air filled with ashes.

"Franz Arthur Madigan, Grand Island, Nebraska, twenty-five, USA Air Force Corporal, currently stationed at Lowry field. He fucked my half-sister, Babs Sullivan, twenty, during Spring break."

I leaned back, waved at campfire smoke, struggled to breathe, and made my voice very deep. "Go on."

Sylvia was on the far side of the fire now. The red of the fire flickered in her dark eyes. "What's to go on about?"

From what I understood of psychiatry, you were supposed to be neutral, supportive, encouraging. "It sounds bad, but there's got to be more to the story. I mean it's bad, really bad, but if you want me to be able to talk to you, I need to know more, I guess."

"She wasn't exactly a virgin or anything, and she's too smart to get pregnant."

"I meant bad for you."

"We'd been 'going steady,' as Franz insisted on calling it, for six months."

Determined not to add to her agony by saying the wrong thing, I sat on the log and nodded my head. "How did you find out?"

"My mom had gone off skiing with her new boyfriend and I'd been over at a girlfriend's house most of the weekend. I came home earlier than I'd planned, let myself in, and heard the back door slam. I even thought I heard voices. Babs tried to tell me she'd been taking out the garbage, but the garbage was still where it always is. I shrugged the whole thing off. About a half an hour later she came up to my room acting all weird and sweet and asked me if I'd help her clean a stain off the Oriental rug."

I wanted Sylvia to know I was listening and to see the somber expression on my face. I got up and then sat on the ground, closer to the fire. "Stain?"

"Babs said she'd spilled milk. But there was this big sticky white gob that smelled really gross and wouldn't come up. I accused her of having had sex on this expensive rug and said she should have at least taken the guy to her bed, because sheets were cheap and easy enough to throw in the laundry. Then she ran off crying to her room and locked the door and wouldn't come out. I kept trying different solutions. Finally I got the cum off the rug, but some of the dye came off, too."

"Okay," I said. "Your sister had sex on the rug. What makes you think it was with your boyfriend?"

"Let me finish. My mom got really pissed about the rug. Babs admitted the mess was hers and that I'd only been trying to get some spilled milk off the rug. She promised my mom to buy her a new rug and that might have been the end of it. But Babs kept acting weird. The next week, she decided to give me about half her wardrobe. That was when I knew for sure what she'd done."

I put a log on the fire, but Sylvia must have seen the skeptical expression on my face. I looked up at her.

"People who betray you usually try to kiss your ass afterwards," she explained. "But there's another thing. They always make a mistake. Something nasty sneaks out of their false good behavior and gives them away."

My legs were hot and stiff from sitting in a cramped position. I went back to the log and looked up at the stars. "I'm not bored or listless," I averred. "My legs got stiff and I needed to cool my eyeballs. What was there about your sister's behavior that revealed this nastiness?"

"Guys are obsessed with tits, so you probably know there are different cup sizes. The measurement concerns the body. The cup size determines the size of the coveted, squeezable objects."

I nodded my head.

"She gave me a bunch of her bras."

"I don't get it."

"She has huge boobs, and as you've noticed . . ." Sylvia repositioned herself for a better view of my response. "I don't."

"I'm trying to remember some line from Shakespeare about the way we magnify our faults. I have noticed, Sylvia, but I wouldn't have noticed and remembered or thought about it if you weren't always so intent on calling everybody's attention to them."

"Okay. I have a complex because everybody else has an obsession. Babs knows full well that I don't need her big cup size. She was calling my attention to her generosity. That would be literal and figurative, I guess."

"Why would she want to hurt you in that way?"

"It's competition. She's three years older and had a different dad. Her dad's never been around. I got my dad's attention. She got big tits. She'd rather have had my dad's attention. There've been times I thought I'd rather have her tits."

"How does your dad figure into all this?"

"Forget him. He's on his fourth wife out in California now. Or maybe in Texas. You don't want to hear any of this, do you? It's too sordid, too ugly."

"You've had to go through it," I said, acting the frontiersman, the hardened cowboy of the movies. "I reckon I can listen to it." I figured the books I'd been reading should count for something and didn't want to admit that any human behavior could possibly shock me.

Next thing, I knew her arms were hurting my ribs. She was breathing in my ear, her hair, warm from the fire, redolent of rich shampoo was in my nose. "Thank you, thank you, thank you." I felt rooted to the ground, but oddly disembodied, some part of me flapping its wings overhead, unable to breathe. I stroked her hair, not out of tenderness, but from a need to touch and hold onto something. The fire snapped and sizzled in the wind. I was a lost kid in a man's body.

"You're so good," she said.

"No," I said. "I'm not good. I'm as confused as you are. But for me, letting it show seems pointless. I don't know. I'm not as trusting as you are."

"You don't trust me?"

"I don't trust anyone."

"That's sad. Do you think you could? Do you ever look for someone to trust?"

"No."

"Should I trust you?"

"You can trust me not to tell other people about anything you say, I guess. But you can't trust me to be wholly honest because I have never been wholly honest or known anyone that I believed was. I don't know how. I have to start by being more honest with myself. But I don't really know how to do that, either."

"What's so great about sex? I mean why do guys crave it so much?"

"I dunno."

"Try to help me understand. I've already promised not to grill you about how many times you've had sex. I'll keep that promise."

She was looking at me closely. I was uncomfortable again. I wanted her to think I'd had a great deal of sex and that maybe a few dozen girls were still longing for me. What I wanted more was to slow down this conversation, drink a little more alcohol, prepare myself for something momentous.

She seemed to sense this. "Do you want to try a little of that rum?"

I had been quite content with her warmth against me, feeling the cool night on my face, smelling the fire, the pines, looking up at the stars. I wanted everything to stop right where it was. A wind kicked up. The fire went white and hot.

The rum was sweet and burned all the way down. We lit cigarettes. Her grief seemed to recede.

"Some day you'll have a wonderful wife."

"I don't think so."

"She'll be blond and have big tits, and because you're married, you'll be able to feel her up any time you want to."

I tried not to smile. "And what about you?"

She laughed and pushed me away. "No, you can't feel me up any time you want to!"

"You know what I meant. What about your wonderful husband?"

"Maybe I'll eventually find some ugly guy with warts on his nose. A lame widower." She snuffled, laughing and feeling sorry for herself.

"A widower? I suppose he'll have fingerprint smudges on his glasses and a potbelly. You've really got a thing about tits, Sylvia."

"No, I don't! Not me! It's just that everybody who has ever been close to me has had a thing about them. Every guy who even interests me slightly turns out to be obsessed with big tits, including you."

"Wait a minute!"

"You can't deny it. I know at least three girls you've gone out with. Everyone of them had bigger tits than most. And Lisa, the one you seem to have liked the best, had the biggest boobs of all! Besides, don't guys have a size thing about their dicks? From what I hear they're always trying to find out whose is bigger, sneaking looks at the other guy's thing over the urinal, prancing around in locker rooms, staring at them in the mirror, and stuff like that. I read that guys actually, you know, make them hard and measure them with rulers and stuff."

This was too much for me. I hadn't taken my own measure, but I'd thought about it. I was fiercely embarrassed and wanted to be anywhere but standing in front of Sylvia Casey, looking at her perfect teeth, smelling rum, tobacco, vestiges of her perfume.

She smiled and wouldn't let me look away. "Well, are you one of the lucky ones?"

I shook my head, sighed, looked at the moon, and prayed for some distraction.

"Oh look, he's embarrassed."

I denied it as best I could. "No. I'm not embarrassed. I'm, I guess, one of the unlucky ones. It doesn't matter. I figure I'm eighteen. I might have a little growth left in me."

"How sweet. And that's where you'd put it, if you were going to grow a little more, invest the growth in your tool?"

"Most guys would," I squirmed. "Like a lot of girls would do with their boobs, you know."

"Yeah, but let me tell you something. It would be a fairer world if guys weren't allowed to hide their dicks in their pants. If penises were as visible as breasts, a lot of men would show a little reluctance to insult girls about their boobs."

"I can't believe we're having this conversation."

She was happier than I'd seen her. "You're shocked?"

I scoffed and she laughed again. "Don't worry. It will be our little secret, okay? There's nobody here to hear us or tell on us. I promise never to tell anybody you admitted to me you have a small dick."

I stared in the fire. "Medium small."

"Don't you find that fascinating, maybe even a little exciting?"

"What?"

"That we can say anything or do anything and nobody will be the wiser as long as we don't feel compelled to tell people who don't deserve our trust."

"I guess."

"You're so enthusiastic," she laughed. "Isn't there something more you want to ask me?"

"I don't want to cause you to experience more pain."

"It's not your fault that you cause me pain."

"That I cause you pain?"

"No, let's not talk about that now. Anyway, I know what you want to know and I'll tell you. You want to know if I had sex with Franz. Plus you want to know how I found out about Babs and Franz, how it is that I'm so sure about the two of them."

"You don't have to tell me."

"But that's the whole point of our being here, telling each other stuff, isn't it?" She hesitated. "Before that whole business with the cum on the rug, Franz told me he had some kind of special duty and wouldn't be able to talk on the phone or leave the base for three weeks. So I wasn't surprised that he didn't call. At first. Anyway, every time the phone rang, Babs would run for it and start a screaming match if I got to it before she did. Whoever it was that kept calling, she'd whisper to them and promise to call them back. One time I was downstairs and she was in the shower and the phone rang and when I picked the phone up I heard Franz talking in the background to one of his buddies. My voice sounds just enough like Babs's to confuse people at times. Anyway, it was definitely Franz, but he denied it and hung up. I was so furious I tore the phone out and chased Babs down the street. The next day I called one of Franz's buddies and said I was Babs. Franz came on the line practically panting and when I caught him thinking he was talking to Babs he was totally furious. He accused me of deception. *Me!* Of course, he denied everything and we had a big screaming match. To make a long story short, a couple of nights later, I was out driving around planning torments when what should appear in front of me but Franz's Pontiac Bonneville. Of course, Bab's was sitting practically in his lap. I raced up behind them with this overpowering urge to bash into them, but Franz saw me coming and took off. I chased them from one side of the city to another at outrageous speeds. I was scared, but I was kind of thrilled to discover that he'd drive that fast, that the two of them would, just to get away from me. Finally, they lost me. I went home that night and carried every blouse and sweater and bra Babs owned out into the front yard and set them on fire."

"Wow."

"That was the big mistake. In the eyes of absolutely everyone after that it meant Franz and Babs were innocent but that I needed therapy, something Babs and Franz were only too happy to agree about. School counselors were enlisted. I got mad and had a couple of public temper tantrums and so now the word at my school is that I flipped out because I felt guilty about having had sex with half the flyboys at Lowry. What's been so weird," she said, "what I really hate is that some of the same guys who sneer at me in the halls at school phone me up at night to sweet talk and ask me out. Every one of them denies any but the purest motives, of course; then they go back to school and spread their bullshit all over again."

She started to cry again. I put my arms around her and pulled her close. The desire to comfort that flowed through me was something I had never experienced before. Our campfire was mostly embers now, and the wind was picking up. I was drunk and tired and yet fascinated by the discovery of this peculiar power I had to listen and provide comfort. I didn't think about having sex with her. What I wanted, I told myself, was simply to lie down beside her in a private dark place until she stopped crying and sighed and drifted off to sleep.

"They're like hyenas, those guys," I said. Even as I said this I pictured the two of us both naked, in bed together, in a room lit by candles. All night long I could stroke and comfort her. Wrapped in each other's arms, we would give and receive comfort. Sex wouldn't enter into it, yet the world would be different when we parted.

"Drive real fast," she said when we were back on the paved highway toward Glenwood. "Turn the heat on high and roll all the windows down and drive real fast."

"How fast is fast?"

"Ninety. At least ninety. Nothing bad can happen to either of us. Not tonight. Not tomorrow." She laughed. "On the other hand, you might not do so good up on the stage tomorrow."

I grunted.

"Do you mind that I kept you from your friends all night, got you drunk, told you all these horrible things? It's too bad you're not attracted to me. I mean, with all that's happened and with all the stories circulating around school I should have sex with somebody. I mean, why not be guilty of what they think?"

I was driving too fast and had to ride the brake hard to get through a tight curve. My heart was pounding and I decided to slow down. "Yeah, I guess so."

"A little while ago," she said, "I thought that you were kind of attracted to me. You know, a little."

I slowed way down. "Yeah, I was. I mean, I am. You're very pretty."

"I know. Cute face and tight butt, but too much of a basket case."

"Don't put words in my mouth that aren't there, Sylvia. Is there any more of that rum?"

"A little. You want me to climb over the seat and get it for you?"

"That would be great."

She clambered over the front seat. The road was under construction. Red and yellow reflectors winked at me in confusing rows, bits of highway equipment were scattered all over the pavement. I slowed down and steered carefully. There were odd noises behind me.

"It's a double surprise," Sylvia said.

I looked at her and the Jeep started for the road shoulder. Her sweater was off and so was her bra. I fought the steering wheel and hit the brakes.

"Christ," she said.

"Shit," I said, whipping the wheel left and right, regaining the road and slowing down. We laughed uproariously.

She stopped laughing first and moved toward me and forward so I could see her breasts without moving my eyes any great distance from the highway. "Well," she said, "At least now you know I don't wear falsies. Are they as small as you thought?"

I didn't know whether to attribute my sudden difficulty breathing to the fact that her breasts, the first real, as opposed to photographed, breasts I'd ever seen, were practically in my face, or the fact that I was still recovering from having nearly driven us into the Colorado River. "God, I can't believe you!" I felt wildly out of control. "No, no. They're beautiful breasts! Just beautiful!"

She spread her arms wide, put her head on the back of the seat and screamed "Yahoo!"

We agreed it was way too late to be seen together, so she dropped me three blocks from the hotel. The center of town was obscured by a glowing white vapor. The nearby hot springs smelled of bad farts and decomposing animals. When Sylvia drove off, I stood listening to the hum of street lamps and the periodic howling of big trucks on the highway. Far away, a dog barked. The stars glowed red and looked to be just out of reach.

When I got to the hotel Sylvia's door was ajar and I smelled her freshly applied perfume. Big, faded, rubbery-looking drapes decorated with covered wagons had been opened wide to admit the moonlight. Sylvia was sitting on a small light-colored woolen blanket or sweater she'd spread on the floor. I sat down beside her and stroked her neck. We sipped sweet rum from cloudy bathroom glasses. It was past time for me to have kissed her, so I did. Her lips were sugary from the rum. We started tenderly, affectionately. She bit my lip, stuck her tongue in my mouth. We laughed and wrestled, competing to remove the other's clothes and retain our own until we were naked, blue-bodied in the streetlight that shone through the window. I was hard and couldn't get enough of my cool body into contact with her great heat. I pulled her up and tried to lead her toward the bed, but she leaned backward, and pulled me down onto the floor. "By the window," she hissed, "I want to see stars. Make me see stars."

I knew nothing. Not even where to find what I wanted. "Lower," she said, "lower."

I was surprised by her tightness, surprised by the element of pain. Jacking off had been nothing like this. She cried out. I hesitated. She hurried me ahead. "It hurts," she gasped. "Oh please keep hurting. Please."

I worried I was too rough. We were doing it wrong. There was too much pain with the pleasure. We reached the point where the pain remained what it was but the pleasure increased. The wildness of the pleasure mounted. I worried I might break my penis in half. She might be injured. But she wanted to be injured, insisted on it. She was bringing it on herself. Everyone in the hotel was awake to our thumping, our gasps and noises, but I didn't care. She didn't care. We were beyond caring. We were exploding into each other and our voices belonged to animals, not to us.

I rolled off her onto my back, gasping and wheezing, slowly falling into the realization that I'd done with Sylvia Casey what I could never do in quite the same way again. We stroked each other softly, unable to speak. Perhaps we dozed. The sky brightened. It was seven by the bedside clock. I had agreed to meet with Mrs. Martin, my drama teacher, for one last rehearsal at eight. I was scheduled to perform at eleven.

"I've got to go," I whispered.

She sat up and put both her hands over my mouth. I peeled them away. "I have a rehearsal in an hour."

She closed her eyes, put both hands over her ears, and shook her head. I stood up to dress, noted with some disgust and wonder that there was blood on my belly and penis and blood on the white wool underneath her. I knelt down beside her and loosened her hands. I wanted her to talk to me, to tell me if the blood meant what all the guys said it did, if we'd done it right, if it had hurt her, tell me if I had pleased her, if she had gotten what she'd wanted. "Are you all right?"

She nodded slowly.

More than ever I wanted her to say something. "Will you be there today? Are we still going back to Denver together?"

She nodded and held her index finger to my lips. I wanted to bite it, to rip my clothes off, to enter her and do it again. She kissed me hard and got to her feet, pushing me toward the door as she kissed me. At the door, she looked in my eyes and moved to kiss me again. I was moving toward her and our teeth banged together. Then I was in the hall, feeling my teeth to be sure they were intact. I was thrilled, alone, and bristling with my own life. I figured I was also probably in some kind of trouble for not showing up at bed check.

Bruce was asleep when I returned to our room, but the door lock snapped loudly and he sat up grinning. It was an accepting sort of grin. He was not a tease and was deeply invested in being enlightened and mature according to standards we both considered mature. I was on fire. Even in the dim unlit morning light coming through the drapes, I felt like I was wearing a button that glowed in the dark with the message, "Just Laid."

I had decided to tell Mrs. Martin that I had a sore throat and was too sick to possibly perform, to stay in bed or at least out of sight during the competition. I had blood, Sylvia's dried blood under my clothes. I was going to shower, nap, and when the sun came up and all the students were safely in the auditorium, slip back to Sylvia's room and have sex with her over and over again before we started back to Denver in her Jeep. We would ride together and take note of how different the world looked. I was raw and sore and bristling with life. I got in the shower and kept adjusting the hot water. I was red and steaming when I emerged. Bruce was wearing a bathrobe. He sat smoking in the room's only chair.

"I don't think you should panic, but you're in a bit of difficulty," he said. "Of course, I'm sure you can talk your way out of it."

"What's going on?"

"You were missed at dinner. People started looking for you afterwards." He laughed and shrugged, convincing me both of his loyalty and detachment. "Eventually, Mrs. Martin got together with that old guy with the weird glasses, you know, that other drama teacher, the guy that looks like a beagle with a toupee. Alas, despite my best efforts to build and maintain a smoke screen for you, people believe you were out all night with some girl from another high school. You can be sure that along with the usual juvenile gossip and envy you were also the subject of discussions about teacher-parent responsibilities"

I smirked and fumbled for a cigarette. I was trying not to swagger or act like James Dean, especially since Bruce was a keen observer of pomp and pretense, but the fact was I enjoyed the prospect of shocking the kids in speech and drama. "I appreciate your efforts to cover for me. Did somebody actually see me with her?"

Bruce laughed. "How the hell would I know? During dinner I tried to tell Mrs. Martin I was sure you were up here napping. But she insisted on coming up to check. I suggested you'd probably gone for a walk and she gave me, you know, the usual harrumph and lifted eyebrow. She loves your bad boy act, Barlow. At the same time, though, and despite the fact that your behavior gives her a chance to exercise some of her histrionic energy, you can expect to run into a wall of bourgeois morality."

"You didn't say anything about Sylvia coming up to you in the hall and you giving her my room number?"

"Get serious. I never volunteer privileged information unless innocent people need to know something to avoid personal harm. Even then, I only say what I see or know. What I know is that the last I saw of you, you were snoring." He laughed again and blew smoke at his reading lamp. "You snore musically, you know that? On the other hand, now that I've heard it, I have to admit I'm glad I didn't have to listen to it all night."

"Bruce," I said, "Uh . . ."

"Tut tut. No confessions or confidences until after I've had coffee and breakfast," he said.

Twenty minutes later, I knocked on Sylvia's door. I wanted to rap loudly enough to rouse her, but at the same time, I worried that my knocking would wake other people up and that they would come out in the hall to see what was going on. At the end of the hall, I found an end table with a stack of magazines and three or four pieces of hotel stationary. I scribbled a hurried note and slipped it under her door. I had the sense that something was wrong as I did.

Her Jeep was missing from the parking lot and a man with crooked teeth at the front desk told me she'd checked out a few minutes before. I sat down in the lounge with the morning paper, ostensibly to read the news, but in fact, to consider my situation. In fact, I paid no attention to the news and just kept staring at the date on the masthead. May first. Next week, a school-wide assembly would be held and Bruce would get up in front of thousands of people to give a speech about how lucky he was to be class valedictorian, a presidential scholar, and be going off on a full four-year scholarship to Princeton. Three weeks later, instead of a diploma, I knew I would be given a blank piece of paper stating that if I satisfactorily completed two summer school courses, I would graduate with a D plus average. My brother-in-law was buying a new car and promised to give me his old one. Rick was renting a beach house in California. I had a lifelong battle to fight against hypocrisy and complacency. I decided not to go to my rehearsal but to give my reading as expected.

I showed up just in time to give my reading, which turned out to be one of my worst.

On the bus home I got plenty of sly looks from everybody except Mrs. Martin. She didn't look at me or speak to me until everybody got off the bus to throw snowballs and frolic at the top of Loveland Pass.

Bruce and I were sitting on the rear bumper of the school bus smoking, watching our cohorts. Bruce was talking about the majesty of the high peaks, the snow and fauna. I was exhilarated and oppressed by the innocence and eagerness that surrounded me. The end of something that might have been important was near and if that was true, I had maybe missed the importance of it in my heedless exhilaration. My life had entered another phase but it would be months before I would have more than a glimpse of that life. Sylvia's phone number, in my pocket with my jackknife and house key, burned my thigh.

Mrs. Martin's filtered cigarette was dark with lipstick. She saw me, dropped her smoke in the snow, put her hands on her hips and said, "Mr. Barlow, I'd like a word with you aboard the bus."

Bruce made a little sound in his throat, signaling sympathy. I withered, tried to shrug it off, followed Mrs. Martin up the rubberized steps, and slumped in the seat nearest the driver.

"No," she said, "let's go all the way to the back."

She crowded me into a corner seat, then swiveled slightly in order to deprive me of the capacity to look away from her furious face. I thought she was beautiful in an adult and volatile, histrionic sort of way. She knew and enjoyed how I felt, loved a good scene, and had carefully stage-managed this one. Unexpectedly, it occurred to me that if I were patient and distant enough, whatever moral energy she had summoned to conduct this conversation would subside. I shrugged and observed that the deprived actress was winning the war against the moralist, the adult, the designated chaperone.

"I had a decidedly unpleasant conversation with a man named Mister Eagleston this morning." She had a way of raising one eyebrow and leaving the other frozen in its original position. I couldn't keep staring at the little smear of mascara just below her eyebrow. I figured that if I could manage to tear myself away from her electric eyes, I could remember how to swallow, breathe, and the worst of this confrontation would be over. Outside, Bruce was admiring a snowman being assembled by half a dozen kids. I swallowed and looked back at Mrs. Martin.

"He was nearly in tears."

"What for?"

"He's worried about one of his students."

I went all James Dean again. "Guess it goes with the territory. A career in teaching."

"Don't give me that ridiculous leer. You *know* who I mean, don't you?"

"How would I?"

"Where were you last night?"

"Walking, I guess."

"With Sylvia Casey?"

"I guess. Part of the time."

"Did she tell you about how she'd tried to commit suicide?"

"I don't feel a need to report all my conversations to adults anymore, I guess."

"I'm not sure you ever did."

"When I was three maybe."

"She's a very troubled young lady."

"Everybody's got problems, I guess."

Mrs. Martin wore pink fingernail polish. She folded and refolded her hands in her lap. The tendons and arteries swelled and subsided. "And you," she said, "you have your problems, too, don't you?"

"Why wouldn't I?"

"One of the maids at the hotel gave Mister Eagleston a letter you slipped under Sylvia's door this morning after she'd checked out of the hotel. I didn't read the letter and I don't know whether Mister Eagleston did. But you were both missed last night. Sylvia's someone many people are a little worried about. You wouldn't happen to know why she checked out so early or why she didn't compete today, would you?"

"She'd had some bad experiences at home and school. She told me not to ask her why she had decided not to perform, and I thought it was okay for her to request that. I have a perfect right to private conversations with friends don't I?"

"All right, Tim. Your point is noted. You'll be graduating soon, leaving me and a few other teachers scratching our heads and disappointed. You're intelligent, gifted, and resolutely determined to frustrate anyone who happens to notice that. What will remain with me for a while is how surprised I felt this morning, how sad I was to learn that you, with your rebellious intelligence and appreciation of drama and poetry, your sympathy for human suffering and injustice, that you are flawed by such a deeply predatory streak. And that you would take advantage of a troubled young lady."

"If you want to believe that, I guess you will."

"Given your unwillingness to talk to me, I'll have to go with a preponderance of evidence."

"Am I on trial? If so, when does the jury selection begin? My peers . . ."

"Your peers are a little embarrassed."

"I think they're cold and wet from the snowman they're building."

"Tim, this girl got mixed up with an older man, threatened suicide. She burned family furnishings."

"Yeah," I said, "but it's not just her that's mixed up."

The bus driver was boarding kids. They were laughing and looking back at us and stifling grins.

"You gotta know who's mixed up," I said. "It's not always the ones you think."

"Okay," Mrs. Martin said, rubbing her hands together and repositioning a pair of gaudy rings. She seemed disappointed that our scene was winding down without the satisfying scene she hoped for. "I hope no harm comes to her because you spent the night with her. I hope no harm comes to you. In fact, I'm afraid for her because she's vulnerable. But I'm afraid for you because you seem to see yourself in opposition to the rest of the world."

I called Sylvia as soon as I got home, but nobody answered the phone. I called her every afternoon and evening for a long time. Three or four times, I drove my mom's Ford and parked it in front of her house. The pink bungalow was always dark and the Jeep was never out front. Concerned that Sylvia's mail might be being read, I wrote her two discreet solicitous letters and waited in vain for a reply. Although it seemed to me that I was the subject of amused curiosity at school, I didn't pay much attention. The fact is, I wanted to talk to Sylvia and I didn't want to talk to anybody else. Not Bruce, and especially not Harley. Still, I knew Harley and Sylvia went to the same school and that he always had his ear to the ground. After two weeks, I finally phoned Harley.

We were at a drive-in on the other side of town, far from our usual haunts. He stirred a giant coke with a pinstriped straw. "I didn't know whether we were buddies anymore or not," he said. "I called you a bunch of times and when you didn't call back, I decided it was up to you."

"Yeah, we're buddies, Harley. I 've just been, you know, caught up in other stuff."

"I know," he said. "Boy, do I know."

I was dying to ask him about Sylvia but didn't want to be in any hurry. "Why do you say it like that?"

"Look," he said, beating me to the punch, "tell me about Sylvia."

"What's to tell?"

"Well, it's cool that you had sex with her and everything . . . I guess."

"Wait! I didn't say I'd had sex with her."

"Yeah, I know. It's part of why I asked you if we were still friends. I mean all this shit's going around school and people are asking and I don't hear from you."

I added sugar to my coffee and lit a cigarette. "What, you wanted to be able to give them the most reliable information?"

"It's not that, man. More like I wanted to stick up for you. You know, in some cases. Especially with all the shit that's flying around. I mean you did have sex with her, right?"

"Right. I did."

"You heard from her at all?"

"No, as a matter of fact I haven't. I've tried to get in touch with her a bunch of times, but nobody's ever around.

"She's not living there no more, man. I heard she's in some psychiatric hospital in Connecticut or somewhere."

"Shit! You're kidding."

"No, I'm not. Sylvia always was a screwy chick, but she just fuckin' flipped out."

"What are you talking about?"

"I can't believe you haven't heard any of this."

"I can't believe you're not telling me."

"What, the whole story? You haven't heard anything? Guys don't come up to you in school and stuff?"

"No, why would they?"

"Okay, here's the story I heard, man, and it's probably got a little bullshit mixed up with a little truth. They say that she had some older navy boyfriend guy who had sex with her mom, if you can fuckin' believe that!"

"Shit. Harley, she had an air force boyfriend who had sex with her half-sister. That's what she told me."

"Well, you would know better. I mean people get shit mixed up, you know that. I'm just telling you what I heard. They say that her boyfriend had sex with somebody in her family and so she went up to Glenwood Springs and had sex with you to get back at him."

"How would they know that?"

"Letters. Like I say, she flipped out. I heard she wrote twenty letters about it. The class president got one, the head girl, her speech teacher. They say she even sent letters to your school so everybody at your school would find out, too."

"Jesus Christ!"

"I never saw one of the letters, but I talked to a guy who claimed he did. Apparently, she was claiming to have been a virgin . . . "

"She was, by the way."

"They say she made you have sex with her on her boyfriend's old letterman's sweater and delivered it to him all covered with blood."

"Are you serious?"

"I'm just telling you the story, man. Feel free to deny any of it. I'll keep your secrets, you know that."

"So that's what that woolen thing was!"

"What?"

"Never mind. I just realized that a part of this story could be true. I remember some little white woolen blanket. Go on."

"So she sent it to the guy, all bloodied up, before she left school, and disappeared. At least that's the rumor."

I felt sick to my stomach.

"Of course some people say she wasn't a virgin. She just wanted people to think she was, so she cut herself or got some piece of steak or something and smeared it all over the sweater."

"Bullshit! Fucking bullshit."

"No, no, I believe you. Take it easy. Anyway, she did a bunch of wild stuff at school, which is all a little vague and I didn't see. Then if the story is correct, she smashed the boyfriend's car up with her mother's Jeep. Word is her mom moved her back to New England somewhere and put her in a hospital up there."

I felt used and abused. My house was empty on Saturday afternoon, so I made several calls to mental hospitals in Connecticut. I spent the rest of the weekend in my room, trying to figure out a way to get in touch with Sylvia, wondering what I should feel. The problem was partly solved for me the following Monday when a group of guys from the football team confronted me in front of school. They were big and muscular and obedient, good boys who made efforts in school, and showed up for practice on time. Ordinarily, they ignored me. I was tall and thin and argumentative in class and told myself I was inured to their athletic accomplishments. We moved in different worlds. The gist of my encounter with them was that they wanted to force me to admit I'd had sex with Sylvia Casey. I decided there was no longer any point in denying it; whatever damage could have been done had been done. They were not interested in her or me. They were only interested in details of the act, which I refused to provide. While they conceded me one or two points for boldness and honesty, the jocks made fun of me for having screwed a girl with small breasts. Their contention was that somehow my having had sex with a girl with small breasts was just glorified masturbation.

That I knew something they seemed clueless about insulated me to some extent to their contempt. I concluded that my hecklers were envious, that they would have done as I did, little boobs or no.

I was hurt and worried about Sylvia for a while, but without realizing it my slow grind toward adulthood was about to come to the end. My roller coaster car was nearing the top of a steep ascent. In time I embraced the most sordid possible view of her crisis and her doings because it came with the comforting supposition that someone so creative would be destined to thrive, wherever she ended up. Then there was the beauty of her revenge: bestowing her virginity on me, tucking her boyfriend's letter jacket under her butt and, before disappearing, from his life and mine, mailing it, bloodied, to the jerk.

My Very Own '49 Dodge

"You'll like the kitten-soft way it travels. . .the way the new
Oriflow Ride cradles you over even the roughest roads."
Dodge Advertisement, **Life***, 1951*

Rick Kissler, who graduated a year ahead of me, had entered into a pact in which he agreed to enroll in college and seriously consider medical school for a year or two in exchange for a year of partly subsidized independent living. With full parental consent he had driven out to California in the TR-3 we'd crashed into a Colorado snow bank. Monthly letters to me described long lazy days on the beach, followed by nightly guitar parties fueled by beer and wine and pot and girls. In September he'd be packing up to go to college. Until then, I was invited to live rent free with him in the beach house he'd rented in Mission Beach near San Diego. I had only to make my way west.

With Rick's most recent letter to me folded up in the back pocket of my pants, I was standing outside watering the lawn one afternoon when my brother-in-law, Ray Mullen, pulled up in front of my house to drop off the '49 Dodge he'd promised me for a high school graduation present. Telling me all about the special deal he and my sister Leslie had just gotten on a newer-but-still-used Oldsmobile, he followed me into the kitchen.

I ran water in a bucket and gathered soap and sponges. Soapsuds were not pixie dust, as I was about to find out, but some primitive part of me believed that with a quarter cup of dishwashing detergent and an application of elbow grease I could cast a spell on the old beater and awaken a measure of automotive reliability. Ray tried to let me know that it had issues, but when I just upped the hot water rate and started whistling, he sighed and brightened. I thought maybe he was going to tell me about his own first car.

My dad would be home from out of town later that night to remind me that there would be no driving the Dodge until I'd scraped together money I needed for car insurance. Until he popped my bubble, though, I was going to get my hands on my car and do a little something, however primitive and absurd, to prepare it for the future, my future.

Ray let the screen door slam behind him and followed me outside to watch and make small talk while I hosed it down. "It used to be blue," he said, "A long time ago. Course, the blue was almost gone from it by the time I bought it."

I was already lathering the driver's door. "Yeah. It seems like there's little traces of blue left."

"It still runs good, though, even if it looks like something spewed out by a volcano."

"A cigarette ash was what I was thinking. About its color."

I worked my way around to the front of the car. Ray came up behind me, placing one of his polished loafers with tassels on its front bumper. By now he seemed to understand what I was doing and spoke with a hint of sympathy and regret. "Your dad told me to give him the keys."

"Yeah," I said, scouring dead bugs off the headlights. "I know."

"I guess he's worried you'll drive it without insurance."

"I guess."

"Where's he at, anyway?"

"He's due back from a sales trip tonight."

"The other thing he told me I should tell you is that this car is no hot rod. If you race it, you'll do it in in no time. It's got a lot of miles on it already."

"I'm not interested in hot rods any more, Ray."

"You've got to remember to check the oil, too. It takes maybe a quart a week, depending on how much you drive it."

"Okay. I'll remember."

He looked down the street and waved at an approaching car. "Here's your sis, Tim. If I go ahead and leave the keys with you, you won't put me on the spot with your dad, will you?"

"After giving me your car? No way. I'll put the keys on his bedside table before I turn in tonight."

Leslie pulled in behind the Dodge. She honked three or four times until my mom and brothers appeared to admire their new lime green barge of an Oldsmobile. While Leslie allowed my youngest brother, Jeff, to climb in and play with the power windows, I politely agreed with Leslie that it looked very comfortable and then went back to hosing down the Dodge's old tires. Ray, who didn't seem to me to be all that keen on the new Oldsmobile, followed me and absently used the toe of his shoes to test the wall of one of the Dodge's retreads. "That rear door doesn't open," he said. "The radio and heater don't work. Apart from that, it's still a good car."

I didn't tell him I would soon be driving it in California where I heard tell you never needed a car heater. Music was something Rick could provide from his guitar or the record player in the beach house that awaited me, but I didn't bother Ray with that either.

"I can see that," I said. "It's a good car and I thank you for it."

Between me and California there would be a high school graduation in two weeks, a few private times, I still hoped, with a restored and returned Sylvia, and maybe half a summer spent caddying at the Denver Country Club where I planned to accumulate my California grubstake. "A reliable work car," I said to Ray, rehearsing my deception loud and clear for my mom's benefit. "I just need a reliable work car so I can get back and forth every day between here and a job in the real world."

Keeping well away from the garden hose I'd turned on the Dodge, Leslie stopped pacing back and forth in her high heels and looked at me with raised eyebrows. Her strange smile, which stopped just sort of a wink, convinced me she saw through my deception. Having made her own escape from the world of Bert Barlow three years before, her expression suggested she would not begrudge me mine.

Dinner still wasn't ready when Ray and Leslie drove off in the Olds, so on the pretext of walking to the neighborhood drugstore for cigarettes, I stopped off at Gene's Hardware and had an extra set of keys made. I put them in the watch pocket of my pants and before dinner positioned the set Ray had given me beside a lamp next to my dad's bed.

The next day, I showed Bruce my keys. We were outside the boy's gym, smoking through the last few minutes of our lunch period. Maturely avoiding any conversation that might lead to a discussion of Sylvia or the wrath of Mrs. Martin, Bruce was telling me about the summer job he'd landed at a downtown sheet music store. I nodded my approval. Into the warm spring afternoon I blew a perfect smoke ring. Four guys still wearing their hair in pompadours watched my smoke ring dissolve and sauntered toward us in a mood that began in timidity and gathered menace. The ringleader, a muscular kid named Brad, spit in the grass and looked us over as if we were both covered with caterpillars.

"You guys think you're pretty goddamned smart, don't you? A couple of eggheads."

"No," Bruce said managing a smile. "I think of myself as curious and lucky."

Brad wasn't buying this. "Luck, my ass. You guys think you're hot shit actors, always being in plays and carrying books around and talking big words. And now, you're going off to a rich kid's school on a scholarship. Look at him. He's going to be the star of a school assembly today, and he's going to walk up on stage in a fucking shirt with clown faces on it."

Bruce had withstood aggressive scrutiny before and faced it now with cheerful aplomb. "It's true. I'm a sucker for anything associated with a circus."

One of Brad's buddies, a greasy kid named Nick who wore heavy taps on the heels of his engineer's boots, was doomed to have to repeat his senior year. A little intimidated by Bruce, he saved his evil eye for me. "That must be why you go around with Barlow the Clown, right, because you love the circus?"

"Nah," Brad said, waving Nick off. "One look at Barlow and you know he's got a part-time job working in a cornfield as a fucking scarecrow. S'posed to be the new cool look, huh, Barlow? Shit-stained beatnik who lives in an alley? What university are you going to Barlow?"

"The University of Soft Knocks."

Bruce chortled. His friends looked a little nonplussed.

"Where the hell's that at?"

"Knocksville, Tennessee."

Bruce laughed and coughed out clouds of cigarette smoke.

"My ass," Nick said. "There ain't no such place."

"There is so," I insisted. "There's even a famous fort beside it. I'm sure you've heard of Fort Knock-ups."

Brad hunched his shoulders and rocked a little on his knees in an effort to restore some of the menace. "Ah, forget this shit," he scoffed at Nick. "Neither of 'em knows dick all."

Nick jeered, "Clown shirt's going to put himself on the stage and lord it all over us in a few minutes, so we don't want to muss him up. On the other hand, Beatnik Scarecrow . . ."

My hands were sweating because I had seen one kid who'd challenged Nick's right to rule the world by force. Scared, I shifted so I could hide a fist behind my thigh and assess the situation. With graduation at hand, fawning teachers were never very far away from Bruce. If only one would arrive now. A group of junior girls had stopped talking to listen. I had to watch out for Nick's attack and not let him take me down. I might have to throw a few punches, nothing too hard or lucky that might make him lose face and earn me a brutal beating, just self-defensive punches, giving ground, warding him off. Behind Nick, the front range of the Rockies was the color of a ripe plum. Beyond those mountains was California, beach life, one that could be lived free from idiots. My Dodge was out in front of my house.

Brad made a little noise in his throat, put a hand on Nick's shoulder, and put himself ever so tentatively between Nick and me. "Well, Mister Superiors, we say neither of you don't know shit from Shineola. What do you think about that?"

Giddy with the conviction that the perfect wiseass remark would buy me time and might save me pain and humiliation, I said, "I know one way you could find out."

Bruce looked at me with an expression of surprise on his face. I looked back at him hoping for inspiration. I had no idea what to say next. Nick adjusted his position slightly and leered. "How's that, scarecrow?"

I flipped my cigarette into a bush and in the process managed to put another step between me and Nick. "Well . . ."

"Yeah," Nick said. "We're waiting.

"I guess if we're talking about knowing shit from Shineola I'd put some gloves on my hand and make up a couple of brown sandwiches. Then I'd ask Dr. Jackson to choose the one he preferred." Dr. Jackson was an assistant principal known for his mean face and rigid approach to school discipline. I stepped back another half step from Nick. "Obviously, the one not chosen would be the one with the shoe polish."

The prospect of the old sourpuss eating a shit sandwich earned me whoops of approval, even from Nick.

Brad was pleased, but he had more on his mind than Dr. Jackson. "I've got a question that will prove that you two guys are a pair of useless freaks of nature."

Bruce understood that he had to endure at least one more test before he could graduate. He looked at me in order to see if I agreed that it was probably in our best interest to fail. "Shoot," he said.

"Where's the water pump on a Corvair located?"

Bruce sputtered. "Huh?"

The first bell rang and Nick was impatient. "Come on, Brains. Prove you know one worthwhile thing. Where's the water pump on a Corvair?"

Bruce sighed and grinned. "I don't know."

"What about you, Barlow?"

"I'll take a flying guess."

Brad grinned. His buddies could hardly contain their anticipation.

"Somewhere just to the right of the fan belt."

Brad and Nick howled and spun in a circle. Their companions laughed and mocked and flung themselves around like tap-dancing marionettes. One kid held his hands over the top of his head as though he feared his brain might ooze from his skull. "There ain't no water pump on a Corvair, you dumb shits!" Brad shouted for the benefit of all in hearing distance, "a Corvair's got an air-cooled engine!"

Graduation passed in a blur of indifference. I was at the country club caddy shack bright and early the next day, and every day after, taking an extra job shagging balls on the driving range at twilight so I could save the money I needed. I dreamed of joining Rick and sampling an unsupervised life on the beaches of Southern California.

Meantime my dad drove my immaculate but tired old Dodge around the block and concluded that it needed brake work, tires, a clutch adjustment, and a tune-up. Minor but urgent repairs ate up everything I earned in June and it was July before I began to save money. The summer was passing me by. Early in August, I bought a postcard in a neighborhood drugstore addressed it to Rick, and scribbled, "I'll be there in ten days."

A week later at two-thirty in the morning, with my billfold bulging with the money I hadn't "wasted" on car insurance, I pushed my knapsack out the window of my basement bedroom, climbed up on a rickety chair, and crawled out on the wet lawn. To avoid waking my parents, I rocked and pushed the Dodge from its curbside berth and, as it gathered momentum on a downhill stretch of street, hopped in, turned the ignition key and popped the clutch.

I headed due south, hoping to be in New Mexico by the time my parents woke and noticed the Dodge and I were gone. One thing Arkansas had taught me was that the cops weren't all that keen on tracking down runaways. With that in mind, I altered my route and started west across the length of southern Colorado. Jacked up on coffee, cigarettes, and freedom, I thought I could drive to San Diego in a single sitting. My euphoria lasted until late that afternoon when I began yawning and slapping my face.

With the sun going down near the "Four Corners" where Colorado, New Mexico, Arizona, and Utah abut, I steered southwest across the flat expanse of high desert. The sun was blinding.

Eyes gritty and burning, I inched up on a big truck until the trailer blocked the glare of the late day sun. The road was flat and straight and mesmerizing. I woke with a lurch that took me across the road center divider. I had nosed dangerously close to the trailer. The suction created by the forward thrust of the truck had kept the Dodge on the pavement. The Dodge was humming along at sixty-five. From the orange sky now swashed with purple, I estimated that I might have been asleep for, maybe, five minutes.

"Shit," I said, hitting myself in the head with the heel of one hand. "I could have been killed." I was wide awake for a quite a while after that.

The moon was rose-white and went red before it set. In the hot dark night enveloping Tuba City, Arizona, I pulled off the highway onto a silent residential street. After pissing in the dark gravel, I curled up in a blanket on the back seat and fell asleep.

The next morning I was in a roadside restaurant finishing up a mess of cornmeal pancakes, gooey with syrup, when I noticed a sign posted on the kitchen door. "Dishwasher wanted. No Indians." Sipping the tepid rusty liquid that passed for coffee, I scanned the place looking for someone with whom I might share my indignation. I was the only white customer in the coffee shop. Three middle-aged men I took for members of a Navajo tribe wore nearly identical straw Stetsons. They sat impassively in a booth behind me, refusing to look at me or speak and dipping wedges of toast into pools of yellow egg yolk. In a shabby hall near the door, two teenage boys in western shirts jiggled and rocked a pinball machine. A chubby younger girl with a sisterly resemblance to one of the boys watched them without interest. I sat for a time, unable to imagine why Indians would patronize the place and why they wouldn't catch my eye. I wanted them to see how sharply I resented their oppression. It didn't occur to me that I might be overvaluing my sympathies or that there might be no other breakfast spot for seventy miles. Finally, feeling noble and lonely, a martyr doomed to anonymity, I paid my check and headed for the parking lot.

The gravel crunched underfoot. The morning smelled of peppery mesquite, creosote, and cactus. An Indian woman sat in a battered Cadillac, nursing a baby and ignoring four older kids who squirmed and tussled in the back seat. Half a dozen Navajo or Hopi men in big hats, and dramatic belts sat in a shady patch of dust and passed around two quarts of beer. I slowed my pace as I walked past them, figuring that if they wouldn't speak, I could at least give them a glimpse of how much the injustices of the world offended me, too. Parked next to the Dodge was a rusty green GMC pickup sporting dusty mud flaps, a cracked rear window, and a long radio antenna. Attached to the antenna were a small American flag and a pennant that read, "Be Proud of Your Indian Heritage."

Lighting a cigarette, I tossed my jacket in the trunk, slammed it, and continued west. As the morning got hotter, the Dodge engine heated up and the gas stations where I could add water to the radiator became fewer. Finally, I crossed a high bridge and looked down into Needles, California. But for the rich blue of the Colorado River, the world had become a hot, colorless place. Gray and blue mountains shimmered in an umber haze.

I gassed up, downed two bottles of soda in a series of parched gulps, and filled the pitted radiator with cold water. I allowed myself to think of Rick and the girls I'd soon meet, and looked at the gas station attendant waiting expectantly to be paid.

My billfold wasn't in any of my pockets. Neither was it behind the seat where it had been known to fall. It wasn't on the floor or on the sloping dashboard, tucked up behind the sun visor, or in the glove compartment. A warm dyspeptic carbonation roiled in my stomach. Beads of sweat trickled through my thin sideburns. I ransacked my pockets again and again. I could picture my billfold, emptied of its vital contents, tossed down in the dust near the restaurant where I imagined it had been recently discovered.

What was the name of the restaurant, the town? There were honest people everywhere, weren't there? Then it occurred to me that the billfold might not even be at the restaurant. I'd stopped elsewhere for water. My money might be in the sour bathroom where I'd stopped to piss. It might have fallen out of my shirt pocket when I stopped to fill my thirsty radiator. There'd been another stop where I'd checked the tire pressure ,worried about the lack of tread on the tires, and bought cigarettes. Worst of all, my money might even be in the hands of some Indian-hating cafe owner or rat of a gas station manager. Did I have enough gas in my tank to drive all the way back to Needles? What if I rediscovered the restaurant but not the money? Could I arrange to leave my backpack with the gas station attendant for security and head back to retrace my steps? Could I work off the gas and oil debt if I couldn't find the money? Virtually on the outskirts of San Diego, would I be tossed in jail and sent home in humiliation? I took a series of deep breaths.

In a panic over the prospect of jail, and maybe more so over the prospect of being required to call and tell my dad that I'd driven the Dodge to California without car insurance and lost all my money, I felt more desperate than I'd ever been.

The attendant was about my own age. He looked neither happy nor unhappy, just nonplused. He shifted his weight from foot to foot. Apparently, nobody had prepared him to deal with a customer unable to pay for gas already pumped. Maybe I could deal with the kid.

"I lost my wallet," I said.

The kid looked at me with a perplexed disinterest that suggested he didn't care about my wallet, only about the money. The more he stood there looking like he didn't know what to do, the more sure I was that it was necessary for me to act boldly, preserve my pride, take my life in my hands.

A geometry of light bulbs on a bank sign across the street registered the temperature at 104. I was sweating, broke, scared, and way too far from Mission Beach. However I managed to do it, I was going to have to get to Rick's in San Diego on the seventy eight cents in my pants. Before I could try that, though, I was going to have to do something about money I owed for gas and oil. My stomach boiled and sweat ran down my back and chest.

"I'll give you the car," I told the kid. "You pay for the gas and you can have it."

There were smaller beads of sweat on the kid's forehead and he kept moving his left hand from a back pocket to a splotch of grease on the back of his neck. He was rubbing it in the pores of his nose. "I dunno," he kept saying, as much to himself as to me.

Other cars were pulling in to gas up now. I needed to cement the bargain before anybody else who might be working inside came out to find out why the attendant wasn't pumping gas. "It's yours," I said. "I don't have the money for the gas and I don't want to cause trouble."

"I dunno."

"It runs fine."

"I dunno."

By now I imagined that my options had been reduced to walking away from the car or going to jail and getting sent back to Denver. I affected nonchalance and grinned. When the kid made no move, I dragged my knapsack out of the backseat. Having already ransacked it three times, I knew the billfold wasn't in the pack, but I made a show of rifling through it again anyway. The kid didn't look any more or less prepared to make a decision when I'd finished, so I poked my arms through the knapsack straps and looked up at the Bank of California sign. By now it was 105.

"I drove it all the way from Denver and never had any problems with it, other than overheating a little in the desert."

"I dunno. Maybe."

"Maybe" was my cue. I took one step toward freedom and then another. When the kid didn't move to stop me, I dropped the keys in his shirt pocket. As he reached to retrieve them, I started down the driveway toward the heart of California.

117

Geography classes hadn't prepared me for the vast deserts of California, nor had one or two Jack Kerouac novels managed to convey the migraine-inducing tedium of hitchhiking across the Mojave Desert in August. I stood on the outskirts of town in the comfortless shade provided by a mileage sign at the edge of town and watched and groaned as each car or truck passed by. Straw-hatted men in string ties waved and grinned at me with exaggerated bonhomie as they powered air-conditioned Lincolns away from the crap table heavens and girly ranches of western Nevada toward the white-hot sun over Barstow. Bovine truckers in mirrored sunglasses sat high in their pinstriped Kenworths and Peterbilts, shifting gears, shaking their heads, and mugging sarcastic regrets. Empty flatbed trailers clattered into the westward haze. Then there were the all-American families heading, I imagined, for Disneyland, floating by in station wagons, iron-jawed dads at the wheel, moms in kerchiefs and curlers. In backseats, their kids turned around to flip me the bird with pudgy, popsicle-stained fingers.

There was a refrigerated drinking fountain just inside the door of a filling station across the road. The third time I crossed the pavement to drink from it and rinse the sweat from my face, an old man with a patchy white beard and a twitching, sunburned nose appeared from a room in back.

"What in THE hell," he demanded, "are you doing standing out there in that sun? Hasn't your mommy or daddy ever used the word 'sunstroke' around you before?"

Dribbling cold water, I wiped my chin with the back of my hand. "Think I'll get one?"

"Kid, do dogs shit tootsie rolls? Unless you find yourself in a cool place with a little shade, I don't have any doubt about it at all." His anger suddenly spent, he looked curious, friendly. "Understand, Junior, you're welcome to all the water you want. I'm not trying to say you can't come in here and drink at the fountain." He stepped back from the door and glanced toward a greasy chair. It was his way of inviting me to sit. "Not saying that at all. Wherever it is, water's the right of every man out here."

I drank again, but I didn't move toward the chair. "Thanks."

"Don't you have anything to say? For yourself, I mean?"

"I appreciate the water," I muttered.

"Well, hell," the old man said, "water's just water. Hold your horses a second. There ain't that much traffic out there now anyhow." He plucked a key from his belt and opened the door of a coin-operated soda machine. In a single motion, he handed me a bottle of orange, waved off an offer

118

of payment, took two quick steps, and hammered the bottom of a vending machine with a boot toe. He lobbed me a bag of disgorged peanuts. "You need some salt, losing all that water."

I looked at the floor when I muttered my thanks, nodded at the man, and went out into the sun again.

I saw the Dodge about fifteen minutes later as it howled toward me and hopped when the kid shoved it into third gear. Briefly, I imagined that the filling station kid's boss was behind the wheel, had come to collect his money or make trouble for me. It was the kid. He didn't seem to see me and downshifted into second gear and turned a corner before I could catch his eye. Two minutes later, I heard a squealing of tires, looked back, and there was the kid again, grinding the Dodge's gears, racing the engine in a way that suggested he hoped he might blow the engine by dark.

I'd liked him when he was on duty. But now there was a sun-browned girl beside him. Seeing him behind the wheel minus his employee's mask of congeniality, I concluded he was a detestable wretch. Gone was the late morning's expression of sweaty cooperativeness, and in its place was a pouty leer just like the one Elvis Presley donned whenever the fresh-faced girls in his movies failed to assess his tough, yet gentle neediness. If he'd been by himself, I might have tossed the empty soda bottle at my feet through the Dodge's open window and managed to conk him in the head. What I really wanted to do was to throw him down in the road and run over him again and again in my Dodge. Okay, his Dodge.

When he and his girlfriend disappeared from my field of vision, I turned back to the pavement, extended my arm, and lapsed again into a resentful pleading with every westbound driver. I had just decided to sweeten my facial expression and make an effort to look a little less desperate when a cop pulled up, honked his horn, and waved me over.

The cop wanted to know what part of Colorado I was from, what I was doing in Needles, and why I had given the Dodge to the filling station kid. He demanded identification, which I said I couldn't provide because I'd lost my driver's license with my billfold. He asked me if my name was Ray Mullen and I said no, remembering that there'd been no title transfer and the Dodge was still registered to Ray Mullen of Arvada. What was my name, then? I shook my head from side to side. The worst thing that could possibly happen at this point would be for me to provide a name and phone number. My parents did not need to know that their eighteen-year-old son was broke, dispirited, and minus his uninsured

Dodge in Needles, California, maybe a 150 miles from the paradise of Mission Beach, California.

The cop groaned and said I certainly wasn't the first person he'd picked up who refused to give his name to a police officer, adding that he was one cop who didn't care to make a big deal out of anything at all during the hottest part of the afternoon. He would, however, take me to a cool, shady place while he ran a check to see if anybody named Raymond Mullen had reported a car stolen or if there were any interesting thieves or runaways on his list of punks. Perhaps, he said blandly, we'd talk about my name again in the morning when the sun wasn't so hot.

Though I hated the filling station kid for trying to destroy the Dodge and for the crime of affecting an Elvis leer, I still considered that I had fairly liquidated my debt for the gas and ought to be allowed to go free. I said as much to the cop in the reassuring presence of a fat lady named Glenda, who sat behind a desk in the red brick building that served as the Needles jail. As if to make it plain he'd lost all interest, the cop turned his back, filled a cup from a shiny urn of coffee near a room marked Lounge, opened the door, and disappeared inside where he adjusted the volume on a television set.

Glenda smiled and said that however the law might be taught out of civics books to high school students in Colorado, the time had come for me to learn that small towns did things differently. The police had confiscated my car, she said, and if it turned out not to be stolen, it would be returned to me. As far as my claim to being a law-abiding citizen was concerned, I had refused to provide my name to a police officer and, having emptied my pockets and established that I didn't have three dollars, I was also guilty of vagrancy. While it wasn't illegal to be poor, it was illegal to be without three dollars on the streets of Needles, California. When I questioned the local vagrancy law, she smiled patiently and predicted that I might be given a chance to discuss it with a judge. Anyway, I should know that I had yet another legal problem. Having been discovered soliciting a ride just a few feet inside of the city limits I was also in violation of a local ordinance against hitchhiking.

A gaunt man emerged from the lounge and yawned, providing me a glimpse of his yellow teeth. He fiddled with a pencil on Glenda's desk and looked at her, rather than at me. "This our Johnny Doe from Collarada?"

Glenda lifted her eyebrows and sighed.

"I'm going to have to put him in the red room."

"Excuse me, Glenda," I said, "before I'm put in the red room, don't I have the right to a phone call or something? Or was that something else my civics book got wrong?"

"No," she smiled. "The problem is, the prisoner's phone is not working."

"I can see three other phones from here."

"Unfortunately, those phones aren't for public use. Who did you want to call?"

"I don't see that that's any of your business."

"You're right," Glenda said, clearly angered. Unwilling to show her hurt, she began straightening her desk. She opened a desk drawer and began rummaging through a small cash box and I heard the rattle of quarters. "The phone was supposed to be repaired today," she explained. "Plus our cook is out sick and it's about time for me to clock out and go home. You're not allowed any choice about food, though I think if you want I can persuade the boys at the cafe across the road to put lettuce and tomato on the tuna fish sandwich you'll be having for dinner tonight."

"About the phone call," I said.

"Yes, well, the reason I asked who you wanted to call was because I was going to offer to make a call for you from my house before I make dinner for my family. Then I realized that would probably not work because you've made the foolish decision not to tell us your name." She couldn't keep the trace of a smile off her face and after a moment stopped trying.

I sighed and looked a little contrite.

A notepad and a ballpoint pen had mysteriously appeared on the edge of Glenda's desk. She seemed to notice the paper about the same time I did. When I reached for the pen I couldn't help but smile. I wrote my name and Rick Kissler's phone number down. The jailer glanced down at the pad and put a hand on my elbow. "Well, Timothy, we'd best be getting on with our business." He opened a door and escorted me down a long dark hall lit by a single bulb.

Glenda's voice called after us. "I almost forgot, Tim. What kind of bread do you want? And do you want lettuce and tomato on your tuna fish sandwich?

"Rye," I said. "Lettuce and tomato."

"Mayo?"

"Pulllllease."

Realizing once he was informed of the facts of the case Rick would wire me the necessary money, and reasonably sure I wouldn't end up back in Denver, I sat down in the big empty room by myself. The red walls, bricked-up fireplace, and makeshift bars in the window reminded me of Sheriff Scotty's Hoosegow, a television studio set I had visited as a Cub Scout in the third grade.

Mornings, during the 1950s, Sheriff Scotty was the clean-shaven mayor of a Denver suburb. Afternoons, he put in an appearance at a local television station, donning a fake beard, rumpled hat, and a tin star as big as a fist. There, once his big-booted feet had gone up on a desk situated in front of a cardboard jail cell, dens of young Cub Scout deputies were shown in. The bright lights were turned up, and the cameras rolled forward. My Cub Scout den had slurped ice cream and swallowed dry cake, fed some goldfish, and cranked up a fake plastic movie camera so that "all the kids out in television land" could watch old cowboy movies. I'd been fascinated by the artificial television set. During commercial breaks Sheriff Scotty ignored the Cub Scouts and joshed with his crew. With the camera back on him, he bickered good-naturedly with the bluff, misguided, quick-draw recidivist who stood behind cardboard jail bars perpetually awaiting the circuit judge who would arrive any day to try him for bank robbery and cattle rustling.

After a while, the guard brought me in a chocolate cupcake with my tuna fish sandwich. The boys at the cafe across the street had forgotten to add the tomato, and the pasty mess of tuna was buried under a half dozen bonus slices of dill pickle.

I'd scarfed the sandwich and cupcake and was in the process of arranging the pickle slices into my initials on the mantle over the fireplace when the jailer announced from the hallway that I was about to have company and escorted two drunken Indian men inside.

The sun had long since set and the single bulb in the middle of the room wasn't providing much light. I hurried away from the fireplace and took up a position in the darkest corner of the room.

The jailer disappeared in a hurry leaving the two men holding on to each other's arms for balance. The larger man let go of the smaller and reached back for the wall. Gaining it, he turned and slid sideways into a sitting position that it took him a minute or two to perfect. The smaller man dropped to his butt and, despairing of his ability to support himself with his arms, put his head back against the wall and laughed quietly. I stood where I was, watching.

Running a hand through his graying crew cut and displaying a mouth filled with tiny, bright teeth, the bigger man smiled. His satiny blue shirt, stained and faded near the armpits, seemed to glow in the dim light of the cell. "Benny is drunk," he said, "so if we want to talk to him, we have to pull his handle."

I was reluctant to show much interest. Grunting, I turned away from them toward the lone window. I couldn't see outside, but I could hear squeaking and banging from a train yard across the street.

The big man's voice was surprising clear for a drunk's. "If you need to help him get on his feet, his handle is that braid he wears."

I turned back and lit a cigarette. "I see."

"No, you can't see it from where you are because it's behind him. Maybe you saw it when he came in."

I sat down under the window, pulled my knees to my chest, and smoked and closed my eyes and wondered why there were no cots in the room. On the beach not all that far away, Rick was probably tuning his guitar. Girls with glorious boobs would be gathered around him in bright bikinis. It seemed to me that they would all be glad to meet a somewhat taller, if paler man who had just gotten out of jail. When I looked up the bigger man towered over me.

He said, "My name is Little Beaver."

He was big, but he was happy and drunk. I felt a little wary, but not threatened. "Okay. My name is Tim."

He tapped himself on the chest. "Little Beaver." He grinned.

"I gottcha," I smiled. "I go by Tim, but on the side I'm the Lone Ranger."

"Could I mooch a cigarette?"

I reached for my pack.

"My friend Benny is too shy to ask."

"So you want two?"

"No. I want one and he wants one. He's got a Zippo so we don't need no light."

Little Beaver carried the cigarettes across the room to his friend and punched and shook him. The lighter flared. Benny burnt his thumb and cussed Little Beaver, but they got the cigarettes going.

"I'll tell you why we're here," Little Beaver offered.

"Drunk and disornery," Benny interrupted. "Drunk and disornery sons of bitches."

"And tired as hell," Little Beaver admitted.

"And tired as holy hell," Benny echoed.

"I'm here for vagrancy," I said.

"Yeah," Benny agreed. "Us, too, vagrancy sons of bitches. Vagrancy in the morning, vagrancy in the evening, vagrancy at suppertime. Tell you one thing, Lone Ranger, when we get out of here, we're going to

Alberta or someplace where there's refrigeration. The beer is warm all over town."

"I lost my billfold," I said.

Little Beaver found this too funny to bear, but he recovered quickly. "Shit, we ain't got no billfolds to lose. Haven't had for a while now. I'm Frank Skyraven."

"Frank," I nodded. "Good to meet you."

"You're a hell of a fellow well met," Frank said, "by your generosity, we're bound to give you some native man's wisdom. Advice about things around here and shit like that. The first secret is don't go to no fucking Betnam. Commies killed my brother over there."

"I'm sorry to hear that, Frank. I won't go to Vietnam. No way. I made up my mind already."

"The other secret is about dealing with the heat. See, your problem in the desert, problem of all your people, really, is you walk with your necks too stiff. You balance your heads on 'em like they were rocks."

I was surprised to see Frank get to his feet with so little effort.

"See, I can tell without ever having seen you even walk," Frank said, "you go like this here." Fred's walk owed something to an old Frankenstein movie and something to a robot. You got to do more like this." Fred walked and looked a little drunk again. "Them muscles along your shoulder blades are for moving your neck a little. If you learn the walk of the loose neck you won't get so damned hot when you're out in the desert sun. 'Course you don't want to move it too much or people will think you're a chicken running back to the henhouse."

Benny made little chicken noises and stubbed out his cigarette.

"Okay," I said, "I'll try to remember that."

The sky darkened and the light went off all but one blue Christmas tree bulb over the door.

Benny and Fred curled up and slept on the concrete floor. I took a shabby throw rug from in front of the fireplace and rolled it up for a makeshift pillow. I fell asleep listening to them snore and woke up at dawn to see Benny, lost and muttering, standing at the fireplace and chewing the pickle slices on the mantle. From across the street, came a sound like a cannon followed by a crashing of metal. In the hot predawn morning trains were being coupled together. A train was moving.

The cell door opened slowly. Glenda looked in. Smiling to discover that Benny and Fred were snoring together, she beckoned me to follow her down the hall.

She pointed to a nest of cold cereal in a plastic bowl beside a small carton of milk on the corner of her desk. "Courts say we gotta feed you before we can let you go," she said.

While I made quick work of the sugary cornflakes, she looked at me with a kind of motherly air that made me uncomfortable. "San Diego is a long ways to go on twenty-two dollars, but I'll guess you'll make it."

"Twenty-two dollars?"

"Your friend wired you thirty dollars. I didn't have any change, so I sent the gas station eight of the seven something you owed them. Here's your keys. Your car is parked outside."

I put my spoon in the bowl and looked up from the half-eaten mess of cornflakes. The office furnishings included a sombrero, spurs and a riding crop attached to the wall, a pair of longhorns, pine paneling, and three or four bad paintings of desert scenes. In the most prominently displayed painting a pinto reared it's muscular body into the red light of a setting sun. The world was filled with everybody else's pictures, everybody else's stories. Everybody was a walk-on or a voyeur in somebody else's dreams.

I drove over to thank the old man who'd given me soda and peanuts and found him on his hands and knees in the bright sunlight, scrubbing a black splotch on the concrete near the gas pump with the help of a brush and a bucket.

"Well, hell," he chortled, "I figured they'd done indicted and shipped you off to Colorado for bank robbery or something. You got a little better disposition this morning from the look of you."

"Sorry for acting the asshole yesterday," I said. "I'd like to thank you for your kindness and pay you for the soda and the peanuts."

"Hell, you don't have to offer to pay somebody back for something like that, Kid. You could be a little friendlier to old men, though. I mean, just because somebody strikes you right off as a nosy old lizard with too many questions, don't mean his intentions are bad."

"Yeah. You're right and I'm sorry."

"That's some old beater. I don't quite figure how you got it down from Colorado in all this heat."

"It was fine until I got into western Arizona and managed to lose all my money."

"Lost your money?"

"My billfold with everything in it. I'll be all right, though. My friend in San Diego wired me thirty bucks last night."

"You're going to try to drive that thing to San Diego on thirty bucks? Better let me make a couple of calls and see what I can get you for it. Take a bus over there."

"It runs fine. It just overheats a little."

"Yeah, I reckon it would overheat."

"You think it will get me through the rest of the desert? This woman over at the jail told me that it was going to be a hundred and fifteen in Barstow today."

"Yeah, and hotter still out there, between there and here." The old man spit on the faded stain and tossed the worn brush in the bucket.

I winced. "Think it'll make it?"

"No, I can't say that I do. Tell you what, why don't you pull it over there by the door closer to my tools and hoist the hood."

"I ain't got much money."

"Well, hell, I ain't no a banker, neither. You walk over to that ugly red shack down the street and get us a couple of coffees and the old doctor will pop the hood on your old jalopy. Hot coffee will cool you in the heat. Tell Jessup over there to put it on my tab."

When I came back with coffee, the old man had arranged half a dozen wrenches and screwdrivers on the car's greasy engine block. He shook his head and sipped his coffee. Finding it agreeably sour and hot, he made a face and cleared his throat.

"What's the verdict?"

"Well, that thing is about terminal, Kid. The tires got about as much tread as banana skins. Under the hood you got thin hoses, rusty clamps and rotted belts, a bad thermostat. It's got low compression and a couple of dozen oil leaks. You got a decent battery and a reasonably solid tranny and clutch, so I'd guess Corky over at Sam's Auto Salvage would give you thirty-forty bucks for it." He stepped to one side in order to spit in a dark corner. "You could hop a late morning bus and get where you're going in air conditioned comfort."

"No way," I said, "I drove it this far and gave it away and recovered it. I'll get it to San Diego by this evening."

"No, sir, you won't," he said.

"Well, I'm not going to sell it. Besides, to tell you the truth, my brother-in-law gave it to me. The title's still in his name so I probably couldn't even sell it if I wanted to."

The old man gathered tools from the engine. "Well, you're in a fix then. I can't encourage you to think you'll make it, but if I were in your shoes and had to try, I'd wait till late at night when it cools off, and then

I'd force myself to pray and drive no faster than 45 miles an hour until I saw that ocean fog."

"Hang around here all day?"

"Not precisely around here." He looked at his watch. "In fact, the owner of this station is going to expect me to have done some work I haven't even started yet. Tell you what you do, go off down yonder toward the river and you'll find a small beach. Take yourself a canteen of water or some beer and go for a long swim. Late tonight when the temperature's fallen, would be the time to start. I've got some old bottles out back you can have. Fill them with cold water and add it to the radiator whenever you stop to rest the engine."

"I appreciate all your help."

"You're welcome to it. Just drive real late and real slow and stop as often as you can make yourself. Your adventure ain't over yet."

Down by the river, I parked in a patch of gravel to one side of a dusty road and changed to my swimming trunks. Locusts stridulated in the bushes. Picking my way through boulders and weeds, I tiptoed around clumps of sand burrs and minced to the edge of the water. With the cold water numbing my feet and shins, I waded out, took a deep breath, and flopped forward. Gradually, I relaxed and put my head back in the blue water, allowing the sun to shine on my sunburned face. Hundreds of miles to the east and north the river began high in the mountains under snow-thatched boulders.

There was a road atlas in the trunk and I got out of the water to consult it for the river's source. I walked, soaked and shivering, back to the car. When I opened the trunk and picked up the jacket I'd thrown down on top of the atlas, my missing billfold flopped out of a pocket onto the spare tire.

I laughed out loud. After paying for my breakfast in western Arizona, I'd been so intent on being acknowledged by those Indians drinking beer in the shade, I'd absentmindedly slipped the wallet into my jacket and tossed it in the trunk. A jacket had been the furthest thing from my mind in the baking heat. Standing at the gas pump worried about the prospects of jail and my dad, it hadn't crossed my mind to open the trunk and search my jacket pockets.

Fortunately, the gas station kid had never gotten that far when he took over my car either. After counting the money and finding it was all there, I flipped the wallet into the glove compartment, locked the car, and ran back to the water to celebrate. I whooped and belly-flopped and flailed up river as hard as I could. Gray birds flitted in and out of the parched shrubbery. Somehow, in my mind, recovering the money reduced the risk of crossing the desert. It was all I could do to make myself wait until sundown.

What we know today as the interstate highway system, with its huge, illuminated green and white signs, fast food chains, long exit ramps, twenty-four hour traffic, was an unfinished mess back then. The undivided and mostly two lane road out of Needles was straight and narrow. As evening fell over the Mojave Desert, a smoldering haze covered the pavement. As the sun went down, oranges faded into pinks along the rims of distant barren mountains. The old engine labored and a dry wind blew in through the Dodge's wide-open windows. I settled down to fifty miles an hour, yet the landscape seemed to draw away. The mountains darkened, the sky dimmed, and the little Dodge seemed to stand still in a vacuum of hellish heat.

When the temperature gauge needle climbed, I stopped to rest the engine and add water to the cooling system. Holding a dim flashlight with one hand and pouring with the other, I stood in the growing darkness. There were no birds and no crickets and the radiator spit and gurgled, belching brown water, burning my hands and fingers. Smoking cigarettes and walking restless circles around the car, I waited impatiently for the added water to deliver its expected cooling and, oppressed by the dark and the silence, got back on the road too quickly.

Worse than the silence was the hum, whine, howl, and roar of traffic. Tiny lights glimmered and twinkled at the edge of the horizon, brightening slowly, inexorably, and taking on a whine. The whine became a howl, the world filled with unbearable brilliance, and quickly it was over; another car or truck was approaching Needles. Taillights beamed in my rear view mirror. Engines and tires fell silent and left me alone again in the small, chugging Dodge headed for Barstow. The vastness of the dark was oppressive. My mind began to wander. Since the temperature gauge needle rose inexorably at fifty, I wondered if I wouldn't obtain more cooling by driving sixty and hurrying forward a little into the ostensibly cooling air. Sixty brought no perceptible movement of the temperature gauge, but neither did the slight increase in speed seem to make the car overheat any faster. Sixty-three wasn't much faster than sixty. Although it began to seem possible to drive the Dodge with the temperature gauge on hot indefinitely, I forced myself to keep the speed under sixty-five.

Bang!
Clank!

The headlights went out, the engine died, and the Dodge went into a hard skid. I yanked on the steering and headed for the road shoulder, but everything seized up at once. The rear end of the Dodge was still partly in the westbound lane when its forward motion ceased altogether.

A point of light glimmering in my rear view mirror illuminated my dismayed face. All my lights were out. I stiffened. A car came on. Brakes squealed. Swerving tires warbled hysterically. The big, white Chrysler came to a stop fifty feet in front of the Dodge. It sat there, tires smoldering, giving off clouds of steam and heat in the glow of its taillights. The driver leaned furiously on his horn, then roared off for the coast.

My ignition key was useless. No amount of snapping the switch back and forth restored the headlights. When I opened the car door to get out, stars lunged, white, bluish, orange, stars I'd never seen before, little glimmers in smoky hazes, shining down since the time of Christ.

I worked the gears and tried to push the car off the pavement and down on to the gravel road shoulder, but there was no getting it into neutral, and no budging it from any of three or four positions from which I grunted and heaved. I kicked its rear fender in exasperation and felt myself succumbing to panic. I was doomed to personal ruin. Having blown my engine in the middle of the desert was bad enough: that my dreamy impetuosity might now cause the deaths of others was unendurable.

I wandered the desert floor in search of a rock, a flare, anything that might prove useful in leveraging the dead car off the road or signaling oncoming traffic. I found only sand and gravel and broken beer bottle glass. It occurred to me that I was in the worst night of my life, the night that would mark me forever. Why had I been so hasty, left so early? Why hadn't I been more patient, taken the old codger's advice, driven over to see Corky, the junkman, given him the Dodge for a few bucks and boarded a bus for San Diego? Any moment now a big semi would come roaring up the slight incline. In my panic it didn't take long for my imagination to go into hyper-drive. Two school buses loaded with kids and their adorable puppies would be coming the other way. The truck would swerve, its hinged trailer swinging into the school buses. The sound of the impact would be heard for miles and indelibly burned into my memory. I imagined the wails of bleeding children, the whimpering yips of dying puppies. The Dodge's existence as an instrument of ecstatic personal freedom was over and its new role as killer of the innocent was about to begin. The morning headlines would clamor, "HUNDREDS KILLED IN TRAFFIC TRAGEDY CAUSED BY RUNAWAY TEEN!"

And there, on the front page, for my mom to contemplate over her breakfast coffee, a photo of her son being led away in handcuffs, and visible in the background, a veritable Shiloh of children's bodies and mangled puppies on the pavement.

After each passing car or truck the wave of panic would subside and I would take comfort from the fact that the highway was all but empty. Somehow I might yet manage to escape. My flashlight was fading and my instinct for self-preservation kicked in hard. I squatted down and removed the license plates. Carrying them out into the vastness together with all the incriminating papers from the glove compartment, I put them all in a small hole I dug with a sharp rock. Looking up from my work, I saw another pair of headlight beams bearing down on the Dodge and ran for the pavement, waving the by now all but useless flashlight, it's last glow fading as I staggered toward the road. I was too late. I stopped and clenched, certain that this was to be the disaster that would send my soul, assuming I had one, to perdition.

But the screaming brakes faded with neither crash, nor horn, nor shout of an enraged human voice. There was no follow-up roar of an accelerating engine. From where I stood, I saw a white car's headlights shining brilliantly off into nowhere. My breathing was loud in my chest. Even so, I heard the idling of the engine.

"Anybody out there?"

It was a man's voice. Not a cop's. Not obviously angry. Curious, perhaps even helpful, and friendly. My voice sounded like a groan. Desperate for any human contact, I forced myself to approach the headlights. "Yes."

"What are you doing with the car half on and half off the road?"

A few steps and I was close enough to see two men in the smoky glare of the headlights of a white Oldsmobile '88. They were wearing only boxer shorts and sneakers in the heat of the desert night. One sat on the fender, massaging a knobby knee. The other stood nearby, pulling on a can of beer. "What are you doing out there in the dark?"

"Burying my license plates," I admitted, walking to where I could be seen. "I blew the engine up. I'm scared somebody's going to bash into the car. I couldn't push it and decided I didn't want anybody to be able to trace it to me. That's why I was out there."

The bigger of the men slipped off the fender and went to examine the Dodge. He kicked a tire. "Maybe it's better that you blew it up when you did rather than drive it any further on that front tire. You ain't so dumb that you stole it, now?"

"No. My brother-in-law gave it to me."

The man popped the hood and whistled. "Buddy," he said, "let me tell you. What were once many independent pieces of metal have turned into a fuckin' meteorite. This thing has rolled its last mile. Where you headed?"

"L.A. Actually, San Diego. Actually, Mission Beach."

"You better let us just push it down off the highway before somebody comes along and sends us all flying."

"I can't tell you how much I'd appreciate it."

"We'll give you a ride to L.A., won't we, Jerry?"

"Yeah, but he ain't driving my car. His bad luck may hold a while."

"Thanks," I said, turning away to hide my relief. When I turned back, Jerry handed me a beer. "Dark hot night, huh?"

I fought a temptation to pour the beer over my head. For a long time I'd been oblivious to the heat. I took my shirt off and tossed it with my knapsack in the trunk of their Olds.

I lit a cigarette and watched while Jerry pulled up behind the Dodge, gunned the engine and pushed it well off the road. He pulled back up on the pavement and opened the door. Dave got in the backseat, situated himself in stacks of stools, suitcases, pillows, and blankets. I slid into the front. Jerry drove the big Olds west with all the windows rolled down so the hot desert wind would cool us if it could. A stinging mist of sand blew in through the open windows, but I put my feet upon the dashboard and sipped beer and told my story in little bursts while the wind whipped through my hair.

Jerry and Dave were two truck mechanics from Dayton, Ohio, they said, running out on wives who didn't understand how much better a life California had to offer.

The Olds was steady at seventy-five. Dave rattled ice cubes in the cooler and handed beers forward. It fell to me to fiddle with the radio dial in search of music. I found a Texas evangelist who bragged of knowing the life of a sinner first hand and then a country voice selling tickets to a car raffle for a worthy cause in Oklahoma.

Just outside Barstow, Dave leaned over the front seat to make himself heard.

"Leave off on the radio," he said. "The wind is song and talk enough for now."

The morning sky went red when they dropped me off outside their cousin's house in Culver City, California. They gave me the last can of beer, warm now that the ice had melted away.

An hour and a half later a balding milkman cursed his worthless, complaining customers and the malevolent, petty bosses who ruined his otherwise bearable early morning job. I sat as upright as I could on an empty steel milk crate, barely able to see out the window, craning my neck and savoring my first view of the Pacific Ocean. The truck's rear end howled, glass milk bottles clinked, and I absorbed the bumps, convinced that at last I was about to be released into heaven. The desert was behind me, as were long hours trying to hitch a ride out of Culver City. Around me now were flowers on the hillsides and landscape rich with greens I'd never seen or smelled. Morning sun had broken through the cloud cover. A cottony white fog flowed out of gulches and into the vast, blue Pacific

Its rear end yowling, the milk truck descended some steep hills. The driver made a right turn and pointed behind his truck. I thanked him and watched the truck lurch back into intensifying morning traffic. The morning brightened and warmed as people in Mission Beach were coming outside to sip coffee or run errands. White, pink, and blue, sand-faded bungalows glowed in the sun. Scantily clad, sun-browned and disheveled women stood talking to one another in front of small shops. Unbrushed hair, dusty skins, sandals, scarves, and shorts; fresh, indolent, Mission Beach looked even better than I'd allowed myself to hope it would. The marine air smelled of ammonia, peppery flowers and bushes, tanning lotion, coffee and fried donuts.

An older woman in sunglasses, a leopard skin halter, and a pair of men's slacks smiled at me and provided directions. Each narrow street was just where she said it would be, and before I was prepared for it, I was looking at Rick's Triumph. Its tattered convertible top was snapped on to protect what was left of the torn interior. The front fender still sported the dent from the snow bank in Winter Park. A bottle of contact lens solution was wedged between the driver's seat and the gearshift lever. Three or four finger picks gleamed on the floor mat in front of the passenger's seat.

Rick stood smirking at me from the cement steps of a dirty white bungalow across the street, the box of his acoustic guitar tucked awkwardly under his right arm. He thumped out a few chords to a Woody Guthrie song and sang something about a mighty hard road. Seeing him again after almost a year, I thought of a mangy cat that preferred an independent life in the woods. His red hair was a long indifferent snarl of curls. A white pasty coating, which covered his nose, added to his feral expression. As I came up the walk, he leaned his guitar against a railing and stood to shake hands.

132

"Where did you park?"

I was in an ecstasy of arrival and found it hard to speak. I raised my arm, pointed east, and finally found my voice. "About two hundred miles thataway."

"Wow! What happened?"

"Blew the engine out in the middle of nowhere. A couple of truck mechanics from Ohio helped me push it into a ditch by the side of the highway and then dropped me off in L.A. sometime before dawn."

"I had to drive all over hell looking for some way to wire you money to get here on. You lost your wallet, is that the story?"

"Yeah, but as it turns out, only temporarily. The car's gone for good, but I found my money in the trunk before I abandoned the car, so I can pay you back right away."

"Great! Drag your pack inside. Denny and I were just about to go down to the beach. You can tell us all about your adventures."

"Who's Denny?"

"My roommate for the last three weeks. But don't worry; there's room for your sleeping bag on the floor by the washing machine."

Denny's forehead and nose were pink, but the rest of him was as bronzed as an Inca. He looked a couple years older than Rick, but in fact was faced with another year of high school. He'd be leaving San Diego about the same time Rick did. But instead of heading off for college, Denny would thumb his way back to Santa Barbara and move back in with his parents for his last year of high school. He was filled with enthusiasms and eager for fun and within ten minutes had invited me to go to Mexico. What I really wanted to do was go back to the beach house for a nap.

A desultory curiosity was all I could manage. "Mexico?"

"Yeah, for a couple of days at the end of next week."

"School's about to start up for you. Why go to Mexico now? I mean, anyway, I just got here."

"It's something I agreed to do for Rick, to earn my share of this month's rent."

It seemed too complicated a matter to understand just then and I didn't really feel like paying attention to details or making a commitment one way or another. Then again, I was half asleep and didn't really feel like moving either. It turned out Rick had allowed his folks to believe he'd been working more than he actually had been. They had agreed to pay his college tuition. Coming up with the money for clothes, books, and to pay his first month's rent was his responsibility. He'd planned to sell his car to raise the necessary funds, but it turned out that before he got

133

around to taking out the classified ad, he'd developed problems with the muffler, the clutch, and the transmission. Not wanting to have to sell it for parts and needing the money, he and Denny had formulated a plan calling for Denny to "steal" the car and ditch it in Mexico. Rick would stay in Mission Beach, report the car stolen after the fact, then collect on his car insurance policy. To my surprise, Rick had rationalized this out pretty well. His parents had been insuring their cars with the same company for many years and had never put in a claim. Not only had he been paying out insurance premiums which amounted to more than blue book value on the Triumph, he'd never even made a claim on the dent we'd put in it when we skidded off the road on our skiing adventure. Finally, provided the insurer paid off, he'd reinsure with the same company once he got another car.

Denny worked on me about how much fun we'd have in Mexico. "It'll be cool, Barlow," he said. "Beers are a dime in Tijuana and my cousin got laid down there for three bucks. We can buy some rubbers before we go."

I considered what it might be like to have sex with a strange, desperately poor Mexican girl, who might or might not laugh at my inept performance, and might or might not summon a knife-wielding brother over some language-related or fiduciary misunderstanding. The whole complicated business with Sylvia, what I might have said or done to keep her from going bonkers, if, indeed, she had flipped out, was still weighing on me. Sex now seemed infinitely more complicated than I'd imagined and I'd decided I wasn't going to have sex again for a while. Somehow, I didn't seriously believe I'd be able to adhere to this resolution, and didn't even really believe I wanted to. I wasn't going to buy sex, though, and I wasn't going to engage in it in a strange place that I associated with dirty blankets, agonizing intestinal ailments, cockroaches, VD, and razor blades. Knowing Denny wanted my company, Rick worked a different angle. He had never conceived of my visit in terms of rent and I could do what I wanted as far as Mexico was concerned; he just wanted me to understand that it was one thing to hold to all these lofty philosophical principles while living in your parents' house, using their electricity, and eating food from their refrigerator, and another to make your own moral and independent way in a world that cared only for money.

The next day while Rick was at the dentist's office having his teeth cleaned, Denny and I walked down Mission Boulevard to get a burger and plan our Mexican escapade. I picked up a switchblade knife from the sidewalk, noted that it wouldn't open, and thinking that it would give me something to do with my hands at the restaurant, slipped it in my pocket.

Almost immediately, two cops pulled up, got out of the cop car, and demanded that we put our hands on the roof of the patrol car and submit to a search. They seemed glad to discover the knife. At first, I tried to behave contritely, to make it easy for them to keep the knife and let me go. They were taking me in, they said, for possession of a concealed weapon. That the knife had rusted shut didn't trouble the cops a bit.

With Denny in the back seat next to me, I got my first view of the downtown San Diego skyline. I didn't enjoy it much, but I wasn't really all that shook up until one of the cops escorted Denny into a new building and left me in the car with the other cop. I was eighteen. Denny was seventeen. He was going to juvenile hall. I was going to jail by myself. Alone with the more genial cop, I tried again to explain about the knife. When he told me to shut up, I thought about how few steps I'd actually taken after picking up the knife and wondered if the cops had planted it there as a part of some sinister campaign to "clean up" the streets of Mission Beach. I brooded about this possibility all the way into the underground parking garage and all the way up to whatever floor we ascended to in a slow elevator.

Doing my best to sound calm and manly, I phoned Rick and asked him to do whatever he could to secure my release. Hanging up with a sinking, nauseous feeling in the pit of my stomach, I emptied my pockets into a numbered pouch and let a cop blot my ink-stained fingers onto something white. Then it was down the hall, onto another elevator and out into a place of chaos, violence, and depression. While I felt confident that no judge would ever send me to jail for carrying an inoperable knife, I was scared of what might happen to me before I ever faced the judge. I'd never been forced to endure the company of violent, aggressively unhappy men and I fought not to remember all the stories and rumors I'd heard. My stomach was churning, my hands were wet. The Needles jail had been a kind of slumber party in an empty clubhouse. This was a scrubbed loud organized nightmare, and I was scared.

They put me in a holding tank crowded with six beds and more than a dozen men. It was sour with vomit and rank with urine and I seemed to be the only one who noticed this. Everybody stared when I walked in. I stood as tall as I could, tried to look more muscular than I was, and sneered. An old man with white whiskers, slimed with saliva, jail-issued Bull Durham tobacco flakes, and puke, slept fitfully, cuddled up around the cell's only toilet bowl.

All the bunks were claimed, so I stood sullenly in a corner with my arms folded in front of my chest. My legs had gone completely numb by the time I finally allowed myself to sit down. Like everybody else, I was watching intently, while pretending to be half blind and wholly indifferent to whatever went on. Conversation didn't really exist, so my mostly drunken cellmates, at least those who needed to hear the sounds of their own voices, addressed the perfect judge they would soon appear before. Those who spoke gave voice to what we all felt; we were all more innocent of our crimes than the cruel men in uniforms were willing to consider. Apart from these monologues, which we had to listen to and so hoped were reasonably entertaining, the only other source of amusement was provided by anyone who needed to use the cell's only toilet, embraced and blockaded by the comatose drunk.

The favorite method of gaining access to the pot consisted of kicking the old guy in the ribs and arms until he rolled reluctantly to one side. The sleeper responded to the abuse with incoherent curses before, invariably, taking up the old position, this time cuddling the toilet bowl like a teddy bear.

One guy with a cobra tattooed on the back of his neck stood on the wino's forearm and saved the last of his stream for the drunk's face. To howls of inmate approval, the drunk gasped, sputtered, wiped the piss from his beard, then rolled onto his stomach to obstruct access to the pot from yet another angle. Once the laughter died down, it became clear that Snake Neck had marked his territory and assumed the crown. He was the boss of the cell. He looked around to see if anyone wanted to challenge his status.

An arrival named Frank had something to say, and pushed his chest forward like an oxygen-deprived rooster. In just a minute or two, Frank shouted, he was going to be cut a deal by a wealthy and sexy loved one. When that happened every one of his cellmates would rot and stink as all small time assholes deserved to do, but he, Frank Bosco, would immediately have it made. The law would blossom like a flower and smell oh so sweetly for Frank, while the ugly and stupid jailbirds surrounding him who were not coming forward graciously with the cigarette he'd politely requested half an hour ago would be left here to jack off in the shower and burn their little pathetic dicks with lye-laced soap. While we moped and tried to masticate dead bread crusts and fought one another over lima bean soup served in steel mugs, Frank would be with his choice of several beautiful women who would spread their legs and, pussies dripping virgin olive oil, beg him for hot sex. Gorgeous women always did this because in a world of undersized peckers, they had come to understand that ten-and-a-half iron-hard inches which never failed could deliver them to pleasure they'd only dreamed about in the arms of lesser men. Before and after the hot sex, they would feed Frank steak and pie and corn on the cob. And hard liquor. Only the best. Bracing for trouble between Snake Neck and Frank, I was both happily surprised and somewhat frightened when a guard opened the cell and called my name.

The guard was swarthy, with heavy-looking eyelids and greenish bags under his eyes. He seemed indifferent rather than hostile. I knew I wasn't going to be released and worried that the San Diego City Jail might contain people even more unpleasant than Frank and Snake Neck.

"Where am I going?"

"For now, you're going to another cell?"

"Why?"

"You like that one?"

"No."

"Nobody under twenty-one can be confined in a holding tank for more than three hours. Stop right there. That's where you're going."

A small dark Latin man who had been lying on his bunk propped himself up on an elbow and offered me a grunt.

I nodded to my new cellmate and turned to watch the guard walk down the hall.

The man in my cell cleared his throat. "What's your name, Bracero?"

"Barlow."

"I'm Hermando, man. You got any cigarettes, Barlow?

Not wanting to approach too closely, I reached for my pack of smokes and lobbed him one. He made a move to catch it, thought the better of it, and allowed it to land on the bunk bed. "Thanks, amigo."

I lit one of my few remaining cigarettes and wondered if and when I'd be allowed to buy more. Hermando sat on the edge of his bed and blew smoke from his nose. "Listen, Barlow. I gotta tell you something. Right now it's just you and me, but as you can see they got four beds in here. Everything's cool now, but later's gonna be we don't know how many guys in here, and a rush for sleeping space. Climb up on that top bunk over there, across from mine. That way we're both in a good position. You don't let nobody take this bed from me, I don't let nobody take that one from you. This place sucks but we're better than we might be. We're both out of the way, close to the pot, a little light coming in from outside."

"Okay," I said, feeling as though I'd be more likely to need his help than he would to require mine. "You've got a deal."

"Another thing. Don't hit nobody unless he grabs you or swings on you first. But don't let nobody hit you no matter how big without taking a swing on them. But also you gotta understand that if you hit somebody and he bumps into somebody else, then you maybe gonna have to fight them both."

I swallowed hard. "Okay."

I told Hermando about being arrested in Mission Beach for carrying a switchblade knife that wouldn't open. Hermando said he was in because he'd hit his brother-in-law with a wrench in some kind of a dispute involving Hermando's sister. Then he gave me the bad news that it being Thursday of a Labor Day weekend, we weren't likely to be arraigned until the following Tuesday.

Though he couldn't have weighed more than about a hundred and thirty, Hermando was hard-bodied. Small inky crosses were drawn on both hands between his thumbs and index fingers. "Pachuco," Hermando said, indicating the tattoos, and nodding his head. "Don't worry about nothing, Litta White Guy, amigo, because we gonna look out together. You get into a situation you don't know nothing about, just look over for me. I'll make you a little signal."

A man named Mickey Lemon was pushed inside and cursed. He was bruised and his face was marked with dried blood. His nose was swollen too far to one side of his face and his lower lip was as black as an old banana skin. When Hermando gestured sympathetically toward him, Mickey shook his head. Flakes of dried blood fell out of his ears onto the concrete floor.

Mickey told how he "didn't do nothin'," not in Tijuana and not in California. They pulled him out of the car and sat on his hip punching him in the balls and laughing. But Mickey had friends in high and low places, and one day, they, the cops, the border patrol, they would all die. He didn't have to say how or when, in this world of snitches and pussies, but he had friends, guys with guns who didn't care and owed him big. That one cop, that one with the belly, they'd set his billy club on fire, shove it all the way up his ass and burn his prostrated gland until it smoked like old bacon. People don't call Mickey Lemon a punk and hit him in the nuts and live long. Nobody yet. Fuckin' primary law of Chula Vista, and Imperial Beach, California, that one was. Better believe it.

A couple hours later, they moved me to a smaller empty cell with two bunks. I sat on top and worried about who they might lock up with me. A guard brought me a tray of macaroni topped with little golf balls of canned tomato. When I asked him if there was any way I could go back to Hermando's cell, he laughed and refused to speak. Ten minutes later a trustee in a jail blue shirt wheeled a cart down the hall and gave me white bread and butter, two or three ounces of chocolate pudding, and a mug of cool coffee. I polished off the pudding and the bread and butter and smoked the last of my cigarettes, listening to the hollow sounds of dishes being clacked together, gathered up, and wheeled back to the kitchen.

Clanging cell doors and men's voices echoing off cement, and guards squeaking down walkways in new shoes, tingling keys, another prisoner marching past the cell. Somebody called for lights out. I was all alone and the world turned deep blue with night-lights. The voices seemed closer. Now it was a world of grunts and groans and men calling out for the guard, for aspirin, for help, for God, for other voices in the night.

I got under my blanket and closed my eyes, but the voices only got louder. You Honky. Nigger. Spic. Wop. Kike. Suck my dick. Get you, motherfucker. The cops got it in for me. My old lady. My buddy. My lawyer. Tell that guy to shut up or I'll kill him. My money. Didn't do shit. I ain't saying. Kick your ass. You know what your mother did for me, Joe? Then she lapped it up like ice cream. She did. Kill you for that. Out of this hole. Give me a fuckin' smoke. Clang. Wake up. Time is it? Half a hair past a mole. Shaatup. That was funny.

Hours later after even the blue lights went out, trustees came down the walkways dragging broom handles across cell doors, the rattle of a new day. We were lined up on the walks and marched into a cafeteria smelling of toxic soap and fat. Trustees with giant ladles slopped boiled wheat cereal into pewter mugs. There was an empty space at a table where Hermando was sitting and I practically ran for it. He was in no mood to talk, but when I shrugged, dabbed my bread crust in what was left of my cereal, and sipped my sour coffee, he handed me his bag of Bull Durham tobacco flakes and papers and tried not to laugh when I made a mess rolling my first cigarette.

Alone again in my cell, I listened to the sounds of cleanup. Trustees, pink-cheeked from having shaved, pushed wooden carts, swung steamy pails of soapy swill, and slapped at the concrete floors with blackened mops. Steaming disinfectant, stink of lime over bleach, then it was lunch. Hermando was not to be seen. Two guys at my table threw punches at each other over who owned the rights to read a paperback without a cover. When the guards dragged them off, I concentrated on my sand-dry white bread with cheese as tough as caramel, its nugget of gray lettuce, and a sliver of jelly-glazed lunchmeat.

I thought of Rick and Denny, of Sylvia, wherever she was, of Bruce packing for Princeton, my parents with no idea of my whereabouts, and of my brothers. There were dozens of people I hoped were thinking about me who probably weren't. Nap followed nap. The terror, the sharp loneliness, and the agony of boredom gave way to dolor, apathy, naps that ended too soon. The blue nightlights came on again and voices echoed down the cellblock. New voices and old. Angry voices and sad ones. Gimme a cigarette. I'm going to hunt you down. Nigger, honky, your mammy. Can I look at your magazine tomorrow? Out of this hole. Fuggin cops. They got no case. My partner will, that's for sure. Liquor store. They planted the shit.

My life seemed half over by the time Tuesday came, but there were raisins in the breakfast oatmeal and a mountain of stale, unfrosted donuts. Even the coffee was almost warm. Afterwards we marched down halls and flights of steps and herded aboard gray buses. Aboard, I managed to get a seat by Hermando. There were seven roll calls and headcounts and we sat in the dank garage for forty-five minutes, forbidden to talk or smoke. Then the buses went up the ramp and emerged into the sunlight. I looked out on a world that could not have been more perfect, more redolent with promise and possibility. Curvy women and girls in skimpy dresses and halters stood in small groups and laughed together in ways that prompted some of the men to point, grin, and whisper about how badly those ripe, busty bodies wanted to be taken into the arms of a man with a hard dick. Children chased one another in circles, grabbing their own arms and hugging their heads to contain their pleasure at running full tilt or rolling down sunny hills of grass. On the edge of a park, dogs chased balls, children in shorts carved ice cream cones with long tongues, and old men with twisted brown legs squinted at one another over fistfuls of playing cards and polished their sunglasses.

Hermando interrupted my reveries. "We don't know how things are going to work, but be ready for when they let us get off. We don't want to end up at the end of the line and draw big numbers, Bracero, 'cause the judges get meaner and the sentences get longer as the day drags on."

We climbed off the buses and formed a line. The ban on talking seemed to have been lifted and everybody was suddenly an authority on what was about to happen.

"You'll be summoned in alphabetical order," a man in a uniform barked as we filed into the courtroom. "When your name is called, step forward to the table in front."

A man entered from a side door near the judge's chambers and proclaimed court to be in session. We got to our feet and a thin balding

140

man eased himself wearily behind a gigantic desk. His voice was languid, arrogant, efficient. "Adams, John Harrod."

"Harold, your honor."

"You're charged with drunk and disorderly conduct and menacing a peace officer, Mr. Adams. How do you plead?"

"Not guilty, your honor.

As the morning progressed, the judge fidgeted in his big chair and wrung the wooden handle of his gavel like a dishrag whenever he was unhappy with the information he was being provided. When he was satisfied that a perfect justice had been handed out, he twirled his mallet and let it fall on the wooden pellet with a distinctive clack.

The first three sentences seemed unduly severe and perfunctory. "Production-quota justice," I murmured.

Hermando nodded.

"Next case. Alvarado, Modesto Geesus."

"Hey-SOOS, your honor.

"Mister Alvarado, I've seen you before. This is certainly not the first time you've been in trouble, is it?"

"No, your honor, but . . . ."

Hermando sank in his seat and folded his hands in front of his mouth as if he wanted to protect his mustache. "I remember this judge. You gotcher choice, Bracero. If yer gonna say not guilty cause your knife no open, he gonna set a trial date and keep you locked up maybe eight or ten more days. You say guilty, he gonna give you shit, Litta White Boy. Tell eem focking guilty with a explanation.   Stenuating motherfucking circumstances. Talk loud, but polite, an don't sass the man."

The judge about to decide my fate had the face of an old cougar, wore tortoise shell glasses with paperclip-shaped lenses, and had a way of leaning back and wrinkling his forehead in an effort to keep his specs from sliding toward his mouth. The wrinkles in the forehead, the pursed lips, made me think he was trying his best to avoid the stench of the accused. Maybe, instead, he was taking it in, smelling a rat, opening and closing his claws, a cat pawing at a wounded bird.

"Mr. Barlow, you are charged with carrying a concealed weapon. How do you plead?"

"Well, your honor . . . ."

"Not well, your honor, Mr. Barlow. Guilty or not guilty?"

Trained not to put my hands in my pockets in the presence of an important adult, I locked them behind my back. "Guilty, your honor, but I'd like to offer the court an explanation."

"You may offer the court your explanation, Mr. Barlow, but keep it brief. There are many others waiting their turn."

"Your honor, the weapon in question, a switchblade knife. It won't open."

Laughing started up behind me. My neck went red, my hands unclasped themselves and I made one of my middle fingers very visible to the prisoners sitting behind me. This produced another ripple of laughter.

The judge dangled the switchblade for all to see. "Is this the weapon, Mr. Barlow?"

"Yes, your honor. Now if you'll just try to open the blade."

"Mr. Barlow, this court has better things to do than fiddle with illegal weapons."

More laughing. Sure, I thought to myself, butter him up, you bastards. I hope he gives you all twenty years. "Your honor, the blade won't open."

"Mr. Barlow, the court informs you that possession of this weapon is illegal in the state of California. It was made illegal many years ago, having no practical utility, and so far as I understand, the illegality of this weapon is not contingent on whether or not it can be flipped open."

"Your honor," I began.

"The court has taken your point, Mr. Barlow. Have you anything else to say?"

My face was hot, my throat dry. Behind me I could feel the magnetic pull of jail life, desolation, loneliness, and now, maybe a couple dozen men determined to get me for flipping them off. I tried to find my voice and couldn't.

"Very well. The court enters Mr. Barlow's guilty plea and remarks that the defendant is eighteen years of age, and that he describes himself as a recent high school graduate from Denver, Colorado. What are you doing here in California, Mr. Barlow?"

Unable to bring myself to say, `your honor' anymore, I bit my lip to keep from saying a lot worse. "Living with a couple of friends in Mission Beach."

"Why did you leave home, Mr. Barlow?"

"To see my friends."

"Apart from your friends, do you have family in California, Mr. Barlow? A job?"

"No."

"Very well. This court sentences you to thirty days."

I glared and sputtered.

"However, in view of your youth, the fact that you haven't been in trouble in California before, and the peculiar circumstances of your case, provided your parents are willing to send you a bus or an airline ticket back to Colorado, the court agrees to suspend your sentence. Otherwise, thirty days with credit for time served. Take your pick, Mr. Barlow. Twenty-six more days, or a telephone number and your permission to contact your parents so you can go back to Colorado."

"Please contact my parents."

I hung my head in defeat.

Aboard the bus on the way back to jail, my attention vacillated between worrying about the inmates ready to beat me bloody for giving them the finger in court for laughing at me, and how long it would take for the bailiff's phone call to produce the desired results. If my dad was on a sales trip, within a matter of hours my mom would send me a quick ticket home. If he was in town but drinking, she'd have to time the news, weather two or three of his beer-fueled rages and wait till he was reasonably sober and rested. If he was sober when the call came through, and if it was still early in Denver, then I figured the argument would take about four hours and by the end of which he'd be drunk. Hoping for a prompt response, I passed on the tuna and potato casserole dinner and, when the nightlights came on, cast myself on a raft of daydreams, floating off on a sea of unhappy voices.

"Bar-LOW!"

I had been asleep. I wanted to be asleep. "What?"

"Cher ass out here."

I rolled off the bunk and stumbled out of the cell. The world was many colors of sickly green. The guard in front of me stood, white and sickly, under a bluish florescent moon. A few cells down, a man in pain was saying he hadn't done anything. The guard was talking to me.

"Hodja hands out!"

Cuffs. Handcuffs.

"What's going on?" My voice was louder than I expected. "Where am I going?"

"Bus station, motherfucker."

Clang. Bang. Slam. Bright lights. Garage. Middle of the night. Backseat of the cop car, the cops talking. Your old lady's got her viewpoint, too. How many you pumpin' these days? Tell her it means nothing. Take her some candy. Once she's fat enough, she won't care who you pump, long as you keep bringing the candy."

Empty streets. Downtown. Bus station. Smoke of diesels. Headlights.

"Come on, Timothy. Say goodbye to California."

"Well, let's reclaim the bracelets."

"No, we gotta walk him up there to let the driver know that Surfer Motherfucker is goin' home. Cmon, Asshole, up the steps."

I boarded, hands cuffed in front of my groin. A man in an air force uniform stuffing a hard-shell suitcase in an overhead compartment turned to stare. A pair of women in scarves lowered their eyes and whispered. For a moment I saw myself as a thin figure in a Renaissance painting, Christ brought before Pilate. Somebody coughed and my fantasy vanished. The bus driver chuckled with the cops. The handcuffs, with a click, came off my wrists. I rubbed my hands and tried to keep from smiling. One of the cops smiled back.

"Later, Surfer Boy."

I took the first empty seat on the aisle. The woman next to me got up and moved, setting off successions of relocations. The passengers disliked and feared me as a known criminal just out of jail, released on who knew what charges, but I didn't care because the bus door was about to close and leave me alone with three or four dozen people unlikely to bray or brag loudly or call one another names. As nearly as I could guess nobody on the bus had "Born to Lose" tattooed on an arm. I would probably ride all the way to Denver before anybody sobbed in the night or threw a punch or identified a nearby cocksucker at the top of his lungs. To keep from singing, I lit a cigarette from a pack I'd acquired at the canteen the night before.

"Smoking in the back two rows only, Buddy," the driver growled. "Or in the lavatory."

I smiled, waved respectfully, and carried my cigarette to an empty seat in the back row. Since I still had some money in a drawer at Rick's, I'd be able to repay my parents for the bus ticket, which should get me off the hook somewhat. Still, I'd probably have to take some sort of job. I planned to behave myself, apologize for taking off in the uninsured Dodge, save my money, and find a less devious way of getting back to the slippery paradise of California.

Meantime, it was goodbye to oatmeal tasting of industrial soap, lumpy mashed potatoes, untearable bread crusts, mushy green peas, and string beans like tree twigs. Goodbye, gravelly Cream of Wheat, thin soup with soggy celery, and the lingering aftertaste of minerals. The cops had stuffed an envelope from my mom in my pocket and the envelope contained twenty bucks, so at the first rest stop cafe I was going to order a piece of hot berry pie and watch a scoop of ice cream melt all over it.

I dozed. Little overhead lights came on, motion stopped. Bodies groaned and muttered and came slowly to life.

144

"Folks, this is El Centro, California. We'll be stopping here for twenty minutes."

In a cafe in the desert, I followed pie and ice cream with coffee and a peanut butter bar. Back aboard the bus, I reminded myself to call Rick and ask him to send my knapsack and money to my parents' address in Denver. I wondered if I'd ever see Denny again, wondered if Sylvia was back in circulation, and thought of Nancy and Lynn, two girls I might still enjoy a little time with before they headed off to college. I would have stories to tell them, and girls liked to be kissed by guys with attitude problems and personal adventure stories.

I knew I could work them up into raptures of caretaking by enhancing my stories of California adventures. I was discovering that poetry tinged with lonely anguish and tales of freedom with the right amount of injustice had strange effects on girls and seemed to kindle lust and longing. Anyway, it would be a kind of burden for them to arrive on campus still a virgin, then check into a lonely dorm room with nobody special waiting impatiently back in Denver for the Christmas holidays. Not that I planned to be in Denver by Christmas. I didn't know exactly what I planned. I planned to make the best of things and call Lynn and Nancy.

When I woke up the sun was shining and the driver was talking through a dying microphone and a faulty speaker. Passengers were thanked for their patronage. It was seventy-eight degrees outside and passengers were urged to step down carefully. Something about the pinkness of the morning puzzled me. The sun seemed wrongly positioned and the air damper than I expected, less pungent. Could this be Phoenix already? How could it be anywhere else?

At the breakfast counter I lit a cigarette and sipped coffee. A waitress walked past me with a saucer of toast.

"Miss....uh?"

"You want more coffee?"

"Please....What city is this?

"What?"

"Uh, could you tell me what city this is?"

She moved back three steps and lifted her heavily penciled eyebrows. "What city is this? Is that what you said?"

"Yes."

"San Diego."

I was about to explain that it couldn't be San Diego because I'd left there some time after midnight and had been riding a bus all night. "San Diego?"

"San DEE-AAAAAYGO!" The waitress walked slowly away, shaking her head and muttering.

Suddenly it hit me. I laughed and put a stack of nickels on the counter and went in search of a pay phone. An old woman holding a donut like a squirrel would hold a walnut looked up at me when I passed by. "Communication and transportation," I said. "That's all life is, really."

She nibbled and reached for her coffee. "What?"

I looked at her over my shoulder. "That's what life's all about. Communication and transportation."

At the end of a polished hall, I found a pay phone. "Rick," I said, "sorry to wake you."

"Barlow! Where the hell are you?"

"I'm down at the bus station. Can you come get me?"

"What bus station?"

"San Diego."

"I called the jail last night and they told me that you were being put on a bus back to Denver. What's going on?"

I reached into my shirt pocket for my ticket. The driver, intent on bantering with the cops, hadn't torn it, and it bore no expiration date or other incriminating markings. Looking out the window I could see that it was going to be a glorious day at the beach.

"The cops put me on the bus in the middle of the night. I was half asleep, and when we stopped at a coffee place in El Centro, I must have gotten back aboard a westbound bus. Weird, huh? I walked out into the parking lot and got on the El Centro bus headed for San Diego instead of the El Centro bus headed for Arizona."

"Weird," Rick agreed. "Now what?"

"Well, now I got a bus ticket back, the money my folks sent me and my own money in a drawer in the bedroom at your place. Going back to Denver will be living hell, but I don't have to face it for a few days. So can you come get me?"

"Well, I would, but I can't."

"Why not?"

"Because Denny just took off to drive my Triumph down to Mexico."

"So Denny's still around? He didn't get sent home by the cops?"

"No. He's underage. Somebody gave him a lecture about bad company at juvenile hall. I picked him up over there about an hour after you called me on Thursday. He was in juvenile hall for an hour and then he got off."

I had only the vaguest idea about how to make a life for myself in a town where I didn't really know anybody except two people who were about to leave for school, so after three more sunny days on the beach followed by midnight guitar parties, I vowed to call or write Rick and Denny about coming out again next summer and, using my original unexamined bus ticket, I boarded a morning bus to Denver.

From time to time I passed through little spasms of guilt, and for the first time I could remember, I felt I owed my parents something. They had gotten me out of jail and I figured I owed them at least a cautious word of thanks and a repayment of the money they'd spent doing it. I also wanted to find a way and reassure them that hardheaded and rebellious as I was, I could and would find my own way in life without being a further burden to them. Unfortunately, with the summer over and the beach house rented to another party, this would probably mean taking a regular job in Denver for a while, a prospect I wasn't crazy about.

As it happened, less than an hour after I returned to my parents' house, I learned that my dad had been on his employment counselor's barstool again. At six-thirty the next morning, I was hiking through Washington Park, hoofing it down to a job interview with a man named Jesse, a beer-drinking buddy of my dad's and manager of the South Broadway Car-O-Mat. Squirrels in the park watched me pass and birds hopped and chirped on the wet lawn. The sky was blue, the breeze cool, and the elm trees already yellowing in the September sun. By seven-ten, I was face-to-face with Jesse in the noisy Car-O-Mat.

"Your dad told me you just got out of jail after blowing up a car and being arrested in California for carrying a pocket knife you couldn't open."

I sighed and shrugged. "It was a switchblade."

He had his John Wayne act down pat. "Hell, I don't care what kind of knife it was, Kid. Your dad bought me a beer and told me how impatient he's become with you. I invited him to send you over for a chat.

I looked past Jesse through the steamy Car-O-Mat windows. The morning was brilliant and promised to warm up. "My dad told me you need willing workers over here," I said.

"Yes, and I told your dad that my willing workers are all clocked in by seven each morning."

"Sounds okay."

"He said he'll make sure you don't go on reading poetry in your room all night, sleeping till noon, and running off to California in old cars."

I smirked bitterly. "He sure knows how to portray a person in the best possible light."

"Look, Kid, I'm short-handed and a little short on patience right now, but I'll tell you like I told him. I will hire you at one seventy five an hour, but I will fire you the first time you give me any trouble on the job." He looked at his watch and stared peevishly toward a wall inside another room. "There are some aprons on that wall."

"I'd like to start tomorrow."

"Understood, Son. But I need you today and if he hadn't told me I could count on you, I'd have put an ad in the paper. He bought me another beer and said if you didn't show up by today and take the job, he'd pay somebody else's overtime and cough up the money for the newspaper ad himself."

"Yeah, well, the only problem is, he didn't know about my plans for today."

When I didn't return the steadiness of his gaze, Jesse put his hands on his hips, and repositioned himself so his squat body nearly blocked out my view of the exit end of the tunnel. "Son, tomorrow the job will have been filled and your dad will owe me money."

"How about after lunch?"

"It's getting late and I've got a line of cars over there. How about hiking out of here or clocking in and grabbing yourself an apron?"

"I'll need five minutes for a phone call."

"Make the call *before* you punch in," he said, "and be here tomorrow in time to go to work by seven. Make it snappy. It's getting busy now and I need somebody out front." Jesse tossed me a pair of rags, and after indicating where I might stow a sack lunch, which I hadn't brought, pointed to a pay phone near the time clock.

"Do workers get breaks, morning and afternoon and stuff?"

"You want to know about breaks already?"

"No, it's not that. I've got to cancel my lunch, but it's still too early to call."

"Breaks are at ten and two," he said. "Ten minutes each. Now clock in, grab an apron, and follow me."

The Car-O-Mat was a damp, glass-covered tunnel, crisscrossed and counter-crisscrossed with dripping, hissing pipes. Huge growling brushes were hydraulically lowered by steel armatures. Cars were towed beneath them by a length of bumper chain attached to a larger chain that clanked and pulled them through successions of soap, water, and rinse stations.

Small groups of mostly black men ducked in and out of open car doors, going over and through each vehicle with vacuum hoses, squeegees, mops, and rags. On a catwalk nearby, customers sat in a reading area, smoking and thumbing through magazines and newspapers. Jesse led me past all this toward the exit.

When my new partner, Frank, ignored my proffered handshake, I looked into his dim eyes, at the clammy whiteness of his skin, and wondered if working at the Car-O-Mat might be even worse than I imagined. Sullen, without being detectably angry or calculating, Frank was in his thirties and very much on the job, without being at all interested in it. There was a myth, a story somewhere. It was the job of a surly guard to make sure that no shifty young dreamer of a better world somewhere ever escaped the grind and growl of Bert Barlow's "real" world.

Frank and I were stationed on opposite sides of a heavy chain that towed cars through the wet noisy tunnel. Just beyond us on the interior side was a howling, whizzing steel arch that blew filmy waters off cars as they creaked and dripped toward us.

As each vehicle emerged from the arch, a pair of young Mexican-American women, their jaws stuffed with chewing gum, let themselves into front and back seats with an assortment of chamois and rags. Lips glistening with lipstick refreshed on frequent forays to the bathroom, they sneered at me and snapped their gum, slapping their rags against wet window interiors with furious shows of contempt.

"Gringo boy can't do better than this? We better do what we can to keep him from becoming assistant manager."

Once the girls were settled in the car, Frank stepped on and unhooked the small chain connected to the car's front bumper. After lobbing it over a pulley that transported the tow chain back toward the entrance for reuse, he made an about-face, turned, and walked for the parking lot to await the car's arrival there.

As he started down the sloped driveway, I opened the driver's door, gave the car a hefty push, and hopped in to steer it sans motor into an empty space in the lot. After applying the emergency brake, I got out and, leaving the girls to complete their interior work, began wiping the exterior, starting with the driver's half of the windshield and working toward the rear bumper. By the time I was finished, Frank had already completed his half of the car and was already back in the tunnel with time to yawn or stretch before the next vehicle emerged from the blower, and another duo of *Chicanas* piled in. I jogged back to my station at the hideously hot wheezing gate. Frank seemed pleased by my miserable expression.

The noisy tunnel didn't lend itself to conversation. But there were brief opportunities in the lot, and Frank began torment me with job-related information intended to add to my suffering. He explained that while I probably wouldn't last on the job and would eventually get fired and sink a few notches lower in the overall scheme of things, at least I didn't have to worry about losing my job to a "colored" man. Only a white male could replace me, he explained, because Car-O-Mat customers didn't want blacks or Mexicans touching their steering wheels, even if only to glide them into the lot. Frank let me know that he approved of this policy and did not like or trust any member of another race. Then, when I couldn't keep from shrugging and raising my eyebrows, he confided that he didn't like me, either.

In the days to come I decided that my presence contributed to Frank's pleasure by providing him with opportunities to remind me of how squarely in the middle of nowhere I had landed. He was at pains to point out, for example, that the men working deeper in the tunnel hated me because, with my blond hair and pale skin, I had landed the second best job at the Car-O-Mat. What made it second best was the fact that at least I could leave the dim tunnel to finish wiping down cars in the sunny parking lot. In their rubberized suits and boots, the black men deeper inside were always damp and left the cave only at closing time.

Although I was careful to avoid giving these men offense and struggled to devise some way of letting them know I understood and appreciated their feelings, or so I imagined, they returned my friendly glances with aggressive contempt. I felt like an outcast. I was disliked by Frank, by the black men in the tunnel, and by a sneering sorority of Mexican girls with whom I was spending the better part of my life. On top of that, at moments, I could feel the hot fetid breath of the draft board on my neck.

Frank had a mosquito's instinct for my helplessness and proved to be right in all the things he said about the Car-O-Mat. His was the best job because he didn't have to push cars or climb in or out of them, and he had little or no contact with furious *Chicanas*, who sneered and snapped their chewing gum at me whenever I looked at them.

I repaid their scorn. By steering the cars in which they were my passengers into distant parking spaces I could give them longer walks back to their stations. If I was a "stupid *paddy*," as more than one sniffed at me between gum snaps, I was a petty *paddy* as well, coolly adding a few hundred steps to their days of car slavery. I became cold and calculating, ensuring that the most offensive girls got the longest hikes back to the tunnel and worked a little harder than those whose behavior was marginally preferable. That this was unhealthy and unwise and passive-aggressive behavior was clear to me from the self-help psychology books I'd taken to reading at night before falling asleep.

One desperately boring morning, when I noticed four or five of the girls staring at me, I gave in to the temptation to mimic one of my tormentors. Without speaking to any of them, I worked my jaws, imitating the way she popped her gum. When this drew hard, but grudging smiles of recognition, I shrugged and curled my lips in an effort to replicate her standard sneer and was rewarded by a chorus of laughter.

After that, careful not to single any one girl out, I develop a mimic of each girl. By the end of the afternoon, they were laughing and no longer trying to hide their enjoyment.

When things got dreary late the next morning, they goaded me into another comic routine. By afternoon I was conferring shorter walks and they were even undertaking portions of my tasks in order to provide me with more time and inspiration for clowning.

Smiles inside the dripping cavern of the Car-O-Mat could not be allowed to go unpunished. Frank complained to Jesse that I was encouraging the girls to do sloppy work. When Jesse called us all together and spoke sharply to me and rebuked them, I knew it was only a matter of time before the girls devised some means of reprisal. For my part, I developed an imitation of Frank, which the girls couldn't get enough of.

My favorite, Marisol, whispered to me that they were getting back at Frank by sneaking into the lunchroom on bathroom breaks and dropping wads of chewing gum in his thermos of milk and squeezing his cheese and lunchmeat sandwiches into little balls of doughy mayonnaise. Unfortunately, within two or three days, Marisol was caught in the act and quickly fired.

She was replaced by Dolores, a slightly older former employee who seemed to intimidate the other girls and share some secret with Frank. A lean young woman a couple of years older than me, Dolores had hard dark sockets around her eyes and a chilly glance that made me wonder what it would be like to make her smile or touch her firm little breasts. Though the remaining girls and I continued to goof whenever we had a moment, they were plainly scared of Dolores, and she spoke sharply to those she suspected of encouraging my antics.

One by one, my favorites began to disappear.

The replacement girls were her relatives or friends of relatives. One or two of these newcomers sometimes ate lunch with the black men who worked deep in the tunnel. The goofing stopped and I went to work each morning with a sense of dread.

The men deeper in the tunnel rushed around in damp aprons, got wet, tripped over hoses, burned themselves on dryers, scratched themselves with brushes, and all day long listened to the chink, chink, chink of the ceaseless chain that would one day tow us all to a still hotter, more wretched hell than even the Car-O-Mat. Even so, it seemed to me that since we were serving time in a kind of work hell, we should share a special sympathy. I couldn't comprehend why the men didn't seem to understand that their anger was not really with me but with the racism on which my job depended. From time to time, I dreamed of organizing a strike for higher wages and maybe negotiating a policy of rotating jobs. I wanted the men to know they could count on my support if they ever decided to stage a protest. The problem was how to tell them that; they seemed to growl and spit in my direction whenever I got close enough to speak.

One morning Dolores walked by and turned around. "You better watch out now, *paddy*, because you're finally gonna get killed for the way you act."

"What do you mean?"

"Just what I said. You think you're so cool, reading at lunch time, throwing your lunch down on top of everybody else's."

A few minutes later, just as I was about to push a green Pontiac into the parking lot, Jesse came up beside me. "What's this I hear about you and Isaac?"

"Who's Isaac?"

"The guy with the scar on his cheek who works with the vacuum. Did you call him a name or something?"

"No," I said. "Even if I were a racist, I'm not a stupid fool. I don't know Isaac from Joe. They don't talk to me, so I don't talk to them."

Jesse went off to conduct his own investigation. A few minutes later, he ambled into the parking lot and motioned for me to follow. "Isaac's mad and talking about getting you without being willing to say why. You better take a lunch over across the street today."

"I brought my lunch," I said, "and it's not twelve yet."

"Here's five bucks. I'll pay for your lunch across the street. Just bring me the receipt. I've got to get to the bottom of this without you underfoot."

I shrugged and threw up my hands. On the far side of a shiny station wagon, Frank looked up from wiping a hubcap and grinned broadly.

When I came back from lunch, Jesse waved off the receipt and handed me my paycheck. "I'm going to have to let you go," he said.

Excited by the prospect of liberty, I was also furious at having been betrayed. "I didn't do anything."

"Isaac and Oliver say you keep smashing their lunches with your own."

"That's bullshit. I only bring a sandwich and bag of potato chips. What kind of lunch is that going to smash?"

Jesse shrugged.

I told Jesse that Dolores and Frank had somehow manufactured the hostility and proposed that we go back into the tunnel so I could speak with Isaac and tell him that I would never do such a thing.

"Won't make any difference," Jesse said. "Besides, you've been making dirty remarks to the girls, too."

I thought briefly of Dolores and her thin, tight sweaters. "No way," I said.

"That's how it is," Jesse said. "I've got to keep the peace around here with people who will work without clowning. Speaking for myself, I recommend the army. A little training in how to follow an order would do you a world of good."

The last I saw of the Car-O-Mat, Dolores and three of her window-wiping allies stood together in the parking lot, smirking at me over four upright middle fingers.

By then, I had accepted Frank's betrayal as somehow in the order of things. I looked at the girls and felt an immense relief. To my surprise, I positioned my hands, palms-down, over the top of my head. Then I lifted my own middle fingers as if they were horns, shook my head, and stamped. I considered, momentarily, how good it would feel to turn and wheel toward them. Then I trotted away, going only a few steps before lowering my hands. For some reason, I turned and laughed, brought both my hands to my lips, bowed, and blew them all a kiss. Even as I did, I entertained a half-formed thought about how easy it was to forgive, if not love, those you could walk away from.

I was thinking dangerously here, but didn't know it yet.

My dad's showy new Chrysler was parked in the driveway when I arrived home. Rather than going directly inside with the news that I'd been fired, I took refuge in the front seat of his car. In a brown bag under the seat, I found a bottle containing half a bottle of cheap port. Sips from the bright green bottle powered my dad with the ability to talk his way through the resistances of the working classes of western Colorado. Perhaps a few gulps of his particular elixir could help me deal with him. Surprised by the syrupy heat and the rush of well being, I sat comparing my life with his.

The age of giant-finned cars had peaked, replaced by a golden age of encyclopedias. Though he rarely read anything, to hear Bert and his fellow book salesmen talk, encyclopedias were knowledge tonics, Sputnik neutralizers, miracle medicines, and sources of American national greatness.

Rummaging through his glove compartment, I came on the names of sales prospects, "mooches," he called them, scribbled on little white index cards and wrapped with rubber bands. Underneath the cards I found his .25- caliber automatic, the one he told my mom he kept for rowdy dogs who ran at him for trespassing on their owners.

His hair-trigger temper and willingness to speak first and think later worried my mom and sometimes scared his cronies. I thought of the weapon as something he'd acquired to flourish in a confrontation with a local redneck outside a small town bar; there was just no way he'd ever need a gun to deal with dogs.

I'd been riding in the car with him last spring when he'd fired the pistol into the head of a hapless mule deer, a doe who had gone down under the big Chrysler outside on the highway leading into Steamboat Springs. It had surprised me that he didn't seem to blame the deer's stupidity for the damage to the front fender. The next day he'd gotten on the phone and started raging to someone at the highway department about deplorable road conditions. By now, the fender had been repaired, but the newly applied paint, nearly but imperfectly matched to the rest of the car, had turned into yet another heated dispute. Bert took his losses hard and did all he could to ensure that his opponents did, too.

Since there were tax advantages to family vacations that could also be combined with sales trips, I had seen him in action. Among his talents was a knack for dealing with feisty dogs.

His headlight beams on high, equipped with the best tires money could buy, he drove hard and long. His way of life was a succession of sales pitches between intervals of drinking and driving. When it served him, which was fairly often, he could quote a handful of Bible passages to the devout miners and working classes of western Colorado. And he had a nose for the sort of town gossip that might dress up his sales pitches. Bert would jot down the names of school board members and judges on matchbook covers, and shamelessly exaggerate small but locally significant acquaintances into significant friendships.

Gaining the respect of his mooches meant behaving as if the most violent and unexpected weather was never an obstacle to mobility. It meant an instinct for when to mount snow tires and bragging about how little you'd paid for them. It meant evincing a respect for the American flag, the Coors family, and a reverence for snowplow drivers. But perhaps, more than anything else, getting along with mooches meant proving you could deal with their dogs. No way did he need a handgun to handle dogs.

For mooches in his sales territory, one dog was not enough. Three was a minimum and four or five just about right. The Spikes and Aces tended to be the biters and fighters. The ones named Merle or Pearl were likely to be high-strung and prone to barking at every shadow. The Dukes and Maybelles knew everybody for miles around and varied their barks accordingly; in the clarion canine voices of their best dogs, mooches could read a friend of the family, garden-variety stranger, Democrat, or the no-damned-business-being-around-at-all trespasser.

Bert Barlow had the benevolent stranger's approach down pat, knowing instinctively where to stand in relation to a barking pack, modulating his voice and setting off his own deliberately hale racket, selling the dogs on the idea that they were holding at bay a stranger they needn't attack. I'd watched all this from the cars in which I waited for him. While the dogs howled, got tangled up in their ropes, or sought improved defensive positions, my dad occupied and stood his ground and hollered out a bottomless friendliness toward any and all critters within earshot. He began by persuading the animals that there was absolutely nothing sneaky or mean about him. I can still see him standing in muddy yards, making broad gestures with his arms to the mooches slowly emerging from their houses and trailers. There was something operatic about the way he stood, descanting his respect for private property, his understanding that all good country dogs were trained and loved for their willingness to bark and yelp and snarl. Yes. Yes, indeed, a certain canine clamor was welcomed by Bert Barlow, God-fearing American cold warrior, hale but loving dog master, fan of all devoted rural womanly homemakers. At least that's the way things started out.

Once the dogs had been pacified and he'd been invited inside, Bert ignored all impediments and invitations to make himself at home in the living room and made a beeline for the kitchen in search of coffee. As I'd heard him explain to trainee salesmen, a warmed-up cup of mediocre coffee followed by a claim that it was the best coffee he'd ever tasted was an important gain in the elaborate transaction to follow. In fact, he held that the worse the coffee, the more certain it was that the woman who'd brewed it would succumb to his praise and eventually conspire with him to obtain her husband's signature on the dotted line and buy an encyclopedia set on one of three offered time payment plans.

On good days, when he left with a check payable to the American Encyclopedia Company, my father knew something of what heaven must be about. Even more satisfying, though, were other, off-the-record ways of selling books. Credit wasn't always what it might be, so, bucking his advisers, Bert Barlow was known to accept post-dated checks, giant jars of honey, IOUs, engagement rings, family heirlooms, even bills of sale for horses. Many items could, at need, be developed into down payments. He knew his mooches for people who paid their debts and when he was on a roll, he'd pull off three-and-four-way trades. One family told him they couldn't take on the expense of making payments on a set of encyclopedia because their young son wanted a horse. Bert took a Shetland pony in lieu of a down payment from one family and gave it to the boy who wanted a horse when his family signed up to buy a set of books. One morning just before graduating from high school, I'd walked out of the house and seen four new tractor tires tied to the Chrysler's roof.

For all of this, between my dad and lasting prosperity was the compatible sales partner he never quite managed to find.

Flushed with a few glugs of his port, I walked into the house, relaxed after a day spent drying cars and, to my surprise, felt almost glad to see him at the kitchen table.

"I want you to give notice at the carwash," he said, looking up at me over a glass of beer and a plate of ham, cabbage, and potatoes.

I'm sure I beamed with delight. Maybe I wouldn't have to confess to being fired. He wasn't the only one who could withhold information and use it to his own advantage. Quickly, though, my pleasure turned to anxiety.

"Why?"

"You don't want to spend your life earning minimum wage, do you?"

"No. I guess not."

"You've had courses in drama and speech," he said, chewing a mouthful of ham. "In fact, if I remember, they were among the few passably good grades you got. All those drama awards ought to be good for something. You've got an appointment with Mitch on Monday morning."

"Who's Mitch?"

"Don't worry about it. He's the sales manager of the *Encyclopedia Genericus*."

"The *Encyclopedia Genericus*?"

"Once he's got you trained and you've made a sale or two for him, I'll bring you over to the *American Encyclopedia*. There's lots of money to be made selling books now. In fact, in a little while, you'll probably be able to buy a car and rent your own apartment." He gulped beer and looked at me with an absence of irritation that seemed to surprise us both.

Monday morning I donned a sports coat and tie and took a bus to a rented studio apartment almost entirely given over to ashtrays, mismatched coffee cups, and folding chairs.

Mitch was about thirty-five and wore a modified crew cut rigidly shaped by a floral waxy dressing that imparted a sheen to his forehead and the tops of his ears. He favored plaid sports jackets, tasseled loafers, tight, knee-length hose, and big finger rings inset with nuggets of colored glass. Smiling frequently, he spoke from the right side of his mouth, exuding, I thought, a don't-mess-with-me-I'm-from-Vegas insouciance. After handing me a badly typed copy of a sales pitch, he introduced me to my training partner, Derby.

Derby and I were to take turns reading the script back and forth, committing our sales pitch to memory for use in the field. Eager, Derby snacked on breath fresheners and kept a small bottle of drugstore aftershave in the inner pocket of his sports coat. Pink-necked, partial to mustard-colored slacks, and given to biting his fingernails to pink stubs, Derby rocked back and forth on a precarious folding chair and recited what he could remember of the sales spiel in little outbursts of prepositional phrases and dependent clauses. When it came time for him to listen to me, he slouched sideways, jingled his car keys, and tapped his foot.

Addressed to Mr. Joe Jones, the sales pitch began with the assertion that just about everyone at the *Encyclopedia Genericus* had already heard of the singularly remarkable Jones family. On discovering what an admirable and exemplary clan they were and how smart their children were, the company had hoped to give them the books and pay each family member a significant amount of cash for endorsing the encyclopedia. But alas, *EG's* legal advisers had only the week before delivered the disappointing news that it wouldn't be possible to make cash payments to the Joneses, owing, the script continued, to some arcane governmental laws regulating payments and product endorsements by households. Unable to award cash, *EG* had nonetheless decided to give the Joneses a free set of the *Encyclopedia Genericus*. For the endorsement to be valuable, of course, family members would have to demonstrate a reasonable willingness to occasionally fly first class to faraway places, stay at the best hotels at EG's expense, hobnob with television producers, and generally be praised for their knowledge of the modern world. Every hundred words or so, the script tossed off the not-so-subtle suggestion that *EG* might eventually employ one or more Joneses to participate in a future television advertising campaign. They could be and would be well remunerated for any such participation, of course—whether or not the Jones family went on to become famous. It went without saying, and yet not quite, that the Joneses would need to be highly informed about "today's changing world." Happily, this could be made easier thanks to an annual *EG* yearbook that, unfortunately, *EG* was prevented by the government from giving away. In fact, to really stay on top of things, the Joneses would want to subscribe to up-to-the-minute special bulletins published and, for a nominal fee, mailed to "television-commercial-eligible" families such as the Joneses each month. The books were free, a true gift from EG. The yearbooks and bulletins were going to cost them the equivalent of forty bucks a month.

Mitch assured me that flattery and slight exaggerations were necessary to sell books, that families would never see through the spiel, and that, in any case, it was good for patriotic Americans to fund scientific research by paying a little more than retail for a set of encyclopedias. When I said that triple the retail value of the books over five years didn't seem like a little to me, Mitch smiled and said he understood. It was a long way from high school to the business world, but we all had a role to play in winning the Cold War. Aggressive sales, through which we would be stimulating the economy, were a good way of serving our country. In fact, everybody was in sales, if you looked closely enough, Mitch said.

The *Encyclopedia Genericus* was in the business of pressing sales prospects for the kinds of decisions that could only be made by a *Mr. Jones. Mrs.* Jones, referred to in the script as "the little lady of the house," was regularly and methodically flattered on the appearance of "her" home, even as she was encouraged to remain in her rightfully silent wifely role. In the hope of persuading Mr. Jones to make the best decision for his children, and then stick by it, the script sprinkled little pinches of invidious itching powder on predictable family tensions, reminding Mr. Jones that the whole world knew who *ought* to have the power to make decisions in the household, even if Mrs. Jones, in her enthusiasm to be a supportive wife, occasionally forgot. Buried deep in the sales pitch was the implication that even suckers duped into paying out more than double retail could always manage to hang on to a beleaguered manhood by refusing to heed any second thoughts or wifely entreaties to renege on signed contracts. It seemed to be the duty of the

158

American male to occasionally pay too much for some product in order to avoid a loss of manliness. Meanwhile, it would be the obligation of sophisticated salesmen, like me and Derby, to explain the future to folks who were working too hard to see it coming.

Roughly, the future amounted to this: provided America successfully pacified Vietnam, got Castro the hell out of Cuba, survived the threat of nuclear war, and contained communism, these things called computers and space travel would work miracles in the American way of life. Meantime, apparently until some of these developments began to unfold in earnest, it was essential that every publisher and working adult run around in little science-worshipping circles, scattering the rich birdseed of knowledge before "our precious young people."

Derby professed a patriotic eagerness to tell a prospect whatever proved necessary, as well as a willingness to let me know when I was straying from the straight and narrow. Derby didn't know about my dad's plan to persuade me to defect, and he, too, saw that I could be potentially useful. He was willing to befriend me, he said, because, unlike the other encyclopedia salesmen he'd met so far, I wasn't an alcoholic.

After a week, during which time I tormented Derby by encouraging him to deliver his sales pitch in ways that would keep me amused, Mitch congratulated Derby on his progress, told him he'd see him Monday morning, and invited me into the small room serving as his office.

"Timbo, my young friend," Mitch began, "let's you and me make a little plan."

I waited for him to stop dinging his coffee cup with his heavy rings. "Sounds good."

"Pardner, let me ask you something? What kind of car are you drivin' these days?"

I shuddered from embarrassment. "I don't have a car yet. My mom lets me drive her Ford sometimes."

"You know what kind of car I'm driving?

"I guess I never thought about it."

"A year-old Caddy."

I hated feigning an interest I didn't feel.

Mitch sighed and assumed an expression of uncharacteristic modesty. "But only a Fleetwood."

"Well, that's all right."

"How much do you suppose my payments are, Pardner?"

"A couple hundred a month, maybe."

Mitch smiled and shook his head. "Zero. Zilch."

"You paid cash?"

"Didn't pay a red cent, Pardner! I won it in a sales contest!"

I looked down at my hands in search of a suitably enthusiastic response.

"Timmy, my guess is that since you're a young man, you probably don't want to drive a Caddy, do you?"

Being called Timmy made me cringe. "I guess not. Not if I had my choice, anyway."

With a big hand, Mitch waved off my adolescent diffidence. "You got a world of choice, Pardner. You're a little bit of a smart aleck, but I was too at your age. And you're a bright cookie." Mitch chuckled to himself. "You get a kick out of teasing Derby, getting him in a sweat, don't you?"

"I get a little bored sometimes."

"Sure. He's a little on the dull side and it's boring sitting around here. I know that. But once you get out there in the field, Timmy, if you concentrate, you're going to make some money, make money for both of us. And today I decided I'm going to help you out."

"I appreciate it."

Mitch held both hands up, palms out, in a traffic cop's gesture. "Don't get carried away now. All I'm talking about here is enlightened self-interest. The way I see it, it's in your interest to help Derby, because you may be his boss some day, and it's in my interest to help you, Timbo, because you're going to be a feather in my cap by helping me win this winter's sales contest. But I tell you what, when I *do* win, I'll give the Fleetwood to the old lady, and plop my own glad ass down in a new El Dorado convertible."

Mitch paused. Apparently, he wanted me to think that he was in the process of clearing his mind of an unmanly indecisiveness. "Now that it comes down to it, I'm not even going to wait for the sales contest. I just decided now that on the day you turn in your third order, about two weeks from now, I'd say, I'm going to give you these." Mitch pulled a white rabbit's foot attached to a set of keys from an inside jacket pocket. "You know what these are, Pardner?"

"Car keys?"

"Attaboy, Timbo. These are the extra keys to my wife's blue '60 Chevy Impala convertible. And, on the day I hand them over to you, I'll also drive you over to pick up both the car and the title. You sell three sets of books before the fifteenth of next month, Hepcat, and you'll have your sales commissions in the bank and a little something more." He paused, waiting for me again. "You know what?"

I was far out ahead of him, sitting next to Lynn or Sylvia or some other babe in what had been his wife's convertible under the Laurel trees in Balboa Park in San Diego. "What?"

"You'll have that Chevy. It's got a perfect top and a big ol'V-8 that will make your girlfriends' pussies drip." Mitch gave me a big wink and chimed on his coffee cup with his rings again. "So, what do you think, Pardner? You going to come in Wednesday morning with your script memorized or what?"

I felt hot and red and embarrassed, and not much inclined to speak. I didn't want a girlfriend whose pussy dripped, especially if it was on account of a car. Suddenly, I was in a hurry to put a lot of distance between myself and Mitch and my voice sounded like Wally's on the television show, *Leave it to Beaver*. "Gee, that sounds great, Mitch."

"Come to think of it, I've got a third set," He lobbed me the keys. "Why don't you carry these around with you while you finish memorizing your pitch. The rabbit's foot on the key chain will bring you luck. Next week, I will personally guarantee you your first sale. I'll take you out and show you how to make those sons of bitches sign. Then, once we're outside, I'll hand you your first deal."

I wanted the Chevy so I risked a little effort, concentrating on my sincerity. A salesman was supposed to show enthusiasm. "A '60 Chevy Impala convertible?"

"Turquoise blue. Put that top down, Daddy-o, take the girls to up to Red Rocks for a look at the stars, and you'll have to put a padlock your zipper." He looked at his big, gold-banded watch. In fact, he held it up to the light in hope that one of several diamonds or imitation diamonds might glitter in the evening light coming through the window behind him. "Hell, I'm running a little late. Take your keys and go on home now, Timbo. Derby's a little slow, so I'm going to give him to somebody else to work with. As far as you're concerned, I want that script memorized when you come back here on Wednesday. Think you can handle it?"

"Yeah. I know I can."

"Okay, Pardner, you're on. But I want that pitch to be as smooth as Tennessee sipping whiskey. When it is, I'm going to introduce you to Alexander Graham Bell's bonanza machine. Know what I'm talking about?"

"The telephone."

"Attaboy! Alex Bell is going to look after both of us. We're gonna make a few calls, get us some appointments, talk to some mooches, and make truckloads of money." Mitch grinned in anticipation. "Call me as soon as that pitch is down pat, now."

I finished memorizing the sales pitch on the bus home, just before I found a photograph. The picture was face down in the bus stairwell, smudged by a footprint. Turning it over as the bus pulled away, I saw a tattered color snapshot of a boyish soldier in a marine dress uniform. His big arms were draped around the shoulders of diminutive but beaming parents. My stomach rolled, my daydream of driving Mitch's Chevy Impala convertible to California dissolved. The draft card in my billfold in my pocket acquired an ominous weight. The photo reminded me of the only mail I'd received in the last few days: a summons from the draft board.

Arriving downtown earlier than necessary, I trudged up the long marble steps of the Federal Building, passed under Corinthian columns and through polished doors. Inside, shorn army privates and prematurely balding corporals carried folders and sheets of paper from room to room. Floors were tiled with brown squares, mottled with flecks of yellow and red, frosted over with a residue of military-issue detergent, then left to dry each evening after a hurried mopping. Heavy walnut doors were locked or held open with rubber wedges. Doorknobs shone with the oils of a thousand hands. In the rooms, big windows were painted shut, leaving grimy, whizzing floor fans to recirculate stale air. The walls looked to have been painted with a creamy dried pea soup. Badly aligned recruiting posters were everywhere, applied in haste and without apparent plan.

Ignored by the busy soldiers, I climbed a flight of stairs and, on an upper floor, found a bench. Lighting a cigarette, I studied a huge mural.

Visible through years of smoke and neglect, rows of lean and faded doughboys carried a forest of bayoneted rifles as long as street lamps. In boots shaped like pipes, they goose-stepped under draperies of American flags through a greenish France, an Oz of triangulated meadows lined with lollipop-shaped trees. With their rectangular jaws, regulation noses, thin, machine-tooled lips, and eyebrows shaped like hyphens, one soldier looked like every other. With their steely-dead faces, the soldiers marched off to kill the *Boche* in the War to End All Wars.

I thought of a photo in my grandpa's album of a young Lester Barlow standing somewhere in Chicago in a suit and tie under clumps of bunting. With a whisky bottle in one hand and a cigarette in the other, Lester grinned proudly between two uniformed men about his own age. The first time we came across it, Lester told me in a choking voice that neither man had ever returned from France. Yet something in his recounting made me think he wished he'd done his part, too, without

162

necessarily meeting the same brutal end. I don't know that this was true, but I do know that whatever Lester thought or did, or however much he drank that afternoon before saying goodbye to his friends, he had gone on to live a thoroughly civilian life. His only son Bert was born on the date the American draft went into effect in 1917. Lester had been deferred.

I'd read *All Quiet on the Western Front* and looked at photographs of Verdun and the Somme. What I remembered was mud, barbed wire, dirt, twisted bodies, and nothing of the heroic adventure Lester may have thought he'd missed. The muralist's robots marched in step toward the front line. Their formations were so taut, the bayonets so thick beneath the helmets, I thought of hydraulic Car-O-Mat brushes lowered to scour the land.

Under a coffee table in our front room were stacks of news magazines, full of regularly published somber black-bordered headshots of high school boys culled from high-school yearbooks. The school photographers had caught them tilting their heads just right, arranging their jaws just so, trying to look good for all the girls who would now never open their legs to them; these were the casualties of Vietnam. When magazines could publish them, of course, they preferred snapshots taken at home, like the one I'd found on the bus. I had thumbed through their pages and seen the freshly shorn faces leaning awkwardly away from tinsel-drenched Christmas trees so as not to obstruct the view of the family's most treasured ornaments. There were likenesses of soldiers bending their girlfriends too far backwards, kissing them in front of snow-frosted alpine backdrops. Some wore swimming trunks. Others posed alongside freshly polished Pontiacs and Chevies. Still others sat on faded couches in front of birthday cakes, flashbulbs glowing red in the backs of their eyes. Rowdy among their buddies, still other casualties-to-be hoisted gleaming beer cans, sporting shiny dog tags on bare chests, sunning themselves on the beaches of the world, floppy straw hats pulled down toward their sunglasses, the better to conceal pimpled foreheads.

Having smoked away my time and brooded myself into what I knew to be a transitory fury, with my knees a little wobbly, I walked down the steps to join the waiting would-be inductees.

A slightly older man with a mustache bragged to a small cluster of young men about the career opportunities provided by the army. Some seemed excited by the simple prospect of leaving home for the first time. I scanned the room in search of doubt, ambivalence. Taking a deep breath, I turned to a muscular kid in a purple shirt. "You looking forward to going in the army?"

"Fuckin' A, man! What about you?"

I shrugged and searched for somebody less gung-ho. "Not really, no."

Two black men in pants and sweaters were talking in a corner. When the smaller shook his head sorrowfully and told the taller man he didn't want to join, I took a couple of steps and caught the eye of the talker. "Just don't go," I suggested.

"Whatchu mean?"

"They can't make you go. Not if you don't want to."

"Man, what kind of bullshit you talkin' about?"

"Think about it," I ventured, "are they going to want to carry you screaming on the battlefield? Why should you fight the Vietnamese ten thousand miles away when you couldn't register to vote in Selma, Alabama?"

His taller friend sneered. "What you know about Selma, Alabama? And who asked your sorry ass, anyway?"

The shorter one grinned, pushed his friend playfully, and turned to me. "They ain't going to take you anyway, Honky, because you so ugly you'd scare your platoon."

The laughter brought me more attention than I wanted. A squat Middle Eastern-looking kid in a sweatshirt took a step my direction. "Did you come down here to preach communist propaganda or something?"

"Communism has nothing to do with the war in Vietnam," I said, trying to sound reasonable. "The majority of the Vietnamese are only interested in getting outsiders to leave their country. They're interested in freedom, self-determination, same as you might be if America had been ruled for five hundred years by Canadians and Australians."

Four men in uniforms put an end to my political science seminar by marching into the room and slamming the door. One of the soldiers rattled a sheaf of papers. "Listen up," he shouted, "After I read your name, step out into the hall, and line your asses up behind the arrow of the designated color. Abatta, Joseph, blue arrow. . . "

A few minutes later, I was following a trail of yellow plastic tape into a room crowded with tiny schoolroom desks. There, lifting a thick forearm in the air, a corporal with a hairy throat and booming voice held a pencil stub high above his head.

"This is a PENCIL. Each of you has a PENCIL on his desk. You will leave the PENCIL right where it is. When I tell you, BUT NOT BEFORE I TELL YOU, you will reach for this PENCIL, taking the PENCIL in either your right or left hand. You will not make use of any other pen or PENCIL, but you will employ the PENCIL on your desk. There are several papers on your desk. They have numbers in their right hand corners. You will look down at those numbers NOW in the right hand corner of the paper. When I tell you to begin you will begin by filling out FORM NUMBER X-146A7-B. That is, B as in Boy! You will NOT fill out form number X-146A7-C as in CHARLIE or form number X-146A7-D as in DANIEL unless and until you have been instructed AT A LATER TIME to do so. When I give the word, you will look down at Form B on top of your desk. You will NOT look down at the form UNTIL I give the word. Keep your eyes on me. In the upper right hand corner of the white piece of paper, you will find a number. . . "

Each word was sung in a monotone at a rate of about one word per second. Short sentences were repeated twice. The word 'pencil' was used thirty-eight times. Finally, I unfolded my hands and reached for the yellow property of the U.S. Army. As directed, I made marks in tiny boxes. Two plus two equaled five. A carrot more nearly resembled a wagon than a turnip or golf tee. "A bird in the hand is worth two in the bush" meant that "crocodiles ate fish."

On Form C, I checked boxes indicating that I suffered from fallen arches, whooping cough, cancer, migraines, pneumonia, schizophrenia, polio, bunions, and several serious-sounding diseases I'd never heard of. I indicated that I suffered from glaucoma, had undergone surgery for a detached retina, been diagnosed as legally blind, and suffered from recurrent delusions of persecution and other hallucinations. I noted that I had attempted suicide three times and thought about trying again approximately five times a week. Flushed with satisfaction, I sat back and awaited further developments.

Forms completed and lining up out in the hall again, I deliberately misunderstood instructions and concocted several elaborate, confusing questions. Eventually, I followed the red arrows and entered a locker room where men were stripping to their underwear and tossing their clothes into empty lockers. Undressing quickly, I sat noting body hair, skin tone, odors. Fat faces and pale, skins like smoked leather, gaunt, blue-black necks, bowed legs, misshapen feet, maybe fifty smelly young men reeking of baby powder, athlete's foot medication, liniment, soured lunch, dead macaroni, sweat, and deodorant.

A sergeant with a spoon-shaped torso stormed in, slammed the door, and ordered us to go through yet another door and form a circle in an adjoining room. A pair of soldiers shouted that an investigation was underway to determine who the wise guy was who came up with the idea of running drinking fountain water into their urine cups. I stood up straight and looked down at my bare feet, hoping I would not be singled out as one of the instigators.

A chubby kid still wearing the glasses he'd been told to remove laughed out loud at the news of the prank, bringing himself the attention of the investigators. When the fat kid denied any involvement, the sergeant called attention to the musical clefts printed on the kid's boxer shorts. The guy standing next to me speculated that the kid had probably chosen those particular shorts that morning because he wanted everyone in the U.S. Army to know that he was a musician in a traveling circus who could fart out the melodies of "Mary Had a Little Lamb" and "Pop Goes the Weasel." Everybody laughed, until a mean-looking soldier entered the room and barked for an end to the hilarity.

When we had assembled in the big room and formed the requisite circle, the sergeant with the voice like a dog said, "All right, listen up, you walking assholes! You will now turn outward and lower your drawers. When you have done this, you will bend over and grab your ankles. You will not snicker when you bend over and grab your ankles, and you will be silent. I will be standing here to make sure you remain silent and in the bent-over position until all the inspections have been completed. Do any of you useless chicken droppings have anything to say?"

Eager to be a part of the new life to which they'd nearly been admitted, a few men were delighted to offer the sergeant a "No, Sir!" I turned my back, pulled down my underpants, and put my head between my knees for a unique view of the human race.

A pair of scowling soldiers entered from another door, marched to the center of the naked circle and made a show of stuffing their fingers into green rubber gloves. While one wielded a penlight, the other worried pre-inductee anuses with a gloved finger. When the soldier with the light moved on to the next stooping figure, his gloved partner swiped angrily at each bottom with a wad of cotton, after which, using his polished shoe like a hockey stick, he pushed the soiled puffs toward the center of the circle and moved again toward the light.

After my turn had come and gone, a small, dark-skinned private made his way into the circle of men and began using a heavy push broom to gather the wads in the center of the floor.

A door slammed and an olive-skinned, overweight soldier stood at attention. "Timothy Barlow!"

I pulled up my underpants, straightened up, and looked at him.

"Are you Timothy Barlow?"

"Yes."

"Get dressed immediately and follow me."

Corporal Martinez followed me into the room where I'd left my clothes.

"What's this about?"

Martinez retained his contemptuous expression. "You are to follow me to Room 214."

"I got that," I said, knees rickety. "But why?"

Martinez shrugged and said nothing.

In Room 214, a balding Sergeant Smith seemed to bite his lips. Fingers interlocked on top of his desk, his hands were swollen with muscles. Three or four pale patches just over his forehead might well have been his only soft spots. Resisting a powerful impulse to stand at attention, I told myself that as a civilian I retained certain rights I wouldn't enjoy as a soldier and slouched as an act of assertion.

Smith looked me over and spoke to Martinez. "What do we have here, Corporal? A man, a mouse, or a walking tumor?"

Worried about the prospects of having my ass kicked in some remote back room, I was filled with the sudden impulse to introduce myself as a middling athlete and former Boy Scout. I wanted to say that I was only eighteen, that I might be capable, under some circumstances, of bravery on the battlefield, that I wanted to be admired, that I hadn't been the first to think of running drinking fountain water in the urine cups, and that on the spot I'd just decided to become more cooperative.

"You a troublemaker, Barlow?"

"No. I'm a conscientious objector."

Smith licked his lips and smirked. "You've been misinformed. There's no such thing as a conscientious objector, my young sir." He looked at his nicotine-stained fingers. "There are, unfortunately, among us a few cowards, traitors, and would-be shirkers. Those who we can't persuade to overcome their weaknesses or otherwise beat some sense into, the United States government sometimes sends to prison. You don't look like one of these types, but you could be. My guess is that once we rid you of about half a foot of hair, and persuade you that there is such a thing as duty, we can ride your sorry ass into a certain respectability. You're not an arrogant, ungrateful coward are you, Barkley?"

At that moment, I doubted I ever had or ever would be able to distinguish bravery from cowardice, stupidity from intelligence, right from wrong. My voice sounded impossibly boyish. "I simply don't think it is right for the United States to take part in an ancient conflict thousands of miles from our shores. The French had no business in Vietnam, and neither do we. Millions of Vietnamese believe that they are fighting the United States simply to achieve independence and self-determination. I'm not looking for trouble, but I am looking for someone to admit that the United States ought to stand for self-determination, even when it means a government unsympathetic to American foreign policy."

"You were not escorted to Room 214 to teach me political science, Boy."

I noticed I was standing a little straighter. Putting my hands in my pockets seemed like a gesture of strength and I risked it. "What was I brought in here for?"

Corporal Martinez quivered with eagerness. "Sergeant, can the corporal offer a response to the question?"

"Go ahead, Martinez."

"Sir, Corporal Morris described him as a troublemaker and ordered me to bring him to you. But, Sir, I brought him in here not as a troublemaker, but as a sorry, yellow-bellied motherfucker, Sir."

Smith allowed his face to register pleasure. He leaned back in his dry wooden chair, making it squeak, and folded his meaty hands behind his ears. "Just what sort of trouble has he made, Corporal?"

"From what I understand, Sir, he started off by trying to give a Commie sermon against the war. Then he deliberately read the eye chart wrong, delaying the other men. He pretended to flunk his hearing test, and deliberately tried to confuse the men about where they had been instructed to go, Sir. For example, he advised members of the G Group to follow the red arrows instead of the green ones. He followed the blue arrows when he should have followed the green ones and tried to say he was colorblind. From what we understand, Sir, he's the ringleader of the group who encouraged several men to run tap water into their urine cups, Sir. He's given us all a long day, Sir, so Corporal Kemper thought it would be a good idea to bring him to you." Martinez looked at me and slowed his litany. "The corporal thought it would be good to alert you to the kind of disciplinary problems we might face if some of the men decided to kick his ass, Sir."

My paranoia surged at the prospect of being set on by a group of pre-inductee patriots. It also seemed to me that on the spot Smith might quietly sign a paper ensuring I would be drafted immediately, thereby providing his men with the punching bag they seemed to crave. I fought back a vision of myself getting pounded in a linen closet.

Smith smiled, enigmatically, thanked Martinez, dismissed him, and took to tapping on a small stack of papers with a long pencil. "You're intelligence test shows that you're of average intelligence," he said, "so you can't really expect the army to believe your health is as bad as you've described it, Barkley."

168

"My intelligence test shows I'm average?" I felt like a character in a story by Kafka. "You must have me mixed up with a guy named Barkley. My name is Barlow."

He studied my face for a long time. "What I'm going to do, Barlow, is take care of a couple of other problems right now. I'm going to leave you with a chance to revise your forms. You take this pencil, these forms, sit at that desk and go over them once again a little more carefully. When I come back, we'll look them over and finish our little talk."

When Smith left the room, a corporal who had apparently been standing just outside opened the door, looked both ways down the hall and made for a telephone on Smith's desk. Another soldier entered and started rummaging through a filing cabinet. After a minute, the second soldier found the folder he was searching for and looked from me to the soldier on the phone.

"Is this Water Dick?"

The soldier on the phone covered the receiver with one hand. "Water Dick?"

"You know, the Commie who pisses tap water?"

"I don't know," the soldier said, "and I don't care. Would you please get back out there in the hall and barge back in here only if you see Smith on his way back?"

The soldier with the file looked at me and said, "See you in hell, Water Dick."

I shot back the expected response. "Not if I see you first."

Changing nothing on my forms at first, I drew arrows and military stripes on my papers and listened to the corporal badger his girlfriend. When he'd made his point, he hung up, smirked broadly at the instrument of his deception, winked at me, and closed the door quietly as he left.

Sergeant Smith stormed into the room and tore at a filing cabinet drawer handle. He rummaged among the papers, closed the drawer, reopened it, found something not to his liking, and frowned at me as if he was surprised to find me still sitting there. He left the room without a word.

I got bored and started filling out the new medical report form, falsifying it anew. The phone rang and kept ringing. I went to Smith's desk, picked it up without speaking, and, replacing it, knocked several folders onto the floor. Picking up scattered sheets of paper, I noticed many had to do with me. Curious, but anxious lest I be caught reading property of the U.S. Army, I went to the door and peeked out. Relaxed voices spoke from nearby offices, but the hall itself was empty. With the sheaf of papers still in my hand, I took one step out, saw a bathroom, ducked in, and hurriedly occupied the rearmost stall. Instead of reading about myself, I began to tear paper into small squares and test the forcefulness of the industrial toilets.

When a man came in to whistle and piss, I stopped flushing and waited him out. A few minutes later, I stood beside the door and listened for footsteps or voices. The hall was empty and quiet. There were two closed doors between me and a flight of stairs. Hearing voices in the hallway behind me, I propelled myself to the bottom, opened a steel door, and found myself in a boiler room, dimly lit and filled with heavy machinery. The boiler room had another bathroom, so I went in to calm myself and occupy another stall.

Refusing to allow myself to speculate about the possible consequences of my actions, I sat for a time. Once I understood that I couldn't stay where I was for very long, I did the only thing I could think of, which was take a few breaths of stale air and start for the bathroom door in the hope of discovering a route to freedom. I was walking past a row of sinks when two men in gray uniforms pushed open the door and entered. They were arguing about what was wrong with a particular pulley they'd replaced the week before. When they failed to express either interest or surprise at seeing me, I grunted a greeting, went out and walked a long cement corridor past three women who were tending industrial washing machines. Coming on another flight of stairs, I climbed and emerged in a hallway in a part of the building I'd never seen. At the end of the hall were two glass doors. I hurried toward them. Two inattentive soldiers stood bargaining with each other not far from the glass doors. I suppressed the impulse to run but turned my face away from them in case they'd glimpsed me earlier. There was another mural on the wall, a World War II civilian scene set in a shipyard and heavily inspired by Diego Rivera. To keep my face away from the soldiers, I studied it as I walked toward them.

After the Japanese attacked Pearl Harbor in 1941, my mother's brother Karl persuaded my dad to enlist in the Marines. Unlike Karl, Bert passed the physical. He never talked about his experience, but I had snooped through family papers and discovered he'd been honorably discharged with pneumonia after two months. I didn't know more than that and didn't expect to ever find out more. But I did know that having recovered, my dad had been a welder in shipyards and later done all manner of assembly work.

At family dinners to which fellow salesmen were occasionally invited, I had overheard enough beery reminiscences to believe that deep down Bert Barlow felt that the best part of his life had been spent welding, bolting, and assembling materiel for the soldiers of World War II and, later, the Korean War. He was naturally dexterous and good with his hands. He claimed, and having watched him at various tasks I never doubted, that his co-workers despaired of ever matching the deftness with which he manipulated dangerous explosives, fire, nuts, bolts, and welding tools.

Though recounted only for woozy salesmen, Bert's fondest memories and best stories were set during intervals of abundant overtime in California and Colorado. Wherever he worked he was admired as "Jitterbug Bert" or "Mr. Jitterbug," he bragged, because nobody could move with such fluidity and accomplish so much with so little apparent effort. And, at least in the retelling, he had been more productive still after a few drinks. Fire, heat, industrial machinery, physical dexterity, molten steel, hot jazz music, and anger. Lightning oboe-trained fingers newly dedicated to perfect welds, flawless assemblies, and winning widespread plant admiration. A man with perfect pitch and welding-rod expertise singing arias on the toilet, hoisting blazing torches, sporting black goggles while touting overtime and assembly-line nimbleness amid Tommy Dorsey runs of fluidity and utility. All this, plus beer, was Bert at his happiest.

In my dad's stories, he cast himself in minor but supporting roles, a sympathetic witness or an initially disinterested participant in successions of workplace pranks, invariably undertaken to insure that the lazy, obnoxious, and "phony bastards" got their just desserts. Polacks who held themselves aloof or recited poetry on the job had their lunch pails welded to shop floors; Jews with excessively leftist sympathies had their tools sabotaged and were deliberately humiliated in front of foremen; anti-union Germans ate sauerbraten tinctured with various "industrial-strength" emetics. Mexicans described as idiot enough to sit down next to their lunch pails without removing their welding goggles ended up devouring the chorizo sausages their cohorts had buttered with packing grease; drunken blacks were allowed, even encouraged, to sleep in dangerous places where they were occasionally injured, though never severely. Then, once all the pretentious, dark-skinned, foreign-born shirkers, phonies, lazy pricks, and swelled heads had gotten the painful dose of the real world they deserved, everybody went back to watching Jitterbug Bert perform eye-popping assembly-line feats.

As I approached the edge of the mural, I became aware of a perceptible dimming of natural light. From the corner of one eye, I observed that the soldiers had moved toward the center of the hall. They hadn't exactly crossed a pair of rifles in front of the glass doors, but neither were they any longer engaged in a discussion that distracted them from me. Pretending to study the mural had gained me fifty feet. Thirty feet from the door and fresh afternoon air, I needed a new strategy. Bringing my hand up to scratch my head, I turned my face toward them, adopted a puzzled but relieved expression, and covered the next twenty feet quickly. One of the soldiers, who was black, was looking from me to whatever small objects were pinned over his shirt pocket. His swarthy companion had spread his feet out and folded his hands behind his buttocks in what I supposed was a regulation at-ease position. Above his shirt pocket was a nametag, "Vitali."

"Maybe you soldiers can help me. Do you know where the Real World Auto Insurance Corporation has its offices?"

Vitali squinted at me as if he was staring into a very bright light. "The which?"

"The Real World Auto Company. A guy down the block told me it was somewhere in this building."

"There ain't nothing like that in here." Vitali looked at his buddy. "Crawford, you ever hear of that? The Real World Auto Company or some shit?"

Crawford left off with his lapel ornaments. "You got an address?"

"Naw. I went off and left it at home." I moved slightly to one side, into a position where Vitali would have to take a very deliberate sideways step to keep me from the door I longed to push.

I adopted a weary, resigned expression. "I don't suppose there's a pay phone around here?"

"Back down the hall, turn to the right. It's by the stairs, before you come to the elevators."

I turned my neck slightly, improving my access to the door still further. "Shit, there's one right across the street. Thanks a lot, Guys."

Crawford followed me outside. It was a beautiful afternoon. The federal lawn was green. A man pushed himself down the sidewalk in a wheelchair. Crawford stopped at the edge of the sidewalk and lit a cigarette. He wasn't following me, but he was definitely watching me.

I crossed to the pay phone and went through the motions of dialing. Upstairs, I supposed Sergeant Smith and Corporal Martinez and their men would be conducting a search for me and the missing paperwork. I held onto the phone receiver for a minute or two, but when a postal service truck double-parked across the street and restricted Crawford's view, I ducked into a parking lot, which led to an alley. The alley led to another parking lot. I cut through that and emerged on another street, well away from the Federal Building.

Listening to my dad's work stories, I invariably cast my lot with the prank victims, the pretentious Poles, rigid Germans, sullen Wops, and Torah-reading Jews with dubious loyalties and suspect work ethics. Timmy Barlow, American mongrel husk around an essence of "goddamned Chinaman," dreamy, good-for-nothing Marxist symp and book-reading elitist.

In Bert's real world, most of the damage was done by phonies, namely those professing exotic, unauthorized, or inappropriate interests or views, much like his oldest son. Although in selling books he'd become something of an exile and expatriate, Bert's true homeland was ruled by production-minded gods, strictly administered by furious, vindictive mechanics. It was a complex of overheated buildings, noisy shops, industrial plants, and, of course, Car-O-Mats, characterized by noxious smells, cans of grease, hand tools, machine oil, time clocks, and the automated chatter of calibrated objects.

Even as upstairs in the bathroom outside Sergeant Smith's office I had flushed the explosive toilet again and again, in some corner of my imagination I had been seeing Bert stacking the last of his poker chips, wagering that his oldest son would go down, peeled of the flimsy arrogance he wore like a merit badge, duly exposed as another of life's cowardly incompetents, writhing, repenting, crushed to the inevitable grit that had to be cleaned from the machines by those responsible for the maintenance of the grinding assembly plant of the real world. Bert was betting I would regret overvaluing ideas, convinced that someday I would wish for his knowledge of, respect for, and competence with machinery. My fantasy lasted long enough to develop its own stage set: a rotten card table in the damp Oedipal basement where Bert sat smiling with anticipation and schadenfreude, toying with little phallic plastic towers of poker chips, the door to the draft board and destiny ajar behind him.

Wherever else it led, I was afraid that door might also lead me to the discovery that there was nothing special about me, that I wasn't the moral agent I imagined myself and that I was or would be in the end the biggest coward ever to be carried in tears of terror and shitty pants from a pitched battle where others died.

In a more appealing variation of this poker table showdown, I sat coughing disinterestedly into a handkerchief, a young, tubercular Doc Holliday, lowering my gambler's visor and histrionically pushing the last of my own chips toward Bert's. I was a young outlaw, a poet, I hoped, capable of sudden, potentially violent surprises and important friendships, a dream-slinger with the capacity to appreciate and inspire others to value the moral force of a solitary human conscience. In my mind, of course, I also had the tubercular gunslinger gambler's sense of how much good luck was beyond the door to the real world, though not necessarily how much bad. When I pushed my chips toward the middle of the table and locked eyes with Bert it was in the conviction that the pen was mightier than the sword, the heartfelt poem mightier than the repair manual, the flush after flush of an industrial toilet more powerful than an army of recruiters.

That night, the weather was balmy and the moon full. I borrowed my mom's Ford and drove by Mitch's house. His wife's Chevy Impala was parked about where I expected it to be. Things were quiet on the street, so I parked the Ford at the end of the block and hiked back to examine the convertible. It was in fantastic condition and I coveted it.

An hour later, in the hope of seeing my friend Gordon, I drove my mom's Fairlane down to Café Le Tarot, a coffee house I'd begun frequenting while still in high school. Gordon was sitting at a table near the window, fiddling with a poem about lost love. When I sat down and grinned, he capped his expensive fountain pen. "How did things go with the draft board?"

"Weird," I said. "Very weird. I can't believe what I did."

He looked at me and put down his pen. "I've got some gin and cough syrup stashed out back. Let's take a little break and you can fill me in on the details."

Three years older and deferred on account of flat feet, Gordon had dropped out of college and hitchhiked into town a year or more ago from somewhere in the Midwest. He drank gin for his nerves and drugstore cough syrup for a clearer view of the bright colors necessary to his poetry. He read books of literary criticism, wrote a poem in which he claimed Leadbelly had been a reincarnation of Christ, and had recently been working off and on with a jazz drummer in an effort to set his translations of Baudelaire to the bluesy chords he thumped out on a cheap guitar.

I chased gin with his cherry-flavored cough syrup. The moonlight cast shadows in the alley. A train whistle sounded over and over again.

"I could go to prison," I said.

"Nah, they always talk about throwing people in prison. If it weren't for the threat of prison even fewer people would enlist or submit to the draft."

"Yeah, but I did something."

"Cool."

174

"Something I didn't plan to do. Never even considered in fact."

His eyes brightened. "What?"

"Flushed half a ream of paperwork down the toilet."

"What paperwork?"

"This file of test results and social security numbers. I don't know what all. Most of them had my name on them. I got ahold of this stuff by a fluke, after being left alone in an office to redo forms I'd deliberately screwed up." The memory made me laugh. "I locked myself in this stall, and tore these papers into matchbook-sized pieces and kept flushing and flushing."

"You flushed all your stuff down the pot?"

"Yeah, just about everything that was on his desk. Even the original letters I'd written to the draft board earlier last year. But there were other papers, too. The thing is, I didn't want to risk going back in the office in possession of papers belonging to these other guys. I was in there flushing away like crazy for about twenty minutes. Some guy came in to take a leak and I thought sure I was busted, but the worst part was when I walked out of the head. You know, I thought sure I was going to run smack into this Sergeant Smith or this Corporal Martinez who had just called me yellow-bellied. I was shaking all over."

"You're telling me that you flushed your entire draft record file down the toilet?"

"The thing is I don't know about entire. That's what makes me so goddamned nervous. At first, I thought I'd gotten away with something. Now I don't know. The last couple of hours the only thing I've been able to think of is that there may be other stuff, you know, in Washington or somewhere."

Gordon was sitting on the rear bumper of an old pickup truck stroking his Fu Manchu goatee. "That was a very cool and very politically hip thing to do."

"Yeah, but what if I get caught?"

"I don't think they'll catch you. But to be on the safe side, maybe you should leave town."

"I was thinking the same thing. You know, all I got to do is sell three sets of encyclopedias in the next few days and some guy, this sales manager, is going to give me, fucking give me, a Chevy Impala convertible."

Gordon shrugged. "What do you want with a Chevy Impala convertible?"

"It's a cool car. I'll sell the books, get the title for it, and drive it to San Diego."

"Car ownership sucks you deeper into the system. I speak now as a college dropout, an auto mechanic school dropout, and a radical poet. And telling lies for money, especially hoodwinking people to sell them something they can look at in the library, that kind of crap kills poetry and creativity."

I gulped gin and struggled to keep from gasping. "Maybe it would have a slightly bad effect on my poetry, at least for a while. But it also occurs to me that driving this Chevy convertible would revive the poetry, after a while I mean."

"Plus, what's in San Diego? A bunch of retired navy captains and old people wandering the beaches with their dogs. The sun turns them into prunes. Republican prunes. What you should do, what I'm going to do next week, in fact, is go to San Francisco."

"San Francisco?"

"Don't you have a buddy over in Berkeley? It's right across the Bay. San Francisco is the soul of California. There's this area of town called North Beach where all the beat poets hang out. You can walk right into City Lights Bookstore, man, and the weirdest looking guy in the store is bound to be Ferlinghetti. We could probably meet Allen Ginsberg and Gary Snyder."

"Sounds great, but how would we get there? I don't have much money."

"Opposable thumbs."

"What?"

"This opposable thumb is a development that dwarfs the importance of the wheel and the internal combustion engine combined. I'm hitching out there next week. I've got to do it. I lost my bookstore job downtown and the last poem in my collection is titled "A Walk over the Golden Gate Bridge."

"What would we do for money when we get there? I mean, I've got a sleeping bag and enough to eat on and stuff for a few days."

"Don't sweat it. I've got an uncle who has worked for Western Union for thirty years. He can set us up delivering telegrams. All we got to do is scrape together enough money to buy a couple old bikes. In fact, I've got a bunch of older cousins, so my uncle's probably got some old bikes stored in his garage. There's one other thing I should tell you, and then you won't be able to say no. Over in Berkeley, there's a group of radical lawyers. They encourage all kinds of acts against the draft. And if people get in trouble, they defend them free."

Once I realized that I could live without the Chevy convertible and get back to California without the expense of buying gas and oil, there was nothing for it but to draw up plans. Once we got talking we realized that there really wasn't any reason why we couldn't get on the road by the next afternoon.

The first part of our trip was all rain and wind and sleeping on wet ground. But somewhere in western Nevada our luck changed. We camped overnight with three guys in a panel truck at the foot of Donner Pass and went to a picnic in a capacious back yard in Berkeley. A girl in pigtails handed me a joint, then said, "Hey, man, have you dropped acid yet?"

"No, not yet."

"Well, some guy from the psychology department has two big jars full of LSD capsules. We're going to be handing them out for free tomorrow afternoon at three o'clock at Muir Beach."

"Where's Muir Beach?"

"It's at the known edge of the universe. Get yourself to Mill Valley in Marin County and angels will take you the rest of the way."

CARLESS

Gordon soon acquired a girlfriend he was serious about, moved across the bay to Berkeley, and got involved in antiwar politics, leaving me to what he called my psychedelic frivolities in San Francisco. I acquired an old yellow girl's bike, which I pedaled up and down steep hills delivering telegrams. When I needed a break from the citywide party, at which I unaccountably considered myself a deserving guest of honor, I spent my nights, usually alone, in a sleeping bag on the floor in a doorless walk-in closet as far from the three broken windows in the front room of my rent-free apartment as I could manage. I read by candlelight. Shadows from clothes hung on overhead hooks flickered across the pages of paperback novels and books of poems. I was independent, camped out just a block from Haight Street, a spectator and participant, smoking weed, dropping acid, doing my share of drugs, and wandering from one sideshow to the next.

Rent was free, drugs and food were cheap, and girls plentiful and seductive. On rare sunny days, birds squabbled in the panhandle of Golden Gate Park across the street. Usually, mornings were foggy and I crawled from the dampness of my sleeping bag well before my alarm clock went off to wake me for work. In the bathroom mirror, from which three or four arrowhead-shaped shards were missing, I brushed my teeth and contemplated the waxy pallor of my face. Then, after showering in water so hot it turned my skin pink and warmed my bones, I sat in the kitchen over coffee, smoking cigarettes until the warmth of the match-lit oven and brew revived my sense of endless possibilities.

One groggy morning, instead of my alarm clock, I awoke to a shrill whistle. Investigating, I found Albert Fine in the kitchen. Albert was gay, and in your face about it, which was kind of scary. But he was also brutally funny, the funniest and perhaps the most honest person I'd ever met.

He turned and smiled. "Did anyone ever tell you how good you look when you first get out of bed in the morning?"

Uncomfortably aware of the thinness of my underwear, I said, "Don't get started." I walked to the kitchen window and looked out at the thin fog. "It's six-thirty in the morning, Albert. You know that?" He was staring into my all-but-empty refrigerator, as though he was waiting for something to appear in it." Do you mind," I asked, "telling me what the hell that whistling noise was?"

"Oh, that. I haven't managed to persuade Gordon to forgive you your silliness or give up his breakfast cough syrup, but I'm determined to help you kick coffee. Look at that wretched coffee pot. Can you imagine this sort of crust forming around your poor kidneys? Allow me to present you with your new whistling teakettle. I'm making tea and the water got too hot." He held it aloft.

"Quite nice," I said on the way back to the front room for my pants. He stayed where he was, so I went on talking to him from the other room. "But at the risk of sounding both ungrateful and inhospitable, I wonder if you'll tell me how you got in here?"

Back in the kitchen I watched him pour water over teabags in mismatched cups. "Well, I turned the knob and opened the door, then neglected to lock it again, just like the last person who came in."

He handed me a chipped cup. "Here, try this. It's the best Lapsang Souchong bags money can buy. Careful, it's hot."

I sat in a rickety wooden chair, the legs of which I'd recently stabilized with a pair of long nails. Albert, more than ten years older, settled into a chrome chair. He was small and compact, fragile rather than thin. On good days his deeply inset green eyes twinkled from within a thousand premature wrinkles. Other times, they were red-rimmed and he looked distraught. There were a few gray hairs along his carefully trimmed temples. I thought of a leprechaun in a jacket.

I'd met him rummaging among discarded vegetables at a time when Gordon and I were still sharing our Mission Street digs. The sunny day had rendered the Chinatown produce less than perfectly fresh looking, Albert explained, so the highly competitive Chinatown merchants striving to display vegetables that looked fresher than those of their competitors just tossed them out. He talked of waste and of the salads he could make from the culled carrots and scallions. Sometimes, he said, he made soup and served it to vitamin-deficient vagrants in his neighborhood. We ambled to a nearby park where I watched him wash tomatoes and cabbages in a public drinking fountain. While I enjoyed coffee and a donut, Albert ate a raw onion and offered free produce to passersby.

Though he lived in a tiny apartment in North Beach, after Albert met Gordon, he soon became a regular at our Mission Street digs, almost a third roommate. Whenever he visited, Albert brought healthy food, small gifts, exotic cigarettes, and, in my case, a revised seduction strategy. I rebuffed him again and again, sometimes confronting him with girlfriends. But with Albert, relenting was not at all the same as giving up.

At first I worried a little about his intricate suggestions that I was repressing my homosexuality. Then, in a discussion with Gordon, I hit on a resemblance between Albert and my dad. Albert was bitchy, witty, and attentive, instead of derisive, overbearing, and indifferent; but, like Bert, he loved food, music, mockery, and laughing in the face of those he freely criticized. When I shared this observation with Albert, he acted hurt and went home. Commenting on Fine's abrupt departure, Gordon surmised that Albert preferred to see himself in the role of the seducer, even if he sometimes settled for "the Auntie Mame and mommy act." But he wanted no association whatever with fatherhood. After that, I began to relax. Repressed homosexual or not, I was enjoying lots of casual heterosexual sex in a city teeming with available young women.

Women who visited me when Fine was around, especially those who showed a strong interest, were often made the butts of a sugarcoated derision and ridicule. His outbursts were almost always followed by laughter and oddly convincing apologies. He could be as sweetly appeasing as a puppy or snappish as a guard dog. He could come on like a twinkly-eyed young prodigy or an aging bitch disturbed at her feed dish. He'd had some kind of elaborate therapy in Europe many years before and didn't want to see the world through anyone else's eyes. He tested our sincerity and playfulness, forcing an honesty on both Gordon and me that we couldn't have forced on each other.

"I've been looking for you for days," Albert scolded, pouring tea. "I sold three drawings in New York, got paid, and wanted to buy you a certain sweater. I didn't know if you'd like it without asking, and now it's been sold. I worried that you bought yourself a station wagon and had driven off yonder with that mail person."

"Mail person?"

"What's her name, that poor sad-eyed creature who can't laugh or afford shoes?" Albert delighted in conversations that were like walking an electrified tightrope, wavering on a high wire of ambiguity between mockery and the heart-felt. He was manipulative, too. Whenever people took him seriously, it turned out he was joking. Whenever they laughed, it turned out Albert had been serious. And then he twisted his knife.

"Irene. You've only met her once, and already you've made up your mind you don't like her.

"I like her fine. I'm sure I'd learn to be comfortable enough around her, if only she could find some other target for her covert competitiveness."

I sighed. "Albert, there is no competition! You . . ."

"No! Don't say it! It's a common strategy; her competitiveness takes the form of pretending to be as stupid as a post. Besides, since you need someone who can help you disengage from the snarl of the preposterous ideas you're always weaving, she's certainly not for you."

I bristled. "That's not for you to say."

He toyed with his teabag, hoisted it, and let it drip into his open mouth. Putting it down on the table next to this cup, he said, "What do you consider her chief attraction?"

"Irene's much brighter and more unassuming than you've judged her to be."

"Oh, look at you!" He laughed, I thought, at himself as well as me. "There's no one you hate more than me when I am overcome with truth-telling, is there?"

"You seem to be having a little episode of some sort."

"Well, I've looked for you for fucking days and days, and only just found out from your junkie friends downstairs that you hadn't moved out."

Albert was unshaven. His eyes were red-rimmed from an apparent lack of sleep. I wondered if he'd been grieving again over the recent death of the aunt he'd said he loved more than his mother. "You've been upset again?"

"No. I've been too busy looking for you to be anything but tired. Anyway, I got a letter from Gordon. Also, alas, a very bad poem. He's read way too much Rilke, hasn't he?"

"Did you have a falling out, you two?"

"No," Albert said. "*I* would never lace his cough syrup with LSD and commit against him various psychedelic crimes which have driven a wedge between the two of you." He put his hands together in a mock gesture of supplication. "You don't look like you've been eating right. All that red meat and sugar is so bad for you."

"I don't need a substitute mother."

"Well, I'd rather be someone else, of course. But then again, who does a young scamp with a wet sleeping bag, no electricity, and a jacket for a pillow need more than a mother? Unless, of course, he's a lapsed Papist in search of a sacred holy substitute mother. Albertina, Our Lady of Drug-Deluded Hippies? Or how about Alberta, Our Lady of Sanctimonious Car Vagabonds?"

"Have you been thinking about your aunt again? Prowling the alleys and not getting enough sleep?"

"No. In fact, while I've been out buying you a new pillow and teapot, you've probably been out there having what that Irish blowhard, Dr. Timothy Leary, calls cellular consciousness sex with that shoeless woman Irene, or some of her friends." Fine batted his eyes like the cartoon character Betty Boop. "I brought you some homemade applesauce. Hurry along and shower. We'll have more tea and some applesauce for breakfast." He started for the cupboard. "I don't suppose there's any chance you have bread? We could have toast."

"The bread's moldy. I was planning to go down to Market Street and have coffee and a Danish."

"It will have to be your treat then. That pillow over there in the corner, the accompanying cowboy-decorated pillow case, and the teapot have cost me all I had after I paid my back rent."

"Albert, you don't have to spend on me. But, thank you."

When I got out of the shower, Albert was sitting in the broken chair, smoking one of his Turkish cigarettes, dabbing at tears.

"Uhh, are you all right?"

"Oh you're such a man about tears. If you must know, I stopped myself from thinking about my Aunt Sally by re-reading my letter from Gordon. He won't say it outright, but he wants you to visit him and to repent of trying to poison him. And I think you should. I'm worried about that beatnik chick. If she doesn't kill him with a bomb she's intended for the Pentagon, or give him venereal disease and cause him to be dispatched to a hell without his cherry cough syrup, she may prove liberating. One day she'll tell him that it's either her or the cough syrup." Albert laughed again. "And then he won't be able to lose. He'll be liberated no matter what he chooses."

"I've never met her. Gordon showed me her picture. What's her name?"

"Rhonda or something god-awful. Actually, she's not so bad when she shuts up about justice for the people."

"I bet you're being nasty about her because she sees through your act."

"Yes, my God, poor thing, and with those bulging eyes. Looking at the world through her telephoto lenses, I'm sure she sees a great deal no one else does."

"You're getting charged up all over again."

"No, no, and let it be said that if I liked women and competing as much as you and Gordon do, I'd be smitten by Rhonda too." Albert sulked. "But then there's your barefoot mail woman. I'm tolerated occasionally by her, but spurned by my lapsed altar boy."

"Leave Irene out of this. I have feelings for her I don't think I've ever had for a woman before."

"Surely I'd be remiss for not pointing out to you that you've left the others in back seats or out in the bushes too quickly to develop feelings for them?"

"Irene's special."

"Meaning you can get her at a discount?"

I could feel the blood creep across my face.

"Oh, I don't mean to be so cruel. You might get her to punish me by poisoning my dinner. She's invited me to join you at her place this Saturday. Of course, once the buckwheat groats are fully ingested, I'll be expected to take my leave without complaint so she can take you into her little Kasbah and have some cellular sex with you. But come, enough talk of spider's webs, she-devils, of sandalwood domesticities and diapers yet to be bought and changed. Let us go now, you and I, for our sanpaku cheese and raisin Danishes. They will be our little secret. Something she need never know of us."

The drizzle ceased when I crossed Telegraph Avenue, and the sky was clearing as I mounted the steps to a weathered bungalow about a mile from the U.C. Berkeley campus. I wiped my boots on the doormat, rang the bell, and looked at my reflection in the glass panel of the door. My aviator sunglasses were spotted with drizzle. I folded them into my pocket, Six feet, slim but sinewy under a damp army surplus jacket, unshaven rather than bearded, I hooked my wet blond hair behind my ears and was using index fingers to dab the water out of my ears when a woman opened the door.

"Hi," I said. "I'm Barlow."

"Of course, and I'm Rhonda. So nice to meet you at last." Her mousy hair was suspended in precarious dishevelment by a pair of enameled chopsticks. Cat's-eye glasses perched on her button nose, a fashion statement of some sort, giving her a puzzled enigmatic expression.

"From everything Gordon told me about you, I expected somebody, uh . . ." She shrugged.

"More of a freak?"

"Well, I don't know. At least somebody who looked more like a hippie and less like a liberal pre-law student." She laughed. "Come on in and toss your coat over the banister. Gordon went down to the co-op for cat food and cardboard boxes. I just brewed some coffee."

Gordon had always gone in for long-legged hipless chicks, languorous Maryanne Faithful types, so I was surprised by the broadness of Rhonda's hips. I followed her down a narrow wood-paneled hall into an almost bare kitchen. I sat at a freshly painted green table, watching her pour coffee. The raw muscularity of her hands was in contrast to the delicate bones in her face. Blatantly sizing each other up, we sat awkwardly, stirring our coffee, adding dribbles of milk.

"I'd offer you a towel for your hair," she apologized, "but the last towel's in the hamper and we're the other side of disorganized around here right now." Pinker skinned than she'd appeared in the photograph Gordon showed me, she was pretty in an understated way, despite the way the heavy lenses of her glasses magnified her robin's-egg-blue eyes. Gordon had told me she was active in the peace movement and that there had been occasions last year when FBI agents had followed her to and from the campus. Not wanting to talk about the war if I could help it, I sipped coffee and tried to imagine her screaming slogans at soldiers and cops. She struck me as too individualistic to chant at peace demonstrations. On the other hand, my adventures with LSD and other psychedelics had made me a little slower to jump to conclusions.

She broke another awkward silence first. "I guess it's the rebel in me. I clam up rather than make small talk. Stupid as it may sound, I guess I'm still getting over how you look. Gordon contends that my thinking hardens too quickly and I don't rebound from surprises well. Unhip as it is, I've been sitting here trying to fit the person I see with the person who's been talked about." She laughed. "Last week Albert was here and referred to you as the St. Paul of Haight Street."

"That's the Albert I know," I laughed. "Everyone must fit on his deranged stage not too close to the footlights. He's always renaming people after the characters they'd least like to be."

"Gordon was surprised to discover that you were living in the Haight. He figured you were still in the place the two of you rented on Mission Street, I guess. How are things up there these days?

"I'm not as much the authority on the Haight-Ashbury scene as Albert likes to pretend, but things there are combinations of exciting and ugly.

Not as much love and peace as advertised, but more dirt and disarray, and just about as spectacular and seedy as described in magazines and on television."

"I used to live there a couple of years ago myself."

"The Diggers still serve free soup and salad, and there are still free concerts and exciting things going on in the park, but too many people are taking Timothy Leary seriously. Something spontaneous and fun seems to be disappearing. Last week, for instance, I went to this party given by people trying to start a commune. Everybody was supposed to sit on the floor and speak honestly about their impression of the person sitting next to them. I was supposed to talk about a redheaded woman I'd never seen before. I said that I felt ambivalent toward her, but that I didn't really consider my ambivalence my fault. Then I tried to explain that I wasn't completely ready to join a commune but was just this idealistic, somewhat skeptical pilgrim who feels twenty things at once when meeting a stranger. The thing is, the party is over and people are desperately trying to make a party into a way of life. Anyway, I'm glad to meet you finally because now you won't have to know me through Albert and Gordon."

Rhonda breathed on her glasses and wiped them with a paper napkin. "Gordon just uses Albert for entertainment. He goads him into saying the most outrageous things, some of which are quite hilarious. Still, it's hard for me to imagine why the two of you put up with him."

"Well, I've wondered myself. Albert naturally favors an explanation that takes into account my allegedly suppressed homosexuality. He might be right that I might have to pass through a lot of revulsion in order to find my true self. It occurred to me that having an extremely critical man, similar to my dad, hovering over me and trying to humiliate me satisfies some kind of low-grade conditioned craving. I suppose this makes Albert a two-headed father-and-mother monster: someone who insults me and then worries about me. Maybe I'm not so far from home as I feel after all. But that's just one of several answers. It's also true that Albert makes me laugh and refuses to let me take myself as seriously as I might if he wasn't around."

"Gordon says he moons over you and has a way of making these oh-so public protestations of love. Aren't you bothered by that?"

"Protestations of lust would be more like it. But his little puns and innuendoes don't embarrass or abrade me like they used to, so he's lost interest somewhat. He's still jealous and insulting at times, though. About a week ago my girlfriend Irene almost hit him. I think Albert's paid a high price to become an honest person and craves contact with human

186

beings whose barriers are down. Sometimes he gets impatient and just tries to break them down. I don't think I'm ready for it, but I think that Albert might do very well in a world where emotional honesty counted for something."

"You may be right," Rhonda said. "He seems funny, vulnerable, and prone to popping off about whatever comes into his head. I worry one day he's going to expose somebody's bullshit and they'll beat the hell out of him. People can be so ugly and violent when they're angry." She looked away, sipped coffee, and took a big breath. "It's none of my business, but I've been curious and unable to get the whole story from Gordon."

"What, about me and Gordon, our so-called falling out?"

"Yes. He drops these little hints that it's something he'd like to talk about, but gets all worked up when I ask about it. You tell me, should I mind my own damned business, or can I pry your version of the story out of you?" She laughed and twisted the sticks in her hair.

"Basically, after a long and stupid discussion lasting parts of several days, I agreed to drink an entire bottle of his cough syrup while he dropped acid for the first time. He had a few rough spots, as I warned him he might, but eventually he mellowed out. I thought if we went up to Golden Gate Park he might meet some fellow travelers and let go a little more. These kids were flying a kite and he seemed to be getting into it. Me, I was wasted and woozy from all that cough syrup, and seeing him start to enjoy himself, closed my eyes and nodded off. The next thing I knew, some straight-looking guy with a white jacket wakes me up and asks if I'm Tim Barlow and would I accompany him to this clinic down the street because a guy named Gordon is shouting my name at everybody. Gordon was gone before I got there. The next time our paths crossed at our apartment, I found him burning a bunch of poems in the bathtub. Later he calmed down enough to say that acid had convinced him his poems were "a lachrymose spangle of lies.""

Rhonda sighed. "Thankfully, he's writing again now. In fact, the other night he read me a part of this new poem he's calling, "The Badass Haight-Ashbury Blues." I'm no authority on poetry, but it has this great line in it where he describes the Haight as 'a realm where delusions of cosmic grandeur, like fog from the ocean, waft through the trees each night as the seductive curry-browned breath of Krishna, turning human brains to smelly, pungent, useless stew.' That's pretty close, anyway. Just one more question and then we'd better shut up about it in case he walks in. Why did you try to coax him to take it again?"

"I should have listened to my inner voice and just shut the hell up," I admitted. "I didn't coax him, though. I had eaten some peyote buttons and he was around and he asked if I had any left. Anyway, I wanted him to be at ease, to understand that I might start behaving in a rather loose way. I offered him some. And figuring that if he didn't eat the buttons but stuck around, he'd probably get some kind of contact high, I started reading aloud from *The Psychedelic Handbook* and *The Tibetan Book of the Dead*. One minute I was listening to some raga music, kind of singing along with it. The next minute I heard the door slam and he was gone again."

"He called you "a bookstore Buddha" for that." she laughed. " I used to live up there, not in Nirvana, in the Haight, I mean."

"You did mention it. But Gordon led me to think that you were as down on psychedelics as he is."

"I still smoke a little weed now and then when Gordon goes off on one of his cough syrup jags. I dropped acid a few times, but it was never really my thing; it's too exhausting. Garth, this guy I was living with for a while, he gave me some advice before my first trip. He said, 'Look, Rhonda, whatever you do, don't let the drug make you critical of others or yourself or of your decisions. When universal truth seems to beckon, do yourself a favor. Just go into the kitchen and peel yourself a banana or sniff the contents of your spice shelf.' Whenever I did acid it was just to see the pretty colors dance. I never looked for truth or meaning or allowed myself to get mystical. Maybe that's my loss."

"Your approach seems to work best when you stay at home," I said. "The more other people are admitted into the picture, the more that strategy breaks down and you have to get into the nitty-gritty of human relationships and meanings. When you take your trip out into the world, you have to be able to make sense of yourself to strangers."

Rhonda got up to admit a scrawny gray cat who was scratching at the back door, poured us more coffee, and sat back down again. "I took the bus up there last summer to look for a friend I'd lost touch with," she said. "In the Haight the bus got caught in this long line of cars. Dads, moms, kids in double-parked station wagons, their windows all rolled up, noses pressed to the glass. When I got off and walked around I saw that tourists had discovered empty storefronts and were opening little businesses to sell 'I Am Groovy' buttons and posters with deformed lettering. The merchants and tourists were going the real freaks one better, wearing feathers, sandals, fringed leather jackets, factory-made beaded shirts, and tie-dyed headbands. People had set up tables and were selling incense and organic apple pies, little torts with yin yang symbol frosting and food coloring. Some fat guy with the eyes of a snake was selling kundalini muffins, misspelled with a 'y' for an 'i' and baked in fucking Burlingame or somewhere. Meanwhile, trash was all over the streets, Hell's Angels were grabbing young girls' asses, trying to rub their tits and coax them onto their Harleys. I wandered into the park where a bunch of people were gathered around a stage, so I went over, thinking my girlfriend might be there. A couple of Angels were speaking too close to the mike, blustering about how they were bearing up under the pain of being misunderstood and haranguing all the hippies for being too pussy to fight for their country. One of the bikers got so worked up he pulled a small American flag out of his vest, jumped down off the stage and, holding the flag high, pissed in the communal soup pot. Then, while a fight was breaking out, some of the so called leaders, the bored poets, filmmakers, playwrights and Leary himself, stepped to the mike to lecture about the importance of peace and love and being real. It was disgusting, their excuse making and appeasement of the Angels. At that point, it was all too painfully clear that the people on the stage who thought of themselves as leaders craved the adulation of the hippie hoi polloi and had come over from posh carpeted homes in Marin County to preach transcendence to the rabble. That was the last time I was there. I don't think I'll go back."

I fetched an ashtray from a drainer near the sink and lit a cigarette. "I was there that day, too. I overheard some bikers talking about dragging Leary down and making him drink a bowl of the piss soup. This was also about the same time I admitted to myself that the idea had a certain appeal to me. Mean-spirited as the bikers, but more gutless, maybe, I went off to Fisherman's Wharf for fish and chips. It wasn't anybody's finest hour. The next day I heard the whole business got resolved when a commune calling itself the Hopi and Bopping Solution handed out a truck of cold beer to the Angels."

"Well," Rhonda smiled, helping herself to one of my cigarettes, "I'm sure that gave everybody something to piss and moan about." I laughed and she went to the window, opened it and looked outside. "Stopping the war, redistributing property, working for improved human conditions, those are things I can understand better. I can even understand that there are people entertaining the outrageous fantasy that the Angels will storm the Pentagon and stop the war if there are enough cases of beer waiting for them afterwards. On the other hand, love and peace, as practiced Haight-Ashbury style, getting back to the godhead, chakras, and chanting to become more spiritual, I have no appreciation for. I mean, I have no idea what you might understand that I don't, and I'm not doubting there are some good people doing some good things over there. On the other hand, you're not a woman, and speaking for myself, I don't want to grow vegetables or become an Indian goddess in some bucolic farmland where the commune rules declare I have to ball my brothers more or less on demand."

With no word of greeting, Gordon clomped into the kitchen, snared the coffee pot from the stove, a cup from a drainer, and sat down. He had a welt on his forehead and his left eye was swollen and almost closed. His lips were puffy and split. I thought of a cracked-open plum, food for a bird.

"Jesus, Gordon," I said, "what happened to you?" I looked at Rhonda, who seemed less than surprised by his appearance. She sighed and shrugged. Gordon took a bottle of cough syrup, his favorite brand, from a pocket in his leather jacket.

"Fucking warmongers," Rhonda said.

Gordon shrugged, twisted the cap off his depressive cherry juice, and sipped carefully, avoiding the crusty ooze in the middle of his lips. "Not as painful anymore as it looks. Some hardhats in the Oakland shipyards got carried away expressing their enthusiasm for the war."

"Shit, man, did you see a doctor?"

"Yeah," Gordon managed a wincing smile. "And a dentist, too."

Two of his front teeth were chipped, reddened by his syrup.

"What the hell happened?"

Gordon waved an arm. "I'm in a forgetting mode, trying to get beyond it. Likewise, the bad drug trip." He held up the palms of both hands, signaling there would be no talk of my drugs or his beating.

I shrugged. "Okay. I'm glad to see you, and sorry you're hurt."

"I don't mean to be surly and talking too much hurts my jaw. Everything that's past is over. You're still delivering telegrams and been having all sorts of adventures over in Haight-Ashbury, I hear."

While Rhonda made sandwiches I brought Gordon up to date. At some point she turned around and pointed a knife loaded with mayonnaise in my direction. "Albert was over here for dinner the other night," she said, "with this hilarious story about coming over to your place and finding you looking like a wet muskrat."

Gordon swilled cough syrup and swallowed it. "Then he went on and on about how you have to hang your wet sleeping bag over a chair by a stove."

I felt defensive. "Hey, it gets damp in the apartment, but the price is right." I laughed. "Or, I don't know. It seemed right at the time. Maybe it was a mistake. Nothing's forever."

Gordon winced from the pain of laughing through his swollen lips. "Al said that all the windows were missing in your apartment and that the morning fog was up to his knees in your fucking bedroom."

"Not to protest too much," I said, "but just the bedroom windows are missing. The one in the kitchen's only cracked. A group of junkies living there used to throw things at one another and miss. They'd been paying their rent with heroin and got kicked out when their supply dried up."

"Al said you were living in an apartment over some junkies. Just please don't tell me that you've been shooting up."

I smiled and shook my head, but Gordon was worked up.

"Like I told Albert, I mean, at least if you die from an overdose of LSD, you'll probably croak thinking you have quite possibly saved the universe from its hopelessly lack-love condition. If you overdose on horse, you'll go out knowing for a fact that you have just been excreted from the anus of Shiva and that the world as it is can't wait to wipe your residue from the outer surface of its puckered memory."

"A little on the scatological side," I laughed, "but the poetry has apparently come back. Smack has no appeal to me, Gordon. My mother left me in my high chair a lot when I was a kid, so I got tired of drooling on myself long ago. A lot of things might happen to me, but I'll never own a Buick, and I'll never inject a drug to get high."

Rhonda laughed out loud at this and Gordon smiled and winked at her.

I hesitated, expecting to be made party to the joke.

"Okay, go on," Gordon said. "We're waiting for details about your junkie landlords."

"Over in the park I met this guy named Tom who was shouting at a tree about the machinery of life. He was having a bum trip. I offered him a few calming words. When he told me a little about what had been happening, I told him it might not have been a very good idea to put acid in a syringe and shoot it up with heroin. Since he wasn't ready for any heavyweight ideas about the illusory nature of human existence, I also suggested that the monsters he'd been seeing might actually be angels."

"Christ, Barlow," Gordon said, "do you have that bullshit memorized from your psychedelic handbook collection, or do you just make it up on the spot? I mean, I think all this stuff should be written down and made available for your grandchildren in case insanity turns out to be an inherited condition and they come to wonder what the fuck happened to them."

"Oh, come on, Gordon," Rhonda said. "He was looking out for others. Give him a break."

Very gingerly, Gordon dabbed his mouth with a napkin. "Okay, fine. I mean, credit where credit is due. One of your most obvious skills is the knack you have for walking around whacked out of your skull on scary drugs, saying things that sound deep, or at least strike you as deep, and looking like a house cat with its mouth closed around a living mouse. Oh, by the way," Gordon reached in his shirt pocket. "Here's that hundred bucks I owe you for back rent."

"Thanks."

"Now, if you don't mind, back to Tom, the tree-punching smack head."

"I asked him about what he'd been doing the last week or so and told him that it had been my experience that angels look demonic when seen through a filter of fear and rage. Almost certainly, I told Tom, these creatures want you to stop slapping your girlfriend." Gordon rolled his eyes. "Hey," I said defensively, "I was trying to tiptoe around his fears in way that would get through to him, without, you know, too much pansy-ass psychedelic sanctimony. Eventually I agreed to walk home with him so he could apologize to Sandra."

Rhonda served us chicken salad sandwiches and oranges and handed me a napkin. "Sandra?"

"Tom's chick. She, or somebody in her family, owns the house on Oak Street where I'm living. She was so grateful that somebody had been able to get through to Tom, she said I could live rent-free in the third-floor apartment. In return, I'm supposed to talk to Tom whenever he gets strung out, keep him from breaking things and hitting her. So far, no real problems."

"Sounds really good," Gordon said, smiling and reaching for his swollen lips. "You can buy yourself a gun."

"Well, I see it all a little differently," Rhonda said. "It sounds to me like Tim might be thinking again about the plight of people who've been disgorged by the system. Like I'm not trying to tell you what to do, Tim, I almost never do that until I've met somebody at least twice, but thinking a little less about the condition of your karma and chakras and a little more about the victims of capitalism might be a step in the right direction."

"You could be right," I conceded, "but just to finish up, I moved into Sandra's third-floor apartment overlooking Golden Gate Park about three days later. From the apartment I can pedal down to work in about ten minutes. Of course, it takes me double that to get up the hill home."

Gordon nodded. "So you're living rent free?"

"Yeah, and thanks to free lunches at St. Andrews Church and dinners provided by the Diggers, I'm saving money."

Gordon finished the last of his cough syrup. "Speaking of money, and steering at least temporarily away from Marxism and Hare Krishna acid babble, Albert said you were shopping for a car. That will certainly require money. Or maybe you've met another sales manager who has promised you another Chevy convertible?"

"No," I laughed, "but I was sorely tempted by a Chevy van I saw for sale a while back. I didn't quite have enough money for it. Otherwise, who knows where I'd be right now."

"Rhonda," Gordon said, "things are definitely getting cosmic, karma is coming around full circle and I'm getting a contact high. I mean, this guy came into my life over some Chevy convertible he wanted and I talked him out of acquiring. Now he comes on another Chevy that he might have bought if I had paid him the hundred I owed him sooner. By introducing him to the advantages of hitchhiking, and then by being slow to repay the hundred I owe him, I seem to have become a karmic obstacle in his life. Gordon Ferguson, the Chevy preventer."

I swallowed the last of my sandwich and reached for a wedge of orange. "The fever's gone now, but I had the car fever for a few days, I admit. I couldn't help but think how with that van, I could put a little curtain in the back window, get a mattress for the floor, and have the best of all possible worlds. The highway would open its exciting heart to me any time I had a few bucks in my pocket, and I would have my own little home on wheels wherever I happened to be. I'd have a dry place to sleep when I wanted one, and a conveyance to take me where I sometimes itch to go, anywhere but here, without the obligation of standing around with frostbitten feet hoping some guy with a car is going to stop and pick me up. But like I say, I'm over it."

Gordon stared into his empty cough syrup bottle. A big grin came over his face. "Want to check out our old Buick?"

"Buick?" I looked at Rhonda. "That thing out in the driveway is yours?"

"It's ours," Rhonda said. "We paid our rent and a debt or two and pooled our money. I gave up hitchhiking about the same time I renounced psychedelics."

I followed Gordon out the kitchen door and examined the green and white '62 Buick parked with its nose against the garage door.

"How's it run?"

"Great! But I just got it. Therefore, I guess I should add the words 'so far.'"

"How much?

"Six seventy-five."

"What's with all the boxes in the back seat?"

"Books, clothes."

"You're moving?"

"Yeah." Gordon looked at me. "Back to Denver."

"To Denver? Just like that? No goodbyes? What about Rhonda's school and all the antiwar work you're doing here?"

"She's finished, except for her thesis. She can write that anywhere. We need to get away from the movement for a while. There's too much talk about bombing buildings. Bad stuff's going to happen, especially around the universities. A friend of Rhonda's who's into Tarot cards warned us to go east and lay low. We're scared of the bourgeois life, man, but it's all we know and it's calling us home."

"But Denver, for Christsake."

"It's east, isn't it? A little place on the outskirts of town. We both love the mountains."

"Now I understand why your apartment looks so bare. You're packing up. And why you sent me a telegram requesting a visit."

"Well, how else could we reach you?"

"You look like you're about ready to go. Except for the furniture."

"The furniture stays. We'll go in a couple of hours, I guess. We thought we'd take you out for pizza, little place down the street. Drive you to the bus stop or something. I mean, actually, we'll drive you to San Francisco if you really want."

"No, if you're going to Denver that would be out of your way. I'll just hitch back."

"Who knows? Now that you have more money, you might see another Chevy van and decide to follow us."

Houses, trees, electrical poles, and billboards emerged from evening collars of fog. Tree leaves ceased to drip, the sun appeared from a slit in the clouds, screen doors slammed, and gates creaked and then banged shut. Students emerged from wooden houses to sit on porch swings. Mothers wearing long braids wrestled with toddlers who were attempting to stand upright in strollers and grocery carts in order to celebrate the last few minutes of sun. I hiked through smells of laurel, fermenting soybeans, fish, and fancy teas, and when I could see the bay, turned and extended my right arm toward oncoming traffic.

Almost immediately I was face-to-face with an Asian man whose wind-blown hair and long goatee reminded me of a figure I'd seen on an ancient Chinese scroll. He squinted at me, shut his motorcycle engine off, and smiled. "Going to San Francisco?"

I was remembering Junior Wong, wondering how many years had passed since I'd last thought of him. "Uhhhh, yeah. San Francisco."

"Would you like a ride into the sunset on a fast motorcycle with a drug-addled Chinaman?"

Psychedelic etiquette called for a gracious willingness to remain a bit-player in the wildest fantasies of another. "It would," I began, "depend on whether or not the drug-crazed Chinaman was self-destructive."

"What if he no longer had a self that could be destroyed?"

On that note I flung one leg over the back fender and off we went. The big Triumph jolted, then whined for the Bay Bridge. Low tails of white cloud rushed over the waters. Brilliant pinks, roses, and yellows of sunset glowed behind the San Francisco skyline.

Cars and trucks stretched ahead like an endless jetty. The cycle picked up speed through a cemetery of strange conveyances. A low-voltage current streamed through my tendons and muscles, melting my bones and turning my flesh into a strange gelatin. Overhead, giant green and white signs blew by like clouds.

Past the tollbooth and up on the bridge, we raced between lanes of stalled traffic. These were not the sorts of cars that Junior Wong and I dreamed of driving to China. They obstructed the bridge, frustrated their owners, burned smelly gas, required insurance payments, new tires, and constant attention. They were demonic. You got in them, sat down, waited your turn, moved and stopped at traffic lights and looked both ways at intersections without seeing anything but other cars. You honked, hit the brakes, stepped on the gas, sat stranded in little smelly smokes, and pounded your fist on the steering wheel when you couldn't go where and when you wanted. Mad human animals, little pale, hairless gorillas, inched forward in steel bubbles, dreaming of freedom that didn't exist. I held on to the motorcyclist and twisted for a brief look back. These cars were not gliding toward China; they were idling, gathering fog and wiping it away with windshield wipers. Ahead, backlit by a white glare, the San Francisco skyline glowered, turned red at the bottom, faded to a softer, dimmer light.

And then the Triumph was across the bridge, roaring down a slope, gliding into and then out of a curve. As the motorcycle slowed, the air current eased and I began to acquire the costume of weight and mass. Skyscrapers and buildings focused themselves against a red sky. I stood a moment beside the motorcyclist, then reached in my pocket, and handed him a dollar.

I first met Irene at the famous Fairmont Hotel. With a genial nod of his baldhead, the hotel porter agreed to keep an eye on my rattletrap, balloon-tired bike while I hurried into the lobby of the Fairmont Hotel with three or four banana-colored telegrams. Shiny with sweat, I strode into the lobby and glanced at the clock as a beautiful woman turned toward me in her baggy postal uniform. I slowed my approach for a longer look at the way she toted the mail pouch over her slender shoulder.

Small and slightly feral, dark curly hair wrapped into a ponytail from which it threatened to explode, clear olive skin, and a face shaped like a perfectly balanced valentine, she smiled at me and my knees went unreliable. Her bare feet did not seem to penetrate the plush red carpet and she glided through a haze of cigar smoke and a stand of self-important men in expensive suits. She had thick, marvelously shaped eyebrows, suggesting a young Frida Kahlo without the anger and brittleness. Our eyes met and the lobby filled with golden sparks. She slowed slightly, seemed to note with pleasure that I was in no condition to speak to her, and then floated out the door. My telegrams went down on the desk in a hurry.

Outside, I spotted the red of a feather in her hair and watched her cross the street. When she turned back to wave, holding up a white hand with long fingers just high enough to be seen, I knew that my life was going to be very different. Back on my bike, I lifted my feet from the pedals, let go of the handlebars, and flew like a confirmed immortal down the long steep hill toward Market Street.

It was almost two weeks before Irene and I finally sat down together. Though we could barely speak for staring, I confessed that ever since seeing her I'd been planning my telegram deliveries to arrive at the Fairmont at 10:15 with or without telegrams to drop off. We arranged to meet again that same day after work and sat over coffee staring into each other's eyes while the world emptied itself of all but wonder. When we finally left the coffee shop, we held hands and turned back convinced, without speaking, that it would probably be important to us fifty years later to retain the shop's meaningless ambiance fresh in our collective memory.

We walked and ate dinner in Chinatown and stared and went to her apartment and made love, then walked and ate and stared and went back to her apartment and made love again. For several days we napped rather than slept and went on napping rather than sleeping. Talking seemed like a reasonably painless way to pass the time until we gained strength and

196

healed for more kissing and rubbing, but half my clothes were hanging in the closet of her apartment before we started to talk very much.

We marveled that Irene, too, had been born in Denver, and still more so when we discovered she was exactly nine months younger than I was. The more we talked about our early lives in Denver, the more vividly I persuaded myself I'd had strange moods whenever I'd ridden my bike or driven by one of the houses where she'd lived.

In high school, she'd been deeply depressed, not so much by her parents' divorce, but by having to move with her father to Chula Vista, California. It turned out she'd been living just a bus ride from Mission Beach when I'd been arrested for carrying the rusty knife, and she'd arrived in San Francisco six months before I had.

Shortly before we met, Irene had received a letter from her estranged Mexican mother, who hoped for a rapprochement and encouraged her to return to Denver. Her mother's clan, the Escobar family, owned a Mexican restaurant in one of Denver's oldest neighborhoods. For three weeks before she'd met me, Irene admitted, she'd thought seriously of returning to Colorado. Now, she could hardly bear to think about what her life would be like if she had moved back.

I said that Denver might not be as bad to visit as it had been to grow up in. The more we talked about it, the more Denver seemed the kind of city we might pass through together eventually on one of our 'round-the-world journeys. It wouldn't be that bad. I had friends there.

Irene said she wanted to see her mother and thought maybe we could go there on a vacation in a little while, explain to family and friends that we both had jobs we liked in San Francisco. Working at the post office wasn't that bad; about two-thirds of the mail carriers she worked with dealt grass and acid and made their rounds whacked out of their skulls. Her supervisor was a major dealer who, for fear of being narced, always covered for and never fired anyone. Not only did he leave her alone, but he found little ways of making her job easier.

Still, she wanted to go to art school. On the walls of her tiny apartment were at least two dozen small reproductions of paintings by the French Impressionists. Saturdays, she attended a life drawing class. She showed me a few of her sketches at a time. I thought they were sensuous, innocent, and promising, but what did I know? We wandered museums together and read poetry aloud and I tried to be encouraging. But the more she talked of school, the more I drifted back to the conviction that formal education drained the creative juices.

She sorted and sometimes delivered mail and lived in a studio apartment above Chinatown. I delivered telegrams and lived close to the streets. She insisted on knowing everything about me. Editing my report to downplay the gratuitous sex, meaningless drugs, and some of the obnoxious things I'd witnessed in the Haight, I told her about my rent-free apartment, how I was socking away most of my Western Union paychecks because I also ate free lunches at St. Anthony's Mission and dinner, often, in the park, courtesy of the Diggers. Sometimes there was music, Bay Area rock bands plugging their amps into houses along the panhandle. Pipes were lit, incense wafted, dancing. On any given day in the Haight you could chant with the tangerine-robed Hare Krishna devotees, hang out in the grocery store parking lot, eat peyote buttons with college dropouts from Oberlin or Bard or the University of Washington. You could crash parties given by people you'd never seen before. I downplayed the availability of sex and assured Irene that loveless balling in the bushes could not be compared with the religious ecstasies we experienced.

One weekend we went to my place, dropped acid, wandered the park, danced together, and paused to exchange deep thoughts or share moments of play and joy with marvelous strangers. When we started to come down a little from the effects of the acid, we bought apples and cheese and carried them to my apartment. We were discussing the texture of cheddar, its softness, velvet versus silk, when I felt her mood slip a little. Though she enjoyed the cheese, Irene said she really had to get back on the macrobiotic diet she'd been following. I was dealing silently with her expressed conviction that I should eat better when we heard a loud thump and shouting voices downstairs.

Irene looked alarmed. "What's going on down there? It sounds horrible, like people fighting or something."

"It is horrible," I admitted. "But if we are required to live out our karma in the bowels of Maya, we must grasp the potential for misunderstanding and learn to face a certain amount of difficulty...perhaps even horror."

"It sounds like they're throwing things downstairs. Are they your landlords?"

"In a way. They are also our lost brother and sister, Tom and Sandra, two sad junkies, probably fighting over the last of their heroin."

I got to my feet slowly. My knees were stiff.

"You're not going down there, are you?"

"Yes. I owe it to Brenda to keep them from hurting each other. That's the way I pay my rent." I gathered up apples and cheese and napkins, and with Irene behind me, started down the back steps.

Tom was already out in the back yard. At my urging, he stopped kicking pickets out of the fence and sat down on the steps. Irene went inside with Sandra. After a while, I gave them a ten-dollar bill and coaxed them into promising they'd share whatever dope they were able to score with it.

Irene and I went back upstairs and lit candles. We made love, ate more apples and cheese, and made love again. The nightly fog came in through the windows, the temperature dropped. We crawled naked into my sleeping bag and tried to wrestle each other into mutually comfortable positions. She loved the necessary tangling of our bodies, Irene said, but since the bag itself was a little rank, she suggested that we spend the next couple of nights at her place and have the sleeping bag dry-cleaned. After a time she wiggled out of the sleeping bag to search for her socks because her feet were getting cold and damp. To help her locate them, I lit a couple of fresh candles, then padded to the kitchen to turn the stove burners on. I brought her back a cup of tea, which she drank, wrapped in some of my shirts, half in and half out of the sleeping bag. She looked slight and childlike and said she was still chilled so I tore up a cardboard box in the kitchen and taped panels over the most gaping holes in the front windows.

She suggested we spend the last of the night at her place. I offered that we'd passed the coolest hours of the night already and that the heat from the kitchen was making its way in our direction. I didn't particularly want to pack up and go to her place, I explained, because I had to report for work in three hours and needed the shuteye I wouldn't get while we traveled to her apartment.

She changed the subject slightly. "Well, with some of the money you've been saving on rent, you should go ahead and have some windows put in up there."

"Yeah, okay, that's something to consider. But to tell you the truth, I don't know how long I'll be here, and I'm not really into putting money into this apartment."

"You're not going away, are you?"

"No, not like that, anyway. We'll be together, stay together. It's just that. . ."

"Just what?"

"Well, you know, if we had a car of some sort, we could get out of the city sometimes, see a few other places. I know from a friend exactly how to locate a particular hollowed out redwood tree in Big Sur. This guy spent two weeks there living in it, climbing down the cliffs to swim in the ocean every afternoon, seeing eagles and seals. Plus, there are other interesting places. I have a good friend named Rick up in Davis, another friend named Denny in Santa Barbara."

"So I guess being here for you in this apartment is kind of like training to camp in the tree in Big Sur then? It would be cool to sleep in a tree for a couple of nights, but I'm just talking now about regular life. I'll pay for the windows while you save for a car, if that's what you want."

"No, you need your money for art supplies and tuition. I'll tape up some more cardboard tomorrow and if it looks like you're going to be spending a lot of time over here, I'll have the windows fixed myself."

To my astonishment, she was crying.

"What's the matter?"

"Just the way you said that. I don't know. What do you mean *if* it looks like I'm going to be spending a lot of time over here? I mean, I don't want to be here unless I've been invited."

"Irene, this place is as much yours as mine. Everything of mine is yours, not that there's much that's mine. But you know, the rain's not much of a problem because of the awnings over the windows, and this is as cold as it has ever been here. Anyway, like we were saying, there are some comforts that make us too soft and timid to really enjoy life as it really is. To be a little chilly, I mean, what could be more natural, what could make us more certain we're really alive?"

"I'm already certain we're alive, Tim. Even the beasts of the field seek comfort when they can find it."

Rather than argue, I sat in silence and tried to figure out what it was we were failing to understand or communicate.

Irene propped herself up on an elbow. "Its only a twenty-minute bus ride to my place," she said, rearranging my hair for a better view of my face. "It's dry and warm there, the bed's big enough for both of us, and I've got some miso soup I could heat up."

"I'm so wiped out I don't think I could eat any soup."

When she said nothing, I opened my eyes and saw she was crying again. "What's the matter?"

"Nothing. It just seems like you don't care quite as much about my comfort this week as you did last week."

"Don't cry. I'll get you a sweater. Of course, I care about your comfort."

"I don't really *want* a sweater."

"Come on, Babe. Think dry warm thoughts. Wait, I know. I've got a spanking clean towel. You can get up and take a hot shower."

"Something's wrong. Last week, you jumped at the slightest suggestion I was uncomfortable."

"I don't know," I said. "Maybe last week you would never have admitted you were uncomfortable. You were feeling more adventurous. Maybe you're getting your period. You know what we could do is drag the sleeping bag in next to the stove where it's warmer. I don't know why I didn't think of that before."

"I'm not getting my period and I'd rather be cold than breathe oven gas, even in a drafty apartment."

"You're really having a bad time, aren't you? I mean, I have to be at work in three hours." Having said it, I flashed on the stupid, job-bound middle-aged man I was dedicated never to become. A long period of time went by. "You're quiet," I said. "You feeling more comfortable?"

"No. I'm just wondering what's more important: my health or flattering the vanity of the man I thought loved me."

"If it's come to that, I guess it's up to you to decide what is important to you. Just as it is up to me to decide what's important to me."

"You're right," she said, slithering out of the bag. "What's important to me is to go home."

"Okay." I climbed out of the bag and reached for my pants.

"What are you doing?"

"I'll go with you."

"No. You decided already."

"You're right," I said, smarting, yet wicked with pride. "But your safety comes first. I'll see you home and come back here."

"No," she said. "You won't."

"But I won't sleep for worrying about you alone on the streets the middle of the night."

She was angry now. "Fine, I'll get dressed, borrow some of your clothes, and sit out near the stove while you sleep."

"No, because the oven gas would make you sick."

"You're right. No sense in being a child about this. I'll take a cab."

"I'll get dressed and see that you get one. In fact, I'll pay your cab fare."

"No, just use your share of the money for windows, if they become important to you. Or a car, which I guess you'd rather have than me."

"I guess maybe you weren't all that interested in camping at Big Sur." I was disgusted with myself, but desperate to show that I, too, was subject to hurt and disillusionment.

"We'll save that discussion for another occasion," she said. "I hope you understand that I don't feel like talking or doing anything but getting home and warm right now."

"Okay, but there is no way that you can keep me from walking out there and waiting until you get a cab."

"Since that's the easiest way to end this discussion, I won't object. Then you can hurry back to get the sleep you need."

We walked out together in the fog. We stood in furious silence and disappointment and grief until the gods sent us a cabbie. We looked at each other and could not kiss. I didn't sleep the rest of the night.

After two days I forced myself to go to a pay phone. She cried and blamed herself. I told her to stop crying, that it was all my fault. We met at a coffee house in North Beach where we sat over cappuccino and dessert, pale and haggard, unable to talk without apologizing and becoming confused again. We made small talk between vague, tiny apologies, furious with each other and ourselves, needy hands sneaking toward the hand of the other. After a time I pinned both her hands to the table with one of mine, stared in her eyes, and said I was stubborn.

"You are stubborn," she agreed. "But the problem was one of my own making. I've been eating all wrong for me. Too much sugar and meat and rich food. The thing is, though I love sharing everything with you, I'm much more agreeable when I'm eating right. You probably would feel a little better too, feel less stubborn, if you ate healthier food."

"It wasn't the food," I said. "At least for me. I was just overtired."

"Well, maybe. I don't think you're quite as sanpaku as I am."

"Sanpaku?"

"It's Japanese for spiritually unbalanced. You can see it in the size and shape of the eyes. I've got to start cooking more for both of us."

It suddenly dawned on me that if I didn't manage to assume more responsibility for our lover's quarrel, I was going to end up eating a lot of food that didn't appeal to me. "In no way was it all that much your fault," I said. "I was stubborn and unsympathetic and didn't realize you weren't as used to the cold as I am. The thing is we'd exhausted our patience on Tom and Sandra when we should have saved it for ourselves. Besides, truly conscious lovers require, absolutely require, flexibility. The art of give and take. You were more giving. I was the more taking."

The next night, I picked up a dozen white roses and two bottles of imported beer and went to Irene's for dinner. I did my best to enjoy a helping of plain brown rice, bread so crunchy it hurt my gums and teeth, and a bitter soup made of fish and burdock root. I tasted everything very carefully and encouraged myself to be more open-minded toward all the things she cared about.

I had planned to stay the night at her place and probably would have if she hadn't said how she was looking forward to sleeping at my place and that she'd seen a couple of blankets she planned to buy me. I stiffened a little, thanked her for her generous thoughts, told her how much it would mean to me for her to stay the whole night there, then said I had to check on Sandra and Tom and took a cable car to Market Square.

Back home I couldn't sleep or concentrate on reading. What was bothering me was less my fib about Sandra and Tom or my disquiet that she didn't find the life I'd chosen quite comfortable enough for her, than the loss of the exhilaration I had come to expect just being in her presence. The next evening, I telephoned from the corner to say how busy I expected to be for a few days, then went home bothered by how content she seemed with my announcement.

The next day I met this chick named Susie from Nebraska. Since she was newly arrived with a girlfriend who was downtown job-hunting, I offered to show her a few of the sites in the neighborhood. Some people were playing guitars in the park, we listened and smoked a joint, then danced barefoot together in the grass. After a while I took her home for sex. When she had to leave to meet up with her girlfriend, I took her address, promised to drop by, and spent the rest of the evening by myself, waiting for the onslaught of guilt and remorse that never came. I wanted to be thinking about Irene, but I was thinking about Susie.

I met Irene for lunch in a downtown park a couple days later. She didn't ask what I'd been doing with myself, and I wondered if she didn't ask because she didn't want me to ask the same of her. She sat close and we held hands between bites of brown rice she was eating and the chicken sandwich I enjoyed. I denied feeling as though anything was wrong between us, but in fact I was brooding that maybe my fling with Susie had impaired my ability to see Irene again as the angel I knew her to be.

Irene was extolling the virtues of buckwheat and seaweed while I was thinking about a Mexican restaurant Susie had told me about, imagining greasy tacos and beer and maybe another frolic with Susie on top of my sleeping bag. Maybe somehow, by seeing and screwing and getting over Susie, I would rediscover what I was missing in Irene. I wanted to rediscover Irene, I was sure, even more than I wanted to undress Susie again. I finished my sandwich, somebody in the park lit an incense stick, and Irene said how much she was looking forward to making love with me again, how much she wished she didn't have to go back to work. I kissed her when she said this, but faked the passion, partly to hide from her the fact that I was less than excited by the prospect of another boring heap of brown rice.

The next day I proposed to take Irene to this place I'd heard about in Fisherman's Wharf. I had heard they served brown rice and fresh veggies, I said.

"Only if you really want to." She was starting to cry again, dabbing her cheeks very quietly. Most girls I'd known could cry without sacrificing whatever it was that attracted me to them. But crying spoiled Irene's looks. "Only if you care enough," she added.

"You know I do."

"I know you say you do. The thing is, I believe you. But as soon as I believe you, right away I wonder if I believe you because you're telling me how you feel or because I want to believe you still feel what you once felt. I have to go." She stood up. "I'm late getting back from lunch."

I hugged and kissed her. Worried that my affection was less than wholly convincing, I found myself bending her backward, hugging too hard. Since when did our mutual exhilaration in each other ever require such theatrics? I couldn't be sure, but I thought she asked herself this question as she winced and walked down Powell Street.

At the Mexican place, the tacos weren't much, the beer was too warm and flat, and Susie was nowhere to be found. If she was at her apartment, she wasn't answering the buzzer or the telephone. I stopped off at a coffee joint on Haight Street, where I ran into Albert Fine.

Outside, three teenage boys were panhandling and putting on a show for passersby. Albert paid up, suggested a walk, and we stepped outside. The boys waved their sign at us.

"Please give us some bread so we can buy drugs."

Albert's response was to laugh and dance a little jig. Once he managed to get the attention of the crowd, I knew he'd do something with it. He put his hand in his pocket and moved toward the tallest of the boys. The kid held out a long hand for the change he expected, but Albert took his forearm, pulled it, and towed him into a big, wet kiss, planted squarely and wetly on the lips. The audience howled and laughed and clapped. The kid, too stunned to wipe the drool off his face, went bright red as Albert slipped a dollar bill in his shirt pocket.

"It's for a drug," Albert laughed. "The drug doesn't get you high, but it cures the venereal disease you're sure to contract from kissing dirty old queers on the street. You were wonderful last night, but what would your mother say to such forbidden love?"

The kid was mortified. His buddies studied him with worried expressions.

"This miracle drug also speeds you through the agony of adolescence," Albert said. "Oh, just look at you. Aren't you a stunned and infected little specimen."

The kid dropped his sign and ran across the street as fast as he could. His buddies called his name and jogged after him.

Albert continued to work his audience for a time. Finally he turned to me. "Forget love. It's all about trust. Isn't trust something?" he said. "We die wanting it, or we die conferring it." He had a hand on both my shoulders and looked mischievously into my eyes. I knew he wouldn't try to kiss me but had the idea that he wanted to shake me. "I'm not sure there's anything quite like trust," he added.

I never saw Albert again after that evening, but years later I would remember his words about trust. I would remember them quite a few times.

One of the most difficult things in life is to force yourself to walk away from anything that you think you had. As for Irene, there came a time when it was hard for us to be together, but harder still to be apart. When we quarreled, we blamed the other for being unable to understand; when we made up, we blamed ourselves for being unable to say what we meant. You could go on trying to identify your viewpoint, even fighting over it for hours. Neither of us ever got the viewpoint totally explained or communicated to each other, but it always seemed that we were just a few hours, tears, or phrases from the bliss of our first week together.

One Saturday morning while Irene was attending a life drawing class, I walked the streets of my neighborhood looking for used cars and vans with "For Sale" signs in their windows. The party was long over; the neighborhood was changing and I had stayed too long in it. The vestiges of joy and vitality had been choked with violence, dirt and an overweening opportunism. Most of those who had moved into the neighborhood for its promise of community had long since departed, leaving behind armies of empty strangers in search of an audience.

The Hell's Angels had taken to parking their Harleys in front of the donut shop where, when things got dull or the beer ran out, they knocked the teeth out of the excessively dewy-eyed or butt-kicked and tormented drunks and junkies, who were now everywhere underfoot, ducking the cops, scavenging change, drugs, and food, and talking empty talk to the would-be revolutionaries and button sellers. Top 40 Radio was playing a song about going to San Francisco and wearing flowers in your hair. Lost souls and tourists were clogging up Haight Street all the way to the park, beating the bushes in search of grooviness, unaware that the hunting grounds had been depleted and despoiled, and that the neighborhood was filling up with high school kids and suburban divorcees in costume. Everybody was looking for what had been for a few moments, but was no longer around.

The bored audience had come down out of the bleachers and the roustabouts had taken over the circus. Families were jamming the Haight-Ashbury district, cruising in search of safe areas to park their mobile homes and walk to incense shopping. The grasses of Golden Gate Park were littered with empty beer bottles and the air was filled with soap bubbles and fake joy. Cameras were everywhere. Tourists posed for newer tourists. I had been thinking about this too long, was trying to stop thinking about it, was struggling to be loving and compassionate toward all sentient beings, and was wondering about the reliability of an old Chevy van with a "For Sale" sign on its windshield, when a girl I'd never seen before put her hand on my arm and looked knowingly into my eyes.

She wore a new leather vest over a tie-dyed dress. Her red-tinted sunglasses were shaped into five-pointed stars. Fixed in her hair was a leather diadem, hand-beaded with alternating peace and yin-yang symbols. I thought the costume was excessive but, trying to overcome my "judgment visions" and find a better vantage point from which to view both her and the degenerating neighborhood, I smiled and nodded. She extended a paper plate on which was an arrangement of sugar cubes, each soggy with a dollop of deep blue. Around her long neck she wore a small sign that read, "Free Whee."

"What is this?" I asked.

"Peace be unto you, holy brother," she said, extending me the goodies, "long may you befriend what is and walk among the blessed."

She continued to gaze at me with a rapt expression until I understood that she would not answer my question with a fact. Looking at my watch, I noted that it was six hours before I was due to meet Irene. Taking the blue tinting on the sugar cubes for psilocybin, a psychedelic drug I had heard was around but never tried, I smiled and popped a cube in my mouth.

"Thank you very much," I said. "And be careful. Avoid the area around the grocery store. There were two narcs with cameras over there a few minutes ago."

"Careful is as careful does," she said, smiling and skipping off.

With the sweetness lingering in my mouth, clouds billowing in out of the west, and the wind picking up, I headed back to my apartment for soup and a sweater. An anticipatory edginess came over me. I wanted to clear my mind, order my surroundings, and reaffirm my goodwill toward men before the potent hallucinogen began to take its effect.

Upstairs, I put a Joe Tex record on my thrift store turntable, ate soup with old bread and cherries, and rolled out my sleeping bag and two new blankets, hoping to persuade Irene to come back to my still-windowless apartment after dinner. I set out fresh candles, washed dishes, and watered my small houseplant.

Looking out my kitchen window, I saw Tom, the junkie from downstairs, sitting at a table he'd made from a door and a stack of cinderblocks. Wondering if I had any mail, I went down the back steps.

"Hey Tom," I said, "how's it going?"

Tom handed me a pipe in which there was no hit left for me to take and drank from a can of beer. "It's going by," he muttered, "by, by, by."

"Indeed it is," I agreed, handing him back the pipe. "How's Sandra?'

"Don't know, don't care."

"You doing okay?"

"I am somewhat fucked up if that's what you mean. But I am not fucked-up enough. And since you ask, I am enormously pissed and offended, okay?"

"At me? At Sandra?"

"Everybody. The only time Sandra wants to screw is when I'm too fucked up to get hard. Otherwise, she's a bitch and a half and won't let me near her. The CIA's all over this neighborhood, and you, now you're standing there with that idiot mask of cosmic serenity, smiling at me, Mister-fucking-blue-lips. Just like everybody else walking by."

"Blue lips?"

"Yeah. It's all over now, Baby Blue Lips. I don't suppose you've looked in a mirror lately?"

"In fact, yes. And I can't help but notice that your lips are blue, too. Last time you took psychedelics you said it was the last time ever, until you'd kicked the needle. Remember, Tom, the last time you dropped acid you got a little wigged out."

"Yes, I did get wigged out, fuck-you very much, Mister Cosmic Parole Officer, and having already thanked you for helping me out repeatedly, I'm going to tell you something that you may understand and you may not. You and I have been snookered and fookered, my friend."

"'Snookered and fookered?' How's that?"

"Just look at us, man. Blue-faced and primed all up. You're convinced that the universe is composed of a few personal friends wigged out on Buddha bliss and a zillion confused people waiting for you to help them get into the consciousness game. And that just ain't how it is. No way."

207

"You've been thinking a lot about how things are?"

"No, because I know how they are, Barlow, and they are fucking over. I mean, since you're not stoned by now like you thought a little while ago that you were going to be, suppose you just stand here and think about a little bit about that lump of sweetness one of those CIA hippies handed out to you. Think about it Baby Blue Lips."

"You're feeling negative vibes, Tom. We've got to get beyond them to have good thoughts and feelings, man, to be able to handle this drug. We don't want to get stuck in all that stuff about trees and demons and shit we went through last time, remember?"

"Get off it! Don't you know there's still a war on? That you and I have enemies because I was over in the shit in Nam and saw through the myth of America-the-free and because you weren't? What this blue ink and shit all over our faces means is that I'm probably going to be all right and that your conscientious-objector peacenik ass is probably fucking going to croak. Ha! Maybe I should call a priest. You want the last rights and shit?"

"Not yet," I said.

"You don't know it yet, but they been all over up here, man, right here in your little piece of lysergic heaven. They hate your ass because you counsel peace and an end to the war. But the fuckin' thing you don't see, for all your dancing Buddhas and paisley goddesses, is that though they hate me, they need me. I'm a source of profit, man, because the cash I lay out to shoot heroin every week keeps the fuckin' marines in bullets. And they know I ain't going to make 'em make peace as long as I get my heroin. They don't need you, though, because you're not an addict. You're just some cosmic dreamer peace creep among other cosmic peace creeps. You're going to die as an example, a deterrent to dreamers coming up behind you."

"You're coming on pretty strong pretty fast, man. Maybe we should go upstairs. I got some lemons and sugar for lemonade. Somebody gave me an Otis Redding record."

"We're different tones of blue around our mouths, man. They gave me that ink-soaked sugar cube as a warning, but they probably went ahead and fucking poisoned you."

"You remember talking about this crap last time, the impending sense of gloom and doom, the conviction that evil enemies want to destroy us? It never happened, and you thought it was going to. Remember talking about that book, *The Tibetan Book of the Dead?* What we're experiencing now is the beginning of those horrific bardos, those netherworlds through which the newborn soul must pass. We're about to rush, psychedelic style, and we can duck the worst of the shit if we just sit down somewhere and get a little quiet. What it is about is ego anxiety, the basic fear that if we are no longer in control, controlling others and deluding ourselves about how important we are, we cannot flourish? But we can. We can flourish and learn to look at the past and understand. We've got to live and get on with things, without always measuring how wonderful or horrible we are, without comparing ourselves to others."

"Compare? You don't compare with others at all, bro. Thou art the thing itself. Problem is the thing itself ain't nothing but an addle-brained moron filled with trust. They've busted your little red balloon and poisoned you, Harry Hippie, or tried to. From all the blue lips on the street I'd say there's probably a couple of hundred people going to check out of this vale of tears by sundown. Pretty soon you're going to see that it's a fucking CIA warning to everybody. 'Cool it with the cosmic revolution, kids, because if you don't, we're going to start poisoning your asses, putting arsenic and other poisons in sugar cubes and handing them out to you daisy-eyed dipshits looking for a free high.' People like you will go down in smoke, Barlow, because you think everybody that walks down the street with a bit of beard or a bead is your holy angel friend, when in fact, he's more than likely the fuckin' CIA secretary for the FBI, man!"

Tom stood up and stomped into the house, slamming the screen door, then the other door, throwing bolts, snapping locks, and shutting windows.

Later that evening I sat in the hallway of Irene's apartment building using a soft drink cup for an ashtray.

"Sorry, I'm late," Irene said, looking at her watch. "Actually, I guess you were early."

"I guess."

"What's the matter?"

"Nothin' much."

"Your lips are all black. What have you been eating, blueberries?"

"Yeah, something like that."

"You're lips and mouth are really blackened."

"I know." I got to my feet. "You got any toothpaste in there, an old toothbrush maybe?"

"Sure, come on in."

In the bathroom, I soaped up a washcloth and rubbed my lips until they were raw. I brushed my teeth, getting most of the blue off them. But even bathroom cleanser wouldn't get the blue off my lips. Finding a bottle of mouthwash, I gargled and spit in the sink.

"You look upset," Irene said. "Are you all right?"

"Yeah, I'll tell you about it in a little while."

"You've still got a lot of blue on your lips...and some on your teeth."

"Yeah, I know. Can we please talk about something else for a little while?"

Irene stepped back and gave me a look all loaded up with tender understanding. "If you don't want to be with me tonight," she said, "we can make it another time."

"No, it's not that. Not that at all. In fact, I've been really looking forward to seeing you. Look, if you don't mind walking around with a man with blue lips I'll take you to Chinatown and we'll eat like pigs."

She kissed me. I pushed her ever so gently back and looked at her. At least the blue on my mouth didn't transfer to hers. I shrugged and kissed her again and felt much better. We held hands all the way down the hill.

It wasn't until I finished my spicy shrimp and vegetables in black bean sauce that I felt up to telling her that Tom and I had taken ink-stained sugar cubes thinking we were being given psilocybin. I told her about Tom's outraged paranoia and about my own deepening disillusionment. "I guess I'm getting the message that the impossible bubble has been popped and I ought to be a little less trusting of strangers, and a little more loving and trusting toward the people in my life who deserve my trust and love," I said.

Hearing this, Irene was radiant. I looked at her, certain the powerful exhilaration I'd been missing was about to return.

Three months later I came up with rent money, and Irene and I moved into a one-bedroom apartment down the block from the one where she'd been living on Hyde Street. One morning she got up from the breakfast table, went into the bathroom for a long time and, on returning, very quietly told me that while I was free to do whatever I wanted, she was not staying in California because she was pregnant. She said she had decided not to tell me about her pregnancy until the morning of my day off, right before she had to leave for work. She wanted me to have the luxury of reflecting before speaking to think about what a baby would mean to her life and could mean to my own. Standing briefly in the doorway on her way out, she added that for reasons she would talk to me about that night, she wanted to move back to Denver.

After the self-locking door snapped behind her, I put my head down next to my empty coffee cup on the tiny table in our kitchen and kept it there. Moments later I went to the window and watched her walk briskly toward the bus stop.

Irene was beautiful. But even as she became physically more familiar, she became psychologically and emotionally more mysterious. She seemed too young and unprepared to be a mother, and too strange and lacking in what I considered discernment to sleep next to me for the rest of my life. When I first met her, she'd been surrounded by a coterie of bearded postmen, an odd assortment of eccentric suitors, and wimpy male friends. Most seemed obsessed with feelings and vague intuitions. In talking to a few of them, I learned that many of them tended to see in the placidity of her face and depth of her dark eyes indicators of spiritual wisdom. In a way I couldn't altogether attribute to my own deficiencies of tolerance, I blamed Irene for enjoying rather than dispelling this impression. In fact, while her smile looked mystical, it was often a mask through which it was impossible to see.

She had been a small outspoken child, slapped, made fearful, and forced to acknowledge the will of bigger, stronger bodies in her mother's family, the Escobars. Cousins and friends of cousins in the neighborhood where she had grown up had bullied and tormented her when she'd been a child, she said, punishing her for her shows of honest candor.

In Denver, the Escobars owned a huge old house that had been converted to a restaurant downstairs and to an apartment upstairs for the family matriarch, Gramma Escobar. In addition to cooking up the finest *chiles rellenos* "this side of the Rio Grande," the Hacienda Escobar, as the restaurant was called, served as a family center where aunts, uncles, cousins, nieces, nephews, and their lovers and boyfriends and girlfriends and husbands and wives gathered to serve customers, to play and sing sentimental songs from Mexico, to modify traditional recipes, celebrate engagements and baptisms, drink beer, watch bullfight films, and analyze and aggravate longstanding family feuds.

A family legend, involving gold, kept them together. From Irene I'd learned that many of the Escobars were persuaded that Pancho Villa had befriended Irene's great-grandfather Jose. Per the legend, the latter had provided the kerosene lanterns by the light of which the notorious outlaw had buried a chest of loot under the house foundations. It seemed that several aunts and cousins believed that when enough of the Escobars had said the rosary a few thousand times, the restaurant would no longer be needed for family cohesion. Then, the house would be closed or demolished and even the most despised and alienated Escobars, among whom Irene numbered herself, would live happily ever after thanks to painstakingly and equitably distributed shares of bandit gold. According to family principles of justice, its source was unimportant and any unearthed gold would rightly belong to the Escobars, constituting a sort of *wergeld* for centuries of persecution endured by the family's Mayan ancestors.

Irene held that the family claim to Mayan Indian blood was probably bunkum, and was an expression of bourgeois disdain for the downtrodden Denver-based Mexican-Americans, among whom the Escobars lived a little uneasily. One afternoon at the library I pored over a book on Mayans and became a believer or maybe a desperate investor, not in the gold but in the Mayan ancestors thing. Though darker-skinned and rougher-looking than Irene, the brightly dressed women smiling in the glossy family and historic photographs shared her shapely eyebrows, large dark eyes, and heart-shaped face. When I mentioned this to Irene, she accused me of seeing things not there.

From shared letters I knew that Irene's mother hoped that she would soon permanently return to Denver, waitress at the family restaurant, and enroll part time in college. A few months back, when I observed that this was an opportunity Irene neither relished nor seemed to take seriously, she got testy. "Why should I?" she said. "The job offer comes from the parents of cousins, and in some cases the cousins themselves, who once called me a paddy, hit me with sticks, and chased me down the street with bottle openers."

Obviously something, probably her pregnancy, had changed Irene's thinking about Denver, if not about her mother's family and working in the restaurant. Now, out of the blue and with great ambivalence, she wanted to go back to her tempestuous, if loving, mother, return to the large musical family fold of the frightening and the frightened. Perhaps she hoped Maria, remarried now and enjoying a fuller life, would somehow prepare her for the impending shock of motherhood.

Maternity was mysterious but guaranteed, I thought. But who, I wondered, might prepare me for the shock of paternity? I didn't want to be a father. I didn't want to go to Denver. Yet neither did I want Irene to be a mother or move to Denver without me. Filled with misgivings, and fighting the pessimism that I was sure to make the wrong, irrevocable choice, I carried a notebook containing poems and musings up to Haight Street and drew up a list I called "Arguments for Denver."

1. Because my semen has fertilized a human life.
2. Because there is no lasting human happiness.
3. Because there might be a transient thing called human happiness.
4. Because I don't know what else to do.
5. Because I am tired of sleeping in a damp sleeping bag, then I reminded myself I now slept in a warm, dry bed; the sleeping bag was rolled-up in the closet.

6. Because I am responsible, or maybe because I am weary of being irresponsible.

7. Because I am deluded.

8. Because I am in love and will soon realize it again.

9. Because I am afraid of what will happen if I don't.

10. Because I am sometimes excited by the idea that something good and enduring might happen even if I don't know what it will be.

After a long time I added a last entry.

11. Because I'd like to go trout fishing again with my grandpa.

Persuaded I might add to or elaborate on my list at a later time, I tore it out of the notebook and folded it in my back pocket. It was still there, having been transferred to several other pockets, three weeks later when I tossed it in among the soiled paper towels in the Men's Room at the San Francisco bus station just before boarding the Greyhound bus for Colorado. Irene was saving me a window seat.

I had telephoned my grandpa long distance the night before. He had seemed depressed and said his feet had been bothering him and that the weather had been bad. Trout fishing was only a maybe.

Not surprisingly, he kept steering the conversation away from fishing. "Your mom tells us her name is Irene," he said at one point. "Your grandma and I are looking forward to meeting the woman of your life."

THE Woman. Of your LIFE.

I had not responded well to Lester's curiosity about Irene. Neither had I mentioned the fetus OF MY LIFE, by volunteering that Irene was pregnant or suggesting he prepare for the dubious pleasures of great-grandfatherhood.

I wanted to leave unchecked the friendly, dreamy voice in me which kept suggesting that the magical-psychedelic-super-enlightened-baby-to-be might look deeply into the tormented hearts and deformed minds of its intended parents and decide that it was better to dissolve than miscarry, by which I thought I meant split painlessly back into the netherworld in search of more mature, reliable custodians. Yet it was also being said that babies would be the harbingers of the new consciousness, whatever exactly that was going to be. I liked to think it was possible that some better, fuller life for both Irene and me might come out of parenthood. Although it seemed a good and worthy hope, I found it difficult to sustain for more than a few minutes at a time.

On the bus back to Denver, at a roadside breakfast stop, pancake syrup oozed down my fork onto my hand. When I finished my hotcakes and lit a smoke, my gluey fingers adhered to the cigarette paper and I burned my index finger. Dabbing at the stickiness, I ripped a paper napkin and it crumbled into strange shapes. Tiny rags of paper adhered to my thumb. Back aboard the eastbound bus, I worried these shreds and studied the pink blister on my finger.

Shortly after the bus rolled into a gray wooden town just over the Utah border, Irene and I got off for lunch. She ordered a salad. I asked for coffee and a grilled cheese.

When the waitress brought our order, Irene folded up the magazine she'd been reading, and began stabbing at a drab salad brightened with cherry tomatoes.

"It was an interesting article," she reported. "Did you know that breast-fed babies are more disease-resistant than babies who are given bottles?"

"Uh, no. I didn't."

"Even more interesting, statistics seem to indicate that most Americans who end up in mental institutions and prisons were bottle-fed babies."

"Uhhuh, that's interesting."

"The thing is, my breasts are so small and I'm worried I won't have enough milk."

Irene didn't seem to mind if I looked at women with small breasts but had let me know more than once that she didn't like me ogling the well-endowed. Hoping to spare myself another conversation about the infantilism of the adult male and the meaning of breasts to a man, and ever eager to avoid the topics of babies, and parenting, I spoke without much conviction. "Your breasts are lovely and you'll be fine." I looked out the restaurant window, tapped my fingers on the table and noticed Irene looking at me expectantly, tolerantly waiting for me to change the subject.

"You know," I responded, "I was just thinking. When the bus gets to Ogden, maybe we should layover. I mean, there are buses heading for Denver all the time, just hours apart."

"Why layover? What's in Ogden?"

I shrugged and fingered my water glass. "I don't know. Unemployment, sheepherders, down-and-out Mormons, I guess. But maybe we could take a look at our money and get a good deal on a car, better than anything we could get in Denver, I mean."

"We resolved that issue already, didn't we? Once we're settled we'll have to buy a car. But to buy a car now in Ogden, one we could depend on to get us to Denver, would cost too much money, especially until we have a place to live."

"The thing is, cars'll be cheaper there. We could get a little more car for our money. Plus, we could get to Denver faster. In fact, we could probably cash-in our bus tickets and eat grocery store food the rest of the way."

Irene speared a tomato and smeared it in the pond of dressing in the bottom of her bowl. "Yes, but we might also break down on the highway. I don't mean to be negative, but I've just been reading how prenatal stress on the mother is a significant cause of miscarriages and birth defects."

I shrugged and conceded the argument. "What about the effects on the mother and fetus of prolonged confinement in an airless bus with assorted depressed military personnel and old women who wear plastic flower corsages?"

Irene laughed and patted my hand. "We made a plan," she said, "Can't we just stick with it?"

"Okay," I sighed.

Back aboard the bus again, Irene grumbled about the frigid air-conditioning, wrapped herself in a *serape*, and then fell asleep. I tried to read *Women in Love*, the D.H. Lawrence novel that I had hoped might either teach me what I didn't know about women or myself, or magically rekindle the explosive vanished intimacy that once was between us. Unable to concentrate, I marked my place, closed the book, and tried to remember anything at all that might have led us to the polite, mechanical companionship I began to find stifling. While she slept next to me, her face gently lit by the Utah sun, it seemed a good time for me to begin trying to see her for who she had been and maybe still was. And what was wrong with me that I found it so hard to love her? Something seemed broken in each of us. I couldn't find a deep fault in her; what was wrong between us had to be somewhere within me.

On the other hand, perhaps, her presence or absence in my life had nothing to do with my own shortcomings. Maybe all my faults stemmed from forest-fire hopes and unreasonable expectations. If the Buddha was right in claiming that all existence was suffering, then being a contemporary karma-encumbered human being with an evolving consciousness probably called for nothing so much as buckling down and some sort of hip *sangfroid*, what the sages had once commended as detachment. Yet how could I be sure the sages had been as enlightened as their disciples claimed? Particularly so when I thought I saw it reflected in others: the Buddhist-like detachment I sometimes aspired to often looked like an indifferent passivity. Was the Buddha really blissed out by some cosmic consciousness, or had he simply been a convincing actor, stymied and in need of attention, a sort of early Tim Leary without the ancient glittering eyes? Then again, if Buddha was wrong, and if, for example, his followers were confused, and some sort of concrete happiness did exist, I supposed it must be compatible only with staying put, an experience I had spurned and missed, a bliss conferred only on those who allowed themselves to take root and deny the thousands of better places in the world. Was it possible that all that made one place look better than another was the illusion that a particular locale was inhabited by people who knew the secret of staying put and not feeling disappointed and stranded?

When our bus arrived in Denver late the next morning, Gordon was waiting for us just outside the door of the bus. The exaggerated cap and cab driver's uniform made him look smaller and younger. While Irene stood over our luggage, Gordon followed me to a dusty room to claim boxes and suitcases Irene and I had shipped ahead.

When we could fit nothing more in the trunk and were arranging things in the back seat, I looked at Irene. "You know what's missing? My sleeping bag."

"It's not missing," Irene said. "We didn't bring it."

"*We* didn't bring it?"

"Okay, *I*. In my hurry and efforts to be real I left it on the street. Somebody will get good use out of it."

"You left it in San Francisco?"

"Tim, it was worn out. The stuffing was coming loose from the seams. It smelled of campfire smoke and mildew. We've got plenty of blankets and people to help us find the things that we need. You can get a new sleeping bag, a better one."

"Don't worry about it," Gordon said. "We've got a good mattress put down for you in our second bedroom."

I ignored Gordon. "You should have asked me."

Gordon elbowed me playfully. "Whatever happened to the gypsy monk who hated private property?"

I pivoted away from him and stepped toward Irene. "It meant something to me."

She sighed. "What did it mean?"

"It meant campfires when I was a Boy Scout, desert creek beds, empty beaches. I slept in that sleeping bag everywhere. When I was sent home from San Diego, I paid Rick a fortune to have it shipped back to Denver. I slept in it when I hitched to San Francisco."

Irene said, "I'm sorry. It was torn and it smelled bad. We were limited by what we could send out. You never said anything to me about this mysterious attachment, so I didn't see any point in keeping it. You're right and I'm wrong. I'm sorry."

I shrugged and turned my head away to spit on the sidewalk. "Well, hell," I said. "You're right. I'm the one who should be sorry. It was just another object in a world of objects." Unfortunately, saying so wasn't quite the same as believing it or accepting its loss. I was surprised and disappointed in myself. I smiled at Gordon, patted Irene's arm, and sat in the front seat studying the meter he hadn't turned on, looking out at the city where I didn't really want to be, wondering why I felt so bereft over the loss of an old sleeping bag.

Gordon talked of driving a cab. He was off cough syrup altogether, he said, mostly out of politics, smoking a little pot, and enjoying, as we soon would too, the last bounty from the vegetable garden he and Rhonda had tended all summer.

We traveled east and south to a rural pie slice of land surrounded by burgeoning real estate developments, bordered on one side by a huge empty field belonging, Gordon said with an enigmatic smirk, to a nearby cemetery. Small houses, most of which were in disrepair, stood on three-and-four-acre tracts. The silent fields had once grown truck farm vegetables. Now the untended yards and fields were littered with plows and strange big objects, tools acquired years before in moments of self-reliance. They were rusting now, unnecessary to the way things had developed or failed to develop, too unwieldy and expensive to junk, at least until weather had rendered them a little more useless.

I would learn the houses were occupied by the sons and daughters and grandchildren and great-grandchildren of the truck farmers. Gordon said most of the property owners in the area were waiting for bankers and suburban real estate developers. They were all eager, he said, to put more distance between themselves and their families and the evils of the city, even if the distance was just four or five miles, to move out to a new suburban paradise characterized by self-cleaning ovens, automatic garage doors, and automated porch lights.

The bungalow he and Rhonda were renting, Gordon explained, was one of many that had recently been attracting the attention of hippies and freaks, who all seemed to be looking for some safe place where they could put into practice Leary's utopian, vaguely agrarian call to "Turn on, tune in, drop out."

We pulled into a long gravel driveway guarded by two spruce trees. When Rhonda came out of the yellow house to meet Irene and help us with our things, Gordon explained that his rent was due next week and that he'd be back in time for supper. Then he drove off in his cab, the yellow of his cab seeming, perhaps owing to the angle of sunlight, to tint the color of the dust cloud he left behind.

Once Irene and I arranged our boxes and luggage in the spare bedroom, Rhonda suggested a walk. As we ambled down the gravel streets, Rhonda said that expenses being what they were, she'd had to put aside her antiwar politics in favor of court reporting school. To bring in a little extra money, she'd been giving tarot card readings at local counterculture events. She'd always had this gift, she said, for predicting the future; she'd just buried it under politics.

At one graveled intersection three hippies blowing bubbles in the sunlight greeted us. But at the other end of the street, two men in bib overalls were visibly less pleased to see us. They left off removing the camper top from a rusty GMC pickup to stare at us and mutter unhappily. We were part of an infestation; there was no known spray.

"Excuse my Marxism," Rhonda said, when Irene perceived their hostility, "but it's class conflict, American style. Out here, you're either a hippie or a redneck. The rednecks hate hippies and find lots of little ways of showing it. They're threatened by the fact that a bunch of spoiled college dropouts like us profess to disdain all the middle-class trappings that they themselves never had but still want very much. The locals are as dedicated as can be to keeping neighborhood property values from falling by renting only to white people. Problem is, it's only the draft-dodging longhairs and part-time university hippies who seem interested in living out here. Many of the rednecks own houses that they inherited and need to rent, and only the freaks seem interested. To make their monthly expenses the rednecks are willing to rent to subtly disguised hippies, but object to the more overt hippies their neighbors rent to. The collective fantasy that unites all the locals is that one day the bankers and construction people and developers will arrive, and all the freaks can be thrown out on their collectively unpatriotic asses."

Irene and Rhonda chattered like old friends about people and houses. I was drawn to the cars, the driveways, the yards. The locals seemed to favor black Chevy trucks with fur-lined rearview mirrors and rifle racks in the back windows. Older men with no need of working trucks typically drove smoky Oldsmobiles with bumper stickers advising others to love or leave America, or announcing for all the world to see that their vehicles were protected by Smith and Wesson. Front yards were littered with camper tops, refrigerators sans doors, and bits of kitschy statuary. The men I saw wore heavy boots and straw cowboy hats. Their wives chewed bubble gum, favored bright pants, loaded up on mascara, eye shadow, false fingernails, and draped their monstrous hair curlers with garish scarves. German Shepherds and Doberman Pinschers were the dogs of choice, well-cared-for fighting dogs. Thankfully, most were chained up.

The dreaded longhaired interlopers, I observed, favored VW Bugs or school buses or older vans. I'd seen their like before. Equipped with incense burners, dashboards would be embellished with crudely painted daisies, nuclear disarmament symbols, and yin-yang decals. Instead of Marlboros, they smoked pot rolled in tight little joints or packed in tiny pipes. Instead of convenience store beer, they drank ginseng tea and organic apple juice. They were partial to Afghan hounds or exotic-looking cats with bizarre names culled from the *Upanishads*. The women wore their hair long or braided, decked themselves with bone beads strung with rawhide thongs, and often sported hairy legs. Homemade tables stood in their cutback yards and there were often elaborate fire pits adjacent to vegetable gardens. Houses with doors open to the warming afternoon blared music by The Rolling Stones and Grateful Dead. Army surplus tents housed cousins and former lovers broken down on their way to Oregon or the Sierras. Naked tots with candy stuck in their hair chased shaggy cats into heaps of cans and other rural detritus.

Rhonda and Irene decided to head back to the house for lunch and a nap. I begged off by implying I wasn't hungry, then walked out of the sticks into the burbs to a burger stand where I ate and drank soda at an outdoor table. Afterwards I bought a newspaper and read it all, smoking cigarettes and sipping sour coffee.

Much to my own surprise I fretted about my abandoned sleeping bag. I had slept in it for years. Its stuffing needed attention and it stank, okay, but it stank of me, of the places I'd been; it smelled of dark places where I'd rolled it out, of bodily fluids, my own and those of a few others, of creosote, lavender, cigarette smoke, pot, sunscreen, sweat, chocolate ice cream I'd spilled on it. It had been a cocoon, a placenta, a time capsule. It weighed a ton, yes, but I had never been cold in it. I thought Irene had associated it with a freedom no longer in my future. She had thrown it out because to her it smelled of other women. I decided that, one day, under pressure from me, she would admit to this. I was surprised by my feelings. And lost.

On the way back to Gordon's house, I paused to watch a brown-and-white dog with ears like potholders pursue a tennis ball thrown high in the air by a lanky boy about fourteen. When I turned away, the dog bumped me behind the knee, then hopped back barking and inviting a wrestling match. When I lowered a hand in disinterested friendship I got stung by the dog's hard wet teeth. I pulled back as the boy ran up and kicked at the pooch.

"Rover! Bad dog! Don't bother this man."

Rover scooted off a few feet, then shrugged and slipped back to sniff my boots.

"He's not a bad dog," I said, "though it may be that he's been a little short-changed in the brains department."

The boy looked relieved. "Aww, he's better off without brains, anyway. If he had any brains he'd be unhappy. Isn't that right, Rover?"

The boy was bony and freckled. Adolescence and the hot outdoor air had browned and hardened him at his edges, crowding and impinging on the softer, whiter boy he'd been until very recently. I said, "You live around here?"

"Yep."

"Whereabouts?"

"Yonder. Next to the pink one. Titty pink, George calls it."

"You live in the pink or white one?"

"White." The boy looked at me and then at the dust on his shoes. "Never seen you around here before."

I enjoyed the way his curiosity overcame his caution. "Just been in town a few hours," I said. "You know any houses for rent around here?"

"How soon you gotta move?"

"I'm staying with friends, but if I was lucky to find it, I might snap up the right place."

"Well, there's a dinky cottage over on Beeler Street, maybe half a mile over toward that stand of cottonwoods." The boy wiped the saliva-soaked tennis ball on his pant leg and stuffed it in the back pocket of his pants. "Walk over there with you if you want, point you out the house."

"You don't have to do that."

"I was thinking about going thataway. Kid across the street's got a go-cart."

We ambled slowly in the warm evening sun. Long since bored by the smell of my boots, Rover trotted zigzag patterns through the weeds and dust, never ranging too far and frequently doubling back lest he miss out on some amusing human activity. The high September weeds scraped my boots and pants. "What's your name?"

"George Atkins."

"Pleased, George. Mine's Tim Barlow."

"Little George'd be better, though. My dad's Big George. He's still about two inches taller."

"About this time a couple of years out, I bet you'll be Big George and he'll be Little George."

"Maybe. But mom says if he don't cut back the drinkin', he may not live to see that come about."

"Big drinker, is he?"

"Medium-size man. Drinks like a damned giant."

"What about your mom?"

"Don't drink. Otherwise, I don't got much to say on the subject of her. Talks too much, won't let me feed Rover, calls him vermin, which I don't care for."

"She won't let you feed your dog?"

"Rover ain't really nobody's dog. Or maybe he's everybody's. Dumb old cat food-dish raider is what he is, ain't you, Rover? Sucks on lawn hoses or drinks from street puddles for his water and buddies up to everybody he sees." He laughed. "You ever see a dog eat a banana peel?

"A banana peel? No, don't think so."

"I never did either till I saw him do it. I didn't know whether he liked it or if he was just starved. I gave him an old hamburger and some gravy, then tried him on another banana peel. Still ate half of it."

We ducked under a length of barbed wire and emerged from the field at the edge of a dusty street. Little George pointed. "See that flagpole? Just go on over through that gate by the mailbox and knock on the door. I'm going to go on over this way and see if Paul's got his go-cart running."

"Nice talking to you, George," I said. George shrugged and I turned my attention to a freshly painted flagpole in front of a wooden house with bright green window frames. Old Glory was high enough to catch a breeze had there been one. But the flag looked a little faded. A sign hung on a steel gate brought me up short. "If you are a hippie not willing to fight and die for your country do not perseed past gate."

I felt a wet heat on my hand and noticed that Rover had licked me. Turning, I saw Little George shuffling my way, heavy-footed and raising small puffs of dust. His hands were too big to fit comfortably into the front pockets of his worn-out pants. Between the tops of his stretched socks and the bottoms of his pants were lengths of white shins.

I spoke first. "Nobody home?"

"They're sitting to dinner and the cart's busted anyway. Nobody home for you?"

I tilted my head toward the sign. "Nobody I want to talk to, anyway."

The boy looked from me to the sign. "You a hippie?"

"No," I said, "just somebody trying to make sense of things. As far as I can tell a hippie is somebody who wants to be noticed. I don't care about that. Costume parties are fun, but after the initial surprise of them they're kind of uncomfortable. In my experience there doesn't seem to be a lot of advantage in life to be gained from just being looked at."

Little George considered this with a nod. "There's lots of hippies moving into this neighborhood and I'd like to meet one or two of 'em, if they wasn't too dirty."

"What for?"

George shrugged. "Maybe if it didn't cost too much, I'd buy some pot for my dad to try out. They say it gets you real high but ain't as addictive as booze to most people. Maybe Big George would switch to marywanna."

"I don't have any pot now," I said. "But I'd be willing to give him a little at some point if you were to talk to him and tell me he wanted it." I felt surprisingly parental. "But I wouldn't want you toking up and ruining yourself for school, so I wouldn't sell you any pot to give to him. He'd have to come for it himself."

"Don't take me wrong or contrary," Little George said spitting and looking at the last of the sunset, "but I'm already ruint for school. Anyways, I don't like smoking nothing. I tried and it hurt my lungs."

We were walking together again. I didn't really know quite where I was going and he didn't seem to care any more about one direction than another. I could see that he was thinking about something, so I stayed quiet.

"If you give me a phone number where I could contact you," he said at last, "maybe things will work out for everybody. Big George was supposed to put a water heater into one of our empty houses and ain't got to it yet. When he comes in off his drunk, though, he'll probably be a little short of cash. Even if he don't wanta buy any marywanna, maybe he'd rent you the ol' house, once he gets the water heater in it."

"Your dad has a house to rent?"

"Three, but one or maybe two's already rented. The old man went off to buy a water heater more than a week ago. Usually he's off for about ten days at a time. I could show it to you, I guess."

"That would be great."

"You got some walk in the legs?" Little George said, "We can go over and see if the electricity is turned on."

"Sounds good."

"Well, good ain't exactly it. Okay's better. Bunch of plaster and paint and bad carpenter work on top of an old chicken coop's more like it. How many's gonna be living there?"

"Myself and one other," I hesitated. "The little woman. Irene."

He thought some more. "If Marge sees us comin' my personal advice is just keep walking."

"Marge?"

"My mom. Dad's the owner and he'd be the one rentin' to you. Marge likes Wallace and Nixon about the same. She's pretty organized and has her good side, but I think she'd take you for a hippie with his hair a little cut back, even though, like you say, you ain't one. She'd be against renting to you. George is pretty nice all the time, long as he's not puking, and he'd rent to you in a heartbeat, especially if I told him to."

The electricity was off, but Little George fetched a flashlight from a nearby toolshed. An early half-moon cleared a stand of spruce trees, conferring a white glow behind a pair of thin curtains in the empty front room. I thought the house was just about right for Irene and me.

"You know how much it rents for?"

"Just tell my dad I told you rent was a hundred a month. He was talking about asking a little more, but I'm sure he'd take a hundred for it, especially if you paid him cash. Shouldn't tell you that, I guess, cause he just takes the cash out and drinks it up. But there you have it."

"I appreciate your help, George. It was good meeting you. I gotta go back and join my friends for dinner. Maybe something can be worked out about the house."

Halfway across the field toward Gordon's house, I smelled vegetables and chicken bubbling over charcoal. When I turned back for a moonlight view of the rental house, Little George had disappeared. For some reason Rover was trotting after me.

--

The '53 DeSoto Firedome

"Here's why it takes 80 percent less effort to steer this
new DeSoto, and 50 percent less effort to stop it."
Advertisement, **Look**, 1953

Very early one morning two or three days later, the doorbell sounded loud enough to rattle the front bedroom windows. I jumped up, pulled on my pants, and hurried to the door.

"Sorry for waking you," a man said, pulling from a can of beer. "The young son here says he rented you the house last week while I was out of town on business. Thought I'd drop over and introduce myself, ask for your deposit, and answer any questions you might have. George Atkins."

I took the offered hand and felt the October chill on my bare chest. "Tim Barlow," I said. "As far as renting the house is concerned, your son showed it to me and I was interested. But he couldn't set a price and my wife Irene still hasn't seen it."

Little George stepped around his dad. "Sorry about this," he said. "Wunst he's had about three or four breakfast beers he's ready to take care of business and don't pay no mind to the time, or what had been said, or who might still be asleep."

Wearing a red sweater over a long skirt and carrying a hairbrush, Irene came up beside me. "I take it you're the owner of the house Tim was telling me about?"

I could see that Big George was seriously smitten. He shuffled his feet a little uncomfortably. "Yes, Ma'am. We come over a little early because I've got to get Little George off to school and myself off on some personal business. But if he had thought to tell me you were in a family way I'd have phoned first and left the front door open for you to have a look in. All he told me was he had an interested renter staying over here under crowded conditions. I was just trying to make up for lost time."

"That's all right," Irene reassured him. "We don't want you to change your schedule for us. How soon could I see it?"

"Well, hell, since you're already just about dressed, how about not too far from now?"

Irene pulled on a pair of old shoes and we walked four abreast across the empty field. Rover cantered happily ahead, sniffing the weed roots and flushing birds.

Irene was ambivalent about the sloppy plastering, the badly installed sink, the toilet that didn't flush forcefully enough, and the warped, built-in knickknack shelves. But when Big George sighed and confirmed that he'd rent it for as little as fifty a month, Irene got enthusiastic about the views from the windows and the giant elm tree shading the shabby grass in the front yard. When she asked shyly if there was a place for her to put in a garden next spring, Big George agreed to pay Little George an increased allowance to drag some boards and accumulating debris out of an old hog pen next door. Charmed by Irene, Big George agreed to waive the rental deposit. When she looked pleased and nodded, I signed all but a few of our remaining traveler's checks on a counter beside the kitchen sink. When Big George promised he'd be back to bolt in a new hot water heater that afternoon, Irene and I hurried across the field to announce our good fortune and fix breakfast for Gordon and Rhonda.

Rhonda loaned us the use of her Buick, Little George volunteered his services, and by the next afternoon, we were all moved in. I discovered two dried-out wooden chairs and a couple of cracked old milk canisters in the hog pen. I secured the chair legs and struts with glue and nails, scoured the canisters, and painted and lugged them into the house for provisional tables. The next day, Irene's uncle Ralph borrowed a pickup truck and we acquired a couch that had been gathering cobwebs in his garage. We stopped off at my parents' house, where I picked up my high-school desk, a bookcase, and two boxes of dishes and pots and pans. We were in the process of hanging Irene's Bonnard prints on the living room wall when Little George's mother, Marge, came up the narrow walk and tapped on the front door.

Half a head taller than Big George, Marge tried to suppress her irritation with us, managing only a tight smile as a show of friendliness. Unlike Big and Little George, whose sympathies were generally with the longhairs moving into the neighborhood, Marge took the part of the locals.

"Little George tells me that you're looking for work," Marge said, sizing me up.

"Yeah, I am," I admitted. "It's a little hard to dig up without a car, but I'll find something." It was three miles to the nearest bus stop. "We're not thinking of moving out, though. And I'm only a couple of weeks from a car."

Marge nodded. "A friend tells me there's a furniture company across the street from his office downtown looking for someone to load trucks."

Having had some recent talks about her mother's boyfriend with Little George I figured the friend for Phil, the lover who stayed over whenever Big George was off on a bender. When Phil was around, Little George seemed to avoid the family house, finding odd jobs for himself, often near our house or one of the other rental houses on the property. As I stood facing Marge, I could see Little George standing behind her, trying to transmit some signal or other. Just beyond him Rover was sprawled by the elm tree in the front yard, temporarily indifferent to everything but a right front paw that he licked with some enthusiasm.

"I appreciate your telling me about the job," I said, moving into a position where I had a better view of Little George.

"Well, Phil wrote it all down on this card, and since I was coming over here anyway, I thought I'd hand it to you in person."

Little George was holding an index finger to his lips and pointing toward the dog, mouthing words I couldn't quite make out.

Marge said, "Seems your dog has been digging up my flower beds."

"What? *My* dog?"

Little George was holding the insides of his hands together, seeming to promise me some vast favor in the future in exchange for a little white lie now.

"I'm reluctant to ask you to tie him up," Marge went on, "but maybe you could keep a little better eye on him. Let him stay in the house whenever you're gone."

I hadn't grown up with pets and didn't all that much care for Rover's slathering affections and thought of him as a smelly, hapless, living testament to the relentlessness of doggie sex, a composite of every breed that ever roamed and sniffed and studied strange dogs in search of sweet release. "Uh, yeah, all right. We'll do what we can."

"The other thing is, it seems that everybody who comes in and out of our yard leaves the gate open. If you happen to be passing by and see the gate open, I'd appreciate it if you could swing it shut. My cat got hit and killed by some of those stoned hippies a couple of months ago. The way these drug addicts drive out here. . ." Suddenly she noticed her son. "And, that goes for you, too, Buster. You're the worst offender when it comes to that gate. What are you doing over here pestering these folks, anyway? Ain't you got homework?"

Little George yawned. "Did it in school. Dad told me last week to get on over here and clean their window screens."

"All right," Marge said. "But don't you hang around bothering them, and you get your butt back for dinner at six-thirty. She went out the door and down the steps and turned back around. "And don't beg his dog to follow you home, neither."

To Little George's great relief and Rover's complete disinterest, Rover became my first dog.

In the middle of the night, I heard the far-off wail of a train whistle, the nearer but distinctive tinkle of a spoon in a cup, felt the cold of the bed, and saw a light in the kitchen. Irene was sitting at the table, blending honey into a cup of tea. I'd had a bit of part-time work and my hands and forearms ached from a week of lifting and stacking couches and chairs.

"The baby's kicking."

"Sorry," I said. It was the best I could manage under the circumstances.

"Do you think maybe you could sleep, if you were being kicked?"

"No, I'm sure I couldn't, either." The kindness in my voice cost me an effort. "Maybe a bath would help."

"I don't think so. But talking with you might."

I rubbed my eyes. "Shoot."

"It's four in the morning. You need your sleep."

"It's Saturday," I said, falsely cheerful. "I'll sleep tomorrow or later this afternoon. Go ahead."

"Moving to Denver is like going back to the dark ages, isn't it? From California, I mean?"

"Yeah," I said, determined to guardedly say or do nothing that might indicate that the move back was her idea. "It's kind of like grabbing a bus to Market Street beats the hell out of riding a bike twenty miles to spend a day manhandling cheap couches."

"I'm scared."

Irene had what I thought of as sudden fears and those required a different treatment than the nagging, steady fears. The former mostly went away if I could keep from giving them too much attention. I knew better than to offer this insight to Irene. The latter, the nagging fears, gnawed at me as well.

"How so?"

"Well, for one thing, nobody in Colorado practices natural childbirth. If I'd realized that Denver was so far behind California, we could have stayed in San Francisco, or at least some part of California."

I didn't want her to see 'I told you so' in my facial expression, so I walked to the window and looked through my reflection into the yard.

Leaning against the elm tree was the battered bike I'd been riding twenty miles a day to the Pleasure Palace Furniture Corporation. Twins named Mohammed and Yusef had hired me. A dark, squat man named Hamid taught me to tilt the cheap couches one leg at a time onto rickety dollies. Akbar and Joachim showed me how to interlock units of furniture into stable configurations on company delivery trucks. My grandfather had taught me how to ride a bike. And now here I was, nobody to teach me what I didn't know I didn't know, nobody really to blame but myself for my predicament, our predicament, too far away from any place I really wanted to be. Just where I did want to be I could not have said. Transportation and communication. Junior Wong, where are you?

"I agree," I said. "We'd be better off right now if we were still in California. You with your medical insurance from the post office, me delivering telegrams." By taking a sideways step and turning my head slightly, I was able to see the extent of Irene's irritation reflected in the window.

"And how would you propose to get back there now, with no car, no bus fare and just about flat broke, and me about ready to have a baby?"

"I don't know. Buy a car is probably the thing. I'm sure I could get a job delivering telegrams again, if not at the office where I was, then at another one. Once you've had the baby, you could get your post office job back."

"No, I don't think I could. Once I told my supervisor I wasn't about to have sex with him he started plotting against me. And how would we take care of the baby? I don't even want to consider it."

"Suit yourself."

"Why is it that whenever I want to talk about my fears and feelings all you ever offer me is the prospect of a long cross-country car trip?"

I shrugged. "Some problems are remedied by a change of scene."

"And some are not."

"Okay, but you're the one who just suggested our lives would be better if we were in California. And I'm the one who refrained from reminding you that Denver was your idea." I turned back to face her. "Do you want to talk about my many shortcomings or do you want to talk about your fears?"

"Fears? Well, Tim, I'm afraid of being strapped into some ridiculous saddle, turned upside down, shot through the hip with a pint of knockout medicine while half a dozen doctors and nurses poke me into unconsciousness. I'm afraid of dying when I'm under sedation, and I'm afraid of waking up with a dead or deformed baby. I'm afraid that you won't even like life with a baby. Why is all that so hard for you to understand?"

"Well, let's look into a brighter light and consider the baby first. The way I see it, a fetus that can kick as hard as this one must be eager to be born. Maybe it's defective reasoning on my part, but if you were deformed, do you think you would be eager to be born? Anyway, it's not like the doctors around here have no experience in these things."

"No, it's just like they want fifteen hundred dollars that we don't have to deliver a baby pulled out of me like a freaking molar. And why do you keep calling our baby a fetus?"

"I don't know. The word 'baby' makes people teary-eyed and brings out their worst behavior. 'Our child.' How's that?"

"I don't want to bandy words. I want to talk about the birth of our baby. I'm just trying to tell you how disappointed I am to discover the way things are here."

Suddenly I felt sure I could say something that would please her. At least a little. "I'm disappointed, too. I wanted to be with you, together, when the baby is born, to be with you and with him or her. But that seems to be out of the question."

"Wait," she said. "Where are you going?"

I called from the next room. "For some clothes and a cigarette. It's cold in here." Back at the kitchen sink, I added water to the teakettle that Albert Fine had given me. How long ago had that been? A year? "Women in Africa deliver their babies in the morning and go back to work in the fields in the afternoon. I read about them in *National Geographic*. The doctors in this city, especially that Doctor Smith, treat childbirth like a life-threatening ordeal. No wonder you're scared." Certain now that I'd found the appropriate tone and words, I rummaged for bread in the cupboard. "You want toast?"

"No," she snapped, "I want to know if you're mocking my fears."

"Not at all. We live in this weird culture is all. We think of ourselves as brains trapped in bodies, surprised ghosts pulling strings in these delicate machines that we know nothing about and never relate to. We lack faith in the big intentions of life. Being as caught up in this culture as we are, I'm sure if I was a woman I'd be just as scared as you are."

Irene seemed to relax. "But you have no fears yourself, about the birth of our baby? You think the baby will be all right?"

"I'm a little reluctant to say anything while you're upset and uncomfortable."

"I'm comfortable now and I'll be more upset if you refuse to say."

I felt blackmailed. "My concerns are smaller, less important."

"Okay, make them as small as you want. We'll say that all of your concerns are almost too tiny to be noticed. They're just barely large enough to talk about, how's that? What are they? What's eating you?"

"In a word, money. Fifteen hundred for the baby minimum. And what do we have to our names? A hundred and thirty and change and a meager paycheck coming next Friday. Then there's diapers, cribs, clothes. Not to mention the little matter of getting to the hospital. And what have we got, five weeks, six?"

"I could just as well end up having the baby at home."

"Yeah, right." I stopped myself. "Why did you say it like that?"

"Well, African women do all right, don't they? I just can't stop thinking about this article I read last week about these two women in Oregon. They've been arrested and fined for it three times, but between them they have delivered more than two dozen babies at home with no problems."

I removed my tea bag from my cup and put it down on the table. "You want to bring somebody out from Oregon so you can have our baby at home?"

"Don't put that tea bag there on the table. It will stain the table."

"It might improve its appearance," I muttered.

"Do you mind? It's all we've got right now."

I removed the tea bag and wrapped it tightly around my thumb. It burned, but I smiled at Irene to prove that it didn't. She shook her head slowly and looked into her teacup for a long time. "If you were open to the possibility of a world beyond our comprehension, I'd like to show you some tarot cards."

"Tarot cards? Oh, God, we need tarot cards for this conversation now?"

"I've been trying to tell you that Rhonda did an amazing reading for me and the baby a couple of days ago."

I sighed and flattened a sliver of butter on a slice of toast. "All right," I conceded, "I'll make you a deal. I'll try to be open-minded, but your part is to promise to be patient with any unenlightened reaction I may have while I'm trying to be open to the whole business."

Irene pushed her chair back, went into the front room, and took a stack of tarot cards from a lopsided shelf. I noted that the cards she wanted were already on top of the deck. She arranged them on the kitchen table into a shape that she said represented past, present, and future. I'd never looked closely at them before. Now I studied the crudely drawn and colored illustrations: cartoony minimalist images from populist figurines in a sanitized Revolutionary France. Instead of hair, the characters had manes, instead of feet, curly clunky shoes. Outdoor thrones were covered with vines. Figures from the Prince Valiant comic strip, brave steeds, and skinny figures with bells on ballet slippers skipped through the air. Sleepy lions and wide-bladed swords, dripping chalices and staves and lavish princesses in flowing skirts and robes jumped off the cards.

When they were properly arrayed, Irene said the cards intended us to understand that we needed to sustain a deep faith in the grace and bounty of the natural world. I was apparently represented by a man in an elaborately decorated chariot, a sure indication, Irene claimed, I would soon be doing a great deal of driving without necessarily going far away. A card in which big chalices were falling out of the sky proved that we were supposed to have the baby at home, alone. The natural world had spoken, Irene said. Plus, the chariot meant I should buy a car right away even if it meant grocery money. If I acted in good faith, the cards showed that the car would be perfect.

By three that same afternoon Irene and I were unaccountably slowing down in the 1952 DeSoto Firedome we had just driven away from a used car lot.

I felt my stomach tighten.

"What's wrong?"

"I don't know."

"Why is the car jerking us back and forth like this?"

"There seems to be something wrong with the engine."

"But we just bought it."

"Tell me about it."

"Can't you at least turn off this busy street? Everybody's honking at us."

"I'm trying. They won't let me pull over."

The DeSoto lurched, gasped, and stopped, marooning us in the middle of Colorado Boulevard.

Irene said, "We can't stop here. We're in the middle of the street."

I put the heels of my hands on top of the steering wheel and hammered out an angry rhythm. "Irene, I didn't stop the car. The car stopped on its own. Something's wrong." With Irene offering me multiple suggestions about what I ought to do next, I jumped out and yanked the hood open, more intent on getting away from her than attempting a diagnosis, for which, in any case, I was ill-prepared. Bending over the reeking motor I named the few parts I recognized as an alternative method of counting to ten.

After a minute, I helped Irene out of the car, spread my coat on a bus stop bench, and encouraged her to sit down while I hurried off to search for a pay phone.

A chilly gust of wind blew into the open phone booth. The receiver was cold against my ear, but I cradled it with my shoulder while I fished my pockets for change. Dialing, I looked back at the flashing turn signals of cars seeking to find a way around the stalled DeSoto. Drivers occupying a clear lane on either side of the stalled car raced ahead or skillfully caressed their brakes in order to prevent other cars from bolting in front of them.

A woman answered the phone.

"I'd like to speak with Scott."

"Uh, just a minute. I'll see if he's still around." She muffled the receiver then released it again. "Who's calling?"

"Of course he's still around. He just handed me some car keys twenty minutes ago. My name is Barlow."

"Yeah, but he was, uh, going duck hunting. I think he may have left already. Let me check out on the lot."

Not long before, Scott had bitten down on a long-stemmed briar pipe, clamping it fiercely with his molars so he could talk from the other side of his mouth. When he didn't need his thick fingers for repositioning his pipe, he wiped his liver-colored lips with the back of a hand or adjusted the soiled plastic sheath containing half a dozen ballpoint pens in his shirt pocket

I knew better than to be taken in by Rhonda's tarot cards or by Scott's bluff reassurances about the reliability of the DeSoto. But Irene's urgent desire to have the baby at home both worried and emptied me of anything but an amorphous hopefulness. Unfortunately, and within hearing of Scott, Irene noticed that when read backwards, the car's license plates matched her birthday. Scott subtly encouraged Irene's numerology and waxed eloquent on the joys of parenthood.

Through a fog of drugstore pipe tobacco, Scott told Irene how lucky she was to have a hard-nosed husband, that he had grandchildren who were the most important people in the world to him, and that he didn't mind saying that he had an instinct for what a fine mother she was going to make. The last part of the transaction blurred in my mind. All I remembered as I stood with the cold phone to my ear was handing Scott five twenty-dollar bills and driving the car off the lot and down the alley, Irene grateful and euphoric beside me, sure our luck was about to change.

My imagination whirled and now I saw myself as Huck Finn and Scott as the King or the Duke, slipping the bills in a gaudy money clip, looking around his fake wood-paneled office to be sure he was alone, then dropping to his knees.

"Oh, Lord, I'll never swindle anybody else again. Just please let that sucker and his wife get that thing far enough down the road that he won't be able to get back here until after I'm gone for the day."

In the cold phone booth, I stared at the car keys and wondered if my hands were big enough to get all the way around Scott's neck. Squeezing the icy phone receiver instead of his warm throat, I listened and thought for a moment that I caught a bit of muffled dialog between Scott and the woman supposedly looking for him.

The problem was, I assured myself, Scott did not yet understand the workings of a karma-fueled universe, did not appreciate, for example, the way simple wrong actions might bring him the punishment of a broken leg or a car accident. I felt oddly virtuous not to be wishing these things on him, though I suppose I was; I just didn't want the punishment to befall him without the cognitive flash, the sudden memory, of the DeSoto and the desperate couple he'd swindled.

"Scott's gone for the weekend," the woman said. "He'll be back on Tuesday."

"Maybe you can help me . . ."

"I can help you mop a floor, maybe. I can't help with nothing else. I'm the cleaning lady. Everybody's gone for the day."

"Hah!" I said, thinking I saw an opening. "Then why are you answering the phone?"

"Stop it from ringing more than anything. Like I say, Scott's duck hunting and will be back Tuesday."

"Tell Scott that I just bought a car from him and I'm bringing it back."

"I can't tell Scott nothing. Call back Tuesday."

The line went dead.

A Yellow Cab had stopped for a traffic light. I caught the driver's eye and held up a hand. When the driver pulled over, I hopped into the back seat.

"I need a favor that may be a little beyond the call of duty."

The driver's eyes appeared in the rearview mirror. I fixed them. "My car's stalled in the middle of the street over there. I'll pay you double fare for pushing it to a car lot a couple of miles down Colfax."

The driver shook his head. "The service you want is called towing."

"My friend Gordon drives a Yellow Cab. He tells me there's a bond of professional generosity among cab drivers. Do you know him?"

"Never heard of him."

"He just started driving a few months back. I passed the test a couple weeks ago myself."

"So what do you want from me?"

"I only have a couple of bucks, but I need a push, at least, to get my car out of the street."

"Your buddy driving right now?"

"Yeah, he should be."

"What you're asking for is against the law and against company rules, but if he's a good enough friend maybe *he'll* help you out. You know his cab number by any chance?"

"I forgot it."

"Look, I'll tell you what. You get out of my cab and go back to your car. I'll drive around the block and if there are no cabs or supervisors cars on the street, I'll push your car around the corner, where you can at least park it. Then you can give me your buddy's name and we'll see if we can contact him over the radio."

Gordon had become very enamored of Meher Baba, a Sufi mystic who had attained an exalted state of consciousness and taken a lifetime vow of silence. I didn't understand the reasons for the silence very well. Nor did I quite grasp how, by following the holy man's example, Gordon hoped to strengthen the quality of his poetry. But Gordon said a poet wanting to purify his language had to learn to endure creative emptiness by purging his life of what he called unnecessary blather. Without saying anything about it, I wondered if his taciturnity had anything to do with Rhonda and the tarot cards.

When Gordon arrived he smiled at me and raised one dark eyebrow at the DeSoto. He left his cab's engine running and turned his heat up high so Irene could sit in the front seat and get warm. Then he started rummaging under the DeSoto's hood.

I didn't press him for an on-the-spot diagnosis. He declined to accept any payment for risking his job and pushing the DeSoto home with his cab. Then he hurried back to work.

Irene and I were sitting at the kitchen table finishing cups of cocoa, saying nothing and looking anywhere but at each other. I was staring at the pane of glass in the door when my dad's face appeared on the other side.

"Dad!" In the silence of the kitchen my greeting sounded like the dismayed outburst it was. Going reluctantly to the door, I saw behind my dad to a new long white Cadillac nosed in behind the DeSoto.

"What's with the Caddy?"

"What do you mean, 'What's with the Caddy?' I've been working hard and selling books. I deserve it." Irene looked at him as if awaiting a more complete explanation for his extravagance. "It's a sales tool. When a man in a Cadillac pulls up outside, everybody wants the neighbors to think important visitors have arrived. They fall all over themselves trying to get the Cadillac owner inside the house. Important people have come to call."

"It's quite a sight to behold," I offered, knowing it would be less than he wanted to hear.

"Speaking of sights, what the hell's with that junker in the driveway?"

Irene laughed involuntarily. I scoffed. "Oh, don't worry about it."

"What do you mean, 'Don't worry about it?' I'm not worried about it. It's not my goddamned driveway. I'm just asking you about it."

Irene stood up and ran her hands over her round belly. She groaned and summoned an excuse for her impending withdrawal. "It's nice to see you, Bert, but Tim and I have been out all day and I have to go lie down. My back is hurting me. You guys make yourselves some more hot chocolate or tea. There's spice cake in the fridge."

Bert moved to head her off. "I thought I'd take you guys for a little ride," he said. "You absolutely will not believe how that baby runs. Smooth as a woman of the evening." Much to my irritation, he winked at Irene.

If sexual vigor was rejuvenated in men with new powerful cars and depleted in those with rattletraps, Irene looked like she wanted to remain blissfully unaware of this phenomenon. "The two of you go ahead," she said. "I'll take a rain check. I really have to lie down."

Irritated and disappointed, Bert waved her away and turned back to me. "So what's with that piece of shit in the driveway?"

"That piece of shit," I said, smoldering, "is a car. It's my car. My Cadillac. My symbol of success."

"Goddamned eyesore. Somebody give it to you, thinking you, of all people, might fix it up?"

"No. I bought it."

"Bought it! Jesus Christ, what the hell for? That son of a bitch is a mess!"

"I've been riding thirty miles a day on a bike for too long. My legs are turning to Jell-O. I have to be able to get to work."

Insulted that I hadn't sought his guidance, he stormed around the kitchen. "Jesus H. Christ! Okay, Chinaman, okay. But when that junkyard hot rod leaves you stranded in the middle of nowhere, just don't call me up to bail you out!"

"I haven't done that in quite a while now," I said, hoping he might remember how little he'd seen or heard of me lately.

"How much did they rob you for it?"

"A hundred bucks."

"Hell's bells, for that we could have worked out some kind of deal on your mom's old Dodge Dart." Suddenly he was eager to discover that the DeSoto was even more of a wreck than it looked to be. Turning, he hurried outside.

"Son of a bitch," Bert said looking under the hood. "Missing timing gear teeth and chain, cracks in the block." He stepped back and gave me a nasty look of recognition. "Well, the Goddamned Chinaman strikes gold again!"

"I'll see you later, Dad," I said. "I'm going to lie down."

"What do you mean lie down? Shit, I drove all the way out here to give you both a ride. Your mom's cooking a chicken and roast potatoes and I told her to toss in a couple of extra spuds. Leave this thing to rot. Your mom can drive you both home later."

"I don't want to go for a ride. We've got other plans tonight, and I'm not hungry. I'm going to take a nap. See you some other time." I slammed the DeSoto's hood down and started for the door. He was coming up behind me, so I turned back. "Like I said, another time, Dad."

Hoping for a little companionship, Rover had been shadowing us. As Bert wheeled toward his Cadillac, he stepped on a paw. Rover yelped, cowered, and immediately sought to appease. He was still fawning and wagging his apologies when Bert gunned the engine. Only after the big Caddy had fishtailed through the thick dust of Xenia Street did Rover approach me with a hunkered-down, guilty look.

A month later the moribund DeSoto was still in the driveway, gathering hog pen dust and sticky debris from the overhanging elm tree. Dizzy from the long afternoon bike ride and covered with sweat, I leaned the bicycle against the driver's door, went inside, and found Irene propped up on the couch. She wore a giant gray smock under a faded blue terrycloth robe she could no longer comfortably close around her belly. Her face was pale.

"How are you feeling?"

"Not so good."

"You're still having contractions?"

"I'm having one right now."

"You're timing them?"

Her face contracted with pain. "Shsssss."

"Where's Rhonda? I thought she was going to stay with you until I got here."

Rhonda called out, "I'm in the bathroom." Rhonda emerged a moment later, adjusting a rubber band around her ponytail. "I'm leaving," she said, "but I'm going to be home all day and all night. Remember, the Buick is running fine if you guys need it to get to the hospital or anything." She tuned me out and looked at Irene. "Just remember, we've done eight different readings since the decision to have the baby at home and they've all come out positive. But, it's a changing universe. Sometimes major decisions have to be altered. I left you a spare deck of cards. You can always do another reading and call me up for help with an interpretation."

I offered Rhonda a kiss on the cheek. "Thanks for staying with her until I could get home from work."

Rhonda wrinkled her nose and shrugged before turning her attention back to Irene. "Remember your breathing. Merge with the oneness of all life whenever the pain gets intense. And don't hesitate to call, even if it's the middle of the night."

When Rhonda walked out, a huge stillness entered the small house. Irene moved restlessly on the couch where she and Rhonda had arranged pillows, cushions, and blankets. Feeling lost and useless, I watched Irene, searching her expression for some clue as to how I might comfort and prepare her for whatever was ahead.

"Well," I ventured anxiously, "I guess we're coming to that place in all the cowboy movies where somebody old with bifocals is supposed to come in and start ordering people to boil gallons of water and bring towels."

Irene looked at me as if I were an annoying stranger then shook her head with a worried expression. "I don't know about this," she said.

"Neither do I. But like Rhonda said, if things get bad we can always go to a hospital. Remember, Irene, whatever happens, you and the baby are going to be fine."

"I was starting to say I don't know about this room. It's too bright."

The curtains in the window behind the couch were open. I pulled them together. Encouraged to think I might be useful after all, I removed a bright light bulb from an overhead socket and installed one with lower wattage.

"I'm cold," Irene said.

I took a blanket from the pile beside the couch and added it to the blankets already wrapped around her. In the kitchen, I heated milk slowly over a small flame. Irene groaned. Her contraction had passed when I brought her cocoa and two soda crackers. She took the mug but kept her eyes on me, taking my measure as if I were a witchdoctor with powerful but strange ideas. I resisted the notion she was turning into someone I'd never seen before.

"Here," I said. "Let me put the cocoa down on the floor to cool. I don't want you to burn yourself."

I dragged the only comfortable chair in the room toward the couch and sat holding her hand. A wave of nausea swept through me. The afternoon seemed suddenly very quiet and I felt light, insubstantial. The air acquired weight. Breathing seemed to call for a conscious, vigilant operation of the muscles in my chest.

Irene stiffened with another contraction. Her face was swollen and pale. I wanted to speak to her, to span the gulf between us, but felt unable to talk and breathe at the same time.

An orange glow appeared on the closed front room drapes. I went to the door and looked out the window at the sunset and the night-blackened front range of the Rockies. Across the dusty street, Old Ben's chickens had vacated his front yard. A Shetland pony sought shelter on the lee side of a ramshackle outbuilding. Filaments of its blond mane winked red and pink in the last chill light.

Fetching four candles from a drawer in the kitchen, I lit and carried them into the front room. As the darkness deepened and their flames glowed unsteadily in the drafty house. I held Irene's hand. The air in my chest tasted of burning wicks and candlewax.

"I've got to get out of here," Irene said.

"I know what you mean. I feel the same way."

"No, you don't," she said. "You never will. You could never imagine."

I stroked her cheek, but she jerked away.

"Don't touch me again," she snapped.

"Okay," I said. "Try to breathe more deeply."

"I mean *ever*."

"Okay."

"This is all your fault."

I bristled and swallowed. "I guess so."

She grunted loudly and squeezed my forearm. Her strength surprised me. "I'm sorry," she apologized.

"It's all right. Just breathe," I said. "Don't forget to breathe."

"Fuck you. Shut up."

239

"Breathe," I said, inhaling, following my own instructions. "Just keep breathing."

The house was hot from the small gas heater in the front room, yet I felt chilled. She was sweating. The distance between us could neither be spanned nor ignored; it had to be lived with, minute-by-minute, hour-by-hour. Donning a sweater, I brought Irene a cool washcloth and swabbed the sweat from her face.

"Get me water," she said. "Cold water. Please." Her eyes glowed strangely.

When I came back with water she said, "I'm going to have cats."

"What?"

"Not a baby human being. A baby cat. A bunch of baby cats. I just saw them. I don't want to have them."

"Take it easy," I said, "everything is going to be all right."

While she drank and gasped, I worried. What if the baby was sideways? What if she had a breech birth? What if something inside her tore? What if the interpretation of the tarot cards was nonsense, the natural world indifferent, and the baby split her groin open? All around me manmade objects seemed to recede and float away. With my eyes closed, I had a sense of the two of us naked, exposed to the elements on a black plateau.

"God," Irene was saying. "God oh God oh God oh God."

"It's not time to push yet."

"Shut up! What time is it?"

"Twelve-fifteen."

"No! It can't be."

"Try to breathe and relax."

"Don't tell me what to do. What do *you* know?"

"I love you," I said. "I'm trying to help."

"My back hurts. I want to put my legs up."

I arranged two piles of pillows and folded blankets and stuffed them under her thin thighs. I caressed her knees and put a blanket over her."

"It's hot! Get that blanket out of here."

"Sorry."

"Don't say anything." Another contraction took her. It seemed to go on forever.

"Breathe."

"Oh God help."

"Breathe deeply and merge with the pain. Think of the millions of women who've gone before you, think of the natural order, the life force asserting itself, expressing itself through you." I took a candle from a pile

240

of books on childbirth and moved it toward her knees. She was widely dilated. Her vagina was sweating, streaked with blood. "I think it may be time to push just a little when the next contraction comes."

She arched her back. Her forehead was greenish, wet with sweat, darkened with little bits of grit. Once she relaxed and began to breathe again, I wiped her face.

"The water's cold, Sweetie," she said.

"I'll warm it up."

"Thank you so very much for all your kindnesses." She put her head back in the pillow and sighed. "I'm going to die."

"Nonsense. Put those thoughts away. You're going to have a beautiful baby."

She was biting down on a corner of the pillow. "Ugggg. Shit! Get out of here! I hate you. Sweetie, Tim. Bastard. Uggh."

"I see him," I said. "Her. I see its little head!"

"Breathe, you bastard!"

"Take it easy," I said. "You're doing fine. You and the baby are going to be all right."

"You fugg yourself, Sweetie, Baby. Uggg."

"The head is coming out!"

"Shut up shut up up shut up."

"The head. Look, the head is out! Come on, Irene, it won't be long now!" A pulsing light was going on and off inside me, and not just my head. My voice sounded strange. "It's coming," I said, "Jesus Lord Almighty, it's coming!"

"Yes, yes, get out, get out," Irene said. She arched her back into something like a wrestler's bridge now.

"All right, Baby." I encouraged, "only one more series of squeezes and the legs will be out. You're going to have the baby and be able to rest very soon."

Irene was grunting and sweating, making noises that threatened to become screams yet never did. What I said or did no longer seemed to matter. I had disappeared from her experience and she had been drawn into an agony of concentration like nothing I had ever seen. I could wipe the sweat from her face with a washcloth, offer my hand or forearm for her to squeeze, remain close to her clenching body, but I could not approach her pain. She was at the bottom of a well. My part was to call down to her that help was coming, to say and believe things would be all right, and to be there waiting for the fleshy object between her legs, to watch it turn into a life. I caught my slippery child. It was oily, smeared with blood, glowing blue and red in the flickering candlelight. There was movement, an electrical pulse coming from the tiny chest. It was warm, moving, and as I gasped for breath, seemed to become a tiny person. "He's breathing! No, *she's* breathing! It's a girl!" I shouted. "It's a girl!" I called down the well to her. "Irene, you've just had a baby girl. It's a wonderful girl. You're a wonderful woman!"

Irene went momentarily limp. "No it's a boy," she wheezed. "It's a boy cat, just like the one I had when I was a little girl. Oh, I've got to get out of this. I've got to stop."

"It's a girl, I tell you! And you're all done! You're fine and she's fine, too."

Sweat was streaming down Irene's face and a wedge of shimmery liver appeared at her vaginal opening. She was pushing.

"That's it," I said, "the placenta has appeared. When the placenta comes out you can finally rest. I can see the placenta now. You're doing great!"

"Owwhuhggg!" The placenta emerged with a small splashing sound, staining the blanket under her legs. Irene wheezed once. "Give her to me."

"Let me just cut the umbilical cord. And then you can hold her."

"Give her to me now, you son of a bitch!" The hard fierceness in her face vanished at once and she touched my shoulder tenderly. "You sweetie, you kitty cat."

"Okay," I said, tangling the baby in the umbilical cord. In a small, terrified, accusatory voice, the baby began to cry. I handed her to Irene and sawed at the slithery night crawler of a cord with the cutting blade in my dull pocketknife. I lost my grip on the cord and slit my finger, my blood, Irene's blood, and the baby's blood, all joined together as tears of joy and relief ran down my face. We stayed together for a long time, breathing, not together or in quite the same way, but in concert. A luminous presence made the room glow. Even the furniture pulsated.

While Irene studied the baby for defects, I found my way to the bathroom, inserted a plug in the tub, ran a bath, and adjusted the water temperature. Leaving the water running, I fetched more candles. Once they were lit, I arranged them around the tub.

When I returned to the front room, Irene was holding the baby's face to her shoulder, stroking the thin, blood-matted hair.

"I'm going to give you both a hot bath. A warm bath."

"First bring me a drink of water."

The air in the house seemed fresh, charged with electricity. My mind was still. The water glass Irene put to her mouth shimmered in the candlelight. Folding the baby in a soft blanket, I helped Irene free her arms from the bloodstained nightgown, then carried her, birdlike, light in my arms, into the bathroom and lowered her into the warm water. Then I went back for the baby and placed her carefully in Irene's wet arms. Blood and bits of floating and circulating afterbirth turned the bathwater pink. The baby clenched and unclenched her tiny fists, then breathed easier, and finally seemed to relax in the warmth. Drying the tiny pink body with a fresh towel, I kissed her chest, being careful to avoid the raw umbilical cord stub. I carried her to our bed, and leaving her in a nest of bedclothes and blankets, returned for Irene. She insisted on pulling herself up with the help of a towel rack, but when she got unsteadily to her feet, allowed me to put one foot in the water and carry her, shivering, to the bed.

She took the baby to her breast and we sat again, listening to the tiny, almost contented new voice in the house. Electrical vibrations traveled up my spine, settled in my head, clearing my mind of thought. I looked at Irene in the dim candlelit bedroom. She stared contentedly and blinked back at me. That we were alien to each other's deepest experiences did not trouble us, either because we were too tired, or because the awe we shared and valued depended on our ability to accept each other's strangeness. Being that alone, in the company of another person that alone, marks you, bonds you for life somehow, I thought.

"I'm hungry," she said. "For a hamburger and some cherry pie."

I nodded. "Are you warm enough? Is she warm enough, do you think?"

"I want a hamburger and cherry pie."

There was an all night coffee shop seven or eight miles closer to the city, but it was two-thirty in the morning.

"It will take me about an hour on the bike."

"So what? It takes you longer than that to ride to work each day. And it took me about fifteen hours to have your baby."

"I wasn't saying no, Irene, just telling you that maybe I should wait a bit. Maybe it's too soon to leave. I don't know. Do you want me to call Rhonda and have her come over?"

"No," Irene said, "let them sleep. I want mustard and pickles and cherry pie."

"I'll go," I agreed, "but I don't want to leave too soon or come back to that mess out there."

Carrying stained blankets and towels from the living room to the bathroom, I dropped them into a tub filling with cold water. In the living room, I blew out the candles. I tossed the placenta and the umbilical chord in a grocery sack and carried it outside to the garbage pail. A strong wind was gusting. A white moon was nearly full. The world seemed a place of peace and rest. Rover rose from his post by the elm tree, sniffed the bag, licked my hand, and escorted me back to the door.

"Thank you so much for all your wonderful care," Irene said. "Do you really mind going out?"

"No," I said, surprised that saying so made it true. "Actually, I've got a surplus of energy. It's a beautiful night, we have a beautiful daughter, and I'm suddenly starving, too." I ducked into another pullover sweater and stuffed a pair of thin cotton gloves in the hip pockets of my pants.

Kissing Irene and the baby, I stepped out, locked the door, and rode carefully down the street. The bike's balloon tires were unsteady in the gravel. Rover ran beside me. When he persisted too long, I scolded him and told him to go back and take care of Irene. He followed me to the corner, but turned back when I stopped and pointed toward the house.

Filled with fierce strength, I pedaled hard into a stiff wind, enjoying the resistance. Overhead, the moon breathed and the world looked insubstantial, a flowing composition without weight, an illusion sustained, then dissolved, with geometries of light and shadow.

Intending at first to return home immediately, I picked up a menu near the coffee shop's cash register. My knees were unsteady and I felt faint so I took a seat at the counter, gulping down glasses of ice water while studying the customers, who seemed asleep in their uneventful lives.

I ordered eggs and bacon, wolfing them down, finishing with french fries and ice cream.

I felt generous, protective, and loving toward Irene. Yet I also smarted, felt chastened and exiled by the impenetrable mystery of birth. I had my own experience of the birth and could only claim for my own now that I was miles away sitting in a coffee shop. Ecstatic as those final birth moments had been, a bliss that lingered still, there was another sense in which the birth of my daughter had been like a fight in which I had been required to take a beating for another. Irene had taken the baby from me with a kind of biological arrogance, a sense of entitlement I'd been forbidden to challenge. Having been through the experience of childbirth, Irene had looked into the face of an uncomprehending man. I had felt like a servant who'd been caught rummaging through the lady's jewelry box. I remembered the look on Irene's face and tried not to take it personally. It was a look that had said that I would live and die a child the way all men did, the way that all who did not give birth would do, a look that said that fathers were onlookers and mothers must never let them forget this.

I wanted to accept my life without anger or vindictiveness. I ordered Irene's burger the way she liked it, thought of how when I got home I'd slather it with the pungent mustard in the refrigerator and rub her small feet. I had never till now appreciated either her or the basic life elements: struggle, breath, light, shadow, cool, warmth, and food when you were hungry. Blood rushing through a cold face, strong hands swollen with the power of life.

The waitress smiled at me with more feeling than I expected. To wander a world where women gave birth and men stood by like frightened children, and then went out to sit among strangers who gave them food in exchange for money, was certainly a marvel.

One day soon, after we had a little more money, I would sit down with Irene and we would praise the little unnoticed or unremarked-upon traits of the other. Showering each other with praise, we would take back one by one the hurtful things we had said, unweave the snarl of misunderstandings, thread by thread, give voice to the kind, appreciative things we might have said but didn't. We would promise each other to listen and take a long time before replying. In this way, the strangers we would at times go on being would become familiar, trusted friends. We would tickle and tease each other and have glorious sex again. We would love our daughter and protect her and teach her to grow up strong and wise. A radio in the restaurant kitchen broadcast the sonorous warmth of Stan Getz on saxophone. I let tears run down my cheeks. Several drunks were sneaking furtive looks at me, convinced that like them I'd had too much to drink. I laughed and blew my nose. Tossing my napkin into the nest of my uneaten fries, I picked up the warm sack containing Irene's hamburger stuffed it up under my sweater and pedaled home without stopping for a traffic light and without ceasing to crank at the pedals.

Irene barely touched her burger, even after I'd lathered it with mustard and warmed it up. But she finished her cherry pie while I sat watching her with wordless pleasure on the edge of the bed.

As the sky lightened, I carried her cold fries and burger out to Rover. I stood out on the cold stoop for a time, not wanting to call him, lest I wake Irene up. Lighting a cigarette I inhaled the hot smoke deeply and concluded he was pouting somewhere, not far off. About the time I decided to put the burger in the refrigerator, I heard a commotion near the fence, and walked over in sock feet to see what it was about. Two feral cats had toppled the inadequately protected garbage can, undone the folded newspaper and crouched, sharing and nibbling, one at each end of my daughter's placenta. Inside, my daughter, Serena, slept through her first sunrise.

Irene's voice woke me about noon. "My God," she said, "we've got to get you to a doctor right away."

The responding voice belonged to Little George. "Rover was trying to mount that little black spaniel down the street. And those two big German Shepherds down the block went after them both, Rover and the spaniel. I heard 'em outside my room. Rover was at the bottom of the pile when I got there and I started hitting the big dogs with a rake handle. That's when one of 'em jumped up and bit me I guess. The other one got me by the ankle."

I pulled on my pants and went for a look. Little George was bleeding from a bite to his cheek, and blood had soaked one sock and shoe and was puddling on the floor where he stood with Rover in his arms. Unable to manage Rover any longer, he slid him gently to the floor.

"Christ, you've been bit pretty bad, George," I said. "Irene, please go back to bed and lie down. I'll take care of this. Come on in, George. Let's call your mom."

A tiny scratchy sound came from the back room. Irene hurried for the baby.

"She ain't home," George said, "and I don't know where she is. Off with Phil, I reckon. Rover's the one hurt bad, though. He's the one's got to have a doctor."

"Your dad? Is he around?"

"Naw, he's down in Florida, drinking steady and thinkin' about the old days."

The phone rang. I picked it up and smothered the mouthpiece. "George, get some ice cubes from the fridge. Wrap them in a washcloth and hold it to your face. I'll be right with you. Hello."

In the bedroom, the baby began to sputter and wail. The voice on the phone sounded far away.

"Tim?"

"Speaking."

"You're late for work. Where you at? Why you home today?"

"My wife had a baby in the middle of the night. I told Mohammed yesterday afternoon I probably wouldn't be in. I was about to call."

"Yeah, well, this is Yusef. The boss said to tell you don't come back. We mail your check."

"What do you mean?"

"You too late too often on the bicycle and too slow moving those couches. We hired a bigger guy today. In three hours he can do more work than you do all day."

"Well, shit," I said, "I had to come home yesterday to take care of my wife. We had a baby girl last night, Yusef."

"Yeah, yeah, I know. Congratulations. Take advice and get a thinking job. Your back is not the best tool of your life."

In a quiet fury, I hung up and headed for the bathroom. Irene was in the bedroom, tending the baby. Rover was bleeding from his face and neck on the tiled floor. George sat on the edge of the bathtub, blotting his own blood onto an icy washcloth. The birth-stained towels and blankets were still in the bathwater where I'd tossed them a few hours earlier. The water was rusty brown.

Irene appeared in the doorway cradling the baby. "I'm hurting a little and the baby needs to be checked out. I guess all of us need to go to the doctor."

"Yeah. I guess I'll call Rhonda."

"She's not home. She stopped by early this morning on her way to some important test at school," Irene explained. "She said she'd ask Gordon to come by later."

"You shouldn't be up," I said. "Go lie down with the baby. I'll call Gordon at home and if I can't reach him or Nick, phone for a cab."

I dabbed George's puncture bites with swabs and iodine, holding his head back, warning him there would be pain. When he sat still for it, I dripped medication from the bottle directly into punctured, still-bleeding cheek.

"It don't hurt all that much," he said, biting his lower lip, eyes filling with tears. "I got some grit in my eye is all. The one hurtin' is Rover. He's the one we gotta look after."

Holding the stained washrag to his cheek with one hand, George squatted down and used his free hand to pin and console Rover while I poured and daubed the last of the medication on the dog's bites. The fierce-smelling iodine stained his bloody fur scat brown. The dog howled, the baby joined in, and Irene cursed the world.

As if on cue, Gordon let himself in the unlocked front door. Seeing the drops of blood on the kitchen floor, and me damp and harried in the opened bathroom doorway he said, "What's going on here?"

I walked out to rinse the blood and iodine off my hands in the kitchen sink. "Way too much. Irene let me sleep and before I could get her and the baby to the doctor, Little George wandered over from a bitch fight. Goddamn dog is dying on the floor in the bathroom. George is all bit to hell and bleeding like a stuck pig." Under the flow of cold water from the faucet, I noticed that the finger that I'd slit severing the umbilical cord in the middle of the night was now bleeding, making a pink pond in a soup bowl in the sink. I looked from the bathroom to Gordon. "Everybody's bleeding here, except you and the baby. I hope your cab's out there. We gotta get this show on the road. The only question is where to."

Gordon went to have a look at Little George. "Rhonda's doctor works out of a clinic on Havana Street," he said. "I think there's a vet in a little building across the street."

"You think there will be a doctor at the clinic where we're taking Irene, somebody who'll be able to work on Little George?"

"Yeah. There are about a dozen or more doctors working out of there."

Minutes later a fat nurse clucked her tongue and led George to a room at the rear of the clinic. Three nurses and a doctor gathered around Irene and the baby and escorted them to a small room just behind the reception area. That left two nurses and the receptionist to join in scolding me for putting Irene and the baby at risk. I stood for it only briefly, then slipped outside where Gordon sat smoking Camels in his cab working on his trip sheet. Rover lay bleeding on a pile of newspapers in the back seat.

Gordon put the cab in gear and zipped boldly across the busy street and into another parking lot. Extricating Rover from the pile of bloody newspapers, I carried him inside, staining my shirtsleeves with blood and iodine. Gordon borrowed a sponge from an orderly inside and went back out to wipe the interior of his cab down. He was polishing his steering wheel when I stepped out and lit a cigarette of my own.

"Thanks for all your help, Gord."

"You're welcome. Hey, cheer up. She said your wife and daughter are fine. The kid will be okay, and your dog will probably pull through, too."

"Would you stop with calling him my fucking dog?"

"Don't be so touchy."

"It's the kid's."

"Okay, so cheer up double then. You don't even have to worry about the vet bills."

"Sorry, man," I apologized. "I'm still wasted from last night. I got fired from my shit job, own a car that doesn't run and that I have to pay to get rid of, a dog whose vet bills I may have to pay because I told my landlady the dog was mine to humor the kid he actually belongs to, and I've got twenty bucks to my name. Now, my landlady's going to be faced with a kid who may be scarred for life for rescuing a pooch that she thinks is mine. I've got a landlord hoping to use rent money I don't have, a mother-in-law who blames me for her daughter's decision, which may or may not have been a stupid one, to have the baby at home, and a dad who won't speak to me, which may be a blessing in disguise. To hear me now, you'd never believe that a few hours ago I was blubbering about the cosmic joy of parenthood in an all-night coffee shop, would you? Anyway, I owe you huge thanks and then I go and snap at you over something stupid."

"Well, maybe this will cheer you up. A couple of hours ago I saw a waiting list on the bulletin board at the cab company. There's only three names ahead of yours now. My guess is you'll be driving full time in less than a month. The bad news is that unless you want to cool it here until about five-thirty when Rhonda comes home, you'll have to take another cab home. I gotta go make some money."

"Here's ten for your time and trouble."

"Forget it," Gordon said.

The next day a bandaged Little George used his dad's power saw to build Rover a doghouse from scraps of wood. I stood and watched him spray paint the dog's name on both sides of the pitched roof and helped him carry the precariously nailed structure to a designated site in the hog pen. That afternoon, while standing in front of the kitchen window doing dishes, I watched Marge drive up to the hog pen gate. Little George carried Rover from her backseat into the fenced yard. Mother and son argued briefly while Marge fixed a rope to the dog's collar, and looking toward my house, caught me watching her and made a little wave intended to mask her embarrassment and irritation. She'd disappeared before I could find a sweater and a jacket and make my way outside.

Rover's face, head, and a large area of his flanks had been shaved, exposing the smallness of the animal under the missing hair. Beneath a pasty medication, the dog bites stank of pus. Little George had two bottles of medicine to be dripped three times a day into fifteen punctures in eight bite wounds, and two gray tablets to be mashed into Rover's dog food each evening. Although I had told Marge otherwise, and she had paid George's and Rover's medical expenses, Little George admitted that Marge was clinging to the fiction that Rover belonged to me.

"It's that boyfriend of hers. She thinks Phil's gonna take her and me to live with him in the city. I guess because we won't have no dog there, and no Big George going and coming without warning, she thinks we'll start livin' happily ever after." There was a glint in his eye. "What she don't know," the boy went on, "is that George has a purty good idea about what's going on and done made me and not her the one going to inherit the place. He's got some attorneys and a bunch of witnesses, and the whole bit. Anyway, her and me ain't going quite the same direction on the subject of Phil. Hell, I reckon if my dad was to drown in his sorrows I'd just stay out to here and live offa the rent my mom and Phil would have to pay me." He shrugged and grinned "Would lower yours some, though."

"How old are you now, George?"

"Fifteen." He winced. "In two months."

"You know some things about life for fifteen, that's all I can say."

"Yeah. I know too much about some things and too little about others. For instance, I know this ol' dog is going to be okay pretty soon and ain't going to like this rope. What I don't know is how we can get rid of the rope and let the dog roam like he's used to without Marge comin' unglued."

A week later I put on extra socks, fished gloves from a dresser drawer, and stepped out into the new snow. Hearing the house door close, Rover, whose rope kept coming loose somehow, trotted out of the hog pen gate to greet me. I petted him a minute, then started for Mississippi Boulevard, the paved street leading out of our particular dogpatch toward the city. Giving Rover orders to stay led to the bother of enforcing them or tying him up. I just let him follow me.

Big George, who'd returned a day or two earlier, stopped brushing the snow from the roof of his Oldsmobile and stepped out to meet me and the dog at the edge of the street. "It's a hell of a cold morning for a walk."

"It's not too bad," I said. "At least it's sunny. Haven't seen you in a while."

"Been holed up in Tampa. Thought I might stay there for the winter, but you know how them things go. Congratulations by the way on the new addition to your family. The boy says she's plump and smiles. The little one, I mean."

"Smiles before and after she shits, at least. Plump and smiles and hoots all night like an owl," I grinned. "Like me, she seems to believe the best part of life takes place after the sun goes down and just about everybody else has gone to bed."

"Probably figures it's the best way to see more of her dad. What's her name?"

"Serena."

George nodded approvingly. "Say, I was on my way downtown and thought to offer you a ride. Seems the least I could do after what you did for my boy after that dog fight."

"Didn't do much for your boy, really," I said, "but I wouldn't say no to the offer of a ride."

"Grabya a cold beer out of the trunk of the car if you want. It's still open."

"Thanks, George, but the ride is really all I want. That, and maybe a little patience about the back rent I owe. I'll get caught up pretty quick."

Carefully, George positioned his own open can of beer on the dashboard while he got behind the wheel. The car was cold and I rolled down the window to avoid steaming up the imperfectly cleared windows. The big car smoked when the man goosed it. The tires crunched through the frozen driveway snow, making a sound that made me think of driving over broken champagne glasses.

George turned the steering wheel hard and gunned the motor as he gained the paved street at the corner. Fishtailing, then righting his heavy four-door, he pulled on his beer a long time before balancing it between his thighs.

"Georgie says your old DeSoto ain't running at all."

"No," I said, "and that's one of the things that has made a new job hard to come by. Part of the reason, I guess, why the rent's late."

"What's wrong with her?"

"With who?"

"The old jalopy."

"Bout everything, I guess. After the battery, the timing chain and cracked gear teeth are said to be what's keeping it from starting up. Old age is supposed to be what keeps it from keeping going afterwards."

"The body's a little lacking for paint," Big George said, "but, hey, that car was made from real U.S. Steel at a time when people still took pride in their work. Bet it wouldn't take all that much to get her going again."

"Yeah, maybe so, but not knowing a torque wrench from a plug gapper, I should have left it on the lot for somebody else, I guess."

George swilled and belched quietly but unapologetically and smoked for a time. The heater began to warm the car. I lit a cigarette and thought George looked too thin, too old, too wrinkled. There were stretches of smooth ice on the paved streets. I reached for a door handle and hoped the beer was his first of the day.

"How far you behind in your rent now?"

"Five weeks, about."

George took a pair of aviator sunglasses from behind the sun visor and adjusted them on his sunburned nose. "I got a mind to offer you a trade. Maybe a couple months free rent for your jalopy. The one month you're behind, say, and the one coming due."

"You serious?"

"Sure, why not?"

"No more questions. You got a deal."

"All right. Me and George'll push it out of your driveway over to the hog pen where we can putter on its innerds a bit. I figure we'll take our time, work on it a little here and there. With any luck, the boy'll have a car to take his driver's license test in when he comes sixteen."

"According to what he told me that gives you a little more than a year."

"Yup, I guess that's about it. I know an old boy with a machine shop. We'll make some phone calls around to the salvage yards and stuff. Give me little more time with him, give him something to do to stay out of Marge's hair."

"I figure that gives me about a month before the rent is due again."

"What the hell, make it six weeks. Bring me or Marge a month's rent by the middle of March. I'll tell Marge you're paid up till then." Big George gave me a woozy wink.

Arriving early for my interview with the Yellow Cab Company, I went to the driver's lounge, plugged the vending machines for bad coffee, and then twisted a pair of crushed leathery donuts from a cellophane pouch. In a corner of the room was a stack of magazines. Improbably, I came on a slick visual arts magazine. Thumbing my way through and clearing it of donut crumbs, I found myself staring at a color photograph of myself, blue-lipped and angry-looking, walking down a street in Haight-Ashbury.

That evening Irene placed Serena's bassinet in the middle of the kitchen table while she washed brown rice in the sink. "How did the interview go?"

"Fine."

"They hired you?"

"Yeah."

"When do you start?"

"Next week. Three-thirty in the morning. Gordon's driving the same shift so I'll be okay without a car for a while."

"You don't seem very excited about it."

"Maybe I'll feel more excited later."

"What's the matter?"

I liked to take my time in reporting things and tended to fester in conversations that struck me as veiled interrogations. Irene put the rice on the stove and looked at me closely. "You have this look of having been surprised, like something else happened. Something you didn't exactly like."

"There's more good news, actually. Big George is back from his latest bender and I traded him the DeSoto for rent. We don't owe him anything until Easter."

"Great! Do you think Marge will go along with it?"

"She'll have to, he says, because he's going to tell her I paid him in cash. It's his property and he controls the rent money. That's probably why Marge never got heavy about the overdue rent."

"Was he drunk when he made the deal? Do you think he'll remember?" Irene looked excited. "Maybe I should go over there and tell him thanks, just as a way of reminding him. In case he forgot."

"Drunk? I dunno. I mean, it has probably been ten years since he's been sober enough to blow up one of those highway patrol balloons. But don't worry. I saw Little George when I walked past the house and he trotted out wanting to know if he and a friend of his could come and push the car out of our driveway and into the hog pen after he finished supper. He was that eager."

"So you got the job. You start next week. You traded off the DeSoto. And you have another surprise?"

I sighed and handed her the art magazine pages. She peeked into the bassinet to be sure the baby was sleeping comfortably, wiped the table with a sponge, sat down and read aloud.

"'Known primarily as one of the forerunners of postcard art, and surely one of the wittiest, Albert Fine recently performed, conducted, and documented what he is calling 'a happening without an audience.' For those who missed last month's performance at the Open Augen Gallery in Manhattan, some evidence of Fine's endeavor: twenty-six artist-captioned commentaries are hanging on the walls as a part of an exhibition titled *Trustadelic*.

"Wait. It goes on. 'Fine's photographs logically extend the printed postcard drawings which have established him as one of the forerunners of the postcard art movement. Not surprisingly, these images treat earlier themes for which the artist has become known and offer varied characteristically witty commentaries on themes of reality, representation, secrecy, trust, and voyeurism.

"'According to the gallery press release, Fine disavows "a photographer's aesthetic," and "silly notions of the artist as perceptual hero." Indeed, he "disclaims origination" and created this exhibition by giving six reconditioned cameras and a dozen rolls of film to amateur photographers he met last year in the Haight-Ashbury district of San Francisco. In exchange for the rights to reproduce and exhibit their photographs as his, and agreeing with the photographers to share the proceeds from any sales, Fine allowed the photographers to keep the cameras. But he didn't stop there. To dramatize what he has called the interplay between trust and belief, Fine recruited four volunteers from a Haight Street drug-overdose clinic. Done up in "psychedelic garb," also designed by the artist, the volunteers, two doctors, and two nurses, traversed the famed Haight-Ashbury district handing out ink-stained sugar cubes. The color blue was apparently chosen for its association with the mushroom-derived psychedelic drug, psilocybin. Under the impression they were being offered a free trip, hundreds of Haight Street would-be trippies were soon wandering the streets with stained lips, as per Western Union Car Cowboy, Figure A.

"'Exhibition curator Chetworth Bindle, who wrote the small accompanying catalog for the exhibition, says, "Albert Fine has long used small images and ink to transmit messages about love and trust to clients and various obscure persons the artist has never met. In *Trustadelic* the disappointed ink-stained hippies stand in for the artist's postcards in so far as they transmit inky messages that eschew imposing either the artist's aesthetic or authority to enter moral judgments. Political commentary, though sometimes subtle in Fine's work, is there for the vigorous and the discerning.

"'At the inception of this particular project, Fine, an artist who regularly sends his postcards to notable politicians and Vietnam War hawks, attended a party where he arranged for a well-known Bay Area renegade priest to baptize him Lyndon Johnson. Hence, in the presidential persona, Bindle writes, "Fine, imitating LBJ, was able to harmlessly disfigure innocent strangers in yet another misguided effort to save people from themselves.'"

Irene looked up from the photograph of me. "Do you feel exploited?"

"When I first saw it I felt pissed off."

"Not betrayed?"

"No, not betrayed, and not even pissed off for very long. Embarrassed, yeah. I still feel embarrassed. God knows who will see this thing. Anyway, keep reading. Turn the page. It goes on."

"My God, that's a picture of Albert all beat up."

"Read what it says."

She read aloud. "'It would not perhaps be carrying the political analogy too far to note that Fine's art has still further implications for American foreign policy. The final photo in Fine's exhibition consists of an image of the artist taken after having been beaten up by a neighborhood junkie who somehow learned that Fine had been responsible for the distribution of the stained sugar and accused him of working for the CIA.'"

"Wow," Irene said, "that is really too weird."

"Yeah, and you know who the junkie was? You remember Sandra's boyfriend? The guy who did that to him was Tom, my junkie buddy downstairs."

"How do you know?"

"I don't. Not for sure." I walked to the front door and looked out. Rover was worrying the garbage can. "The thing is, maybe the reason I don't believe in fortune telling is because it's always presented in this good-news-bad-news sort way. What's predicted is always pretty unimaginative. Yet surprises like this seem to awaken a kind of seventh sense in me, a sense that someone out there is laughing at psychics and challenging them to top this."

Yellow Checker Cab Number 231

As a new cab driver with no seniority, I was provided a ten-and-a-half-hour shift beginning at three-thirty in the morning and assigned an old Checker workhorse with 657,000 miles on it. Cab number 231 ran without faltering and had a heater that might have baked potatoes, but it was sluggish off the line and had a bad suspension.

The main challenge was following the radio, making sense of the relentless numeric recitations of cab and neighborhood numbers. When a driver reported "2-3-1's on 4-5," it meant that cab number 231 was located in the neighborhood mapped and designated as 45. The dispatcher's drone of "2-3-1's 5 on 4-5" meant that I was fifth in line for a trip originating in the 45 area.

The driver who had trained me taught me to use the radio to "log on a post," that is to register in a neighborhood, but said nothing about which neighborhoods were better, safer, or more potentially remunerative. On my first morning, I logged on to the post nearest the cab company.

The dispatcher's response was a blasé monotone. "2-3-1, The Sportsman Lounge."

"What?"

"Who's that out there telling me what, over?"

"I didn't hear what you said."

Cab drivers were a captive audience, wholly dependent on a dispatcher's goodwill. Dispatchers provided income and, when bored, a measure of potentially embarrassing entertainment.

"You didn't hear me," the sarcastic voice said, "and I don't know who is talking to me, Boss. So that makes us even." The dispatcher turned his attention to other cabs on the street, reciting what sounded like garbled grade school math problems and solutions.

"2-3-1, did you hear me?"

I fumbled with my microphone and dropped it in my lap. "No, I didn't hear you."

"2-3-1, the Sportsman." The dispatcher took a sharp breath. "6-5-0 is 6 on 1-4." Another pause. "4-7-9 it's 3652 Elati. 2-9-8? Yeah, Boss. She called back. She's in the lobby of the hotel with a white suitcase. 2-3-1 are you sleepy this morning and sneaking a nap on me?"

"Uh, I couldn't hear what you said."

"2-3-1 you have a wonderful tenor but don't talk to me EVER again until AFTER you've told me what your cab number is."

"This is 2-3-1. I didn't hear what you said."

"2-3-1, I said 'The Sportsman' . . .as in Lounge."

"Where's that?"

"2-3-1, I'm not talking to you until you can remember to precede everything you say with your cab number. I got real cab drivers to work with and it's time to put the drunks to bedeebye."

"2-3-1," I stammered. "I don't know where the Sportsman Lounge is."

"It's at 30th and Lawrence, Boss. And take your finger off the button when you're done using the microphone so you don't make me deaf. I got business to take care of this morning, and when you hang on to that button I can't hear my cabs." Sharp breath. "6-1-9 it's 2176 Curtis. 9-4-0's 1 on 1-9. 9-4-0, if you stay way out there near Pike's Peak I figure I'll have a trip for you about Christmas Eve. You're going to have to deadhead in toward civilization, Boss. Even the coyotes haven't moved out that far yet. . . 231, over."

I dived after the microphone. "2-3-1."

"2-3-1, either you're a new driver or you got a bag of sand between your ears."

"2-3-1's a new driver."

"Okay, 2-3-1, you're a new driver. Don't shout into your microphone. Take your finger off the button when you're done talking to me. Sevens, I don't know, she said she'd be out there waiting for you. Honk once, then get out and ring the bell. 1-4-2 it's Denver General Hospital, the emergency entrance. 2-3-1 are you alive?"

"2-3-1's alive."

"2-3-1, you coulda fooled me. The Sportsman Lounge is at 30th and Lawrence. Now put your thumb on that button and let me hear you say those sweet words, '2-3-1 check.'"

"2-3-1 check."

"6-0-6, go to the back room and ring the doorbell that says Maggie. . . 2-3-1, take a deep breath, Son. It's gonna be a long morning."

The bars had closed at two, but as a private club, the Sportsman was permitted to serve until four-thirty in the morning. The slummy downtown street was dark and empty of traffic. The only sign of life was a series of blinking lights out front. When there was no response to the honking of my horn, I left the battered Checker running outside and walked inside.

From a poster on the door I learned that the Sportsman would tolerate no guns, knives, clubs, or heavy objects that might be used as weapons and that management reserved the right to frisk guests before serving them. Guests who didn't like this policy, though I certainly approved of it, were invited to go elsewhere. The hot room smelled of beer and barf. I gagged, cupped my hands around my mouth and said, "Yellow Cab."

Raucous conversations abruptly ceased and seven or eight dark-skinned men stared at me: a pawky rooster crowing an end to their night. Even the bartender glared. I wanted to do my professional duty, but I didn't want to take another step toward the bar, and I secretly hoped whoever called for the cab had already given up and walked home.

"Yellow Cab," I said one last time. "Did anybody here call a cab?"

I was glad when the uneven row of angry drunks just sat there. The fact was, I didn't want to take anybody I could see in the Sportsman for a ride in the silent city in the wee hours of the morning.

Outside, two men were climbing into my cab, one of them settling in behind the steering wheel. The last thing I wanted to do was hang out at the Sportsman and report my cab had been stolen on my first shift. Without thinking I rushed to the driver's side of cab and pushed the man trying to get behind the wheel. "You can't do that," I said. It was only when I saw the look of anger on his face that I realized that maybe I'd made a rash decision and would now have to pay the price for it. On the other hand, I was as scared of being left without wheels outside the Sportsman as I was of the two hoody-looking characters trying to steal my cab.

"Don't push me, Motherfucker!"

As the would-be-thief recovered his balance, his buddy emerged from the passenger side and started toward me. I knew that no one in the Sportsman would come to my aid. I was on my own.

I jumped up onto the car hood and hopped on the sturdy roof of my dieseling Checker. The men spoke to each other in Spanish. The would-be passenger suggested that the best thing to do would be to get in the cab and drive away with me still on the roof, but the guy I'd pushed wore the fierce, aggrieved expression of one who could find peace and honor again only after my death. He moved one way toward me. His friend tried another direction. I took up a defensive position on the roof over the windshield.

"You may get me eventually." I wagged my heavy engineer's boots in their faces. "But at least one of you's going to lose some front teeth before it happens." In defiance and terror, I whooped and did a little jig.

They called me names I couldn't understand and were apparently perfecting their plan of attack when a police car cruising Lawrence Street flashed high headlight beams and roared to my rescue. One of the thugs dashed across the street, flung open a gate, and dashed through it with a big cop in hot pursuit. A second cop jumped out of the patrol car without bothering to close the door and chased the other one in the opposite direction.

I climbed down and stood in the middle of Lawrence Street, my knees shaking and my hands damp with sweat. Streetlights sizzled. Static from the police car competed with the drone from the cab radio. Save for my own heavy breathing, the sputtering radios, and the heavy groan of a truck horn many blocks away, the predawn morning was very still. Maybe somebody had bought another round inside the Sportsman, maybe turned the jukebox up.

The last thing I wanted to do was get back on the radio, remember my cab number, and try to tell the sarcastic cab dispatcher what had happened. The second to the last thing I wanted was a conversation with the responding police officers. The more I thought about it, the more worried I became that my enemies might evade the cops and double-back in an effort to complete their high jacking.

I drove five miles down Broadway to a better neighborhood and calmed my nerves with a cup of coffee from an all-night donut shop. If the cops wanted to talk to me, I figured, they would call the cab company.

Back behind the wheel, with the sun coming up I was dispatched to an all-night Safeway store and helped a daft old woman load five bags filled with frozen dinners into the cab's trunk. After carrying groceries upstairs to her rancid apartment, I was sent to pick up a businessman hoping not to miss a plane to Milwaukee. At the airport, I got in line behind six or seven other cabs to wait for an incoming fare. It was there, when I got out to wipe the windshield down, that I noticed the dimpled pattern my boots had embossed on the cab roof. This worried me and I drove the rest of my first shift expecting that I'd be fired for turning in a damaged cab. Not only had I left the scene of a crime, I'd embossed the roof of my cab. Toward the end of my shift, I heard unexpectedly from the dispatcher.

"2-3-1, over."

I groped for the microphone, heart pounding. "2-3-1."

"2-3-1, I got a message for you, Boss."

"What is it?"

"2-3-1, it says right here that your wife got a ride to your parents' house, so don't go home for her. Instead, just go to your parents.' Over."

"That's all?"

"Is that 2-3-1, forgetting how to use his radio again? 2-3-1 tell me again, Boss. Are you mentally retarded or just numb with happiness that you finally get to go home?"

"2-3-1," I gulped, too flustered to respond, but remembering, at least, to use my cab number. "That's all?"

"Yeah, that's all, 2-3-1, so drive your cab another half an hour or whatever you've got and then go have your dinner. 6-1-9 says what? Right, 6-1-9. 2-3-1, over?"

"2-3-1."

"Driver 6-1-9 says that you're a new driver AND you're definitely mentally retarded."

619 was Gordon's cab number. I was glad he was on the streets and that before long I would be able to tell him about my adventure at the Sportsman. I laughed out loud, convinced that I'd gotten through my first day. Then I remembered the dents in the roof.

The maintenance attendant on duty at the cab garage was filled with good cheer. I parked 231 in its designated stall, checked my mileage figures, and started for the driver's lounge to count my money and compute what I owed the company and turn in my trip sheet. Hiking the lot, I noticed that most of the cabs were banged up one place or another. Walking back to my cab as a casual observer, the roof welts and indentations didn't seem that noticeable. I decided to say nothing about them. I could always claim, I figured, that I'd failed to notice them in the excitement of my first day on the streets.

Nothing was said about the cab either the next day or the day after, and I soon found I could understand the dispatchers, get off an occasional good-humored remark of my own, and turn up at most addresses within the city limits. Still, walking out under the lights of the parking lot to climb in my cab to begin my shift in the darkest hour of the night, I almost never failed to notice the marks on the roof. There were even times when I ran my hand over the roof as if the dents left by my boot heels comprised a message written in Braille. "Transportation and communication."

Life at home consisted of naps interrupted by Serena's crying or ringing telephones. There were late afternoons over a pile of dirty dishes. Dead winter days, diapers hanging in the kitchen because outside it was snowing. Irene sat making pencil sketches of the baby and hanging them on the walls. The fridge was filled with tasted and disliked jars of baby food.

Through the kitchen window, I could look over the weathered fence into the hog pen where Little George often sat behind the partly repaired DeSoto's steering wheel. More often than not, Rover was with him, on his regrown haunches in the back seat, eyes front and center like some preposterous canine potentate on a Sunday tour of his vast doggy estate. As I had done years before, Little George seemed to sit dreaming of days when he would at last be able to drive the DeSoto down the dirt street, out onto the pavements, through the city and into some better world where there were no attack-minded German Shepherds, no alcoholic short-order cooks, suppressive mothers, no house-painter jerks with Clark Gable mustaches like his mother's lover. Dog's life, boy's life, car's world.

The '60 VW Microbus

In March I persuaded the cab finance company to loan me the money to buy a red-and-white 1960 Volkswagen bus. I gloried in it and for a few days life looked better than it had in a long time. No longer shelling out big cab fares for rides to and work, I brought home more money. Grocery shopping and errands became a breeze.

The weather warmed and I managed to get two days off in a row, so I decided to spend one solitary day fishing and drove my bus to my parents' house to pick up fishing gear stored in the basement. My dad associated Volkswagens with people too independent and thrifty to buy encyclopedias from him. Less than impressed, he referred to my van as "an underpowered Kaiser roll for pipe-smoking schoolteachers."

When my mom served coffee and pie, I slyly asked him for details about the newly acquired gouge along one side of his Cadillac. When my parents started arguing about my dad's habit of swigging quarts of beer while navigating the curving two-lane blacktops of western Colorado, I picked up my tackle box and fishing rod and gleefully headed home to pack.

At dawn I drove alone to a mountain lake. Lobelias and penstemons quivered in patches of late morning sun. Magpies hectored me as I walked to the lake. The wind hissed steadily, bringing a rich mountain smell I associated with deep cold groundwater drawn up from granite bedrock into the roots of blue spruce and aspen trees.

Threading beady salmon eggs on a small hook, I cast my bait as far into the choppy waters as I could. Then, balancing my rod between two stones, I hunkered down on the lee side of a big boulder and stared at my line. Black flies interested themselves in the jar of salmon eggs I'd placed on a flat stone. When I spread out my lunch, bees walked my tuna fish sandwich and banana, explored the creamy coffee in a thermos, and then wandered to a bit of dyed feather and bright lure in the open tackle box. With the wind gusting and the sun bright in my face, I sprawled in a bed of red pine needles and listened to the rhythmic gurgle of waters. Fluffy clouds drifted across a blue sky and my mind turned to thoughts of freedom, of justice and its place in my life.

Irene thought it childish of me to rage against Nixon and Agnew, and accused me of refusing to be happy until the state of the world aligned itself with my hopes and expectations. I countered that she lived too deeply in schoolgirl fantasies of enchanted forests and bedtime fairytales. Fairytales were sources of wisdom, she said; it seemed to her highly enlightened to face existence with wide-eyed wonder. I admired, even envied, the pleasure she took from simple routine, but worried because she refused to assess the damage done to all of human life by the self-interested actions of others. I felt I had to remain extra vigilant so that I could defend her against nameless evils. I resented that I had to protect her while she took refuge in a cocoon of motherhood. She seemed eager and able to banish the past.

I was twenty-two years old and had been waiting too long for the present to deliver on the promises of the past. Or were they my fantasies about what the past had promised me? A time of great hope and exhilaration had passed, but I thought it might return, couldn't let it go, and believed it was up to me and an inventive cadre of others to revive a world of faded promise. It was getting harder to cling to the notion that the human race was about to begin a meteoric ascent toward a state of higher consciousness. Still, I hoped and waited with growing impatience.

Self-pity ran in my family and was strong in me. What dark, obliterating karma required me now to rise up before dawn each morning and wrestle through city traffic? What was I to make of my surly cab passengers, most of whom seemed to live only for more of what had already sickened and numbed their spirits? When would the universe begin to resound with joy? But how could creation rejoice in cosmic playfulness while Nixon and Agnew conspired and the war in Vietnam went forward in lies and blood? What particularly festered was a remembered image of a sun-browned kid about my own age, college dropout from Indiana or Ohio, standing up in Golden Gate Park to predict that the day was coming when an LSD-illuminated Martin Luther King, together with Allen Ginsberg and assorted others, would lead the country out of its napalm rages and its race-benighted nightmares. Sophomoric pipe dream though I had known it to be even then, the scenario had been advanced with a hope so compelling and seductive that its fervor had poisoned me with delusions of magic.

Sprawled by the lake, burdened with the self-pity I recognized but couldn't shake, my heart felt as cold and heavy as an anvil. I was shackled by the illusions of my generation: somehow nothing mattered when everything actually did, marooned in a grim psychedelic bardo, numb to the present, suspended in a rage that had only a moving target.

When the sun disappeared behind a mountain, I reeled my empty line in and drove home.

Early that summer I was awarded a slightly later shift. Summer was a long, stifling August heat wave, days of brutal temperatures and intense glare. One late afternoon toward the end of my day, I turned the corner onto California Street, looking forward to getting off the hot roads, sipping a cold soft drink in the cab drivers' lounge, then going home to sit out under the elm tree in front of the house with Irene and Serena.

California Street was an artery leading downtown through the city's predominantly black neighborhood. I shifted lazily into second gear and heard a sudden thump. From the corner of my eye, I saw a dark form ricochet from the hood. A bird? A dog? The cab crossed an intersection and started down the next block before it occurred to me that the small object could only have been a child.

Yanking the hand brake, I put the cab in park and switched on the emergency parking lights. As I trudged up the street, a thin, taunting melody emanated from a bell-shaped speaker on the roof of an ice cream truck. In the street, about three sprinting steps from the safety of the curb, lay a small black boy who'd dashed away from the ice cream truck and was now crumpled on the pavement.

Three more leaping steps and he would have cleared the cab, gained the far side of the street with his ice cream bar still clenched in his fist, and I would have glided obliviously by. One or two seconds either way and he would be safely licking the melting stickiness from between his fingers instead of lying as he was on the asphalt, forming a question mark with one thin arm, his tiny fingers making spasmodic motions. A greeting, a farewell, a question, one I echoed with every step toward the crowd gathering around him.

Why?

Why?

Why?

Everybody was gathering from up and down the block, wringing hands and waving arms and stomping feet and saying what I heard myself saying.

No.

No.

No.

About fifteen feet away from the boy, the sweaty load of my body became too much for me to tow. I dropped to my knees on the hot pavement. All around me, angry voices fluttered like the flames of a bonfire directed at the sky. I was at the bottom of a fire pit, protected by gravity, for now, from the worst of heat.

A big, older black woman knelt down beside me. "Lord," she said, "sweet Lord have mercy."

My knees were in the street. My mind was in the sky. My voice was saying things over and over again. The woman's voice was alongside, around and under my own, lifting it, praying to a God who was always changing and rechanging His mind, a God open to last-minute appeals. The words moved out of her lungs on an electrical current. Under the sweat streaming down my face and neck, I could feel her words rising like glowing, lighter-than-air bubbles. Either I scooted closer to her, or the cool white light that had enveloped her from the beginning spread out to soothe and vibrate in me. Our voices moved together, saying things that could never be remembered. A coolness washed over me. The hairs on my neck and arms stood up. Tingling, reassuring vibrations traveled up and down my spine and filled my head. From a safe, cool height I heard voices all around me saying that I'd been speeding and that I was white and, like all others of my age and race, naturally reckless with their lives and the lives of their children. I looked without comprehending at the small body in the street. Something should be done, something about ass kicking, something about burning. Burn baby burn. Burn for Martin, burn for Bobby, bring some hot wrath on this honky racing down these streets, indifferent to the little lives in L.A., Chicago, Detroit. Burn, Denver, burn.

A siren wailed. Two panicky white cops appeared and pulled me out of the blazing and tingling light, away from the woman, through the baking heat of the evening, and shut me up in the cop car. As they closed me in and turned back to listen to the gathering crowd, the woman's voice rose, "It wasn't your fault, Honey. Just keep praying to Jesus."

Vapors of heat surrounded and distorted the shape of an ambulance. The lights on its roof went round and round. Two men in sweat-stained white shirts loaded the boy onto a stretcher, glided him inside, hopped in, and drove off, making a mournful, desperate music. A man in a loosened necktie squatted down, and with a length of chalk, made a quick contour drawing of where the boy had lain.

On the dry lawns along California Street, the cops nodded and talked a long time with witnesses. Women shook their heads slowly and wept. Men with long fingers gesticulated toward the cab and the car where I sat. Drab official cars, gray and green, disgorged men with tape measures, cameras, and notepads. They called out to one another and paced back and forth between the cab, still idling down the block, and the chalk drawing where the boy had been. A man with sideburns photographed the still-open driver's door of my cab and walked slowly back to speak to a man in a straw hat studying the pavement for skid marks.

At the police station a redheaded detective handed me a soft drink and led me to an air-conditioned room. Two men with empty shoulder holsters sat side by side at a battered desk, poring over papers covered with handwritten scrawl. The absence of skid marks, the position of the boy's body relative to the dent in the cab's fender, together with reports from the older woman and the ice cream driver tended to confirm my story that I had not been speeding or driving recklessly. However, since several eyewitnesses insisted I'd been doing sixty or seventy miles an hour, the detectives said they were obliged to cite me for reckless driving. The man who wrote out the ticket shrugged sympathetically as he handed it to me.

"The truth is," he said, "bad shit happens when people let their kids play in the streets. My advice is to go home, stay home, drink all the beer you can hold, and go to bed knowing that some night real soon you're going to sleep easy because the people who will count in the weeks ahead have done their homework and honestly believe you weren't speeding."

About eight that night the phone rang. The cab company attorney, Mark Davis, said, "Bad news, the little bugger died on us."

At a deposition the next afternoon, I learned that Samuel Waddell had just turned five. Davis assured me that while he believed every particular of my story, we had to prepare for hostile witnesses. As many as half a dozen angry people said I'd been speeding. Although the filing of reckless driving charges was clearly a prelude to more serious vehicular manslaughter charges, Davis said, he had every reason to believe we would win an acquittal.

In this way, the grief I wanted to feel for the boy who would never become a man tangled and knotted itself with my fear of becoming a scapegoat, being singled out and convicted of trumped-up charges, sacrificed by elected white politicians and some gutless judge to appease a mob that might otherwise burn Denver's Five Points to the ground.

Irene slept placidly in the dawn. Serena was between us, her tiny knees tucked up under her round tummy. Adjusting the blankets, I carried my clothes into the kitchen and dressed.

A warm wind smelled of hay and, incongruously, black tea. Inky clouds drifted south. A symphony of crickets lamented the brightening of the sky. I lit a cigarette and sat on the stoop. Rover ambled over to dig his wet snout under my free hand.

As a kid, the sacrament of confession had turned me into a composer of lists. The last words of the dream I'd awakened from had been "sins of motion." There had been the stick through the front wheel of the girl's trike and her fall to the sidewalk. Snowballs I'd thrown at cars might have caused an accident. Then there'd been drag racing my mom's Ford and the high-speed bump that tore the hood from its hinges, the crunch of Lincoln against Mercury at the dealership, the burying of my Dodge's license plates in the Mojave Desert, the disastrous purchase of the DeSoto, and the speeding I'd done every day to earn a living behind the wheel of the cab. The gods of karma were inexorable, so how surprised should I be that people along California Street now wanted to testify that I'd been doing seventy miles an hour? I hadn't been going that fast, of course, but had I really been doing only twenty-five as I'd claimed? How fast had I been going a few minutes before? Had the universe tried to warn me? In the court of law or in the court of my own mind, how innocent was I of the death of Samuel Waddell?

The crickets settled down and the sky brightened. Cars whizzing down Mississippi Boulevard turned off their headlights. Meadowlarks and mourning doves in a stand of cottonwoods across the street predicted another hot day. The August morning lit the upper leaves of Rover's elm tree while I rubbed the little matted knots behind his mud-flap ears. Across the street a screen door slammed and Ben, the retired black truck farmer, emerged from his house, scattering the chickens worrying the gravel at his doorstep. Ben called out a cheery greeting and I lifted an arm high above my head, hoping thereby to convey both goodwill and my preference for silence. Hollering words about the delicious coolness of the morning, Ben dragged a sack from the chicken house and disappeared into his little bungalow.

Rover wandered over to sniff the first splash of sunlight on the bole of the elm tree and Irene came out to join me, saying something I didn't hear. She sat beside me on the step and studied her bare feet, then turned her brown eyes to me, wanting my permission to stay where she was, take an action, ask a question. I grunted, provisionally.

"How long have you been sitting out here?"

"I don't know."

"Couldn't you sleep?"

"I slept okay."

"How are you feeling?"

Having seen Bert lose all sense of time and place to the most trivial frustration, I had cultivated a reluctance to overstate my feelings. From my readings in Zen and other mystical dabblings, I was sure that to do so was to grant them a power and permanence they might not otherwise enjoy. To experience and abide feelings was one thing; to describe them was another. To contextualize them was impossible, an illusion. To wait feelings out, I thought, was to recognize that confusion and conflict were always in the process of passing, even in the dieseling of guilt and grief. Irene had not been observing the progress of the clouds. Originally, they had been the color of a fresh bruise. Now they were a creamy color, almost buttery.

"It's a beautiful morning," I said, "and I feel better now that the sun is up."

"I'll go in and fix you some breakfast."

She went in and left the door open, so I turned around and watched her fetch a frying pan and carry it to the kitchen stove. For a moment I considered asking her if she was feeling more lost than she ever had before, but in the bedroom the baby stirred and sputtered, and I remembered how upsetting Irene found it when I didn't seem to share her conviction that the very presence of Serena, like some slow-acting medicine, was certain to restore and improve our lives.

Irene carried me out coffee, toast, and eggs and then went to finish tending the baby. The toast tasted like sand. I put it down on the step. Rover flinched at it, tentatively, reluctant to presume, willing, if necessary, to exercise self-control. When I pushed it at him with my foot, he inhaled it with two quick snaps, followed by a single motion of his sticky tongue.

I lifted a forkful of eggs to my mouth. Their consistency repelled me and I spit my mouthful into the grass. Rover, jumped up, snared it, and stood grateful and vigilant, just in case.

By the time Irene carried Serena outside, my plate was on the step beside me, glistening with dog saliva.

"Do you want more eggs?"

"No thanks."

"Do you like them like that, with a little cheddar?"

"Yeah. They were good. Coffee's dead perfect." I smiled and, for a moment, wanted to ask if there was somehow some way we could make the baby comfortable and go back in the bedroom and undress each other, hold on to each other's thin tense shoulders, until we recognized the old desire. But there seemed to be a huge gulf between seducing a stranger I could walk away from and needing a woman I had disappointed in so many small ways, if not sexually, every day. Like an old swimmer on the beach I sat contemplating a rough tide. The moment passed, adhering to other similar moments, acquiring mass.

I was cradling Serena in my arms when a Volkswagen bus almost identical to mine turned off Mississippi and started down the dusty street toward us. I saw a familiar shape, a hand rising up in the window in greeting, just before the bus pulled in behind my own.

"I'll be damned!"

Irene asked, "Who is it? Do you know them?"

"I know him. It's Denny, Rick's friend, this guy I used to hang out with in San Diego. Remember my telling you about getting thrown in jail for carrying the switchblade knife that wouldn't open? That's the guy I was with."

"Good," Irene said, starting for the bus. "A little reunion with an old friend will draw you out of yourself a little."

Three, four years? What had it been? There was a new prominence of bone over the eyes and along the jaw that I attributed to the disappearance of the last of his baby fat. Otherwise, Denny looked much as he had when we parted at the San Diego bus station.

A tall pregnant woman in a plaid halter and wraparound skirt emerged from the passenger side and hurried around to greet Irene and the baby. She'd coiled a pair of heavy blond braids around and above her temples, elongating her head and making her thin neck appear unequal to its burden.

Rover got up from his tree, prancing and wagging his hindquarters. Obligingly, the woman stooped, ruffled his shaggy ears and spanked his flanks with an open hand. Stepping back and swiping her hands on her hips, perhaps to clear them of dog hair, she extended a long arm to me. "I'm Omaha."

I marveled at the arm's lightness. "Pleased to meet you, Omaha."

Denny shuffled his feet and patted her firm, rounded belly. "Her real name is Audrey," he said. "You should hear what she's thinking of naming our kid."

"No," Omaha insisted, "my real name is the name that's real to me." She looked first at Irene. "Luckily, we've got three months yet to decide about the brat. Besides, maybe the kid will have ideas of its own. Denny tries, but he's a little slow with new ideas. Anyway, I believe we should all feel free to use any name we want. Whatever has a personal significance."

Irene smiled nervously. "Are you by any chance from Nebraska?"

270

"No." Omaha laughed. "Not Omaha, like the Nebraska city. But *Om*, you know, like the holy breath of the godhead, and *aha* like "surprise." I'm Dylan's gypsy gal, originally from San Jose." She hesitated, as if there was more that might need saying before she could finally be shut of the obligation to explain herself. "Originally," she added.

Denny moved a hank of hair from his forehead and scratched one of his sideburns. "Well, Tim, I gotta tell you Omaha pissed your dad off pretty good this morning, with my help, of course."

"How so?"

"Woke him up."

"Now that sounds like a daunting way to start the day," Irene said.

"Worse for him than us," Denny said. "We've been camping for a couple of days, and I left my watch up at the campground and I assumed it was later than it was."

Omaha, who was provoking Serena's toothless laughter by touching noses with her, glanced up and grinned at me. "He came to the door in his underwear, hair sticking up all over the place, looking as if he was unsure if we were real, or characters in a dream."

Irene took the baby from Omaha and proceeded to burp her. "Did he call you fucking idiots?"

Denny laughed. "No, but he looked like he was thinking about it until your good old mom hurried to the rescue. He was wearing these old boxer shorts, man. The flap was all worn and the whole time he stood at the door staring at us, I kept thinking that if he moved the wrong way his prick might fall out."

I smiled, "Sounds like vintage Bert Barlow. In fact, I'm sure some sort of a display, or maybe a comparison, wasn't all that far from his conscious mind. Physical endowment, aggression, and territoriality get all mixed up in him when a stranger rings his doorbell. He's very grizzly bear-like when he wants to sleep in."

"I guess maybe we're lucky then. If he had been canine and territorial he might have come out and pissed on my boots or something. Actually, he was like a bear. When your mom stepped in, he just kind of growled and retreated. She gave us your address."

"And I bet," Omaha said, more to Irene than me, "you can guess which of us wanted to call first and which one insisted on driving right over."

"Damn right," Denny nodded and winked at me. "After all, why should your dad be the only one to be surprised?"

I laughed. My parents didn't know about Samuel Waddell and I had no plans to tell them. From time to time, I worried they'd somehow find out. "I'm sure once he's fully awake for the day," I speculated, "the phone will ring and I'll hear some choice words about my insensitive, not to say mangy, friends. In fact, now that I think of it, consider yourself appointed to answer the phone for the next few hours."

After a few minutes, Denny went inside to shower. Omaha carried sourdough batter and raspberry compote from a cooler in their bus and started a breakfast of pancakes. Irene filled an old turkey roaster with hot water, carried it out into the sun, and gave Serena a bath in it. I wrestled a stiff hose into position among the last vegetables in our garden and turned on the sprinkler.

I ate and ate. When I lit a cigarette and glanced at Omaha and Denny, their looks were a little too solicitous. I realized Irene must have managed to tell them about the accident. Gathering the plates and scraping the remains of breakfast into a tarnished pie tin that served as Rover's doggy dish, I went inside to shower and change clothes. When I returned a few minutes later with a fresh pot of coffee, Rover was shining the bottom of his scrap plate with his tongue and Omaha and Denny were telling Irene in awed tones about the Woodstock Festival and their summer on the road with two families, the Biancos and the Thunderheads.

While threading new laces in my boots, I did my best to make sense of Omaha's report. From what I gathered, the Biancos and Thunderheads had been living down the road from Denny and Omaha in Eureka, California. Bill Bianco and Ron Thunderhead had bought a pair of retired county school buses and convinced Denny and Omaha to follow them to Woodstock in Denny's VW bus. Afterwards, inspired by days and nights of hashish, music, rain, and dancing at Woodstock, the three couples had formed Grooved-Out Productions and begun drawing up plans to promote a series of smaller "mini-Woodstocks" near Boulder. Bianco's cousin Dominic, who had remained in California, was said to be best friends with a millionaire. Dom's millionaire friend would provide the necessary front money.

Having cased out and discarded Boulder as a base of operations, they'd gone on a scouting mission to check out potential free outdoor concert sites. Denny and Omaha were bringing up the rear in their underpowered VW bus, when they came on the big school buses parked on the road shoulder, smoking and steaming. At the moment, Omaha said, the Biancos and Thunderheads and their five kids were stranded in a high mountain campground up near Bailey. Denny and Omaha had driven to Denver in the hope of finding quick jobs and raising the money to have the buses towed down to the city for major engine overhauls.

"They're big and heavy," Denny said, "but mechanically they're pretty simple. If we can find a place to work on them, we can rebuild them ourselves. A good machine shop, some parts, maybe a hoist and a rack. No big deal."

Omaha sipped the last of her coffee and looked at Irene. "Like I'm over the judgment visions about it now, but at first I thought it was really weird that Denny's ethics permit him to smoke dope but not to deal it." Denny raised his eyebrows and grumbled. Omaha laughed. "I'm cool with it. I'm just like telling Irene that it makes it a little harder for Bill, who's up there now patrolling campgrounds on his motorcycle, attempting to deal to raise some of the repair money."

"He's comfortable with it," Denny said. "And like I said, Om, it's your karma. You want to come down and deal his dope here in town, it's fine with me."

"No. I'm too naive. The narcs would set me up for sure. Besides, I'm a crack secretary. I'll find temp work easy."

"Bill will probably ride his bike down here in a few days," Denny said. "He's smooth and selling the dope should go okay. Hell, from the look of things around here, it seems about like he could just walk the streets of your neighborhood."

"I'd help you out with a short-term loan if I could," I said, tying my laces. "But I've fallen behind in my rent and I just lost my cab-driving job."

"Don't worry about it," Denny said. "We didn't come to touch you up for bread, though maybe you can help us come up with some leads for work."

Irene finished pulling the baby's tiny arms through a sundress decorated with ducklings and tiny pink ribbons. "You're going to be late for your doctor's appointment, Tim. It's almost ten-thirty."

Omaha shook her head and looked at me a little dubiously. "I hope you still know where your head is when you come back, Man. If this shrink doesn't know what's happening, he's just going to put a kink in your brain and blow your mind with terminology." I hadn't said I was going to see a shrink and shot Irene a betrayed look. "That's what they did to my brother," Omaha continued, "filled his head with nonsense, and turned him from a surfer prince into some uniform-wearing stranger who polishes his shoes every night and issues parking tickets for a living."

"It's bad karma to keep secrets from your friends," Irene said. "Isn't that the gist of what you and Gordon agreed about a few days ago?"

"You're off now?" Denny asked.

I shrugged. "A lot of people who didn't really see the accident have persuaded themselves they were in the front row. For some reason, the cab company's lawyer thinks it will make a good impression on the judge that I've been to a shrink in case people start testifying that I was going a hundred miles an hour. I don't quite follow his logic on that, unless he proposes to make a case that I wasn't disturbed before the accident but that I am disturbed now. Tug somebody's heartstrings, maybe. The cab company is paying my legal fees, so I figure I better play along."

Denny registered concern. "You know, maybe we should come back when things aren't so hectic for you guys."

"No," I said, sneaking a look at Irene, seeing her nod. "You are both welcome to stay here as long as you like." I stooped down to kiss Serena. "I'll be back before dinner. Maybe we can come up with a way to make some quick money."

When I returned from the shrink later that afternoon, Little George's DeSoto's hood was open and Denny was draped across its faded fender, grunting and muttering at the motor. As many as two-dozen greasy parts were arranged in tidy rows on a stained tarp at his feet.

The hog pen was a two-hundred-foot-long enclosure bordered by a gray, rotting wooden fence. It had been a long time since it had been home to anything but boards and scrap. Now, apparently, it would be a temporary home to Denny and Omaha; a teepee, tied to the roof of Denny's bus earlier, occupied a long triangle of shade just inside the northern end of the hog pen a hundred feet or more from the old DeSoto. Denny raised up from his work, spit in the dust, and saluted me. "Hey, Tim, how did the interview go?"

"It was a little longer than I expected, but otherwise all right. From the look of things around here I feel like I've been gone a week. Obviously, I've got a lot to catch up on."

Denny's grunt became a smile. "Yep. We've made a good start on just about everything."

"Looks like you've accomplished more on the DeSoto in a few hours than my landlord has in months. I take it you met George."

"Quite a character." Denny wiped a wrench against a pant leg. "He's one of those guys who fixes cars by removing and inspecting parts, then gets worried he'll forget how they fit together before he gets around to working on it again, and so reinstalls the bad parts and has to start all over from scratch." Denny saw me eyeing the beer cans. "Never was very cold, but hey, I think there's still one or two over there in the cooler."

Drowned bugs floated in three or four inches of tepid water in the cooler. The lone remaining beer tasted warm and sweet, but I pulled hard on it anyway. "Where's Irene and Omaha?"

"Across the field for a tarot card reading. Irene said to tell you we're invited over there for dinner about six."

"Okay, now we know about dinner. How about telling me how you happened to get working on the DeSoto?"

Denny inserted a pair of needle-nosed pliers into the maw of the carburetor and grunted. "Well, I've about come to the end of whatever can be done without more parts and better tools. This engine is going to have to be pulled like a bad tooth. George said a while ago he knew where he could get a hoist."

"Where is he?"

"Well, until a few minutes ago he was out here matching me four beers to one." Denny put the pliers in his shirt pocket and reached for a can of beer on the battery. "What happened was, Irene went grocery shopping while Om and I rolled out our sleeping bags and took a nap with your daughter. I heard George out here banging around and, figuring from what Irene had said he must be your landlord, came out and offered him a hand. He decided I should take over for a few minutes while he went out for beer. We drank beers and puttered and I told him a little about what was going on. When I told him I might be able to expedite things with the DeSoto a little, he agreed to rent us the hog pen as a place where we can work on the buses. The rest is pretty much what you see. The gals are over there talking babies and tarot cards, George is sawing away in the teepee, and I'm smeared with grease and getting hungry." He looked to the tent and shook his head. "I guess the thing to do now is leave him to nap, toss the parts in the car trunk, and close it up in case it rains."

"George is asleep in the tent?"

"Beer and sun got to him, I guess.

I sighed. "Well, all I've got to say is, good luck going to bed in there tonight. And good luck with all the rest of it, too."

Denny looked at me, nonplused.

"What I mean," I explained, "is that I hope things go smoothly, but they may not. Landlord George has a way of disappearing on long binges. When he does, his old lady Marge comes around to worry about and remind us about what all her Nixon-admiring neighbors are thinking of her tenants. Little George and the dog hang out in the car."

"Marge? Little George? Live in the car?"

"No, not quite. Marge is Big George's wife. They have a kid named Little George. When Big George leaves on a bender, every other week or so, Little George comes around to hang out in the DeSoto with the dog. Marge is a little tense and the presence of two giant yellow school buses in the hog pen is not likely to strike her as a neighborhood improvement."

"Sounds a little awkward," Denny admitted, gathering up beer cans. "Anyhow, George told me his wife and son were in Indiana till school starts. I had to promise him we'd have the buses out and the fence reinstalled before they get back." Denny started lofting the empties, like basketball free throws, into the open cooler. "I take it the shrink decided against electric shock treatments. Was he bearable, or was he one of those guys with a lot of theories and a pushrod up his ass?"

"A little strange, perhaps, but okay. When he shook hands his hand felt so warm I started off the interview wondering if maybe he kept a warmer in his pants pockets. He told me he had a cousin who did acid with Leary and Alpert in the old days, but that he himself preferred champagne and a good novel. He'd read the deposition I'd given in which I said I might write a book someday and wanted to talk about literature. At first that made me a little paranoid, thinking he was going to take the measure of my psyche by comparing whatever I said to some pool of data about normal people somewhere. Maybe he did or maybe he's doing that now. On the other hand, he had some interesting ideas of his own. I don't know what kind of a shrink he is, but he was incredibly good when it came to projecting himself as a keen, unflappable audience. We never really talked about the accident."

"Wasn't that the whole purpose of your appointment?"

"I thought so. Since we didn't, I thought at the end that he was going to broach the subject of fees and tell me that I needed to see him every week. Instead, he thanked me for sharing my insights and said he was going to read a couple of the novels I'd talked about and hoped, someday, to read one written by me."

With serious charges against me I couldn't drive a cab, even had I wanted to. Neither could I stop bringing in income. Bright and early two mornings later, Denny and I stood on a cracked, concrete warehouse floor, listening to a guy named Gus explain why Texarkana Cluckers were the best frozen chickens in the country. Denny chewed gum and rocked from side to side. I held a pair of cotton work gloves behind my back, twisting, working the grime-stiffened fingers as if they were udders.

Gus, who was chewing on a black cigar stub, was bald on top and unkempt at the temples. His thinning red hair was streaked with gray. It curled and bushed out, commingling with the darker hair in his ears. A circus clown without makeup or mirth. Denny inquired about chicken farming and methods of freezing, and then with perfect timing, asked for and got a twenty-five cent an hour wage increase for both of us. Then Gus led us to a rickety worktable piled high with crowbars, hammers, screwdrivers, and dustpans. Brooms and hand trucks leaned against a crumbling brick wall.

Gus looked at me. "You guys ever do any mining?"

"Never," I said.

Gus chortled. "How about ice fishing?"

"A little," I admitted. "I didn't really like it because my feet got cold."

"Whelp, it won't be your feet getting cold," Gus laughed. "Come on outside."

Four long refrigerated truck trailers were butted up against a loading dock. When Gus unlatched the first pair of heavy doors and swung them wide, I stared at a wall of ice in which were embedded thirty-pound boxes of Texarkana Cluckers.

"I see what you mean," I said, testing my lower back with a swaying motion.

"Soon's you finish this trailer, I'll come out and open another. You'll find it goes a little slow at first. But the ice begins to thaw once the doors have been open a couple of hours and by then you'll find the rhythm." He looked at me, then at Denny. "Let's understand each other. If you're afraid of hard work or if you're looking for variety, I don't blame you, exactly. But you're shit out of luck, at least around here."

"We're interested only in cash," Denny said, winking at me, talking out one side of his mouth, doing some kind of W.C. Fields imitation. "We may look like just so much soft human tissue, but we're really a couple of ice-chiselin' box-chuckin' machines. Come on, Tim. Are you a hard-rock-minin' chicken-chuckin' motherfucker, or are you a hippie-dippy mouse?" Denny was enjoying himself. He spit on the dock and swaggered. "Chickens for cash, I say. Every day the same cold thing."

Gus smiled without enthusiasm. "Take turns loading hand trucks five cartons high. Wheel them to the conveyor ramp and shoot 'em on down those rollers yonder. The guys in the basement will take 'em from there."

We used the mallets like clubs and wielded huge screwdrivers like swords. Once we'd cracked the ice walls, we pried the boxes loose with crowbars. Individual cartons snapped free with small explosions of icy shrapnel, stinging our exposed skin.

Gus watched us for a time, then retreated to an enclosed office where he sat at a desk behind a window, fingering cigars and occasionally talking on the phone.

About ten, a secretary from the front office carried out some rock-hard donuts and cups of thin coffee. Denny and I sat on the sunniest patch of the dock and wrung the smelly cold water from our torn gloves. There was blood under my cuticles. My fingernails were dough-soft and my cold hands a cotton candy pink. My donut tasted like chicken skin. So did my cigarette. So did everything I put in my mouth for the next five days.

On Friday, in addition to the cash, Gus awarded us each with a carton of Texarkana Cluckers. We drove home with the windows open to the balmy evening sun. From down the block, and before we saw the crowd and the bright yellow school buses, we could already smell the charcoal, the mesquite, the roasting meat and marijuana.

"Looks like we're late for the party," I observed.

"I don't know about you," Denny said as we got out of his VW outside the house, "but I'm so hungry I could eat a chicken."

"Not me," I said, "After all that chicken, I've been thinking of going back on a macrobiotic diet."

Freshly dressed, radiant, and wearing a pink flower in her hair, Irene met me at the door and kissed me affectionately. I stared at her with raised eyebrows.

"I know, I know," she laughed. "It all happened a little fast. About the first thing Bill and Ron did when they got here was give Big George a beer, tell him what a great guy he was, and ask for his permission to build a couple of fire pits in the hog pen. The next thing I knew, George was sitting out on the steps with his very own six-pack and Bill and Ron went off on Bill's motorcycle to invite everybody in the neighborhood to a cookout."

I felt myself scowl. It was one thing to have the two families living in school buses right next door and another to have an impromptu festival of peace and love under the elm tree in my front yard. I didn't like feeling this way, but I did.

Irene led me slightly to one side and got up on her tiptoes to speak in my ear. "In a way, I think we have to think of them as renters. In fact, maybe we should think of it as their party to which we've been invited. Not long ago, Omaha and George drove down to the market. She said George spent two hundred dollars on food, and that was before going to the liquor store. You know George. As long as Marge isn't around, the more beer and the more people to drink it with, the happier he is."

Women I'd never met before were bustling between the stove and refrigerator, talking about organic onions, watermelons, ripe tomatoes, what might be used for seasoning on the chicken, and where to put trays of newly arrived pies and brownies. The answer seemed to be, in the living room, somewhere near the bags of baking potatoes, loaves of bread, and mountains of corn on the cob. Obviously, some of our neighbors weren't quite as poor as they looked. On closer examination, most of them didn't look so much poor as they did costumed.

I decided to shower, only to discover that the bathtub was filled with ice, beer cans, soda, and jug wine. Opening a can of beer, I soaped and scalded my hands over the sink, lit a cigarette, and sat on the edge of the tub, bare feet in the ice, persuading myself to meet and welcome my new temporary neighbors and enter in the spirit of the cookout. It was harvest time. A community-minded humanity celebrated the harvest: this was an ancient rite. Throwing a little water on my face, I toweled off and stepped into the crowded kitchen.

People were still arriving. Bearded strangers, women from down the block towing mangy toddlers. A boy about eight was squatting down by the refrigerator sponging up spilled lemonade under the watchful and encouraging eyes of his mother, a woman who lived across from Gordon and Rhonda. A small girl whose diaper consisted of a crookedly pinned dishtowel scanned the room in search of her mother and whimpered about the pain of a stubbed toe. I kissed her smudged forehead, held an ice cube to her dirty toe, and handed her a plastic cup in which I poured two fingers of pulpy lemonade. Denny appeared in the open doorway and beckoned me out to the hog pen.

The four new adults and five kids now camping out near Denny's teepee hurriedly arranged themselves in some mock military formation in front of one of the buses to conduct some sort of greeting ceremony. They were all scrubbed and freshly scented from showers, taken in my house, I supposed, before the ice and beer had arrived. I smirked as Bill Bianco led the group in a cheer, in which I was touted as a "mighty frozen chicken warrior and savior." After a moment I accepted Bill's offer of an elaborate glass water pipe filled with pungent hash.

Brightened by the reception, by the gulp of heavy smoke, and by the news that everyone would wait on me hand and foot because the party was in my honor, I allowed myself to be led to a folding chair. Bill's wife Tessa presented me with a jar of herbal salve for my puffy hands. I was rubbing it into my swollen fingers and sampling a small bowl of chili when Denny reappeared with a big tray of the mostly thawed chicken.

"A lot of it is still frozen," Denny said. "But Irene and Rhonda insist we should thaw and cook all of it and give away whatever we can't keep."

Bill Bianco and Ron Thunderhead were roasting a huge leg of lamb on a spit over one fire pit. Tessa Bianco and Donna Thunderhead stirred a pot of bubbling chili over the other.

The two men were attempting to rotate the leg of lamb without burning themselves. Blisters of fat spattered over the glowing coals as they succeeded. When it was offered, I chewed on the first sliver of meat, though I focused on the men preparing it.

With his shoulder-length curly hair, long goatee and waxy, curled mustache, Ron Thunderhead seemed to have styled himself after Wild Bill Hickok, though Thunderhead lacked the hat, the wide-bladed knife, and pearl-handled revolvers favored by the assassinated gunslinger. It seemed to me that the rangy gunfighter would have disdained the fringed, shin-high moccasins and the shiny silver necklace.

Bianco, who wore his black hair in a topknot, seemed unable to make up his mind about whether he should favor an Italian Renaissance prince or a seventeenth-century samurai. He led me by the arm to see the huge restored Indian motorcycle he'd won in an all-night poker game three weeks earlier. He had the long arms and the muscled thighs required to manage the big cycle, though he was too small and elfish to impress many of the hulking bikers I'd seen in California. He struck me as affectionate and emotionally demonstrative, a charming boy growing a beard to go with his bike.

"This mighty steed," Tessa Bianco informed me, "was our downfall. If not for its weight and that of the trailer, we'd probably have made it up that pass without blowing the bus engines."

Bianco laughed and scratched his hairy throat. "No way, Baby. If you hadn't been bugging me to hurry on up the pass and get down to a campground so you could start lunch, we'd still be doing fine."

The Monday after the weekend-long party, I stood in the hog pen with Bianco, Thunderhead, Denny, and Gordon, sweating and laughing over a primitive winch until the bus's yellow nose tilted skyward and Bianco and Thunderhead could stoop and begin work on its grimy underbelly.

In the days that followed, Bianco and Thunderhead bickered and labored over and under both buses, searching for tools, dropping micrometers, and lobbing fouled plugs and tubes of gasket sealer to one another. Thunderhead and Denny, aided at times by Gordon and Bianco, did most of the mechanical work. Some afternoons Bianco washed up and rode his Indian motorcycle into the city to sell small amounts of pot, returning home with pears or basil and fresh tomatoes for Tessa's sauce or ice cream for the kids.

By day, the women sat at the kitchen table over tea, peeling carrots and slicing apples, stirring, tasting, and seasoning whatever happened to be on the stove, planning meals and manipulating towers of containers wedged in our small refrigerator or in one of several coolers outside. They coaxed the kids to take naps, organized activities for them, talked about astrology and tarot cards, and made skirts and dresses on the one working sewing machine.

Sunset was a time of campfires and hearty meals. While the kids sucked on fire-blackened marshmallows and consumed copious amounts of ice cream, the rest of us passed joints or hash pipes, occasionally sharing peyote buttons Bianco sometimes took in trade for his marijuana. When the stars came out the women retreated to the kitchen or the tents, towing kids to bed, gathering dirty dishes while the men tinkered with the fire, succumbed to fits of hilarity, discussed the future of the revolution, and speculated about the exact nature of the conscious universe. No subject was too large, no lack of formal knowledge or precise terminology proved a handicap. When the kids had been bedded down, the women made apple strudel, sautéed mushrooms, spice cake, bottles of jug wine or mead. Conversations about the threat posed by Nixon and whether or not there was a real state of consciousness called satori gradually gave way to descriptions of the taste of homemade cinnamon rolls or fantasies about the things we would buy and journeys we would all begin to make after Bianco's cousin Dominic masterminded the financing for the first successful Grooved-Out Productions concert. Education played a role; there were some nifty yogi tricks and the sitar that Thunderhead thought he'd like to study and master once he finally got to India. Omaha wanted to learn Catalan and live in Spain. Donna hoped to travel through South America and dreamed of a small fishing fleet there. Irene talked about Gauguin and Tahiti or Cezanne and pleasant cottages in the south of France.

I humored them all, but saw myself as a weary overmatched boxer, waiting out the effects of a left hook that had hit me out of nowhere. Until I could shake off my particular swoon, I didn't feel that I could trust my judgment; my whims and desires came and went so fast they only fanned my growing discontent. As I confessed *mano a mano* to Denny one night, the only thing I was sure I wanted was a kind of magic Euro-Rail pass through time, an infinitely adjustable ticket which would allow me to dawdle over my earliest verifiable conscious experience, undoing my own mistakes, coming again to manhood in a world without taxis or unsupervised children. For a time I welcomed the diverting fantasies and the commotions, the bawling kids, the constant comings and goings, the errands, both necessary and whimsical, and the long nights of diverting talk. Thoughts of taxicabs, of my pending trial for manslaughter and reckless driving, and the yawning vacant life yet to be conceived and made with Irene and Serena left me feeling that I lacked both the tools and the inspiration to make a decision of any kind. What I enjoyed best and what troubled me most about Irene's talk of Tahiti, France, and remote islands of Greece was my too-vivid ability to see how happy she'd be in those places, with Serena, but without me. There'd be no one to make remarks about her fairytale visions or to accuse her of sentimentalizing a handful of nineteenth-century painters and writers. Though I didn't say so, I didn't hold out a lot of hope for the future of Grooved-Out Productions. But life was strange, and if indeed some millionaire was ready to bankroll concerts and pay Bianco's cohorts fabulous profit shares, I planned to work hard and earn my share, if only to see everyone else off on the excursions of their dreams.

I knew better, of course. "Scenes" like this were like wildflowers: blooming pungently and spectacularly, short-lived, vulnerable to quick decay and subject to the imposition or onslaughts of ordinary of events. Already the days were cooler and the nights longer. Marge would soon return with Little George. The buses would be repaired and driven off.

One afternoon when most of the work had been done on the buses and the house teemed with harried mothers and wrestling children, I boarded the shade-sheltered Thunderhead bus in search of a place to nap.

Ingeniously roped-together trunks, guitar cases, and strands of wooden beads served as room dividers, but the interior stank of pot resin, cat piss, apple vinegar, turpentine, and a cloying frangipani incense that left on everything an oily, smudgy residue no soap or open window could ever quite expunge. Opening a rear window in the hope of fresh air, I flopped on a mattress in the back of the bus.

I awoke to snuffling sounds. Parting a madras curtain, I saw Tessa, sitting in a little patch of sunlight near me. The rims of her eyes were red and she was wiping her nose with a handkerchief. "Oh, hi," she said with a laugh that didn't hide her embarrassment, "I thought I was alone. I'm sorry. I guess you thought you were alone, too. Were you taking a nap?"

Groggy and uncomfortable, I felt obliged to stay with her until I was more awake and all traces of her embarrassment had vanished. That tears might have a different meaning to a woman of thirty than a man of twenty-two was obvious to me, even then. "Yeah." I smiled, sheepishly, "a nap." Until that moment, Tessa's permanently flushed cheeks and throat had made me think of old *Saturday Evening Post* magazine illustrations in which a buxom younger Mrs. Claus catered indefatigably to the wants of a cranky Santa. Tessa excelled at listening to Bill and other opinionated men, at comforting dirty children, and at accommodation. At that moment, though, she seemed less a mother and a wife. She was a thwarted misunderstood stranger with a private self.

"Don't worry about me," Tessa said. "I'm just a little homesick."

I looked solemn, or hoped I did. "For the house?" I speculated, "And, I imagine, the bookstore in Eureka?"

Tessa's family had given her and Bill a small piece of property in northern California. Over time, they had parlayed the property into a small house and a relatively prosperous bookstore in Eureka. Then, like so many others, Bill and Thunderhead started taking and dealing LSD, leaving the store to Donna and Tessa, after replacing an inventory of travel, cookbook, and photography books which sold with radical political, psychological, and eastern religion books that didn't. The room over the renamed "Stoned Truth Bookstore" became a crash pad and eventually a source of community irritation. A group of businessmen had offered to buy them out. Bill and Ron had decided that the future was in music, anyway, so they pressured Tessa into accepting the initial offer, bought a couple of school buses, and took off for Woodstock. Tessa's wet handkerchief now made Woodstock seem very different. Still, her willingness to stand by Bill and make the best of the decision impressed me. Such fast loyalty was, I suppose, something I missed in Irene.

"It's just a bad day," Tessa said, folding her handkerchief into triangles and putting it in a dress pocket. "When I came back from the grocery store I saw that Lorry had put a sandwich with honey on top of my jewelry case and that Bill hadn't kept the cats out of the tent, so there was cat piss on my favorite sheets." She laughed and blew her nose again. "Soap and water solve so many problems, though, don't you think? I'm embarrassed. You have real grief and I just have some petty disappointments, homesickness, and extra domestic chores."

Her eyes were a jade flecked with yellow. It seemed to me that if I wanted to make the effort, I could look through them into her mind where there was a huge absence of cultivated resentment and thoughts, neither hidden nor fiercely defended. She loved her husband and children and preferred strawberry ice cream to any other flavor she had yet tasted. In her, life seemed so simple. She smelled of laundry soap, moisturizing cream, and something floral and piquant.

"What you want is real enough," I said. "And in contrast with what I want and what everybody else does, what you want seems very attainable. Bill and Ron and the rest of us talk all night as if wishes or hopes were tools for making things happen. They're pretty, these little bubbles, but sometime I think they're just tantrums against the possible."

"Oh, what a beautiful thought. You have such a way with words," she said, patting my hand. "Yet you're not having things easy right now."

I flushed. "I'm just trying to find some understanding," I gulped. "The last few days it has occurred to me that what happened to me could have happened to just about anybody. That realization has begun to change the way I see things. I think I'll start a new growth cycle soon. Grow up a little more at a faster rate." I was surprised by what I said and a little embarrassed to observe that my surprise was evident to her.

"Okay," Tessa smiled. "You want me to know that you're not feeling sorry for yourself. That's admirable, probably even heroic. But have you ever just let yourself blubber? You know, poor me? I mean, I'm a great believer in the idea that just because you get drunk doesn't mean you have to become an alcoholic, and just because you let it all hang out doesn't mean you have to become infantile. I don't like those scary drugs that you guys do. But I've gotten drunk and cried and felt better afterwards. For me there's nothing like the release I get from crying. I suppose crying's what gets me back to feeling satisfied and keeps me so complacent most of the time. You and Bill and the guys think you have to figure things out. Once something happens and I realize life's a mystery that I'll never get very far toward solving, the tears come, and I feel good enough again to stop caring about figuring things out. Just now, to tell you the truth, I feel great. Happy and optimistic about everything again."

"Something won't let me think that self-pity could be enough," I said. "I mean, I do feel sorry for myself. But my dad and grandpa wallowed in their misery too much, so I can't enjoy it very long before it occurs to me that I'm just like them, those I didn't want to be like at all."

"Maybe you underestimate the power and simplicity of love, particularly self-love," she said. "I'd be lost without a certain amount of self-love." She reached for my wrist and captured my right hand between both of hers. Her nails were cut back and slightly smudged, but her hands were warm and plump. Staring at my free hand and not knowing quite what to do with it, I gave it to her and worried about where our conversation was headed.

"The buses are about ready to roll again," I predicted, "and I think maybe your journey back toward the life you once loved may begin by letting Bill wear himself out trying to shake loose money for concert promotions. Even if something actually comes of the millionaire patron, it's going to take some time. Meanwhile, there are plenty of houses for rent in Denver or Boulder. And when Dom comes out with the books you left in storage in California, you'll have rented a house where cats don't piss on the sheets and ants don't bite the kids, and the beginnings of a book inventory. Reality is on your side. You don't really have to worry about having to live much longer in a bus or a tent." I laughed. "Of course I didn't derive any of that from tarot cards."

"And you," she said, "will be found not guilty. You will learn to trust your instincts, find that some possibilities keep coming back to you, shining a little brighter than the others. You will find your way. Madame Tessa has spoken."

We were leaning forward to hug, each of us sitting awkwardly. I put my forehead against her throat. Her hands moved through my hair and along the nape of my neck. I closed my eyes and she moved one of my hands to her throat and urged it, I thought, toward her bosom. A warmth traveled from my chest downward, raising the hot knot of an erection. When I shifted to make room for it, she eased herself back onto a row of cushions. Outside, it was very quiet. There were small sounds in her throat, but she was not saying any words, not reminding me that the bus door was open, that Bill or Irene or anyone could come bursting in on us, not saying that she wanted me to stop or resisting, not at all nervous-seeming or worried. I wanted to stay where I was, absorbing her warmth and comfort. I wanted my erection to subside and to ease my way out of any sexual danger without embarrassment for either of us. Yet maybe more than this, I wanted to be sure she was pulsing a little against my hardness, that she was as aroused as I was. She purred and rolled a little to one side, releasing the tension from one leg. My hand moved up her thigh, which was firmer than I expected it to be. There was an answering throb, a warm dampness moving under her thin cotton panties. I was worried, frightened, excited. A soft sound, in the dust outside, became a crisp pounding on the bus steps. We flung ourselves apart as five-year-old Lorry Bianco stared at us.

"Mommy!" There was an uncertainty to her voice, a disturbed edge.

"Hi, Lorry!"

"How come you're hugging him, Mommy?"

"Well, he was feeling a little sad, Lorry. Don't you think it's nice to give somebody a hug when they're feeling sad?"

"Yeah."

"Well," Tessa said, "will you give me a hug?"

"Why? Are you feeling sad?"

"A little. I'm sorry for getting so mad at you about the sandwich."

Lorry shrugged it off. She looked at me, big-eyed and dirt-streaked cheeks under a mess of robust auburn hair. She rubbed her hands on a tie-dyed shirt already stained with what looked to be ketchup. She took several steps toward us, opened her mouth, and put an index finger on her dangling tongue. She leaned and whispered to her mother, but she was looking at me. "I don't know if I want to hug you now."

Tessa looked a little taken aback. "Why is that?"

"Because you hugged him."

"You don't like it when your mommy hugs other people?"

"I don't know." Lorry gave the matter some consideration. "I don't want you to hug him."

"Why, Lorry? Don't you like Tim?"

"Yes."

"Well," Tessa said, winking at me, "I bet Tim would like it if you gave him a hug."

Lorry scowled at her mother then looked at me.

"I'd like that any time, Lorry," I said. "You don't have to do it, though, if you don't feel like it."

"Well, I will when I'm six, you know."

"That will be nice," I said with exaggerated solemnity.

"Or maybe sooner. Maybe I'll hug you next Thursday."

Tessa scooped Lorry into her arms and tickled her. "Are you Mommy's little coquette, Lorry?"

"No," she said. "I'm your Coca-Cola. I want you to make Dylan stop calling me names."

"Dylan called you names?"

"Yeah, and he said that if I didn't stop talking to him he'd tell Rover to bite me."

"Oh, he did, did he? Well, I will talk to Dylan. You can be sure of that."

"Rover wouldn't bite you, Lorry," I explained. "Rover likes you. In fact, Rover would bite any bad dog or bad person who tried to hurt you."

Tessa stood up. "I've got to talk to Dylan and Donna, then start some gravy for tonight's pasta," she said.

Days passed. Exhilarated kids screamed in the yard, tracked dirt or mud through the house, whined, and left the toilet unflushed. Every day a new talus of dishes stood in the kitchen sink, and visible through the window behind the stacks of plates, wet clothes flapped on a rope tied between the two school buses. The kitchen smelled of burning cereal, cinnamon, and fried eggs. When they weren't working on the buses, Bianco and Thunderhead were off on the motorcycle, dealing small amounts of grass, meeting local rock musicians, talking to club owners. Even so, a lack of cash was beginning to make itself felt.

One night I set my alarm clock and secured it under my pillow so its ringing wouldn't disturb Irene or Serena. I awoke at dawn. Gusts of wind creaked in nearby cottonwoods and made banging and rattling noises among the flotsam in the yard and hog pen. I switched off the alarm to prevent it from ringing, snared my clothes from a nearby chair, and hurried into the kitchen to dress. Outside, a meadowlark called. In the hog pen a pair of crows walked hungry, scavenging circles around last night's fire pit. I got in my VW bus, started the engine, and chugged slowly to the end of the block. The sun was rising east of Havana Street. When I turned the corner and headed northwest, patterns of pink and orange shimmered in each mirror.

Downtown, I parked in front of the labor pool office, bought coffee from a greasy spoon across the street, registered with the day dispatchers, who might or might not assign me a day's work, and sat down on the curb, silently talking to myself. Why were the joys of fatherhood so ephemeral? It was the first of a chain of whys.

The prospect of change, almost any change, promised relief. The sun was bright but cold. Somewhere, tired men were arriving at jobs they hated, innocent men in prison were eating oatmeal from tin plates, free men were driving away from malcontented lives. Why did anyone remain anywhere they were unhappy when there were so many places to go, so many possible fresh starts and amazing strangers waiting for new friends? While I was about to be making two bucks an hour to unload and stack bags of coffee beans, it might be raining in Baja, where what was left of Rick's Triumph would be slowly rusting in the scrub where Denny had parked it. My abandoned Dodge would have become a tarantula's nest in some junkyard outside Barstow; my discarded telegram bike had probably been sold at police auction; my cab would be back on the streets with a new headlight and fender. Waves of courage, cowardice, capitulation, boredom, and an urge to gamble came and went as I sipped coffee. Transients with stained whiskers and bad breath approached and hit me up for cigarettes. Wanting to be left alone, I parceled out smokes with no show of friendliness. A shadow moved across my shoulders.

"Bub," a man's voice behind me said, "you want to go to work today? They need some help at the Old Glory Potato Chip Company."

I stood up and repositioned myself. The man stepped back, breathed heavily, coughed, shifted his weight, and set off a jingling of keys on his belt. When he turned into the low sun to assess the men behind him, the lenses of his glasses flared as though a flame would consume his face. He looked back to me again and the flash vanished. "Clean and oil some kind of potato scrubbing machine, the card I'm reading says. Box bags, load trucks, fill orders. They need five guys for a week and you seem to be the only one around here with transportation. The guys have already said they'll pay you gas money to pick 'em up down here mornings and drop 'em off downtown when you get off. Pays better than those frozen chickens and should be a hell of a lot easier on the hands and back."

Surprised that the man remembered me from the week before, I sipped the last of my coffee and spit the grit in the bottom of the cup into the gutter. "I'll take 'em and bring 'em back today," I said, "but I might be gone tomorrow. I may have to leave town." I was kidding myself, but the prospect of an abrupt departure made me feel better. The idea that I could up and go and find a better world was a dram of whiskey to a drunk, I thought.

I drove south down Broadway, sitting next to a man whose grin exposed too few teeth. His gums were the ruddy, nearly the color of supermarket beefsteak. The hand he offered was hard as a hoof. "Ed."

"Tim," I answered.

The men in back exchanged names they wanted to be known by and lapsed into silence. It was a bittersweet quiet. A necessary pact had been made. There would be no bragging, no fawning, no faked friendships, no talk of past or future, no questions, no show of disrespect, no sighs, not even deep breaths. For a few moments at least, for me and for everyone in the bus, the only thing that mattered was the coming payday. That and the hope that one day we would have the luck or strength to paddle and rise from the backbreaking labor of the shit jobs before us.

It turned out that the clamor of the drier and the brushes at the Car-O-Mat was nothing to the drone of the stainless-steel machinery at the Old Glory Potato Chip Company. Inside the lunchroom, only the manager, Adam Grant, talked, and then only minimally. Real conversation was impossible. To be heard, you leaned forward and shouted into an offered ear. In the lunchroom nobody wanted to hear anybody's story or really anything but the reduction of machine noise. Fifty people sat at folding tables, the only nearby sounds the delivering hum and regurgitation of the sandwich dispenser, the clunk of the pop machine, and the crisp chewing of free Old Glory potato chips for all.

My co-workers failed to meet me at the designated rendezvous site the next few mornings, though one or two lasted three or four days. I stayed on, burdened, depressed, and yet relieved to be in an environment where conversation was undesirable and scarcely possible. The work was mindless, unhurried, unchanging, and largely unsupervised. My mind disappeared when I worked and reappeared, briefly, on breaks, nothing much to say for itself, taking in the sounds of stale sandwiches being chewed, loud swallows of soda. Finished, I'd light a cigarette, put my head on the tabletop, and doze until the buzzer sounded, then I filed out along with everybody back to the howling, clattering plant floor.

When things got busy or production lagged owing to some mechanical breakdown, the manager roamed the floor waving his arms like semaphores or tapping people on the shoulders, leading them like captive Hollywood Indians from one work station to another. I enjoyed loading the trucks with the huge weightless boxes of potato chips. But more than anything, I treasured the profound interval of silence that settled over me when the machines shut down.

It was a stillness that often lasted for more than an hour.

One evening I pulled into the driveway and saw that everything was different. The yellow buses were gone, the hog pen fence was rebuilt, the fire pits were filled in, and even the tracks left by the bus tires had been carefully effaced from the gray hog pen silt.

Doing the dishes after dinner, I looked out the window and saw Little George sitting in the DeSoto. Studying him, I saw myself years before in Irv Blocker's car lot. Behind me Irene was working on a drawing and talking about how much she wanted to go back to school, about the paintings she would make once she was enrolled there, and how she hoped cynical art collectors would buy them, despite their brightness and fundamental optimism.

The '55 Chevy Stake Bed

Returning home early one afternoon after Saturday overtime, I ran a bath and scrubbed the sheen of potato chip grease from my hands and face. In the kitchen, I made coffee and heard the first low rumble of thunder. Thick clouds had blown up out of the south and the air smelled of rain. Lighting flared over the front range of the Rockies. Diapers and towels on the clothesline flapped violently in gusts of wind. Running outside as the first drops began falling, I gathered armloads of clothes and tossed them into a heap on the table and hurried for the ringing telephone. The wind blew the door open. Snaring the phone receiver, I kicked the door shut, and stood by the sink, trying to catch my breath.

"Is this Tim Barlow?"

"Yes, it is."

"Whoopeedoo!"

"I'm glad you're pleased."

"Well, take it as personal as you like. The fact is I'm trying to reach Bill Bianco."

"He's not around. In fact, he's moved."

"Yeah, well this is his cousin Dominic Sospiri. I'm somewhere getting an ass kicking from hailstones. What I mean is I'm out here in the boondocks with bad directions and all Bill's first editions and art books are getting soaked in the rain."

"In the rain?

"Yeah, you know, hail turns to rain. Sorry, I didn't mean to be sarcastic. It's been a long drive and now I'm lost and getting hit by freezing golf balls."

"Okay, where are you exactly?"

"I don't know. Hang on a sec."

His phone receiver banged against a hard surface. I heard a garbled shout, followed by the sound of voices and a steady patter of hail. Dom came back on the line. "Alameda and Sheridan, a guy said. I'm just south of there, parked in some little boarded-up shopette."

Outside my window the rain spattered on the steps and roof. "Okay. You're forty minutes away," I said, "Rather than try to give you directions when you're already lost, I'll come meet you. Do what you can to find some shelter for the truck. I'll meet you at the shopette."

"What are you driving?"

"A red and white Volkswagen bus."

"All right. Look for a man with wet red hair and a scraggly beard or a '55 Chevy stake bed truck with broken stakes. The color of dried pea soup, piled high with cardboard boxes. I've got to get out of this."

Without letting me know until after the fact, the Biancos and Thunderheads had moved into a big, ramshackle brick house on the edge of a largely black neighborhood where rents were relatively cheap. An hour later, after I deciphered their directions and Dom followed me, I pointed him to a parking place out front of their house, made a U-turn, and parked across the street. The clouds were gone, the sun was out, and hailstones steamed in puddles at the edge of the street. Nobody was home, but Dom produced a front door key.

The old truck's gray, cracked stakes were pulled inward by crisscrossed ropes. A dozen soggy cardboard boxes had worked free and tumbled out of the ropes into a jumble. The soaked knots in the rope were as hard as small rocks. Hail was melting in crevices between cartons and the uppermost boxes looked ready to dissolve.

"I lost my tarp this morning in a horrendous Wyoming wind," Dom explained as I handed him down the first carton.

"It can be windy up there," I conceded, fighting another knot.

"Fuck the ropes," Dom said. "Use this knife."

While we carried boxes into the downstairs hall, he rambled about his adventures. "I was fighting to keep the truck on the road and didn't notice that the tarp was gone until I stopped for breakfast in Laramie. What a landscape! It was like God was a frustrated painter in the middle of making this major ten-million-acre canvas, got interrupted, and just let the whole thing fall down to become Wyoming: God's wadded canvas, all rock and wind and monstrous trucks."

When the books were off the truck, I went to my bus for cigarettes. In the hall, Dom was standing beside a stack of bathroom towels, wiping water from the cover of a damaged book.

"You're going to use clean bath towels to dry them?"

"You bet. Anything for a cousin, you dig?"

I laughed. "What about the cousin's wife?"

"What, Tessie?"

"Yeah. She does the laundry."

"Sweet on Tessie, huh? Better watch out. Anyway, she ain't going to do this batch. Billy Ju-sep-ee Bianco's going to launder these towels. And I'll be there watching to see he uses the right amount of detergent, too."

I laughed. "Every family to its own unique insanity, I guess."

"Bastard was supposed to wire me money for a closed truck and get me a plane ticket back. Instead, he spent his wad rebuilding the buses and buying chrome doodads for his new motorcycle." He looked at me. "You look cold. You doin' all right, man?"

"Fine," I said.

"You'd think they'd have the heat turned on, but I guess teepee life has hardened 'em all. Let's build a fire in that fireplace and you can dry out."

"I'm okay," I said.

"I know you're okay. But let's double that okay with some fire and mescal." Dom pulled a bottle from his pack, swirled its contents, then swigged. "This is some wild hooch."

I burned my lips on the bottle, before I even tasted the mescal. When I'd recovered, I said, "that banister looks to be solid oak, and those stakes on your truck are so rotten they wouldn't ignite. So what are you proposing to burn, other than our intestinal tracts with this psychotic turpentine?"

"All right, Tim!" Dom laughed and clapped me on the back. "A fellow wise ass at last! So very pleased indeed. When I talked to Tessie on the phone a few days back she mentioned a bunch of wood they'd brought over from your place. I bet it's down the basement. You ransack the kitchen for some glasses, and I'll go down there and see what I can find."

A few minutes later, Dom stepped away from the fireplace and gestured me toward the heat. He gulped from his bottle and rubbed his eyes. "So, Tim," he said, breathing on and staring at his hand as if the mescal might change its pigment, "now that I've told you the story of my recent life, what do you have to say for yourself?"

The mescal had deposited a bed of glowing coals in my sinuses. I rubbed my forehead. "I'm only here to listen," I said. "The only reason I came to your rescue is because Bianco promised me you had ideas for money making and could keep me from working any longer at the Old Glory Potato Chip Company. Thanks to you, I'm told, we're all about to become wealthy rock concert impresarios. Your cousin plans to become the Bill Graham of the Mile High City."

"Filling your head with bullshit about rock and roll and the coming revolution, huh?"

"With the backing of your friend, Gary, we're going to start the Open Air Rocky Mountain Avalon Ballroom of the Front Range. Dance all night with hundreds of thousands of hippies in alpine meadows, and vacation in Tahiti. So I've been told."

"Glen, not Gary. Glen Spillwell," Dom said, "can squander his own fortune. And no doubt he's proving it even as we speak."

I laughed. "My impression was that there were several Glens, a kind of trinity maybe, three Glens in one millionaire. Bill's Glen, Tessa's Glen, your Glen."

"Well let's start with Bill's Glen. That's easy to do because he's only an apparition. Bill gave him some acid one day and ever since then has been insisting against accumulating evidence that Glen's just looking for an excuse to give him money, for investment purposes, of course. Actually, it all happened a little differently, though Bill's been trying to hound Glen for seed money ever since. Not that you seem to be a believer, but my take is that we can forget about rock concert promotions. The cash cow's got friends of his own now, and he's become more interested in adding to his store than promoting love and peace."

"Bianco said he inherited millions."

"I don't know how much, just that it happened about three years ago. Ever since, he's been ducking a sister and a nephew who think he got their fair share as well as his own. He hides from his relatives and their lawyers, skis, buys and rides in hot air balloons, and has sex with top-of-the-line whores." Dom poured mescal in my glass and said, "Enough about him. When's your trial?"

I gasped and looked accusingly at the glass in my hand. "Trial?"

Dom laughed. "Where I come from we talk about everybody. Listen, Tim, if you want southern Italians to dig you, you've got to blow off some of that Scandinavian diffidence and speak from the guts."

I shrugged. "Middle of next week."

"Scared?"

"Yeah. I look around and see a lot of politicians and people who wouldn't mind sacrificing some white kid in the interest of appeasing a couple of centuries of black rage. I'd be a fool not to be a little scared."

"Yeah, well, I'll come down to the courthouse and testify. You can be sure of that. Listen, in my opinion, nothing combats lies and delusions like laughter. What we got to do is introduce some laughter into this whole thing. Before and after."

"Laughter?"

294

"I'm kidding about testifying, but I'm really serious about laughter. You've got to clear your sorry heart so you can emit one or two good belly laughs when these people start up with their bullshit. Anyway, before we get on the subject of laughter we should chow down on a couple of sirloin steaks and salads. I'm buying and we're going to see how much beef you can pack into that bag of bones you call a body."

"Thanks, but I'll have to take a rain check on the steak, Dom."

"Prior commitments?"

"Yeah. It's the Day of the Dead and I'm already running a bit late."

"Day of the Dead?"

"Irene's half Mexican and her family owns this restaurant called the Hacienda Escobar. There's a bunch of family birthdays about this time of year, including the Grandma matriarch's, so the family throws an annual bash on the Day of the Dead. In fact, if you could settle for *carne asada* with pulverized garlic, you could come with me. Gramma makes unbelievable guacamole."

Dom poured himself more mescal and shook his head. "I don't eat Mexican food."

"You don't like it?"

"It's not really that."

He seemed strangely reticent. I wasn't about to let him off the hook. "Allergic reactions, food poisoning, bad experience with the trots, racism, allergy to jalapeno peppers?"

He shrugged and fiddled with the fire, but when he turned back I was still looking at him, the picture of patience.

He muttered. "Superstition, I guess."

"Aha, superstition! The diffident Scandinavian puts the superstitious Italian on the spot and learns that the man who believes in the restorative power of laughter is secretly afraid to fart."

"All right," Dom said. "All right, I'll be a sport. Five years is long enough. But you'll have to drive me back here after dinner."

"Plan on tying one on?"

Dom put his empty glass on the mantle and headed for the door. "I'll tell you more later." After days of solitary driving, Dom was an eager audience, particularly when it came to the history of Hacienda Escobar, so he got the whole story.

"The big old two-story wooden house and restaurant was situated along the banks of Cherry Creek, originally built in the nineteenth century," I explained, "after a fire and a flood had destroyed much of early Denver. Pedro Escobar, the family patriarch, said to have been a friend of Pancho Villa's, died too young, shortly after the Japanese attacked Pearl Harbor. With eight partly grown children, his wife Lucia, known for her cooking, turned the home into a restaurant.

"Irene's maternal grandmother, Lucia Escobar, is seventy-six and Gramma to everyone, including a handful of trusted priests who never pay for their meals. Lucia's oldest son, Ralph, lives in a small house behind the restaurant and helps her with the cooking. She is slowly going deaf now and lives in an apartment over the restaurant with a milk-colored Chihuahua named Cha-cha. Even in summer, bald little Cha-cha, who is pink under his thin fur, wears a shamrock-colored vest and trembles with jealousy whenever a family member approaches Gramma to kiss her wrinkled cheek.

"Together, Gramma and Ralph decide which of dozens of young relatives wait tables, bus, or wash dishes. Their decisions," I continued, "seems to turn partly on who is regularly attending Mass and receiving the sacraments. But religious devotion wasn't everything and nobody is ever fired for petty theft, though Gramma and Ralph will quietly, if temporarily, replace thieves and make sure they talk to a priest before allowing them to return. By a process known only to them, Gramma and Ralph find new hardship cases in the family and schedule them for work, easing out those whose problems had grown old and boring.

"On special occasions like tonight," I explained, "Ralph will probably pound out simple melodies on a dining room piano that looks to have been salvaged from a pond. Various family members will be called on to sing solos, and just about anybody in a brilliant dress or starched white shirt with string tie and sombrero can be coaxed to step forward with a guitar or song. Some Escobars sing quite well, others only passably and passionately. Some songs of love and loss require an ensemble.

"The kitchen is a warren of hormones from which chubby, randy teenagers in thick mascara or oiled hair and tomato-stained shirts and blouses will serve steaming platters of *refritos* and *chiles rellenos*. Service is exceptionally slow because the wait staff needs time to bicker with cousins, make deals and dates, give and receive gropes, and step outside for a kiss or a feel or a smoke or a sulk. Gramma does her part not to detect these episodes, remaining at the oblivious heart of the kitchen and personally perfecting the appearance of each heaped plate of food. She is stone deaf to the bad language of the great-great-grandsons.

"Every night at ten twenty-five, Gramma emerges from the kitchen in a fresh apron, but the same smudged eyeglasses. Ralph steers her through the restaurant by an arm to say goodnight to family and customers, distinctions that increasingly fail her. It is said that she prays alone by her bed each night and falls asleep promptly at eleven, no matter how loud the music downstairs.

"In summers there is an outdoor patio, red-tiled and wood-fenced, on which real foliage is kept dried and strangled by snarls of waxy plastic red roses which rot and turn brown in winter. When the weather cools, the patio doors are closed and locked. Confined to one of three dining rooms, observant customers might notice the greasy plaster walls, stained, unpainted and cobwebbed in their upper corners. Inhaling the history of the place, I told Dom I could almost persuade myself that there might indeed be, as family legend had it, Pancho Villa gold buried under the foundation of the old house.

"The tables are mismatched and rickety and there are chairs of so many different sorts that on slower nights regular customers wandered in search of a favorite stable chair. Tables were covered by plastic cloths with various floral and fruit patterns, most cracked and peeling from repeated scrubbings, and faded by nightly applications of hot water and lemony detergent. On the tablecloths candles burn in fingerprint-smudged colored jars and mismatched bottles.

"In the hall there is a glassed-in display case of rosaries and an accumulation of gifts from assorted Spanish-speaking monsignors and important priests in the archdiocese. A permanent nativity scene, in which Walgreens' Easter basket stuffing serves as straw, occupies a dusty circle atop Ralph's piano. In the most secular room of the house are framed autographed photos of former mayors, Denver's most famous folksinger, Judy Collins, and a print, crudely torn from a book and captioned in Spanish, of the outlaw nationalist Pancho Villa, putative amigo and posthumous family benefactor.

"Dining room walls are decorated with year-round dusty Christmas tree lights, each shabby chord its own fire hazard, and in the upper corners of each room are crepe paper remnants of celebrations gone by.

"Irene loves Gramma and, in a more tortured way, her own mother as well. But she grew up too fast and too violently among too many horny older male cousins and tends to see the family's dark side almost exclusively. While I am aware of the mice and the cockroaches in the kitchen and have become familiar with some of the feuds and affairs, the lecherous uncles and rumors of molested relatives, I see a pathetic comedy, a neurotic pageant leading nowhere at all. Where Irene is appalled, I am mostly amused."

Dom and I finally arrived, and that night Irene was in a good mood and enjoyed Dom's banter, even as she worried about getting Serena home to bed. Dom, despite his proclaimed ambivalence about Mexican food, polished off two platefuls, drank beer after beer, danced the Mexican hat dance with one of Irene's cousins, and charmed Gramma with a few Spanish phrases, slapping his chest with both hands and exclaiming in some amusing hybrid of Spanish and Italian about the quality of the food.

When Gramma finally went upstairs, Irene looked at me and said, "We should go, too, I think."

"Yeah, I guess so."

"No, Irene, wait." Dom grew animated. "Gramma and Ralph made me promise we'd stay on a while. There's some poet washing dishes in the kitchen who wants to recite. I think they're afraid his feelings will be hurt if there aren't enough people in the audience."

"I gotta go, Dom," I said.

"Irene," Dom said, smiling, "if he won't be too crabby in the morning, and if I pay for your cab home, would you consider letting him stay for the performance?"

Irene smiled at him. "I'm sure I could get you out of the obligation to stay if you'd rather go," she offered.

"To be really honest about it, I'd love to stay."

By midnight, when the restaurant was nearly empty. Somebody put on a Manitas de Plata record, and Carlos the poet emerged from the kitchen in fancy hard-heeled boots to stomp and, via a Lorca poem, mourn the death of someone who had died for the revolution.

By one in the morning Ralph and Carlos were sitting at our table, drinking from a bottle of rum and speaking Spanish, while Dom and I sipped beer and devoured the chips and salsa Ralph felt obliged to keep replenishing.

At one point, Carlos stood up, turned his back, drew a sharp breath, and wheeled back toward us. His brown eyes smoldered in his face. No sooner did he begin reciting another poem than rum and wild gestures of his hands and shoulders caused him to stagger backwards into another table. When he'd regained his balance and backtracked to the beginning of the poem, he slumped back in his chair and gestured for Ralph to translate the poem into English.

In bland, homely English the literal-minded Ralph scratched his balding head as he explained that in the face of death a man ought to chew rocks until his teeth cracked and tear his hair and curse God, and accept only the comfort of a certain unnamed woman. Ralph nodded with a distant appreciation of this and looked like a man who would rather die than admit it was hours past his accustomed bedtime. Carlos poked him and said a few more earnest words.

Ralph turned his attention to us and tried to look like he wasn't stifling a yawn. "Carlos says that in his village it is the custom for every man to recite a poem about death before going to bed on the Day of the Dead. He said he doesn't want you to feel challenged, because he already knows you are real men, even though not of his culture. Still, he would be very happy if you could recite for him maybe a little something about death."

In Italian, Dom recited a few verses from Dante and then a couple bits from a longer poem by D'Annunzio. Carlos said he didn't understand more than a few words but that he could tell from the sounds, the way that a guitarist knew when his guitar was properly tuned, that this was very good poetry indeed.

Dom spoke broken Spanish to Carlos, pushed his chair back a little, and grinned drunkenly at me. Carlos gave me a reverential look. For a minute I thought he would stand up and bow. Ralph smiled blandly at me, "Your friend says that you are a poet."

"My friend only met me for the first time today, so he wouldn't really know."

"Your friend knows all the gossip," Dom said. "And repeats it at times."

Ralph did his best to get me off the hook, but Carlos insisted on some kind of recitation. Tired of my own excuses, and convinced nobody was going anywhere until I said something on the subject of death, I did my best to remember a little ditty I'd written recently.

Death Chant for Guy the Hippie
On the occasion of his funeral in Haight Street, I offered up this
epitaph.

"Here lieth Guy the hippie,
barefoot, oh so very trippie;
he died from love of diurnal spacies;
for coconut donuts he shopped at Tracy's.
We lifted for him this supermarket hearse
in case God's cops shout out, 'disperse!'
Now in our graft and sullen cart,
we kipped it from Safeway,
split, depart.

Ralph knitted his brow and began translating in the most serious tones. Noting the expressions of the old men and the earnestness of the questions Carlos put to Ralph, I smiled an impostor's smile in my beer.

Finally Ralph said to me, "Carlos believes you are a very talented American poet. Though you are young, he predicts that someday you may write great poetry. However, this cannot happen, he claims, until you have more direct experience with death. Then he said it is obvious to him that your friend knows something about death, even though he himself is not a poet." Carlos, in very formal language, begged Dom to tell him how it is that death has already made its mark on such a young man.

"Okay," Dom said, looking at me, "this will also give you a sense for why I almost didn't come here tonight." He pulled on his beer and wiped his lips. "Four years ago, I did like many of my fellow American college students were doing, I tried the drug LSD. At the time I was living in California, attending college, and working toward an advanced degree in psychology. Anyway, I went with my friend Glen Spillwell into the California mountains."

"*The* Glen?" I interrupted.

Dom winked and nodded. "*The* Glen," he acknowledged, looking back at Carlos. "Maybe Carlos has seen Indians high on peyote. We were stoned and had visions of our own human helplessness in the huge chaos of all created things. We shared our thoughts and were persuaded that our lives would never be the same."

Carlos stuffed a hand into the breast pocket of his stained sport coat and passed around a box of thin cigarillos. Dom and I accepted the offer. Ralph lit one of his menthol cigarettes with a lighter and said, "Please continue."

"At the time we were working as bus boys at a Mexican Restaurant called the Sonora Matador. Both of us were scheduled to work that evening and were a little anxious because we were still high on acid and didn't want to call attention to ourselves by being late. We stood out on the highway and hitchhiked. Three Mexican migrant workers stopped for us in a battered '52 Ford with one headlight. They pulled way over and got out of their car to stretch. They were drunk but friendly and a little curious. Glen spoke Spanish with them and learned they were on their way down the coast to pick garlic and artichokes. They said they had been cheated of some of the money they'd earned on the last job and had spent the last of their money on beer and gasoline. They would give us a ride no matter what, but they hoped we might come up with a little money for food because they were getting hungry and weren't sure when they would eat again.

"Glen told them we only had two dollars and change between us, which was the truth, but that if they would give us a ride to the Sonora, we'd slip into the restaurant and bring them out some rice and beans and maybe some chicken.

"They were extremely pleased to learn that we worked in a Mexican restaurant and made a big deal about clearing the back of the car of empty beer cans and other stuff so Glen and I could have the whole back seat to ourselves. We weren't very comfortable, because the back seat had been taken from some other car and hastily installed without the right tools." Dom looked over at me. "Imagine sitting in one of those rickety old-fashioned porch swings while roaring down a bumpy highway in a car with a nonexistent suspension system and dubious brakes at a speed that, maybe because they were so hungry, rarely dropped below 90."

Ralph translated for Carlos, then ground out his cigarette as Dom continued.

"The steering was crazy, the tires bald, and every time we hit a little bump, Glen and I would bounce toward the low roof and look again for something to hang on to. It was late afternoon, maybe four o'clock, and little patches of fog drifted across the highway. We were trying to let them know that our being late for work wasn't that big a deal when everything, the whole fucking world, just vanished, disappeared," Dom paused and looked at Carlos. "Just the way this candle flame disappears."

Dom blew out the candle, dropped it with a touch of melodrama, and put the bottoms of his fists on the table. Ralph, looking a little more wakeful, took care to ensure that Carlos had followed the story down to the significance of the extinguished candle.

"For a time," Dom said, "I was fully conscious, but I don't know what I was conscious of. I didn't remember my name, how to speak. Nada. I was in a green place, surrounded by the smell of flowers. I felt the presence of God and worried that He was going to turn out to be just as touchy as the God they had taught us about in grade school. I didn't want to look on God or on Paradise because I figured that to do so would somehow make worse the torments I knew must be coming. I kept my eyes closed and waited for God to get bored. It was easy to do because I felt so tired of everything that it took to stay alive."

"What persuaded me, finally, to open my eyes was curiosity at the smell of my own fart." Dom laughed. Ralph shook his head wistfully and brought Carlos to a big grin.

"When I finally opened my eyes, I remember experiencing a powerful sense of disappointment that I couldn't see anything but fog. It occurred to me that I might run away, so I felt my body, to see if I still had one and decided that I did have my body, even if it was numb and partly still in some other world.

"Glen appeared out of nowhere and sat down beside me. Neither of us could speak or make sense. After a time I noticed that his shirt had been ripped and he was wearing two sleeves and a collar and a little pennant of blood ran down his back. He was smeared with mud and his teeth were pink with blood. I didn't think of the car or the Mexicans, but it occurred to me that if the two of us went downhill through the grass and bushes toward the sounds below we would eventually reach some necessary understanding.

"I had a bad feeling of not wanting to understand, but I took Glen's hand and we started down the hill. We stumbled over this very mysterious object that seemed to have something to do with who we were and what was going on, but I had no way of recognizing it as a car seat at the time. We climbed over a fence and walked down to the edge of the highway.

"Ambulances and tow trucks and highway patrol cars were everywhere, and Glen started crying out and yelling about the all the flashing lights. A tow truck driver, his face grimy and bearded, considered Glen and said, 'Where the hell did you guys come from?' Glen was whooping crazy and making strange noises, and the guy backed way off and looked at me and said, 'Oh Christ Almighty! Then he turned and ran back toward a group of cops.

"When the tow truck driver said, 'Where did you guys come from?' it was like remembering how to talk in a heartbeat instead of taking three or four years. The tow truck driver seemed to have asked me the hardest question anybody could ever ask. At the moment it seemed so unanswerable that I fell down laughing. I remember a cop coming over and slapping my face because I couldn't stop and he couldn't listen any more. I couldn't feel the slap or anything except his frustration, and what a relief it would be if I could simply laugh until I slept. This was not one of those druggy convictions that seem so profound but can't be remembered five minutes later, Barlow, but the beginning of an understanding that laughter, as a response to life, is both a rejection of confusion and a refusal to accept any indirect authority handed down by people too humiliated to admit their own confusion. Meanwhile, Glen was jumping up and down and screaming, 'They're dead, they're dead, they're all three dead!'"

302

Ralph seemed to forget he was translating. He rocked back and forth a little in his chair. Carlos looked at Dom, then at me, then jerked his head at Ralph. Ralph still didn't talk right away. Outside, tarps on the patio tables flapped in the wind. There was a small sound from the dark kitchen, maybe mice gathering loose beans, shreds of grated cheese. Ralph looked tired. Shaking his head from side to side, he spoke Spanish while Carlos worked his eyebrows with an index finger.

Dom pulled on his beer for a long time. "A very matter-of-fact long-haul driver who witnessed the accident explained that the Ford had passed him at about 100 miles an hour, hit a bump, somersaulted through the air, and smashed into a concrete bridge. During the somersault, one of the back doors flew open, at which point, though the driver never saw us, Glen and I apparently rode or followed the seat sixty, or seventy feet through the air and landed near each other on the landscaped hillside, just uphill from the back seat. The three men in front were killed instantly."

The poet nodded his head and spoke earnestly in Spanish. Ralph looked reluctant to translate. Finally he spoke, "Carlos says, 'The dead are restored to innocence while the guilty wander deserts in search of peace.'"

Dom said, "What we did, Glen and I, after being treated for concussions, was live on in stunned confusion, me laughing and rejecting everything and trying to explain myself, Glen listening to rock music records on drugs as if he expected some kind of jinn to come out of the vinyl and tell him why he was still alive. I had a girlfriend who did what she could on our behalf. Understandably, the families of the men wanted nothing to do with us. We had some kind of memorial service for them, something we made up, totally, and Glen borrowed money from his Aunt Lilly and sent it down to Mexico to help with burial expenses. I'm not sure that the families ever got the money. We tried to come to terms with guilt and awe. Glen went into therapy, then took some Scientology courses. We eased ourselves out of school. We never returned to the Sonora Matador, and since then, until tonight, the night of the Day of the Dead, I haven't eaten Mexican food."

It was my turn to speak. "Tessa said that an aunt left Glen a fortune while you guys were living together in a trailer in Oregon. Was it the same aunt he borrowed from?"

"Yeah. Unknown to Dom, she restructured her will after the accident so that he inherited ninety percent of what she had. He thought it might be a couple of hundred thousand. When the lawyers went through her assets, though, it came out to a lot more. Glen never said how much more, probably because he was afraid if I knew how much I'd ask him for a share. Though the inheritance effectively twisted our friendship, it didn't end our connection.

"He hired some lawyers and a public service agency and built a community center in the dead men's hometown and gave some money to churches in the area so Masses would be said for their souls until the turn of the century. Then he started enjoying himself."

Carlos wanted to know if Dom, too, was rich.

"Rich in confusion and in my dedication to laughter, maybe. For about a year I lived high on the hog while Glen and I partnered and worked on my idea to start some place called "The Funny Farm." I hoped people would come and learn to laugh, but we had different ideas about the place and lost our focus a little. We bought cars, flew first class to various humanistic centers around the world. Searched out Zen masters, the whole bit. All the while, though, he was also giving money to these violent left-wing causes including the Weather Underground. We had a big fight about that and some other things, so while I was in Kyoto, he wrecked the car he gave me, slept with a girlfriend of mine, gave her a bunch of money to go start a new life somewhere, and fired me. So, Ralph, to answer Carlos, I'll have about sixty-five dollars once I've paid for the beer and food we've been putting down, plus some travel expense money I probably won't be able to collect from my cousin for a while."

"No, no. You have been a guest of my family tonight," Ralph insisted. "Especially after such a story. Where is the friend now? The one who betrayed you?"

"Paris or Florence, last I heard. He's spending his fortune trying to break altitude records in hot air balloons, which I think is his way of acting out that he's still up in the air about so many things." Dom laughed. Ralph smiled and made a bobbing gesture. Ralph's movement was probably supposed to help Carlos appreciate Dom's figure of speech.

When I returned from the bathroom, Ralph was firmly resisting any payment from Dom and wiping down the table with a stained sponge. Carlos was sitting where he had been, looking into his rum glass and humming to himself. When Carlos realized we were leaving, he clasped Ralph's wrist to be sure the older man listened carefully.

"Si, si." Ralph agreed. "Carlos said the meaning of the story is that if we must travel by car, then we must be certain the cars are as new as possible and kept in good repair."

Hearing the mice run through the kitchen, I nodded, and said, "*Buenos noches, señors.*"

Serena was sucking fitfully on her baby bottle. I held her, leaning against the sink, making little cooing noises in my throat to ease my hangover and coax her into a better mood. Irene sat at the rickety kitchen table, rubbing a drawing tablet with a stub of black chalk. A chipped vase on the kitchen table contained a fistful of bristling late flowers. Next to the vase, three drying red peppers were going brown, cracking, and exposing clusters of blond seeds. I looked from the table to Irene's drawing. She turned her head slightly toward me. "Could I make a suggestion?"

"Sure."

"Maybe you could consider moving Serena to your other arm or taking your cigarettes out of your shirt pocket. She's probably a little put off trying to nurse from a bottle of milk with her face snuggled into your cigarettes. Tobacco and milk don't necessarily go together."

"She's never fussed about it before," I said. "In fact, when I was very small I liked it that my dad smelled of cigarettes. The real problem is, her bottle is stopped up." I pinched the rubber nipple, bit down on it, then dabbed a drop of warm milk on my wrist. Serena went back to work, puckering and swallowing audibly. "Gulp that down, Princess." I looked back at Irene. "Are you pissed about Dom paying for your cab fare home last night?"

"Not at all. He was obviously having a great time and I was glad to see you showing flashes of your old self. I just want to say that based on a Tarot reading and some other things, I don't think you need to be quite so anxious about the trial."

I grunted. "That's easy for you, or should I say you and Rhonda and the cards, to say."

She shifted in her chair. "Feeling sorry for yourself?"

"Yeah, probably a little. I mean this whole business is supposed to be about finding justice for Samuel Waddell, but really it's kind of a soap opera about race revenge and appeasement. I hate the idea of going to jail period. But the prospect of going to jail as a scapegoat to pay down hundreds of years of injustice to black people is intolerable."

Irene folded the flap of her tablet down over her drawing. "You can't personally control the racial attitudes of everybody on earth any more than you can end the war in Vietnam. Besides, nobody but you seems to think you'll go to jail at all. Gerald suggested that you should take an hour or two before going to court to reflect on the simplicity of the case. Reduce it to its bare essentials."

"Who the hell is this Gerald I keep hearing about, and how does someone I don't know presume to speak so authoritatively on the subject of my trial?"

"I don't say this to be critical, okay? You were a little crocked and distracted by your new friend, Dom, but I escorted Gerald over and very deliberately introduced you last night."

"Oh, that guy with the neatly trimmed beard wearing that brass peace symbol around his neck who acted like we were old friends?"

"He's been very helpful to my family and me."

"And now he's trying to be helpful to me, too."

Irene was irritated. "Maybe *you* don't want to talk about the accident, but it doesn't mean *everybody else* won't or can't. When I have a problem, I have to talk with *somebody*."

Determined to hide my jealousy and not feel accused or coerced into addressing, yet again, the subject of my habitual reticence, I turned and looked out the window. Irene gave me a moment to snuff out my cigarette and picked up where she'd left off.

"He's an art teacher at City U. He serves on the Community Relations Committee."

"Meaning he teaches you art and poses as a friend, but works for the people who are going to tear down the family restaurant?"

"Well, you could put it that way. The fact is, he wants to be helpful. He and my mother have done quite a bit of research together with an eye to easing things for the family and making it easy for me to go back to school."

"Ralph started to talk to me about Gerald and the whole business last night, but then he hurried off into the kitchen and got distracted by the poet."

"Maybe he was suggesting to Carlos that he keep his hands off my ass."

"Carlos had his hands on your ass?"

Irene sighed. "Let's just say he was working his way down to it."

"Meaning?"

"I ended his lechery very quietly by telling him in my best Spanish that I was married, had a baby, and didn't like to be touched."

"So you handled it?"

"I handled it."

"Okay, so now tell me how Gerald figures in your going back to school and why I should consider him a friend. Closing the restaurant is a bad idea."

"There's no choice. It's urban renewal, eminent domain, whatever. Everybody in the neighborhood has to leave. The university is expanding. New classrooms and administration buildings are going up all over the block."

"So your family should hire a lawyer, get all they can from the city, and reopen the restaurant as close as they can to the original one. Anyway, I don't see how all this adds up to school for you. Unless, of course," I laughed, "you are vested enough to also get your fair share of Pancho Villa's gold. . ."

"Very funny. Just don't share your humor with anybody else in the family, right now, okay?" Irene was watching me diaper Serena. "Anyway," she said, "the city has set up this thing called the Dislocation and Vocational Retraining Fund. According to Gerald, everyone economically displaced by the demolition and rebuilding will qualify for free tuition at City University and, maybe, a small stipend."

"Too bad *we* won't be economically displaced."

"We will be if *we* work in the restaurant."

"Yeah, but we don't."

"Well, *I* do. And you *can*."

I stuck myself with a safety pin. "Ouch. You do?"

"Starting tonight. That's why we don't have much time. If you want to buy a white shirt and tie for court, we should go do that now. I've got to buy a peasant blouse and some little corsage. I'm due at the restaurant at six."

"So that means I'm baby-sitting?"

"Three evenings a week."

"How will you get to work?"

"I guess you'll have to take me until we can move into the city."

"Move into the city?"

"Apparently. Gerald says that in order to qualify for free tuition we have to live in the city, which means we'll have to move out of here as soon as possible. The only other catch is that we have to earn at least forty percent of our income from the restaurant. Plus we have to have been employees for at least six months."

"I doubt you can earn that much in three nights a week."

"True, but Gramma loves taking care of Serena, and she and Ralph have agreed that you could work as kitchen manager on Friday and Saturday nights."

"Kitchen manager?"

"Yeah, I don't know quite what they have in mind since Ralph isn't about to give up control of the operation. It's just Gramma and Ralph's generous way of making sure we're earning enough to qualify for the free tuition, I guess."

About three in the morning, unable to sleep, I went out in the yard to smoke and brood about my upcoming trial. A car with crooked headlights made its way up Mississippi Boulevard and slowed. My old DeSoto, the one I'd given George for back rent, roared up the paved boulevard. It turned too fast, skidded in the gravel, and started up the street toward me. The interior light was on for some reason, and I could see Little George behind the wheel. Rover sat in the back seat, upright and regal on his canine haunches, looking like some doggie duke of Arapahoe County out for a joyride.

Not wanting to wake Irene or Serena, I didn't call out when Little George raced by, but stood at the edge of the street in an effluvium of noxious white smoke watching the DeSoto turn right at the end of the block and head south again. When a light cold drizzle started to fall, I went inside and made coffee in the dark kitchen. Carrying my cup to the couch, I sat listening to the sound of the cold rain falling on the steel awning over the front room window until I fell asleep.

Serena had a cold, so the next morning I knotted my necktie, accepted a guilty kiss from Irene, and stepped outside, glad, in a way I couldn't explain to myself, to be going alone to court.

The DeSoto was back in the hog pen and a fine sleet glistened on my bus. Determined not to speculate about what might happen in court, I worried briefly about George, well under age to be out joyriding all night. Before long, to rhythms of my windshield wipers and the accompaniment of tires hissing over rainy streets, I was improvising an imaginary innocent-man speech in a courtroom crowded with blacks and whites who, at the end of my peroration, burst into applause and dedicated themselves anew to social justice for all. In the hall, righteous soul brothers were shaking my hand and inviting me to their churches.

A sharp metallic snap, like a pistol shot, launched me back into the real world of clogged morning traffic. Bobby was dead, Martin was dead, morning commuters hated one another, and I was shaking off racial daydreams a mile from the courthouse where I was about to be tried and found guilty of ridiculous reckless driving charges. Now it looked like I might be held in contempt of court because my clutch gave out on Speer Boulevard minutes before I was due in court.

The little rear-mounted engine raced uselessly in the compartment behind me. I punched the door and turned to give the honking cars behind me the finger. I rapped my forehead three times on the rim of the steering wheel. Then, with my turn signal clicking, I stepped down into an icy puddle, soaking my newly shined shoes and clean socks. Pushing and steering with an extended right arm, I managed to get the bus down the block into an available parking place. With passing traffic spraying me with icy water and less than fifteen minutes to get to court, I plugged the parking meter with coins from my pocket, looked around in search of a city bus, realized I no longer had the required correct change for bus fare, and started running for the courthouse.

Soaked, thighs burning and quivering under my wet slacks, I mounted the courthouse steps with minutes to spare.

I hurried into the men's room to dry my clothes off with fistfuls of paper towels. Two men were shaking their pricks over a blackened urinal and discussing the cost of filing certain documents. They moved toward a mirror where they stood grooming themselves and watching as I hung my wet sports coat over a toilet stall. Blue dye from my jacket had leaked through the torn lining of my sports coat and stained a shoulder of my white shirt. I dried my neck and throat while one man adjusted his tie and the other whistled and shaped his breast pocket handkerchief. I heard them laughing when they stepped out into the hall.

Inside the courtroom, a woman court reporter, wearing brightly framed glasses on a chain around her neck, looked up at me from a sheaf of papers. In a corner of the dim and virtually empty room, I spotted Mark Davis, the cab company's attorney. He was sitting on a corner bench with one of the men from the bathroom.

At a small dismissive hand signal disguised as a greeting from Davis, I took a chair politely away from their animated conversation, but decidedly within view. Soaked shirt cold on my back, wet hair plastered to my skull, I sat impatiently watching rain and sleet run down a row of big windows along one wall.

The man next to Davis wrinkled his nose, tapped his foot impatiently, looked from me to Davis, and raised his voice in calculated anger. "You're out to lunch, Marky. Twenty thousand will just get you the mayonnaise on this one. Just the dressing."

Davis had a legal pad on his thighs and rolled an elegant fountain pen between a thumb and index finger. When I looked at him, he winked and wiggled two fingers on his free hand, flashing me a jade ring, manicured nails, and an irritable smile.

"Look, Ernie," Davis responded, "You and I've got better, more productive things to do than dicker. It's up to you to let your people know that if they want to tell their sordid little tale in court they are simply going to have to be prepared for consequences."

"Wait a minute, wait a minute, fuck the sordid tales, Marky. There's nothing at all unseemly about honest misunderstandings not expressly and contractually addressed. . . as any judge and jury in the state will quickly agree."

Davis raised his eyebrows at this and shook his head. An overweight man in tight uniform trousers walked across the room. The butt end of a pistol protruded from a stiff, chocolate-colored holster. I thought he was about to call for order and got to my feet, but he jingled a ring of keys and headed for a door at the back of the room.

Davis watched the guard, rubbed his graying temples with both hands, and said, "Ernie, Ernie, my people are getting a little tired of motion after delaying motion and all this bluster and bullshit. I suggest you go back to your office and tell them what we both know but they don't: that it's a little unpleasant to be on the witness stand patently drooling after more money. Frankly, your problem right now is simply that you haven't held the conversations necessary to reduce your clients' expectations to a reasonable level. Otherwise, I got news for you, Ernie," Davis resumed. "We are going to go to court and we are going to rumble, and we, as in both of us, are going to cost our people a lot more than they expected to pay. Because of your own intransigence only, we are going to help half a dozen people discover new thresholds of embarrassment and disappointment. And when it's all over, I will win, you will lose, and you and I alone will know that it all happened as it did because of one thing. You are still smarting from Smegley v Vargas when, though both the judge and I tried to save your ass, you insisted on dragging the Smegleys down into martyrdom."

With a *hauteur* clearly intended for the imaginary jury, the man accepted a folder of some sort from Davis and let it fall into the dark lining of his opened attaché case. Tilting his chin as if he could smell a judge, he snapped the briefcase shut, grabbed Davis's extended hand, and hurried from the room. A door opened and a uniformed man stepped in front of the bench.

"All rise."

Davis walked over and put a hand on my wet shoulder. Withdrawing it quickly, he wiped the hand on the pocket of his suit coat and with his manicured fingers folded in front of his groin, stood answering a few crabby inquiries from the bench.

I'd been expecting newspaper reporters and a room filled with angry blacks, but there were fewer than two-dozen people in the room. There followed a few moments of shuffling and passing papers, a shifting of chairs. Good mornings were mechanically exchanged, spectacles were removed and polished and repositioned. Nobody looked at me or even long at one another. Davis seemed surprised by the contents of a manila folder he'd been handed by another man in a suit. I wanted a room filled with high-minded people, not a dozen efficiency-minded individuals who were only just now familiarizing themselves with the details of the case before them.

The judge looked sharply at the prosecutor. "How dare your witnesses be tardy, Mister Findler?

"Ah, your honor. My assistant has stepped out in the hall and is making phone calls at this moment. My understanding is...."

"Your witnesses are your responsibility, while your understanding is not the court's concern, Counselor." The judge's thick eyebrows seemed to twitch to his anger. "Bailiff, get phone numbers and addresses from Mr. Findler and send drivers if necessary to get those people into this room. In twenty-five minutes they will be held in contempt of court. This court is adjourned until then."

"Your honor," Davis interrupted, "the defense would like to move that..."

"Mr. Davis, the court will entertain motions in thirty minutes."

Davis and I walked the hall together. He wore a checked jacket and an excess of cologne, and kept his brow furrowed with a calculated expression of compassion. "Let me share my concern, Jim."

I walked stiffly, enraged that Davis had been negotiating another case when he should have been reviewing mine, that he'd been surprised by details of the case, and even more by the fact that, for the tenth time he'd called me "Jim."

"Somehow, some way, and for some reason, the district attorney has found witnesses prepared to say you were speeding and driving recklessly. Samuel was black, the witnesses are, I imagine, black, and the judge is black. I think we should go *nolo contendere*, which means not entering a plea but throwing ourselves on the mercy of the court."

It occurred to me that Davis wanted me to ask for mercy so that he wouldn't *lose* the case and so perhaps keep his account with the Yellow Cab Company. I seethed. "I am not inclined to do that."

Davis looked at me with professional patience.

"I am not going to plead *nolo*," I said, "because I am innocent. I understand that I might be made a scapegoat, be found guilty of the charges in order to reduce feelings of outrage in the black community. The court can do with me as it will, but I am not going to do or say anything to encourage anyone to believe that I am anything other than completely innocent. I had just turned the corner and the car was still in second gear."

An hour later the sole witness to finally appear gave a preposterous account of the accident. He said I'd been going over seventy, remembered my being in a lane which I hadn't been in, mentioned squealing brakes and skid marks, and said I'd shown no remorse. Photographs, police evidence, and depositions from other witnesses contradicted this testimony. Unprepared as he was, Davis caught the witness in a dozen inconsistencies and then launched an improvised speech portraying me as a man of feeling and intelligence, detailing how after the accident I had gone down on my knees in the street to pray. He even mentioned my love for my daughter, "Sara."

The judge scolded the witness, warned both attorneys for coming to court inadequately prepared, and apologized to me. Once the judge said I was free to go, I did. I offered Davis one ungrateful accusatory look while he stood to arrange his papers. As I stalked off he turned around in the expectation that I would stop and wait for him. No way was I going to contaminate my exhilaration with the anger I'd feel as soon as he tried, as I knew he would, to take credit for my acquittal. I bounded down the courthouse steps, and walked quickly through the rainy morning to my broken-down bus.

Gradually my joy and relief at having been freed gave way to the knowledge that I was stranded miles from home and would soon have to come up with money for a new clutch and go to work in wet clothes.

It turned out to be worse than that. My bus was gone. I made a series of phone calls.

"Hello, is this Tessa?"

"Yes, it is. Hi, Tim. I've been thinking about you all morning. How did it go? They found you not guilty, right?"

"Yeah, so that was a relief."

"You don't sound all that relieved, though. In fact, you sound like you're in the dumps."

"I'm happy to have been acquitted. But I have a couple of other less serious unexpected problems, I guess. I'm cold and wet and feeling kind of sorry for myself."

"Did you have any breakfast? I mean, if you want to swing by I could heat you up some delicious stuffed shells."

"That sounds great, Tessa. But the thing is, I'm late to work and my bus has been towed away. I was just hoping Dom was around and could maybe give me a ride. I've got to go and do my potato chip thing whether I feel like it or not."

"Gee, I'm sorry. Dom left early this morning. How do you know your bus was towed and not stolen?"

"Well, it's been a long morning. First, the clutch went out on the way to court and I had to run downtown in the rain. When I got back here and saw that there was still time left on the parking meter, I knew. For reasons I'm unable to understand, after the accident, the cab finance company stopped cashing my payment checks and won't say why. I called them up just now and they admitted they had towed the bus away. Then they gave me the phone number of their lawyer and hung up. That was what gave me the idea to call Dom. You know, this is the kind of absurd humor that is right out of his Funny Farm fantasy."

"Just tell me where you are or where I can meet you and I'll drive the big bus down and get you to work."

"You don't have to do that."

"Everyone else is gone. But even if they weren't, I'd want to. Besides, I want you to taste my shells."

I was in a parking lot, tossing pebbles at a billboard when Tessa honked and bounced the heavy yellow bus into the driveway. She shut the engine off before opening the door. No longer a camper and makeshift living quarters, the school bus had been all but emptied of its domestic furnishings. On one of the seats near the front, Tessa had piled a thick, fluffy beach towel, a pair of Thunderhead's pants, a rough flannel shirt, thick woolen socks, and a pair of Dom's shoes. Atop the pile were a small stainless-steel thermos and a warm brown paper sack, smelling of garlic.

"Thank you, Tessa," I said, emotionally, hugging her hard and kissing her cheek.

She seemed anxious, animated. "Sorry about the plastic ware, but I was having a hard time finding a lid. Anyway, the shells have three kinds of cheese and a sauce that I've been improving for a while now. The coffee's fresh and black, though I forgot the damned sugar."

"I don't take it anyway. Thank you so much for coming."

"After all you guys have done for us? Are you kidding?"

We were both looking at the clothes.

"You must be freezing. Take that towel and the clothes in back. I'll sit up here and hide my eyes so I don't," she laughed, "see anything I'm not supposed to."

Toweling off my hair, I shrugged, turned my back, and peeled my wet clothes off in a hurry. Tessa ignored her promise not to watch. She said, "I guess I should have thought to bring you some underwear, too."

When I turned back, she handed me a thermos cup of coffee. "Cab credit union decided to repossess my bus this morning. But hey, I'm not in jail."

"At least I remembered that you like it black. Didn't add milk to the coffee, I mean."

I sat down next to my wet wadded clothes. She pushed them to one side and sat down next to me. I poured and sipped the coffee and considered my reflection on the surface of the steaming liquid. It was incongruous but at that moment I felt disappointed she hadn't brushed her hair or put on lipstick. Yet as I looked up at her, I detected what I thought was a faint whiff of perfume. It had to be fresh. I sipped and smiled at her and wondered whether she'd sit so close if Irene or Bill were present.

"Maybe I should get up and start driving so you're not any later to work than you have to be."

"It's all right."

"You'll need your potato chip wages to get your bus back."

"I suppose."

"I'm sure Bill and Dom will help you put the new clutch in." She moved a little closer. "It's good to see you."

I squirmed at the mention of Bill. "You, too."

She reached for my coffee and sipped it.

I wondered why she seemed so tense. "So tell me, how are *you*?" I said. "How's the new house, I mean?"

"Oh, fine. I don't miss teepee life, but I kind of miss you and Irene and the baby. You know, the warmer nights, the cookouts."

"How's Bill?"

"Pretty much the same." She stopped herself. "He says we don't need Glen's money to promote the first event. He's been talking to this guy who owns a realty company and a big chunk of land near Longmont. Bill wanted us to have the first event before Christmas, but there won't be time now. He's a little disappointed that you and I and Dom and Irene aren't more into it, but he and Ron get together and make themselves crazy with how much money we'll be making soon. The kids really like their new school."

"I heard that Omaha had her baby."

"Yeah, Corvella, they're calling her. They're out in California with her folks for a while. They're coming back out after Christmas. Om promised she'd send us all baby pictures."

"Bill thinks I should be more involved in the Grooved-Out Productions idea. He finds it so amusing that it could be abbreviated as

314

'GOP.' I guess he thinks legions of Republicans will be incensed. I mean, I never quite know what to do or what he expects."

"He craves enthusiasm and wants lieutenants to do his bidding. I tried to tell him you've got your own ideas."

I smiled. "Maybe you can help me remember what they are. I've kind of forgotten."

"Well, you would, wouldn't you? All that worry about the trial. What did Irene say about your acquittal? Was she surprised?

"Frankly, I haven't called her yet."

"Oh." Tessa hesitated. "Do you want some more coffee?"

"This is the last of it."

"I'm sorry. I should have brought the bigger thermos. Do you want to stop somewhere on the way?"

"No. I'm fine. These shells are truly delicious, Tess."

"I should start driving. I just like to watch you . . . You know, I'm kind of goofy. I like to watch people enjoy my food. Is everything okay with you and Irene?"

"Yeah, she's fine. Because of her family she's in contact with this art teacher named Gerald. She thinks he's going to help her family and get us both enrolled in school on these special scholarships they're giving out to people being displaced by the new construction.

"That sounds really cool." Tessa looked at me, her face registering expectation.

"The reason I haven't called Irene yet is because I don't feel like hearing her I-told-you-so attitude again. I have a little trouble dealing with that in her and just want to enjoy the fact that I don't have to think about the trial any more without thinking about how she's going to be right yet again. I'm sure it's partly my fault for not giving Irene the credit and praise she deserves, but she seems to believe that life contains too few opportunities for her to be right about things. Then, of course, the other reason I've put off calling her is knowing that she'll be flipped out about my bus." I looked at my watch and sighed.

Tessa patted me on the knee and flopped into the driver's seat of the bus.

The bus was loud inside and the Old Glory Potato Chip Company parking lot was small and crowded with cars. Tessa turned into the lot, parked, and shut the engine off. Instead of opening the door, she came back and sat beside me. "I know you've got to get to work," she said, "but my whole day would be ruined if I didn't tell you how much we miss hearing from and being with you guys, maybe me more than Bill, and I wonder, you know if it's because, well, you know, that afternoon I got a little carried away."

"No," I said. "It was me who got carried away. Anyway, it has nothing to do with that. We've been caught up with the baby and the restaurant and now, plans for school. We'll have you guys over soon. And then when Denny and Omaha get back, we'll have a big party with babies and the whole business."

"I wrote you a letter last week, but I tore it up."

I lit a cigarette and inhaled the acrid smoke. "You wrote me or us?"

"You."

I thought of Bill and Irene and squirmed and studied the red and white stripes on the employee entrance door of the Old Glory Potato Chip Company.

"I didn't send it because I felt like it could be misunderstood and maybe it was garbled. I was thinking mostly about you and about hope, and how sometimes the faith we have in our lives falters a little and we try to fight that faltering and make things worse. Clichéd though it is, I just want to say, Tim, that we can't go back in time. I can't go back to my little California house with its hand-sewn drapes and wood stove, and you can't go back to the Haight or wherever it is you think you might like to go. You can't go back to the time before that little boy died and Irene maybe couldn't understand how you felt." Again, my nearest hand was between hers. She had more to say. "I think life becomes a party sometimes, complete with happiness and dreams and balloons. When the party is over, the first thing you have to do is get up and pop all the balloons, one at a time. If you don't, people will hang around long after the party's over and everybody will get all sad and start talking about how great the party was, and offer up opinions about how soon we can do it again or how it might have been better and before you know it, everybody is lost in the party they feel they half missed. Last week I asked myself what was it about you that got under my skin and decided that you remind me of my grandfather. Something about you is the same." She laughed and shook her head. "He kept dimes in a coffee can until he had enough money for opera tickets. By the time I was old enough to pay much attention to him, my grandma would no longer go to events with him because afterwards he'd stay there after performances were over clapping and clapping and get mad at people for leaving."

"For me," I said, "it's not so much the ending of something as prolonging and enhancing its anticipation. When something good happens I can walk away from it all right, but the anticipation I felt before it started often seems better that what actually happened. And the sense of its loss lingers on and on."

"How do you mean?"

"Christmas morning when I was about five, you know, probably old enough to remember a couple of other Christmases, I woke up at dawn, tiptoed halfway downstairs, and just stood there for a long time leaning over the banister. I could see and smell the Christmas tree and the bulging stockings nailed to the mantle. I had planned to go down and sneak a look at my presents, but when I got to where I could see the whole setup I stopped and sat down on the step. The morning got brighter and brighter and I hoped my parents and sister and younger brother would never come down. I think I found myself frozen by the understanding that the presents couldn't be as good and satisfying as they looked like they could from where I sat, that nothing bought or sold could ever match the anticipation and the mystery of what might be. It turned out to be a perfectly miserable Christmas for me because I realized then and there that the best part of most experiences was in the anticipation of them, the allure they held before they had completely taken form and rendered the imagining and enhancing of them moot. A few years ago in San Francisco a friend asked me what I thought was the worst thing about human life. I said that I thought that the worst thing about it was that from what I could tell everything big and good happened in your first twenty years, and then could never be repeated or experienced again in the same way. Whatever is good we all want to repeat, but whatever we repeat only gets more hollowed out to taint the original memory. The only things that can retain value and meaning are those we're willing to forget, but somehow don't."

"That works both ways, though, because we can also teach ourselves to forget about the bad things that probably make us want to remember in the first place."

Somebody was banging on the door of the bus.

"Hey, how about moving this monster out of the middle of the damned parking lot?"

I jumped to my feet, went to the door, and saw Evvie, empress of Old Glory Potato Chips."

"Barlow." Evvie recognized me and shouted through the door. "Aren't you a little old to be coming to work in school buses?"

Tessa got to the driver's seat and opened the door. "I'm sorry," Tessa said. "I'll pull out right away."

I said, "This is my friend Tessa Bianco. Evvie, I don't know your last name."

Evvie was fiftyish, broad-shouldered, a former Olympic swimmer and gym teacher. Her physical appearance convinced me there was a price to be paid for many lunches and too many free bags of Old Glory Potato Chips; she was taking on the oleaginous pallor of the company's low-salt variety, though not its crispness. She wore tight black slacks that squeezed her butt into fatty bubbles. She had no job title I was aware of, but thanks to her bossy style, her loyalty to the company, and seniority, she all but ran the place. "Don't worry about my last name," she said, pointing to a nearby red and white Chevy Camaro. "Worry about blocking me in and keeping me from my dental appointment."

When I walked down the steps to join her in the lot, Evvie shifted to make room for me, then mounted the bus for a better look at Tessa. "There aren't any more openings, honey. You should have gotten here earlier, before they hired that other bozo."

"I'm not applying for a job," Tessa explained.

"Well, I wish you were, and I wish you'd been here a couple of hours earlier." Evvie turned to me. "You're basically all right, but why did you have to send that laughing hyena down here? Godamned loudmouth that Dom is!"

"Ah," I said, "so they hired Dom?" Looking, I saw his stake bed truck parked in a remote corner of the lot.

"Yes, and he's been making an ass of himself ever since." She turned back to Tessa. "Thinks himself a clown. Seems like all these EYE-talian men think they're studs or clowns." Evvie ran a hand through her thin, short, graying hair, but succeeded only in adding to its limp shapelessness. The sun winked out through thinning clouds and Evvie reached into a jacket pocket. Behind the silver-tinted aviator glasses soon perched on her nose, she looked like a highway patrolman trapped between genders.

Tessa was having a hard time starting the bus and offered Evvie cab fare to the dentist. I took the keys and failed to get it going. The plant manager, Adam Grant, appeared in the Old Glory doorway and started toward us. Dom followed him outside, bounded up the bus steps, and touched by him, the motor roared to life. Tessa hugged and thanked him and, once he hurried back inside the plant, kissed me on the lips.

The bus rattled out of the lot. Evvie's Camaro roared and emitted a burst of white smoke.

Dom punched me on the arm. "Guilty or not guilty?"

"Not guilty."

"Congratulations!"

"Thanks."

"Where's your bus?"

"We'll talk about it later."

"Yeah, well, thanks to you, or maybe no thanks to you, I'm employed. But granny Gestapo there reminds me of photographs of those women who served in Nazi concentration camps. She seems to have dedicated her life to making sure nobody ever laughs around here."

"I can see you two have really hit it off," I said.

Inside, Dom returned to the delivery van that he'd been loading with big lightweight cartons of chips. Adam directed me to the dreaded miasma of warm water and the huge, throbbing automated peeler. An avalanche of white potatoes bounded from the peeler's stainless-steel maw, landing on a rubber conveyer towing them toward the slicer. With a paring knife in one hand, I snared a stained potato, cored an eye or a black spot, and tossed it back into the river of rumbling spuds. Armed with identical knives, five other workers stood opposite and alongside me, doing the same thing. We were alone in the world, our minds on automatic, stupefied by the howl of the peeler and the click click click of the slicer, breathing dead air, acquiring patinas of grease, our lives and the product flowing away from us for three twenty an hour.

Three days later the Old Glory machinery broke down and the plant went very still. I was stacking boxes of salt against a wall and heard Dom inside the employee lunchroom, presumably practicing on co-workers the sort of therapy he'd eventually provide to residents of his "Funny Farm."

"Hey, I mean, is life sour as all that?"

I imagined a dozen pair of sullen eyes peering glumly at him over sandwiches and lunch pails.

"What's the big deal? Don't you realize there's nothing more stupid that we could do with our short time on earth than wave saltshakers over bits of steaming potato? I mean, we're all going deaf from noise out on the floor and can't talk, but you still manage to concoct feuds just to keep from dying of boredom."

"That sounds like the beginning of a speech about communism." It was Evvie's voice. "Is that what they teach you out in Brooklyn?"

"What it is," Dom said, "is the voice of your own consciousness hammering at the door of your self-induced comas. Why you don't dig me, I think, Evvie, is because I bear witness to our collective humiliation. I speak in the voice you've tried to muffle in yourself."

"If you find this job humiliating and you hate working here so much, why don't you go back where you came from or find another job? And

319

until you do one or the other," Evvie suggested, "why don't you leave us in peace and shut the hell up once in a while?"

"If I did shut up, what would be left? Outside this room, it's the roar of the machinery. In here, only the sound of ham sandwiches being chewed. The thing is, all of youse, you gotta take a look around. I mean, in a few years, maybe less, unless we lay off these potato shits, we're all gonna die, our hearts transformed into these grease-swollen oil pumps."

"All we ask is that you go before us, Dom." It was a man's voice. I supposed it belonged to Vlad, a man with thin, wispy red hair, the captain of a neighborhood bowling team.

"Yeah, that's cool. But what if later on I'm waiting for you, sitting down on your favorite bowling bag beside those pearly gates, the first heavenly being to ask you what it was like to spend most of your life on earth pouting and going deaf. And how were those vacations you took in that Winnebago where you couldn't afford the full tank of gas and so went back where you'd been before?"

"Go to hell, Dom."

"For me hell would be a job where people like you handed me a form saying I was forbidden to laugh. Laughing is the key to getting out of potato hell."

It was Evvie's turn. "From the smell that comes out of the men's room when you go in there we kind of thought marijuana was the key. Maybe you think if we all took up marijuana smoking we might find the kind of happiness you're such an expert in. Aren't you supposed to be able to get high from smoking banana peel? Want me to save this one for you?" I smiled to picture Evvie waving her banana peel at him.

That evening, carrying most of a six-pack of beer and a bag of Old Glory chips to feed the geese, Dom and I sat down on a bench in Washington Park. A fleet of geese and ducks on the pewter-colored lake steamed noisily toward us. The sun cast a cold yellow light through the uppermost branches of maples and elms on the far shore of the south lake. Thanks to an inch of snow that had fallen and melted earlier in the day, the park lawn was a brilliant green over a slippery muck underfoot. Of the snow, all that remained were a few patches of white between tree roots.

"You seem to be using the factory as a kind of laboratory to test your theories and techniques," I observed.

"So what's wrong with that?"

"I dunno. Maybe nothing. I mean, you can be very funny. But I think you still need to understand the difference between mocking and humiliating people, and making them laugh. Maybe what's funny to you

320

comes across to those people as just so much native New York truculence. I mean that business with that guy about his Winnebago. . .

"What? You heard that?"

"I was working right outside the lunchroom. What I was saying is that those people haven't gone home tonight resolved to start laughing at themselves or even laughing at you. They're thinking about how they'd like to murder you."

"Yeah," Dom conceded, "I guess today didn't go over so hot. But you missed out on yesterday. I had 'em falling out of their chairs when I was imitating the way Evvie drives her hot rod around. Where'd she get that street machine anyway?"

"I heard she repossessed it from a son-in-law. Anyway, my advice is if you need the bread and you want to stay on, cool it a little. Especially toking up in the men's room. Around here they send people to jail for pot. I know a guy who got five years for simple possession."

Dom waved me off. "Listen, man, whatshisname, that guy who wears his coat all the time no matter how hot it is, he gets up each morning and wonders what I'm going to say. He told me as much. When I walk into that lunchroom, people know they're going to feel less bored. They can't admit it, but I enrich their lives."

My hands were cold, so I held my beer between my knees and stuffed my hands under my armpits. "Entertaining them's one thing, insulting them's another." I gave him a sarcastic look. "But you don't need the job, anyway, right?"

"Meaning you'd like to keep your ass out of the frying pan, is that it?"

"I don't know what I mean. But small though they are, I like those paychecks right now."

"Hey, instead of encouraging me to leave, you should encourage me to stay on. Without a car it's going to take you a lot longer to get to and from that dump when I'm gone. Of course, you should get away from there, too. Maybe go back to school. Get some kind of part time gig."

"School does seem to be in the works."

Dom broke a handful of potato chips into bite-sized shards and scattered them among the geese and ducks. "I probably won't be there much longer. Glen wrote me a letter saying he was going to send me a big check to shop around and buy him some mountain real estate. Still, seeing's believing, I guess."

Birds waddled through muck, circled our bench, chased each other away, stabbed and snatched at the potato chip flakes. "Millionaire Glen," I scoffed. "I always thought he was Bill's fantasy."

"I didn't contact Glen, though. And that's an important distinction that might be lost on Billy. Glen met some rich guy in Paris who is convinced that Crested Butte is going to be bigger than Aspen. Supposedly they want to pay me to scout around for a chunk of land within an hour's drive or so of there. If I can find a hot springs on about a hundred acres or more, Glen says he'll fund the Funny Farm." Dom lit a cigarette and looked serious. "But back from fantasy to reality, speaking of the next few days rather than some remote future, I'll agree to cool it at the factory if you promise not to fuck my cousin's wife. Or maybe I should say fuck her again."

I was a midnight mule deer, caught, apparently, in the glare of my too obvious and guilty fantasies.

Dom shook his head and frowned. "Well, if it's really all that alarming, I'm worried maybe I'm too late."

I lit a smoke of my own. Still, I said nothing.

"What is this about, Tim? Am I too late? Is this tit for tit? Did Bill fuck Irene or something and you get back at him?"

"Get serious!"

"Hey, I am. I don't mean to be insulting. This is my first serious conversation this week."

"You're out of your mind."

"Come on, Barlow. I hear the mooning when you're not around. Bill talks about Irene and Tessa counters by talking about you. I don't know whether she has the hots for you because she wants to pay him back or if she finds you irresistible. But if you're a friend to me and to them and their kids, you'll back off and stay away from her."

"The only reason we were together that afternoon was on account of my bus. I called you for a ride, but you were out and she answered the phone."

A wind kicked up and I zipped my jacket. The ducks and geese at my feet scurried and scolded each other. They were as annoying as panhandlers. Why didn't they fend for themselves? I hated potato chips. "Bill talks about Irene?"

"He's got the hots for Irene in a way that he has the hots for any woman connected to any man he might compete with. Some people say that that's some kind of tortured gay thing. I say, think it over; maybe Irene's sending you signals and you need to treat her better, kiss her on the mouth like you did Tessa that day." Dom looked at me. "I've never been married, but I've gotten it on with married women whose husbands I never met, so I'm probably way out of line, aren't I?"

322

"Matter of fact, yeah. Wasn't it you who told Irene's cousin, little sweet sixteen, Gloria, that you'd like to show her how Italians kiss?"

"I looked to see if she was wearing a ring. Is she married, shacking up, having kids, your little Gloria?"

All I had left was my sarcasm. "No, but I'm sure her dad doesn't think she should lose her virginity until after she's gotten her driver's license."

"Look, man, much as Bill would like to poke Irene, and much as he enjoys tormenting Tessa with his open-marriage talk, and much as I think he's already fucked Donna, I also think, knowing his uncles, that he'd shoot to kill anybody who balled Tessa." He flashed the obnoxious New Yorker grin. "That would be all right maybe, but he might miss you and hit Tessa."

"Sex is a long way from a little sympathy and kindness."

"Yeah, well, in my opinion, it is not. I have an instinct for this shit. I'm talking from a family pathology. My dad did it to Bill's mom. Bill's sister Tina did it to my brother Nick the night before he got married. I have four older brothers and they've all been porking each other's girlfriends and fighting about it ever since I opened my first copy of *Playboy*. It's *coitus everywhereyoucanus,* and it's the main reason I don't go home for the holidays anymore. I don't want to know about or suspect any of my relatives of screwing around. They're all so afraid of losing points in the sexual competition they're caught in. The prevailing idea is to screw somebody else's mate before somebody else's mate screws yours."

A goose with a tumor on its head was hissing and flapping and doing all it could to keep a trio of mallards from the empty potato chip bag at our feet. I kicked the sack toward the water, and turned my back on Dom. Across the lake a boy in a bright red ski parka romped with a pair of Irish Setters.

"It's simple," Dom went on. "Just resign yourself to the fact that you'll never know, and you don't need to know, what Tessa feels about you or anybody else. Just decide never to ask about her feelings or be alone with her again." He stomped his foot and half a dozen ducks squawked and waddled toward the water. "Hey, man I'm just trying to keep you out of the cosmic sick ward. Let Tessa fuck Thunderhead if that's what she's about. He's the logical instrument of her revenge anyway. That way all four of 'em could become betrayed hypocrites with nobody to blame but themselves."

I drank the last rinse from my beer can, whirled twice like a discus thrower and flung it as far into the lake as I could. When I turned around, an angry/guilty polluter of the park I'd always professed to cherish, the goose with the tumor was in the center of a circle of ducks, shaking the empty sack, flapping its wings.

The next day, the machine that sealed potato chip bags was clogged with glue. The machinist had partly dismantled it and my job was to crawl over the mechanism to attack gobs of glue with a stiff, wire brush, sloshing blackened serrated edges with noxious, soapy water. The peeler machine, thirty feet away and still deafening, howled and spewed a river of spuds.

From the corner of one eye, I saw Dom clambering up on the conveyor belt in front of the peeler. He looked tall and ridiculous under the hot overhead lights. He stood momentarily among the skinned bounding potatoes, then dropped to his knees and brought his prayerful hands up under his nose in a parody of a grade-school holy card, Christ's agony in the garden, begging for forgiveness in a Gethsemane of raw, jumping potatoes.

Knowing that Dom was stoned and wanting to distract him before Adam Grant discovered his stunt, I climbed down from the sealer just as Evvie hurried into position right behind Dom. She cocked her arm as if she were about to fling a softball from third to first base. I started to run, recognizing that the steel glint in her hand could only be the tool of her temporary trade, her paring knife.

I broad-jumped a toppled cart. When I landed on a greasy spot on the floor, my right foot shot sideways and I staggered into a small wagon loaded with saltshakers. Pushing off from the cart, clipping a footstool and taking it sharply against my shin, I managed to make contact with Evvie's arm as she was flinging the knife at Dom's broad back. My arm came down on top of her head, my knee struck her hip. She felt soft and fell hard. One of my knees was in her round belly when she hit the floor and I found myself looking dead into her open mouth, staring at her fillings and bridgework, smelling her lunch and bad strong coffee.

People pummeled me with elbows and hands and maybe a fist or two. I tore myself free, wheeled to see a flying potato hit Dom on the chin. He executed a judo throw on Twyman the machinist. Vlad, wearing his ubiquitous bowling team jacket, threw a wild haymaker at Dom, but Dom slipped the punch and kicked Twyman in the groin. As Twyman went down, somebody pulled my hair and hit me in the neck. The next thing I knew, everybody had hands on everybody, shaking, restraining, threatening and shouting fiercely, mutually, stupidly, that the fight was over. The electrical power went down with a growl and a hiss and suddenly all of us could hear every shouted word. People with reddened, strained faces stood gasping in the stillness.

Not too many minutes later, Sergeant Jim Coogan removed his cap, establishing right off that he'd long ago paid the price of a once-healthy head of hair to the stresses of police work. Placing his hat on a long Formica-topped table, he sat behind a large complementary bag of Old Glory Hot Cha Cha Chips with Sour Cream flavoring. Chewing carefully, he produced a steel-bound notebook.

His partner, Sandoval, a thin, subordinate cop with a long nose, stood over Coogan's shoulder asking us questions and abridging overly elaborate answers so that Coogan could record the essentials without neglecting his chips.

More subdued than I'd ever seen him, Dom sat near the door, his back to the wall, everybody's villain. Two younger cops, each with a small bag of barbecue chips, stood on either side of him. I pressed a wet washcloth to a small but surprisingly deep cut on the back of my right hand, and sitting next to Coogan, studied the blocky letters he drew in his book.

"Barlow, Timothy J. Mnr ct bk of rht hand. Curedwoode, Mrs. Evylyn R., brkn glsses, scrch on lft neck and thrt. Sospiri, Dominic V., Brklyn, NY, nse bld. Kolonsky, Vladimir, Amer cit, swln wrst. T. Twyman, kicked groin."

Fingering her broken glasses, Evvie looked tired, but self-assured. "In fact, the episode actually began," she said, risking an accusatory glance at plant manager Adam Grant, "when Adam hired this marijuana-puffing bozo who wants to be a clown when he grows up."

Coogan wrote the word "pot" in his notebook and drew a connecting arrow to Dom's name. Coogan decorated his arrow with feathers while Sandoval got up on his tiptoes, elevating his nose toward the ventilation system, as if he thought Dom might have sneaked a toke within the last hour and, as if with its perpetual stink of pickles, baloney, and green banana, the lunchroom might yield the resiny scent of weed.

"It culminated," Evvie continued, "when Vlad, who has worked here without trouble for twelve years, playfully lobbed a potato at Dominic, deliberately missing him."

Flushed, worried about his job, Vlad caught Adam's eye. "Yeah. Playful," Vlad muttered in his own defense. "No harm whatever. No intent to injure."

Impatient, Evvie cut Vlad off. "Dom waited until Vlad was distracted and bounced a potato off the top of his head. When Vlad looked stunned, Dom laughed and climbed up on the conveyor belt." She looked furiously at Adam Grant. "Knelt right in the middle of all those damned potatoes that people are going to eat. Something in me snapped, then, thinking of our customers. It never happened before."

Sandoval raised an eyebrow. "And that's when you attempted to stab Sospiri?"

"No, that's when I considered throwing a paring knife through his back and into his heart. Next thing I knew, Tim, who watches the bathroom door whenever Dom goes in there to smoke his pot, jumped on me."

I gave Evvie an outraged look. "Considered? You did throw it, Evvie. You might have killed him."

Evvie softened a little. "Actually, I take that back. I don't want to say anything against Tim. Let's just say he thought I was going to throw it and it was dislodged from my hand on impact, giving the appearance that I had thrown it. I don't know, I might have been going to throw it and might even have even been in the act of throwing it."

Coogan had eaten his way to the bottom of his bag of potato chips and took to pinching for crumbs. "Now we're starting to get a different twist on things," he observed, looking at Evvie. "I'm getting the idea you want to let the whole thing drop."

"Well, I don't want Tim to have any problems over it. I mean, the better part of me is glad he stopped me. I don't want a jail sentence."

Coogan put his ballpoint beside his cap and wadded the empty potato chip sack into a ball. Observing that all eyes were on him, including those of his junior officers, he rubbed his lips and chin into a serious expression. "Now, what about this pot you've been accused of smoking, Mr. Sospiri?"

"It was Italian seasoning," Dom said, deadpan.

The two cops standing near Dom laughed loudly. When Sandoval glared at them, they sobered up. I looked at Dom.

Dom met my worried glance with a wink. "See, I don't get enough Italian cooking these days. My mama could tell you that going without the right meatballs makes me a little crazy."

Coogan rolled his eyes. "Let's not turn this into a sideshow. What is your current address, Mr. Sospiri?"

I thought of the peyote buttons Bill Bianco was known to keep in a bell jar in the cupboard next to containers of herbal tea, of the yellowed marijuana roaches half-smoked in ashtrays scattered all around the house.

"He's staying with me," I said, "till he can afford a place of his own."

Evvie, who had no idea whether or not Dom was living with me, seemed to see a way out of the imbroglio. She was nodding her head up and down with the self-confident energy of a quiz show contestant with the correct answer. She rotated to face Adam Grant, rather than Coogan. "The Old Glory Potato Chip Company doesn't want to be written up in the daily papers as a place where employees kneel and tromp around in our product," she insisted. "Nor do we want to be known as a place where employees use drugs. I mean, I think Dom has to be fired for violating safety procedures, but Adam, you know, the more I think about it, the more I'm inclined to think Dom's telling us the truth. Hell, how would I know marijuana from spaghetti spices? He probably *was* smoking sage and parsley in the bathroom. Just like he says."

Adam found Evvie's argument highly persuasive.

Coogan sighed and seemed to scan the room for another bag of chips.

That evening, I had planned to walk a couple of blocks and take a city bus to the Hacienda Escobar where I was scheduled to bus tables and wash dishes. Dom's weathered Chevy truck was parked in front of the factory when I emerged from my shift. I climbed in and raised an eyebrow. "Champagne? You're celebrating getting fired?"

"Hey, what we're celebrating is the saving of a human life. You're my hero. I owe you big, and this is just the beginning."

I smirked, shook my head, and swigged from the nearly empty bottle he handed me. It was warm but still bubbly. A second unopened bottle was on the seat between us. "You're a crazy son of a bitch, Sospiri."

"Whazat?" Dom's nose was a little swollen. His breath was sour from drink and his voice sounded peculiar. "Crazy's just an argument about differences in the standards of behavior. You know, in some tropical countries when somebody freaks out, they just dig a steep pit and dump him in it. Every few hours somebody comes by and looks down in the ditch. When he's sane enough to beg them to let him out, they consider him cured. After all, only a crazy person would stay in a pit if he could talk somebody into letting him out. Anyway, I think you say I'm crazy because I act while you sit around and worry about things."

"I've heard heedless impulsiveness called poor impulse control."

"You're right and *they,* the callers, are also the controllers. But we'll talk about that some other time. Right now, I have only the loftiest things to say about you and your friendship. You can ask for anything you want. Anything at all, except Tessa. Just ask."

"Are you in love with her? Is that why you're so protective of her?"

"No, I'm not. I do love her, though. And I'd like to protect her. She's a better person than any of us."

I said, "Anything I want?"

"Anything.

"All right. Item one, shut the fuck up about Tessa already. Item two, slide over. You're drunk as a skunk and I'm demanding driving privileges."

"Let's have a look at that cut on your hand."

"It's no big deal."

"How did it happen? The knife?"

"I don't know. Somebody said the knife sailed past your head."

"Just think how guilty you'd feel right now, if instead of making her miss my back you caused her to throw it through my temple or into my ear and brain or something." Dom laughed.

I lit a cigarette. "What brain?"

He laughed. "Okay, fair question."

"You sound like you've got a head cold. Did you ever get a broken nose from a thrown potato before?"

"I don't know if it's broken or not, but frankly, I like the shape of it better now. Anyway, about the celebration, when it became clear that Adam was worried that I was going to drive from the plant to the newspapers, I got a little bargaining in. I got two weeks' wages on top of what I had coming."

"You're a real scamp, Dom, but we'll have to celebrate later," I said. "I've got dishes to wash."

"What? At the restaurant? Tonight?"

"Yeah. Irene's already there."

"I'll pick you up when you get off. The three of us will celebrate."

"Yeah, well, you better sober up first or Irene won't ride with you."

Dom climbed out of the truck and walked around to the passenger's side while I scooted behind the steering wheel. As I reached for the ignition key, Dom snared my wrist. In one quick motion, he ripped the Band-Aid from my hand, ducked his head and kissed it, more like banged it, with his face. With my free hand, I shoved him off balance. "What the hell are you doing, you drunk moron?" The back of my hand was wet with blood, most of it not my own. Hardly any of it was. Blood was running freely from Dom's nose again.

"Blood brothers," Dom said with a look of drunken triumph. "We're blood brothers now."

I was furious. "Yeah, well, I got news for you. I don't want to die because you blew bloody snot in my cut. This ain't no cowboy and Indian's movie set or psychedelic mob rite, and I feel like smacking you in the fucking mouth."

Dom got himself quickly to the far side of the cab. "What for?" he laughed, "tearing your bandage off, or kissing your hand?"

"Fuck you. I'm supposed to go to work at the restaurant now, serve food to people? With blood all over me?"

"Impulse control," Dom reminded me. "You have it. I lack it. Therefore, looks like I get to keep all my teeth." He wiped his nose with the inside of his wrist and chugged from the champagne. "Actually, if all our racialist ancestors were on to anything with their blood purity stuff, we'd be more alike now. You know, blood as a medium of temperament and all that. Soon you'll become more hot-blooded, develop an unexpected ability to laugh, and I'll start brooding about everything and get the hots for married women."

"You're bleeding all over the seat!"

"Forget the seat," Dom said, rummaging through the glove box for a pack of tissues and tilting his head back. "I don't want to get blood in our champagne. Let's go to a filling station and wash up."

An hour later, I dropped Dom off at the Biancos. Tessa came to the door to let him in and motioned for me to get out of the truck, but I begged off, blowing her a kiss and honking the horn.

Irene stood next to a big stove in the restaurant kitchen. Gerald was holding her shapely chin with his thumb and index finger, bobby pin in his teeth, the better to affix a gardenia in the bushy hair on top of her head. The quickness with which he pulled back and she stepped away from him brought me a stab of jealousy.

"We were starting to worry about you," she jumped, freeing her chin. "Did you have to work overtime?"

"No," I said, "not really."

"You smell like wine."

"Dom bought some champagne. An unexpected celebration."

"Where's Dom?"

"Gone home to sleep it off, I guess. We have use of his truck till tomorrow night."

There was a commotion on the back steps. Irene's uncle Ralph absorbed a swinging screen door on one shoulder. Grunting behind a cardboard box filled with clinking beer bottles, he staggered into the room toward the largest of three refrigerators. He lowered the carton to the floor, and as the screen door slammed behind him, stood up and put a hand on either hip. "Wall, halo, Teem."

I shook Ralph's hand and squatted down by the box to feed him the bottles to put away. While he arranged them into tight military formations on the cold refrigerator shelves, I looked up at Irene, now checking at her reflection in the window over the kitchen sink, improving on the gardenia's placement in her hair.

Gerald stepped toward me. "A party of two dozen people from City University Planning Commission are coming at seven," he said. "We're going to be busy tonight."

I eyed him. "*We* are?"

"It looks that way."

"Have I been replaced or something?" I enjoyed his discomfort.

"What do you mean?"

Irene took an interest in the conversation and stepped toward both of us.

"I mean," I said, "I didn't know you worked here. I thought you were an art professor."

Irene came to his rescue. "He is."

"Oh, I see what you mean," Gerald laughed. "I don't work here. Forgive the royal 'we.' Gramma makes family of all of us, I guess." His blond curly hair was carefully trimmed and painstakingly disheveled. Thin, dry skin on his forehead and cheeks muted clusters of freckles that refused to fade away. The polished boots, the herringbone tweed slacks, the army fatigue jacket, all struck me as elements of a costume carefully calculated to win the sympathies of City U students dreaming of a sociologist's revolution, clean and painless. The carefully twisted mustache, waxed and torturously shaped, put me in mind of some *fin-de-siècle* Prussian martinet. A friend to the Kaiser. *Echt Deutsch* with fencing skills. Had he gone to Princeton? He could see I didn't like him and I didn't care. What did he want with those the cool, assessing fish-gray eyes behind the Trotsky glasses? His own restaurant? Tenure? Irene? What did Irene think he wanted? Art, I was sure. A loyal handful of truly talented, receptive students who would appreciate him. But appreciate him how? In what way?

"Gerald's life drawing class was just over," Irene explained, "and he wanted to stop by because Gramma promised him her recipe for molé. What did you do to your hand?"

"Just a little cut is all."

"You can't wash the dishes with a cut hand," Gerald offered.

My look was less than friendly.

"All that chorizo grease and salsa will kill you," he hastened.

"I'll be fine," I said to Irene.

"No, I think he's right," she insisted. "Let's see how deep it is."

"It's all right. I don't want to take the bandage off again. I'll just wear rubber gloves."

"I've got a better idea," Gerald said. "I'll wash dishes and wait tables and you can go home."

By the terms of the finally negotiated, elaborate eminent domain agreement with the city, the family restaurant was to be demolished so City U could be greatly expanded. Irene, as an immediate relative of the owners, was entitled to a small cash allowance and free tuition at City U. As a restaurant employee, think occasional paid dishwasher, I would be entitled to reduced tuition. Thing was, we did have to live within the city limits to qualify.

We found and rented a second-floor apartment about a fifteen-minute bus ride from the developing campus, enlisted the help of a few friends, and arranged to borrow Dom's truck. Our Saturday moving day coincided with an eightieth birthday party Gordon and Rhonda had planned for Ben, the retired black truck farmer who lived across the road.

After putting Ben's leftover birthday cake in the refrigerator and washing and drying every dish and surface in his dim kitchen, Irene, Omaha, and Rhonda piled into Rhonda's Buick among boxes of candles and cleaning supplies. Denny and Bill crossed the street to ready the truck and lug out the furniture, while Gordon and I followed Ben to a shed behind his house.

Behind bags of sand and chicken feed and under a bale of wire, just where the old man thought it would be, we discovered a battered old hand truck. Gordon wheeled it outside, followed by Ben, carrying a small oilcan and an old rag. While Ben squatted in the dust to lubricate its battered wheels, Gordon said, "How does it feel to be eighty, Ben?"

Ben used the steel frame of the hand truck to pull himself upright. His skin was a dusty coffee and his hair, except for darker tufts that bloomed from his pear-shaped ears, approximated the color and texture of lamb's wool. Overalls exaggerated the length of his torso and made his hips and legs look fragile. If he carried any body fat at all it seemed to me to have gathered around his lips. Otherwise he was knots and twists of tendons and arteries. When he turned his head slightly, I noted the forcefulness with which the blood pumped through his carotid artery.

"I can't eat as much cake as I used to," Ben said, nodding his head slowly. "And I spend too much time worrying about my hens. And I forget things. When I woke up this morning I knew it was my birthday but thought I was going to be seventy-seven. One of your wives had to do the arithmetic for me."

"She has to do it for me, too," Gordon said.

Ben chuckled. "Course both numbers are older than I thought I'd ever be."

"Well you're hearty enough," I offered, wondering why I felt obliged to protect old people from the discovery that I perceived them as old, and why I spoke to them so loudly and in such tones of calibrated cheerfulness.

Across the road, Denny and Bill were pounding with hammers, constructing a makeshift ramp to wheel the old refrigerator that I had bought from Big George up into Dom's stake bed truck. Their banter, though not their actual words, carried in the cold, dry air.

Ben looked toward the truck with small rheumy eyes and started to whistle. Abruptly he left off and looked at me. "I almost forgot I told the boy I'd speak to you about the dog."

"There's a leash law in the city," I said a little defensively. "And there's no fenced yard connected to our apartment."

Ben nodded and licked his lower lip.

"Between school and work, Irene and the baby and I are almost never home."

"I told the boy that if you agreed and that if the dog left my hens be, I'd keep him fed and watered. The boy said he'd help me with a heavy errand now and again."

"That sounds like a perfect arrangement."

"Yes sir, he sure loves that old car you gave him." The old man tapped the toe of an old boot in the dust. Speaking more than a few words at one time seemed to wear him out.

The electricity in the new apartment wouldn't be switched on until the first of the week, but there were plenty of candles and I was anxious to have everything upstairs before dark. I lit a cigarette and sighed. Ben watched me blow a long stream of smoke, shook his head and said, "Not too good for the boy to be drag racing that ol' car down the street, though."

"I spoke to him about not driving it before he got his license," I said, "But you're telling me he was racing it down the street?"

"Yes, he was racing your friend, the driver of that truck all right. Would have been Wednesday or Thursday, I guess. It kind of slipped out of mind until I saw the truck y'all are driving."

Gordon was untangling a stained canvas belt attached to the hand truck frame. "Tim wouldn't race him down the street, Ben."

"No," Ben reflected, "I don't believe he would neither."

332

Gordon looked at me. "It was the guy who owns the truck. A goofy friend of ours named Dom. I'm going to see him later and tear into him about it."

Ben nodded. "Still kind of wish you boys would have another piece of cake. Maybe take some to your helpers yonder."

"They already had some, Ben," I reminded him. "Little George and Rover will help you finish it off. I'll get your hand truck back in a day or so."

A minute later, I was pushing the borrowed hand truck toward the house we were about to empty out. I turned to Gordon, who was coming up behind. "What was all that about Dom and Little George?"

"Well, I saw 'em, too. I was sitting at the stop sign when they went by. They weren't breaking the sound barrier, but they weren't doing bad considering the heaps they were driving. The worst thing was they were taking up both sides of the road. Fucking Dom, all that curly hair thrown back, laughing his fool head off and egging the kid on. I thought about following them, but they were going the other direction and I was late for work."

The restaurant was due to be torn down in seven months, and thanks to a padding of our restaurant hours, timely phone calls, and some help from Gerald with the paperwork, Irene and I were both qualified to receive free tuition at City U. We'd been having sex again and had managed to get through the first two weeks of school, dealing with the long commute by riding buses, cadging rides with Gordon or Dom or Rhonda. Our new apartment would be only a mile and a half from school and two miles from the restaurant. But the image of Dom and Little George racing down the street darkened my mood. Out of all proportion, I thought.

"Have you ever observed runs of luck? Your own personal streaks of good and bad luck?" I asked.

Gordon shook his head. "I know you and Rhonda do, but speaking personally, I don't like to think in terms of luck. I'm a man of action and reaction, I guess."

"I don't swallow Tarot cards," I said, "but for a long time I've felt like I could see or hear my good luck running out just before it does. When the last of a run of good luck is at an end, it's like the echo of a broken engine."

"In your own way," Gordon observed, "I think you're as preoccupied with what's going to happen as Rhonda is. I'm not going to judge you, but if you started to enlarge the present somehow, live for the moment, and forget what happened or might happen, you'd do better. I doubt if I'm the only one waiting for you to grasp that."

"You're right," I said. "Sometimes I feel like a parachutist. I've got to make a landing to get on with whatever it is that I'm doing, but a wind keeps blowing me. I feel myself moving and I look down and just don't seem to be gaining on the ground."

Gordon opened the gate. I looked at Denny and Thunderhead studying the piles of boxes and furniture in the yard. "You think we'll manage to get everything in one truckload?"

"We've got plenty of rope," Thunderhead said.

Gordon laughed. " Yeah, and when we're done, I hope there's enough left over to hang Dom for drag racing Little George."

Denny rode in the back of the truck, seated a little precariously in a stuffed chair. He had taken up that position in order to keep the tilted couch from falling into the street on the drive to the apartment.

Bianco rode shotgun. He lit one of his cigarillos, rolled down the window, and said, "Rhonda told me you got fired, Gordon."

I looked at Gordon. "You didn't tell me you got fired by the cab company."

Gordon grinned. "Yeah. Tuesday night, I guess. I picked up this middle-aged woman at the Oak Cask Bar on Broadway." Gordon looked at me and winked. "You know how it is. It was closing time, the first of the month, everybody flush and ready to drink away their sorrows. I walked in and this little old lady wearing a red wig slumped over a bar glass looked up and nodded. She was extremely woozy so I led her out to the cab, propped her up in the back seat, and asked where she was going. But she nodded out and wasn't able to give me an address. At first I was amused, but then I started to get very uptight, thinking about all the fares I was missing. There was cab business everywhere. Every once in a while I'd reach around and try to shake her awake. Whenever I did, she would say, 'My son, you're a beast.'"

Bianco laughed, "I bet she wasn't the first woman to call you that."

"Actually, what she was saying turned out to be that her son was a priest."

Bianco and I laughed.

"Go on," Bianco said. "This is getting good."

"Regulations require drivers to transport incoherent drunks either to the police station or the nearest hospital. Thing is, if you do that, depending on your location, it takes about an hour out of your shift. Anyway, while I was fretting about the business I was missing, I heard the dispatcher over the radio telling some other driver that a certain bar was located near the Cathedral of the Immaculate Conception over on Colfax."

I raised my eyebrows. "So you took her to church?"

"Hey, it would never have occurred to me if she hadn't said her son was a priest. It even seemed like one of those sweet, if remote, possibilities that her son might be up there reading the epistle and look down from the pulpit to see his mother sawing away. I guess it was Rhonda's influence. Rhonda, I figured, would appreciate my decision in a big way. You know, smile and nod, and see it as evidence of my highly evolved soul."

"It was spooky in that old church, dark and smoky with all those fluttering, what do you call them, Tim, those candles in these cups in front of the statues?

"Novena candles."

"Yeah the whole place smelled like these ancient fires. Anyway, I'm carrying this little old lady who couldn't have weighed more than about eighty or ninety pounds and the floor is creaking underfoot. Not having been a Catholic or spent much time in church, I felt like I'd walked onto some Vincent Price movie set. I laid her down in a pew toward the front of the church, got her into a position where I thought she'd be okay. Only when I decided to prop her purse up under her head did it occur to me that I could remove my fare. I didn't want anything extra, but I felt like, you know, I should have something for all the time she'd taken up. I unsnapped her purse and saw that in addition to a fistful of loose coins, she had eight twenties, a one, and a five."

"A couple of twenties," Bianco said. "She'd never remember, and you were certainly entitled, fare plus TLC. Forty and no more. It would start to be ethically dubious at forty-one dollars."

"I approached it more modestly," Gordon said. "Four dollars cab fare and a twenty-five percent tip. I took the five, left her the single and the eight twenties, closed her purse, propped it under her dirty head. I went outside feeling pretty good about everything until I saw that a cop had pulled in behind my cab and was in the process of writing me a ticket for being illegally parked. Naturally, the cop wanted to know what I'd been doing in church at two-thirty in the morning."

"Praying for the soul of a dead uncle," Bianco suggested. "Something like that. That's what I'd have told him."

Gordon laughed, "Yeah, but the cop was suspicious. When he reached for his flashlight I realized he was going to walk me into the church, probably to check the poor boxes. I decided I better tell him the truth,

335

right down to how much money I'd taken and how much I'd left in her purse."

I shook my head. "Was he able to bring her round?"

"We couldn't find her."

Bianco laughed. "I can't believe this story."

"Neither could the cop." Gordon smiled. "He shone the flashlight in my eyes and asked me if there was anything I wanted to change about my story. I said no, that the woman must have somehow gotten up and moved. Then, before we could go up and check behind the communion rail, two more cops came rushing into the church with their guns drawn."

"Whoa!" I said.

"Luckily, the cop shouted out he was a police officer. Even so, it was one hairy moment, I tell you."

"Did you find the woman?"

"Sure," Gordon said, "She was curled up and snoring away behind the pulpit. The cops shook her and coaxed her until she said her son was a priest, and finally, I persuaded one of the cops to open her billfold so that at least he could confirm the amount of money in her purse. When that had been done, the original cop, a guy named Martinez, asked me to produce the five I'd taken from her. All three cops laughed about the whole thing and advised me to sign for my parking ticket and go back to work."

"Wait a minute," I said. "If the cops let you go, how did you get fired?"

"Supervisor. When I went back outside, a cab supervisor was just pulling in behind the police car. He took an instant dislike to me. The cops came out after a minute or two and told him that I was a good guy and honest and the whole bit. But by then both supervisor and I were trapped in this mutual paranoia. He examined my trip sheet on which we have to record our fares and asked me why I hadn't written my most recent trip down. I said I'd just forgotten. Then he got on the radio, audited my meter, and discovered that I hadn't thrown the meter down for the fare."

"Why didn't you say that your meter was accurate and that the driver of the earlier shift had failed to record one of his trips?" I asked. "I mean, anybody can forget, or make a simple mistake. The other driver of your cab would probably have found a way to cover for you and keep himself out of the frying pan."

"Yeah, maybe so. I don't know," Gordon admitted. "It might be that I'm too honest, but it's probably that I'm too stupid. Yet it seemed by then that the supervisor was going to get me one way or another."

Bianco chewed on his cigarillo. "So what are you going to do now?"

"Well, I don't know. Help wrestle that refrigerator and ugly couch upstairs." Gordon winked at me and elbowed Bianco. "Actually, now that Barlow's back in school and got more work than he can handle, I was thinking about applying to work for you. I'd be a hell of a rock concert promoter."

Bianco laughed. "I think you would, too. The problem is our cash cow has all her udders locked up. Dom's buddy Glen is only interested in doing something for Dom. But that's Dom's story. He's bringing pizza over later and will tell us all about it."

"Funny how we were going to make a revolution," Gordon reflected, "and now we're all becoming businessmen." The stove had been connected and the phone turned on, but for light we had to make do with those candles and flashlights. I looked out the kitchen window at the falling snow, found odds and ends of kitchen stuff in a crumpled box, and boiled water on the stove. The doorbell rang and I heard Dom's voice, and then together with an assortment of cups and glass jars and a small carton of milk and a bag of sugar, I balanced the teapot Albert Fine had given me on a wooden tray and started through canyons of boxes toward the front room. Blunted shadows flickered over the freshly painted walls of the apartment, and an aroma of pizza commingled with a pungent fog of cigarette, pot, and incense smoke. I closed my eyes and envisioned myself a washed potato, bounding and bounding toward the peeler and some new strange life.

Bianco and Gordon were separating pizza slices with a pocketknife blade. Delighted to have found an audience in Dom, Rhonda sat on her bare feet studying an arrangement of Tarot cards. Dom squatted beside her, ostensibly engrossed in her prognostications.

"I see a journey," Rhonda said, "but not a long one. Then I see a restlessness, a going back and forth over the same territory for a while."

Stoned as usual, Dom was all eyes for the images on the cards. "No fair," he protested. "Bill told you."

"Hey, Cousin," Bianco said. "I didn't say a thing!"

The picture of Rhonda's glowing apprentice, Irene sat on a bed pillow, looking over Rhonda's shoulder, nursing Serena and studying the arranged Tarot cards.

"I see a woman," Rhonda continued, "maybe more than one. Or maybe it's the female principle, yin." In order to be sure she was understood, Rhonda looked up from the cards. "Since we're all combinations of male and female, maybe it's just your female energy, longing for comforts like home and stability. It's hard to say."

Dom looked nonplused.

"Oh, well, Dom, it's all simple enough, isn't it?" Omaha said. "If you're going away, of course, we'll all miss you. Yang and yin, guys and gals alike."

I served Irene a slice of pizza, relieved her of Serena, and leaned toward Dom. "What's this about going away?"

"His millionaire buddy came through yesterday," Bianco explained, handing me a slice of pizza. "He's off to become a jet-setter, a privileged man of leisure. Hopefully, he won't forget his friends, family, the dream of Grooved-Out Productions, and the concerts which could make us all prosperous."

"What's this about, Dom?"

Dom turned slightly toward me, put a hand in the inside pocket of his jacket, and produced an envelope. "A one-way ticket to Aspen," he said with a grin. "First stop on the way to the Funny Farm."

Omaha was eager to share her social commentaries. "There's already a Funny Farm in Aspen. Everybody in Pitkin County, except the waiters and bartenders, is rich and crazy. If you want to move into that town you have to own two Irish setters and a yellow Jeep convertible. And they hate hippies, unless they happen to be fake hippies, you know, slumming European skiing champions, preferably Swiss or French."

Thunderhead had his own interests. "You're flying one way to Aspen, Dom? You want me to drive your truck up there?"

"Up and down those mountain passes in this snow and shit? Get serious. Anyway, the gig comes with transportation. Glen's going to be heading back to Europe and leaving me his Land Rover to scout out real estate."

Irene asked. "You're going into real estate?"

Thunderhead handed Dom a joint. He drew hard on it, held his breath momentarily, and shook his head. "Glen and a couple of his cronies want to buy land in and around the town of Crested Butte, which they're convinced is going to be bigger than Aspen. They're also interested in a couple of other areas west of Gunnison. Supposedly, among the things I'm going to do is explore, take notes, and photographs, and prepare a report of some kind. Glen and his buddies sent me a few bucks along with this ticket. They're giving me a pair of first-rate skis and boots, a decent salary with expenses, and we're going to work out the details of the plan in some chalet they're renting on the Crystal River."

"What are you going to do with the truck?" Thunderhead inquired.

Dom looked from Thunderhead to the mess I was making of the pizza I was trying to share with Serena. "I'm giving it to Barlow, the guy who

338

made the rest of my life possible. He's finally come to terms with the fact he's never going to get his VW bus back."

I swigged the Chianti and almost choked. "You're giving me the truck?"

"Yeah. It's out front. I'll get you the registration and title as soon as I've heard the rest of my fortune."

Rhonda smiled, eager to resume her reading. "The Aspen trip is perfectly visible, actually. In fact, there's the forest. There's your ally, the Fool, which is usually Tim's card. You are in for a benign change of circumstances and it shows that those life improvements will rub off on Tim. At least some of them."

Dom looked at Irene and me. "Can I crash on the floor tonight? And will you drive me to the airport tomorrow morning?"

I shrugged and nodded. I was gaining a truck but losing a crazy and much-needed ally. I missed him already.

Dom laughed. "Pricks sent me a ticket for six a.m. tomorrow. They want a breakfast meeting so they can get in a full day on the slopes afterwards, I guess."

The next morning I dropped Dom at the airport, gave Irene a ride to school in the newly acquired stake-bed pickup truck, and returned to the new apartment to unpack. Balancing plywood sheets on sawhorses, I constructed a pair of makeshift study desks, prepared some rice and beans, hung clothes in closets, and stacked books in towers near still-obstructed bookcases. While Dom was probably sitting down to lunch in front of a fireplace, drinking champagne and schmoozing with millionaires, the phone was ringing.

"Timothy? This is Benjamin Ewell Johnston."

"Oh, hi, Ben. I was planning to drive that hand truck back out there to you tomorrow, but I guess I could do it this afternoon if you need it."

"No, I don't guess I need it. Probably never use it again."

"You feeling all right, Ben? You sound a little under the weather."

"Well, I'm lower than I thought to be. I'm feeling each of my eighty years and it's kinda mournful and forlorn out here today."

"I've got some beans and rice on the stove and the roads aren't too bad. I could drive out and bring you over for dinner. Drop off your hand truck at the same time."

"No, I'm not hungry or needful of friends or anything like that, Tim. I guess I'm worn out from sitting under a load of bad news for these two hours. Right now I'm makin' myself call to tell you that the boy died last night."

"What boy? Your son?"

"Little George."

"Jesus Christ!"

There was a long pause. I looked around the room, searching for a way out of my life.

"Little George and your dog, that ol' tramp dog. They both died in a car accident last night."

I sat heavily, crumpling a carton of bedclothes. "Son of a bitch! Please tell me you're kidding!"

"Can't say so. Wish I could. No, I'm not."

I squeezed the receiver and put the back of my head against a cardboard box. "What happened?" I hoped Ben would spare me the need to ask more questions. I heard him breathing a raspy whistle more suggestive of congestion than grief.

"According to what Mister Phil told me . . . ."

"Mister Phil?"

"The house painter gentleman."

"Gentleman? You mean that paint-spattered moron who's been pumping Marge? Asshole is what you mean!" I was in a rage out of all proportion to my interest in Little George's mother and her tawdry love affair. "That house painter son of a bitch used to send the boy outside without a coat for hours at a time to sit in the goddamned car by himself! If it wasn't for Phil, Little George wouldn't have gone out and sat in that car, wouldn't have started driving it before he was ready." Immediately I regretted my outburst. "I'm sorry, Ben. Please go on."

"Don't have a lot of facts and it happened real late. The painter tole me that the boy and the dog sneaked the old car off and got to driving it kinda fast. You know that big cottonwood grows down there near Alton Street, where the street ice don't melt so good?"

"Yeah, I remember it."

"They're figuring the rain and snow over the ice sheet made the pavement a little slicker than it might have been."

"Who's they?"

"I don't know. Them that does the thinking about these things. Did you ever meet Cecil that repairs washing machines and small motors? Pink house by the cottonwood? He told me he heard the crash and came outside in the middle of the night. Way he figured afterwards, the boy skidded on the ice patch, ripped out all those mailboxes and a length of chain fence, and then the old car wrapped itself around the tree. Cecil figured if the boy could have somehow dodged that cottonwood, he'd have skidded on into the empty field and probably just scratched and dented the car."

"Shit! Son of a bitch!"

"Surely," Ben suggested, "the Lord was calling him home."

The traffic hissed on the one-way street outside. The refrigerator clicked and groaned. The lid over the boiling beans rattled.

"It's all a little hard to figure for a tired-out old man," Ben said. "I been sitting here looking at your phone number for a long while and now that I've done called you, I believe I'll take my soup. If I don't have my soup by three and get to bed by eight, I won't sleep again till eight tomorrow night. And I do feel like a sleep is what I need."

"Thanks for calling Ben. I don't know what to say. I can't even talk. I'm rocked hard by this. Rocked. You can't imagine. I'm the one that gave his dad the DeSoto in the first place."

"Oh, I guess I can imagine a little. About all the strength I have right now is for imagining, and I don't want to use it all up." The old man made a humming noise. "Your missus is gonna be sore from hearing it, too, always feeding him like she was. I can see and hear they got all kind of misery across the street now. Cars pulling up all over. People shouting and screaming on the porch. They say the older George is flying in from Galveston tonight. Hard to know who to feel the worst for."

"George," I heard myself. "You poor dumb kid."

"Well, I don't know much more, and don't know any more that's any good. Except that it must be good not to experience a lot of pain if you're going to go to the Lord anyhow. The wash machine man said the boy was dead of a broken neck right off."

I was pounding the bottom of my fist on a scrap of wood.

"What's that noise?"

"Nothing, Ben. Nothing."

"They say the dog was cut up and yelping. If the thing had happened any closer to my place I'd probably have heard him myself. By the time the ambulance came into the driveway, they said Cecil had put the dog down with a little handgun he keeps for prowlers."

I was standing up now, pressing my forehead to the wall.

"About all I'm living for," Ben said, finally, "is to take care of my chickens. But that boy hadn't hardly started living. Seemed like he just wanted to go off in a car and find him some kind of place to start a life. Only other thing that crossed my mind of any account is that if you and your friends decide to come to the funeral, maybe you could bring a little supper afterwards over here, being as how we're outside the family but still inside the circle of grieving ones. I don't know about it yet, though. I'll see how strong I'm feeling when the time comes."

"That might be the thing," I said. "That might be it. Yeah. Yeah, we'll do that, Ben. Sure, that's what we'll do." I kept saying such things long after the line went dead.

What I remember of the early evening and later night was walking the streets, the oblique angles taken by the snowflakes that were falling again through the yellow cones of street lamps, the snow melting in my hair and icy water running down my back. When I got home in the wee hours the apartment was cold because Irene had opened all the windows to expel the odors of burned beans and rice.

The apartment still stank of burnt food when I woke up at dawn with a sore throat and a fever. I took some aspirin, made myself coffee, and walked out in the frigid morning for a newspaper. The sky was a deep blue and the frozen snow squeaked underfoot.

Serena was drooling her oatmeal and banging joyously on her high chair when I returned. Between bites offered to the baby, Irene was downing a poached egg. She was late to anthropology, but started in on Big George and Dom, blaming them for Little George's death. I tossed the paper on the couch and said that even if I wasn't running a fever, I wouldn't want to talk about anything so ridiculous. She accused me of an impossible eagerness to pardon men who lacked self-control.

I countered with the argument that she was blaming Big George and Dom for the longstanding offenses of her alcoholic father. What about us? We bought the car. We gave the car to Big George. I knew Little George was driving it and didn't come down hard enough on him for it. As I coaxed Serena to finish her apple juice, Irene announced there was no way she was going to Little George's funeral, not after having lain awake all night imagining herself pouring a cheap bottle of bourbon over Big George's head, dreaming of ways to make Dom suffer, if she ever saw him again, which she hoped, frankly, she wouldn't.

Before going to bed that night, Irene and I had an even nastier argument. Why was it, I wondered, that for all her talk of reincarnation and rebirth, she could deal with the stone weight of a real death only by blaming its occurrence on the negligence of others. For her, I said, accusingly, ideas were toys, baubles to be examined and put quickly away. Little George was dead now, I said, my voice wavering strangely, and to me that was a sad, naked fact out of reach of any blame or idea. A bare pit with no comfort at all. Irene stormed into the bathroom and left me to deal with Serena, who was crying, I supposed because she feared and hated our raised voices.

342

Two mornings later, still feverish, I put on a faded thrift store suit and started the truck. Another snowfall seemed imminent; the morning was gray and grim. The neighborhood chapel a few hundred yards from where Little George had died was unheated and stank of disinfectant. At the end of a tunnel made of red and white flowers, I saw a dark, wood-stained casket. A threnody of organ notes, impersonal and ancient, oppressed me.

I didn't want to receive or offer any comfort and sat in back with Gordon and Rhonda and Denny and Omaha. I nodded at them. They might have been strangers. The Biancos had decided not to attend. Ben, too, had a fever and was unable to attend. Irene had refused to attend, and nobody had heard from Dom or knew how to reach him.

Lagging behind the cortege of cars, I drove the truck to the cemetery. Once the pallbearers, uncles, professionals, and people I'd never known wheeled the casket to the grave site, I got out and walked up a small hill, sipping from a bottle of sour cherry cough syrup.

Big George wore huge sunglasses, his forehead and cheeks almost translucent from the bitter wind. He rubbed and squeezed his hands, or let them hang stiffly at his sides to claw the cold air. Marge was a fierce apparition in lipstick and rouge, a de Kooning painting, obfuscated by grief and the white cold weather. She made eye contact with me, vaguely accusatory, then blinked and found Big George's nearest hand, less to hold, I thought, than to stop his little spasmodic motions. Pink and blue of cheek, Phil, the housepainter, stood directly behind Marge. Staring at him I thought of a corrupt Spanish priest who'd been told too often he bore a resemblance to Clark Gable. He wore a rented tux with a midnight blue velvet lapel. His slicked-back hair shone with extra wax and when he showed me a smile of perfect teeth, I realized that I, too, was being assessed and evaluated.

I was all too visible: long blond hair, the decision to stand slightly off, ankle deep in snow rather than in the shoveled clearing closer to the other huddling mourners. I knew what I looked like; nose red from blowing it, about three inches of white shirt sleeve protruding from the arms of my ill-fitting black suit coat; the too-large faded pants gathered pouch-like around my thin hips, belt more drawstring than anchor. The jacket was tight where it should have been loose, baggy where it should have been snug, and the cough syrup bottle made a bulge in a pocket of my suit coat. Half choked by a bright red necktie, cold-reddened hands folded in front of my groin, I discovered my voice and added it to the reluctant ensemble who stood blinking and muttering the Lord's Prayer.

Only the minister seemed immune to the cold, eager perhaps to lift so many heavy hearts toward Jesus. A wind gusted and I fought an urge to cough. My dry eyeballs ached in their sockets and the bones in my face felt fragile and paper-thin. The cough would not be relieved by little noises I made behind pursed lips, so I took a few lateral steps toward a tree, obscured myself from view, tiptoed through a patch of crunchy snow and walked slowly back down the cleared walkway to the truck. Collective murmurs of prayer followed me downhill, calling me back to the gravesite.

I slugged from the syrup bottle and allowed myself one small cough. A wind brought me a sharp whiff of pine, as the cold air and chemical tartness of the medicine numbed my mouth and lungs.

The distant barking of a dog made me think about Rover, wonder whether he'd been cremated or buried. I was struck by the fact that Rover, that adoring knuckle-gnawing mutt, had metabolized protein unbearably intimate to me, to Irene, and Serena. I shook if off with a shiver and looked back up the hill. Two-dozen people still huddled up there beside a naked sapling. Carefully closing the truck's door, I started the engine and coasted toward the cemetery gates, the chink and rattle of the truck's failing rear end disturbing the heavy silence behind me.

When spring came I installed a small latched gate at the top of the apartment stairs to keep Serena, who had started to walk and explore, from tumbling to the landing below or wandering into the busy one-way street.

Dom sent me a postcard saying he was scouting land all over the west, staying temporarily in eastern Utah, and would write or call as soon as he had a permanent address.

I was enrolled in school, had a hauling business with the truck, and a part-time job at the student cafeteria. Irene had art classes, a part-time job at the child care center, shifts at the family restaurant, and an address book filled with the names and phone numbers of art-student friends, including Gerald's. On good days I thought I was growing up, developing a respect for learning, and possessed of reasonable parenting skills. On bad days it seemed to me I was sleeping with a woman I didn't know very well while the world filled up with untrustworthy strangers.

Irene quietly sneered and Gramma and Ralph smiled and shook their heads, but the perdurable rumor that Pancho Villa and the late Joachim Escobar had buried a strong box filled with outlaw gold under the foundations of the Escobar family house refused to die. In the weeks before the restaurant closed for business, several believing members of

344

the immediate family were said to have met and signed a pact among themselves that Gramma would receive 51 percent of any discovered treasure, with the remaining going to the individual whose claim had been staked nearest to the site of the anticipated discovery. Irene said her Uncle Eduardo and Aunt Cecilia had hired attorneys and talked with both the city and with executives at the demolition company.

To my surprise, Irene volunteered to help organize the Escobar Fiesta, the final enchilada dinner to be given at the Hacienda Escobar for family, valued customers, and a throng of invited city bigwigs.

Having cultivated media contacts and used various academic committee positions at City U to his best advantage, Gerald assured the Escobars that there would be ample television coverage of the destruction of the old house, and even predicted that new quarters for the restaurant would easily be found. Gerald's promises made Gramma smile and pat his hand approvingly. To me, Gramma seemed happy with the financial settlement from the city and totally disinterested in starting another restaurant. Yellow tulips were blooming from Gramma's flowerbeds when I went to pick Irene up one afternoon from a planning committee meeting.

"We finally got a date," she announced. "They've scheduled demolition for the twenty-third, so the fiesta will be on the twelfth. Gerald's got television coverage all lined up. Anyway, to change the subject, as a representative of Basic Visual Design, I've been delegated to ask you something. How would you feel about letting half a dozen of us paint your truck as a part of the fiesta? After buying the paint, we'd take up a collection among ourselves so you could get a fee for letting us do it. Plus, you'd probably get more business and certainly the truck would get noticed."

"No way."

"Stop and think about it a minute. Gerald says that since you're a former employee of the restaurant, the television people might do a story on you and your hauling business. You could get free television advertising. In fact, Gerald's already got Katie Caper interested."

"Who's Katie Capon?"

"Caper. She does late night weather and news stories on Channel Nine. Even if there's no spot for such a television story, Gerald's sure you'd get interviewed on the radio. There will be more than a dozen radio stations there. The thing is, if you want to be on TV, you'll have to practice being light-hearted. Katie likes to laugh on camera."

"Let her hire a fucking clown."

"Aren't we cheery." Determined not to be brought down, Irene brushed at my shirtsleeve. "A little gritty and dusty, too."

"I just carried eight old mattresses down four flights of stairs," I said, wishing we might not talk about Gerald for a while. "My shoulders are sore and I don't feel like being light-hearted."

"I was just trying to say that people want these little television stories to be amusing, you know, cast a ray of hope. Even your friends would agree that you can be funny when you want to be. You're just a little overly serious at times."

"Yeah," I said, "And Gerald's a fucking hyena."

"Hyena?"

"Lying up in the bushes, using the demise of the restaurant to advance his career as a community organizer. What else would you call him?"

Irene was miffed. "A realist. Someone who accepts that the past doesn't live forever and that people have to go on with their lives."

"You know, Irene, it bothers me that you're so eager to participate in this stuff. We're talking about a family business that involves real people. When the pot of gold is given up on, a lot of people in your family are going to be completely cast adrift by all this."

"Well, you have your own little viewpoint, your own little corner, your own relationship with Gramma and Ralph and stuff. But you weren't around there as a kid to get punched and poked and fondled, so you don't really know very much about the restaurant or about the family."

The sudden chill scared me. "Okay, you're right," I said, "I understand and accept your feelings." She seemed to breathe a little easier. "But please understand," I added, "that I don't want to be on television or in any way connected to the closing of the restaurant. And painting the truck is out. Over and out and done with…and finished."

"You just want to throw a rock at the hyena, I guess. He likes you, says he admires your independence, your refusal to buy into ideas that have made things worse instead of better. The thing is, no matter how hard he tries to do things that help us, you deliberately misunderstand him."

"I understand him too well. From what I've seen nearly all of his goodwill disappears when you lift up his mask. On the other hand, for a careerist nostalgia merchant, a carrion-sucking, media-courting vulture, he's not bad."

She looked at me strangely.

"Maybe I'd like him better, if you didn't like him so well."

346

"I doubt it. I don't think you could like anyone who was a true friend to me. But never mind. It's your truck and your decision, Tim. Purely as a favor to me, though, you might be able to concoct a reasonable reason for not wanting the truck painted."

"All right. Tell him and your design student cronies that I don't want to play the clown or seem to be a kind of merry prankster leader in some hippie-dippie-looking truck. Every day I have to go out and ask for work from Nixon-lovers who hate anything they can possibly associate with antiwar radicals. My dad always claimed that his new Cadillac paid for itself in a year and a half in sales he wouldn't otherwise have made. I used to scoff at this, but now I realize he was right. Already some people won't give me hauling jobs for fear the truck will break down before I can get it out of their neighborhood."

"Okay," Irene said. "I accept your answer and will deliver it to my art class in a modified form." She softened her tone. "But would you do me a favor in the next few days? When you have a few minutes?"

"Sure, as long as it doesn't involve Gerald or the restaurant."

"When you go to the store, pick up some soap and a scrubber of some sort, and see if you can get rid of those horrible spots on the seat."

"I don't get it. First you ask me to let your art class slop paint all over the truck and now you're bugging me about stains on the seat."

"They just bother me. In a way that nothing about the outside of the truck does, that's all. What are they, dried grease or soy sauce or something?"

I laughed. "Blood. Dom's and mine. They're from the night last fall after that business at the potato chip factory. He made himself my blood brother by banging his bloody nose into a cut on my hand."

Where I thought she might laugh, Irene sighed. "Deformed by cowboy and Indian movies. John Wayne and Barbie dolls. That's what's really wrong with our generation. Okay," she said. "Once the restaurant has closed I'm going to get out the sewing machine and make some slipcovers. That won't ruin your business, will it?"

Among my parental pleasures at the time was taking Serena to the grocery store, positioning her in the shopping cart's kiddie seat, and showing her off to the little old ladies. She was old enough to sit up, yet still too young for product recognition. I handed her packages and, once she'd examined them, she'd hand them back to me to arrange in the bottom of the cart. I knew from watching other parents that the day would come when she, too, would lose all interest in the texture of lettuce and scream for the bright packages of jelly-filled cookies and boxes of sugary cereal.

One day I filled the cart and handed Serena a can of tuna fish while I waited in the checkout line. Then, in a hurry to get home, I arranged the grocery bags in the back of the truck, propped Serena up on the seat next to me, and backed out of the parking space. It was early evening, just after rush hour, and traffic patterns in the lot were complicated. Seeing an opening into the exit lane, I turned the truck quickly into the available intersection and the truck door swung wide. I reached for Serena to keep her from falling, but my hand slipped off the steering wheel. Groping for the brake, I hit the gas and the truck lurched. As it did, Serena toppled onto her shoulder and sledded for the open door. I snared her by one tiny ankle. She was crying, but she was safe.

The door to the truck was open. I was blocking traffic. Women were watching me and wagging their fingers. Drivers were honking. I had neglected to close the door tightly and turned too fast and nearly lost my daughter. I closed the door and held Serena, crying, against my shoulder. After calming her with a cookie, I sat tickling her chin, and promising her another cookie after dinner.

That night I awoke to the roar of engines and the shrill trilling of tires. Another drag race down Corona Street toward 6th Avenue. Drag races took off from the light on 8th Avenue, observed the light change at 7th Avenue, and flew down a steep hill toward Sixth. I listened as the engines roared and the racers crossed 7th Avenue, power-shifting, straining toward sixty, gambling on the short green light at the bottom of the hill. I sat up, listening for the sudden explosive collision, but the engines faded and I was wide-awake. Was there or wasn't there a script, another dimension, a timeless rebalancing and retributive principle of some sort? Like some antibiotic-resistant bacteria at the base of my brain stem, Rhonda's arguments for patterns and karma lived on. Was it Samuel Waddell, the sound of the engines, a wet diaper? Why did Serena suddenly start crying?

The night before the fiesta, Gramma Escobar cooked the restaurant's final dinner. Shortly before her bedtime, she emerged from the kitchen long enough to laugh and shrug off a standing ovation. Gently coaxed by Ralph, she sat a few moments, smiling at the center of admirers who wished her well in words she didn't hear very well. She sipped, without finishing, a small glass of champagne, and then her youngest son, Eduardo, won the right to drive her to her new condominium, while Ralph distributed the last bottles of beer from the almost-empty refrigerator.

Purchased with resettlement funds from the city, Gramma's new home was a freshly painted tenth-floor condo with air-conditioning, an electric stove, a dishwasher, and garbage disposal.

The media coverage of the fiesta was something of a disappointment. One television channel did a thirty-second story, but to Gerald's hand wringing and dismay the focus was more on the expansion of City University than the demise of the family restaurant. The next day, the daily newspapers mentioned what they called a neighborhood block party. There were no photographs, just architectural renderings of the gymnasium to be built on the site of the old family home.

A few days later I cut English Lit to watch the demolition of the restaurant. Huge yellow and orange machines with tank treads smoked blackly and stank, crunching and pushing the old house into a jagged pile of rubble. While Gerald took photographs of the fallen walls, Ralph sat on a folding chair using a checked handkerchief to dab the tears from his eyes and wipe the white dust that accumulated on the lenses of his heavy glasses. Ralph said that Gramma had appointed him the official family crybaby because on such a hot day she decided to stay home to enjoy her air-conditioner and garbage disposal.

Feeling sweaty and uncomfortable, I drove off after a while and returned with beer. Ralph and I drank quietly while some of his younger brothers and sisters went to work with picks and shovels in the hope of striking it rich. By then, all that remained of the Hacienda Escobar was a big mound of splintery boards in a haze of ancient plaster and dust. A few minutes more and the big machines scooped the heap into huge trucks and drove off down the street.

No gold was found, though middle brother Hernando unearthed an old horseshoe he subsequently offered the local historical museum. A few weeks after the museum declined the horseshoe bequest, I helped Ralph hang it over Gramma's fake fireplace, at a respectful distance from the badly painted dime store *pieta* she had won a few years earlier at a parish bingo game.

I was sitting at my desk in the hot apartment, dripping sweat on my geology notes. From the kitchen came the sound of running tap water and the irregular knock of a knife on a cutting board. Irene's voice startled me. "Where's Serena?"

"Isn't she out with you?"

"No. I thought she was with you."

"Maybe she's in her room."

"Did you remember to hook the screen door when you came in?"

I sat listening for the small voice that so often chattered and sang to itself or the padding of small feet on the wooden floor. I closed my book and heard the drone of rush-hour-traffic outside. I started toward the open front window for a glimpse of the street but changed my course in response to the sudden howl of truck brakes. Bracing myself with one hand along the stairwell wall, I took four steps at a bound, straight-armed the screen door, and sprinted toward the edge of the street as the sound of brakes faded and the black maw of a richly lacquered tow truck came to a stop only feet away from Serena's flushed face. Except for the now-soggy diaper I'd folded over her small hips a few minutes earlier, she was naked, standing in the middle of the street waving, of all things, a toilet plunger!

Sweaty, agitated, and caked with grease, the truck driver scooped her up with a hairy forearm, snatched at the plunger, and flung it onto the grass. As he did, I tore Serena from his arms like a football and ran back up the steps into the apartment where Irene, pale and shaking, took her from me. Serena started to cry.

Outside, horns were honking and the air was filled with angry rush-hour voices. My daughter safe, I hurried down to the street. The driver stood at the door of his glossy truck. He got his head right in my face, broad, sunburned, his yellow, unbrushed teeth smelling of onions and coffee, and shouted that bad things happened to careless parents. Finally, he took a step back, spit on the pavement, and with the big arteries in his neck and temples jumping with blood, hopped into his truck and roared away.

Chagrined, I picked up the toilet plunger and carried it upstairs. Perhaps Serena had been inspired to direct traffic by one of the tattered books being read to her at the college day care center. I could wonder about this now, with her safe in the house, and I could shut out from my mind how she'd appeared to me as I ran for her: a pudgy parody of a tarot card, called, I thought, The Princess of Wands, a little blissed-out mutant refugee, escaped from Rhonda's prized deck hopping around and turning over tables and chairs in my over-heated imagination. Even as I ran to take Serena from the driver I had thought of Samuel Waddell, the universe as some retributive engine of justice, idling, waiting on my moments of carelessness. After dinner, I was more rational. Vague crimes or mistakes unwittingly committed did not trigger tit for tat, a death for a death. Karma was a twisted dogma intended to frighten its adherents into a passive and dubious integrity. What mattered, or at least what could be acted on, was observable to the reasonably alert: I didn't have to atone for crimes I'd committed in former lives. I only had to remember to hook the door when I came home.

The night was even hotter. I'd been rearranging my pillow in search of a dry patch on which to catch a dream. Just as I drifted off, the doorbell rasped and then rasped again. My first coherent thought was of the tow truck driver, off-duty, returned to settle the score, mete out the punishment on which he'd been brooding. Pulling on a pair of pants, I stumbled to the closet and groped in the dark until I found a softball bat.

Irene murmured, "Don't go downstairs."

"Maybe it's one of my brothers. Maybe there's been an accident. Anyway, the doorbell is going to wake the baby up." Leaving the stairs dark, I turned on the porch light and descended slowly, the bat concealed behind one leg. Hearing behind me the sounds of Irene's bare feet, I half turned. "Stay back," I called to her. "Stay upstairs."

A man's voice, muffled, called to me through the glass. "Tim, it's me. I got to talk to you."

Parting the curtains I saw Ron Thunderhead. My fear turned to irritated curiosity. I unhooked the screen and Thunderhead followed me upstairs. Irene fetched him a glass of water and he sat in a living room chair, his long hair disheveled, the front of his shirt dark with sweat.

He downed the water and wiped his mouth while Irene went to comfort the crying baby. "Sorry I had to wake you guys, but I had nowhere else to go. Bill's been busted."

"Busted?"

"Fuckin' cops broke in the house, threw him in the car, and punched him twice. I couldn't help him or warn him."

"When did this happen?"

"Our house, about eight o'clock. I was on the way back from the hardware store and had parked my bus a couple of blocks away. As I was walking up the street, I saw all these cars, headlights off, driving real slow. Two cars pulled up out front and sat there with their engines running. A couple of cop cars pulled in behind them. Before anybody saw me, I jumped into an unlocked Oldsmobile parked across the street. When it seemed safe, I peeked out and cracked the window. By then, there must have been ten cars and about fifteen narcs, some of them uniformed, some not."

Having given Serena a bottle and coaxed her back to sleep, Irene appeared in the bedroom doorway. She closed the door and sat on the floor. Wrapping a long skirt around her legs, she pulled her knees toward her chest, shook her head, and made a pair of small fists with which she rubbed her eyes. "What happened to Tessa and Donna and the kids?"

"They weren't home. Anyway, the cops tried to push the front door open. One of them shouted something about a search warrant, then two of them kicked the door in. About ten cops rushed inside. Three or four stayed out on the front porch, watching the street. After a few minutes, this fucking fat guy comes out of the house with a grocery bag of stuff that he then proceeds to show the other cops. I wasn't close enough to see what he had, but I could tell from the way they were laughing that some of it was dope. After that, a pair of cops led Gordon out."

"Gordon!"

"Yeah. Handcuffed, hands behind his back. Marched him to an unmarked car and drove him away before I could exhale. Man, I was hyperventilating."

"What was Gordon doing there?"

"He came over to help build some bookcases for that storefront Tessa's been wanting to rent. What was weird was that if it hadn't been for him saying he needed a new drill bit and some sand paper, arguing for the importance of quality, I'd have been at home and gotten busted myself."

I was outraged. "Shit, Gordon doesn't use anything at all! He's not even drinking cough syrup any more. He probably hasn't had three beers all month!"

"Yeah. Bill was yelling just about exactly that when out of nowhere, this big bastard with a crew cut socked him right in the face. When Bianco yelled and kicked at the guy, some other guy gut-punched him right on the front porch. They sat him down on the steps for a minute and it got real quiet. That's when I heard one of the cops say my name. I think they got Gordon, thinking he was me."

Irene looked up, angry. "That's just great."

"No, wait a minute, Irene," Thunderhead said. "Tim, there's something I want you both to understand. If I had realized at the time that they were mistaking Gordon for me and not just busting everybody who happened to be inside, I would have given myself up right then and there. I swear. I was scared and shocked and didn't put it all together until it was too late and he'd already been driven away. They'll find out he's not me soon enough. Hopefully, they'll let him go when they do."

"Nobody's judging you," I said, perhaps a little dishonestly. "Go on."

"There's not a whole lot more to say. The cops eventually walked Bill to another car and drove him away. The fat cop with the grocery bag got in a green Ford and followed them. That left five or six cops coming and going in the house. I started getting worried about the owner of the car I was hiding in, figuring he might come out and I'd be done for, so I eased

352

myself out, ducked down, and went from car to car, keeping myself hidden. My plan was to make my way back to my bus. But before I could get to it, I saw this big tow truck arrive to haul Bill's bus away and realized the cops might conceivably know that I own one, too. When I'd gone a couple blocks, I heard the sound of a big motorcycle. Since there were no cops with motorcycles at our place, I'm pretty sure they confiscated Bill's Indian, too. The narc mentality being, "Well, we don't know if these dope-puffing commies will actually be found guilty and sentenced or not, but at least in the name of police procedures we can steal and trash some stuff they're likely to value.'"

"What exactly did the cops find at your house, any idea?"

"Not a lot. Just enough dope to bust some peace creeps. Two or three ounces of pot. Maybe a small jar of peyote buttons. They probably got off with our address and phone number book, too. They always do. That may mean trouble for quite a few people."

"Son of a bitch," I said. "Son of a bitch."

Thunderhead laughed nervously. "Luckily, you guys, at least, don't have to worry."

"I don't know about that," Irene said. "We don't have any dope around here, but even so, if the cops came with a search warrant, even if they didn't break in, we could still be evicted from this apartment as undesirables." Irene looked warily at me. "Isn't there some sort of charge like 'harboring a fugitive?'"

"Yeah, there is," Thunderhead admitted, "and you guys have to do what you have to do. But what I was saying is you aren't listed in our phone book. That's the only reason why I came here. We were looking all over for your address and phone number the night before last to invite you over for supper. Bill thought I'd written it down, I thought Donna did." Thunderhead smiled. "You guys are safe. It's everybody else I'm going to have to try and get in touch with."

Irene sighed and went to the kitchen to make tea. I made my way to the bedroom for a shirt and my cigarettes. Behind me I heard Thunderhead pick up the phone.

"Don't call your house," I said, turning back. "The cops may still be there. They may have the line tapped. Maybe they're monitoring the phone."

"It's all right," Thunderhead insisted. "It takes them a while to trace a call. I'll hang up immediately if anybody but Tess or Donna answers."

Nobody answered.

Later that morning, leaving Thunderhead to make a few phone calls and nap on the couch, I went down the back steps to the truck. Irene followed me, toting Serena. The air was filled with a promising scent of flowers and mulch. Squirrels dallied in the sun at the base of the locust tree. Robins bobbed for worms in the lawn. Our nearest neighbor, an old Greek woman, was rustling among her marigolds and tomato plants. She called to the baby in Greek. Irene held Serena up to be seen and touched, and Serena rewarded the old lady's ardor with a curling motion of her fingers and a "bye-bye."

Irene settled herself in the truck. "I still say we should have called Rhonda last night," she sulked.

"And what if the cops were there and answered the phone?"

"They wouldn't be there if they were convinced Gordon was Thunderhead, though, would they?"

"We have Thunderhead's report, but we don't really *know* what the cops think."

"So we shouldn't believe him?"

"We should avoid jumping to conclusions is all."

"Well, we should have gotten word to Rhonda somehow, before now, like this. We should have called."

"Calling this morning would have been just as risky as last night, maybe more so. Now, by popping in on her like this, even if the cops are out there, we can pretend to be making an ordinary late-morning social call."

I rolled down the window of the truck and did what I could to discourage Irene from talking. Little George was dead. Dom was getting rich, out of touch, who knew where. There was a filthy basement I was scheduled to clean for fifty bucks later that afternoon. I would have to attend art history class early in the evening and then take a geology exam for which I was unprepared. I was falling behind in my other classes and couldn't say why I was in school. Bill and Gordon were in jail. Thunderhead was an unwanted couch guest. Irene was growing more cool and distant, perhaps mirroring my own state.

In the park, which I went out of my way to drive through, the grass was green and soft; somewhere on this perfect morning, hopes were being realized, poets were walking in the foothills. Mystics and visionaries were praising the Zen suchness of all things, while I was damning the fact that I wouldn't have one moment to myself, not even the ten minutes I needed to fend off the self-pity that welled up in me. My imperfectly suppressed desires for a few such moments were making me a problem to Irene and Serena, to my friends, clients, and professors.

Caterpillars turned into butterflies, but parents turned into pack mules. I looked quickly into the truck's rear view mirror. Serena's scowling stuffed camel glared back at me.

Rhonda's front door was open to the air, but all the curtains were drawn and we found her sitting alone behind a single candle, the ubiquitous Tarot cards scattered and a copy of the *I-Ching* open on the table before her. Little shadows quivered over her pale swollen face as she looked up. "Listen to this," she said. 'Six at the beginning means one sits oppressed under a bare tree and strays into a gloomy valley. For three years, one sees nothing.' Shit, you guys, even the *Book of Changes* offers no hope. The cards are even worse. I'm scared, and I've got a bad feeling about all this stuff."

Irene put an arm around Rhonda's shoulder. "I brought over some cantaloupe and cherries. They're really ripe and sweet. Gordon is going to be okay."

"I'm not really hungry right now, but thanks for thinking of me. There's leftover coffee on the stove. It's probably not very fresh. Tessa and Donna were drinking it with brandy all night."

"So they were here then," I said. "You weren't all alone with your troubles."

"They just left about an hour ago. We've been on the phone with Ralph Mitkin, this lawyer Gordon and I know from our activist days in Berkeley. Mitkin told us that from what he was able to find out, last week the cops busted some high-school kid who'd bought some grass from Bianco and Thunderhead. The kid knew where they lived and the cops put the house under surveillance."

I poured coffee and sliced cantaloupe. "From what I gather," I said, "the bad luck for Gordon seems to have been that the description in the search warrant was so vague. Gordon has longish hair of about the same color as Thunderhead. Then there's the mustache. He's shorter and heavier, but they busted Gordon as Ron. Of course, that's all conjecture."

"Maybe so," Rhonda said, "but I doubt it. Gordon had a billfold with all kinds of ID, so there were plenty of good reasons for not taking him for Ron. Where the hell is Thunderhead now anyway?"

"At our place sleeping on the couch, or trying to." Irene was coaxing Serena to eat a small wedge of melon. "He's going to call a lawyer later."

"How come he let Gordon take the rap for him? He should have turned himself in."

"He told me he didn't realize that the cops were mistaking Gordon for him, or even that his own name was on a search warrant until after

355

Gordon had already been driven to jail. Thunderhead promised to do whatever becomes necessary to keep Gordon from taking the rap for him. But if Tessa and Donna went home, I'm worried they might be caught up in the whole business."

"No, they're all right. Mitkin talked to them. It turns out they weren't named in the search warrant. It seems the cops didn't know about them or the kids, though that's a little hard to understand if they actually had the house under surveillance. Things were better for them than they hoped, but worse than any of us imagined for Gordon. The last time I heard from Mitkin he had gotten through to somebody at the DA's office. It's all so incredibly messed up." Rhonda started to cry. She blew her nose on a tissue and flung the wadded paper at her tattered copy of the *I-Ching*. "The cops are claiming that not only did Gordon have a hash pipe in his pocket when they searched him, but that he committed an armed robbery and held up a dry cleaner's a couple of weeks ago."

"Armed robbery? That's ridiculous," I said. "Believe me, that won't stand." My conviction failed me as soon as I said it, so I turned away and lit a cigarette.

"It looks bad, Tim. They put him in a lineup early this morning and he was apparently identified as 'probable' by one of the robbery victims. The DA and the cops are taking the position that the proceeds from the robbery provided Ron and Bill with the cash they used to buy dope." Rhonda began to cry again. "They really believe Gordon robbed that place."

"Whoa!"

"My God," Irene said.

Rhonda straightened up the scattered cards. "Meanwhile, earlier when Donna and Tessa decided to go home to clean up the mess, but just before they got off the phone with Mitkin, the cops pulled up outside. A bunch of them barged in here with a search warrant and started throwing things around looking for the pistol they said Gordon used in the stickup. Luckily, Mitkin was still on the line. No doubt because they knew I was on the phone with a lawyer they didn't hassle me and even made some effort at cleaning up after themselves. They were only here about twenty minutes and they didn't say anything at all to Donna and Tessa, apparently still not connecting them with Bill and Ron. Naturally, they didn't find any pistol."

An hour later I started toward home. Every time I stopped for a traffic light, the truck's temperature gauge needle moved visibly toward red.

"Let's stop and get some ice cream," I suggested. "Seeing Serena eat ice cream always cheers us up. We could take the ice cream to the park for a few minutes before I go on to class."

In Washington Park Serena sat on the edge of a shaded picnic table to bite her chocolate ice cream bar. Irene ate sherbet with a blue plastic spoon. I licked a double cone.

Irene said, "I think I might be pregnant."

I confined my reaction to a single raised eyebrow and two or three energetic assaults on my ice cream. "Your period late? It's not the first time."

"You're going to have to do better than that, Tim." Irene's calm was icy. "I'm more than five weeks late."

"And you're just now getting around to telling me?"

She smiled coolly and looked at her spoon. As when she got pregnant with Serena, she'd obviously spent some time preparing her announcement. She had things to say and didn't want to be deflected from them by any of my reactions. "You can take that back if you want...."

"I do. I do take it back."

"Provided you say something, anything, honest and right away."

"I'm scared."

"Thank you. So am I. Remember making love a couple nights ago?"

"Sure."

"I was going to tell you then, but you fell asleep."

"I guess I was tired."

"Sure. You'd been working really hard. Anyway, what I started to say was that after you fell asleep, I lit a candle and put it on the dresser and sat up watching you. You looked sweet and boyish and I remembered then when we first met. How it was. We used to make love by candlelight a lot."

"Back in the ice age," I ventured cautiously. "The good ol' days."

"Yes, maybe. Before Denver and Serena and Denny and Bianco and Gordon and cab-driving blood brothers and potato chips and Samuel Waddell and Little George. You had such spirit. I thought of you as my pirate prince, my Man from La Mancha."

I was playing for time. "Before the Chicago Convention, before Martin Luther King and Bobby were shot, before Charlie Manson's groupies slashed to the sounds of the Beatles, before Woodstock, Kent State, and the Hell's Angels' murder of that kid at Altamont. Love before Nixon."

Irene raised her eyebrows and waved her spoon. "Your big bad world," she said quietly. "Your burden."

I swallowed ice cream, convinced it was arrogant of her to dismiss the impact of recent history.

Irene continued, "I also remembered watching you while you were telling me about the bulldozing of the restaurant, and you looked like, I don't know, scared and wild, like a rat caught by a farmer in the corner of a shed."

"Something in me doesn't want the past to disappear until it has been dealt with and understood somehow. Final permanent things happen too quickly. Things should happen more slowly. If I was in charge of the world, I thought about this after George's funeral, dead bodies would be kept on ice until everyone agreed it was time to bury or cremate them."

"You seem to feel that you have more past than anyone else."

"What's that supposed to mean?"

"I don't think it's the past. I think it's the future that was scheduled to arrive and never quite did. You bought too deeply into every improbable hope and fantasy of each tripped-out acidhead and freak who crossed your path. You're a cynic, you say, but that's just your insulation talking. You're angry and confused because the world is forever punishing you for your wild hopes. The tiniest things, the taste of an ice cream, the simple closing of a gate, you have a hard time with such things. You know, when something is over, there's a mechanism in most of us that immediately goes to work creating a sense of scale so that we can measure our happiness or disappointments, put them side by side with other events, compare them, and go on forward into time. But your mechanism for doing that seems faulty somehow. Disappointed, you don't really evaluate your perceptions, but just sort of mope around until some new fever of raw hope overtakes you. Lately those enthusiasms have been fewer and fewer." She wiped dried ice cream from Serena's chin. "We need to look at us."

"Okay."

"We're twenty-four, overwhelmed by our lives, distracted by our friends, or should I say your friends, living in some bubble that's overdue to burst. We're not doing very well, you and I, and I need to figure out what to do with my life. In order to do that, I need your help."

I had a sense of myself searching for a shovel with which to begin digging furiously to unearth the right response. I chewed ice cream and nodded to myself like a daft old man. If she was pregnant was it my fault or her fault? Did I love her? Would I love her more or less if she had another baby? Would having another baby make her more pleasant and lovable, or more compliant or more rebellious? I was waiting out the obtuse, bratty egotism of my most obvious, most self-serving responses. Her brown eyes were on me and I couldn't stay silent forever. I knew the right answers and wished for a desk so I could write them down without anybody looking in my eyes 1. I love you. 2. I'm glad I'm going to be a father again. 3. I will love you more after you have a second baby and will make all the necessary sacrifices much more cheerfully. Irene was watching me attentively and I felt the difficulty of immediately meaning what I hoped I could think over and mean eventually.

"I love you," I said, "but I'm scared and confused and overwhelmed. I can see a brother for Serena. I don't know what to say. I'll do better. I need some time to get used to the idea of having another baby. We need to think about ways of being closer, you and I." I kissed Irene very lightly on the lips and held her hand on the way back to the truck.

When I hoisted Serena onto the seat and closed the truck door, I glanced down at the pavement and saw a rusty brown puddle that could only have come from the truck's radiator. The truck ran hot and rough on the way home. Having other things on my mind and knowing Irene did, too, I didn't think about the truck for a few days or what its demise might mean to my hauling business.

On my way to the City U library to research a paper on the King Arthur legend, I was tapped on the shoulder by a man in a slate-hued suit with a modest necktie. Heavily framed black glasses exaggerated his protuberant ears, which were misaligned and spatulate, and made me think of monkey footprints. His gaunt cheeks were freshly shaven and pink. Shorthaired. Only the tiny bright eyes were vaguely familiar.

"Would you let somebody who looked like a speechwriter for George Wallace buy you a cup of coffee?"

I smiled involuntarily at the familiar voice and shook my head. "You've overdone it, Thunderhead. With the disguise."

Gone was the curly Wild Bill Hickok hair, the waxed handlebar mustache; ditto the wire-rimmed glasses *a la* Joyce or Trotsky. Gone the fringed jacket, leather vest, battered hat, the woolen scarf, and sadly, the sense he was my friend, anybody's friend. He was a haunted man, a ghost with a past who I wasn't especially glad to see.

We walked the hall in silence and climbed a flight of stairs. While I dragged my knapsack of books to an untidy table in the student cafeteria, Thunderhead inserted coins in a machine and carried over two plastic cups of the steamy brown beverage that passed for coffee.

I sipped the hot beverage and said, "Nice suit."

"A hundred bucks from a department store clearance rack."

"I'm surprised you were able to find me."

"I just got off the phone with your old lady. Congrats on the pregnancy by the way."

"Thanks."

"I didn't mean to disappear on you guys. It was more a matter of legal advice than anything else. Anyway, how are things around the apartment? Any interesting discoveries or anything?

"What's to discover?"

"I don't know. Just forget it. I hunted you down to let you know that yesterday I heard from reliable sources that charges against Gordon are about to be dropped."

"Great!"

"Yeah, and my days of looking over my shoulder, well I hope they're about to come to an end too, thanks to a couple of sharp attorneys. Tell you the truth, when the heat is finally off, I've decided to enroll in law school, save other people the kind of shit Bianco and Gordon and me have been through. Anyway, to get back to the point, my lawyer talked to the guy who's representing Gordon. The upshot was a haircut, a dye job, and new image for me. My lawyer persuaded Donna to come in with family photographs. Tessa and Rhonda even managed to turn up some shots of Gordon and me standing together beside the bus. Donna and Rhonda then gave depositions that I was me and Gordon was he, or however the fucking grammar's supposed to come out. Donna testified honestly that she didn't know where I was and hadn't heard from me, so there was no problem with perjury or anything. The best thing, though, was that the guy from Berkeley, Mitkin, flew into town with a guy from the antiwar movement who looked a whole lot more like Gordon than I do. Yesterday afternoon, the dry-cleaning guys who'd been held up identified not Gordon but the other guy as the one who held them up, proving they don't know what the fuck they're talking about. Of course, the guy that got fingered could account for his whereabouts on the day of the robbery. The latest negotiations have Gordon pleading guilty to being an accessory to possession or some damn thing. He should be out in a day or so."

"That's good. What about Bill?"

"Man, I'm afraid they're going to grind him up into hamburger. Tessa's got some hometown ravioli spumoni guy from Buffalo on the case, but I don't think he's doing the job. The pigs have photographs of Bill dealing on the street, straddling his beautiful, unique motorcycle.

Unfortunately, there isn't another bike like that Indian for five hundred miles. People are talking about him doing some serious time."

"How long?"

"Five years? I don't know. It's too depressing to think about for more than fifteen seconds at a time."

I shook my head, thinking of Tessa and the kids. "What about you?"

"I just met with my attorney at a garage where I've been hiding out. The cops have plenty of pictures of me, too, and they've also taken fingerprints from my bus, which they've impounded. They want my sorry ass in a big way, and I got to get myself out of the area. Wait for the cops to get busy on other drug busts."

"Poor Bianco," I said.

"Yeah, I'm hip. But we had some conversations about this stuff before, man, Bill and me, and we agreed that if one of us got busted he'd do all he could to keep the other one out of it. Meantime, I'm going to make some bread to help his family out. Even if Bill does some time, he'll charm his way through it. He's got an advanced degree and he'll finagle some teaching or social work, get himself out on good behavior pretty fast. The cat has some charm, man, and charm will get you far in life, whether you're in stir or not. Speaking of charm, what about you? I hear you're making all 'A's in school, but don't have much money."

"Between Irene and me we have four part-time jobs, eight classes, and we're pretty much living hand to mouth. School is about to shut down for Christmas, and since most of our income comes from school jobs, we'll soon be leaner than ever. The hauling's been pretty slow, plus the old truck is overheating and running rough."

"If I wasn't laying low, I'd help you out with it. What's wrong with it?"

"It starts up just fine and runs okay until it gets hot. Denny's been meaning to take a look, but he's been pretty busy. Last time we talked he suggested that I should put an ad in the paper, ask for four-fifty and accept maybe three hundred."

"Does it smoke bad?"

"Not much."

"How often do have to add oil?"

"At least once a week. I'm thinking of taking an ad out this weekend, selling it to finance a few Christmas presents and get us through January if I can."

Thunderhead smiled broadly. "Well, I've got to get me and Donna and the kids back to the Pacific Northwest, so I'm your man for the truck," he said. "Sometimes there's just no escaping karma."

361

I scowled and gave my best bitter look. "I'm under oath to kill the next person who mentions the word karma. Anyway, you don't want to buy that truck."

"I don't know about that. Look, man, I was there when Dom gave you the truck. I even suggested it."

I snorted. "That's the first I've heard of that."

Thunderhead backed off with a smirk and a shrug. "Not that Dom would ever listen to me, of course. But I'm telling you, man, that if that truck could talk it would tell you that it had done all it could for you and that now it wanted to serve me. A sort of liberty wagon, get me and mine out of the reach of the long arm of the law."

"I don't want to sell you that truck," I explained, "for the simple reason that I'd feel guilty asking you to pay what I need to get for it. Anyway, it would break down long before you got anywhere near Seattle."

"Nah. What you don't know is that along with being a quite respectable mechanic, I'm a master at automotive hobbling," Thunderhead said. "How much will you take for it, and how long can you give me to come up with the money?"

"Like I said, I want four and can't possibly take any less than three.

"I can dig that, man. I mean, it would be nice to get five. But there's no way that you're gonna get three hundred, especially just before Christmas. See, like your thing is words, man, books and words. But my thing, at least one of them, is salvage. In an age of planned obsolescence, I'm into fixing things. Death to the American dream of planned obsolescence and that kind of thing. Anyway, don't sweat it. If you can't help me out, maybe I'll pop over this weekend, get it running so good you won't want to sell it anymore."

"Already I don't want to sell it," I said. "But I need the money to pay my rent."

"Hey, I'd just like to come over. I'm missing Donna and the babies something fierce and figured if I can't see my kids, maybe I can risk a glimpse of your little angel. You can call Donna up and I can have a little chat with her. In fact, Santa Thunderhead's got a couple of little presents for Serena. It sounds like you're going to need them to keep her believing in the old North Pole elf gift giver."

Thunderhead arrived with a pint of brandy crammed into a small toolbox with wrenches and pliers. We stood under the open truck hood, sipping, passing the bottle, fiddling with spark plug connections and fan belts. Thunderhead had a couple of rags in a back pocket. These he spit on from time to time and used them to rub blackened parts as he talked. "Last night I went into a convenience store, man, and this cop looked at me and my heart just started hammering in my ribs. I thought I was done for and felt like I was going to fucking faint. I've just got to get out of town, get Donna and the kids safe, and start putting together some bread to help Tessa. She's such a saint, man. If I wasn't so much in love with Donna and if my best friend wasn't already with her . . . ."

I looked at him sharply and decided Dom had it all wrong. Tessa would never sleep with Thunderhead. "How's Tessa holding up?"

"From what I hear she has her good days and her bad. Word is that if Bill does time she's going to move back to Buffalo for a while. Both she and Bill have big families there who can help her take care of the kids. Even so, I'll have to send her something each month as soon as I get settled in Seattle. I don't know how all that's going to shake out," he said, "because like I was telling you, I don't hardly have the money even to get us there."

I saw that I was supposed to give up the truck, if not for Ron and Donna's sake, then for Bill's or Tessa's. I was supposed to take whatever few bucks Thunderhead said he could raise. The pressure to hand over the keys was already irresistible, but I thought I might push it away. "Maybe you can find something cheaper than this."

"That's not gonna happen. All the old trucks around town, either the owners want too much for them or they need too much work. It's not the work I mind, you know, just the time. The more I see of this Chevy, the more I'm convinced that if I'm going to make it out of town okay, it'll be in Dom's old truck."

"You don't want to get out on the highway and find that you need valves and rings, Ron. I'd hate to think of you guys broke and stranded in Idaho in a winter blizzard or something."

"It's a chance I'll have to take. Like I said, before I bought the school bus I used to earn a big part of my living helping people keep their old vehicles alive. Without spending much money, I can keep a rattletrap running longer than anybody on the planet. Like I know the characteristics of all the different brands of gunk to pour in the gas tank, all the nitpicky adjustments to make to this and that. With a couple of cheap parts from a wrecking yard and a tool kit beside me on the front seat, I could drive this thing all the way to China."

China.

"It will break down before you get there. What will you do then?"

"It's possible that it will break down, but you know what? I don't think so. The other thing is that as long as I'm already on the way back to

Seattle with Donna and the kids, if and when the truck did break down, my folks know what's happening and would wire me the money to get us the rest of the way. They're cool that way."

"Maybe they'll help you put together the money you need to get the right vehicle for the drive."

"I already asked them. They won't actually send me the money to get started. My old man knows what's happening and feels sure that if he gave me the money to leave here he'd be caught and found guilty of obstructing justice and be sentenced to life in prison or some shit. He's a little goofy, got all these strange rationalizations, and doesn't respond well when somebody points out logical inconsistencies in his ideas. But he'd kill for my kids, same as I would. But I hear you, Tim, and once I get back to Washington and get some money coming in, I'll forward you some of what I can't pay you before I take off. We can work out some little time payment plan or something."

Upstairs, Irene served us tea and biscuits with honey while Thunderhead soothed her with the understanding that this particular Christmas was going to be a time of privation for all concerned. Everybody who dug Gordon and the Bianco family would just have to make some extra sacrifices. But the next Christmas would be lavish. His parents owned a roomy place with outbuildings on Whidbey Island near Seattle where we could all gather with the kids, including Gordon, who would go free any day now, and Bianco, who might have to serve a month or two on a trumped-up possession, but who could probably eventually beat the charges of dealing. We would all gather around the fireplace on Whidbey Island and drink champagne and brandy and laugh at how badly a good year could end. And who knew but by then the world might have already discovered what a great undiscovered painter it had in Irene. Anyway, now that Gordon was about to go free, there would be a major legal push to free Bianco. The cops had their little law enforcement games, but Thunderhead told Irene that as he'd been saying for a long time, conscious people like Bill Bianco and Tim Barlow had spiritual missions. They had spiritual force, powerful karma the world would not be allowed to trifle with for very long.

The ringing telephone woke Serena from her nap. While Irene talked with a fellow art student, I went to Serena's crib and picked her up. On the way to the bathroom with the soggy mess of her diaper, I discovered Thunderhead in our bedroom.

"What do you need, Ron?"

"I was just wondering if maybe you borrowed a gray sweater of mine."

"No," I said. "I don't borrow things without asking."

"Of course," Thunderhead said, clapping me on the back. "I figured maybe you borrowed it after asking and I just forgot about it. No problem. It will probably turn up some time, though I guess it's also possible I left it in the bus and the cops got it."

The sun was setting a chilly pink when Thunderhead handed me six twenty-dollar bills and a fifty-dollar food stamp coupon and drove my truck away. The next day most of the loot was gone for groceries, a Christmas tree, and an armload of presents. What remained of the money went into a coffee can on top of the refrigerator.

Six weeks later, I received a stained envelope with a Seattle postmark and no return address. Inside was a color photograph of Thunderhead and his family standing in front of the old Chevy truck. Visible through plastic tarps, supported by broken and patched wooden stakes and snarls of rope, was a towering assemblage of cribs, boxes, sculptures, elk antlers, kids' bikes, a washing machine, a mattresses, and duffel bags. Scrawled on the reverse side of the image were the words, "Luckily, the wind never blew!" I turned it over for another look. Thunderhead stood with his arm around Donna, bib overalls bulging with road maps. His beard was growing and the Trotsky glasses were back on his heavy nose. He was posing as some post-psychedelic Old Man Joad, as if he'd been photographed gloating and lounging on a movie set during a hip remake of John Steinbeck's novel *The Grapes of Wrath*. Standing beside him, Donna looked pale and worried. As unkempt and mangy as ever, the Thunderhead kids stood on the truck's hood under a Jolly Roger flag that had been attached to the truck's otherwise-useless radio antenna. In a brief letter, Thunderhead wrote that the truck had served them well. All he'd done, he claimed, was to install a thermostat, tighten the tappets and add crankcase gunk. The letter did not say where or how to reach him, contained no word about any payment plan, made no mention of Bill and Tessa Bianco, didn't inquire about Gordon, who'd been released on Christmas Eve, and didn't even wonder, as I did, what had become of Dom Sospiri.

Two weeks later, Tessa called to let us know that Bill Bianco had been sentenced to five years at Canyon City Penitentiary.

I didn't think very much about Thunderhead again until just before Irene had the new baby. Having spent bus fare on sour vending machine coffee and phone calls home to check on Irene, I stuffed my notes and books in a tattered knapsack, filed out of class, and walked out into a rainy April evening. By the time I got home, the temperature had fallen and the rain was turning to sleet and snow. Hearing neither Serena's running footsteps nor her shrill excited greeting, I removed my water-saturated shoes on the landing, draped my soaked socks over the banister, and trudged upstairs.

Irene was sprawled uncomfortably in a nest of pillows on the couch. On the floor nearby was an unfinished cup of cocoa. A book titled, *Your Toddler* Can *Cope with the New Baby,* was spread face down on a copy of her favorite novel, *Justine*, by Lawrence Durrell.

I studied Irene's pale, swollen face as I massaged the cold water out of my hair. Wiping wet hands on my pants, I asked, "How are you feeling?"

She flopped heavily into another position. "Terrible. Not only is my back killing me," she said, "but I have a headache. Would you please go to the store and get me some aspirin?"

"Sure."

I started toward the bedroom for a dry pair of socks. She called after me. "Dry off and change your clothes so you don't catch cold. Otherwise, they'll never let you in the delivery room tomorrow."

I hollered back. "Where's Serena?"

"Rhonda drove over and picked her up already. Serena seemed perfectly happy to go over there, and that way, Rhonda can get some work done at home, instead of having to hang out over here. The only thing is, we'll have to find another way to get to the hospital. The rain's supposed to turn to snow tonight."

I rummaged in a drawer for dry socks. Remembering some old sneakers and a pair of battered galoshes that could be pulled over them, I groped in the dark closet. Noting that one was much heavier than the other, I reached inside and removed a small, chrome-plated pistol. Dumbfounded, I carried it, muzzle down, into the front room.

"What the hell is that thing?"

"Well, I don't know. I just walked out here hoping you'd tell me how this pistol came to be stuffed inside one of my galoshes."

"Your galoshes? A pistol in your galoshes? You're kidding! How would I know? Where did it come from?"

"It was in the one that belongs on the left foot. "

She looked at me in disbelief.

I looked at the weapon. It was a cheap, plastic-handled .25 caliber semi-automatic. It looked like a convenience store punk pistol that might have been mail-ordered from an ad in a pulp magazine. I removed the clip and shook the chambered round into my hand. "All loaded up, too." Five cartridges gleamed in a little blot of oil on the palm of my hand.

"Get it out of here," Irene ordered. "My God, Serena might have found it! She could be dead. Any of us could."

I was baffled, silent, and Irene was indignant at my unresponsiveness. "Would you mind," she said, when I continued to shake my head, "returning to the subject at hand?"

My irritation got the better of me. "There isn't any subject at hand, Irene. I just found a pistol in one of my galoshes. Neither of us has any idea how it got there. It's weird as hell, but I've accepted it, and that's how it is. So there's no fucking subject at hand. In our different styles we're just considering the appearance of something that obviously bothers us both." I carried it toward the kitchen.

She hated it when I walked out of the room when either of us was angry. As often as not, her immediate inclination was to discipline me by starting the offending conversation all over again, from the beginning, as if it had never taken place.

"Where did it come from?"

"No idea, Irene," I said. "No idea at all."

It was true when I said it, but it became false two seconds later. Suddenly I did have an idea, something I didn't want to share with Irene on the evening before she was scheduled to go into the delivery room and have a baby. Thunderhead.

"What are you going to do with it?"

I closed my eyes, placed the weapon very carefully on an upside down frying pan beside the dish drainer, and then turned back. Positioning my hands on either side of the doorway, I managed a bland expression. "Any suggestions?"

"Throw it away."

"It's not a toy or a piece of trash," I said. "You can't just throw it away."

"Well, what do you plan to do with it?"

"For the time being, I'll put it way up on top of the cupboard. Up inside that silly little electric crockpot that we never use."

"What about the bullets?"

"They can't be tossed out, either. Maybe I'll put them temporarily in the coffee can with my pencils." The idea pleased me in a strange way. "Serena can't get near either place. Once I've done that, I'll go to the store and get some aspirin, come back and heat up some of that vegetable soup." I walked toward her smiling. "I propose that we forget all about the gun until after the baby is born. Then we'll talk about it rationally on a good day and arrange to have it removed from our apartment, okay?"

Almost any other time she'd have been offended by my patronizing tone. Now, she just grunted and shifted her position on the couch. Even so, when I returned from the bedroom carrying my galoshes and sneakers, she was waiting for me.

"It's your dad's idea of a joke," she offered. "It's his way of bringing to our attention that the world is a violent place and everybody should keep a gun. I think you should call him up right now and tell him to come over and get it. Hiding a pistol on the floor around a toddler who talks with her mouth full of every inedible thing she can lift to her face! Jesus, he's impossible!"

"He would never be so stupid as to leave a loaded pistol where Serena might find it. No way does it come from him."

"I never thought I'd see you stick up for your dad." she harrumphed.

"Irene," I said, flush from the effort of tugging on the ill-fitting galoshes, "it didn't come from him."

"He keeps a gun in his car and guns in the house."

I held my hands up and brought them toward my ears. Then I lowered them to my thighs and smoothed my still damp pants. I sighed and sat down. "Remember last summer when I asked my dad if he had any salmon eggs, so I could go fishing for an hour or so in the park without having to go to the sporting goods store?"

She rolled her eyes and looked at the ceiling. "No. But I remember a few minutes ago when I asked you to go for some aspirin."

"Okay, just let me finish. My dad didn't say anything for a long time. Finally, he fetched his tackle box. Inside were three, maybe four, already opened jars of eggs, any one of which would have been fine. But he insisted on giving me the new jar, the one with the price tag still on the lid. You know why?"

She rubbed her eyes and shook her head.

"I'm almost finished. He insisted I take the new jar because with the price still visible he could charge me retail and be sure he also got the correct sales tax."

"Okay, he's stingy, but I don't see what that has to do with that stupid gun."

"In the real world there's no such thing as a free lunch. If my dad's going to charge me sales tax on a jar of salmon eggs, he's sure as hell not going to give me a free pistol. Try to sell it to us? Yeah, okay, maybe."

I fought off the chilly night air by chanting my anger as I ran to the grocery store. The snaps on my galoshes jingled like Christmas bells.

"Blue lips, reasonably priced rock concerts, Wild Bill Hickok, and Ron Thunderhead, stick-up artist and attorney at law."

I remembered that Thunderhead had asked me about surprising discoveries at the new apartment and seemed relieved when I'd been nonplused. While we were making the deal on the truck, I caught him at the door of the bedroom closet on the pretext of looking for a lost sweater. Rightly or wrongly the pistol was his. He'd probably hidden it in the boot on the morning he was hiding from the cops and Irene and I had driven out to Rhonda's, just before taking to the streets.

Out of breath, I stood in the middle of the supermarket aisle, eyes scanning a row of toiletries for aspirin tablets. I hadn't managed to follow all the intricacies of the case, but I knew the various attorneys had been in touch with one another and had managed to communicate with Thunderhead when he'd been on the lam. I had no patience with anti-marijuana laws, and deplored the irrational vindictiveness I associated with their enforcement. But gun crimes were another matter. I'd have done what I could to harbor Thunderhead, especially when he vowed to turn himself in before allowing Gordon to take the rap. Now, with the discovery of the gun and the belief bordering on conviction that Thunderhead had held up the dry cleaners, his promise to turn himself in before allowing Gordon to go to prison rang hollow. Ostensibly, once the heat was off, Thunderhead had returned to the bedroom where he'd stashed it earlier. Maybe he wanted to hock it for gas money.

"Or maybe you wanted it to hold up another dry cleaner's, you fucking asshole." I snorted loudly.

Two boys in stocking caps at a nearby magazine rack hurried away. Only then did I realize that I'd been talking aloud. I snared the smallest box of aspirin, squeezed it in my fist, and carried it to a cashier. The younger of the two boys grabbed a woman's coat sleeve and tiptoed up to her face to whisper, "Mommy, there's that man who was saying bad words."

The woman glared at me and hurried to put her own broad backside between her progeny and the wet, unshaven man, looking back and forth between the boys and his own reflection in the illuminated supermarket window. Catching a sight of the wet crazy man the mother saw, I took half a step backwards, increasing her margin of safety.

I opened my eyes in the chalky light. Powerful gusts of wind rattled the loosened bedroom window, sending shivers through the faded madras curtains. Easing myself out of bed, I went to the window. Outside, it was snowing hard. The lilac bush, all but ready to bloom earlier in the week, was squashed and deformed under a white mound of snow. From somewhere down the street came the sharp crack of a snapping tree limb followed by the muffled thump of a heavy fall. Lightning flared, imparting a brief afterglow to the snowflakes in the air.

I listened for a sound of traffic, but heard only the wind followed by a rumble of thunder and more creaking and snapping of tree branches. According to a clock by the bed, in four hours Dr. David Korkov was scheduled to induce Irene's labor. A jar in the kitchen contained seven dollars and change, enough under ordinary circumstances for a cab to the hospital. But would cabs or even buses be in service in weather like this?

Irene slept on. Her legs were splayed out and her knees bent as if she were sprinting through her dreams. Her pajama top had ridden up, exposing the small bottoms of her breasts and the massiveness of the belly over her hips. I'd studied and stroked the belly a few days before. It was hard as a watermelon and her skin was stretched taut as a drumhead. Dark purple and blue blood vessels fanned out in all directions. Tiny rivers and tributaries of life, branches, Irene's and the baby's, were plainly visible just beneath the waxy skin of her tummy.

Moving slowly, I climbed into bed next to her and pulled up the covers. Outside the thunder boomed. Trees groaned and cracked. A bright light over a neighbor's garage combined with a nearby streetlamp to illuminate a long rectangle on a wall near the window. Faint shadows of snowflakes streamed ceaselessly through the glow. Flickers of lightning alternately erased and restored them. People, too, were on the move, receding, before a shaping force stronger than their own intentions. Such a perception, I thought, should be accompanied by some mystical bliss, some flicker of the peace that was supposed to surpass understanding.

I rolled to one side. Irene groaned and flopped, inserted her knees behind my thighs and began drawing back some of the warmth I'd extracted from her body. Outside, the thunder and lightning receded.

For some time now, the raw formless hopes of a generation had been going up in a choking smoke of sandalwood incense, cordite, napalm, rock concert campfires, and blown engines. Chagrined by having lingered too long, the last dreamers, among whom I had to number myself, were slipping off in search of something to take the place of those hopes. What was wanted was a self to realize, a cause to join, an untapped market for sandals or earrings or tribal festivals themed to what no longer quite existed, maybe never had existed. The many had become the few; the few were becoming fewer and more desperate. Strange, how you didn't really have to be one of the believers to burn with the fever of delusional hope, how you didn't have to hope to be hopeful. The lamps had gone out not to be lit again in our lifetime, and a spectacle, a glorious, hopeful pageant had mutated into a circus of narcissism at a national flea market.

On a bunk in a cell in Canyon City, Bill Bianco was observing different lightning bolts perhaps, or sleeping his way into another dreary morning. Pregnant and without financial resources, Tessa had sold the last of the books Dom had hauled out from California and moved back to Buffalo where she and Bill had family. Thunderhead, armed robber that he now seemed to be, was in the Pacific Northwest, the Chevy stake bed parked outside a rented house in West Seattle. Gordon had passed a civil service exam and, now that all criminal charges against him had been dropped, had gone to work as a mail sorter at a post office branch halfway to Boulder. Dom, who probably still didn't know about Bill and Tessa, had sent me three postcards, apologizing for being without a permanent address, promising phone calls that never came, and visits that never happened. The mail a few weeks earlier had also brought me an Albert Fine original, a postcard bordered with simple line drawings of "Band-Aids" and spoons on one side. An all-but-indecipherable paragraph talked about being snowbound in an adobe house with five dogs on a New Mexico Indian Reservation. A month before, I had learned from a mutual acquaintance that my high school friend Rick had given up sports cars, guitars, chicks, and LSD, and gone to India with a begging bowl. I shuffled memories of friends and felt sleep, a warm tide, tow me under.

I awoke before dawn, convinced that keeping secrets and thinking about the secrets of others had made me old before my time. Secrets and friends who drifted off in indifference, these were the causes of stooped shoulders, grayed hair and thinned bones. Secrets: the weight of what we knew and decided others should never know.

The shadows of snowflakes had all but disappeared from the bedroom wall. Beside me, Irene stirred. I felt a small, insistent thump against my butt. Irene's murmur seemed to fill the room. "Did you feel that?"

I did, but I couldn't speak.

"The baby's kicking," she said.

She didn't say where the baby had kicked me. Perhaps she didn't know. My life, her life, its life. A life-to-be had kicked me in the ass.

Hearing a loud, cracking sound, I jumped from bed and ran to the front room window. A huge limb from the largest maple tree on the block had snapped and crushed the roof of a station wagon directly across the street. Looking down the block, I saw more torn and fallen branches. Only the saplings and the cone-shaped spruce trees escaped breakage. Parting the curtains for a view of the other end of the block, I saw torn power lines, dangling and disappearing in snow. Suggesting a dead giraffe, an apartment house awning lay toppled, its supporting pipes akimbo in the slush. An elm tree limb as thick as my waist snapped and fell, detonating an explosion of snow in the middle of Eighth Avenue. The streets were empty of human activity. Other than the breaking of trees, the only sound of the morning was one of tires, whirling, humming, going nowhere. Irene appeared beside me in her bathrobe. "We'd better leave earlier than we'd planned on," she suggested.

Sorely tempted to call the hospital and reschedule her appointment, I looked at her and wondered how she could be so fragile and vulnerable, yet so puffed up with determined ferocity. I shrugged, pushed my shoulders back, and started to dress. For me, I decided, it would be the perfect day only if I could manage to prevent Irene from falling down in the knee-high snow and getting hurt. She disappeared and returned in the duck slippers Gramma Escobar had given her years ago. She shuffled into the kitchen to make coffee. In the bedroom, lightning flared and the light bulb winked. From the kitchen, Irene shrieked and laughed. Thunder rattled spoons in the dish drainer.

I gulped burning coffee and went down to find our downstairs neighbor's snow shovel leaning where I'd last positioned it, against the side of the house. The heavy, gray slush was littered with leaves and twigs and bits of bark. I bent for my first load of snow and slowly warmed to the task. Covered with sweat and looking back up the street after a few minutes, I saw I'd cleared only a narrow path. I'd have to walk ahead of Irene. Ignoring the predicaments of stranded drivers who called to me for a push, I went back to shoveling. They had cars and health plans. I was working with a borrowed shovel and carfare.

Later, outside in the still blowing snow, Irene clasped my forearm with an iron grip and studied the shovel I carried in my free hand.

"Why are you taking that thing?"

"I only got as far as the corner. Unless you think you can wade through knee-high slush, there's still shoveling to do. Maybe you should go back upstairs and wait."

"We'll be late."

Big flakes of snow spattered us. "Doctor Korkov wouldn't want you wade through all the slush and chance a fall. I'll just tell him that I had to shovel." I risked a small joke. "Maybe he knows a chiropractor who can treat me while you're in the recovery room."

She shook her head. "I don't want to go back upstairs and deal with coats and sweaters again," she said. "I'll follow behind as you shovel."

My back burned. The sweat from my efforts joined the icy slush falling in my hair and ran down the back of my neck, over my face, and into my ears. Periodically, in an effort to clear the straightest possible path, I dragged smaller branches out of the way.

Tree limbs continued to snap, dropping big and small branches loaded with green leaves and ice all around us. I positioned Irene as far away from dangerously laden branches as I could, and between grunting and groaning, listened for arboreal warnings. If, after an initial creaking, a branch didn't immediately spring and toss its load of slush high into the air, there usually followed a softer tearing of inner tissue and a violent crack as the branch gave way. For every vehicle making even an uncertain headway on the street, dozens of cars sat going nowhere, gunning stinky engines, drifting more and more deeply into heavier mounds of slush. Tires whistled and howled.

By the time Irene and I reached Downing Street, I found it hard to stand up straight for the pain in my lower back. I gouged a rough path to the curb where I hoped a bus might come, stabbed the blade of the shovel into the snow, and spread my hands on my lower back, working my stiff flexors as if they were dry hinges. I lit a cigarette, cupped my hand around it to protect it from the still falling snow, and squinted down the street. "Maybe we'll get lucky. Maybe even if there's no bus, somebody will stop for us. Maybe there will be a bus." After such an effort to be optimistic, a tender moment surprised me and I put one arm around Irene's shoulders. "Cold?"

She was, but she smiled and shook her head. "Thank you for your work," she said. "Thank you for your understanding."

I shrugged.

"Is that a bus?"

I stepped down off the curb. "I don't think so."

"It is," she said. "It's a bus. It's our special bus. I can feel it."

I raised my eyebrows and once again she caught me in a gesture of pessimism.

She was shivering. "You'll see."

I did and I kissed her.

Staying well toward the middle of the street, a red-and-white city bus inched toward us. I tossed my cigarette in the slush and watched the bus creep and drift toward us. When its door opened, a warm, vaguely unpleasant antiseptic public smell swam out at us. The boarding steps loomed like a small mountain.

"Take your time," the driver called down. "Looks like the three of us are the only ones in the city going anywhere this morning." He laughed, a smile glowing in his dark eyes. "And I don't know how much farther we're going."

When we gained the top of the steps, Irene smiled and said, "Thank you."

The driver beamed at her and shook his head, seemingly amazed. "Whoohee, you are one pregnant lady," he said admiringly. The windshield wipers groaned irregularly, sounding like a jump rope rhyme waiting to be brought into language. I laughed and wiped my wet hair and face with both hands.

Irene looked very pale and anxious. "Tim," she said, "I forgot the bus fare."

"I've got it."

The bus driver winked at me. "You're not a lawyer, are you?"

"No," I said.

"That's good," the driver said, "because I'm not an obstetrician."

In no mood to deal with obscure humor, I grunted. While Irene sat down, I dug into my pockets for coins. My hands were wet and cold and all but useless. I kept fishing up nickels and dropping them on the floor.

The driver chuckled. "Not a lawyer, not a communist, just another spaced-out paleontologist on the way to China, huh?"

"Yeah," I grumbled, finally finding the coins I wanted, dumping them in the box.

"Look at him," the driver said. "Paleontologist wants to go to China, still on the wrong continent, and he's about ready to leave his shovel behind. He's got the wrong kind of shovel, too." The laugh got my attention and I turned around to study the driver, slowly. He looked vaguely familiar.

"How you going to excavate your dinosaur bones without so much as even a snow shovel, Timmy Barlow?"

"Shit. Junior Wong!"

"Jefferson." He hesitated, then chuckled. "Okay, still Junior to family and a few honored old friends. How you been in your life so far, Tim?"

"Fine, fine. Good God, I can't believe this! How did you recognize me? I still look the same?"

"You used to be clean shaven."

"No, but I mean you recognized me."

374

"You've got a dreaminess that looked familiar. But she called you by your name, and then there was your cussing. You say 'shit' just like your old man used to, with plenty of conviction about it." Wong shook his head and smiled at Irene. "Ever meet his daddy, Mister Burke Barlow, opera singer guy with a hot temper?"

"Bert," Irene corrected him. "I take it you guys know each other."

"Yeah, I know this shrimp thief," Wong said.

"Shrimp thief?"

"That's what my brother used to call you. You used to try to steal his shrimp and make him cry."

I said, "Irene, this is Junior Jefferson Wong. He taught me to read when I was four years old. He's the one to blame for many of my big ideas. Jefferson, this is Irene."

"Irene and Timmy, the goddamned Chinaman. That is to say, honorary, honorable goddamned Chinaman."

"You knew that?" I was embarrassed. "You knew my dad called me a goddamned Chinaman?"

"Quiet speech wasn't really his thing, was it? How is he anyway?"

"Same as ever. But forget him," I said. "I want to hear about you."

"I thought you wanted a bus ride."

"Yeah, of course. Communication and transportation, right?"

Wong nodded his head. "Sometimes you gotta do one, sometimes the other. You gonna leave that snow shovel there in the snow bank?"

"No, it doesn't belong to me. I guess I better take it along." I hopped down and brought it aboard. "Irene," I said, grinning, "Junior and I were going to drive the speed of light to travel through time. Thanks to some weird version of relativity Junior cooked up, we thought we could get back to the age of dinosaurs."

Irene was cold and scared, wanting something from me, looking at me and knowing I was once again on the verge of being overwhelmed by the past. Even so, she smiled. "Nice to meet you, Mister Wong."

"He taught me to read and was in the process of setting up an experiment to teach me about how brakes worked," I said. "That's where we left off, more than fifteen years ago."

"I'll be happy enough to pick up where I left off. The first thing is, for us today, you don't have to worry about stopping if you can't get going. Even time travel has to begin with two miles an hour." Jefferson eased the bus from the curb, the rear tires whizzed, the rear end drifted, but the engine slowed and the bus righted itself and inched forward.

I looked at his face and heard, or imagined I did, an echo from my own past. "I can't believe it," I said "All morning I've seen about five vehicles actually managing to move, and I haven't seen one cab or bus. Five minutes after we arrive, you, of all people, pull up in a completely empty bus."

Wong nodded, concentrating on the approaching intersection.

"There are a lot of things I'd like to talk to you about," I said.

"Such as?"

"I don't know. For starters, your life and what you make of it, your grandmother, your dog Low Foo Doy, your brothers, the old neighborhood. What I remember of those days that you might have forgotten. What you remember that I don't."

"I'm okay in a bus lane," Wong laughed. "But I'm no good in Memory Lane. My grandmother has died, but maybe I should give you my dad's phone number. Or Marshall's. They run the big memory banks in the family. Me, everything I can forget, I do. And everything I can't forget, I try not to remember."

"Okay," I said, a little stung, "But why then did you bother to recognize me? You could have said nothing."

"Well, I don't want to be warped about it. We need a memory, like a muscle, to remember dentist's appointments and birthdays. You have to remember to brush your teeth and how to tell time, but in my opinion memory should be kept on a low-calorie diet. My grandma, she's dead ten years now. Before she went, though, she and my dad talk, talk, talk about the past. And he still wakes up every morning, my dad, and thinks about his village in China, his school days, before the Japanese and the war. Every day he compares his here and now with his then and there, and decides his life here is no good. Every day he's picking the scabs of his memory and bleeding. Everything you say to him is just a reminder of how much better things used to be in China. He overlooks that as a boy in China he had tuberculosis and no medicine and a cold room with no heat to share with six brothers and sisters, no food to eat. Memory is the big liar and the big thief. But, hey Tim, you were car crazy, so why don't you tell me what kind of car you drive?"

"Christ. Don't get me started on cars again. You wouldn't believe my life with cars. The fact is, I don't have a car at the moment, Junior. There I go. Jefferson. What about you?"

"Me, I drive a Studebaker Avanti. There's not many of them around and it's a real quality car." He looked at Irene. "Is the baby going to be a girl or a boy?"

"A boy," she said.

"Yeah, I think so, too. But I bet Tim thinks it's going to be a girl."

"Yeah, I think it's a girl," I said. "And I'm going to watch her be born this morning."

I was wrong on both counts. Irene's water broke while we stood shivering at the hospital admissions desk and Matthew Lester Barlow was born, red and healthy, while I was struggling into a cap and gown outside the delivery room.

The '63 Chevy Biscayne Station Wagon

*"Take a pencil and map out your Magic Circle fun right now.
You've got the car, and if you're missing out on this kind of driving,
you aren't enjoying half of what your car offers you."*
*Ethyl Corporation Advertisement, **Look**, May 12, 1959*

Shortly after Matt was born, Irene was awarded a one-time "studio" grant by the City U Art Department. After completing a great deal of paperwork, we got permission to use the money to rent a three-bedroom house not far from the apartment where we'd been living. Once we moved in, Irene converted the largest bedroom into a studio, and I took a part-time job at the University of Colorado's Medical Center.

At work the day after Matt's first birthday party, I banged into and toppled a bulletin board with an overloaded cart of medical supplies I was pushing. In replacing the scattered notices, I discovered that several fleet vehicles were being sold in a sealed-bid auction. News of the sale of had been concealed by recent postings. Restoring the bulletin board, and papering over the auction notice again, I submitted bids on several vans and a station wagon. When my offer of less than two hundred dollars for a white '63 Chevy Bel Aire Biscayne station wagon turned out to be the highest, I drove the car home the following week. Its tires were bald, but mechanically the Chevy was perfect.

Though I'd still been in high school when it rolled off the assembly line, I discovered that the station wagon had retained much of its cachet as a family car. Seeing us emerge from it, strangers in our middle-class neighborhood stopped glaring at Irene and me as if we were unkempt student revolutionaries and bad parents, and started smiling and making small talk. Owning the Chevy was transformational in other more important ways as well. Wrestling strollers and kids on and off city buses became a thing of the past. With shopping, laundry, and travel to and from work so much easier, Irene and I managed to take the kids for occasional afternoons of sledding or kite flying. We were busy with school assignments and holding down four or five part-time jobs between us, but we were increasingly better organized and, for me, there were even times when our cooperative punctuality and efficiency began to look like the beginnings of a roadbed that might lead somewhere.

A poem of mine was published in a local literary magazine and, about the same time, Irene won the blue ribbon for best painting in the City U Student Artist Show. The night before the exhibition opened, we celebrated our successes by hiring a babysitter and splurging on dinner at a Greek restaurant, where we both drank wine. Coached by a middle-aged couple in peasant costumes, we even stumbled and laughed our way through a few basic dance steps.

The winning painting was to be exhibited on a prominent wall outside the student café. The next afternoon on my way to work I got my first look at the four-panel oil portrait of our family that Irene had titled *Seasons: An American Family Now*.

The smallest panel, *Spring*, depicted 18-month-old Matt swinging a toy car at an improbable edifice of building blocks. His blue corduroy overalls were stained with fruit juice, his blond hair unruly, his enthusiasm characteristically transparent, and his laughing, wide-open pink mouth showed new pearly teeth.

In another panel, *Fall*, five-year-old Serena, pink with baby fat and wearing a gauzy blue tutu, was the central figure in a group of chubby preschool ballerinas. The basic composition was derived from a photograph I'd taken a few months earlier at the City U childcare center, a converted house trailer. The original was taken in harshly lit fluorescent glare, but Irene had imbued the new background with the cold, chalky light of a Degas painting. I was sure her inventive use of light was one of several art historical references that won her the first prize and the premier exhibition spot in the student show.

Individually and together, the other two panels troubled me. *Summer*, the largest and most prominently displayed, was an unorthodox, full-bodied self-portrait of Irene at her easel. A pair of my old jeans bunched around her small waist with a hank of clothesline, making her ass appear rounder, larger, and more voluptuous than it was. Six or seven paintbrushes, which she'd fanned out in a back pocket, endowed her with a kind of peacock's tail and a sexuality that surprised and shocked me. Apart from the tail, what I disliked most in the *Summer* panel, but said nothing about, was that a wedge of one of Gerald's color photographs, which hung on a wall in Irene's studio, also appeared in the upper right hand corner of her painting.

Winter, the second largest panel, featured a greenish upper body portrait of me as I might have been painted through the windshield of the station wagon by a none-too-favorably disposed stranger. The Chevy's hood and front end were prominent, and the car's white lacquer confidently reflected the pinks of a cold late afternoon light. Irene got the

380

hazy wildness in my eyes just right, but I was unhappy with the out-of-focus smeariness of my face. Irene defended it as homage to James Ensor and Georges Rouault. When she pressed me for an opinion, I said that while I could see its merits as a painting, it was unflattering as a portrait, adding that if Emil Nolde had chosen to paint the clown Canio in *I Pagliacci*, he would have produced something quite similar. What I disliked most about the panel, though, was the hands she'd hooked over the steering wheel. They were fatter and more sensuous than mine. And they were grasping the wheel in a way almost to the point of being grotesque.

For the next little while every day on my way to work the lunch rush in the student café, I looked dispiritedly up at the wall at what represented my graspy hands on the steering wheel. On good days I told myself things weren't as bad as I imagined. On bad days I was sure that her art school cohorts were whispering to one another or lingering in the food line to study my hands as they filed by the steam table where I regularly flipped grilled cheese sandwiches and handed out greasy sacks of french fries.

If I could see those paintings again, now, with all their props and little domestic details, I might remember more of our lives between Matt's birth and the spring fishing trip I took the week of graduation. Unfortunately, years later, Irene couldn't pay a heating bill during what she came to refer to as her "Japanese period," and burned the painting's wooden stretcher bars one night for firewood. When times continued hard, she cut the canvases into squares and rectangles and knocked off a series of lilac and tulip landscapes set against a snowy background of Long's Peak. She told me she then sold the lot for between twenty and forty bucks apiece to Decor To Go, a downtown poster and painting warehouse. She rather gloated about having buried our domestic life under heaps of flowers, scattering the evidence to the new Denver suburbs, increasingly occupied by oil executives and lawyers, or to doctors' waiting rooms and cheap motels from Alaska to Florida.

All of that was ahead of me the week that Dom called while I was finishing up my last term paper. He told me how good the trout fishing was within half an hour's drive from the house that he'd rented in the small western Colorado town of Paonia. The weather was warm in Denver when he called. Ready for a break and wanting to see him again, I agreed to do my best to bring Irene and the kids over to Paonia to celebrate my graduation with a few days of fishing.

Unfortunately, Irene hadn't forgiven Dom for drag racing with Little George, for being Bill Bianco's cousin, or for having inspired what she regarded as my misplaced loyalty. She had more than a semester to complete before earning her own degree and, though she, too, would be off school for a couple of weeks, she wouldn't hear of driving west, even for a long weekend between the spring and summer terms. When I coaxed, she got mad and said she didn't want go fishing, live barefoot in the woods, or study "the laughter that heals" under Dom's tutelage. In a somewhat improved mood a few days later, she cited the sore throats and colds the kids would surely get in a big, under-heated house in the woods, then reminded me she was scheduled to work several waitressing shifts at a neighborhood nightclub. Finally admitting she wanted to stay home to paint and maybe invite a few other artists over to see her new work, she encouraged me to organize my fishing gear and go by myself.

When Serena overheard our discussion and whined about wanting to go fishing with me, I took her to the drugstore for flashlight batteries, bought her an ice cream cone, and told her she might be old enough to go next year. Back at home, I knotted a balloon and played peek-a-boo with Matt. The following afternoon, instead of attending graduation ceremonies in Boulder, I scraped the hardened bits of dead night crawler and shriveled salmon eggs from the bottom of my long-unopened tackle box, stuffed warm clothes and battered pots in an army surplus duffel bag, and inserted one of my grandpa's handmade spinning rods with a gleaming new reel into my new, rolled-up sleeping bag.

In the months to come, I put myself through a lot of alcohol-fueled might-have-beens, speculating about how different things could have turned out if I'd bought decent tires instead of a new spinning reel and sleeping bag. I told myself that I should have, by then, evolved into a person who would have bought the tires, borrowed the sleeping bag, and made due with the old reel. That person might have started driving through the Black Canyon earlier, later, or even the day before I eventually did. The pay phone in a certain restaurant might have been out of order. I would one future day be perched over a beer glass in my barroom blackness, angling for an understanding I could learn to live with. Another dark, still night I would throw rocks at the moon and listen as they fell kerplunk in the lake in Washington Park.

But all the drinking and rock throwing were months away when I climbed the stairs to Irene's studio. The evening sun beamed through the window, imparting red highlights to the curly hair she'd wrapped with a kerchief. I remember kissing her cheek, more than a little sullenly, then clomping downstairs, carrying the last of my gear out to the car, a pouting baccalaureate with a drugstore cigar tucked in the breast pocket of my army field jacket, my grandpa's battered slate-colored fishing hat resolutely pulled low on my forehead.

I bought a can of beer in a convenience store forty miles out of town. In the darkness below the summit of Kenosha Pass, I lowered the station wagon's tailgate and sat dangling my feet, sipping from the cold can. I fired up the stogie and puffed out smoke signals, pungent doodles addressed to any watching gods or members of my tribe in the valley below: "Baccalaureate conditioned as goddamned Chinaman seeks escape from real world. Willing to relocate. Any better world, come in. Over," read the puffs. No answer.

I'd gone to City U because it was all but free, because a college degree vaguely promised relief from a life otherwise condemned to unloading frozen chickens, patrolling city dumps, or working in potato chip factories. I chose four years of confused fatherhood and study, because I knew there was a lot to learn and thought I could teach myself to endure teachers and administrative regulations. My initial enthusiasm was dimmed by my realization that having a family to support meant choosing between good grades and poverty, or acceptable grades and reductions in family hardship. Too quickly I discovered that with a supply of yellow highlighters and an innate ability to mimic the tone of academic papers heavy on ponderous, qualified sentences and sonorous, respectful tones, I could avoid classrooms, write elective essays for others in the wee hours of the morning, shed one part-time job for another, and, at least, earn more dollars to argue with Irene about. Now, given my unremitting fear of selling out, my untenable political ideals, and my invidious capacity to metabolize raw hope and expectation, I had a degree and one or two amorphous hopes. But I had no life plans, no resume, no career or desire for one. Nor, later that night, did the midnight stars provide me any inspiration. The bluer winking stars, I remembered, were said to be the hottest. The red ones were cooler, but guttering, slowly burning out. Black holes, fierce, cosmic fists of purest gravity, were towing our galaxy through space to purposes everybody could imagine but nobody could really observe. A wind came up. My cigar went out and unraveled. I tossed it at a big rock and got back in the car.

I parked near a promising stretch of water in time for dawn fishing on the Taylor River and studied the now-overcast sky for signs of change and a promise of warmth. I built a fire, made coffee, smoked, and waited in vain for a primitive sense of well being to kick in. Refusing to stay by the fire, put on warmer clothes, or drive into the town of Gunnison for breakfast, I mounted my new reel, found a flat rock, and dragged a wet fly through the river.

Late that afternoon, I carried my gear uphill and made a simple camp in a clearing a hundred feet over the river. I cleaned two rainbow trout in a gravel sink I dug with an ax, built up a big blaze, then let it burn to coals while concocting a sauce of mustard, onion, and almond flakes. I fried the fish with small pieces of bacon, added my sauce, and ate the tasty mess on a pair of hamburger buns toasted on a rock. A trio of chipmunks circled warily, squeaking at the heat and frightening themselves. I downed a can of tomato juice and gathered firewood for the coming night. The wall of gray clouds opened slightly and a cold yellow sun glazed a nearby butte. Out of the north, clouds smothered the sunset and a gray fog eased down the valley toward me through a stand of spruce. Below, the river flowed incessantly, a dark Tao from which I derived no comfort. Later, a wind hissed through the forest and blew the fog away. I slept fitfully, enduring strange dreams.

I looked forward to seeing Dom. But I didn't look forward to admitting that I was miserable or to hearing him sound off on any of a dozen subjects he would certainly bring up to improve my frame of mind.

My idea at this point was to outlast my frustrations and rage and regret, and draw healing from hours of staring numbly at my monofilament fishing line, taking in the smell of pines, dawdling around the fire, and at night, position my head on the damp ground and study the glittery indifference of the stars. Now that Irene had seemingly given up on hearing anything from me, I was down to maybe one or two more chances to persuade her that I was worth listening to again. But I didn't feel capable of any persuasion and didn't know what I might have to say. She had Gerald and a circle of friends encouraging her, I felt sure, to withdraw her faith in me in favor of whatever it was she could make out on the far side of the cool impacted indifference that had grown between us. Clear nights on my back in the open, sleeping bag pulled to the damp end of my nose, moonlight and silence; that was what I had fantasized about as I packed for the trip. But what I got was gray days, intervals of intermittent drizzle, and lackluster fishing.

In search of primitive mindless discipline or order, I quit fishing early every afternoon and went in search of flat stones to perfect my circular fire pit. I improved my bed, adding rust-colored pine needles and fistfuls of crushed aspen leaves. There was a temporary pleasure to meals, corned beef hash scooped from a can, fresh trout, carrots, brown rice, celery, gluey supermarket biscuits from explosive paper tubes, sweet oranges, fresh cherries, organic honey, and condensed milk for midnight coffee. But the pleasure disappeared with the food. Night fell, clouds hid the stars and, when visible at all, the moon glowed only as a faint halo. I woke to the sound of wind rushing through the valleys, the creaking of lodgepole pines, the small cries of animals I never saw, and the trickle or roar of the river, depending on which direction my head was turned.

Even my nightmares seemed to belong to someone else. Nixon and Agnew and George Wallace pulled guns on children and chased them down filthy alleys. Marines attacked kittens with machetes. Dragons gave birth to carbuncular birds in soggy, sewer-like caves. Snowplows tore holes in mountains and filled valleys with mine debris and pig guts. Militant Black Panthers, demanding justice for the disenfranchised, kidnapped Matt and Serena. Thunderhead was selling cosmetics and bombs from the back of my old stake bed. I wandered lost and wounded, strangers came and went, begging money, food, shelter, whatever I didn't have. Enraged by my lack of resources, they spit on me and I awoke to a predawn drizzle with smoke-reddened eyes. I pissed against rocks, certain that when I put my head back down I could hear the big trucks on the highway miles and miles away. Dozing, I dreamed that Junior Wong and I flew a mechanical dragon toward China. A giant floating poster of Mao came to life and laughed at us. Our flying contraption got tangled in wires and I woke again, sharp stones poking me in the back.

By the cold fire pit, a camp bird snacked on blackened bits of last night's fried potatoes, tipped my coffee pot over in the ashes, then shit on the cardboard lid of my oatmeal box before flying off into the forest.

On the sixth desolate day, I tossed my still-damp sleeping bag and gear in the back of the station wagon and drove the tight, curving dirt road toward Gunnison. The temperature dropped, the mountains receded, the land opened out, and the sky turned a hard blue.

Breakfast was ham and eggs at a crowded coffee shop on a wide street in the middle of town. While waiting for my order, I bought two postcards. On the one I addressed to Serena, I wrote about a pair of chipmunks, Squeak and Yeek, who bickered every evening around my cooling fry pan. Addressing the other card to Grandpa Lester and Grandma Nina Barlow, I described a fat brown trout that got away from me and reassured my grandma that I was looking forward to taking her to see a ceramics exhibition scheduled to open in Denver in a few days.

Lacking postage, I stuffed the cards in the pocket of the extra shirt I put on, and then, with the Chevy's heater on low so I wouldn't fall asleep, I drove west on Highway 50, shortening the distance between me and Paonia by taking 92 north over the Black Canyon of the Gunnison River.

I thought of a thousand things I wanted to tell Dom, who listened well in person but always seemed so distracted on the phone. I'd start by filling him in on whatever details he didn't have about Bianco's bust and the story of Gordon being taken for Thunderhead; some of this he would already know, either from letters Bianco was allowed to write or from having talked with Tessa. Dom knew I'd sold the truck to Thunderhead to help him make good his escape, but I had never had enough of his attention during our brief phone conversations to tell him about the pistol I'd found in my closet. I wanted to give and receive as much factual information as possible, and ease into telling him how lost and rootless I was feeling.

When a gust of wind threatened to blow the car off the road, I emerged from my reveries and began observing the road's ascent and narrow switchbacks. Stunted trees and shrubs bobbed and bowed to the broken rocks they grew among. Another icy blast roared and beat against the windows, rocking the car. Rounding a curve, I saw the slate-colored Gunnison River several hundred feet below. It wasn't the steep rocky walls that gave the Black Canyon its name, but the deep areas in the twisted canyon bottom where the sun never shone.

Long before, gangs of men had laid railroad track on narrow, rocky shelves they blasted and built up along the river, slaving and fighting and breaking their bodies for trains that would rarely make it through the deep, impassable snows or obstructions of falling rock. The trains and tracks and men were soon gone, just as the Indians predicted they would be. How strange that now the softened ancestors of those men could drive past, high above their work and bones, in station wagons and Jeeps. They could pull over and look down with binoculars on all that abandoned labor and check into motels that night, cameras containing images in which the river was a luminous green ink, a motionless signature gouged in granite, promising nothing. Today, though, there were no tourists, no photographers. But for the rising wind, I might have been on the moon.

In intervals of calm, I heard my own breathing and the thin grip of smooth tires on the road. Then the howling wind seemed to lift the car and set it down again, leaving me gripping the steering wheel as Irene had painted me, hands like meat hooks, dragon claws. I thought of her painting of me. What had she foreseen? I felt sick to my stomach.

At the end of a long curve I looked into the blackest cloud I'd ever seen. As it raced toward me, a snowflake the size of a quarter fell on my windshield. Giant, icy, wind-driven splats followed, quickly filling the air.

In a matter of minutes, snow covered the ground and the edges of my windshield. The road faded and blurred and I steered carefully, hugging the rocky walls, keeping well away from the canyon edge. It had been a long time since I'd seen another vehicle. What did everybody else know that I didn't?

The tires were unreliable and it occurred to me that in a moment of doubt, or panic, or excessive speed I might glide off the pavement into the abyss. The wind died, or at least the noise of it did, and I had to slow down and squint through melting flakes on the windshield. The curves and undulations of the highway exaggerated themselves. I rounded a curve and slid toward icy oblivion. I backed off on the gas. The tires stopped whining, but the car's rear end fishtailed toward the chasm. The pavement was at least ankle-deep in slush. Every small ascent or descent, every incline, became a challenge or a threat. To gain the top of a slope required a momentum that was increasingly difficult to obtain without sliding and skidding dangerously. There was no road shoulder, no end to the blowing snow. The temperature continued to fall.

This was June. How much could it snow? How cold could it get? How many more miles before the road ceased to climb? How long could this canyon be? I told myself that at any minute the road would begin to descend, reducing my task to one of riding the brake and managing to keep my forward momentum from sweeping me over the edge and into the abyss. It would be drier and warmer off the mesa. Dom had told me that the first buds were on the apple and cherry trees in the orchards outside Paonia, but I was in another world: the far north, Siberia. The car's outside mirrors and back windows were useless, and the windshield wipers were losing their battle against the wet, white onslaught.

Two-thirds of the way to the top of a particularly steep slope, my tires began to spin in the slush and the station wagon started to fishtail. Risking a collision with any vehicle that might be coming up behind me, I backed up to get a run at the hill. The problem was visibility; in the dense blowing snow I could no longer back up far enough to gain the necessary momentum. The bald tires hummed and whistled, urging the car in every direction but forward. I got out of the car. My hands were clammy. My hair was wet with slush, but sweat was running down my back. Stepping too quickly, my feet shot out from under me and I went down in deep slush. Squatting in wet snow, I used my hands to dig holes under and in front of the rear tires. Getting up, I fell again, bruising my knee. I got back in the car, cussing. In those few short minutes, the windshield had already covered with too much snow for the wipers to move. After clearing the windshield with my red ungloved hands, I got back in the car again. Switching quickly between first and reverse, I managed to rock the Chevy free from the rut, but I still could not get to the top of the rise. The clutch began to feel flimsy and the car went nowhere, except maybe ten or twelve feet more toward the inside road shoulder where once again a touch of the accelerator pedal sent the car sideways. In a rage, I hit the gas, turned the steering wheel hard, and skated into a deep drift just off the road.

Again I got out to dig, and again I fell, cracking the protective crystal on my wristwatch. I wandered the road in search of a stone or any natural object I might insert under a tire for traction. I found only heavy rocks, impossible to lift. By now the snow was over the top of the rear tires. Somehow I had gotten myself in the worst possible position for the worst spring blizzard of the century. My watch had stopped and my clothes were soaking wet.

Getting back in the car, I changed to the few dry clothes I had and began unrolling the sleeping bag that I hadn't bothered to dry before breaking camp that morning. Thinking that I heard the sound of a car, I jumped out of the car and fell again. I brushed off the snow as quickly as I could and listened to the silence.

Back in the car, I started the engine and turned the heater on high. I was spreading the wettest of my clothes out over the tops of the seat when it occurred to me that I could be completely buried in snow in a few hours.

At least Jack London's fictional fools had died in the wild many miles from human habitation in temperatures well below zero. How humiliating it would be to be found dead of exposure in the settled and comparatively temperate state of Colorado! Men in the nineteenth century, even in our own, had eaten their sled dogs in search of the Pole. So, I scolded myself, what was wrong with my mind that I was thinking panicky thoughts, imagining my death and ready to give up the ghost in a June blizzard only a few miles from grassy fruit orchards buried in cherry blossom petals? I tried to remember the name of the grandson in Thomas Mann's novel, *Buddenbrooks*, so pampered, so beleaguered, so overwrought that he died of a toothache? Before I would allow it to come to that, I would manage to get the car free, somehow, and drive it, even if it tumbled over the edge of the canyon. Better to be thought the victim of a tragic accident than be discovered dead in a car with bald tires, looking like a frozen plucked chicken in a wet sleeping bag. There was a point between the middle of my ears, a microscopically small speaker from which I thought I could hear the sound of my dad's laughter. Then the wave of panic passed. I removed my socks and put them on the dashboard. My feet were the color of strawberry ice cream. Rubbing them, I lit a cigarette. I had gas and damp newspapers. Somewhere in the forest was burnable wood. Up there somewhere would be an overhanging rock. Would I ever find a sheltered place in such a furious, blinding blizzard? How long would daylight last? I had lost all track of time and my broken watch offered no reliable guidance.

Something dark moved behind me. I jumped, honked the horn, flung open the door and ran barefoot through the snow, shouting and waving my arms like semaphores. A Ford Bronco passed me by, slowed and stopped fifty feet ahead. I stopped too, expecting the driver to back up. When the Bronco stayed put, I sprinted toward it, a madman, my bare feet burning in the slushy snow.

I appeared on the driver's side.

"I'm stuck in the snow," I shouted. A dead blank behind mirrored sunglasses, the driver's face nonetheless managed to register only an impatient disgust. Worried that he might drive off, I got one hand on the door handle and the other on his closed window. "I know I look stupid. My clothes got wet. I'm normal."

The driver gunned his engine slightly.

"I'm stuck down there," I repeated. "My tires are bald and I can't get out of the snow."

He rolled down his window as if to afford me a look at myself in his shiny glasses. I saw Irene's painting of me and stamped my foot as if to erase, forcefully, the panicky clown, the pink, wide-eyed, blond-stubbled refugee from a loony bin.

The man looked at his watch. Lowering the volume of the music, he flinched and said, "Hurry up!"

I ran back to the car, grabbed socks and boots and an armload of what was nearest, then staggered for the Bronco. Halfway there, I stopped, felt for my wallet and laughed. Who said I didn't learn from experience? I was still laughing when I got into the Bronco. With a contemptuous sneer, the driver adjusted the speed of his windshield wipers.

"Boy, am I glad to see you," I said, gushing. "Thanks for stopping."

He gunned the engine and the Bronco went sledding over the pavement. He shifted gears with an angry forcefulness and worked the steering wheel hard. I held on to my locked door as he raced through the deep snow, skidding and counter skidding, climbing and descending.

He didn't bother to look at me again, but barked, "Where you headed?"

His question sounded like a challenge to my right to go anywhere at all. I told myself that I should be grateful, but I felt humiliated. "Paonia."

"Shit."

I wondered if he meant this as a response to my destination, an assessment of my character, or an expression of frustration that in the heavy snow the Bronco had yet again refused to instantly obey his will. We skidded toward a guardrail. I reached for the dashboard, as though hanging on to it might make it possible for me to survive a rocky drop of fifteen hundred feet. When the Bronco roared back onto the pavement, the driver tossed his silver shades on the seat. He was thirtyish, sunburned, with arrogant little blue eyes, thin lips, perfect teeth. Just as I was about to suggest a reduction in speed, he cranked up the volume of his music and set little muscles in his neck and jaw twitching.

"Goodbye Mom, it's hard to die,
When all the birds are singing in the sky."

I had long ago decided that I wanted a particular Bach fugue played at my funeral. Now, via karma that Rhonda had warned me about, this hollow-headed ski jock had been sent to mock my grandiosity. We schussed through a foot and a half of slush, skidding first toward the vast hole over the river and then toward the rocky walls and snow-covered trees, power gliding down the mesa at breakneck speed.

"We had joy, we had fun,
We had seasons in the sun . . . ."

He rammed the Bronco into a lower gear and watched calculatingly as it drifted toward a giant boulder.

"My tires had no tread left," I said, searching for an improved connection to the man at the wheel.

He sneered, grunted, and upped the volume.

"Goodbye Pa, it's hard to die
With all the birdies singing in the sky."

In a sudden rage I decided that the next time he looked at me with such contempt, I would hit him in the jaw as hard as I could. If we left the road, I would jump across the seat and go down pounding him until the sharp rocks below put an end to both of us. Nancy Sinatra seemed supportive of my decision.

"These boots are made for walkin'
And that's just what they'll do
One of these days these boots
Are gonna walk all over you."

The Bronco skidded. The tires grabbed and the car jumped back toward the middle of the pavement, missing a tree by a few inches.

I'd rubbed some feeling into my pink hands and decided that though hitting him would be the thing to do if he drove off the road and we started the long fall to the river below, I wasn't going to hit him otherwise until he stopped. And it seemed imperative that until we did, I never again show anxiety or fear. If we died, I would use whatever influence I might have garnered in my recent incarnation to convince the gods that my killer deserved great enduring supernatural pain prior to and throughout his next life. I put my bare feet up on his dashboard, daring him to ask me to remove them. I decided he probably wouldn't do this for fear it might lead to conversation. The road finally began descending, seemed to widen and become a little straighter. The snowflakes had become smaller, less wind-driven. My voice surprised me.

"You must really miss skiing now that the slopes have closed for the season."

The driver grunted. His fingers were on automatic wiggle and the muscles along his jaw were working incessantly.

"The gods have just sent me a message," I continued.

He looked at me and twitched.

"If we die on this mountain in your Bronco," I said, "I will be reborn as a downhill Austrian skiing champion. But since you're behind the wheel, you won't fare so well. A clairvoyant friend told me she knows for a fact that amphetamine users killed in car wrecks are invariably reborn as cockroaches."

The driver shivered. The dry corners of his mouth gave way as he smiled to himself and I was still talking.

"Not cockroaches in Aspen, who live off prime rib fat and drink what they find at the bottoms of brandy snifters, either. Cockroaches in poor countries. Haiti or sub-Saharan Africa."

Patches of wet pavement began appearing on the road. The driver was slowing down, either because he didn't like cockroaches and didn't want to become one, or to pull over and demand the fight his nervous system seemed to crave. I was pulling my wet socks back on and reaching for my boots in the knowledge that he wouldn't move on me until he'd stopped the Bronco. He slowed and twitched and reached for a flask, some kind of sheepskin-looking sack.

I could feel the heat of his beverage from where I sat tying my bootlaces. He replaced the cap, started to screw it back, then extended it to me. "Fuckin' cockroaches eat everything man."

I gulped his brandy and laughed. The snow had turned to drizzle. Ahead and below was a wide, flat, rainy expanse of wet green. We approached a major intersection. I saw a few buildings. A highway snowplow going the opposite direction started up the canyon.

The driver twitched again. "Fuckin' cockroaches make my skin crawl."

I handed him back the flask. The road straightened and the land, green, wet, with a very gray sky, opened out before us. Old pickups were cruising down the road we were approaching, then a solitary school bus. The ski jock blinked and looked troubled. There was no contempt when he looked over at me and he used a turn signal when he pulled over to pass the school bus.

We rode in silence for a time and then he slowed and came to a stop. "Paonia's a half a mile down that road," he said. "Here's where we part company."

"Obliged," I said. The rain, hard and steady, soaked me again. I looked back at the driver. He reached across to close the door as I stretched to do likewise, expecting one last exchange. The Bronco's headlights came on and it jumped forward, spraying me with gravel and puddle ice, roaring down the road, away, maybe, from the cockroaches.

Hatless, my watch broken, and my knee bruised, I shouldered my knapsack, stuffed my hands in the damp pockets of my army field jacket, and took the muddied road downhill from the highway into Paonia. My knapsack and jacket absorbed the cold weight of the steady rain, yet compared with the snowy canyon, the air was warmer and brighter here. Rain ran down the back of my neck and flittered in the marshy fields. The untended yards at the edge of town smelled of weeds and wildflowers and little buds of fruit-to-be. A small tin containing lead fishing weights rattled in my pocket as I walked. Soaked, my feet squished in waterlogged boots.

The freezing gale, the huge sudden blowing snowflakes, and the too-soon-accumulated snowdrifts over the top of the Chevy's hubcaps receded like yesterday's hallucinations. Tucked away somewhere, maybe in a damp pocket in my backpack, was a phone number and a street address. Not that they would necessarily be current. Dom was ebullient and overwhelming, so I felt sure that even if the number had been disconnected or the address relocated by now, if I could locate the hub of nighttime social activity in Paonia, he would sooner or later show up, or already be there holding forth. At the edge of town were rows of jeeps with ski racks. Pickups, mud-spattered and angle-parked in front of wet, dimly lit buildings, were guarded by big dogs that sat on their haunches and barked as I walked past.

Fixed to the wooden outer walls of shops were wet posters announcing theatrical performances, rock concerts, and church suppers. The prints were mostly homemade or silkscreens, a year or two old, stained and curling at the edges. The town air smelled of burning, soggy wood. A woman about sixty, wearing a thick yellow sweater, looked up from her book out the window as I passed the library. A man in a checked shirt with a blond ponytail emerged from the Hotchkiss Co-Op. He dumped a heavy saddle on the tailgate of his GMC pickup, rolled it back toward the cab, and flashed me the ubiquitous V-sign.

I nodded. "Is there a pay phone in there?"

"Yup, but it's out of order."

"Know of one anywhere close?"

"Well, the most reliable one would probably be over at Pat's Pantry House."

"Pat's Pantry?"

"Those winds blew the damned sign down last week. But if you go on down to the end of the block there and hang a right, you'll see a winking neon thingmajig in the window."

"Thanks.

"Gotcherself a little moisturizing did you?"

"Yeah, got my car stuck in spring snow up the canyon. Do you happen to know a guy named Dominic Sospiri?"

The man closed the tailgate of his truck, rubbed his hands together, and methodically kicked the toes of his new boots against the bumper. He rubbed his nose and looked at me closely. "I can't say so, though I might pick him out of a group. He that guy from Brooklyn? Bearded with sort of reddish hair, talks nonstop about baseball and real estate, laughs and smokes a little too much reefer?"

"That's the guy."

"Friend of yours a long time?"

"What?"

"Way you asked, I figured you for somebody'd known him quite a while."

"Long enough, I guess. Why?"

"Curious is all. You know, some cats, the more they talk, the more they interest people. Then at a certain point the interest of others seems to make 'em nervous and they hunker down. I heard he works for some group of rich real estate investors and wouldn't mind an introduction. I got some land I ain't doing nothing with and wouldn't mind a conversation. Maybe talk to him about what he's looking for."

I didn't think of Dom as a "cat." In fact, I didn't know many people who referred to other people as "cats;" "dude" at that point was futuristic. The boots on the guy's feet, which he kept scraping on the bumper of his truck, looked wrong somehow. I shook off my umpteenth surge of paranoia that day and looked with a shiver in the direction of Pat's Pantry. "What's your name? I'll tell Dom you were helpful. Maybe we can hook up some time. Or maybe you and Dom can, anyway."

"Cool. I'm Mike McKinley. Great-great-nephew a bunch removed from the ex-president. What's yours?"

"Tim Barlow." When I offered my hand, he made some kind of fancy motion with it.

He was hip, but I was cold and suddenly interested in being dry and eating food. "Thanks for your help, Mike."

The rain had become a thin drizzle and a little wedge of blue was opening up in the sky north of town. I walked slower, noting the sheets of weathered plywood over many windows. I considered Mike's penmanship on the blank side of the card he had given me and, turning it over, considered the card's origins. "Sherman's Security Systems, Sherman Grantison, Crested Butte, Colorado." I flipped the business card into a nearby trashcan and hurried toward Pat's.

The first bit of bright color I saw in the dingy town was a luminous rendering of a martini glass winking and dumping, then reacquiring its contents again and again. A hand-drawn sign on the door read, "Pat's Pantry House, Burgers, Beer, Bar."

The opening of the door triggered an old cowbell. Greeted by a wall of warm wood heat, the snapping and popping of a recently tended fireplace, and the aroma of charring meat, I had the sense of having left my troubles behind on the mesa and crossed the threshold into outermost heaven. Though I could see the welcome bathroom door at the end of a hall, I stood soggy and dripping a moment, soaking up the heat from the fireplace, feeling my blood jump toward the warmth of the blaze, sorting smells of bacon, chicken, and maybe biscuits or bread. Half a dozen scattered customers looked up from their coffee or beer. A small vapor of steam issued from my wet coat. A skinny old man winked at me before turning back to a slab of uneaten pie. Two men in sheepskin-lined coats sat at a bar sipping tap beer from promotional glasses. They nodded at me, then went back discussing the doings of a local named Wally.

A woman stooping over the illuminated window in a jukebox straightened up, turned, put her hands on her hips, and smiled at me. Conscious of dripping on the probably recently mopped wooden floor and trying not to shiver, I took a few steps toward her. "Somebody told me there was a pay phone in here."

"Back in the little alcove on the way to the kitchen."

I had the sense of being in a country where many women spent a lot of time cleaning floors. Men who undid those chores, especially well-meaning strangers, ought to notice what they'd done and offer amusing, if not altogether sincere, apologies. "I brought my own pond."

"I see that." She flashed me an accepting smile and looked at my feet. "And a little gluey acreage under your ruined boots."

While I headed for the bathroom, she turned back to the jukebox. The coins registered and I heard the click and whir of her selections.

The bathroom door was stenciled with a cowboy hat and mustache reminiscent of the Spanish painter Juan Miró. As a soap dispenser started working its magic on days of fishing dirt and streaks of mud, I heard Neil Young singing about a yellow moon on the rise. I rubbed my soaked head with paper towels that left shreds of paper in my hair. I was at the mirror trying to comb out this papery residue when somebody knocked at the door. Unable to understand why it was necessary to knock on an unlocked bathroom door, I growled, "I'll be out in a minute." The door opened slightly and a thick white cotton towel waved at me from the end of a forearm.

Recognizing the bracelet on the wrist of the jukebox woman, I said, "Thank you very much."

"You're very welcome."

I was looking forward to eating, to depositing the demanded quarters in the pay phone and speaking to my daughter and sitting by the fire till my socks and feet began to dry. With any luck at all, there would be time to admire the jukebox woman while I sat eating and waiting for Dom to appear and take me to his house.

Groping in my wet pack for a marginally drier shirt, I found one, buttoned it, and went for the phone. I dialed Dom's soggy number, hung up after twenty rings, then carried my gear to an empty table in front of the fireplace. The blaze had been built up again. Closing my eyes I faced the heat of the fire until my cheekbones tingled. When I opened my eyes, the woman was putting coffee on the table. I swallowed a fierce surge of gratitude. "Thanks."

"I don't want to say you look like an escapee from hell," she said, "knowing the same might be said of me. But you look tired and mad." She placed a tarnished pewter pitcher of cream on the table and scooted a sugar dispenser toward me. "Mad in the sense of being pissed, I mean."

There was an appealing softness to her. Trying to take her in, read her intentions, still moved by her kindness in providing the towel, the coffee, the brighter fire, and the smile, I fumbled for a suitable response. "You should apply for town therapist."

"Well, to hear me talk, you'd think I was considering it, wouldn't you?" She laughed. "I'm not always this forward or curious, or this slow to give my name. I'm Molly." I accepted her hand.

She was tall and thin, older, maybe a little. Her face was a pale, slightly feral triangle at the heart of a recalcitrant mane of curly raven-black hair. Her brown eyes, red with reflected light from the fireplace, looked at me with an amused expression. I thought I saw an anger in her, tinged with sadness. When she caught me noticing what another might have overlooked, her full, almost sullen lips parted in a surprised smile, shutting out if not banishing her darkness. Maybe she smiled because she caught me gawking at the slender length of her neck and the low-slung shapely breasts behind the camisole under her white blouse. In any case, holding on to her hand too long, I embarrassed us both and deliberately pushed my chair back to make its legs squawk on the wooden floor. "Mine's Tim Barlow," I said, "and you're right, Doctor Molly. It has been one long and trying day. Days, in point of fact."

"Yeah, you don't look like somebody whose troubles are only a day old, Tim."

"I lost my car this afternoon in a blizzard up on the mesa."

"Lost it?"

"Stranded it in a foot and a half of snow's more like it, I guess."

"Yeah. Hell of a freak storm up there, we heard. Did you have to hitchhike down?

"I finally got a ride with some drunk meth freak. He almost drove us off the road about seven or eight times, then dropped me off at the edge of town."

"Poor baby."

"You always mock your customers?"

"*I* don't have any customers."

"You mean you don't work here?"

"Wait. Could we backtrack? You thought I was being sarcastic, just now? I think that was the beginning of our misunderstanding. I answered you too sharply. It's been a crazy day for me, too. I'm sorry. I overreacted when it occurred to me that you were humoring me, waiting for me to take your order."

"Okay. Fair enough. Please sit."

"I can't just now because I've got a couple of things to do behind the bar. See, I kind of do work here and kind of don't." She flashed a smile. "Sorta."

"I'm a little confused."

"Me, too. What I'm trying to tell you is that on any other afternoon someone named Karen would have greeted you at the door and told you right off that the lunch rush was over and the dinner rush had not yet begun. Karen couldn't come in today, so I came over to help with lunch. The lunch rush ends at two. Now it's dinner and I'm still here."

I smelled meat and good food in the kitchen and, giving her what I hoped was a devilish grin, showed her my broken watch. "It's still pretty close to two."

She laughed. "The clock we go by says it's four. That's basically the start of dinner you're smelling. Special discounts if you order before five.

"So you're off duty now, just kind of hanging around to play the jukebox and disappoint any poor wet pilgrim who happens by in search of a cheeseburger, is that it?"

"Okay, Poor Pilgrim" she laughed, "you go back to the kitchen, tell Mitch about your car, and ask him if he's willing to grill you a cheeseburger and ring the bell when it's done. I'll take care of my business at the bar, fetch you a cold beer if you want one, and traipse back to the kitchen if and when Mitch agrees to cook."

"Thank you, Molly. I'll go talk to Mitch, whoever and wherever he is."

"He's my father-in-law and he's in the kitchen."

"Okay, I will ask your father-in-law Mitch to make me some food, Molly. A beer, if you're still willing to bring one, would be a treat. A real treat."

"Are we getting our signals crossed a little again?"

"No." I insisted. "We think only the best of each other and know that each of us has had a hard day. We understand that any and all little misunderstandings arising or dissipating probably have to do with the bad weather."

"Electromagnetic disturbance in the atmosphere?"

"Something like that."

"It's partly my fault for being forward and anxious and teasing you a little." She looked expectantly at me.

"And partly mine for. . . "

"I don't know. Maybe just walking in today. Now rather than earlier."

"This conversation was easier when I thought you were a bored waitress, flirting for tip money."

"It'll probably get easier again once you've had some food, assuming you can persuade Mitch to cook something other than a big dinner on the dinner menu." She started toward the bar, but turned before she got there. "Mitch is thataway."

I was on my feet. "So am I."

In the kitchen a florid man with a bald head was scraping down the grill. "Are you Mitch?"

"Last fifty-four years."

"Molly sent me. Can I get you to make me a cheeseburger with all the trimmings?"

"She's here extra for me, so yeah. Anybody Molly wants me to feed today, I take it as an order. How you want it cooked?"

I provided him with the particulars and rummaged through my pockets. "I don't suppose you've got change for the telephone."

"Local?"

"Local and long distance, alas."

"You'll want to go back to the register and ask Molly. If she's shy of coins tell her there's three rolls of quarters under the counter near the shot glasses."

I traded Molly damp paper bills for a fistful of coins and went back to the pay phone. Dom still didn't answer, so I dialed home. Serena picked up on the first ring.

"Hello," she said, her subdued voice filled with pride at her growing telephone skills.

"Hi Serena, it's Dad."

"Hi, Daddy."

"How are you?"

"Fine."

"Do you miss me?

"Yes."

"Let me talk to your mom."

"She said I can't bisturb her. She's taking a nap and said not to knock or come in or talk to her."

"What are you doing?"

"Fine."

"No. What. I asked you *what* you were doing."

"Taking a nap."

"You don't sound sleepy."

"Mommy and Gerald are getting up at four-flirty."

"Mommy and Gerald are taking a nap?"

398

"Yes. They said if I don't make any noise or come in the room they're going to take me for ice cream when they get up."

My throat constricted and my breath wouldn't come. I made a couple of strange noises and managed to speak again. "I've got to go, Serena."

"Okay. Bye."

"Love you."

"Love you, too. Bye."

As I was hanging up I heard a faint, alarmed voice, unmistakably Irene's. In the kitchen my burger sizzled. A voice on the radio near the grill was shouting out lists of local appliance store bargains. Outside a car door slammed. Steel guitar strings introduced a Jerry Garcia complaint. I took a back corridor to the bathroom, closed myself into a stall, sat on the seat and, hands shaking, lit a cigarette. When it began to burn my fingers, I threw the butt down the toilet and went back to the phone. I dialed information for Gerald's number in Denver. His phone rang and rang. I went back to the bathroom, opened the window for some cold, fresh air, and smoked another cigarette, listening to the rattle of rainwater in the gutter on the roof.

Numb, I returned to the table. Molly sat sidesaddle in a wooden chair, curling her bare feet in front of the fire and sipping a beer of her own from a heavy glass mug. My cheeseburger was on the table, at the base of a mountain of french fries. A frosty mug of beer glimmered in firelight. The dry wood in the fireplace sparked and snapped. My stomach was in an uproar. I slumped into my chair and put my hands flat on the table and looked down at them as if to stop them from shaking.

We sat in silence for a while for a long time.

"I'll clear it all away if you want," she said.

I reached for my beer and managed a gulp without spilling any.

"My mom used to say the best way to get your hands to stop shaking was to cease biting your tongue. Course, we were female and nobody ever told us to take it like a man."

"Huh?"

"She claimed that unsaid words got jammed up in the hands and caused the shakes," Molly shrugged. "I see you've had some bad news. Maybe I should disappear for a while."

"I phoned home just now and found out that the mother of my kids was in bed with another man."

"Oh, God! I'm so sorry."

"I was jealous of her friendship with the guy, but expected that she would get over it. Now I feel stupid for refusing to consider that she might actually have sex with him."

"She told you this over the phone? How cruel."

"She didn't tell me anything. My five-year-old daughter answered the phone and said they were taking a nap. Just before I hung up, I heard Irene's voice asking my daughter who was on the phone."

"You didn't actually talk to Irene?"

I shook my head. "I would have called back, but from the sound of her voice, Irene's voice, I felt no need. It's like being hit in the stomach, I guess." My hands needed activity. I picked up french fries and tossed them one by one into the fire, then watched them twist and burn like dying worms. "I can't believe I'm telling you all this. You must think I'm an incredible chump."

"I don't."

"I guess maybe I hoped you'd point out the flimsiness of my evidence."

"I'd like to, but I can't. I have a cousin in New York, a marriage counselor and a therapist who claims that a key difference between suspicion and knowledge is that suspicion produces rage or terror, and knowledge produces a biological reaction."

"I'm sorry. I'm not following you very well."

She leaned toward me and spoke quietly. "There's a recent context, unfortunately. Two weeks ago, I learned my husband had been balling my younger sister for two years."

The fire snapped.

"Nine days ago they both disappeared."

"Disappeared?"

"Vanished. She has some adobe house outside Taos. She doesn't have a phone there. Just a waterbed and a big record collection."

"Mitch, who cooked this cheeseburger? That would be his son?"

"Mitch and Patricia Turnquist, proud owners of Pat's Pantry House, thirty-five years of marital fidelity, they say. Long-suffering mother and father of Peter Turnquist. Esteemed in-laws of Molly Turnquist."

I lit a cigarette and looked at my smoking hand till it steadied some. "I'm surprised you'd ever walk back in here."

"I'm the daughter they never had. For years I've been closer to them than Peter has. Sweet substitute parents, both of them. Are you going to manage to eat something of that cheeseburger?"

"I don't think I can."

"Maybe I'll go out to the kitchen and bring back something to wrap it up in."

I shook my head and she glanced around to make sure no one was looking, then lobbed it in the fire. "Don't mind me. I try to make things a little nicer for Mitch these days. I'd like him to think you ate it with gusto." The flames consumed what I couldn't.

"Would you like my company for a while yet, Tim?"

"Yes."

"Okay, let's make a little plan. Pat is going to come in the back door for the dinner rush any minute. The best thing I could do right now would be go to the kitchen and cheer Mitch up and stay to say hello to Pat. Just around the block there's this place called the Hotchkiss Co-op. I could meet you there in fifteen minutes."

Outside the rain had stopped and the sky cleared. The air was chilled and breezy, but sweet with the smell of pungent growing things. In front of the co-op I dried the wooden bench with a sweater from my knapsack. A swarm of birds rioted in a nearby cottonwood. Three young boys and a girl pumped down the street on bikes, splashing through the deepest puddles they could find.

I remembered the day when I'd taken Thunderhead's pistol, deposited it in a lunch bag, and put it in a truckload of tree branches and soot, burying it in a deep stinky mass of garbage in the city dump. I wondered if I could dredge it up, covered with shit and sludge and fat, wait outside Gerald's apartment, fit its slender, filth-coated muzzle into his mouth, and shoot the rancid rot into his brain and out the back of his head. Different bullets would make different messes. I thought of JFK's spattered head and the rabbit my grandpa had blasted to bloody meat on the hillside many years ago. Irene's life would be spared because of Serena and Matt, and because, one day she would come undone with the realization that no man would ever love her like I might have managed to do, once circumstances improved a little.

I encountered special problems thinking about Irene's suffering, though, realizing that I'd been resentful, that I'd ignored a hundred signals, rebuffed her and put her off. Had I failed her into betraying me? It wasn't long before it became impossible to keep separate the pain I wanted her to feel from the pain and guilt of wanting her to feel it. I closed my eyes until I thought I could hear her small voice calling and calling my name and the splashing of the bikes in the street suggested the sounds her small hands might make in a flood, paddling with the current, drifting away from me.

I got up and walked up and down the street. Like it or not, I was free. Like it or not, I was not free. Irene had tried to set me free the only way she could. No, that was giving her too much credit. She had thought only of herself. Not Serena, not Matt, not me. She wanted to hurt me. Irene

401

had planned my agony down to details and then carefully set it in motion. She had more strength and wisdom and faith than I did. We needed to be apart. I needed to leave her and there was only one way she could think of to make me leave. Well, she could get on with her life, get on with Gerald if she wanted to, but I would take the kids. The kids were mine. They would go with me. Wherever I went.

Where the hell was Dom? Dom, of course, would say, or maybe have the grace to refrain from saying, at least for a while, that he'd seen it all coming and tried to warn me. Sooner or later, he'd get on my case about Tessa and tell me to stop feeling sorry for myself. He'd predict that I'd have gotten to Tessa before Irene got to Gerald if Bill hadn't been busted and if Tessa hadn't left for Buffalo. He'd say I should have treated Irene better, that it was too bad about the kids, that I should go back and kick Gerald's ass while Irene watched, and then with or without her and the kids, come back to Paonia where we could fish most of the summer and he could tell me what to do with my life. He'd be full of ideas about what I should do and tell me how we could get plenty of nooky in Grand Junction or Crested Butte. He'd fire up a joint, talk about the Funny Farm, go on about the wreckage of the Ford and the deaths of the Mexican migrant workers, about lying up there on the Berkeley hillside smelling his own fart and knowing he was alive, strolling down to the pavement, looking at all that wreckage, the migrant worker blood, dripping through the torn metal car doors, the police looking on, studying his shocked facial expression. He'd probably even recite his favorite line of T. S. Eliot's. "Wipe your hand across your mouth, and laugh; the worlds revolve like ancient women gathering fuel in vacant lots."

The sun was setting. The kids were pedaling away from me, home to dinner maybe.

I was standing in the mud with my mouth open, making wounded noises, trying to establish ethereal contact with the Zorba, the Zen Master, the Funny Farm Therapist within. I was emitting little animal moans and trying to laugh when a strange car slowed under a streetlamp and honked. Desperately afraid she'd seen me acting strangely, I misled Molly with the impression I'd been laughing at the sight of her red Volkswagen beetle.

"Do you hate the color?"

Seeing her made me feel better. "Hate's too strong a word. It looks like a halved tomato with windows."

She smiled. "The motor's been rebuilt. The clutch and brakes are fine, but some kind of strange problem makes it cold as hell in winter. Of course, it's not exactly a professional paint job, I have to admit that."

"Hand-painted? With fingernail polish?"

She laughed. "I used two hardware store brushes. It would look less gobbed and bubbly if I had waited for another day and worked in better light. Look close, and, along with everything else, you can find a little grit adhered to the surface."

I wrestled my backpack onto the back seat, sat down in the bucket seat next to hers, and closed the door. The little Volks chugged down the main street toward the highway. "I like it better knowing that you painted it yourself."

"Peter, who is colorblind, bought it for me with his usual air of having made a decision that could not be improved on and brooked no further discussion. It used to be a horrible green. To this day, he's never commented on the fact that I painted it red."

"To this day?"

"Don't worry. He and Nadine are long gone. If they're not hunkered down without a phone near Taos, I'd guess the Caribbean. Maybe South America. Some place where drug arrests are few and far between."

"Ah. Drug problems?"

"That's a long story and will keep a while, I guess."

The red Volks was heading into a pink sunset.

"Where we going?"

"Anywhere you'd like."

"Anywhere?"

"Well, my neighbors, Amy and Dirk, are out of town. For three days I have responsibilities. Dogs to feed. After that. . . ." She let go of the steering wheel and wagged her arms as if they were wings.

"After that?"

"I'm free."

"What about now?"

"I'm almost free now."

"I mean going now."

"Well, we could go out drinking and spend a whole bunch of money maybe neither of us really wants to spend. I have a nice big house all to myself on the edge of those mountains over there. You probably want to start with a bath, change to dry clothes, anything you wanted from Peter's closet. Tomorrow we can go for your car if you like. Of course, you might have, I don't know, some other destination. You might also think I'm crazy."

She seemed supernaturally beautiful, an angel sent to talk me through a nightmare. "Molly, there's no place I'd rather go. Nobody I'd rather be with."

"You know why I'm so happy to hear you say that?"

"Why?"

She laughed nervously. "Suddenly, I'm scared to say it."

"Take my example. Just blurt it out."

She pulled over to the side of the road and parked in front of an assembly of rusty mailboxes. The little engine behind us coughed and went quiet. A horse in a field a hundred feet away considered us momentarily, then lowered its head in the wet grasses. The evening was very still.

"When I came down here today, I had a premonition. I knew I was going to meet you. Not somebody like you, either. You."

"I'm lost."

"I know. We both are. Maybe that's the point."

"It's strange," I said. "Peter, Irene, the whole business."

"Whether or not you go in for this sort of premonition, I want to reassure you that I have never, ever done what I'm doing now. I'm not in much better shape than you are emotionally, but I feel safe with you. On the basis of my premonition, or whatever you want to call it, I'm sure I won't regret taking you home."

She started the Volks, steered it up on the pavement, and when she shifted into fourth gear, reached for my hand. We looked longingly at each other, felt a bump, and the Volks headed off the road toward a rail fence. She mad a little cry of alarm, flung my hand away, yanked the wheel, and got us back on the road. We laughed together and felt good. The silence that followed was softer.

After a while I said, "I'm thinking about my car. Do you, does Peter have any tire chains?"

"We can look around. But to tell you the truth, I don't think we'll need them. It's supposed to be sunny and warm tomorrow."

Molly lived in an octagon-shaped house constructed principally of planed railroad ties and large timbers that Peter had scrounged from abandoned mines in the area. His first significant drug deal, at least the first Molly knew of, had been with a pair of contractors building ski condos in Snowmass. Peter provided them with quantities of pot and coke, they sent him over drivers with cement mixers and flatbed trucks with cranes. On an elevated circle of rocks and concrete, architects and woodworkers had started from what looked like some Lincoln Log fantasy and ended up with a hippie space station. Hidden from the driveway was a greenhouse Molly called her "legal herb garden." Eventually she led me to a bathroom dominated by a tureen-shaped tub inlaid with marble pilfered from nearby mines and a huge hot water heater, custom-painted with multicolored cosmic eyeballs by one of Peter's artist customers.

"It gets pretty steamy in there," Molly said, "so if you're planning to shave you might want to do that first and take your bath later."

Clean, shaved, warm, and dry, I met her in the kitchen and accepted a glass of red wine. The fireplace was bright and there was a smell of food. Somehow she looked different, too, more beautiful, shy and anxious. "Hello, Stranger."

All I could manage was, "Smells good." More smiling and mooning. "Anything I can do for you?"

"Just come over here. Crowd me a little."

"A nice idea. What's cooking?"

"Chapattis, chicken soup with veggies. There's cheese, some pear chutney, more wine. I don't know."

"You've been crying," I observed.

"Good crying." She let go of a pot handle in a big hurry. "Shit!"

"You burned yourself?"

"Almost."

"I really have to thank you for this, Molly."

"No. I mean, I wish you wouldn't. I wish . . . "

"I'd just shut up?"

"No. I just wish you'd understand."

"I wish I would, too."

"Maybe we could just kind of stay close to each other without talking for a while. There's a lot to say, I know. But I just want to be quiet with you, just stay close, kind of underfoot."

I hugged her until the soup boiled and the first batch of chapattis burned. She lit candles and put them on the table. We moved our chairs close and sat hip to hip. I ate three bowls of soup and went out to the porch for more firewood.

The candles were moved to a table in front of the couch. We ate homemade pear chutney on chapatti, sipped one of Peter's rare brandies, and sat watching the flames and coals in the fireplace. Irene, Serena, Matt, Dom, the car, and the blizzard seemed a long way off. An owl hooted in the trees behind the house.

I'm tempted to conclude that the best moments in a human life are lived and cherished from within giant, gravity-defying bubbles. When you're inside, adrift in the promising air, you can't see the cold, sharp, encroaching world. Too many of these, too much inside bliss, and you begin to doubt that the world can be all that encroaching, cold, or sharp.

Later that night the nearly full moon climbed over a skylight and poured a pearly white light on a night-blue bedspread. Breathing irregularly, as if I was somehow lifting and lowering the weight of its dusty light with the muscles of my chest, I opened my eyes. A stranger's long hand was draped over my forearm.

I remembered the scent of Serena's freshly washed hair, the milky almost floral smell of my son's laugh, and supposed that the invisible weight on my chest was the understanding that for the first time in their short lives my children's lives were diverging from my own. Because of what I'd done and not done, said and considered silently, they were already drifting off in confusion, uncertain and displaced in ways they would not be able to understand or characterize for years, if ever. They had flourished for a time, but now, rather than grow slowly, simply, and painlessly into themselves, they would be shoved and buffeted by complicated events and adults who feared to say too much about those events. I sensed the price the kids would pay for my mistakes and saw too well what lay ahead for Irene and for me. Our lives were uprooted, our shelter sunk in a sand of memory and possibility. Ahead were years of Tarot cards, canceled plans and recitations, middle-of-the-night lists of intricate tasks fated to go badly wrong in the lives of unprotected children. In ways we never had before, Irene and I would wrestle in the dark with shapes we could not name. Innocence had fierce, unpredictable enemies. We would try to fight them in the blackness, at distances measured in miles.

What was the name of this inner voice in me, the voice drunk on rancor, set on judgment, telling me that I was justified, innocent, unfairly punished? It was a voice given to moments of lucidity, ursine grunts, and swallowed howls of pain; it was stern and harsh and filled with puritanical rage at the very suggestion of human need and weakness. It tried to pass itself off as a conscience, but it was not a conscience. It was a hungry, roaring animal king, a regal ape with bloody incisors. Every wronged self-serving liar in the world had a voice like this to listen to, and horrible things happened to those who listened too well and too long. I wanted to jump from my body, but I didn't see how I could manage this with this woman so still beside me.

Molly was the color of chalk. I saw a wet streak under both closed eyes, a dark spot on her pillow. Her voice made me jump. "Do you think I'm a slut?"

Memory and sorrow vanished temporarily, and I turned into the wronged ape king again, tumescent, and filled with animal ardor and the wish that Molly would put on silken midnight blue panties, red, waxy lipstick, green eye shadow, heavy perfume. She had given me more pleasure and more forgetting than I had known maybe ever, but now I hoped for her to move her hands over me, bite, whimper of unendurable desire, block out all thought and memory. "No." I sighed. "I do not think you're a slut."

"Would Irene think I was a slut for having sex within twelve, say fifteen hours of meeting a man I picked up in a bar?"

"Was that who you were crying for? Irene?"

"Probably not."

I laughed bitterly. "Right now she'd probably feel grateful that we'd made love. I think she'd favor any woman who could relieve her guilt a little. I'm just guessing, though. She has women friends who don't like men much. She might be filled with a sense of entitlement."

Molly frowned and wrinkled her forehead.

"What would the word 'slut' mean to Peter, assuming he knew it referred to you?"

"It would mean," she said, trembling in my arms, "that I was more like my sister Nadine than he ever dreamed."

"You'd like him to think that, wouldn't you?"

"Not only that, I'd love it for him to listen to all the steamy details of the night I discovered it was true." She laughed, then started crying again.

I pulled her face to my shoulder. Her tears warmed my bare arm. I stroked her silken, curly hair.

"I was faithful to him for nine years, almost ten." She sat up for a better view of me. "You're the first person I've slept with since we got married."

"I believe you. I understand. I'm grateful."

She looked at me again, probing without speaking. When the tension reached a certain level, I said, "Maybe you're fishing, hoping to discover if I've been faithful to Irene?"

She nodded.

"If I say I haven't been faithful, then you'll persuade yourself you mean nothing to me. If I say, yes, I have been faithful, you'll blame yourself for wrecking my chances for reconciling with Irene. Come on now," I said gently, "put your own happiness, your own life, front and center."

"Oh, my. I'm afraid you've taken me for someone more saintly and less selfless than I am, Tim. You will do what you will do, but I won't encourage you to go back to her. I couldn't bring myself to do that even if I thought you should. I will stay out. Way out."

"I have been faithful, but only barely, and more for a lack of convenient opportunities than anything else. I guess for a while now I've hoped for better opportunities. Is that what you wanted to hear? Or is my response sullied by your learning that I may be just a less successful opportunist than Peter?"

"It does spoil it a little," she admitted. "But in another way, it was the perfect answer because it persuades me that while you're around I can talk to you about things Peter would never sit still for. Most of all, though, it robs me of the moral high ground I guess I thought, till now, that I held against him."

"Meaning what?"

"I've been making myself feel better, or worse maybe, by telling myself how much I've been the wronged woman. Now I've met you, and suddenly I have to wonder if I would have tried to seduce you even if I'd met you before Peter ever got involved with Nadine, before Irene took up with Gerald. At the very least I'd like to believe I could have, but I doubt it, too. Peter was the second. You are the third man. I've never been so. . . I don't know. I just never knew it could be like that."

"Neither did I." This was true and I hoped to persuade her of my honesty with a kiss. When she trembled and moved slightly away and stroked my face, it occurred to me that what she wanted more than anything right then was just to go on hearing my voice in the house where she said she'd been betrayed. "Molly, when you said you never brought a man home before, I believed you. How could I think badly of you? You offered me healing, even though you yourself are badly bruised. I haven't doubted or backed away from anything you've said to me. Though nothing outside this room is quite as we would like it to be, this room, this moment is perfect. You were, you are, the best lover I've ever had, too."

In moonlight still pouring down through the skylight, her face glowed with a pure pleasure I'd never seen before.

"Ever?"

"Ever."

A kiss increased her happiness. This was utterly new to me, to kiss someone into a greater happiness. I kissed her again. She gasped, kicked off the covers, and rolled on top of me.

When we were wet and spent and the moon had moved away from the skylight, she arranged the blankets around us and rolled on her side. "An apprentice slut?"

I laughed and let my head fall back on the pillow. "A journeywoman," I said. "A master woman of the craft. A trollop in triumph."

408

"Now that you've made a wanton woman of me, I wish I could make a believer of you, persuade you that I knew I was going to meet you today."

"If I could manage to believe it, what would it mean to you?"

"To us."

"To us?"

She sat up and arranged the blanket around her breasts. "Nothing's certain, but it could mean a lot. Despite the painful circumstances under which we've met, our meeting *could* have some deeper significance than you've assigned it."

The owl was hooting again.

"Oh, I'm not talking about what it *does* mean or *will* mean, which is up to me and you. But if I'm right, it could mean renewal and opportunity. If I'm wrong, then it probably means there's only tonight and tomorrow, and maybe a day or two after that. And then for me, the way I feel now, fifty years of remembering that we once met in a time of sorrow that was otherwise perfect. Kind of like that Bogart movie. We'll always have Paonia."

The wind picked up and small man-made things outside made metallic sounds.

"I'm scaring you," she said, laughing. "The poor guy's heartbroken, worrying about his kids, the man he wants to murder, the woman he wants to torment, and this floozy picks him up in a bar, takes him home, feeds him, rips her clothes off, then keeps him up all night screwing and pressing him for a committed relationship. I'm sure that very common drama is playing out somewhere tonight, Tim, but not here. That's not what this is about. I will always think *something* prompted our meeting. Something more than your bald tires kept you from going wherever you thought you were going, then made sure you walked in on my life."

Having kissed her because she'd been pleased, I now kissed her again and again because she pleased me; kissing her out of simple befuddlement seemed false. As if I could take back the befuddlement, I wiped my fingertips over her full lips. "I can't fully share an experience I didn't have, Molly. But, if only because life amid chaos, retribution, and arbitrary cruelty *should* be balanced by grace and mercy, some built-in mechanism of design and redemption, if only because you've got me happily numbed under your spell, I'll do my best to believe it," I promised. "I'll make it my pleasure to enjoy doing my best."

"You make me so happy."

She kissed me, then pulled back, the vigilant lover undeceived by the tiniest equivocation. "What's the matter?"

I listened for the owl but heard only wind. In the stillness it seemed important that I make an effort to risk honesty and not conclude that much of what occurred to me was too much trouble to explain. "For me happiness comes in intense, short-lived bursts and disappears again. For a while now I've doubted that it exists in any sustainable sense. If it did exist in the sustainable sense, only the fierce or the stupid could or would do whatever's necessary to hold on to it. Maybe it's just that the only people I've met who claimed to be happy struck me as determined to see things in a self-interested way, excluding what's around them in ways I can't manage, and don't really want to. They always have to get up and turn off the television set or fold up the newspaper or pretend that injustice or cruelty are misjudgments more than anything else. It's hard to walk away less than fully satisfied from anything or anyone who once pleased us. It's hard to face the fading of anything that pleased us earlier. That's the way I understand what you said. But all I meant was that I'm very pleased, very happy you are willing to hope. Whatever endures between us, if anything ever will, won't be something static or unchanging. It won't be something we can have only if we manage to keep other people away from it."

She bunched the blankets around me and climbed from bed. There were no walls separating the bed from the kitchen. The moon now angled through a sliding glass window. She had disappeared into a pocket of darkness near the open fireplace. A wooden match, when she struck it, flared and outlined her against the window glass. A burner on the stove hissed and turned deep blue. "I'm making coffee," she said, flickering in bluish tones. "I'll carry it into the bath if you want to sleep. I'm too alive, too full of wonder with what has happened to sleep anymore."

We sat on the couch in front of the fire, wrapped ourselves in blankets, and smoked cigarettes. I had a powerful hope that I could dismantle my life as it had been and put it back together so that it moved in rhythm with Molly's life. It all seemed a matter of talking, of educating each other. The owl was back in its tree, hooting a steady encouragement to these predawn fantasies. A pale light came through the windows and, sexually sated, we were full of talk. No anxiety was too vague, no discussion quite irrelevant, no subject taboo. We were naked, trembling children lost in the forest. We were adults on the edge of immortality. We talked in autobiographical snippets. Ghosts from our pasts came and went. Irene, Gerald, Peter, Molly's traitorous sister Nadine. Parents, ancestors, children, Matt and Serena, children yet to be.

When late morning sun angled through Molly's kitchen window, it glanced off a pair of potted plants. Scents of mud and grass, of marjoram or rosemary wafted through the half-opened front door. Outside, small birds trilled competitively in a stand of apple trees bordering the driveway. A dog barked, then ceased. There were house sounds: the groaning of the washing machine, the clicking of an automatic dishwasher next to the kitchen stove, a faint hiss from the coffee warmer on a counter. I dragged a wooden rocking chair toward the kitchen phone, poured coffee in a mug from an overhead cabinet, lit a cigarette, dialed, and waited in vain for Dom to pick up.

In a bookcase across the room, inserted between *Loving and Being Loved by Your Garden Herbs* and a paperback copy of *The Hobbit*, I discovered a wooden box of maps. Unfolding the most useful one on the counter, I got my bearings and wrote on a discarded envelope directions I hoped would take us to the address Dom had mailed me: a house number on Deer Run Drive. Molly's ancient hairball of a cat hopped up on the counter to insert its head under my free hand.

Outside, I sat with my bare feet in the sun and watched Molly at a wooden table, writing furiously in a notebook.

An hour later, Molly turned the car off Deer Run Drive onto a muddy driveway. She parked the Volks behind Dom's, or rather Glen's, Land Rover, then followed me through the long grass. The house looked dark and damp, top-heavy under an accumulation of rust-colored shingles. Judging from a pile of boards, an unfinished section of siding, and a table-saw covered with a tarp, the sagging wooden porch had been under recent repairs. I banged on the door, rang the bell, and called out. Molly occupied a porch swing, making it squeak with girlish enthusiasm, while I walked around, squinting through small curtain openings into darkened rooms.

Coming up behind me, she put a hand on my shoulder. "If you want to leave him a note with my phone number, there's probably an old pencil in my glove box."

Molly's Volks probably couldn't push or pull my stranded station wagon from the deep snow along the canyon, so I rummaged through the unlocked Land Rover, in search of tire chains or a jumper cable. I found a small set of screwdrivers, a ratchet set, and a working flashlight, but no registration, no insurance papers, no chewing gum papers, not even a hamburger wrapper wadded up on the floor. The Dom I knew was always surrounded by disorder, so the tidiness surprised me. Given that I'd seen him lock his car when he was walking fifteen feet to a convenience store, it seemed unlike him to leave the ignition key in

Glen's expensive toy, especially if he wasn't going to be around to watch it.

"I found a stub of a pencil," Molly said."

"Oh, thanks."

"Something wrong?"

"A little strange, anyway."

"How so?"

"First of all, he's supposed to be expecting me some time this week and isn't home and doesn't leave a note. Well, okay, he can be a little forgetful, drop the details once in a while. On the other hand, Dom's a guy who leaves half-eaten sandwiches on car seats and keeps fistfuls of rubber bands on the floor so he can leave messages to himself on sun visors."

"Maybe he's been driving important clients around or something. Anyway, people tend to take care of their cars up here."

I laughed. "Digging at me about my bald tires, are you?"

"Not me. If it hadn't been for those tires I might not have met you."

"Never to my knowledge has Dom left his car unlocked."

"Well, people move up here and start to shed some of that big-city paranoia."

"Maybe, but being from Brooklyn, he has more paranoia than most to shed, believe me. He washed his car here earlier this morning, but there's no sign of him and no recent tire tracks in the driveway."

Molly laughed. "If this was the beginning of some husband and wife detective series, my line would be something like, 'My dear, whatever makes you so sure he washed it, and here, earlier this morning?'"

"His tires are clean, despite the muddy driveway so he must have hosed them off. Other than ours, there are no recent tracks in the driveway. Therefore, he washed it here and then cleaned up after himself. There are no rain streaks on the windshield, yet you told me it had been raining down here for almost three days before I arrived."

"The cheese!"

"The what?"

"Our picnic cheese is wrapped in white butcher's paper. You can leave him a note on that, and I can stuff the cheddar in some tissue in the bread bag. Anyway, maybe we can push his door open. For all we know, he could be asleep inside with the television on."

All the doors and windows were locked so I wrote him a note, leaving Molly's phone number, asking him to call. I pinched the paper in the screen door so the wind wouldn't blow it away.

Molly pulled out onto the highway and headed toward the Black Canyon and my Chevy.

"I bet the two of you will have quite a reunion dinner."

I looked at her, unready for the loss of her enchantment, not trusting the spell I was under to last. "You have other plans?"

"No, but I have lots to do around the house. I don't want to smother or mother."

"What does that mean?"

"You need time with Don. Isn't that why you originally came up here?

"Well, yeah, that and some time by myself."

She pulled up to a stop sign short of the highway and looked over at me. "Don't misunderstand me, Tim. I'd love to join you and maybe I will. I just don't want to crowd your friendships is all. Guys don't like that, I've already learned."

The sun was bright. The canyon, as we began our climb, smelled of pine and a thousand growing things I couldn't name. In such shirtsleeve weather I might have been looking out at the rock formations, the swarms of birds bubbling in and out of bushes, or monitoring the lazy drift of fluffy clouds across the Continental Divide. Instead, as the little red Volks labored up the two-lane road I brooded over the meaning of "smother or mother." At her coaxing, my guard had come down and I'd drifted into fuzzy musings about the future, thinking about how Matt and Serena would respond to her. Irene was three hundred miles away, maybe going somewhere with my kids and Gerald, while I was ascending into a neurotic hell with a beautiful woman I'd met less than twenty-four hours before. What was wrong with me or Molly or life that Molly could go from intensely intimate lover to perfect stranger on the magic carpet of a simple remark? Was I in love or just sex-starved, broken, and benighted? How had I gotten myself into this? More to the point, needy, neurotic lunatic that I clearly was, how was I going to get out? For some time, Molly had been talking blithely of how nice the weather had turned out and what she'd brought along for our lunch, leading me to realize, suddenly, that I was all alone in my derangement. "Back at Dom's you said something about not wanting to smother or mother."

"Ah," Molly nodded, "and you thought I was warning you that I would not be a stepmother?"

"Well, I know we should be a few thousand hours from any such discussion. We're crazy. Or at least, I am."

"We are crazy. But what I said referred only to you and Don."

"You keep saying Don and I keep saying Dom."

"Okay, so Dom, then. Do you feel better now?"

I sighed and laughed at myself. She looked warm and normal, happy and content. It was cooler above the valley, but a warm wind blew through the canyon. Except for a few patches around tree trunks and in the shadowy crevices between rocks, the snow was gone.

"Is that it?"

It was. The white Chevy was parked at an odd angle, smudged and streaked with a residue of dirt. Twenty-four hours? The station wagon looked like it had been there for years.

It started right up. I rocked it from first to reverse to first, and it jumped eagerly out of the mud and up onto the pavement. It was damp smelling and messy inside, hot and close from the beating sun, but it was ready to go, at my service. I parked in a drier, sunnier spot a few yards down the road. Molly nosed in behind me in the Volks. While I spread my damp sleeping bag and some damp clothes where they might dry on the roof of the station wagon and secured them with small rocks, Molly wandered up the hill with a picnic basket.

I caught up to her after a few minutes. From a rocky shelf we looked down on the ribbon of the Gunnison River. Today the waters were blue, silent under layers of wind. Far below us and yet well out over the water, a pair of hawks cruised the air currents, steering clear of the jagged, rocky walls, patrolling, pleasure-gliding through sun and gusts of changing air.

The tourist traffic on the pavement had increased, but from where we stood its sounds were lost in the warm wind. After climbing for another fifteen minutes, we came on a flat, grassy area, high and warm, bordered with toadflax and bellflowers. Sweating, I hung my shirt on a tree branch and sat down on a blanket beside Molly to feast on cold chicken, sour apples, celery, bread, olives, cheese, and the last of a berry pie. Big blue jays argued, chipmunks hopped, flies buzzed, and big, whipped-creamy clouds rode across blue sky as we shared one of the last bottles of Peter's expensive champagne. We talked, kissed, made love, and napped naked under the warm sun, at least I did, sitting up quickly when I heard a slide of loose gravel and a thump of a falling stone.

"What was that sound?" Molly asked. I was on my feet and she sat, waiting for my report.

There followed a snapping of twigs and a woof, and I saw two dogs straining against leashes, held back by one of three men. One man carried a rifle or a shotgun. Another wore a holster on his hip. The man in front looked vaguely familiar. He saw me, naked and wildly surprised,

414

and called up to us, "Y'all stay right where you are, and everything's going to be all right."

I rushed for my clothes.

"I said to stay put now!"

I looked at Molly, the fragility of her long thighs as she got to her feet, shoulders hunched to cover her breasts, hands cupped, making a bikini of her fingers. Studying the deliberate, now-closer men, I tried to read their expressions, to play for time. "What the hell do you think you're doing?"

"Police. I want both of you to get up and walk slowly, just as you are, toward that rock up there. We want to look through your things."

"Get the hell out of here," I said. "You've got no right to bother us."

"Shut up," the oldest of the three said. "Do what you're told and you'll be fine. We'll toss you your clothes once we've looked through them. We didn't come up here to do you harm, just ask you a few questions."

The man with the shotgun tied the dogs to a tree and leaned the shotgun against it. The other two examined the contents of the picnic basket and went through our clothes. Only after everything we'd carried up the hill had been spread out on the blanket, did the oldest man, short, overweight, wearing a cheap necktie, stand up and make a show of averting his eyes.

His younger, broader, pot-bellied companion leered disapprovingly but lustfully at Molly in a way I hated. He was the one who spoke first. "Okay, my hippie friends, I'm carrying your articles of clothing over to that rock. Get yerselves dressed and come on down here."

"Shit," Molly said, "I know who you are! Leave us alone you fucking intruding bastards!"

I reached for her shoulder. "What the hell's going on, Molly?"

She didn't answer me. "Fucking bastards."

"Y'all hurry up and come on down here."

"You have no right," Molly called down to them, "to be up here harassing us." She had dressed quickly. Buttoning my shirt, I climbed down to stand next to her.

"Narcs," she whispered. "Peter." Then she started yelling at them again.

The bald man asked her to watch her language. When the specter of rape and violent death-by-strangers began to recede, I recognized the man who'd talked to me outside the Hotchkiss Co-op and laughed without wanting to, "Is it Mike or Sherman?"

"Mike. Where'd you get Sherman?"

"The business card you gave me."

"Oh, that." He smiled and shrugged. "Michael McKinley, Mister Barlow, FBI." He introduced the others, too. Rothman, another Fed with different affiliations. Winslow, beer-bellied and with the hots for Molly, claimed to be with the Delta County Sheriff's Department. The three men looked warm from the ascent, but all business.

"What the hell is this about?"

"Peter," Molly said, leaning toward me. "It's about Peter."

Rothman, bald, shortest of the three, sat on a rock, drank from a canteen, then studied every scrap of paper in my billfold, driver's license, student ID, my last few dollars. "This is not an arrest, Mister Barlow. Not yet at least. We'd like to ask you a few questions."

"He doesn't know anything," Molly insisted, "and I've told you all I know. Twice."

"Mrs. Turnquist," Rothman said, stressing her marital status, "there are illegally parked cars down there registered to each of you. Picnics and alcoholic beverages are not allowed up here, and this is nobody's bedroom. We have grounds for taking you both in, but we'd rather ask you and your friend a few questions in the hope we won't have to do that. You've got a choice here. You can sit quietly and answer a few questions or we can put you under arrest."

"I think my range of choices is greater than that," Molly said, "and I'm sure my lawyer will agree."

McKinley squinted and licked his dry lips. "During the last conversation I remember, your lawyer agreed we could ask you questions as we developed them and, on that basis, we agreed to bring no drug charges. Although it's conceivable that we may do so, we don't have to charge you in any drug matter to arrest you, Mrs. Turnquist."

Winslow pulled his sagging uniform pants up over his belly. His head was too small for his chest and thick neck, and too round for the bushiness of his scraggly sideburns. His straw hat was too far on the back of his head. "Anyhow, Molly, since we last talked to you, the surprised and faithful wife, you've raised some new questions in our mind."

"I bet," Molly said, glaring at him a little fearfully, I thought. "I just bet."

Rothman held up a hand and stepped toward me. "Mister Barlow how long have you been a friend of Nick Sospiri?"

"I don't know anybody named Nick."

"Nick," Molly said, "Goddamnit! Shit!"

McKinley shook his head as if he'd caught me in a regrettable lie. "Think about it, Mister Barlow. Just yesterday afternoon you asked me if I knew where he lived."

416

"I asked about my friend Dom."

Winslow hawked and spit on a rock. "Dom, Nick, whatever you call him, we don't care. We want to know how long you've known him."

I ignored Winslow and looked at McKinley. "What the fuck's Dom got to do with all this?"

"Dom, Tim," Molly said, trying to clue me in. "Your friend DomiNICK Sospiri."

"Mrs. Turnquist," McKinley said, "I'm asking the questions and he's answering them without your coaching. Mister Barlow, if you just cooperate you're gonna be fine. How long have you known him?"

"Four or five years or so."

"When was the last time you saw him?"

"Is he all right?"

McKinley shook his head wearily. "I do not know, Mister Barlow, and I only care in a purely professional sense. I asked you when you last saw him."

"He came through Denver for a weekend last summer, stayed at my place."

"Pricey juice, Tim." McKinley nodded, squinting at the empty champagne bottle. "Did you smoke a lot of dope with him at that time?"

"No, but if I had, I wouldn't be likely to say yes, would I?" I looked sharply at Molly, scared for Dom now. She mouthed, "He's all right."

Winslow gave Molly a stern look. "This is no nude beach in south France. You go coaching him, Molly, we're going to take the both of you in and lock you down."

Rothman waved Winslow away. It was his turn. "You ever been arrested, Mister Barlow?"

"A bunch of years ago, just after high school. I did twelve hours for vagrancy trying to hitch a ride in Needles, California."

"Ever been arrested on any kind of drug charges?"

"No."

"We're gonna check out all these things that you tell us, Tim," McKinley warned.

Rothman had been fingering my billfold in search of secret compartments. "Ever been to Mexico, any islands in the Caribbean, Canada, France, Switzerland? Do you have a passport? Ever been to Aspen? Crested Butte?"

"No passport. Never been out of the country. I've been through Aspen and Crested Butte."

"Have some friends in those towns, do you?"

"None that I know of."

"Why were you looking for Sospiri?"

"He invited me to go fishing."

Winslow looked like a man unable to contain his secret much longer. "How'd it happen you left your car up here?"

"How do you know I did?"

Winslow lost his patience. "Because we followed your hippie asses up here from Sospiri's house, that's why."

Rothman raised an eyebrow and frowned at Winslow. Rothman had the look of a patient man who preferred to understate his authority and provide a minimum of information. He stepped in front of the sputtering Winslow. "What's your car doing up here?"

"I got it stuck here in the blizzard yesterday."

"That jibes with why he was so wet and miserable and looking for a pay phone yesterday afternoon," McKinley told Rothman.

"How did you get down off the canyon?"

"Hitchhiked."

Winslow peered into a small paper sack containing our chicken bones and apple cores. "How long have you known Molly here?"

Winslow had posed the question, but I answered McKinley. "Since yesterday. I met her yesterday."

Winslow registered his irritation with me and his impatience with McKinley by kicking at a rock.

Rothman took over again. "Have you ever been to Paonia before?"

"No."

"How long have you known Peter Turnquist?"

"Never met him."

"What's your relationship to Nadine Shepherd?"

"Never met her."

"Do you have any outstanding airlines reservations, Mister Barlow? Any travel plans at all?"

"No. None other than going back to Denver."

"You married, Mister Barlow?"

"Yes."

"Children?"

"Two.

"Ages?"

"Five and almost two."

"Employed down there in Denver?"

"Not at the moment."

"How have you been supporting your family?"

"I just graduated from college. Up until two weeks ago, I held three part-time jobs. I've got pay stubs and there are employers who will vouch for this."

The men had settled into their roles. McKinley was the sympathetic professional; Rothman, the authority from on high, the almighty federal agent, uncomfortable in the wide open spaces; Winslow was the local cop whose internal voice never failed him when it came to distinguishing good law-abiding tourists from the bad Commie lawbreakers. He looked at Molly lasciviously and turned toward me. "Your wife know about the picnic today?"

Careful to turn my face far enough but not too far away from Winslow, I spit to get his taste out of my mouth. "I tried to telephone for permission, but she'd stepped out of the office. Why? Do you want to tell her?"

Rothman and McKinley withdrew a few steps for a muttered conference. Taking advantage of their momentary inattentiveness, Winslow lit a menthol cigarette and made another effort to advance the investigation. "Problem I have with your story, Barlow, is this. Sospiri and Turnquist and Shepherd all three vanish into thin air eighteen hours before they're due to get busted on major drug charges. Sospiri leaves your name and phone number in the house. Records show he made recent calls to you in Denver. Then you pop up in town right after they all disappear and are found up here in flagrato delectation, or whatever you call it, with Mrs. Turnquist, wife of one of the fugitives. Before this, damned if both of you don't go over Sospiri's house this morning, try to break into his house, open up the Land Rover, and take a bag with ten thousand dollars in cash and about eight thousand dollars of cocaine."

I'd heard and read about this kind of police work. "That's bullshit!" I shouted, on my feet moving toward Winslow. "Worthless fucking narc bullshit and you know it! There was nothing in that Land Rover but a flashlight and some tools!"

"Tim, be careful!" Molly said. "That's *old* bullshit about the money and the dope, and there are lawyers at least who know it's bullshit. The missing money and dope has already come up. Tim, they're trying to get something out of me that I don't have by going after you."

Winslow shook his head. "We were watchin' you the whole time, son, and we talked to people back up the road who said you'd hid that bag of cash and dope on your way up here."

"Yeah, well, why don't you go over there with your dogs and find it then? Wherever you do find it, I'll come around to help you stick every dime of it up your monkey's ass!"

I slipped Winslow's punch easily, but Rothman appeared out of nowhere and blind-sided me with a short right hook. While I struggled to find my balance, McKinley got an arm under my chin and used one of his knees against the back of my leg. Molly screamed as I went down. McKinley's forearm shifted under my chin and I fell through a dark tunnel, down and down at a high rate of speed. Before I hit the bottom my head began to ring. The darkness went red and I felt a fierce itching I couldn't scratch because of handcuffs pinching my hands behind my back.

Molly was crying and McKinley was telling her I'd be all right. "It's called a blood choke," McKinley told Molly as he pulled me to my feet. "Makes for a quick, painless sleep, saves teeth, lawsuits, and wear and tear on the knuckles. You all right, Barlow?"

There was echoing in my head and my ear burned from Rothman's punch, but I wasn't about to say so. McKinley dumped everything taken from our pockets into a canvas bag. Winslow was taking advantage of Molly's distress, pretending to have difficulty getting her wrists into his handcuffs even as he shifted and squinted through her shirt buttons for a view of her bare tits.

"Talk to me, Molly," I pleaded.

"No," Winslow said. Positioning himself between us, angling for an improved view of her breasts as he clapped a hand over her mouth and urged her toward the dogs and down the mountain. "Not anytime soon, anyway."

Rothman and McKinley came up on either side of me. Rothman beamed with the knowledge that he'd shown his younger underlings that he still packed a punch. McKinley looked sympathetic, maybe a little troubled.

"Mike," I said, "you escort her. Please."

To my surprise, McKinley shrugged, nodded at Rothman, and intercepted Molly and Winslow.

Rothman marched me down the hill, while Winslow untied the dogs. Behind me, Molly and McKinley started arguing about something I couldn't hear. When I turned around to look at them, I stumbled over a rock and nearly fell on my face.

"Best keep your eyes where you're going," Rothman advised me.

My station wagon was already gone. I watched a tow truck pull Molly's Volks around a curve and disappear. Rothman eased me into the back seat of an unmarked green Plymouth and started back toward Molly and McKinley. The Plymouth was hot from the sun, but I ducked my head and twisted and saw Molly descending behind Winslow and the dogs. Her cuffs had been removed, a sight that suddenly awakened my suspicions. Winslow closed the tailgate on the dogs in the back of McKinley's pickup then swaggered up to the Plymouth and settled in behind the wheel. Positioning a big arm on the front seat, he turned to me.

"If I'd punched you back there, you'd still be up there on your ass having hippie visions."

With my hands cuffed behind me, my head ringing, and the afternoon champagne roiling in my stomach, I assured Winslow that I knew how lucky I was to have slipped his haymaker. Rothman climbed in the Plymouth next to Winslow and glanced back at me.

Molly came running toward us. Preoccupied with quieting the dogs, perhaps, McKinley didn't seem to notice her at first and was a little slow in giving chase once he did. Molly arrived at the open window, leaned in and tried to kiss me. "Call an attorney named Stuart Meacham in Grand Junction," she shouted. "I'll see you tonight."

Head throbbing, wrestling with lingering suspicions, I looked at her and said nothing.

She was breathless from her run. "I love you. Believe in me. I'm sorry."

McKinley arrived to lead Molly back toward his pickup. The Plymouth roared, jumped, and kicked up sand and grit. For a time, I sat twisted in the seat to watch for McKinley's truck coming up behind us. After a while, head still ringing, I slumped on the seat, mulling the tension between the men in front.

I decided that Rothman was missing his wife and family and the indoor comforts of whatever eastern city he lived in. He sat so he could look at me and avoid Winslow. Winslow's slit, glassy eyes appeared in the rearview mirror, glittering with aggressive benevolence. If he'd been more articulate or self-aware he might have reflected that, drug-dealing, atheistic Commie bastard that I was, at least I was from the west. I represented a degradation of his values, but the two of us recognized the preeminence of those values. I had been told about the divinity of Jesus Christ, and maybe more to the point, hadn't spent my driving life on commuter trains or in traffic jams on cramped eastern parkways, paying turnpike fees every fifty miles. Unlike Rothman, who studied me with uncertainty, Winslow looked satisfied, comfortable in my presence.

When I told Winslow I wanted to smoke, he flashed a yellow-toothed grin, lit one of his own and told me to go ahead. He kept his wrinkled sunburned eyes in the rearview mirror, perhaps hoping I might ask for help, which he might or might not provide in exchange for my help in his one-man range war against Rothman. Winslow watched while I put the edge of my feet on the seat and pulled my narrow hips through the loop made by my arms, got them around my boots, and managed to fish a cigarette from my shirt pocket. A match was another kind of problem. When Rothman noticed that Winslow seemed to be hoping I'd ask for a light, he plucked the cigarette lighter out of the dashboard and held it orange, then a faded rusty-brown, toward me.

The country outside the car was agricultural. The air stank of refineries, crops, and horseshit. I wondered where exactly I was going, what I was being charged with, but relishing the silence, decided not to ask. When the cigarette got short, I awkwardly tossed it out the open window. Pressing the door button, I watched the window rise and thought about how long it had been since I'd slept as deeply as I wanted to sleep. I closed my eyes. Winslow was talking about the miles and miles he'd driven with his prisoners and I fell into a dream. I couldn't tell Winslow's talk from my dream, and didn't really care to.

Gordon had written a poem about there being three gods: parents to children; doctors to the aged; captors to their prisoners. My ear was ringing and there was a little grit of blood inside it. I was going to jail. Either I had a concussion or there was something broken in me; it seemed that the harder it was for me to go where I wanted, the more I wanted to be on the road, going anywhere.

The car stopped, the door opened and, under escort, I walked through a nearly empty parking lot toward a low, winged, red brick building, navigating patches of manicured lawn, passing a monumental pole on which the national and state flags hung limp under a hazy, smelly afternoon sky. I went through a series of rooms. Metal doors slammed. Winslow and Rothman vanished. Uniforms were gray, walls were green, and I couldn't stay awake, couldn't remember the questions I ought to be asking, what my rights were, or why I was there. There were metal baskets to empty my pockets in, except they'd already been emptied, papers to sign with a pen nearly out of ink, and tissues to wipe the ink off my fingertips. There were more metal doors and everywhere posters exhorted good behaviors and forbid various actions. The gray scrubs were too big and belts were not issued. The sleeves of a faded blue shirt were too short and couldn't be buttoned around my forearms. The deeper I went into the building, the meaner the prisoners and guards looked, and the greater the load of jingling keys guards wore on heavy belts. I passed down a hall and heard the voices of men, smelled cream of mushroom soup and soap. Then I was alone in a yellow room with a toilet, a sink, and a towel, shiny and devoid of nap. Four pewter-colored, disinfectant-smelling blankets were folded on a cot that stank of bug spray. I lay down and watched the late afternoon light that came through a small overhead window. An ocean of sleep was ready to wash me away, take me down, show me its power. The air conditioner made one kind of sound when it shut down for the night, and the heater, when it came on, muttered and hissed.

Once or twice I was taken out to walk in a fenced yard where men were tending flowers and pruning bushes with screaming, smelly engines. There were halls with red, glowing lights over heavy steel doors, noisy buzzers, and at times, from a distance, the cheery musical voices broadcast by televisions. In my cubicle was a Bible. It seemed a crude code: God was the highest cop of all. A complete manipulative maniac.

There was another room with a metal chair and a plastic ashtray. Coffee and donuts and men in neckties scoffing at what I said or patting me on the shoulder and giving me cigarettes. There was a certain amount of kindness on display here and there, but I didn't trust it, not from the group of men in bow ties who gave me a pack of cigarettes, not in the men in cowboy boots who put me in a lineup and asked me stupid questions through a booming speaker. I remember standing beside other men in a blinding white light, a wretch among wretches, a little less lost, singled out and inserted in the Old Testament. God was on the other side of a miasma of cigarette smoke, booming questions suggested by muttering angels.

"What do you want to do, Barlow?" Or maybe it was, "What do you want to do with your life, Barlow?"

"Sleep."

They let me sleep again for a quite a while, and when I woke up I knew I was in jail for a crime I didn't commit. I knew I had to protect Serena and Matt and somebody named Molly whose touch was vivid and healing, but had faded somehow. I ate heavy wheat cereal from a plastic bowl. The trustee gave me extra coffee and everything important started to come into focus. I remembered backwards from the questions I'd answered, getting from Winslow and Rothman and McKinley to Molly. Every time I got to Molly I felt better and better and remembered more, and I wondered whether I'd been given some drug that had knocked me out and made me say things. Or maybe I'd been exhausted for lack of sleep, had a concussion with delusions. Or what?

The television came on. I took another nap and woke up to more coffee. I asked the trustee about my situation, but he didn't know anything. I was sitting down, thinking about constitutional rights, charges, crimes, phone calls, lawyers, and the magic words I had to remember when the door opened and a man with tufts of silver hair that seemed to have roots in his generous ears, wished me good morning in a drawl that seemed to go on forever.

"Mistah Timothy Barlow?"

"Yes."

"Good morning to you, Sir. My name is Stuart Meacham."

The hand I took was fat and warm, but I wasn't ready to trust its owner. I put my hands back in my pockets and stepped back.

"Molly Turnquist asked me to do what I could do for you, Mister Barlow, and belatedly, I have managed to effectuate your release this morning."

"Who are you to Molly? Is she all right?"

"A friend. Yes, she's been worried about you, but she's fine. I spoke to her at nine last night." With me glaring at him, Meacham seemed at a loss for what to say.

"Who are you?

"Well that's a tale for a long telling. I am Peter Turnquist's godfather."

"I want out of here but I don't want to talk to fucking Peter Turnquist's attorney!"

"Sir, I did not say I am Peter's attorney. I'm not. And you certainly do not have to talk to me. I appear before you to expedite your release as a courtesy to my client, Mrs. Turnquist."

I sighed. I was awake. "Thank-you for coming. I'm sorry for being surly. I've been very confused by all this."

"I imagine you have, Mister Barlow. I have been a little confused by the matter myself."

"What have I been charged with?"

"For reasons I have not been altogether successful discovering, sir, it appears you were never charged with anything. Initially I was told there were minor violations having to do with littering and picnicking in an unauthorized area." To cover a moment's embarrassment, Meacham glanced at his watch. "There was a vague third charge of some sort, predictable given the individuals we're treating with, maliciously cooked up, no doubt, to besmirch Mrs. Turnquist's reputation, and yours, of course, as well."

"They never mentioned any charges at all to me. I thought I was going to do ten years on drug-related charges. They think I'm involved in some drug ring."

"If the authorities ever genuinely believed that, and Mrs. Turnquist and I doubt that they ever did, they no longer maintain it. They've presented me with paperwork, showing you were free to go within about twenty hours of your arrest. Administrative error's their claim."

Meacham and I ignored the guards who followed us through buzzing doors and bright rooms, waited for the administrators and trustees to gather my things. They provided me with a little grocery cart for them and hit buzzers until we stood in a big, glassy room that looked out on the parking lot, occupied casually by combinations of official cars, among which I did not notice Molly's red Volks. Meacham said something about my "need for some respectable nutrition," and with my sleeping bag bundled under his arm, opened the door to the parking lot. I wanted to ask about Molly, about my car, about who Meacham had talked to, and what he knew of Dom and Peter. More than that, I wanted to push my face in Serena's clean blond hair, pick up my son, feel his tiny ribs in my hands, toss him skyward toward the ceiling of my house, and watch him descend, pale hair splayed out, laughing and trusting. Of course, I wanted to do all this without seeing Irene or Gerald.

Meacham seemed to notice my emotional mood. He put a hand on my shoulder and gestured toward a long gray Cadillac.

"It's very good of you to come, Mister Meacham," I said. "I can't tell you how much I appreciate your trouble."

Meacham folded the sleeping bag neatly on top of a golf bag in his trunk. I dumped the rest of my stuff and looked at him expectantly.

"Regretfully, I have only a few minutes before I have to drive to Craig. Molly has arranged for you to take a car service to her home, where, I'm sure, you will learn more in a short while than I could tell you in a month. However, I do have time for a cup of coffee, sir, and if you'd like to pay a visit to a pancake house nearby, I will tell you the little I have been able to piece together."

Meacham talked of the weather and local golf courses while he watched me finish a huge breakfast of orange juice, eggs, bacon, and pancakes. With the last pancake crumb in my mouth, I sipped coffee, lit a cigarette, and looked at him. He was glassy-eyed, sixty or more. Poodle white curly hair stood out in tufts from the side of his head. I decided the redness of the face was not sunburn. His hands were manicured, puffy, and he held them around his coffee cup much as a priest might hold a chalice. From occasional sighs and the exposed blood vessels of his nose, I judged his religion to center around drinking. Drinking with individuals of good manners and breeding.

"Mister Barlow, as an essentially weak person with a stern moral upbringing, I have trained myself to pursue no unnecessary knowledge for its own sake. Professionally I'm trained to avoid learning from others what might become a source of vexation to me or a trouble to them."

"Meaning you don't want me to say anything at all about who I am or what I've done or haven't done?"

"Mister Barlow, I prefer to provide you with what I have been led to believe without learning anything you might know and for which, as a mineral rights attorney and something of a bumbler in the courtroom, I would have no good reason to know." A very small smile. Winking would have violated his courtly bearing.

"You're not going to learn anything you don't want to know from me, Mister Meacham, because I don't know anything to compromise you. I am very confused."

"Your confusion may linger, I'm afraid. Much of what I know was gleaned from some rather overstated and underreported stories in the area newspapers around here a couple of weeks ago. These articles, I believe, would be available to you at newspaper offices or certainly libraries. Briefly stated, the authorities are alleging that Peter Turnquist and Dominic Sospiri and several others are involved in a medium-to-large-scale drug buy, bankrolled abroad and managed by a pair of odd real estate developers in Florida.

I sighed and lit a cigarette. "I gathered some of that from the questions I was asked. Stuff about passports, pilots' licenses, hidden bank accounts. A whole lot of baloney."

"Your misfortune may have been a double one, Mr. Barlow. You were a friend of Mister Sospiri's, which you never attempted to deny. According to another attorney who made a couple of calls on our behalf, you are also thought to resemble an associate and fugitive who may or may not have left the country with Mister Sospiri, Mister Turnquist, and Miss Shepherd. Thank God your fingerprints got you out of that one."

"Dom has left the country?"

"That's what the authorities believe at the moment."

I didn't think Dom could be entirely guilty of, or innocent of, what he was being hunted for. I wanted to think he had been gradually drawn into dealing by the mysterious patron Glen and his jet-set crowd, lured by promises of financing for his Funny Farm. "I don't know Nadine or Peter, but Dominic's my friend. What is he charged with exactly?"

"I'm afraid I didn't delve, but more than a dozen offenses, Mr. Barlow. Among other things they allege he was renting various private landing sites in Colorado and Utah where small planes loaded with drugs from Mexico and South America could be unloaded in secrecy. I'm afraid even rumors of large quantities of drugs imported from other countries

426

tend to excite paranoia on a federal level, Mister Barlow, making it hard for a small-time mineral rights attorney to obtain up-to-date information on what they know or suspect."

"They claimed that Molly and I had removed a rather large amount of cash and drugs from a Land Rover parked on the property of the house Dom's been renting."

"According to attorneys with more experience than I have in these matters, this an unfortunate ruse often used in drug-related arrests. Quantities of cash and drugs disappear and are used to incriminate the innocent or leverage cooperation, even perjury. Fortunately for you, no cash was ever produced or claimed missing. Four days, of course, is a slow softening."

"Four days?"

"Yes, the matter was called to my attention four days ago on Friday morning. I was in court in Pueblo. A more-connected, knowledgeable criminal lawyer might have gotten you released sooner. Judges are reluctant to criticize rights violations when drugs are involved and federal attorneys are slow to return phone calls. Then, of course, attorneys with other accused clients are slow to move whenever it comes to any action that might put their own clients at risk."

"Since you said Molly had arranged this whole business, I assume she wasn't held as long."

"No. Mrs. Turnquist was released later that evening, after your automobiles had been thoroughly searched. Unfortunately, the switchboard denied you were being held, denied having access to the paper work, and said you were due to be released. She had no way of getting directly in touch with you." Meacham was sneaking looks at his watch, so I nodded my head and stood up, not so much because I wanted him to get to Craig on time or was satisfied with what he'd been able to tell me, but because suddenly I wanted to see Molly in a bad way.

A few minutes later, I loaded my gear in the back of the Intermountain Alpine Transit Company's blue Jeep, the so-called car service. While the driver, a guy named Lars who worked for the ski patrol in the winter, described the broken legs he'd set recently, I sat watching the clouds scud, eager to be with Molly, but also fighting off a dread and the magnetic pull of home. I had constructed a dozen provisional plans while staring at the four walls of my cubicle and I wanted to hear what Molly would say to each scheme.

Although Molly had prepaid the fare, Lars was happy to take a five-dollar tip. I schlepped my stuff to her front porch, noticing the brand new tires on her red Volkswagen. Wondering where my Chevy was, I hoped that it hadn't been completely trashed by those who'd searched it for dope. Rain started to fall. I called Molly's name in the dark house. I turned on lights. A note, sealed in an envelope, was on the table.

Dear Tim,

First and last, I love you. I never meant to be dishonest. You and I got ourselves into such a state, felt that violent need to connect quickly at the deepest possible level, and the things that did not get said just sort of ambushed us. Wanting you as I did and do, literally, symbolically, physically, mentally, spiritually, and every other possible way, I withheld details about Peter and the agents who'd been hounding me. I thought the whole thing was over and wanted to be close to you, wanted us to share the experience of being us, together. I had every intention of telling you everything, but there was always something that seemed more immediate and more important; hence your evil surprise at the canyon. While I speak only for myself and what I withheld, I worry now that maybe there are things you didn't tell me. Were you in some way involved with Dom, at least? I don't really want to believe you were, and would forgive you if you were, but you see what loneliness and paranoia and guilt can do. My faith in the experience I had just before meeting you remains strong. If you can muster some faith in us, then I believe what you are about to read will strike you as a challenge, a beginning rather than an end.

Peter was in construction when we first met. He got lucky, the banks were generous; he started building houses and making money. After a while he hooked up with some peculiar characters and life began to change. I was corrupted by the money, used it to fix up the house and asked few, if any questions. Things, including his behavior, got worse. I blamed his new friends and protected his parents from finding out what he was doing. My sister Nadine once worked in a bank. Soon she was helping Peter with finances and I was working only to perfect my plants and my blinders. Interesting that you knew your friend as Dom and I knew him, but only slightly, as Nick. He had a friend in common with Peter, a rich ski enthusiast, some vague character named Glen. Glen had friends with planes and ski lodge connections. While I tended my herbs, and let Peter and Nadine take care of selling condos, they suddenly stopped building. I don't have all the facts by any means. I learned later that private planes loaded with drugs were landing on ranches. Peter and Nadine said they had to do some traveling to Florida and other places. They had to travel together because Peter couldn't deal with numbers. We all have our shortcomings and blind spots. I couldn't face the truth about my sister until I had my nose rubbed in it.

I smoked a little pot, but Peter brought coke around and started using heavily, arguing that it was necessary for sales and that he would stop using when things slowed down. As has been pointed out to me too often in the last little while, I've been an accessory and they could probably send me to prison for it. Instead, of course, the narcs hope I will serve as bait for Peter's return.

I don't have any reliable information about what led to the aborted bust. Frankly, I was completely hysterical about having found out about Peter and Nadine when the whole thing went down, and failed to appreciate how quickly this house would be crawling with people asking questions and making accusations. They claim that Dom, Nadine, and Peter all caught a flight out of Aspen headed to Florida. Apparently, they're combing Miami for them right now. They could be busted tomorrow or never. They could be hiding in any very comfortable place in the world. I do not know where they are or where they might be. Frankly, at this moment at least, I don't really care. And, Tim, you know I'm not just saying this for the eyes of the narcs who may see this letter before you do.

When you read this, Natasha, your favorite cat, and I will be on our way to, or already in, California, where I will spend the summer visiting college friends. By September I expect to have a teaching job in an elementary school not too far from the ocean. Think somewhere near Ojai or Santa Barbara. For the foreseeable future I will be praying every night at bedtime to hear from you. Peter's father will have an address and phone number for me as soon as I'm settled, as will, I'm sure, every narc in the country.

Also thank you for understanding my need to have something of yours in my hands and under my care. The Volks has a higher blue book value than your Chevy. Sell it if you need a bigger car. For my part I promise to take good care of it and give it over to you again. The title in the Volks has been signed over to you. Also, I bought the new tires I promised I would, and got new tires for the station wagon as well.

I know you must feel relieved to be out of jail. Please don't feel horribly abandoned by me. The most selfish part of me wants to stay right here and never let you out of my sight. But that would be the most destructive thing I could do. You need to think about your life and the lives of your family at a little more distance than I would ever be willing to give you had I stayed. And I need to get away from being followed and hounded by law enforcement. A part of you will always be with me and I pray all the rest of you will be with me someday, too. It is after dawn now. I am crying to think of the miles between us when you read this. How I ache for you. How I hope you can believe, and can know, that I love you.

Molly

The '60 Volkswagen Beetle

"And you're still pushing a hood in front?
When all that could be behind you?"
Advertisement in **Life**, *April 5, 1963*

I flashed back to a recent Sunday dinner at my parents' house. My dad had cooked a ham and prepared some sort of raisin-based gravy for the mashed potatoes. He was drinking a lot of beer and Irene was stressing about the kids and going on about the perils of sugar consumption. As we sat down at the table I tried to signal her to tone it down, but she ignored me. My dad rolled his eyes and responded by serving Serena a baked yam filled with a frothy marshmallow concoction as big as his fist. Forbidden by Irene to dig into her white mound, Serena began to cry. Irene began to pack Serena up for home. While she organized our departure, my dad and I stood shouting at each other from opposite sides of the dinner table. No disappointment or disagreement or betrayal or likely character trait or flaw was too small or too ancient to exaggerate. My dad was no reader of books, but he was far from illiterate, and stress and anger sharpened his tongue. Recalling some earlier holding forth of mine about the American Transcendentalists or maybe a dispute about the unfairness of the Vietnam War draft or the tyranny of authority, he zinged me as Irene and the kids and I were leaving.

"Scofflaw Quixote!" he shouted. "You'll never amount to anything because you're a wishful thinker and a Scofflaw Quixote!"

Reverie done, I folded Molly's letter and put it in my pocket, then stowed my gear on the back seat of the Volks and turned the engine over. At the edge of her driveway I stopped and got out to take a deep breath. A left turn would take me west toward California. A right would put me on the road back to Denver. The temperatures were warmer than they'd been on my arrival and the air smelled of the cherry and apple orchards surrounding the property. Unable to decide which way to turn, I backed up and parked. I spent the next day-and-a-half dabbling in self-pity, while wishfully thinking and closely watching the driveway from the dining room table, waiting for Molly to pull up in the Chevy with a change of heart.

While I waited, there was plenty of time to think of Gerald and Irene. Gerald was older and slightly heavier, but I was taller and younger. Under purely competitive circumstances, I guessed that we might be fairly matched. But the advantage of any encounter, I felt sure, would have been all mine, since I wasn't concerned about winning or losing. A good ass-kicking, or at least a couple of brain-damaging punches from Gerald, would have been just about as welcome to me as feeling the bones in his jaw under my knuckles.

The possibility that Serena might have misunderstood or made up the story about Irene and Gerald taking a nap didn't find a foothold in my imagination until the sun went down and I gave up on waiting for Molly. After a long slow drive back to Denver, instead of going home I parked in front of Gerald's apartment building. In the darkness, his doorbell was lit up like a miniature lantern. I took a deep breath and reached to grab the ignition key, but pulled back to reconsider. If he were to come to the door and I started hitting him before he could talk, how would I know when to stop? If he were to come down and peek through the door curtain and open the door already talking a mile a minute, how could I bring myself to hit him until I'd heard some of what he had to say? How far would I let him excuse himself before delivering my first punch? My neck wet with sweat, my hands shaking, I lit a cigarette.

Smoking with the window down, it occurred to me that things between Gerald and Irene might be more serious than I'd thought. Irene might have made, or be in the process of making, a choice of her own. However I might begrudge it, she had that right. How would I fare if it came to that?

Gerald had attended a prestigious school in the East, had lived for a time both in Florence and Paris, and spoke Spanish, Italian, and French. I remembered much of my altar boy Latin and had earned a minor in German at City U. He had a Ph.D., a professorship, a new Datsun, and access to the mother of my children. I had a B.A., a dread of going back to work at the Old Glory Potato Chip Company, a rage that scared me, and an obsession with a mysterious woman who, having stolen my station wagon to drive to California, left me her old VW Beetle in trade. How much was my passion for Molly a diversion or a shunt for my anger with and disappointment in myself and Irene and the lives we had fallen into, dragging with us two small children?

To keep such questions at bay I decided to ring the doorbell and ask Gerald a direct question. "When did you first have sex with Irene?" I could imagine him standing barefoot in his doorway, wearing not pajamas but a bathrobe, saying, "Well, be honest with yourself, Tim, and

432

you can probably figure it out. When did you first notice she was losing interest in you? Wouldn't it have been about then?" No, I decided, he wouldn't say it, not, at least, quite that way. He would notice my dilated eyes and the stiff, twitching muscles along the sides of my neck and behave as if he wanted to keep his front teeth. Still, I worried that in some diplomatic, insidious way he'd duck the issue and trick me into putting painful questions to myself. Vivid enough already were the litanies of her excuses, the delays, assurances never delivered on; worse were the long sighs and midnight motions of duty. I didn't want to be called on to try and remember the last time Irene seemed to enjoy sex with me.

It was possible that the moment I called home, Irene was indeed napping as Serena had said she was, dozing with her hair spilled over Gerald's chest because of what the two of them had done a few minutes earlier or done during my hours of fishing the Taylor River. I didn't believe Irene innocent, but neither did I believe she'd had sex with Gerald for the very first time on the afternoon I called. In the end, I think what had kept me sitting in the car was the realization that I might have gone to bed with Molly without ever knowing Irene was involved with Gerald. To lose control of the woman who had mothered my children, and of my tight-fitting armor of moral outrage, seemed too much to bear.

But just after 2am, I leaned hard on Gerald's doorbell, then shoved my hands in the roomy pockets of my fishing pants. Clenching my fists in my pockets would at least give him a chance to say something brief and persuasive. I shifted my weight back and forth, unsure whether I was going to confront him with a sock or a sob. Even so, I burned to know what I would do or say when we were eyeball to eyeball. I rang and rang, but there was no sound or motion from within.

Aware of the brightness of the porch light and in no mood for another encounter with the cops, I crossed the street to a pay phone and dialed Gerald's number from a dark, empty grocery store parking lot. A light came on in his window, but went out again after a minute, so I went back across the street and spent another ten minutes ringing his bell before I gave up.

In school when researching a paper for a History of World Religion course, which I'd signed up for because it fit so neatly between intervals of a part-time job pouring coffee and serving fries at the student union café, I had read a twentieth-century essay about the cruelty of a God who forced us to prepare for what never happened and then made us endure what we had never prepared for. Who had written it or what its title might be, I couldn't have said, and can't still. I thought about certain

433

passages in the essay again while I parked in front of my house, where I vomited out the window and then sat stroking my car key until I was confident I could face Irene without raising my voice and waking the kids. My boots would come off in the hall, the sock feet would mount the steps to the dark bedroom, the wronged husband would stand quietly, doing a little meditation breathing. He would turn on the light in the hall and illuminated in the doorway ask, "Have you been having sex with Gerald?"

On the sidewalk outside my house I barfed again in the grass and drove to an all-night gas station where I bought some mints and prepared a few sweet and soothing words to say to Serena in the event she somehow answered the phone again. When Irene came on the phone, I planned to announce in a very flat voice that I would be home in ten minutes. Informed of this, she would tell Gerald to leave, if indeed he had gone over there after my calls.

The phone rang and rang. Minutes later, I let myself into the house.

The rooms had a dead, airless smell. Noting the tightly closed drapes, hearing the echoing of my first steps, I understood why the phone had gone unanswered. On the kitchen table, I found Irene's note. Irene, Serena, and Matt were out of town, she wrote, and she would "be in touch" in a few days. A plastic bottle containing a few swallows of apple juice was about all that was left in the fridge. I closed the bone-white door and put my face on the cold Formica table.

At dawn I carried my stuff from the Volks into the front hall and went out to walk the streets. The sky brightened and mourning doves cooed in the maple trees. Boys wrestled with overloaded bikes and launched newspapers at porches. There were whitewashed wooden boxes under windows. Old women emerged from immaculate houses to water the bright flowers in boxes on their porches, eyeing me warily.

At seven, Denny, my friend since San Diego and now a father himself, agreed to meet for breakfast at a diner on East Colfax. I hurried toward his truck, but when he leaned to the far side of his pickup to tie the shoelaces of his three-year-old son, Lincoln, I fixed a brutally false smile on my face and clapped him on the back. Over hash browns I downplayed meeting Molly and my subsequent arrest, told him about Thunderhead's pistol, about Dom and how the feds were looking for him in Miami. I admired Denny's skill at urging orange juice on Lincoln. Denny was less shocked and concerned than I'd expected him to be and seemed to understand the whole business as just another story about bored cops and bureaucrats trying to justify their overtime. He mentioned a letter he'd received from Gordon and Rhonda, who had moved to Santa Cruz a few months earlier, talked a little about his wife's decision to enroll in law school at Denver University, downplayed the success of his own thriving cabinet-making shop, and regretted having to rush off to deliver Lincoln to child care. We agreed to get together for beers some night soon. But when I thought of it again, I decided I preferred my loneliness to sharing my misery. I didn't call him for a year and a half, and we were both pushing forty before I laid eyes on him again.

I avoided the house that had been my home and started spending a lot of time over beer glasses in smoky, hellish bars, wondering what had become of my friends and all my faith in them. After closing time, I drove the streets, discovering new all-night convenience stores, thumbing through magazines, and buying little doodads that I didn't need or want. By day I slept in the sun-warmed grasses of Washington Park.

One morning, having stared dumbly at the masthead of the morning newspaper I remembered with a jolt that it was the day I'd promised to take my grandma to the ceramics show. I went home to shower, shave, and change clothes. Not wanting to surprise Irene at home or be surprised by her when I was in the house, I had taken to inserting a matchbook cover between two lightly drawn pencil lines in the screen door in such a way that it would fall if the door was opened. When I found the bit of cardboard where I'd placed it, I went inside, checked the mail, and discovered the postcard I'd written to Serena about two weeks earlier, on the morning I'd breakfasted in Gunnison. Still a little woozy from the night before, I couldn't understand why it had taken so long for the postcard to arrive.

Clean and looking better than I felt, I made tea and reread my card to Serena over and over, fascinated by my capacity for sentimentality and penchant for tickling her innocence. Abruptly, it dawned on me why the card had taken weeks to arrive and was postmarked in Santa Clara, California. I had inserted the card in my shirt pocket without a stamp. Suddenly I realized that Molly had found it in my Chevy and mailed it from California only recently.

The phone rang, and irrationally sure it was Molly, I jumped.

"Timmy?"

I sighed and softened my voice. "Hi, Grandma. Are we still on for this afternoon?"

"Yes, if you still want to go."

I forced a little eagerness. "I'm counting on it."

Her voice was hushed and a little hurried. "I can't talk long."

"What's going on?"

"Well, your grandpa's been feeling a little down, I guess, ever since we got your postcard yesterday."

"You got my postcard? Yesterday?"

"Yes. I thought it was sweet, but it seemed to make him sad. Even though he hasn't been up for anything more than walking across the room for a while now, he hated to think that you went fishing without him, I guess."

"How's his sore foot?"

"Not so good. Listen, I bought some smoky sausages when we went to the store the other day. You remember them, that kind you used to love so much when you were little?"

My voice was absolutely chipper. "You did? You bought smokies?"

"And some of those peanut butter cookies."

"Peanut butter cookies!"

"If you have time, I thought you might come over for lunch. Before we go see the pottery, I mean."

"Sure, Grandma."

"Uh-oh. He's coming up the stairs. I don't want him to know I called you. Just pretend I never called, okay?"

"Okay, Grandma."

"And there's a package for you here, too. A big one."

"A package for me? There?"

"Bye."

On the drive across town, I rehearsed in my mind half-a-dozen stale anecdotes intended to convey how happy Irene and the kids and I were, how glad I was to have finally graduated from college, and how much I was looking forward to getting a job that I could settle into, just like my grandpa had. I loved my grandparents, but it burdened me to be so sure that only lies about my life could please them.

Arriving, I kissed my grandma and glanced at the return address on my package: Paonia Laundromat. My grandma suggested that I open it right away. Since I hoped it would contain at least a letter from Molly, I feigned disinterest, assuring her that it contained only a load of clothes that I'd gone off and left in a washing machine. The postcard that I'd written to Lester and Nina too many days ago to count now was taped to the outside of their refrigerator. I glanced at it before skipping down the basement steps to where Lester was tinkering with his gun cabinet.

In five minutes we were polishing and cleaning his rifles and shotguns and he was admitting that he sometimes wondered why I never called and asked to borrow them. While my grandma worked upstairs to prepare us the perfect lunch, the old man updated me about the diabetes-related infection of his foot. Sensing how depressed he was, I talked in cheery, class-president tones about the wonders of modern medicine. He lamented that his hunting days were over, while I told him, truthfully, that I'd seen deer in manageable foothill country not far out of the city. He said he was sorry my school and family had been keeping me so busy and asked me if I needed to borrow any money. I said I was sorry, too, that I didn't need money, and then started trying to talk to him about my life in a way intended to help him appreciate how much he'd influenced it. He brightened a little over lunch, particularly when I mentioned that Matt was already learning to throw a rubber ball the size of a baseball.

Nina and I wandered for an hour through the ceramics show. Remembering her little paleontologist of long ago, she insisted on buying me an ashtray with a tiny *Brontosaurus* painted on it. When she got tired of standing we went to a nearby teashop.

"Grandma, do you know how lucky we are?"

"No. How lucky?"

"I don't mean everybody. Just you and me."

She beamed with the implied exclusivity. "What makes you say that?"

I took a long gulp of tea and turned my head to hide the liquid in my eyes. "We are the only two people I know who have never disappointed each other." Suddenly, I wasn't quite sure she understood or agreed with me. "Have I ever disappointed you, Grandma?"

She shook her head and smiled. "No."

"I didn't think so. I can't tell you how happy it makes me to hear you say that. You have never disappointed me, either."

I lit a cigarette and unwrapped my new ashtray.

Lost among her own thoughts and memories, maybe, she didn't absorb what I was trying to tell her. From my grandpa I'd learned to spot her worries as they seemed to take shape and to redirect them before her hands trembled, her face paled, and she succumbed to them herself. As far as she was concerned, I could do no wrong. She had stuffed crumpled dollar bills in my little boy's pants pockets when no one was looking. But much more importantly, she had bestowed on me a steady, willful blind love. It had taken a while, but I had learned to return it. All that was required of me was that I remember her soft fragility and keep my inner darkness and cynicism cloaked. That all personal information I shared had to be coated in advance with sugar didn't trouble me at all.

To keep Nina from noticing my stress and the intensity of my feeling about our conversation, I dumped my little chrome teapot on the tablecloth and got a grip on myself while she explained "my accident" to the waitress.

She was having a good time, so I ordered more tea. Her white hair, so tightly wrapped round her skull, glistened in the afternoon sunlight. The sun showed dull patches on her worn blue satin dress. Her glasses were covered with a thin glaze of partial fingerprints and she was so deeply involved in her own memories that she didn't notice me staring at the variety of wrinkles on her face and neck.

I drove home and, pleased that Irene had not yet returned, sat on the couch to open my package. It was carefully wrapped, hastily slathered with stamps and masking tape, and addressed to Mr. Timothy Barlow c/o Lester and Nina Barlow. That it came with a Paonia return address and a Santa Clara postmark similar to those on the late-arriving postcards did not surprise me. I recognized the shirts right away. Near the bottom was a white tee shirt and a pair of my underpants, both tattooed with lipstick kisses. Smiling, sighing, and removing them, I uncovered a thick envelope containing three thousand dollars. On motel stationery, Molly had composed a rhyme.

"Half from Mitch, half from Molly. Now you're rich, hope you're jolly."

I hurried to the phone, and after a brief conversation with an operator, dialed quickly.

"Pat's Pantry."

"May I speak with Mitch, please?"

"Mitch is on vacation. May I take a message?"

"Pat?"

"She's with him."

A desperate twinge of hope. "Is Molly there by chance?"

"Who the hell is this? Peter, is that you?"

"No. My name is Tim."

"Yeah, well, you've got the wrong number, Tim."

The line went dead.

Over a solo dinner in a fancy hotel that night, I fit things together as best I could. Molly had found the postcards I'd written to Serena and my grandparents, then taken them, along with my Chevy and clothes, to California. Apparently, the narcs hadn't been lying about the missing ten thousand dollars, but how Molly had come by it and why and under what circumstances was hard to get at. That Mitch had agreed to give me any money was a mystery, but maybe I'd find out. What did come back to me as I downed the last of a bottle of champagne was Mitch's expression that afternoon in the kitchen when I asked him to cook me a cheeseburger and he'd said he'd take as an order any suggestion Molly made to him.

Until I saw Molly again, I'd have to make do with that recollection, that and Molly's telling me how Mitch had built the huge kitchen and a cellar underneath the restaurant by himself, thirty years before, at a time when he'd had more time than money.

The next afternoon I rented a one-bedroom apartment overlooking a dismal shopping mall parking lot six or seven miles south of the Emerson Street house and a safe deposit box at a bank across the street. Denny seemed to be the last real friend of mine who hadn't left Denver. I loved him honestly enough, but I didn't want to be in the presence of his great talent for life when my own knack for living seemed so hopelessly clumsy. Rather than call him, I rented a truck and hired two college kids to carry a few pieces of furniture from what was becoming Irene's house to my apartment. I spent fifty bucks on picture frames so I could display some of my favorite snapshots of Matt and Serena on my desk, and then worked the better part of three days and nights scrubbing every visible surface in the apartment.

Dead drunk a few days later, I dialed home and Irene answered. "Welcome home," I said.

"Where are you?"

"Why do you care?

She sighed. "Put it that way and I guess I don't."

I had all I could do to hold the receiver to my ear and keep breathing. "How's Gerald?"

"I don't know."

"Is he there?"

"He's in Paris. On sabbatical."

"That where you were?"

"As a matter of fact, no."

"Just fuck 'em and leave 'em, huh? That his strategy? Wreck homes and head for Europe?"

"Are you drunk?"

"Yes. Are you in love?"

"Why would you care?"

"Why wouldn't I?"

"You've been showing you haven't for a long time."

"My kids might care."

"Your kids?"

"Ours, I meant. Our kids. Can I talk to them?"

"They love you."

"I'd rather hear it from them."

"I'd rather they not hear anything from you until you're sober."

"I'll call back," I said.

The next night, a bit less drunk, I did. "I want to talk to Serena."

"She's in bed."

"Matt?"

"In bed."

"Can I come over?"

"No."

"I want to talk to you."

"You are."

"When did you first have sex with Gerald?"

"I don't want to go into it."

"I don't either, but I don't have a choice."

"But I do have a choice."

She proved it by hanging up.

I called again the next morning. "The only thing I have to know," I said, "is when, where, and how often?"

She hung up again.

I drove to the house. She was gone. I called that night. "Where, when, and how often?"

She was quiet a long time. I pressed the phone to my ear, hoping to hear her crying. After a minute, she spoke very calmly. "That's a pointless discussion. Serena cried for you this afternoon."

"Put her on."

"You'll remember she's a child?"

"I'll remember everything."

"Hi, Daddy. I want you to come home."

"I know."

"But you have to get well first."

"I do?"

"Yes, because you're sick and you have to be somewhere there are no kids making a lot of noise, where people can take care of you."

"Oh, is that it? I'll be able to visit you soon."

"When?"

"Tomorrow."

"Tomorrow?"

I heard Irene's voice. She came back on the phone.

"I'll drop them both off at your folks at two if you'll promise to drop them off there again by four."

"Keep my parents out of this."

"Too late. They're already in it. Your dad called the other night. I said I didn't know where you were, that I hadn't talked to you since you went off fishing, which was certainly the truth."

"I don't know where you were the other night, either. I'm not sure I want to." I was drunk again and nodding my head up and down. "But you know why I was wherever I was, don't you?"

"Don't let's get started. Your mom called yesterday. I told her we'd been having problems, that we were living apart temporarily."

"Temporarily?"

"Everything's temporal, isn't it?" There was a cruel teasing in her voice.

"Aren't you glib?

"Tim, sober up. Do you want to spend time with the kids or not?"

"Yeah, but I want to pick them up at home. Not at my parents' house."

"I don't trust you. You've been drinking. You're filled with what you think of as self-righteous anger."

"I never ever more than raised my voice with you, Irene."

"Yes, but you've never been like this before, either."

"I'm not going to pick them up at my parents. I'll wait for them out on the front porch or in the car and you can send them out. You won't have to see me."

Irene and I collaborated on some childproof fiction about why we had to be apart and the summer became a painful haze of visits with the kids, alcohol, and pot smoke. Irene went back to school, having at least another semester to complete.

After Labor Day I walked Serena to her first day of kindergarten. Matt had started saying a few things that I could understand on the telephone. I gave Irene five hundred dollars to buy a battered Oldsmobile from a friend in the art department and agreed to make small child support payments. Eventually, I kept the kids overnight at my apartment two of the four nights a week that Irene worked waitressing at a local nightclub. On the phone, we were crisp and clear and businesslike. We made little pronouncements of our intentions and then hung up before the other could ask questions or start another argument. On those occasions when we had to occupy the same room for a few moments, we refused to look at each other. One night when I was too drunk to care, Irene let slip that for the kids' sake she might consider counseling toward some kind of reconciliation. The next morning when I brought it up, she said she'd changed her mind. Meantime, I carefully pumped Serena for information. Gerald was not in the picture it turned out but there was a man who came over sometimes. His name was Oliver and Serena gave him some of her candy. He was never there in the morning when Serena got up.

To stop brooding so much and spiraling down, and to increase my grubstake for a new life, I found a vacant parking space in the Old Glory Potato Chip Company and walked inside. Evvie, who'd gotten remarried and become the new manager, happily hired me back and put me in charge of shipping.

One Saturday morning after I picked the kids up from Irene's, Serena unsnapped a plastic handbag Irene had bought her from a thrift shop and handed me a letter without a return address. Disappointed to discover that it was from Dom rather than Molly, but also eager to see what Dom had to say for himself, I read the letter while pretending to listen to Serena struggle through a song she was learning in school.

He apologized for not being around for my visit, saying that some friends of his had gotten burned in a major drug deal and that he'd had to make himself scarce. He said that for the time being he was living in a tool shed behind a gardener's house on an estate in San Marino, near Pasadena north of LA. He'd made some mistakes and learned from them, and luckily, he wrote, he had a good lawyer. The narcs had "lost" amounts of drugs and more than ten thousand dollars and completely botched the case, so that even as I was reading, he wrote, big shots in the DEA were being forced to accept that they would have to choose between Dom, assuming he could be found, and revelations about their own shady dealings and incompetence. Dom claimed that, through his lawyer, he'd been offered two years probation if he would come forward and name names. Dom had always evinced a fierce loyalty and I knew he wouldn't do this, even before I read his words of reassurance. He was convinced the government would cut him loose. He inquired about Irene and the kids, said he had a few bucks salted away, and would like nothing better than to spend Christmas in Denver with the four of us. About this possibility and about everything else, I should write him at a Pasadena post office box.

That night I wrote him a twenty-three-page letter on yellow legal paper. Dom already knew about the death of Little George, about Thunderhead and what had become of his old truck, so I started with the bald tires on the snowy Black Canyon, meeting McKinley outside the Hotchkiss Co-op, and my encounter with Molly, the wife, I reminded him, of Peter Turnquist, his partner in dope. Gerald, the phone call to Serena, sex with Molly, the arrest on the mountain, my time in jail, Molly's departure for California, the tea with Nina, and my separation from Irene. I tried to keep my language plain and did my best to seem to be feeling less sorry for myself than I was, erasing little outbursts of self-pity wherever I detected them. Partly to convey how well I was holding up, I told him what I knew about Evvie's remarriage and her ascendancy at the Old Glory Potato Chip Company. The next morning, I added a postscript of questions. Where were Peter and Nadine? Was he in contact with Peter? Had he ever met or did he have any news of Molly? How, if he knew, could I get in touch with either Molly or Peter?

A week later, Dom replied that Peter and Nadine had told him they were headed to Buenos Aires, though he knew for a fact that they'd bought first-class one-way tickets to Jakarta, Indonesia. He'd met Molly three or four times in and around Paonia, he wrote, but didn't really know her or have any idea where she might be. By then, I was involved in my own search for her. Not having a phone in my apartment, I kept rolls of quarters in the glove box of the Volks and fed them by the dozens into pay phones in my neighborhood.

Mitch talked to me twice, but there was just no way that I could convince him that I wasn't a cop or get him to talk about Molly. I thought maybe that mentioning the money Molly had sent me might make him believe I was who I said I was, but when I did, he insisted he didn't known anything about any money. Eventually, I coaxed his wife Pat into giving me the phone number of Molly's attorney. Kindly Stuart Meacham made a few inquiring calls on my behalf, but he finally recommended I contact a private detective agency in Denver. I sent Meacham a thank-you card and a fifth of Scotch. The other fifth I drank that night.

Not far from my apartment, I discovered a dumpy neighborhood honkytonk called Sancho's Keep. There was nothing literary or medieval about the place, unless maybe the pervasive smell of urine over disinfectant, but the beer was cheap and cold, and the ready companionship of fellow drinkers was suitably loud and undemanding. Thin and unseeing as Quixote himself, and with my little red Rocinante parked out back, I could have benefited from the sage amiability of a Sancho Panza, had there been one. The owner was a retired barber named Abe. There was a lot of George Jones on the jukebox and under his spell I regularly sought my Dulcinea in any woman willing to talk to me for ten minutes at a stretch. Among the candidates were three or four divorcees who often stopped at Sancho's every midnight for nightcaps, after having clocked out from the nearby Gates Rubber Company.

To keep any conversation silly and not serious, I sometimes introduced myself as Don Coyote or Don Key Coyote, saying that having expanded my consciousness, I now wanted to contract it and descend the evolutionary ladder in the general direction of, say, Spiro Agnew. I didn't mind that my rambling natter fell on mostly deaf ears. What I wanted, or told myself I did, was just to sit stupefied in an alcohol mist in front of a television set and get midsection to midsection with some God-fearing female who had never heard of Timothy Leary or the Grateful Dead. My short-term goal was a brief interlude, urgently biological and meaningless, with some fallen cowgirl who otherwise snapped her chewing gum, teased her hair, and did her nails in front of the TV. To that end, I perched on a barstool among a dozen fellow drunken knights in whom I had only a competitive interest. It didn't take me long to conclude that the women from Gates Rubber who minced around Sancho's in fringed white boots knew more about how to get what they wanted than the knights errant who hoped to win them. I played the game with a little more disinterested misery and guile than most of my rivals, and buoyed my interest by keeping a journal in the voice of a self-help book titled *Scoring While Dead Drunk*. My working theory boiled down to this: the randier a woman looked, the heavier her eye shadow, the more hoisted and tanned her cleavage, the more likely it was that she had the skills to select from her potential suitors the man most likely to listen to her protracted tales about her miserable ex in exchange for a single, chaste, goodnight kiss.

My favorite would-be Dulcinea was Beatrice, a supervisor at Gates, who wore her ash blond hair in roughly the shape of a Nazi helmet and called herself Beatie. One night at her suburban ranch-style home, she made vodka gimlets while I went through the motions of professing interest in tales of the pipe-fitter husband she'd finally worked up the nerve to throw out. I was sitting in an atmospheric red light looking at our reflections as we sat slumped over her wet bar in a family room decorated with drawings made by her kids. We flirted promisingly and carried our deadly watery drinks to a stained couch in front of the television. But just as she began to notice how inherently sweet I was, her twelve-year-old daughter appeared with a sore throat. While mother and daughter repaired to an upstairs bathroom for a gargle and aspirin, I squatted near a stereo and thumbed through racks of dusty Elvis, Patsy Cline, and Nat King Cole records.

Nat was on the turntable when Beatie returned, drinks were freshened, and we started dancing closer and closer. Unfortunately, her nine-year-old son then came down to tell her about a bad dream. While Beatie followed him back to bed, I brightened the lights enough to peruse her bookshelf, where bowling and Pony League baseball trophies were needed to support the scarcity of books. There was one book about the hidden messages of the Dead Sea Scrolls, two or three illustrated volumes on home decoration, a collection of Rod McKuen's poems, a paperback on the importance of Christian positive thinking, a stack of *TV Guides*, and a tattered book of crossword puzzles.

Rhonda had always told me that my Tarot cards, whenever she read me, showed that I wasn't much good at accepting pictorially encrypted messages from the gods. My retort had been that however bad I was when it came to following inspired guidance, I was even worse at overlooking or ignoring it; my carefully fortified unbelief was desperately fragile. I would rather have seen meaning everywhere, like messages from God on toothpaste billboards, than no meaning anywhere.

When Beatie came back downstairs, I told her that I had a headache. Indeed, the rumblings were already there. One little effort at honesty soon led to another and I finally heard myself saying that I was sorry that her kids were having sore throats and bad dreams and doing without on account of their deadbeat dad, and that I didn't want add any falseness or empty hopes to anyone's life. Beatie said I was sweet and walked me out to her front porch, which was illuminated with a pale blue flickering that rendered her face alternately pink and green. I told her I was going to cut back on my drinking and advised her to look out for some of the bums who hung out at Sancho's. She laughed and tossed her head, and I saw that she was competent and much less hideously enticing and more appealing than I'd seen through my predatory squint. I thanked her for the evening. She brought her green face up to my cheek and kissed me. The warmth of her lips went very deep. When she stepped back I half expected her to go on receding into the void like some Indian peyote goddess. But she just opened the front door, put one foot inside her house, turned and said, "Happy Thanksgiving."

"Oh, yeah," I said. "Thanksgiving. Same to you."

The evening was chilly and the stars were bright. I breathed deeply, moved my head and shoulders reflexively, and some dirty weight or other slid from my chest, like some smelly hide of a robe I'd picked up in the gutter for warmth.

The next afternoon, I drove Matt and Serena to dinner at my parents' house, where I'd been assured in advance that Irene and my marriage and my future would not be a subject of any kind of conversation. With three different drinks within reach, my dad was sitting in his lounge chair cozied up to one of his new speakers. *Aida* was cranked up so loud that Serena put her hands over her ears and hurried to her grandma in the kitchen. Most of the rest of the family stood there not-all-that-quietly complaining about how loud the music was and what, if anything, might be done about it without spoiling Thanksgiving.

I served apple cider to the kids and added milk to a cup of coffee I poured myself. After a few minutes, Serena went back out to the living room and charmed my dad into lowering the volume.

When we were ready to eat, I helped Serena settle Matt in a booster chair at the small kids' table in the kitchen, while my sister's two daughters, also at the kids' table, started arguing about which of them would get the biggest slice of pie. Matt lost no time in inciting little-girl laughter by rubbing his food-coated hands in his hair and banging on his plate with a spoon. After making an effort to calm things down a little, I left the supervision of the kids' meal to my sister and mother, and joined the adults gathering around the dining room table.

Bert moved his drinks in an order known only to him to and attacked the turkey with a carving knife. Abruptly, he slammed the serving fork down on the platter and glared at my mom. "Well, Jean, once again, thanks for the goddamned shoe leather!"

My grandpa Lester made a clucking noise with his tongue and said something about couldn't we "one day a year," while my grandma Nina winced and muttered to herself. Noticing how quiet it was around the table, Nina tried to smile and observed that the bird looked just perfect to her.

Bert gave his mother a look of unadulterated disgust. He looked up at the chandelier, called briefly on the gods to give him patience, and when they proved slow to respond, flung the serving fork across the room, imbedding its tines, like an accomplished circus performer, in the back of one of his new speaker cabinets. My younger brother Michael decided to wait out the storm by wandering out to the kitchen for another glass of beer. Too young for beer, and oddly inured to his father's outbursts, my youngest brother Jeff couldn't keep from admiring the way the fork wobbled in the walnut speaker. I decided to collect Matt and Serena and take them to my apartment, hesitating only when Bert hoisted the twenty-five-pound bird, carried it around the table, and dropped it like a bomb on Nina's plate. "Since it's to your liking, Mom, you can eat the whole goddamned thing!"

I rushed to my grandma and pushed the bird off her broken plate onto the tablecloth, ready to defend her at any cost. "Happy Thanksgiving, Dad," I shouted. "I'm sure that chief among the many blessings we all feel today is the knowledge that none of us will ever have to endure another Thanksgiving here ever again!"

"Don't come over here and give us your speeches in front of my grandkids, you ungrateful cocksucker!"

When I saw him reach for the gravy boat, I hurried back to my place at the table and altered my position so that if and when the gravy boat missed my head it wouldn't break the window and shower us all with a shrapnel of glass. Losing gravy to his shirt, Bert cocked the gravy boat behind his ear, but lost a heartbeat perfecting his aim. Taking no such trouble, I let my dinner plate fly from where I'd snatched it. A giblet hit him in the throat and the blood of canned cranberry sauce appeared on his white shirt. Luckily, the plate itself sailed past his head, as did a gob of mashed potatoes that adhered to the wall, stuck there like a rubber-tipped dart from one of my old dart guns.

Bert dropped the gravy boat to the floor and came for me. While every adult voice in the house called out for forbearance, we stood just out of reach, rage-to-rage. I was on the balls of my feet, looking into his shining eyes, observing the dark, exposed capillaries in his nose, smelling beer, thinking suddenly and unaccountably about how we were gathered unthankfully together, three generations of Barlow men, when from the corner of one eye, I saw the fourth, Matt, wide blue eyes, terrified and too scared to cry. Little buttons of sweat glistened in Bert's hairline. My grandma was crying and wondering why somebody didn't call the police. My grandpa was talking about killing himself. My brother Mike was telling me to cool it. My mother had one hand on my arm and one hand on Bert's. The storm had passed. She was the last one to realize it was all over.

On her own initiative, or maybe I'd said something, Serena gathered our coats and squatted down to zip Matt into his parka. As the sun was setting, the three of us drove to McDonald's for cheeseburgers and strawberry shakes where I promised Serena she never have to go to another family dinner at grandpa's unless she wanted to.

After dropping the kids at Irene's I took a late night walk through Washington Park and began to formulate a plan to extricate Matt and Serena from the cycles of self-pity and disappointment and rage that cursed the Barlow line.

The next day there was another letter from Dom. He'd come into a little money, he said. He proposed to send me round trip airfares, so that over Christmas break the kids and I could fly out and he could take them to Disneyland and Knotts' Berry Farm and wherever else we could think of. Or, he added, if I wanted to stay in California to make a new start, he'd fly Matt and Serena back to Denver, and have them delivered to Irene's door at any prearranged time in a limousine. Technically still a

447

fugitive, Dom said he planned to phone his lawyer that week and find out if he'd been cleared and if he could now walk the streets under his own name. Dom's idea sounded like the mystical new beginning, the pilgrimage I needed to make. I didn't want to do it on Dom's drug money, but over my Thanksgiving cheeseburger I had decided I wanted to raise Matt and Serena by myself. Probably in the back of my mind was the conviction that Molly would eventually reappear to save us. I wrote Dom that I basically liked his idea and that the kids and I would be on the scene in the not too distant future.

I'd stood up to my dad and acquired a basic tolerance for working class people who shared none of my real interests. I'd slow danced miles to George Jones with divorcees who worked at Gates, acquired a measure of respect and compassion for many people who felt trapped and many who didn't know they were trapped. I had done the working class bar scene. Feeling a need to keep moving in a direction that seemed forward, I took an evening job delivering pizzas in my Volkswagen. When Irene was working at the nightclub, the kids sometimes rode around with me, eating cold pizza and singing songs they'd partly memorized from my Dave Van Ronk and Bob Dylan albums. Delivery tips were invested in ice cream.

The promised plane tickers never arrived, but in January there came a letter from Dom saying that he was pretty much off the hook, off drugs, and had rented a house in Topanga Canyon where he was finishing a screenplay. He still hadn't been officially cleared of drug charges and had no phone, but the heat was off, he insisted, and he was pretty much going where and when he wanted. This time he included an address; I could either write back and he could forward me a phone number when he got one or I could just show up on his doorstep.

When February came the weather turned bitterly cold. I wrote Molly's lawyer a letter containing Dom's address and sent a postcard with the same info to Pat's Pantry. I paid a kid who was studying auto repair to tune the Volks, adjust its valves, and repair its sticking accelerator pedal.

I gathered boxes from neighborhood supermarkets, removed the front passenger seat from the Volks, and heaved it up and into the dumpster behind my apartment. I worked with empty cartons until I found eight boxes that could fit on the back seat, on the floor in front of the back seat, and on the floor where the passenger seat had been without obstructing my view. I packed my prized books and albums, made a small bed from a length of foam rubber and cut up three woolen thrift store blankets for bedding. I rigged a place for a baby seat on top of a wooden box in front, secured the baby seat by driving a pair of nails into the wooden box and tightened it with a pair of bootlaces. The seat wasn't as steady as I wanted it to be, but I calculated that a little weight in the boxes coupled with some strategic shimming would do wonders to stabilize Matt's ride west. From such a position, he would be able to look out at the changing landscape. Serena had to stay in school for now, but I vowed I'd come get her once Matt and I were settled.

Very cold, I removed the child seat contraption and went upstairs, had a shot of brandy, and began organizing my stuff. After a few minutes, I called Irene to let her know that it was three degrees outside, that it would be about the same inside the Volks, and that Serena should be warmly dressed for our planned one-on-one private birthday celebration.

Serena asked me about the missing front seat in the car and I told her that I'd removed it without offering an explanation. We drove from the old house, Irene's house as we were now calling it, to a neighborhood restaurant for burgers and soda. For dessert there was cheesecake. I took a small box of pink candles from my coat pocket and inserted them carefully in her cheesecake.

"Daddy, what are you doing?"

"Shh. We can't talk loud because we don't want people to notice us. Tomorrow's your birthday, isn't it? I'm fixing you some birthday candles."

"But are you going to sing 'Happy Birthday' tonight?"

"Yes. Don't you think you and I should have our own birthday party, even though we're in a restaurant and you won't be six until tomorrow?"

"Yes!" she laughed. "That way I'll have two birthdays."

I lit the candles and sat close to her.

"Daddy, how come you came over here by me?"

"I want to sit next to you. That way we can sing quietly."

"Why do you want to sing quietly?"

"Well, did anybody else in this pizza place buy you a new dress or even give you a little present?"

"No."

"So, they aren't invited to our party. And I don't want them to come over here and watch us, do you?"

"I don't know."

"Okay, you sit back, close your eyes, and make a wish. If you can blow all the candles out without breathing twice, and if your wish is a good one, it will come true, but only if you remember that you're not supposed to tell anyone what you wish for."

"Not even you?"

"Not even me. Close your eyes now."

She leaned back and gulped air. Her cheeks puffed out, looking like she was holding a small-inflated balloon in her mouth.

"No, wait. You're supposed to wait until after I've sung 'Happy Birthday.'"

"Well, hurry up, because I don't want that pink candle to melt on my cake."

I pulled her close and sang in her ear. Her blonde hair smelled of discount store shampoo, of bubble gum, and of Irene's fruity hand cream. "Happy Bir. . ." My throat contracted.

"Daddy? Why did you stop singing?"

"Ah. Um. I forgot some of the words."

"Well, hurry up and remember."

"Okay. "Happy Birthday dear . . . ."

"Daddy, how come you're singing it like that?"

"Like what?"

"Making your voice sound all funny?"

"Does my voice sound funny?"

"Yeah. Sing it right. And hurry up, so I can blow the candles."

"It's okay, you can blow the candles out and get your wish once somebody starts to sing. Go ahead and blow the candles out."

"No, I want you to finish singing first."

"Okay, but I'll have to wait a minute."

"Why?"

"Um, a frog bit me in the throat."

"A FROG BIT YOU IN THE THROAT?" She laughed, goading me, prepared to flop off her chair in an outburst of convulsive giggling.

"Shhh. We don't want people to hear. I'll finish singing while you blow the candles out. Ready, set, go."

I helped her blow the candles out and hurried through the song.

"You still sang it funny."

"Well, I had to help you blow the candles out. Did you make a wish?"

"Yeah. I wished that you. . . ."

"Don't tell me or it won't come true."

". . . would come back home and live with us."

"You did? That's what you wished?"

"Yeah. Will you?"

"I don't know. Not right away. But you know what?"

"What?"

"Even if I can't live with you right away, I will live with you as soon as I can and I will always love you."

"But I don't want you to love me. I want you to tuck me in at night and buy me dresses and give me rides on your shoulders."

I twisted my spoon and made a shape in my ice cream.

"Daddy, you're playing with your food."

"You're right. I tell you not to do it, so I shouldn't do it, either. But Serena, I can't live with you for a while."

"Come back on Sunday then."

"Even though it's making me sad to say it, I can't come back Sunday or the next Sunday or the Sunday after that."

"Why, Daddy?"

"Can you keep a secret and not tell anybody?"

"Yeah."

"ANYbody?"

"Just Mommy."

"Not even Mommy."

"Okay."

"I have to go away for a while."

"Can I go, too?"

"No, because you need to be in school and I have to try and get some money. But you know what? Once I get some money we'll find you another school and then you can come and live with me."

"And Mommy and Matt too."

"Matt can come. Your mom? Depends on what she wants."

"She wants you to grow up. That's what she told Lenny."

"Do you want me to grow up?"

"No, because you're already grown. But I want Matt to grow up so he doesn't cry all the time and stops pooping in his diapers."

"I hear you can change his diapers."

"I'm not going to do it anymore, though. He kicked me when his diaper was off and made me stick him with a pin, and then he got mad and kicked me again. Sometimes he pees on me and laughs. Daddy, I don't like this cheesecake."

"Okay, just eat your ice cream then."

"I don't want it. I want to go home."

"You want to go home already?"

"Yeah."

I buttoned her sweater and zipped her coat tightly against her throat. After paying the check, I came back and sat down next to her. I didn't want to drive her to my all-but-empty apartment where she'd see all the piled boxes. Neither was I quite ready to say goodbye. I didn't want to just disappear, so I coaxed her into playing the game of secrecy. A little more effort would probably be necessary to keep her quiet until the next afternoon.

"No matter what happens, Serena, I want you to remember one thing."

"What?"

"I want you to remember that I love you, just as much as I love Matt. I love you just the same. I don't love him any more and I don't love him any less than I love you. I love you both just the same. When I get some money I will take care of you both the same."

She looked at me and wrinkled her nose.

"Do you like the two dresses I bought you for your birthday?"

"Yes." She nodded, her eyes wide and blue.

"Think about how I love you whenever you wear them, okay?"

I tried to swallow but couldn't, so I looked out the window. Three or four inches of snow had fallen the week before. The snow began to melt one afternoon, then the temperature dropped precipitously. Now the snow was topped by slabs of glassy ice.

"Daddy, I want to go home now."

"Okay."

"Will you tuck me in and tell me a story?"

"Sure."

Irene heard me pull up in front of the house. She pulled the drapes in her studio back and squinted down at me. I had hoped to avoid looking at her, prayed that her face would remain fixed in its coldness and that she'd manage to keep hidden whatever sadness and regret she might feel. Her eyes were jet-black and her face gray and hostile when she opened the door. She stepped back to admit Serena, then forward again. With a small gesture, I acknowledged her power to admit and refuse visitors. A great warmth seemed to rush out of the darkened hall behind her.

I looked at Serena, then at Irene. "She asked me to tuck her in," I said, facial expression as neutral as I could manage.

Irene stooped to remove Serena's mittens, but she didn't step back to admit me.

"He promised to tuck me in and tell me a story."

"He did?"

Serena put an ungloved hand against the barricade of Irene's hip and, with a determined forearm, eased her mother to one side.

"Thanks," I said to Irene. For a moment, I doubted what I was about to do. I felt defeated, temporarily empty of anger or resentment.

Irene grunted and started up the stairs toward her studio.

"Brush your teeth," Irene said, stepping inside the brightly lit room and holding the door to close it against me. Maybe Irene felt a greater need for privacy now that I was no longer living there. Serena had her own room and Matt slept in a crib in Irene's studio. I knew he was in there, awake, and I deliberately called to him as I escorted Serena into the bathroom and put toothpaste on her brush. I heard him jabbering at me, so while Serena brushed, I went to the closed door and knocked.

Irene's voice was cold. "What?"

"I promised Serena that I'd tuck Matt in, too."

"It's not a good time."

There was no way I wasn't going to tuck him in. "I'll only be a minute. I solemnly promise not to nose about, ask any questions, or look at any of your paintings."

My bedtime story for Serena was about the origins of the word "daddy," which were unknown to a little girl who lived with her mother and brother in a cheesecake house on the edge of the forest. The mother was beautiful and the father was handsome and the little girl was smart, always asking her daddy to supply her with the meanings of words. One day the father went into the forest and didn't come back. The little girl was very sad and asked her mother every day about her daddy. Of course, the mother didn't know why the father had disappeared. After a day or two of sadness the little girl went into the forest by herself and there she met Sequester, the King of Squirrels, who told her the origins of "daddy." "Da" meant a man who loves his children and "dee" meant someone who always returns no matter how long he is gone because he always loves his children no matter where he goes.

Serena was more interested in a description of Sequester than the actual tale. I told her that I didn't have too much background on him, only that he was an ancient and wise squirrel who could eat four nuts at a time while whistling. Then I pulled the blanket up under her chin. Kissing her goodnight, I turned out the light.

Irene emerged from her studio, passing me in the hall without speaking or looking at me. I hesitated and thought of suggesting that she take a good look at what a beautiful wonderful little boy our baby son had turned into.

"Please hold it to two minutes," she said, as my heart went hard as steel. "He needs his sleep."

"How's he going to get to sleep while you're in there painting?"

"I'm done for the night."

"He's not sick, is he?"

"No. He's just been running around all day. Try not to get him all dancing and excited, okay?"

I called to her as she went down the stairs. "Where's Oliver?"

"No idea."

Matt stood in his crib, bouncing up and down in a pair of pajamas decorated with tropical fish. I lifted him out, hugged him to my chest, and felt the wetness around his bottom.

Disposable diapers!

The one essential element missing from my plan.

After changing him, I stuffed three plastic-coated diapers from Irene's closet under my coat, while Matt cheered me on with a little hopping dance on his mattress. I wrestled him into a dry pair of bottoms, laid him down, covered him up, and then called down to Irene, "Shall I turn out the lights?"

"Don't bother. There's something I need up there."

We met on the stairs again.

"Why don't you say a special good night to him?" I suggested. Unwilling to be either utterly hostile or at all friendly, Irene grunted. "I think I'll say a special good morning instead."

Back at my apartment, I turned the heat up high and went back to work outside. Carrying down my boxes and wedging them into predetermined positions in the Volks, I left the box containing Matt's extra warm clothes for last. Upstairs, I put the finishing touches on a letter to Irene, slipped it into a back pocket and heated a pan of eggnog, finishing off with a generous brandy pour. A little more than half of my blend I poured into a thermos. The other half went to a plastic baby bottle. I enlarged the opening in the nipple of the baby bottle to allow for the thickness of my concoction, which I then wrapped in a red snowsuit that I'd bought for Matt the week before. On the way out I shut off the heat, turned out the lights and trudged downstairs. The snow squeaked underfoot and cracked where it had been frozen.

Irene's house looked dark, so I drove her alley to see if she was maybe up reading in the back bedroom. Thinking she might not yet be deeply asleep despite the darkened house, I drove to a bar on Sixth Avenue and drank two cups of sour hot coffee. Returning again by way of the alley, I circled the block and parked out front, then let myself into the house, grateful my old key still worked. Slipping my boots off by the door and mounting the wooden stairs, I hugged the banister to avoid the squeaky middle of the steps. Irene's bedroom door was cracked, rather than ajar. I stood beside it briefly, conscious of my short breath and laboring heart, then tiptoed to her studio.

Matt sputtered and kicked momentarily. I'd tried him out on the eggnog over Christmas, so the eagerness with which he bit down on the warm, sweet nipple didn't surprise me. I kissed him and whispered,

"Suck that good stuff down, Boy." While he worked the bottle, I stuffed him gently into the giant quilted snowsuit and held him until his eyelids began drooping. Then it was glide sock-footed downstairs, step into boots without bothering to lace or tie, and open the door to the frigid blast of night air. A little amazed at myself, I listened and noted the click of the lock in the front door behind me.

Helping Matt hold on to his bottle, I positioned him in the back on the foam rubber pad, tugged little mittens over his hands, and wrapped him like a mummy in overlapping blanket fragments. The little Volks engine chattered, and with a frozen sound suggestive of driving over broken glass, pulled slowly away from the curb.

I'd thought of buying a better car with a working heater, and would have probably done just that if I hadn't decided against it on a day when the temperature was sixty degrees. I wanted to have money to rent a small apartment of my own when we got to LA. Dom had written that he had the goodwill of a couple of television writers who had some contacts and had agreed to help us get into script development. If this promise amounted to anything at all, I would need at the minimum a television, telephone, and a better typewriter. I hated the idea of wasting money and time watching television, but I liked the idea of making fifteen grand for writing a single sitcom episode. Also, and I kept this from myself as best I could, I liked the idea of arriving in southern California in a red Volks that Molly would certainly recognize if, somehow, she happened on it. Wishful thinking, Scofflaw.

For days I'd been a slave to isobars and temperature tables in the daily newspaper. All the passes through the Colorado Rockies were closed or open only to four-wheel drives or vehicles equipped with chains. To the south, Raton Pass had been closed by record snows and cold. Obliged to avoid the high passes by crossing the Continental Divide in southern Wyoming where it had been crossed so many times by generations of pioneers, I felt confident that after turning west out of Cheyenne I'd be faced with about fourteen hours of bitterly cold driving before descending into Salt Lake City where the weather would be warmer. It would be at least fifty degrees once I got over the Nevada border and started along the desert floor to Las Vegas. Life would be a little cold and rough, but only for a day or so.

With Molly's new tires, and a rock-hard sheet of ice under a dusting of new snow, I anticipated better traction and a higher rate of speed. Heading north on the Valley Highway, I discovered that I had overestimated how much body heat the two of us would generate in the little Volks. The bitter cold was something that I hoped we'd both quickly adapt to, and now I saw that I hadn't given enough thought to visibility problems. In the heater-less Volks, I'd have to drive with my front window slightly open. Not far out of town my gloved hands began to go numb on the steering wheel, and I kept looking back at Matt, wondering if maybe there was a better way of doing what I was trying to do.

Big trucks roared past us blowing smokes of powdery snow all over the front of the car. Driving, I scraped constantly at the thin sheets of ice that formed on the inside glass of the Volks. As if body weight might make a difference to the plodding Beetle, I hunched over the wheel and leaned toward the Wyoming border.

With a thumping sound in back, Matt rid himself of the baby bottle. When I recovered and offered it again, he pushed it away. Despite talking to him, patting him, I failed to distract him. He wrestled in his woolen cocoon. My rendering of "Pop Goes the Weasel" was good for about five miles. Then he started to whimper. Doing "Old MacDonald" with special attention to the animal noises got me another few miles, but Matt was crying and angry by the time we reached the outskirts of the town of Fort Collins.

The woolen blankets weren't as warm as I'd supposed they'd be and the cold, unheated tile floor of a Conoco station was no place to change his diaper. It was, however, a place where I could get at him and make sure he was dry. Where had I put the damned baby powder?

"Daddy, cold. Daddy, cold."

"I know partner. I'm going to fix you right up. Want some candy?"

"Yeah. Home."

"I'm going to take care of you, Spunkhead. Get you some candy, get you nice and warm. We're going to have fun."

Feeding a candy machine inside the filling station, removing the candy, and handing it to Matt, I looked at the attendant. "Is there an all-night coffee shop somewhere around here?"

The attendant blinked, moved a massive lump of Skoal toward his rearmost molars and spit at a lidless oilcan. "Bout fi mal. Jeffson Street exit."

"Jefferson?"

"Yep."

I carried Matt toward the heat vent and held him in front of it. We jabbered and handed little rubbery shapes of sugary animals back and forth. I identified them and named their colors. The attendant smoked cigarettes and muttered to himself.

Rather than put Matt in the back on the foam pad again, I positioned him in his car seat, securing him with blankets and the homemade rawhide seat belts attached to nails I'd driven in the boxes. If it had been less cold, or if it had been daylight, or if the ice hadn't formed so quickly on the windshield and restricted Matt's visibility, he might have ridden a long time in that position. He started to fuss again almost right away.

"We're on our way to Disneyland. You'll see Mickey Mouse, Goofy. We'll ride in teeny boats through a tunnel and you'll go gaga over these singing dolls. You'll have cotton candy, ketchup on your hotdog. There will be lots of doggies, an ocean, baby girls in strollers, and old ladies with blue hair to drool over you. You can watch television till midnight and have fruity tooties for breakfast. I'll get you a cowboy potty chair. You'll be a surfing champion and have the best tan in your first-grade class."

He listened for a time, but when he lost interest in my pep talks, he didn't want to hear anything but the sound of his own unhappy cries.

The bathroom in the coffee shop had plenty of warm water. I sat him on the sink and washed and dried him with steamy paper towels until he stopped crying. Truck drivers stood at the urinals and craned their necks to watch me soak his feet where they had hoped to wash their hands.

We went to a booth well away from the drafty front door. A waitress in a mustard yellow uniform with big pockets in front jingled her tip money and stared at me.

"Coffee."

She rattled her money. "For him?"

"Side of bacon, hot chocolate, strawberry ice cream."

She raised her eyebrows.

"Bacon first."

She scowled. "Bacon first."

"Otherwise, he'll just fill up on the ice cream."

"I see."

"Fatty food, " I explained. "He'll burn that fat. It'll keep him warm."

"That's heart attack food. You want him warm, you take him home and put him to bed."

"I am taking him home and putting him to bed. It's just that home isn't exactly around the block, know what I mean?"

"I know the customer is always right. How do you want his bacon cooked?"

"Practically burned."

"Practically burned it is."

Matt was pink and laughing and calling me Daddy over and over again when he saw that bacon. A couple more minutes and he was trying to use chips of burned bacon as a spoon for his strawberry ice cream.

The waitress came over and poured me more coffee.

"How far is it to Cheyenne?"

"Don't know. A hundred miles or so I guess."

"Can't be. From Denver it's only a hundred miles."

"Guess so," she admitted. "I live in Greeley and I'll be leaving here in fifteen minutes and unlocking my door in forty-five. What world did you say you're from?"

"Nether."

"What?"

"Netherworld."

"'Nother world is right."

Matt's hot chocolate was no longer warm and when I tried to get him to drink he drooled it and spit it in his ice cream. He'd lost interest in the ice cream, too, except as a medium for a drawing he was making with a bacon shard in the melted pool of it on the stainless-steel counter of his high chair.

"One tough day, maybe, two, Matt. Then we'll come down out of this amazing canyon and start across the Nevada desert where the temperature will be a lot warmer and we'll be able to ride comfortably wearing only thin jackets. "

Enthusiastically, Matt bobbed up and down in his high chair. "I go go go go."

"We'll drive down the strip in Vegas and you'll get all saucer-eyed when you look up there at those winking, shooting lights in the shapes of bowing cowgirls and gunfighters and playing cards. You'll just get out of that car and put your head back and you won't want to stop staring at all the lights. We'll have steaks for a buck apiece and you can drown yours in ketchup if you want."

"Home now, home now. Home now."

"We'll wander through the casinos where glamorous floor girls will hold you in their arms and kiss you all over and teach you how to pull the gleaming arms of slot machines. "

"I go home, Daddy. Home."

"Dom and I will take you out on the Santa Monica Pier. You can shoot real guns and we'll play pinballs and old men will show you the ugliest fish you've ever seen in your life. We will build castles of seashells and starfish and we'll go in the water. It's not as cold as they say. I'll teach you to pinch your nose shut and the whole world, once made of water, will fall over our heads. It will make a huge loud noise, scare the hell out of us, and then we'll bob back up to the surface and start laughing."

An old woman at the counter had moved her coffee several seats toward us. When I looked at her with the offended look of someone whose privacy had been unreasonably invaded, she raised her coffee cup and grinned. "Take me with you," she said.

"Yeah, right," I said, picking up a napkin and turning my attention to the mess Matt had made.

"I don't want to go tonight, but wherever you're going I'd hell of a lot rather go than he would."

I had no response to this. But Matt did. "I go bye-bye."

The old woman got to her feet. There was no resemblance, physically, but something in the way she walked, or in the way she would have walked if she hadn't been so drunk, made me think of my Grandma Nina. I watched her pay for her coffee and listened to a conversation at the cash register. A truck driver was complaining of the twenty-five-below-zero temperatures between Laramie and Rawlins, where Matt and I would be driving about sunup, I figured. The roads were slick. Nothing but winds and heavy trucks. Matt could say cold and potty and a few other phrases, but he couldn't say frostbite or hypothermia and I didn't want him to learn those words or have any of those experiences yet. I'd probably run out of disposable diapers long before then and it would be the middle of a frigid day before I ever found a town where I could buy some.

The woman wandered back and put a quarter on the counter. I ignored her but Matt waved to her and said, "I go bye now."

She nodded her head, looked askance at me, and stirred at the coffee no longer in her cup.

The afternoon when I had driven my grandma home from the ceramics show she told me about the weekend that she'd kept me at her house while my mom had been in the hospital delivering my brother Michael. What made her chuckle to herself was the memory of taking me home again to have a look at the little brother I wouldn't have much interest in for some time. I'd been about Matt's age, running down the hall and into the kitchen. Seeing my mother there, my grandma said I'd mounted my red-and-white tricycle and pedaled it furiously around and around the room chanting, "I'm home. I'm home. I'm home."

When I put out my cigarette, Matt was saying, "I go bye-bye now," and the waitress was standing over me with a hot pot of coffee she maybe wanted to pour over my head.

"I've got to get him home."

459

The waitress smiled, relaxed in neck and shoulder, and half-filled my cup.

"To his mother."

The waitress nodded.

"Where he wants to be."

She stepped back and scratched her head.

"Because he said so."

She took a pencil from her ear and started writing out a check.

"I don't want him to grow into somebody who feels sorry for himself because he feels he's never listened to, and then gets angry that he isn't listened to, and starts thinking there must be something wrong with him because nobody's paying any attention." I had gulped the coffee and was bundling Matt in his snowsuit, gathering our stuff. I put tip money on the table and the waitress led us toward the cash register, which opened with a little ring as soon as she pressed a button.

"This boy is going to make genetic history."

The waitress counted me out my change with one eyebrow raised high. Her hand was warm when she gave me the money.

"He's going to become the first known member of his bloodline to listen to what others say and retain the capacity to say what he wants."

"How do you know what he wants now?"

"He said so."

"And you listened."

"Yes. Finally. If you're listened to early in life, I think you probably don't have to insist so hard about being heard later. That make any sense at all?"

"Not much. It might, though, if I wasn't too tired to listen."

"Good night."

"Drive careful."

The temperature hadn't actually risen when I settled Matt in the Volks and turned back to Denver, but it felt warmer. The car rolled more easily, the crunch under its tires didn't sound so harsh. Oncoming drivers dimmed their brights more readily, and Matt rode happily in his makeshift seat chanting about daddy and mommy. He was dozing against my chest when I unlocked the front door of the house. I moved soundlessly up the stairs to the bedrooms. His blankets were still warm and his diaper still dry. His fat little cheek was soft where I kissed it. After covering him up and going back downstairs, I reclaimed the note I'd left on the kitchen counter for Irene. I tried to modify what I'd written, confessing what I'd nearly done, but then gave up and carried both efforts to a burner on the stove. I let them flare and curl in the stainless steel sink, then rinsed the blackened remnants down the drain. Counting out ten hundred-dollar bills, I placed them and my surrendered front door key, under a cup containing Irene's unfinished tea.

I tiptoed down the front porch step and paused for one quick backward look. It was too cold for the big moment that might have been, too cold to sigh, even. I squeaked across the frozen snow on the sidewalk and started the little Volks, its engine chattering to life.

When I got out beyond the city lights, the road consisted of two little black valleys scored in the impacted snow by the repeated passage of wheelbases wider than my own. The snow was not deep, but where it covered the pavement it was rock hard and my tires drifted up and off these long icy shelves, marking my forward progress with bumps and skids. With each road jolt the boxes of pots and books shifted behind me.

I'd tossed my stocking cap in the dryer the week before and now it was too small. It pressed my ears to my skull and squeezed my forehead. It itched, took on weight, and felt like a jousting helmet.

A salt of snow fell for a time, so I drove with the ice scraper in my lap, reaching up every four or five miles to scratch at the thin patterns of translucent ice that formed on the inside of the windshield. My fingers went cold and numb in the woolen gloves, partly because I removed them to smoke cigarettes, donning them again only after I'd stubbed out another butt in the tiny ashtray. The cold, the glare of oncoming traffic, the challenge of driving, and the roar of passing trucks made anything but nattering impossible. There was a kind of comfort in hearing the sound of my own voice not quite drowned out by the engine.

First there were the "what ifs." If I'd spent my small nest egg on a better car with a working heater, I told myself, I'd be west of Cheyenne already, Matt sleeping soundly in the back. I might be listening to some cowboy radio station out of Texas instead of the loud monotonous chatter of the little motor behind me. I could have left Matt behind with Irene and taken Serena who was easier to care for and a few years closer to being able to take care of herself. With a warmer car, I might have arranged for the kids to spend the night with me and taken them both.

My nose ran and I wiped it on the back of my hand and, as I did, fought the sense that I was driving through the unraveling threads of what had been my life. At the center of my just- jettisoned plan had been Matt, destined in my care to grow into the first young smiling Barlow male, happy and free: the baby boy, then the school kid and man, at peace with himself and the world, his life spread out like a field of flowers in the near-heaven of Southern California where people were more tolerant and where it wouldn't be five below any time soon. My

461

plan had promised to break the chains that bound the other Barlow men to compressed lives of shouts or swallowed sobs, warped them into strangers to one another, deaf to cooperation. The Barlow males, among whom I reluctantly included myself, tended to be raging archeologists of hypocrisy and pretense, dark knights on dubious journeys through scarcely endurable communities.

Irene would be all right. Gerald would return from his sabbatical. If things didn't work out with him, there would be other men. There had always been eager manly eyes on her; and now she would be free to evaluate the attention of strangers and acquaintances. Meantime, she would have to hustle a little harder as a cocktail waitress. She would finish her BFA, find a way to exhibit her paintings, maybe even go on to graduate school. As the big-eyed darling of the entire City U Fine Arts Department, she would face no shortage of academic advisors and maybe win some scholarships. She had a sister, a mother, aunts, and friends to help her look after the kids. Once I settled down somewhere, I'd write her a letter and make an appointment for a telephone conversation with the kids. I'd send her more money as soon as I could.

One day, Molly would write to Pat and Mitch, and they would forward my letter on to her, wherever she was driving my old car. Maybe Molly would write my grandmother. My grandma, I felt sure, would remain my ally even when she wouldn't be able to defend me against the judgments of others or ease the pain and sorrow felt by Serena and Matt in my absence. I did not like to think about this pain, but I had gone too far to run from it entirely, and too far toward some imagined glory to settle into some diminished, more-responsible life.

Though he was voluble and self-dramatizing, Dom was a steady friend and would remain one, I felt sure. That didn't mean believing everything he said, I reminded myself. I was tempted to believe that Dom really did know screen and television writers who would help us get started in the business and that we could or would make oodles of money. I could fly back to see both kids every other weekend, and maybe build or buy a house near Santa Monica beach for myself and them. It was also tempting to hope I would hear from Molly within a month or two. She might even turn out to be living nearby. Memories of that afternoon on the rim of the Black Canyon, our bodies naked and warm in the sun, were there for me like a drug any time I wanted to think about them. Hopefulness was hope contaminated with wishfulness, and I needed to train myself to work and plan and recognize real hope, while avoiding the cheap sugar rush of hopefulness. If religion was the opiate of the masses, then hopefulness was the drug of choice of the overly imaginative.

Maybe I could have worked harder and made a plan and put the sorrows and betrayals of the past behind me and gone on living in Denver, but sometimes a clean break worked faster and better. Nobody seemed to know very much about anybody's past out in California. And maybe, thanks to all that dry sun and opulence, the past didn't seem to carry the same weight.

Many years before, I'd run up the back steps to the porch on Emerson Street where the turtle had been killed. I tripped over a lip of rotted molding and fell across the trunk lid that my dad had removed from his Mercury, its license plate still attached. The scar left by that plate never disappeared from my forearm. Before it scarred, though, while it was still an interesting wound, I had sat out on the porch with Junior Wong, dreaming of travel to China. Once there, I planned to show my gash like some sort of merit badge to gatherings of interested and mysteriously humane admirers.

Wounds bled and scabbed and healed and sometimes scarred, and that was that. I didn't want to be blameless any more than I wanted to be blamed. I wanted to come upon and cherish the natural permanence of things and become a friend to those who managed real hopes they never allowed to decay into hopelessness.

The highway curved and a shaft of moonlight lit fields of snowy emptiness north of Fort Collins. At one point the Volks lost traction on a patch of ice and I had to brake carefully to keep from sledding off the road. Junior Wong had described brakes as these little hands that emerged from hiding when they needed to stop the turning of the wheels. He went on to claim that if you kept your foot on the gas pedal and brake at the same time, the little brake hands eventually got worn out like tiny broken fingers. The concrete steps where we sat after the killing of the snapping turtle radiated the heat of the afternoon sun to our little butts. We were both fairly convinced that the Hudson Hornets of years to come would be fast enough to transport us back through time. The challenge would be to apply the brakes in the right geological age. Junior's oldest brother had taken him to the planetarium where Junior had sworn to me that he'd looked at a star that had first started shining toward him when carnivorous dinosaurs still ruled the world. We agreed that one day we would drive out of some beam of light the Hudson controlled and touch down on a dry spot in a jungle and get the holy hell scared out of us by living dinosaurs.

But Junior had changed. The last I'd seen of him was that morning Matt had been born. I had this scar on my arm that I hadn't looked at for years, and Junior had no memory of that glimmer of starlight or even of our talks of time travel, because he claimed never to think of the past. To him, he'd said, memory was a liar, an improviser, a huckster and dealer in might-have-beens or should-have-beens. I still hoped to find a middle way, a way of living in a continuum as a whole-hearted man who could make a lasting peace with truth and losses; own everything and complain of nothing.

Before me flickered the green and white lights of Cheyenne. My hands ached and fingertips burned with the beginnings of frostbite. My nose dripped and froze in my nostrils. My legs and feet had gone dead. Let the truckers drive all night to wherever it was they were headed, however much they were earning per mile, and whatever they were hauling. Part of renouncing hopefulness had to do with developing patience. I was going to have to start pacing myself a little.

I turned into the driveway of the Blue Yonder Motel, took my foot off the gas, and sat a moment in the vast silence of the Wyoming night. Once inside the stale and overheated room, I refused to turn on the television set. It wasn't just that I hoped to train myself to tolerate missing my kids so I could arrive securely and permanently on the other side of an ache that I'd never felt before. It was that I owed it to myself and to my children to feel my sorrows unbuffered by distraction or self-pity.

The next morning I filled my thermos with free motel coffee, tugged my stocking cap over my ears, and drove away from the pink sky behind me. I clenched the steering wheel in both gloved fists. It was too cold to snow much, but the morning wind blew a dry smoke of powder across patches of pavement. I talked to myself as cold miles accumulated, trying to stifle every wish without losing the hope that made each one possible.

ACKNOWLEDGEMENTS

Forty years ago I began learning that writing a novel is a prelude to the trickier rigmarole of selling one. To get published by a respectable "house," it came to seem like you had to be able to pat your head, rub your tummy, and kick yourself in the ass at the same time, and continue doing so longer than I could ever manage. My decision to self publish comes too late for my mom, son Michael, and friend Harris Nolan. I thank, first of all, my daughter, Rohana, for her patience and forgiveness. For years Mary Bond partnered with me and supported my struggles, financially and otherwise. A shout out to my friend, Phil Normand, often exasperated, sometimes exasperating. For about five decades Phil has goaded and spurred me, and only occasionally given up on me. Greg Lee and Karen Brooks helped me get paid to freelance and edit. Most people with attention disorders like mine aren't lucky enough to have a patient and clear-minded stepson. Thanks, Calin Berk, for your tech support with this and other projects. And thank you to Marvin Berk of WestGroup Creative for tweaking the overall format, covers and spine. Finally, for twenty-five years Lee Noonan has been an enthusiast, critic, personal editor, supportive companion, and a beloved wife. For the last decade she's also been a business partner in WriteXpression (www.writexpression.com). *Lurching toward Yonder* is my tale, but it has been groomed and shaped and clarified by Lee.

Made in United States
Orlando, FL
16 November 2022

24629804R00283